STEPHEN JONES lives in London, England. He is the winner of three World Fantasy Awards, three Horror Writers Association Bram Stoker Awards and three International Horror Guild Awards as well as being a sixteen-time recipient of the British Fantasy Award and a Hugo Award nominee. A former television producer/director and genre movie publicist and consultant (the first three *Hellraiser* movies, *Night Life, Nightbreed, Split Second, Mind Ripper, Last Gasp* etc.), he is the co-editor of *Horror: 100 Best Books, Horror: Another 100 Best Books, The Best Horror from Fantasy Tales, Gaslight & Ghosts, Now We Are Sick, H.P. Lovecraft's Book of Horror, The Anthology of Fantasy & the Supernatural, Secret City: Strange Tales of London, Great Ghost Stories, Tales to Freeze the Blood: More Great Ghost Stories* and the *Dark Terrors, Dark Voices* and *Fantasy Tales* series. He has written *Creepshows: The Illustrated Stephen King Movie Guide, The Essential Monster Movie Guide, The Illustrated Vampire Movie Guide, The Illustrated Dinosaur Movie Guide, The Illustrated Frankenstein Movie Guide* and *The Illustrated Werewolf Movie Guide*, and compiled *The Mammoth Book of Best New Horror* series, *The Mammoth Book of Terror, The Mammoth Book of Vampires, The Mammoth Book of Zombies, The Mammoth Book of Werewolves, The Mammoth Book of Frankenstein, The Mammoth Book of Dracula, The Mammoth Book of Vampire Stories By Women, The Mammoth Book of New Terror, Shadows Over Innsmouth, Weird Shadows Over Innsmouth, Dark Detectives, Dancing With the Dark, Dark of the Night, White of the Moon, Keep Out the Night, By Moonlight Only, Don't Turn Out the Light, H.P. Lovecraft's Book of the Supernatural, Exorcisms and Ecstasies* by Karl Edward Wagner, *The Vampire Stories of R. Chetwynd-Hayes, Phantoms and Fiends* and *Frights and Fancies* by R. Chetwynd-Hayes, *James Herbert: By Horror Haunted, The Complete Chronicles of Conan* by Robert E. Howard, *The Emperor of Dreams: The Lost Worlds of Clark Ashton Smith, Sea-Kings of Mars and Otherworldly Stories* by Leigh Brackett, *Clive Barker's A-Z of Horror, Clive Barker's Shadows in Eden, Clive Barker's The Nightbreed Chronicles* and the *Hellraiser Chronicles*. He was a Guest of Honour at the 2002 World Fantasy Convention in Minneapolis, Minnesota, and the 2004 World Horror Convention in Phoenix, Arizona. You can visit his web site at www.herebedragons.co.uk/jones

Also available

THE
MAMMOTH BOOK OF
BEST NEW
HORROR

VOLUME SEVENTEEN

Edited and with an Introduction by
STEPHEN JONES

CARROLL & GRAF PUBLISHERS
New York

Carroll & Graf Publishers
An imprint of Avalon Publishing Group, Inc.
11th Floor
245 W. 17th Street
New York, NY 10011-5300

www.carrollandgraf.com

AVALON
publishing group incorporated

First published in the UK by Robinson,
an imprint of Constable & Robinson Ltd 2006

First Carroll & Graf edition 2006

ISBN-13: 978-0-78671-833-7
ISBN-10: 0-7867-1833-1

Printed and bound in the EU

CONTENTS

ACKNOWLEDGMENTS

I would like to thank Kim Newman, David Barraclough, Rodger Turner and Wayne MacLaurin (sfsite.com), Mandy Slater, Hugh Lamb, Pamela Brooks, Brian Mooney, Lisa Morton, Del Howison, Jo Fletcher, Gordon Van Gelder, Douglas E. Winter, Amanda Foubister, Richard Dalby, Peter Crowther, Sean Wallace, Jay Lake and, especially, Pete Duncan and Dorothy Lumley, for all their help and support. Special thanks are also due to *Locus*, *Variety*, *Ansible*, and all the other sources that were used for reference in the Introduction and the Necrology.

Congratulations to

Ramsey Campbell

and

Forrest J Ackerman

on the occasions of their
60th and 90th birthdays, respectively.

INTRODUCTION

Horror in 2005

IN JANUARY, FORMER Oxford University Press editor Michael Cox reportedly received the largest-ever advance for a British debut novel. After a "frenzied" telephone bidding war, John Murray paid £500,000 for *The Meaning of Night*, described as a murder-mystery set in Victorian London that took the author thirty years of planning and six months to write.

The Author's Guild and three individual writers sued Google in September, seeking damages and an injunction to stop the Internet search-engine's ambitious plans to digitise all the world's books and put excerpts up on its "Google Print" database (the name was later changed to the less-inflammatory "Google Book Search"). Authors, publishers and distributors complained when Google said it would go ahead and post extracts unless publishers provided a list of specific titles to be excluded.

Meanwhile, in the UK, W. H. Smith's CEO Kate Swann announced that she would "improve efficiency" by levying a system of fines against publishers for late delivery of books. Not surprisingly, the publishers refused to co-operate, claiming that such a system was illegal without their agreement.

An attempt by UK bookseller Waterstone's to take over its smaller rival Ottaker's was delayed in December when the Office of Fair Trading, backed by the Society of Authors, ruled that the £96.4 million deal would have to be examined by the Competition Commission.

Under an EU ruling, the UK announced that it was introducing artist resale rights, which meant that each and every time a piece of artwork is sold through a gallery or auction house, the creator would receive a *droit de suite* royalty. Many people disagreed with the ruling, including artists, arguing that the UK has the biggest art resale market in Europe and the new law could ultimately affect sales, with markets eventually moving to the US to circumvent the ruling.

In Canada, total Halloween sales were projected to be $1.1 billion – up 50 per cent from five years earlier, and for the first time rivalling Christmas as the biggest holiday season for retailers.

As a result of pre-orders that were "substantially higher than originally anticipated" for *Harry Potter and the Half-Blood Prince*, Bloomsbury announced in March that profits would be above industry expectations. Published on July 16th, the sixth adventure of the boy wizard enjoyed first-day sales of almost seven million copies in America and more than two million in Britain.

In America, where 13.5 million copies of the first edition were printed by Scholastic, sales topped $100 million, which was $17 million more than the combined box-office take of that weekend's top two movies, *Charlie and the Chocolate Factory* and *The Wedding Crashers*.

In fact, the book sold twice as many copies – 6,397,000 – in the US in its first two weeks than any other book during a whole year, and author J. K. Rowling was estimated to have earned £1 million per hour in royalties during the first twenty-four hours of the title's release.

Rowling was quoted as saying that children should be scared by books so that they can deal with fears in later life. "We need to fear and we need to confront fear in a controlled environment and that's a very important part of growing up," explained the author.

Meanwhile, in the English town of Skellingthorpe, in Lincolnshire, a primary school scrapped its "Harry Potter Day" to coincide with the launch of the book after the headmaster received a letter from the local rector, the Reverend Richard Billinghurst, who warned that the event was "a couple of steps from real evil".

In America, freelance writer Anne Hiltner, who unsuccessfully attempted to sue Stephen King fourteen years earlier for stealing her manuscripts, brought a new $500 million lawsuit against the author, this time claiming to be the inspiration for his character Annie Wilkes in *Misery*. Maybe Hiltner should have taken a closer look at King's story "Secret Window, Secret Garden"?

Meanwhile, King's short novel *The Colorado Kid* appeared as part of Dorchester's "Hard Case Crime" series of pulp books, and a new illustrated edition of *'Salem's Lot* included fifty pages of alternate and deleted scenes, two related short stories, a new Introduction and atmospheric photographs by Jerry N. Uelsmann.

With an initial print run in the US of 600,000 copies, Dean Koontz's *Forever Odd* was a follow up to the author's 2003 book *Odd Thomas*, while *Velocity* was a new serial killer novel from the same author.

Neil Gaiman's short novel *Anansi Boys* was a semi-sequel to his earlier best-seller *American Gods* and concerned a young boy who discovered that his estranged father was an ancient Spider-God. The book debuted at #1 on both the *New York Times* and *Publishers Weekly* best-seller lists.

The attractive UK hardcover, published under Headline's Review imprint, was padded out with "exclusive material" that included a deleted scene and notebook extracts with new prefaces by the author, an interview with Gaiman, and often hilarious questions for reading group discussion. A beautifully designed signed and slipcased edition that also included all the extra material was available in the UK for a very reasonable £40.00.

Gaiman's earlier books – the novels *American Gods*, *Stardust* and *Neverwhere*, and the collection *Smoke and Mirrors* – were reissued by Review in handsomely re-designed paperback editions containing the author's preferred text and exclusive extra material such as interviews, introductions, web links and more reading group questions.

DreamHaven Books issued a new paperback edition of *Now We Are Sick: An Anthology of Nasty Verse* edited by Gaiman and Stephen Jones. Re-edited and re-designed, the book featured a cover by Gahan Wilson and interior artwork by Clive Barker and Andrew Smith.

For Christmas, DreamHaven published Gaiman's Hugo Award-winning Lovecraft/Holmes story "A Study in Emerald" as a facsimile broadsheet newspaper, illustrated by Jouni Koponen. A 200-copy edition signed by the author was also available.

F. Paul Wilson's *Infernal* was the ninth in the "Repairman Jack" series, while James Herbert's *The Legend of Crickley Hall* was described as a new spin on the ghost story.

In David Morrell's new novel *Creepers*, a group of urban explorers broke into a run-down hotel awaiting demolition and uncovered a festering evil.

The agents of Chaos attempted to lure a woman carrying a very special child back to a bizarre dreamland of the dead in Jonathan Carroll's witty new novel, *Glass Soup*, a sequel to the author's *White Apples*.

Child of Darkness was the third in the "Gemini" series credited to the long-deceased "V. C. Andrews"®, while *April Shadows* was the first volume in a new Gothic series. The author was still probably Andrew Neiderman, whose own novel *The Hunted* was about a killer stalking hunters in the woods.

When a comedian's son was killed by terrorists, he uncovered a darker mystery in *Innocent Blood* by Graham Masterton. A deaf social worker helped the police in Masterton's *Unspeakable*, while *Darkroom* was the sixth volume in the author's "Jim Rook" series. *Manitou Blood* was the busy Masterton's fourth novel about the evil shaman Misquamacus, who turned his victims into vampires by spreading a plague through New York.

In Lisa Tuttle's *The Mysteries*, a private investigator looking for a missing woman found himself involved in ancient Celtic myths and folklore in the Scottish Highlands.

In her seventh mystery, parish priest Merrily Watkins was called in by the police to investigate sightings of a dead boy in Phil Rickman's *The Smile of a Ghost*.

Dance of Death by Douglas Preston and Lincoln Child was a sequel to *Brimstone* and featured characters from the authors' other series of books.

Blood of Angels was the third in Michael Marshall (Smith)'s loosely connected trilogy of serial-killer novels featuring the sinister Straw Men organisation.

A number of old foes also turned up in *The Black Angel*, the latest "Charlie Parker" novel by John Connolly, in which an abduction of the streets of New York involved the private detective in a centuries-old supernatural mystery.

A strange piece of graffiti on the window of a London restaurant led to a series of gruesome murders, the mysterious Nomads' Club, the rituals of a lost tribe and a secret history of espionage and mind-altering patterns in Paul McAuley's latest thriller *Mind's Eye*, which had its roots amidst the chaos of post-war Iraq.

Dead Simple was the first novel in a new mystery series by Peter James featuring Detective Superintendent Roy Grace. The horrific death of a missing groom's four friends pitted the loner policeman against a sadistic killer.

Reputedly completed by Dean Koontz, *The Glory Bus* (aka *Into the Fire*) was the latest posthumous new novel from Richard Laymon, about a group of disparate and desperate characters on a journey into the dark heart of the Mojave Desert. In the UK, Headline Books began reissuing Laymon's earlier novels in double omnibus editions beginning with *The Beast House/After Midnight*.

Graham Joyce's *The Limits of Enchantment* was set in the 1960s and was about a young woman who might have been a witch.

A sequel to the acclaimed *A Choir of Ill Children*, Tom Piccirilli's *November Mourns* was about a former convict investigating his teenage sister's mysterious death who was haunted by ghostly visions.

In Christopher Golden's atmospheric *Wildwood Road*, a man found himself looking for an enigmatic ghost-child while trying to recover the woman he loved. The ever-busy Golden also collaborated with Thomas E. Sniegoski on *Tears of the Furies*, the second novel of "The Menagerie", whose members investigated people being turned into stone in and around Athens. In collaboration with actress Amber Benson (*Buffy the Vampire Slayer*), Golden also wrote *Ghosts of Albion: Accursed*, a Victorian supernatural novel based on the animated BBC Internet serial.

A series of covert tests released the ghosts of psychiatric patients and caused a twelve-year-old boy to unleash his latent psychic powers in Scott Nicholson's latest Appalachian Gothic thriller, *The Home*.

Joseph Nassise's *Heretic* was the first volume in a new dark fantasy series, "The Templar Chronicles", as the Vatican's last defence in the war between good and evil took on a cabal of necromancers searching for a lost holy relic. The book was subsequently podcast free over thirty weekly audio episodes read by the author, sponsored by The Horror Channel and The Podcast Network.

Under the Leisure imprint, a man was drawn by his repressed memories into the mysteries of his past in Tim Waggoner's *Like Death*, while a disturbed young man moved into a very strange apartment in Tim Lebbon's *Desolation*.

In *The Reckoning* by British writer Sarah Pinborough, a group of old friends relived the nightmare of a summer twenty years before, as an evil influence spread out from an old house to infect the small town they grew up in.

Evil was also spreading out from an old mansion in *The Abandoned* by Douglas Clegg, and people started going through bizarre changes in James A. Moore's *Rabid Growth*.

A man plagued with visions consulted an occult expert in Michael Laimo's *The Demonologist*, a stolen gold coin carried a gypsy curse in *Grave Intent* by Deborah LeBlanc, and an Italian teenager became a vampire in nineteenth-century Paris in Jemiah Jefferson's *Fiend*.

Thomas Tessier's *Finishing Touches* combined the title novel with the novella "Father Panic's Opera Macabre".

Mistress of the Dark was the latest novel from Sèphera Girón, *Flesh Gothic* and *The Backwoods* were two new novels by Edward Lee, and Simon Clark's *The Tower* was yet another haunted house tale.

Stephen Laws' 1993 vampire novel *Gideon* was reissued by Leisure as *Fear Me*, and the imprint also reprinted *City of the Dead* by Brian Keene, *Come Out Tonight* by Richard Laymon and *The Girl Next Door* by Jack Ketchum (Dallas Mayr), the latter adding a new author's note and two stories (one original).

Christine Feehan's *Night Game* was about the GhostWalkers, a Special Forces squad called in to fight the paranormal.

The Smiling Affair by Jeremy Sheldon featured paranormal investigator Jay Richards, while Lee Killough's *Killer Karma* was about a ghostly detective.

John Taylor investigated the origins of the Nightside and discovered a clue to his missing mother in Simon R. Green's *Hex and the City*.

The Good, the Bad, and the Undead by Kim Harrison (Dawn Cook) was a humorous sequel to the author's *Dead Witch Walking*. It was followed by *Every Which Way But Dead* featuring the same witchy private investigator.

Renegade witch Eve Levine was sent back from the afterworld to battle evil in Kelley Armstrong's *Haunted*, and Jack the Ripper stalked a virtual theme park recreation of nineteenth-century London in Hervé Jubert's *Dance of the Assassins*.

Better Read Than Dead and *A Vision of Murder* were the second and third books in Victoria Laurie's "Psychic Eye" series featuring psychic Abby Cooper, while violet-eyed empath Natalie Lindstrom unearthed a cursed treasure in Peru that led to murder in *Golden Blood*, the third volume in the series by Stephen Woodworth.

Charlaine Harris' *Grave Sight* was the first in a new series about Harper Connelly, who found the bodies of dead people by talking to them, and a couple could sense the dead in T. G. Arsenault's *Forgotten Souls*.

If Angels Burn and *Private Demon* were the first and second volumes in the "Darkyn" paranormal series by "Lynn Viehl" (Sheila Kelly, who also writes under a number of other pseudonyms).

A psychic child tracked down a secret society of cannibals in *The*

Epicure, and a small Pennsylvania town was gripped by evil in *Ashes*, both by "H. R. Howland" (Holly Newstein and Ralph W. Bieber II).

Set in the 1950s, John Farris' *Phantom Nights* featured a mute boy haunted by the raped and murdered nurse who befriended him.

A recently released mental patient confronted a supernatural evil in T.M. Gray's *Ghosts of Eden*.

Steel Ghosts by Michael Paine (John Michael Curlovich) was set in an abandoned Pennsylvanian steel mill, and Nora Roberts' ghostly novels *Black Rose* and *Red Lily* were the second and third volumes in the "In the Garden" series.

A music festival was held at a haunted house in *Matty Groves* by Deborah Grabien, the third volume in the "Haunted Ballard" series based on traditional folk songs, while an up-and-coming singer found she was being haunted in Tananarive Due's *Joplin's Ghost*.

The ghostly Aunt Dimity was consigned to the sidelines in *Aunt Dimity and the Next of Kin*, the tenth volume in the "cozy" mystery series by Nancy Atherton, while *Innocence* by Kathleen Tessaro was another ghost novel.

A pregnant woman believed she was carrying the spirit of a murder victim in *The Unwelcome Child* by Terese Pampellonne, and a paediatrician's miracle cure had an unforeseen side-effect in James M. Thompson's *Dark Moon Rising*.

Dying of cancer, loser Tommy O'Brien still had time for one more horrific mistake in Brian Keene's *Terminal*, a letter-writing job turned into a nightmare in Bentley Little's *Dispatch*, and a woman searched for her long-lost grandfather in Christopher Nicole's *The Falls of Death*.

A mystery writer encountered a strange woman in *Within the Shadows* by Brandon Massey, a deaf and blind boy could hear whispers of evil in Chandler McGrew's *In Shadows*, and a group of old college friends faced off against something nasty in Craig Spector's *Underground*,

Originally published in Japan in 1998, Koji Suzuki's *Loop* (*Rapu*) was the third and final book in "The Ring" trilogy, translated by Glynne Walley.

A seaside town was plagued by a mysterious disease and strange creatures in *The Town That Forgot How to Breathe* by Kenneth J. Harvey, while a palaeontologist uncovered a fossil older than the Earth in Robert Masello's *Vigil*.

The new proprietors of a seaside inn discovered that local disappearances were linked to the legend of a century-old creature prowling the Atlantic coast in Chris Blaine's *Drowned Night: A*

Novel of the Abbadon Inn, the third book in the series after *Twisted Branch* and *Dark Whispers*. "Blaine" was a house name for, amongst others, Matthew Costello and Craig Shaw Gardner.

Twisted Souls was the latest novel by Shaun Hutson, while *Follow* was written by Rick Hautala and published under the pen name "A. J. Matthews".

Mark Wm. Simmons' *Habeas Corpses* was the third novel in the humorous series that began with *One Foot in the Grave*.

Jewell Parker Rhodes' mystery *Voodoo Season*, a sequel to *Voodoo Dreams*, once again featured the great great granddaughter of voodoo queen Marie Laveau.

Suspense and Sensibility or, First Impressions Revisited was the second volume in Carrie Bebris' series featuring Jane Austen's Mr and Mrs Darcy investigating the supernatural.

In Ann Lawrence's dark romance *Do You Believe?*, a woman searched for her missing sister with the help of a horror writer. A biographer discovered that her subject, Lord Byron, was still alive in Melanie Jackson's supernatural romance *Divine Fire*, and *Carved in Stone* was the first volume in Vickie Taylor's paranormal romance series about shape-shifting gargoyle Nathan Cross.

Day of the Dead was an erotic supernatural novel set in Mexico and featuring Vivid adult movie star "Mercedez" as the main character. Author "Desirée Knight" turned out to be Nancy Kilpatrick.

A strange book from her father's library led a young girl to investigate the secret history of Vlad the Impaler in *The Historian* by Elizabeth Kostova. Publisher Little, Brown reportedly bought the debut novel for $2 million and, predictably, the 642-page volume quickly sold to the movies after being on the US best-seller lists for eighteen weeks

Tim Lucas' clever and meticulously researched *The Book of Renfield: A Gospel of Dracula* was an alternate version of Bram Stoker's 1897 novel, as seen through the eyes of the fly-eating madman, R. M. Renfield.

Octavia E. Butler's *Fledgling* was about amnesiac Shori Matthews, the survivor of a death squad massacre who discovered that she was a vampire genetically modified to survive in sunlight.

Set during the Inquisition, *State of Grace* was the eighteenth volume in Chelsea Quinn Yarbro's popular historical series about vampire Count Saint-Germain.

The Priest of Blood was the first volume in Douglas Clegg's new

trilogy "The Vampyricon", in which mediaeval warrior Aleric discovered his destiny in a pagan temple in the Holy Land. An extract
from the book appeared in a free sampler from Penguin's Ace and
Roc imprints, containing excerpts from seven novels by different
authors.

A witch and a vampire teamed up to protect musicians and their
fans from a psychic soul-sucker in *Children of the Night* by Mercedes
Lackey, *Already Dead* introduced Charles Huston's vampire investigator Joe Pitt, and Liz Maverick's *Crimson City* was the first in a
series set in a Los Angeles overrun by vampires.

Pale Death by David Thurlo and Aimée Thurlo was the third book
featuring Native American Nightwalker police officer Lee Nez.

The alien Reapers were confronted by pockets of resistance in E. E.
Knight's *Tale of the Thunderbolt* and *Valentine's Rising*, the third
and fourth volumes in "The Vampire Earth" SF series, and *The
Bitten* and *The Forbidden* were the fourth and fifth volumes in the
"Vampire Huntress Legends" series by "L. A. Banks" (Leslie Esdale
Banks).

The vampiric Marquis de Sade was not the only one leaving bodies
drained of blood in Mary Ann Michell's *In the Name of the Vampire*.

Seize the Night, *Sins of the Night* and *Unleash the Night* were the
sixth, seventh and eighth volumes in the "Were-Hunters" and
"Dark-Hunters" series by Sherrilyn Kenyon (aka "Kinley MacGre-
gor").

A vampire stole a woman's memory in *Be Mine Forever* by
Rosemary Laurey. Savannah Russe's *Beyond the Pale* was the first
book of "The Darkwind Chronicles" introducing vampire spy
Daphne Urban, and *Bite Club* was a gay debut novel by Hal Bodner,
set in West Hollywood. All three titles were published in hardcover
by the Science Fiction Book Club.

Chicago wizard Harry Dresden was being blackmailed by a
vampire and searching for a dangerous book of magic in *Dead Beat*
by Jim Butcher, the seventh book in the "Dresden Files" series, and
vampire detective Jack Fleming found himself working for the mob
in P. N. Elrod's *Song in the Dark*, the eleventh volume in "The
Vampire Files".

Containing a new Introduction by the author, *The Vampire
Genevieve* was a hefty omnibus volume that also included the novels
Drachenfels, *Genevieve Undead*, *Beasts in Velvet* and *Silver Nails* by
Kim Newman writing as "Jack Yeovil".

Nancy Collins' 1995 "Sonja Blue" novel *Paint It Black* was
reissued as a single volume by Two Wolf Press. The book also

included a preview of the author's new werewolf novel, *Wild Blood*.

British imprint Orbit released *Quick Bites: Fiction to Sink Your Teeth Into* as a free paperback sampler containing vampire novel extracts by Laurell K. Hamilton, Kelley Armstrong, Charlene Harris, Tanya Huff, and Barb and J. C. Hendee.

In her fifth humorous Southern mystery, waitress Sookie Stackhouse was surrounded by supernatural suitors while investigating a killer of were-creatures in *Dead as a Doorbell* by Charlaine Harris. *Dead by Day* was an omnibus of the author's latest novel and *Dead to the World*, published by the Science Fiction Book Club. Television rights to the series were sold to HBO.

A woman's Christmas was spoiled when she turned into a vampire and received death threats from a fairy in *The Midnight Work* by Kassandra Sims, and vampire and werewolf buddies helped a restaurant owner with her zombie problem in A. Lee Martinez's humorous *Gil's All Fright Diner*.

In Tanya Huff's *Smoke and Mirrors*, the second volume in the series about TV researcher Tony Foster, the cast and crew of a vampire-detective show were trapped inside a real haunted house.

How to Marry a Millionaire Vampire was a humorous romance novel by Kerelyn Sparks about a female dentist and a vampire who had lost his fangs, while a fledgling bloodsucker got advice from a suicidal vampire in *Bitten & Smitten* by Michelle Rowen.

Susan Sizemore's *I Hunger for You* was the third volume in the vampire romance series that began with *I Burn for You* and *I Thirst for You*. All three novels were collected in the omnibus *Crave the Night*.

Undead and Unappreciated by MaryJanice Davidson was the third volume in the chick-lit vampire series featuring queen of the vampires Betsy Taylor, who discovered that her illegitimate daughter may be the spawn of Satan. In the fourth volume, *Undead and Unreturnable*, Betsy's Christmas and forthcoming wedding were disrupted by a serial killer. *Betsy the Vampire Queen* was an omnibus from SFBC that reprinted all four novels.

Dark Secret was the latest volume in Christine Feehan's "Carpathian" series of novels. A vampire fell in love with a human in *Fangs for the Memories* by Kathy Love, and other vampire romances included *Night's Kiss* by Amanda Ashley (Madeline Baker) and *Sex, Lies and Vampires* by Katie MacAlister (aka "Katie Maxwell"), while *Waltz with a Vampire* by Maggie MacKeever was a Regency romance.

Despite its title, *The Remarkable Miss Frankenstein* by Minda Webber was yet another vampire romance novel, featuring the niece of the notorious doctor. The author followed it with *The Reluctant Miss Van Helsing*, in which the heroine fell in love with a vampire.

Two by Twilight was an omnibus collection of two novels in Maggie Shayne's "Wings in the Night" series, *Run from Twilight* and *Twilight Vows*.

The vampire romance anthology *Bite* contained another "Anita Blake" story by Laurell K. Hamilton, a "Sookie Stackhouse" tale by Charlaine Harris and a "Betsy Taylor, Queen of the Vampires" story by MaryJanice Davidson, along with an Arthurian tale by Angela Knight and a story by romance writer Vickie Taylor.

MaryJanice Davidson's *Derik's Bane* was the first volume in the "Wyndham Werewolf" romance series about shape-shifter Derik Gardner, who was assigned to kill a nurse who turned out to be a reincarnation of Morgan Le Fay.

Carrie Vaughn's debut novel, *Kitty and the Midnight Hour*, introduced werewolf radio talk show host Kitty Norvill, who discovered that her show about the paranormal was popular with depressed supernatural creatures.

A female werewolf and a sidhe warrior teamed up to battle a vampire in Angela Knight's *Master of the Moon*, and *Moon's Web* was a werewolf romance novel by C. T. Adams and Cathy Clamp.

Hal Duncan's first novel, *Vellum: The Book of All Hours*, was set in the near-future and dealt with the forthcoming End of Days and the final battle between Heaven and Hell.

Children were being murdered to create magic potions in Richard Kunzmann's debut thriller *Bloody Harvest*, and something evil was protecting the new kid in town in *Cruel Winter* by Anthony Izzo.

In Justine Wilson's first novel, *Blood Angel*, a rock singer spread evil in his wake, while a female realtor protected three bachelors from a sexy shape-shifting demon in Lexi Davis' *Pretty Evil*.

A witch fell in love with her enemy, an evil warlock, in *Charmed & Dangerous* by Candace Havens, and M. A. C. Petty's debut novel *Thin Line Between* was set in a haunted museum. It was the first book in the "Wandjina Quartet".

Although not published as genre fiction, Bret Easton Ellis wrote an alternative version of himself into *Lunar Park*, as the protagonist who got a second chance at life that still went horribly wrong.

A psychic woman possibly killed with her touch in Russell Ho-ban's *Come Dance with Me*, a psychic tried to prevent the death of his daughter in Anthony Doerr's *About Grace*, and a female detective teamed up with her psychic partner to track down a serial killer in *Last Girl Dancing* by Holly Lisle.

A. N. Wilson's *A Jealous Ghost* had an American graduate student in England reliving the events of Henry James' *The Turn of the Screw*, while *Kornwolf* by Tristan Egolf was about an teenage Amish werewolf.

John Crowley's *Lord Byron's Novel: The Evening Land* was about a lost Gothic manuscript supposedly written by the notorious poet, with notes by his daughter Ada.

Lovecraft: Tales was a classy hardcover collection of twenty-two classic tales by H. P. Lovecraft, edited by Peter Straub for the prestigious Library of America imprint. *Shadows of Death* reprinted sixteen stories and four fragments by Lovecraft, along with an Introduction by Harlan Ellison.

Count Magnus and Other Ghost Stories collected fifteen stories and two essays by M. R. James, and *The Terror and Other Tales* was the third volume of "The Best Weird Tales of Arthur Machen", containing thirteen stories and an essay on occultism. Both volumes were edited with Introductions by S. T. Joshi.

Issued as part of the "Lovecraft's Library" series from Hippo-campus Press, M. P. Shiel's *The House of Sounds* collected seven stories and the 1901 novel *The Purple Cloud*, with another Intro-duction by Joshi.

Leonard Cline's 1927 Gothic novel *The Dark Chamber* was reissued by Cold Spring Press with an Introduction by Douglas A. Anderson and an Afterword by the author. From the same imprint, Anderson also edited and introduced *Adrift on the Haunted Seas: The Best Short Stories of William Hope Hodgson*, which collected seventeen stories and four poems.

From Red Jacket Press, *Roads* was a boxed facsimile reproduction of the 1948 Arkham House edition of Seabury Quinn's short Christmas novella, with illustrations by Virgil Finlay.

Edited with an Afterword by Stephen Jones, *Sea-Kings of Mars and Otherworldly Stories* from Gollancz's "Fantasy Masterworks" series collected twelve classic fantasy and science fiction stories by Leigh Brackett (including a collaboration with Ray Bradbury), along with an Introduction by the author. Dan Simmons' classic 1985 novel *Song of Kali* was also reissued in the same series.

In March, Sotheby's in London sold ailing film director George Pan Cosmatos' collection of English and America literature, including Horace Walpole's *The Castle of Otranto* (£2,400), William Beckford's *An Arabian Adventure* (aka *Vathek*, £660), Mary W. Shelley's *Frankenstein; or The Modern Prometheus* (£66,000), John W. Polidori's *The Vampyre: A Tale* (£1,440), Wilkie Collins' *The Woman in White* (£6,600), Arthur Conan Doyle's *The Sign of Four* (£3,360), Oscar Wilde's *The Picture of Dorian Gray* (£1,680), H. S. [sic] Wells' *The Time Machine* (£2,040) and *The War of the Worlds* (£1,020), Bram Stoker's *Dracula* (£9,600), Aldous Huxley's *Brave New World* (£3,600), John Wyndham's *The Day of the Triffids* (£1,020) and Anthony Burgess' *A Clockwork Orange* (£1,680). Condition varied, and not all were first editions.

In early June, the Roald Dahl Museum and Story Centre opened its *Charlie and the Chocolate Factory* gates in the late author's home village of Great Missenden, in Buckinghamshire. The museum included an archive of Dahl's work, interactive exhibits and a reading centre.

Lord Loss and *Demon Thief* were the first and second volumes in "The Demonata" young adult series by the very popular "Darren Shan" (Darren O'Shaughnessy).

The first three titles in a new series by R. L. Stine, *Fear Street Nights: Moonlight Secrets*, *Midnight Games* and *Darkest Dawn* were set in a bar called "Nights".

Raven's Gate was the first volume in Anthony Horowitz's "The Gatekeepers" series.

The Hollow: Horseman and *The Hollow: Drowned*, by Christopher Golden and Ford Lytle Gilmore, were the first two volumes in a new series about a group of teenagers who unknowingly set in motion a curse in the town of Sleepy Hollow.

A hip-hop rock legend found himself on a train travelling with the newly dead in Sean Wright's *Dark Tales of Time and Space*, a novel aimed at older teenagers and published by Crowswing Books in a 1,000-copy paperback edition, a 470-copy hardcover and a 30-copy slipcased edition.

A boy searched for his missing brother in *The Devil's Footprints* by E. E. Richardson, and the spirit of a murdered teenager discovered that her killer was about to strike again in *The Innocent's Story* by Nicky Singer.

Incubus was written by Keith Brooke and published under the pseudonym "Nick Gifford". A Native American legend became real in Joseph Bruchac's *Whisper in the Dark*, and a strange maze led to a different reality in William Sleator's *The Last Universe*.

Red is for Remembrance was the third volume in Laurie Faria Stolarz's series about a Wiccan teenager who dreamed about murders that had yet to happen.

Witch Season: Winter was the fourth and final volume in the series by Jeff Mariotte, while *The Witch of Clatteringshaws* was the eleventh volume in the "Wolves of Willoughby Chase" series by the late Joan Aiken. The volume included story notes by the author's daughter, Lizza Aiken.

The Seer: Last Dance and *The Seer: Witch Bell*, both by Linda Joy Singleton (aka "L. J. Singleton"), were the second and third books in the mystery series about psychic teenager Sabine.

Cate Tiernan's *Balefire: A Circle of Ashes* was the second book in a series about teenage twins with supernatural powers, and *Midnighters 2: Touching Darkness* was the second volume in Scott Westerfeld's series about a young girl discovering her paranormal powers, who was hunted by the creatures of the dark and the light.

Tales from the Dark Side: Blood on Snow was the first in a new series of ghostly novels aimed at teenagers by Tim Bowler, illustrated by Jason Cockcroft. A boy's grandmother trapped ghosts by feeding them in *A Gathering of Shades* by David Stahler, Jr.

Meg Cabot continued her series about a girl who could talk to the dead in *The Mediator 6: Twilight*, and a boy attracted the attention of a long-dead girl in an abandoned house in A. M. Jenkins' *Beating Heart*.

A boy was the only person who could see the ghost of a young girl in Laura Whitcomb's debut, *A Certain Slant of Light*, while Eileen Rosenbloom's first novel, *Stuck Down*, chronicled the exploits of a dead teenager.

Stephanie Meyer's first book was the YA vampire novel *Twilight*, *Bloodline* by Kate Cary was a semi-sequel to *Dracula*, and *Kissing Coffins* by Ellen Schreiber was the sequel to *Vampire Kisses*.

High School Bites was the first in the "Lucy Chronicles" by Liza Conrad, while a group of women accidentally infected with a parasite were turned into vampires in Scott Westerfeld's *Peeps*.

Vampire Plagues: Paris, *Vampire Plagues: Mexico* and *Vampire Plagues: Epidemic* were the latest volumes in the Scholastic series by the pseudonymous "Sebastian Rook".

Got Fangs? and *Circus of the Damned* by Katie Maxwell (aka "Katie MacAlister") were YA romances aimed at teenage girls, in which psychic adolescent Francesca found herself the object of an amorous vampire's affections and accidentally raised a Viking ghost.

Vampirates: Demons of the Ocean featured two shipwrecked twins involved with a ghostly galleon crewed by vampires in the first of Justin Somper's six-book series.

James McCann's *Rancour* was about a werewolf who hunted vampires, and a werewolf's teenage offspring moved to Maine to be with him in Henry Garfield's *My Father the Werewolf*. Stephen Cole's *The Wereling: Prey* was the second volume in the werewolf trilogy about two teens trying to escape a family of lycanthropes.

By These Ten Bones by Clare B. Dunkle was a young adult werewolf novel set in medieval Scotland, while Edo van Belkom's *Lone Wolf* was a sequel to *Wolf Pack* and involved four teenage werewolves.

Wicked Odd: Still More Stories to Chill the Heart was the fourth volume in Steve Burt's self-published series of young adult horror collections.

Invasion of the Road Weenies and Other Warped and Creepy Tales collected thirty-five original stories by David Lubar, and *Bonechillers: 13 Twisted Tales of Terror* was a young adult collection from D. W. Cropper.

Adventure Classics: Edgar Allan Poe Collection featured nine stories and four poems and came with a snap-together model of a pendulum, while *Tales of Terror* collected six illustrated stories by Poe, along with an Introduction by Michael McCurdy and a CD.

Edited by Ted Thompson and Eli Horowitz, and featuring eleven stories (three reprints) by Neil Gaiman, Kelly Link and others, *Noisy Outlaws, Unfriendly Blobs, and Some Other Things That Aren't as Scary, Maybe . . . Depending on How You Feel About Lost Lands, Stray Cellphones, Creatures from the Sky, Parents Who Disappear in Peru, a Man Named Lars Farf, and One Other Story We Couldn't Quite Finish, So Maybe You Could Help Us Out* was certainly the longest-titled anthology of the year. Published by McSweeny's Books with an Introduction by Lemony Snicket, proceeds from the book went to 826NYC, a non-profit tutoring centre in New York.

Looking for Jake, the first short story collection from Arthur C. Clarke Award-winning author China Miéville, contained fourteen stories (three original, plus a new graphic tale illustrated by Liam Sharp). Regrettably, the book lacked an Introduction or any story notes by the author.

From Dinoship, *Dead Travel Fast* collected ten previously published short stories and novellas by Kim Newman with new afterwords by the author, and Chuck Palahniuk's *Haunted* collected a number of linked stories based around a group of writers trapped inside an old movie palace.

Brian Lumley's *The House of Cthulhu: Tales of the Primal Land, Volume I*, was a reprint collection of ten previously published Lovecraftian stories with a new cover painting by Bob Eggleton.

Hotel Midnight: A Collection of Short Stories from Robert Hale contained twelve stories (nine reprints) by Simon Clark, along with an Introduction by the author.

From Thunder's Mouth Press, *The Emperor of Gondwanaland and Other Stories* collected eighteen reprint tales by Paul Di Filippo, including collaborations with Don Webb and Barry Malzberg, while *Different Kinds of Dead and Other Tales* contained fifteen stories by Ed Gorman.

Named after the eponymous California bookstore, *Dark Delicacies* co-edited by Del Howison and Jeff Gelb certainly attracted the Big Names. Out of the nineteen original tales, the best work came from such old hands as Ray Bradbury, Ramsey Campbell, Gahan Wilson and, especially, Clive Barker. Other authors represented included Whitley Strieber, F. Paul Wilson, Roberta Lannes, Brian Lumley, John Farris, William F. Nolan, David J. Schow and the late Richard Laymon, while Richard Matheson contributed a very brief Foreword. Unfortunately, despite this stellar line-up, the anthology did not turn out to be "the most significant horror anthology in the past twenty-five years", as Gelb claimed in his overly enthusiastic Introduction.

Co-edited by Nancy Holder and Nancy Kilpatrick, *Outsiders: 22 All New Stories from the Edge* was a mostly-original anthology (one reprint) struggling to find a unifying theme. That didn't stop it from containing some fine work, with an impressive line-up of names that included Neil Gaiman, Steve Rasnic Tem, Tanith Lee, David J. Schow, Caitlín R. Kiernan, Jack Ketchum, Elizabeth Massie, Kathe Koja, John Shirley, Poppy Z. Brite, Brian Hodge and Joe R. Lansdale, amongst many others.

Lost on the Darkside: Voices from the Edge of Horror was the third in editor John Pelan's series of original paperback anthologies from Roc. It contained fifteen modern horror stories by such authors as Tony Richards, Maria Alexander, Ramsey Campbell, David B. Silva, Mark Samuels, Michael Reaves, Jeffrey Thomas, Jessica

Amanda Salmonson, Joseph Nassie, David Niall Wilson, Gerard Houarner and the editor himself.

Edited by Martin H. Greenberg, *All Hell Breaking Loose* contained sixteen satanic stories from such authors as P.N. Elrod, Tom Piccirilli and Dean Wesley Smith, with an Introduction by John Helfers. *In the Shadow of Evil* co-edited by Greenberg and Helfers featured fourteen stories in which Good was defeated by Evil, from Tanya Huff, Gregory Benford and others

From Oxford University Press, *Late Victorian Gothic Tales* collected twelve stories with an extensive Introduction and notes by editor Roger Luckhurst. Edited by Gary Lachman, *The Dedalus Occult Reader: The Garden of Hermetic Dreams* collected nineteen stories and novel excerpts.

What Dreams May Come contained three supernatural romance stories by Sherrilyn Kenyon, Robin Owens and Rebecca York, while *Hot Spell* conjured up four supernatural romance stories featuring vampires, demons and other creatures by Emma Holly, Lora Leigh, Meljean Brook and Shiloh Walker. *Sex and the Single Witch* was another supernatural romance anthology containing work by Theresa Alan, Carly Alexander and Holly Chamberlin.

Edited by Greg Wharton, *The Big Book of Erotic Ghost Stories* contained twenty stories (seven reprints). *Blood Surrender* was an anthology of sixteen erotic horror stories (three reprints) from Nancy Kilpatrick, Maria Alexander and others, edited by Cecilia Tan.

Published by the Science Fiction Book Club, *The Fair Folk* was an original hardcover anthology edited by Marvin Kaye that featured six new novellas about elves, not all of them benevolent, by Tanith Lee, Megan Lindholm, Jane Yolen and Midori Snyder, Patricia McKillip and Kim Newman (featuring Charles Beauregard of the Diogenes Club).

Transgressions edited by Ed McBain contained ten novellas by leading crime writers, including a ghost story by Stephen King inspired by the events of 9/11. Other contributors included John Farris, Walter Mosley, Joyce Carol Oates and McBain himself.

As always ably edited by Ellen Datlow, Kelly Link and Gavin J. Grant, *The Year's Best Fantasy and Horror: Eighteenth Annual Collection* from St. Martin's Griffin contained forty-four stories, plus seven summations of the year and the usual list of "Honorable Mentions".

The Mammoth Book of Best New Horror Volume Sixteen collected twenty-one stories and novellas (including two by Neil Gaiman), along with an extensive overview of the year in horror by editor Stephen Jones, a detailed "Necrology" by Jones and Kim Newman, and a listing of "Useful Addresses".

The two anthologies overlapped with just two stories, by Stephen Gallagher and Tina Rath.

Editor Ellen Datlow's weekly *Sci Fiction* posted excellent stories online throughout the year by Steve Rasnic Tem, Pat Cadigan (a vampire story), John Sladek, Kim Newman (a Richard Jeperson novella), Fritz Leiber, Gahan Wilson, Tom Reamy and others. However, in November, parent company SciFi.com announced that after more than five years it would be discontinuing the prestigious site at the end of the year, despite the webzine winning Datlow the 2005 Hugo Award for Best Editor.

February marked editor Judi Rohrig's two-year anniversary as editor and publisher of the informative weekly electronic newsletter *Hellnotes*.

Issue #609 of *Amazing Stories* was made available as an exclusive download from Paizo.com. It featured fiction by Ben Bova, Robert Sheckley, George Zebrowski and Sarah A. Hoyt, plus articles on the movie *Constantine*, Clive Barker's *Renaissance Man* project, and the film of Ray Bradbury's *A Sound of Thunder*. Downloads were free to subscribers.

The Australian webzine *Horrorscope* began including reviews of magazines from around the world, including *Weird Tales*, *Book of Dark Wisdom* and *Crimewave*, while also running interviews with Australian authors such as Kaaron Warren, Paul Haines and Brett McBean.

Shadow Box was described as a "fusion of flash fiction and dark art lashed together with multimedia nastiness". The e-anthology edited by Shane Jiraiya Cummings and Angela Challis was the first release from Australia's Brimstone Press and contained seventy mostly original stories, with profits going to charity and supporting The Australian Horror Writers Association.

Darkness Rising 2005 was a hardcover print-on-demand anthology edited by L. H. Maynard and M. P. N. Sims for Prime Books. The attractive-looking hardcover featured twenty original stories by Steve Duffy, William P. Simmons, Cyril Simsa, Mark McLaughlin, Peter Tennant, Scott Emerson Bull and Paul Finch, amongst others.

Also from Prime, *In the Palace of Repose* was a stunning debut collection of nine stories (seven original) by Canadian writer Holly Phillips, with an Introduction by Sean Stewart.

The Empty House and Other Ghost Stories was a print-on-demand edition of Algernon Blackwood's 1906 collection from Wildside Press/Prime Classics Library. *The Bowmen and Other Legends of the War* reprinted Arthur Machen's 1915 collection of five stories, and *The Room in the Dragon Volant* was a reprint on the 1872 novel by J. Sheridan Le Fanu.

Wildside Press also continued its series of facsimile pulp magazine reprints with the September 1st, 1919 issue of *The Thrill Book* and the first issue of *Sinister Stories*, dated February 1940.

From the same imprint, *Dark Duets: Musical Mayhem*, contained fifteen fictional collaborations (eight original) between Michael McCarty and Mark McLaughlin, P. D. Cacek, Charlee Jacob and others. Bentley Little supplied the Introduction.

Fewer stories and a larger typeface would have benefited *Poe's Progeny*, edited by Gary Fry and subtitled *An Anthology of Contemporary Stories Inspired by Classic Dark Fiction*. Available from Gray Friar Press with an Introduction by Michael Marshall Smith and an evocative cover illustration by Robert Sammelin, the book contained thirty stories connected to writers or sometimes spurious "themes" ("genre character", "the movies", "modern master") by Mike O'Driscoll, Mark Morris, Tim Lebbon, Joel Lane, Chico Kidd (a Luís da Silva adventure), Nicholas Royle, Stephen Volk, Adam L. G. Nevill, Simon Clark, Donald R. Burleson, Ramsey Campbell and others, including the editor.

From the same editor and imprint, *Bernie Herrmann's Manic Sextet* contained six dark novelettes by Mike O'Driscoll, Paul Finch, Donald Pulker, Andrew Hook, Gary McMahon, Adam L. G. Nevill, Rhys Hughes and Simon Strantzas.

The fifth volume of *Polyphony*, edited by Deborah Layne and Jay Lake for Oregon's Wheatland Press, featured thirty-one original stories by Iain Rowan, Bruce Holland Rogers, Jeff VanderMeer, Forrest Aguirre, Ray Vukcevich, Leslie What and the late d.g.k. Goldberg, amongst others.

Lake also edited *TEL: Stories* for the same imprint, an original anthology of twenty-eight eclectic stories (two reprints) by such authors as Ian Creasey, Tim Pratt, Dean Wesley Smith, Greg Beatty, Forrest Aguirre, Jeff VanderMeer and Gregory Feeley.

From Raw Dog Screaming Press, John Edward Lawson's *Last Burn in Hell* was a modern horror novel in which a man recalled his life while dangling over a lava pit. Also available were volumes #7 and #8 of *Bare Bone*, edited by Kevin L. Donihe and featuring fiction by Gary Fry, John R. Platt, Donald R. Burleson, Robert

Dunbar, C.J. Henderson, Gary McMahon, Michael A. Arnzen and Charlee Jacob.

Published by Two Backed Books, an imprint of Raw Dog Screaming Press, *The Book of a Thousand Suns* collected fifteen disturbing stories (nine original) by former World Class Heavyweight kickboxer Wrath James White. From the same imprint, *Tempting Disaster* was an anthology of stories exploring sexual taboos, edited by John Edward Lawson and featuring contributions by Jeffrey Thomas and Michael Hemmington.

John Shirley's 1988 novel *In Darkness Waiting*, about a small Oregon town invaded by insectoid evil, appeared in revised and updated trade paperback and hardcover editions from Infrapress, with a new self-congratulatory Foreword by the author.

Horror Between the Sheets was an anthology of twenty-three stories drawn from *Cthulhu Sex* magazine, with contributions by Mark McLaughlin and others.

From Hippocampus Press, *Tales Out of Dunwich* edited by Robert M. Price was an anthology of ten Lovecraftian stories (one original) from Jack Williamson, Richard A. Lupoff, Nancy A. Collins and others.

Published by Elder Signs Press, Tim Curran's novel *Hive* was a sequel to H. P. Lovecraft's *At the Mountains of Madness*, set in a series of caverns discovered beneath the South Pole. *Horrors Beyond: Tales of Terrifying Realities* was available from the same imprint, edited by William Jones. The anthology contained eighteen Lovecraftian stories (one reprint) by Curran, James S. Dorr, Gerard Houarner, C. J. Henderson and Richard A. Lupoff, amongst others. Both books boasted impressive cover artwork by Dave Carson.

Also out as a print-on-demand title from Elder Signs Press, *Terrors* was a collection of sixteen stories by Richard A. Lupoff, several of them pastiches of H. P. Lovecraft.

Chuck Palahniuk had nice words to say about *Angel Dust Apocalypse*, a collection of twenty stories (eleven reprints) by Jeremy Robert Johnson from Eraserhead Press.

Available from Chimericana Books, editor Mike Philbin's *Chimeraworld #2* contained twenty-three original tales by Steve Lockley & Paul Lewis, Kurt Newton, Quentin S. Crisp, Ken Goldman, Suzanne Church, Tony Richards, John Meany and others.

Edited with an Introduction by Charles R. Dinkins, *Modern Witches, Wizards, and Magic* from Kerlak Enterprises contained sixteen magical stories (ten original).

Gaston Leroux's *The Phantom of the Opera* was newly translated by Jean-Marc Lofficier and Randy Lofficier, who also contributed an original story. Available on-demand from Black Coat Press, the book was illustrated by forty-seven artists. From the same imprint, *Tales of the Shadowmen 1: The Modern Babylon* collected fourteen pastiche pulp stories by Robert Sheckley, Brian Stableford and others, while Paul Féval's 1878 novella *The Wandering Jew's Daughter* (*La Fille du Juif Errant*) was translated and introduced by Stableford.

Carrie Masek's *Twice Damned* from Mundania Press was about a Nazi-created vampire who learned that others of his kind had also survived. Available from California's Midnight Library, J. F. Gonzalez's *The Beloved* concerned a race of emotional vampires co-existing with humans.

Watchers: Culloden! was the third volume in William Meikle's trilogy, available from KHP Industries/Black Death Books, while the hunt for a lost heirloom by Glasgow private investigator Derek Adams led to Lovecraftian horrors in Meikle's *The Midnight Eye Files: The Amulet.*

The Blackest Death Volume II edited by The Staff of Black Death Books was an anthology of twenty-four original horror stories.

KHP also teamed up with Demonic Clown Books to publish Steve Vernon's Wild West horror novel, *Long Horn Big Shaggy*, along with *Night of the Loving Dead*, James Futch and James Newman's novella about zombies and the Mafia.

Rough Magic by John William Houghton was an occult thriller from Unlimited Publishing.

The Apartment Building Next Door collected six horror stories and six poems by Joseph R. Grych, available from AuthorHouse.

From Phosphor Lantern Press, *Songs & Sonnets Atlantean: The Third Series* was the final collection of poet/performer Donald Sidney-Fryer's 44-year extension of the type of verse and prose-poems achieved by the California Romantics. Terence McVicker supplied the brief Introduction.

From classy small press imprint Hill House Publishers, *The Cat's Pajamas: Stories +5* was a beautifully designed and expanded edition of Ray Bradbury's 2004 collection, with amusing illustrations by the author. It was limited to 1,000 numbered and fifty-two lettered slipcased copies, all signed by Bradbury.

Also from Hill House, the first of the publisher's holiday Christmas Books was a beautifully hand-crafted edition of Fitz-James O'Brien's 1858 story *Little Red Kriss Kringle*, limited to just fifty hardcover copies and issued in an illustrated envelope.

In January, Jeff VanderMeer's Ministry of Whimsy Press ended its short-lived association with Night Shade Books after its founder confirmed that he wanted to direct his energies towards his own writing and editing projects.

Meanwhile, Night Shade's "Lost Wellman" series kicked off with two attractive hardcover volumes by the late Manly Wade Wellman. *Strangers on the Heights* and *Giants from Eternity* each collected two pulp magazine novellas that had remained unpublished for decades.

Terry Lamsley's 1996 collection *Conference with the Dead* was reissued by Night Shade in trade hardcover and as a signed, limited edition that included an extra story.

Ramsey Campbell's new serial killer novel, *Secret Stories*, about an author who committed murder to overcome his writer's block, appeared from PS Publishing in a signed hardcover edition of 500 trade and 200 deluxe slipcased copies, with an Introduction by Jeremy Dyson.

Mark Morris' latest novel, *Nowhere Near an Angel*, was about a man whose punk-rock past came back to haunt him. With an Introduction by Stephen Gallagher, it was also available in trade hardcover and deluxe slipcase, signed by both contributors.

PS also published a limited edition of Graham Joyce's *TWOC*, a comedic supernatural thriller in which a teenage car thief was haunted by his dead brother after a fatal crash. Rob Grant supplied the Introduction.

Don't Turn Out the Light was the latest volume in the revived "Not at Night" series of anthologies edited by Stephen Jones. It contained seventeen stories (nine original) by Ray Bradbury, Richard Matheson, Terry Lamsley, David J. Schow, Charles L. Grant, Peter Atkins, Roberta Lannes, John Burke, Basil Copper, Hugh B. Cave and others, plus interior illustrations by Randy Broecker. It was published in a 500-copy hardcover edition signed by the editor and 200 numbered and slipcased copies signed by all the living contributors.

With an Introduction by Christopher Golden, Joe Hill's first collection, *20th Century Ghosts*, was probably the most talked-about book debut of the year and set to become a modern collectible. Containing fifteen often remarkable horror stories (two original, plus another hidden away in the Acknowledgments), it was available from PS as a 1,000-copy trade paperback, a 500-copy trade hardcover signed by the author, and a 200-copy slipcased edition signed by both Hill and Golden.

Little Machines was the long-awaited new collection from Paul McAuley. Boasting a wraparound dust-jacket by the legendary Chesley Bonestell, it contained seventeen previously-published stories, along with a brief Introduction by Greg Bear and an Afterword by the author.

Available from PS Publishing in editions of 500 trade hardcovers and 200 slipcased editions signed by the author, Ray Bradbury's classic 1960s collections *R is for Rocket* and *S is for Space* featured new Forewords and Introductions by Arthur C. Clarke and Tim Powers, and Ray Harryhausen and Michael Marshall Smith, respectively. Both books also came in 100 special slipcased sets signed by all the contributors, along with a bonus new Bradbury collection, *Forever and the Earth: Yesterday and Tomorrow Stories*, containing eleven reprint stories originally dropped from *S is for Space* and various correspondence and notes. The books were also profusely illustrated with the magazine artwork that accompanied each story's original appearance.

One of the best anthologies of the year was *Taverns of the Dead* edited by Kealan Patrick Burke, containing twenty-seven stories (nine reprints) about pubs and drinking by Ramsey Campbell, Jack Cady, Neil Gaiman, Thomas Ligotti, Roberta Lannes, Christopher Fowler, Charles L. Grant, Peter Straub, David Morrell, C. Bruce Hunter, Chaz Brenchley, Tim Lebbon, Chet Williamson, Terry Lamsley and others. F. Paul Wilson supplied the Introduction.

CD also published Burke's novel *The Hides*, about a boy who helped the dead find their murderers. It was published in a 750-copy signed edition and a leather-bound lettered edition of twenty-six copies.

Edited by Peter Crowther, *Fourbodings: A Quartet of Uneasy Tales from Four Members of the Macabre* contained four novellas by Terry Lamsley, Simon Clark, Tim Lebbon and Mark Morris. Along with the twenty-six traycased copies, there was a 1,000-copy signed edition.

Hornets and Others collected seventeen horror stories (two original) by Al Sarrantonio, while *Zero* was the fourth book in F. Paul Wilson's *Sims* quartet about chimpanzees genetically modified with human genes. Both books were limited to 750 signed copies and twenty-six lettered.

Ray Garton's *Scissors* was about the return of a childhood nightmare and had a 1,000-copy trade edition from CD.

In the Cemetery Dance novella series, a meteor shower interrupted a lakeside vacation in *Blue November Storms* by Brian Freeman, while Geoff Cooper's *Retribution* was part of the author's "Brackard's Point" series. Both were available as 750-copy signed hardcovers.

The arrival of crows in the coastal town of Black Stone Bay, Rhode Island, presaged a much more powerful evil in James A. Moore's Halloween vampire novel *Blood Red*. It was published by Paul Miller's Earthling Publications in a 500-copy signed and numbered edition, and a fifteen-copy lettered edition signed by all the contributors, including cover artist "Edward Miller" (Les Edwards) and Simon Clark, who contributed the Introduction.

Home Before Dark: The Collected Cedar Hill Stories Volume 2 contained nineteen tales (two original, the others revised and corrected) by Gary A. Braunbeck along with related items about the haunted town. Illustrated by Deena Warner, it was also limited to a 500-copy signed and numbered edition and fifteen traycased lettered copies.

In Erik Tomblin's original novella *Riverside Blues*, a wife who disappeared half a century earlier mysteriously returned to her husband. It was published by Earthling in a signed edition of 300 numbered softcovers and fifteen lettered hardcovers, with an Introduction by James Newman.

China Miéville's 1998 novel *King Rat* was reissued by Earthling in 400 numbered slipcased copies and a fifteen-copy lettered traycased edition. The handsome-looking volume included an original Introduction by Clive Barker, a new Afterword by the author, and black and white illustrations by Richard Kirk.

From the same imprint, *Song of Kali: 20th Anniversary Edition* was an attractive signed hardcover of Dan Simmons' classic novel, with a new Introduction by the author. It was available in an edition of 400 numbered and fifteen lettered slipcased copies.

From Fedogan & Bremer, *Weird Shadows Over Innsmouth* was a follow-up to editor Stephen Jones' 1994 anthology *Shadows Over Innsmouth*. It contained eleven Lovecraftian stories and novellas by Brian Lumley, Ramsey Campbell, Kim Newman, Michael Marshall Smith, Paul J. McAuley, Hugh B. Cave, Richard A. Lupoff, Caitlín R. Kiernan, Basil Copper and others. With a wraparound dust-jacket by Bob Eggleton, the book featured interior artwork by Eggleton, Randy Broecker, Les Edwards and Allan Servoss and was available in a trade hardcover edition and a 100-copy signed and numbered slipcased edition.

To tie-in with his Guest of Honour appearance at the World Fantasy Convention in Madison, Twilight Tales released a trade paperback edition of Robert Weinberg's *The Occult Detective*. It reprinted seven stories featuring psychic detective Sidney Taine, with an Introduction by Stefan Dziemianowicz.

Illustrated by Shelley Jackson, *Magic for Beginners* was the second collection of Kelly Link's short fiction from Small Beer Press. The book contained nine stories (three original) and came with glowing quotes from *The Village Voice*, *New York Magazine*, Michael Chabon and China Miéville, amongst others. A set of playing cards, also illustrated by Jackson, was used to promote the book.

Published by Westwood St Thomas School/Beccon Publications in a 125-copy numbered hardcover edition signed by all the contributors (which quickly sold out) and a 800-copy paperback edition signed by the author, *Black Dust & Other Tales of Interrupted Childhood* contained three reprint stories by Graham Joyce, selected by editor Bob Wardzinski along with an Introduction by Mark Chadbourn, additional contributions by Jeffrey Ford and Jeff VanderMeer and an Afterword by the author. All the contributors to the book (including designer Michael Marshall Smith, the printer and the publisher), donated their work for free to raise as much money as possible to establish a bursary for students at the Nqabakazulu Secondary School near Durban, South Africa.

From Side Real Press/Northern Gothic and produced with funding from the Arts Council of England, *Phantoms at the Phil* was a book and CD recording of live ghost story readings by Sean O'Brien, Gail-Nina Anderson and Chaz Brenchley at the Literary & Philosophical Society of Newcastle-upon-Tyne in 2004. Limited to 300 numbered and signed hardcover copies, the slim volume included an introductory essay by Ramsey Campbell about his own spooky encounters.

Al Sarrantnio's *The Pumpkin Boy: A Tale of Halloween*, the latest entry in the author's "Orangefield Cycle", was the third volume in the Endeavor Press Novelette Series. Nicely illustrated by Keith Minnion, with a cover by Alan M. Clark, the book was available in a 200-copy signed limited edition and a $100 lettered edition.

From Necessary Evil Press, *Pieces of Hate* was a new novella by Tim Lebbon, in which Gabriel and the demon Temple from the author's *Dead Man's Hand* found themselves involved with cut-throat pirates. With an Introduction by Brian Keene and artwork by Caniglia, the slim volume was limited to a signed and numbered edition of 450 softcovers and twenty-six hardcovers.

Boasting an impressive cover illustration by John Picacio, *Adventure Vol.1* edited by Chris Roberson was the first volume in a new series of adventure pulp anthologies. It contained seventeen original stories by Mike Resnick, John Meaney, Lou Anders, Kage Baker, Paul Di Filippo, Kim Newman, Michael Kurland, Michael Moorcock and the editor himself.

From Welsh imprint Pendragon Press, Stuart Young's *The Mask Behind the Face* was an attractive collection of four stories (two original) with an Introduction by Mark Samuels.

From the same imprint, Mark West's *In the Rain with the Dead* was a first novel about demonic lust that came with enthusiastic quotes from T. M. Gray and Brian Keene, and Liz Williams supplied the Introduction to *An Occupation of Angels*, a new novella about celestial invasion by Lavie Tidhar.

Published by Cold Spring Press, *The Shadow at the Bottom of the World* was a "Best of" collection containing sixteen stories and an Introduction by Thomas Ligotti. Edited with a foreword by Douglas A. Anderson, most of the stories had been previously collected and were arranged in the order they were written.

Produced by Biting Dog Press in hand-crafted editions, Jack Ketchum's Indian fable *The Transformed Mouse: A Parable from the Panchatantra* was available in a 250-copy signed and numbered edition and a twenty-six copy lettered edition, while Edgar Allan Poe's *The Raven* was limited to just sixty-five numbered copies with wood engravings by George A. Walker.

From Ash-Tree Press, *Sea Mist* contained seventeen stories and was the fifth and final volume in the "Collected Spook Stories" of E. F. Benson, edited by Jack Adrian and covering the period 1927 to the author's death in 1940.

Mr. Justice Harbottle and Others: Ghost Stories 1870–73 was the third and final volume collecting the supernatural fiction of Joseph Sheridan Le Fanu, edited by Jim Rockhill.

The Watcher by the Threshold collected all the major supernatural stories (twenty-eight) by John Buchan, with an Introduction by Kenneth Hillier, Secretary of The John Buchan Society.

First published in 1919, *The Motion Demon* collected the railroad stories of Polish author Stefan Grabinski, translated by Miroslaw Lipinski and available in an edition of 500 copies.

Harry Ludlam's short novel *The Coming of Jonathan Smith* was originally published in 1964 and was the fourth volume from the "Ash-Tree Press Classic Macabre" paperback imprint.

A man discovered that his dead father had been involved in a blood ritual that had released something evil in Shane Ryan Staley's novel *The Cleansing*, published by Bloodletting Press,

British short film writer and director Frazer Lee was the author of

Urbane and Other Horror Tales, a collection of four reprint stories and six previously unpublished short screenplays, issued in trade paperback format by Robber Baron Productions with a blurb by Tobe Hooper.

Coming in at a hefty 400 pages-plus, the second volume of editor Mark Pilkington's *Strange Attractor* was an impressive-looking volume featuring fiction and articles celebrating popular culture by Graham Harvey, John Coulthart, Roger Dobson and many others.

D.F. Lewis' fifth "nemonymous" anthology, *Nemo Book 5*, contained twelve stories whose uncredited authors would be identified in the next volume. Among those revealed to have had stories in the 2004 edition were Jay Lake, Keith Brooke, Allen Ashley, Gary McMahon and Andrew Hook.

Edited by Vincent Sneed, *Dark Furies: Weird Tales of Beauties & Beasts* was an anthology from Baltimore's Die Monster Die imprint of fifteen mostly original stories about women and monsters, with an Introduction by Adam P. Knave. From the same imprint, *The Midnight Hour: Saint Lawn Hill and Other Tales* collected eight stories by James Chambers about radio personality Madeline Night, with illustrations by Jason Whitley.

Gauntlet Press published *Duel & The Distributor: Stories and Screenplays*, which collected two stories and scripts by Richard Matheson, with a Foreword and Afterword by editor Matthew R. Bradley and an interview with actor Dennis Weaver.

Edited with a Preface by Stanley Wiater, *Collected Stories Volume 2* contained twenty-nine of Matheson's short stories written between 1953–58, while *Woman* was a new psychological horror novel by the author, also from Gauntlet. At the launch party in Los Angeles in June, Matheson described it as his "first true horror novel since *Hell House*".

From Overlook Connection Press, Jack Ketchum's *Offspring*, a sequel to his 1981 novel *Off Season* (also reissued in an unexpurgated edition with a special Introduction by Douglas E. Winter), included a new Author's Note and Afterword. It was available in a signed limited edition, a 100-copy Sterling Edition, and a fifty-two copy lettered edition in a handcrafted black wooden box set with pewter bones for $500.00.

F. Paul Wilson's story *The Last Rakosh*, a "Repairman Jack" tale set in a travelling carnival, was expanded to novella length for its first trade hardcover publication, while *The Tery* from the same author was a SF novel about mutation run amok.

The Silence Between the Screams collected five horror stories (four original) by Lucy Taylor. A 1,000-copy signed edition was issued under the author's preferred title, *A Hairy Chest, a Big Dick, and a Harley*, with interior illustrations by Glenn Chadbourne and variant cover art.

Mort Castle's 1980s novels *The Strangers* and *Cursed Be the Child* were reissued in signed 300-copy hardcover and trade paperback editions.

A tenth anniversary edition of Phil Nutman's *Wet Work* included the original short story, a new Afterword by the author and an Introduction by Douglas E. Winter. Also from Overlook, *Smothered Dolls* by A. R. Morlan and *Matinee at the Flame* by Christopher Fahy were new collections of short fiction. All three titles were available in trade paperback, as 500-copy signed hardcovers or twenty-six copy lettered editions for $300.00 apiece.

In Guy Adams' novel *More Than This*, published in paperback by Humdrumming, children were vanishing in the crumbling seaside resort of Gravestown, and thirteen-year-old Gregory Ashe was befriended by the The Magician, a mysterious stranger who could see beyond the limits of reality.

The Tales of Inspector Legrasse from Mythos Books contained H. P. Lovecraft's "The Call of Cthulhu" and a further six stories about Inspector Legrasse's battle against the Cthulhu Mythos by C. J. Henderson.

From Subterranean Press, Caitlín R. Kiernan's third collection of short fiction, *To Charles Fort, with Love*, contained thirteen excellent stories, including the original "*Le Peau Verte*", along with a Preface by the author and an Afterword by Ramsey Campbell. The signed edition was limited to 250 numbered copies and came with a fascinating chapbook entitled *A Little Damned Book of Days*, in which Kiernan reprinted accounts of weird and unexplainable personal encounters.

After being delayed for a couple of years, Subterranean finally published David J. Schow's collection *Zombie Jam* in a signed, limited edition of 750 numbered and twenty-six lettered copies. Featuring eight walking dead stories along with a new Introduction and Afterword by the author, the book was nicely illustrated by Bernie Wrightson.

The Drive-In: The Bus Tour was a new horror novel from Joe R. Lansdale, available as a 1,000-copy signed edition, a 350-copy deluxe edition with added artwork, and a twenty-six copy lettered traycased edition.

Mad Dog Summer and Other Stories collected eight tales (one original) by Lansdale. A 250-copy deluxe slipcased edition was also available containing extra material. Lansdale's *The King and Other Stories* contained the titular story and seventeen short-shorts (some having previously appeared on the author's website), illustrated by Glenn Chadbourne. It was published in a signed edition of 750 numbered hardcover copies and a fifty-two copy lettered edition.

Charles de Lint's *Quicksilver & Shadow* collected seventeen early stories, while *The Hour Before Dawn and Two Other Stories from Newford* was a slim hardcover volume containing one new tale about a haunted private detective with photo-illustrations by the author.

Mr. Fox and Other Feral Tales was an expanded version of Norman Partridge's 1992 collection, containing eleven additional stories, an excerpt from an unpublished zombie novel, a Foreword by Edward Bryant, and a new Introduction by the author. It was released in a signed and numbered edition of 750 copies, and as twenty-six signed traycased copies containing an extra three stories (two original).

Originally published as a BBC online serial, *Ghosts of Albion: Astray* by Amber Benson and Christopher Golden was issued in an edition of 750 numbered and fifty-two lettered editions with illustrations by José R. Nieto.

Bradley Denton's *Laughin' Boy* was a satirical novel about some very different types of superheroes, while Ray Garton's *Night Life* was a belated sequel to his vampire novel *Live Girls*. It was published in a 400-copy signed leather-bound edition and a thirteen-copy lettered edition that sold out before publication.

Edited with an Introduction by Stefan R. Dziemianowicz, *The Fear Planet and Other Unusual Destinations* contained twenty previously uncollected stories by Robert Bloch and was the first volume in "The Reader's Bloch" series. It was available from Subterranean Press in a signed edition of 750 copies and a twenty-six copy lettered edition with cover art by Gahan Wilson.

From Robert Morgan's Sarob Press of Wales, Tony Richards' *Ghost Dance* was a collection of nine stories and novellas (two original), with an Introduction by Graham Joyce. John Glasby's horror novel *The Dark Destroyer*, about something old and terribly evil being awakened, was also available from Sarob in limited and signed slipcased editions.

Basil Copper's *Solar Pons: The Final Cases* from Sarob contained five novellas finally appearing in the author's definitive texts after more than thirty years, along with a reprint Sherlock Holmes story. It was limited to 220 hardcover copies and a deluxe edition of fifty-five copies.

Also by Copper and issued under the Cauchemar imprint in a numbered and signed edition of only 150 copies, *Knife in the Back: Tales of Twilight and Torment* was a slim volume collecting eight horror and suspense stories (six original).

From Telos Publishing, the new edition of Stephen Gallagher's 1987 body-hopping serial killer novel *Valley of Lights* also included a host of bonus material: a new Afterword by the author, a film location diary, an interview with Gallagher by Stephen Laws, and the connected short story "Nightmare, With Angel". It was published in both trade paperback and limited hardcover editions.

In the "Telos Original Novellas" series, Lee Thomas' impressive vampire tale *Parish Damned* was set in a small American seaside town invaded by the undead, while Simon Morden's science fiction/horror story *Another War* involved the discovery of two men who vanished a century before and a machine that could travel between the dimensions.

Published in hardcover by Robert and Nancy Garcia's American Fantasy imprint, *Invisible Pleasures* collected eighteen stories (four original) by Mary Frances Zambreno, with a short Introduction by Jane Yolen and a superb cover painting by Douglas Klauba.

Expanded from a short story, Charlee Jacob's novel *Dread in the Beast* was published by Necro Publications in a 400-copy signed trade paperback and 100-copy hardcover edition. Edward Lee supplied the Introduction.

Thicker Than Water from Tigress Press contained nine original vampire stories by Cullen Bunn, J. P. Edwards, Curtis Hoffmeister and Mark Worthen, while from Shocklines Press, *Dead Souls* collected ten stories (six original) by David G. Barnett with an Introduction by Gerard Houarner.

All Eve's Hallows was the first novel in Dean Wesley Smith's exploits of "The City Knights", a thousand-year-old secret organization charged with protecting humanity from the creatures of darkness. Published in trade paperback by Phobos Books, a young female ex-marine confronted the evil sprites that were spreading destruction throughout New York City.

Death Sentences: Tales of Punishment and Revenge collected five stories by Matthew Warner (two original), with an Introduction by Gary A. Braunbeck. It was limited to 250 signed copies from Undaunted Press.

Edited by Harrison Howe, *Dark Notes from NJ* from the Garden State Horror Writers Press was a softcover anthology inspired by the songs of New Jersey musicians. The book featured fourteen original stories, by John Passarella, Mary SanGiovanni and others, including the editor, along with a Foreword by Brian Keene. The inclusion of musician biographies was a nice touch.

Published by Crescent Books, with support from the Scottish Arts Council, *Nova Scotia: New Scottish Speculative Fiction* was an anthology of twenty-one new stories and a poem edited by Neil Williamson and Andrew J. Wilson, with an Introduction by David Pringle. Contributors included Ken MacLeod, Hal Duncan, Jane Yolen, Charles Stross, John Grant, Jack Deighton and both editors.

Limited to 100 copies, *Assembly of Rogues* from PurpleRage Productions/Rainfall Books comprised a paperback anthology (thirteen stories), music CD, and DVD interviews with Ramsey Campbell, Mark Morris, Graham Joyce, Tim Lebbon, Paul Finch, Peter Crowther, Mark Chadbourn, Simon Clark, John B. Ford, Paul Kane and others.

Paul van Heuklom and Craig Hargis' *Little Girl Blue* from PublishAmerica was an irreverent and humorous novel about New Orleans evil which one commentator apparently described as "Clive Barker on crack".

From TripleTree Publishing, *Ghosts at the Coast: The Best of Ghost Story Weekend Vol.2* edited by Dianna Rodgers was an anthology of twenty-five original stories, and A. S. Mott collected five new ghostly tales in *Haunting Fireside Stories*, published in softcover by Canada's Ghost House Books.

The Grinding House, from Australia's Canberra Speculative Fiction Guild (CSfG) Publishing, collected a mixed bag of nineteen stories (four original, including the title novella) by Aurealis Award-winning author Kaaron Warren, with a brief Introduction by Donna Maree Hanson.

Founders Peter Atkins and Glen Hirshberg took their Rolling Darkness Revue on the road for a second year in October to five California bookstores. Once again combining music with fiction readings, guest stars on the "Darkness Rising" tour included Michael Blumlein, Nancy Holder, Robert Masello, Robert Morrish and Tamara Thorne. Earthling Publications produced a 250-copy chapbook of mostly original stories, and there was also a T-shirt and button badge available.

Issued by Earthling as a slim no-frills chapbook produced exclusively for the World Horror Convention in New York City, *Blood Tide* was a prequel to James A. Moore's novel *Blood Red* from the same imprint. The publisher also released two other chapbooks at the convention, *Little Lost Angel* by Erik Tomblin and *After the Elephant Ballet* by Gary A. Braunbeck, and all three titles were limited to just 250 copies.

Gary Braunbeck also had a chapbook out from Chicago's Endeavor Press. *We Now Pause for Station Identification* was limited to 500 signed copies.

From Borderlands Press, the initial volume in the *Dark Voices* series was *Horn of Plenty* by Thomas F. Monteleone. It came with an audio CD recording of the author reading the story.

Published by Shocklines Press in a numbered and signed edition of 225 copies, Steve Rasnic Tem's *A Small Room* was about a woman's secret life. *The World Recalled* was another bizarre story by Tem, issued both in chapbook and hardcover format by Wormhole Books with illustrations (many in full colour) by the author.

Two Twisted Nuts, from Novello Publishers, featured two testicular terror tales by Jeff Strand and Nick Cato and was limited to 500 copies. From the same publisher and limited to 250 copies, *Right House on the Left* included three hysterically haunted tales by Steve Vernon, Mark McLaughlin and L. L. Soares, along with an Introduction by James A. Moore.

Christopher M. Cevasco's Lovecraftian short story *Dark Heresy* was published as an individual chapbook by Paradox Publications, limited to just fifteen copies signed by the author, while *Through a Glass Darkly* was a chapbook by Angeline Hawkes-Craig from Naked Snake Press.

The second and third volumes in Iguana Publications' series of chapbooks were *Requiem for the Radioactive Monkeys* and *Bone Ballet*, both edited by John Weagly and featuring stories by J. A. Konrath, Tina L. Jens, Wayne Allen Sallee, James S. Dorr, Martin Mundt and others. Both booklets were limited to 100 copies apiece.

Revenant: A Horror Anthology edited by Armand Rosamilia was a thin volume containing five stories, while *Beastie and Other Horrific Tales* collected six original stories by Rosamilia, both from Carnifex Press.

To celebrate his fiftieth birthday, *The King of the Hill* reprinted Paul McAuley's eponymous fantasy story along with an Introduction by Kim Newman and numerous congratulatory messages. It was limited to just fifty numbered copies.

From Iowa imprint Sam's Dot Publishing, *Eeku* was a slim

collection of "dark scifaiku" by Karen L. Newman, illustrated by 7ARS (Theresa Santitoro) and Sandy DeLuca.

From PS Publishing, editor Peter Crowther's perfect-bound *Post-Scripts* magazine had three editions and featured more excellent short fiction from Chaz Brenchley, Gene Wolfe, Stephen Volk, David Herter, Garry Kilworth, Stephen Baxter, Lawrence Person and the remarkable Joe Hill along with interviews with Lois McMaster Bujold, Richard S. Prather and China Miéville. Ramsey Campbell contributed a guest editorial to the fifth issue, which also added a new subtitle to the masthead: *The A to Z of Fantastic Fiction*. Issues of *PostScripts* were also available in signed, hardcover editions limited to just 150 numbered copies. Subscribers to the magazine also received a special Christmas chapbook by Gene Wolfe.

Weird Tales managed just a single issue in 2005. At least it featured new stories by William F. Nolan (the first of two parts), Jack Williamson, co-editor Darrell Schweitzer, Clark Ashton Smith, Jack Ketchum and Fred Chappell.

In May, John Gregory Betancourt's Wildside Press bought *Weird Tales* outright from Warren Lapine's DNA Publications and took full control from issue #337 onwards. Betancourt re-joined George Scithers and Schweitzer as co-editor of the title, after the trio had originally re-launched the magazine in 1987.

From Wildside imprint Prime Books, the premier issue of *Fantasy Magazine*, edited by Sean Wallace, featured fiction from Tim Pratt, Jeffrey Ford, Jeff VanderMeer, Nick Mamatas and the excellent Holly Phillips.

Another new magazine launched in 2005 was William Schafer's *Subterranean*, published by Subterranean Press. The first two issues included stories by Norman Partridge, Mark Morris, Kealan Patrick Burke, Peter Crowther, Harlan Ellison, Charles Coleman Finlay, Michael Bishop, Robert Silverberg, Joe Hill, Charles de Lint and Jack McDevitt, along with a novel excerpt from Joe R. Lansdale, a teleplay by George R. R. Martin, an interview with Thomas Ligotti, and some excellent illustrations. The second issue was a Caitlín R. Kiernan special, with two stories and an interview with the author.

DNA Publications' long-delayed second issue of *H. P. Lovecraft's Magazine of Horror*, edited by Marvin Kaye, was a Richard Matheson special. It featured a previously unpublished short story by Matheson, plus an article about his movie adaptations and an interview with the author, along with stories and poetry by Tanith Lee, Ray Russell, Jean Paiva, John Glasby, Chris Bunch and H. P. Lovecraft.

Gordon Van Gelder's *The Magazine of Fantasy & Science Fiction* published stories by Alex Irvine, Esther M. Friesner, Ron Goulart, Claudia O'Keefe, M. Rickert, David Gerrold, Marc Laidlaw, Scott Bradfield, Steven Utley, Arthur Porges, Bruce Sterling, Joe Haldeman, Terry Bisson, Gene Wolfe, Elizabeth Hand, Jeffrey Ford, Delia Sherman, Geoff Ryman, Sydney J. Van Scyoc, Gardner Dozois, Alan Dean Foster and many others, along with the usual review columns by Charles de Lint, Elizabeth Hand, Michelle West, James Sallis, Kathi Maio, Lucius Shepard, Paul Di Filippo, Robert K. J. Killheffer and David J. Skal. There were also "Curiosities" columns from Roberto de Sousa Causo, Connie Braton Meek, Bud Webster, Steven Utley, David Langford, Paul Di Filippo, F. Gwynplaine MacIntyre, Darrell Schweitzer, Douglas A. Anderson and Dennis Lien.

The April issue of Shawna McCarthy's *Realms of Fantasy* looked at the fantastic art of Gary Gianni and included a new vampire story by Gene Wolfe.

Richard Chizmar and Robert Morrish published three issues of *Cemetery Dance*, featuring fiction by Stephen Laws, Scott Nicholson, Sèphera Girón, Kealan Patrick Burke, Joel Lane, Eddy C. Bertin, Tim Waggoner, Kim Antieau, Tom Piccirilli, Michael Cadnum, Adam-Troy Castro and a very brief novel excerpt from Stephen King. There were also interviews with Laws, Girón, Chelsea Quinn Yarbro, the late Richard Laymon, Tamara Thorne, Carol Serling, Robert McCammon and Melanie Tem, plus the usual departments and articles by Bev Vncent, Thomas F. Monteleone, Paula Guran, Michael Marano and John Pelan.

Andy Cox's TTA Press managed to turn out two more editions of *The 3rd Alternative* before announcing that the title of the magazine would be changing to *Black Static* with issue #43. Along with a guest editorial by Joel Lane, these issues featured fiction by Scott Nicholson, Chaz Brenchley and Conrad Williams, an interview with Phil Rickman, and columns by Stephen Volk, Allen Ashley and Peter Tennant.

Also from TTA, *Crimewave 8: Cold Harbours* contained seventeen often dark stories by Scott Nicholson, Kristine Kathryn Rusch, Steve Rasnic Tem, Stephen Volk, Joel Lane, Joe Hill, Jay Caselberg, Darren Speegle and others.

TTA also published six issues of *Interzone*, which underwent yet another design change – this time for the better. As the title passed its 200th issue, along with the fiction and usual columns, there were interviews with China Miéville, Susanna Clarke (by her husband, Colin Greenland!), Sarah Ash, Richard Calder and Ian R. MacLeod.

Celebrating its tenth anniversary, the usual two issues of Patrick and Honna Swenson's *Talebones* featured fiction and verse by Nina Kiriki Hoffman, James Van Pelt, Ray Vukcevich and others, along with an interview with Ben Bova, plus all the usual review columns. Jason B. Sizemore's new digest publication, *Apex Science Fiction & Horror Digest*, also featured review columns and interviews, plus fiction from James P. Hogan, James R. Cain, Lavie Tidhar, Ken Rand, Tom Piccirilli, J. A. Konrath and Bryan Smith.

James R. Beach's *Dark Discoveries* entered its second volume with two issues featuring stories by James Newman, Jeffrey Thomas, Michael Laimo, Paul Finch and Shaun Jeffrey, along with interviews with Thomas, Laimo, Graham Masterton, Brian Keene, Craig Spector, Michael A. Arnzen and Shane Staley of Delirium Books.

Issue #4 of Marc Shemmens' *The Horror Express* was billed as a "Tim Lebbon Special", and contained two stories, a bibliographic article and an interview with the author. Dean Koontz and Amy Grech also contributed stories, and there was the usual book and film reviews and poetry. The following issue contained an even more impressive line-up of contributors, including stories by Neil Gaiman, Graham Masterton, Bentley Little and Lavie Tidhar, plus interviews with F. Paul Wilson and Shaun Hutson.

The fifth issue of Trevor Denyer's *Midnight Street* showcased author Tim Lees with two stories, an interview and a bibliography. There was also fiction from Gary Fry, Simon Clark, Marie O'Regan and Allen Ashley, an interview with Simon Clark, and a free twenty-page bibliography of Clark's work, compiled by Tony Mileman.

The third issue of the revived *Argosy*, edited by James A. Owen, featured stories by Steve Rasnic Tem, Zoran Kivkovic, Charles Coleman Finlay and Richard A. Lupoff.

Horror Garage included interviews with Thomas Ligotti, Adrienne Barbeau and Matt Schwartz of Shocklines.com, plus fiction by nobody you probably ever heard of.

The second digest issue of *Allen K's Inhuman Magazine* continued the title's pulp inspiration with new and reprint stories by Joe R. Lansdale, Elizabeth Massie, Michael Laimo, Ramsey Campbell, Thomas F. Monteleone, Brian Lumley and others, all illustrated by editor Allen Koszowski.

The three issues of William Jones' Lovecraftian-inspired digest *Book of Dark Wisdom: The Magazine of Dark Fiction* featured fiction and poetry by David Niall Wilson, Bruce Boston, C. J. Henderson, Amy Grech, A. A. Attanasio, Lavie Tidhar, James S. Dorr, J. Michael Straczynski, Tim Curran and John Weagly, amongst others, along with a regular column by Richard A. Lupoff, interviews with Ramsey Campbell and Douglas Clegg, plus a couple of full-colour covers by Dave Carson.

I'm not sure what Lovecraft would have made of Michael Amorel's *Cthulhu Sex Magazine*, billed as "The Magazine for Connoiseurs of Sensual Horror". The latest two issues contained the usual mix of stories, verse and artwork, much of the latter quite impressive.

Edited by Christopher M. Cevasco, the two issues of *Paradox: The Magazine of Historical and Speculative Fiction* included fiction and poetry by Paul Finch, Carrie Vaughn, D. J. Cockburn, Darrell Schweitzer and Jane Yolen, plus an article about history in the works of Robert E. Howard by Patrice Louinet.

Gordon Linzner's *Space and Time* #99 included fiction and poetry by Darrell Schweitzer, Hugh Cook, Uncle River, Mark McLaughlin and W. Paul Ganley, along with the usual variable artwork.

John O'Neill's always handsome-looking *Black Gate: Adventures in Fantasy Literature* featured fiction from Iain Rowan, Paul Finch, Jay Lake, Muray Leinster and Charles Coleman Finlay, amongst others, along with an interview with Charlene Harris, an interesting overview of the history of Ace Doubles by Rich Horton, and all the usual columns and departments.

Shar O'Brien's *NFG* continued to bill itself as "Writing With Attitude" with fiction and poetry from America, Britain and Canada.

The London Vampyre Group's *Chronicles* changed to a large-size format with full colour covers and included an interview with Kim Harrison, plus articles on the J. S. Le Fanu's *Carmilla*, *Dark Shadows* comics, *Mona the Vampire* and methods of Goth dancing!

The latest incarnation of *Amazing Stories* was put on hiatus with the February issue by Paizo Publishing. A spokesperson claimed that the magazine was "unexpectedly successful".

According to the *UK Press Gazette* in June, accusations of plagiarism were levelled against British horror film magazine *The Dark Side*, edited by Allan Bryce, after a high number of reviews appeared to have been lifted from horror film websites and allegedly recycled without permission, payment or credit. Although Bryce admitted to the theft, and offered to pay a nominal fee to the fans whose thousands of words were appropriated, it was rumoured that "now sacked freelance writer" Gordon Booker was actually a pseudonym for the editor himself.

Canada's *Rue Morgue* continued to be the horror fan's essential guide to the genre. The glossy monthly magazine featured interviews with Douglas Clegg, Jack Ketchum, Tim Lebbon, Thomas Ligotti,

Edward Lee, Stephen Jones, Michael Slade, artist Caniglia, Japanese film-makers Shinya Tsukamoto and Takashi Miike, Jess Franco, composer Graeme Revell, John McNaughton, Michael Rooker, the late Amando de Ossorio, Stuart Gordon, Mick Garris, Bruce Campbell, Clive Barker, Jake West, and the Brothers Quay, along with articles on H. P. Lovecraft, werewolves and pulp magazines.

Clive Barker was one of the guests at *Rue Morgue*'s hugely successful Festival of Fear: Canadian National Horror Expo, held in Toronto over 26–28 August. Other celebrities who attended included Tony Todd, Linda Blair, Elijah Wood, Gunnar Hansen, Ken Foree, Crispin Glover and Elvira Mistress of the Dark.

While disgruntled subscribers still waited for their copies of the long-promised Mario Bava book to appear (publication date was delayed yet again, despite an announced September release date), Tim and Donna Lucas managed to squeeze out eight of the scheduled twelve issues of *Video Watchdog* magazine. Along with the usual DVD, video, audio and book review columns, there were interesting articles on Ray Harryhausen, Universal's lesser-known monsters, David J. Schow's overview of *Day of the Triffids*, Edison's silent *Frankenstein* and an appraisal of the first *Looney Tunes* boxed set. However, we could perhaps have done without the dull interview with Yutte Stensgaard, Larry Blamire's pointless look at 1950s sci-fi heroes, and more inflated Jess Franco coverage.

Richard Valley's *Scarlet Street* came up with a Val Lewton special that included interviews with elusive performers Simone Simon, Elizabeth Russell and Russell Wade.

Empire magazine's *The Story of Sci-Fi* supplement featured contributions from Kim Newman, amongst others.

Stephen King's usually insightful column "The Pop of King" in *Entertainment Weekly* included the author's thoughts on book critics' ignorance of popular fiction (by way of Tom Wolfe's latest novel), Bret Easton Ellis, DVD extras, *Lost*, Halloween and George A. Romero's *Living Dead* series, but more often than not it was simply lazy lists of the author's favourite things. At least the magazine also included a fascinating article by Dalton Ross on the making of 1966 cult movie *Manos: The Hand of Fate*.

The Halloween issue of *Publishers Weekly* included a short feature by Peter Cannon on specialist Burbank bookstore Dark Delicacies and its co-proprietor Del Howison.

The Bulletin of the Science Fiction and Fantasy Writers of America featured interesting articles on copyright, literary criticism, starting your own podcasts and blogs (God forbid!), writing a book a year, editing your own stories, game novelisations, a tribute to Andre Norton, and the Authors Guild lawsuit against Google over potential copyright violations, along with all the usual columns.

Locus featured interviews with Neil Gaiman, Clive Barker, Susanna Clarke, George R. R. Martin, Tim Pratt, Paul McAuley and MonkeyBrain publisher Chris Roberson, amongst others.

The three information-packed issues of Barbara and Christopher Roden's square-bound *All Hallows* included fiction by Rick Kennett, Reggie Oliver and others, articles on Montague Summers, Edgar Wallace, Robert Murray Gilchrist, "The Monkey's Paw", Censorship in Australia, *What's the Matter with Helen?*, *The Monster Club* and *Night Tide*, short interviews with Chico Kidd, Guillermo del Toro and Joel Lane, plus the usual columns by Ramsey Campbell, Roger Dobson and Richard Dalby.

Now a chunky annual anthology, David Longhorn's *Supernatural Tales 9* contained sixteen original stories by Dallas Goffin, Tina Rath, Barbara Roden, Jim Rockhill, Gary Fry, Nina Allan, Paul Finch, Michael Chislett and others.

Issue #26 of Eric M. Heidman's *Tales of the Unanticipated* was a perfect-bound issue packed with fiction and poetry by Stephen Dedman, Gerard Houarner, Uncle River, Judy Klass, Mary Soon Lee, Laurel Winter, Bruce Boston, G.O. Clark and others, including "Edgar Allen Pooh"!

From Kelly Link and Gavin J. Grant's Small Beer Press, the three issues of the literary magazine *Lady Churchill's Rosebud Wristlet* featured fiction and poetry by Bruce McAllister, Stepan Chapman, Amy Sisson, Diana Pharaoh Francis, David Connerley Nahm and Mary A. Turzillo. There was also a non-fiction piece on *The Tenant*, and an offbeat comic strip by Lawrence Schimel and Sara Rojo.

Heather Shaw and Tim Pratt's near-identical publication *Flytrap*, from Tropism Press, included fiction from Karen Meisner, Jay Lake, Jeff VanderMeer, Jeffrey Ford and Sonya Taaffe, poetry by Daphne Gottlieb, and entertaining columns about writing by Nick Mamatas and Jed Hartman.

Edited by John Benson, the two issues of *Not One of Us* included fiction and verse by Terry Black, Kevin L. Donihe, Sonya Taaffe and others,

Published free of charge to promote the website, the quarterly print issues of *Whispers of Wickedness* contained stories and poetry by Peter Tennant, Rhys Hughes, James Harris, Gavin Salisbury and others, along with centrefold news sections. The magazine went to better-quality covers and binding with its Winter 2005 edition and added non-fiction columns to the contents.

Harlan Ellison's personalzine *Rabbit Hole* featured an advance look at the final issue of Dark Horse Comics' *Harlan Ellison's Dream Corridor*, a short piece by Terry Dowling about updating *The Essential Ellison*, and a brief tribute to the late Chris Bunch, along with all the usual news about HE.

Machenalia was the newsletter of The Friends of Arthur Machen and featured news, articles and letters about the author.

Under editor Debbie Bennett, *Prism: The Newsletter of the British Fantasy Society* turned out six bi-monthly issues packed with information. Meanwhile, the Society's magazine *Dark Horizons* had a new editor, Marie O'Regan, and a new look as the content was expanded from just fiction and poetry to include columns and reviews. Contributors included Tony Richards, Mike Chinn and Bob Covington.

The British Fantasy Society 2006 calendar was an improvement over the previous year's attempt. Once again edited by Paul Kane and Marie O'Regan, it included short-short horror tales by Kelly Armstrong, Clive Barker, Ramsey Campbell, Simon Clark, John Connolly, Christopher Fowler, Neil Gaiman, Stephen Gallagher, Muriel Gray, Stephen Laws, Graham Masterton and Poppy Z. Brite, along with artwork from Bob Covington, James Ryman and others. The regular BFS Open Night meetings continued in London, with the Christmas event in early December attracting record numbers.

Exhaustingly edited by S. T. Joshi and Stefan Dziemianowicz, *Supernatural Literature of the World: An Encyclopedia* was an impressive and indispensable three-volume hardcover set from Greenwood Press that formed an A–Z guide to horror fiction and its practitioners. Along with a Foreword by Ramsey Campbell, the esteemed line-up of contributors included Mike Ashley, Leigh Blackmore, Everett F. Bleiler, Rusty Burke, Donald R. Burleson, Peter Cannon, Scott Connors, Paula Guran, Melissa Mia Hall, Don Herron, Ben P. Indick, Stephen Jones, Robert Morrish, D. H. Olson, John Pelan, Robert M. Price, Jim Rockhill, Barbara Roden, Christopher Roden, David J. Schow, Darrell Schweitzer, Brian Stableford, Peter Tremayne, Lisa Tuttle, Hank Wagner and Chet Williamson, amongst many others.

Once again edited by Stephen Jones and Kim Newman, with an Introduction by Peter Straub, *Horror: Another 100 Best Books* was a follow-up volume to the Bram Stoker Award-winning 1988 compi-

lation, featuring 100 original essays by an all-new line-up of contributors.

Gina Wisker's *Horror Fiction: An Introduction* was a critical
guide to the genre covering themes and major authors, published
as part of the "Continuum Studies in Literary Genre" series.

Stephen King is Richard Bachman by Michael R. Collings was an
updated look at the story behind the author's alter-ego, available in
trade hardcover and a 400-copy limited edition signed by Collings,
from Overlook Connection Press. In *Stephen King: Uncollected,
Unpublished* from Cemetery Dance Publications, Rocky Wood with
David Rawsthorne and Norma Blackburn compiled an exhaustive
guide to around 100 "lost" works by King that also included a
chapter from the author's unpublished 1970 novel *Sword in the
Darkness*.

Stephen King's The Dark Tower: A Concordance: Vol.II by Robin
Furth was a reference guide to the final three books in the series,
while *The Illustrated Stephen King Trivia Book* edited by Brian
Freeman and Bev Vincent contained more than 1,000 questions, with
illustrations by Glenn Chadbourne. It was published by Cemetery
Dance Publications as a trade paperback, hardcover, and a fifty-two
copy lettered traycased edition.

Compiled and edited by Tim Richmond after a decade's research,
*Fingerprints on the Sky: The Authorized Harlan Ellison Bibliogra-
phy* was a fully illustrated reader's guide published by Overlook
Connection in trade hardcover, signed limited edition, and a $500.00
lettered slipcased version with additional DVD.

Although written during its subject's lifetime, John Gawsworth's
biography *The Life of Arthur Machen* finally saw print from
Tartarus Press and was available as part of the annual subscription
to The Friends of Arthur Machen.

Jason Colavito's *The Cult of Alien Gods: H. P. Lovecraft and
Extraterrestrial Pop Culture* tied contemporary alien mythology into
Lovecraft's stories and concepts, while *H. P. Lovecraft in Popular
Culture: The Works and Their Adaptations in Film, Television,
Music and Games* by Don G. Smith was a critical bibliography
from McFarland & Company.

*The Lovecraft Lexicon: A Reader's Guide to Persons, Places and
Things in the Tales of H. P. Lovecraft* was an encyclopaedic guide by
Anthony Pearsall. Originally published in 1991 and translated by
Dorna Khazeni, *H. P. Lovecraft: Against the World, Against Life* was
a critical essay by French novelist Michel Houellebecq that came with
an Introduction by Stephen King and two stories by Lovecraft himself.

Edited with an Introduction by S.T. Joshi and David E. Schultz, *Letters from New York* collected letters written by H. P. Lovecraft while he was living in New York and was the second volume in the "Lovecraft Letters" series from Night Shade Books. Also edited by Joshi and Schultz, and available from Hippocampus Press as a print-on-demand edition, *Letters to Rheinhart Kleiner* collected letters from Lovecraft to one of his earliest correspondents, along with an essay by Kleiner and poems from both writers.

Edited with a Preface by Michael H. Hutchins for PS Publishing, *A Reverie for Mister Ray: Reflections on Life, Death, and Speculative Fiction* was a hefty collection of nearly seventy essays and reviews by Michael Bishop, with an Introduction by Jeff VanderMeer.

Bradbury Speaks: Too Soon from the Cave, Too Far from the Stars was a collection of thirty-seven essays (twelve original), and *The Bradbury Chronicles: The Life of Ray Bradbury* was an authorized biography by Sam Weller, billed as "predicting the past and remembering the future". The book included notes, an index and a selected bibliography.

Wonder's Child: My Life in Science Fiction was a softcover reissue by BenBella Books of Jack Williamson's Hugo Award-winning 1984 autobiography, with an additional twenty years of new material, a portion of the author's diary from World War II and a new Introduction by Mike Resnick. The 97-year-old Williamson even had a new SF novel out in 2005, entitled *The Stonehenge Gate*.

More Giants of the Genre, from print-on-demand publisher Wildside Press, collected twenty-three new and reprint interviews by Michael McCarty with Whitley Strieber, Laurell K. Hamilton, Joe R. Lansdale, Graham Masterton, Stephen Jones, Charles Grant, Terry Pratchett, Ingrid Pitt, Harlan Ellison, William F. Nolan, John Carpenter, Richard Matheson and others, including controversial mentalist The Amazing Kreskin.

Lorna Jowett's *Sex and the Slayer: A Gender Studies Primer for the Buffy Fan* was a critical examination of *Buffy the Vampire Slayer* published by Wesleyan University Press. From McFarland, Jess Battis' *Blood Relations: Chosen Families in Buffy the Vampire Slayer and Angel* examined the concept of families in the TV shows.

Facts on File/Checkmark Books published Rosemary Ellen Guiley's *The Encyclopedia of Vampires, Werewolves, and Other Monsters*, which featured a Foreword by Jeanne Keyes Youngson.

2005 was the year of Peter Jackson's *King Kong*. Christopher Golden wrote the tie-in novelisation, while Matthew Costello's *King Kong:*

The Island of the Skull was an official prequel to Jackson's remake. Russell Blackford's *Kong Reborn* was a sequel to the original movie, with scientists cloning a new "Eighth Wonder of the World".

Delos W. Lovelace's 1932 novelisation of the original *King Kong* was reissued by a number of publishers on both sides of the Atlantic. The Underwood Books edition included four illustrations by Frank Frazetta, Dave Stevens, Jon Foster and Ken Steacy, and the Grosset & Dunlap edition featured four pages of stills from the original RKO movie. The Random House trade paperback included a new Preface by Mark Cotta Caz and an Introduction by Greg Bear, while the compact edition from Gollancz, with a new Afterword by Stephen Jones, was only the second time that the book had appeared in hardcover in Britain.

With a Foreword by James V. D'Arc, *Merian C. Cooper's King Kong* was basically a pointless expansion of Lovelace's novelisation (including inconsistencies) by artist Joe DeVito and Brad Strickland for St. Martin's Press. *Kong: King of Skull Island*, a sequel from the same team, appeared from Dark Horse Comics/DH Press with an Introduction by Ray Harryhausen.

Other film tie-ins included *Constantine* and *Doom* by John Shirley, *Serenity* by Keith R. A. DeCandido, *Aliens: Original Sin* by Jan Michael Friedman and *Underworld: Evolution* by Greg Cox. Matthew Stover's novelisation of *Star Wars III: The Revenge of the Sith* reached #2 in the British best-seller charts, and Yvonne Navarro's 2005 novelization of *Elektra* was re-issued as a hardcover by the Science Fiction Book Club (SFBC).

Vampire Hunter D and *Raiser of Gales*, both by Hideyuki Kikuchi, were the basis for the Japanese *anime* film series. Translated by Kevin Leahy and illustrated by Yoshitaka Amano, they were published as trade paperbacks by Dark Horse Comics/DH Press.

The first titles in the Dark Horse "Universal Studios Monsters" spin-offs series included *Dracula: Asylum Book One* by Paul Witcover, in which the Count exerted his influence over Dr. Seward's Sanatorium, and Michael Jan Friedman's *The Wolf Man: Hunter's Moon*, in which the cursed Lawrence Talbot found himself pursued by a cult of werewolf hunters.

The biggest publisher of film tie-ins was British imprint Black Flame/BL Publishing, whose deal with New Line Cinema resulted in a number of different franchise series. Hockey-masked serial killer Jason Voorhees found himself competing against a couple of moralistic murderers in Jason Arnopp's *Friday the 13th: Hate-Kill-Repeat*, and the series continued with Scott Phillips' *Friday the*

13th: Church of the Divine Psychopath and Paul A. Woods' *Friday the 13th: Hell Lake.*

Pat Cadigan adapted the futuristic sequel *Jason X,* and followed it up with *Jason X: The Experiment.* In the same spin-off series, a sinister doctor attempted to clone Jason in Nancy Kilpatrick's *Jason X: Planet of the Beast,* but he was back for *Jason X: Death Moon* by Alex S. Johnson.

Sharp-fingered dream-killer Freddy Krueger was the subject of *A Nightmare on Elm Street: Suffer the Children* by David Bishop, *A Nightmare on Elm Street: Dreamspawn* by Christa Faust and *A Nightmare on Elm Street: Protégé* by Tim Waggoner.

New Line's *Final Destination* films, about teens trying to cheat Death, were the inspiration for *Dead Reckoning* by Natasha Rhodes, *Destination Zero* by David McIntee, *End of the Line* by Rebecca Levene, *Dead Man's Hand* by Steven Roman and *Looks Could Kill* by Nancy A. Collins.

Aimed at younger children, *The Adventures of Sharkboy and Lavagirl: The Movie Storybook* by Robert Rodriguez and his eight-year-old son Racer Patrick Rodriguez featured illustrations by Alex Toader and was apparently better than the movie that inspired it.

With the TV show finally coming to an end, *Mystic Knoll* by Diana G. Gallagher, *Changeling Places* by Micol Ostow and *Picture Perfect* by Cameron Dokey took the *Charmed* series over thirty titles.

Lost: Secret Identity by Cathy Hapka was the first volume in the inevitable TV tie-in series.

The Triangle by Steve Lyons was a novelisation of the Sci Fi Channel miniseries about the Bermuda Triangle, and *Roger Corman's Dinocroc* by Thompson O'Rourke was based on the TV movie from the legendary producer.

Battlestar Galactica by Jeffrey A. Carver was the first tie-in novel based on the Sci Fi Channel's highest-rated series ever, while *Battlestar Galactica: Redemption* by actor Richard Hatch and Brad Linaweaver was inspired by the original 1970s TV series.

Buffy the Vampire Slayer: Spark and Burn by Diana G. Gallagher showed that there was still life in the spin-off book series, and Nancy Holder's *Buffy the Vampire Slayer: Queen of the Slayers* was set after the show had ended.

Dean Koontz's Frankenstein Book One: Prodigal Son by Koontz and Kevin J. Anderson was based on the author's original concept for the USA Network pilot that he disowned. Ed Gorman collaborated with Koontz on the second volume, *City of Night,* and Charnel

House published a 750-copy signed edition of Koontz's unused script, along with twenty-six lettered editions costing a cool $1,600.00 each.

Published as part of the Black Flame/New Line Cinema deal, *The Twilight Zone: Upgrade/Sensuous Cindy* by Pat Cadigan, *The Twilight Zone: Chosen/The Placebo Effect* by K. C. Winters and *The Twilight Zone: Burned/One Night at Mercy* by Christa Faust each contained adaptations of two shows from the 1980s revival of the series.

The success of the BBC's revival of *Doctor Who* saw three new hardcover novelisations, *Monsters Inside* by Stephen Cole, *The Clockwise Man* by Justin Richards and *Winner Takes All* by Jacqueline Rayner, all enter the UK best-seller charts.

Hellboy: On Earth as It Is in Heaven by Brian Hodge was based on the comic book series created by Mike Mignola.

Lucien Soulban's *World of Darkness: Blood In, Blood Out* and Greg Stolze's *World of Darkness: The Marriage of Virtue and Viciousness* were both based on the White Wolf role-playing game *Vampire: The Requiem*.

From HarperCollins imprint William Morrow, *MirrorMask: The Illustrated Film Script of the Motion Picture from The Jim Henson Company* by Neil Gaiman and Dave McKean was a hefty oversized hardcover that included material from the fantasy film of the same title. The UK edition published by Headline/Review had some subtle differences and was, if anything, even more attractive.

Published by BenBella Books, *King Kong is Back!* edited by David Brin was subtitled *An Unauthorized Look at One Humongous Ape* and contained nineteen original articles about the King of Skull Island by Adam-Troy Castro, Keith R. A. DeCandido, David Gerrold, James Gunn, Robert Hood, Paul Levinson, Steven Rubio, George Zebrowski and others, including Bob Eggleton, who also contributed the illustrations.

Edited by Karen Haber for Pocket Books, *Kong Unbound* collected fifteen essays about the original film by Jack Williamson, Richard A. Lupoff, Esther Friesner and others, along with a Preface by Ray Harryhausen and an Introduction by Ray Bradbury.

From Titan Books, *Tim Burton's Corpse Bride: An Invitation to the Wedding* was a beautifully produced, full colour behind-the-scenes guide to the stop-motion animated film, with text by Mark Salisbury and a brief Introduction by Burton himself.

The Art of Batman Begins: Shadows of the Dark Night by Mark

Cotta Vaz was a nicely-designed but overpriced showcase from Titan, featuring concept designs, storyboards and stills from the latest attempt to revitalize the *Batman* franchise. Denis Meikle's *The Ring Companion* looked at Hideo Nakata's original film, the sequels and remakes, and its influence on other J-horror titles.

Also from Titan, *The Art of Wallace & Gromit: The Curse of the Were-Rabbit* was a look at the making of the Aardman Animation film by Andy Lane and Paul Simpson, while Brian J. Robb's *Counterfeit Worlds: Philip K. Dick on Film* explored the many and varied adaptations of the troubled science fiction author's work.

The British Film Institute continued its series of "BFI Film Classics" with a look at Carl Theodor Dreyer' silent *Vampyr* by RSC dramatist David Rudkin. *Telefantasy* by Catherine Johnson studied the place of fantasy, SF and horror in British and US television, and "BFI TV Classics", celebrating key television programmes and series, was launched in December with critical readings of *Buffy the Vampire Slayer* by Anne Billson and *Doctor Who* by Kim Newman. Both small-size paperbacks included notes, episode credits and indexes, and were profusely illustrated with stills.

From Tomahawk Press, Tony Earnshaw's *Beating the Devil: The Making of Night of the Demon* was an in-depth look at the making of Jacques Tourneur's classic 1957 film, based on M. R. James' "Casting the Runes".

Alec Worley's *Empires of the Imagination: A Critical Survey of Fantasy Cinema from Georges Méliès to The Lord of the Rings* was an illustrated guide to fantasy films from McFarland & Company, with an Introduction by Brian Sibley. Also from McFarland, *Earth vs. the Sci-Fi Filmmakers* was a further collection of twenty interviews with veteran personalities conducted by Tom Weaver. *The Mexican Masked Wrestler and Monster Filmography* was a useful compendium from Robert Michael "Bobb" Cotter, while Bonnie Noonan's *Women Scientists in Fifties Science Fiction Films* was perhaps aimed at an even more exclusive readership.

From Telos Publishing, *Back to the Vortex: The Unofficial and Unauthorised Guide to Doctor Who* was a hefty reference book by J. Shaun Lyon with a very brief Foreword by TV producer Philip David Segal, while *The Handbook* by David J. Howe, Stephen James Walker and Mark Stammers was an unauthorised guide to the production of the original *Doctor Who* series.

David McIntee's *Beautiful Monsters* was an unofficial guide to the *Alien* and *Predator* film series from the same imprint. Unfortunately, because these titles were unauthorised companions, the books suffered from not having any licensed illustrations.

British publisher Chrysalis sold its books group in 2005, which included fantasy art imprint Paper Tiger, to a management group. The new company was called Anova Books.

Nicely produced in a square hardcover format, *Arts Unknown: The Life & Art of Lee Brown Coye* from NonStop Press featured more than 350 illustrations by the legendary regional and pulp artist, beautifully reproduced in colour and black and white, with text and a selected bibliography by Luis Ortiz.

Spectrum 12: The Best in Contemporary Fantastic Art was, as usual, edited by Cathy Fenner and Arnie Fenner for Underwood Books. Among the 273 artists featured were Donato Giancola, John Picacio, Dave McKean, Brom, Gary Gianni, Michael Whelan, Charles Vess, Leo and Diane Dillon, Todd Lockwood and Kent Williams, along with a comprehensive review of the year and a profile of Grand Master recipient H. R. Giger by Harlan Ellison.

Edited and written by J. David Spurlock, *Grand Master of Adventure Art: The Drawings of J. Allen St. John* was a stunning collection of black and white drawings, many of them based on the work of Edgar Rice Burroughs.

Available from Rizzoli as an oversized art book, *Clive Barker: Visions of Heaven and Hell* contained more than 300 drawings and paintings with commentary by Barker and an Introduction by Joanna Cotler. A deluxe slipcased edition was also available for $250.00.

The World of Kong: A Natural History of Skull Island used designs from the new movie to create a nature guide to the many strange creatures that inhabited Kong's home. Weta Workshop also produced a 500-copy print of New Zealand illustrator Gus Hunter's concept art from *King Kong* as a signed full-colour lithograph, matted and framed with a brass plate and shell cases fired by actors during the filming.

IMAGO was a disappointing selection of colour artwork and previously unpublished drawings and preliminary sketches by Jim Burns, issued in an interesting hardcover format by Heavy Metal and Titan Books.

A group of toys defended their young owner from *The Pluckier* in the first illustrated novel by artist (Gerald) Broom.

Grips Grimly applied his macabre artwork to "The Black Cat", "The Masque of the Red Death", "Hop-Frog" and "The Fall of the

House of Usher" in *Edgar Allan Poe's Tales of Mystery and Madness*, while *Edgar Allan Poe: The Fall of the House of Usher and Other Tales of Terror* collected four stories adapted by Richard Margopoulos and illustrated by Richard Corben.

Compiled by Doug Ellis for his Tattered Pages Press imprint, *Virgil Finlay: The Art of Things to Come* was a spiral-bound portfolio of rarely-seen illustrations that the legendary artist produced for the Science Fiction Book Club's bi-monthly newsletter between 1959–70. It was published in an edition of just 100 numbered copies, of which fifty-five were distributed amongst the Comic and Fantasy Art Amateur Press Association.

Published in compact hardcover format by Fantagraphics Books, *Muzzlers, Guzzlers and Good Yeggs* collected four true crime stories by cult artist Joe Coleman, whose work has been described as "a blend of Breughel and the E. C. horror comics of the 1950s".

Although disappointingly not compiled in chronological order, *Batman: Cover to Cover* was still a superb full-colour selection of more than 250 of the greatest comic book covers featuring the Dark Knight, from DC Comics. It also featured written contributions from Brian Bolland, Neil Gaiman, Chip Kidd, Denny O'Neil, Alex Ross, film director Christopher Nolan, 1960s TV Batman Adam West, and the voice of the animated Joker, Mark Hamill.

In an effort to combat falling sales and escalating costs, both DC Comics and Marvel revamped their lines, bringing in new creative teams to work on high-profile titles. DC once again tinkered with its whole universe with its *Infinite Crisis* series, while Marvel did much the same for *X-Men* with its *House of M* sequence. Marvel also got Stephen King involved in a *Dark Tower* spin-off, while *Lost*'s co-creator Damon Lindelof scripted a Wolverine/Hulk team-up.

In January, Stan Lee won his lawsuit against Marvel Enterprises, Inc. for breach of contract, after the company rejected his claim for a 10 per cent share of earnings from film and TV spin-offs featuring the characters he helped to create. The 82-year-old Lee was set to earn millions of dollars from the US district judge's ruling. However, Marvel announced that it planned to appeal the court's decision. Around the same time, the company entered into long-term publishing deals with four book imprints to exploit Marvel characters.

Grant Morrison's revisionist *Seven Soldiers* miniseries featured a group of DC Comics' lesser characters, such as Zatanna, Shining Knight, Klarion the Witch Boy and Mister Miracle.

The Matrix creators The Wachowski Brothers scripted the third issue of *Doc Frankenstein*, illustrated by co-creator Steve Skroce and published by Burlyman Entertainment.

From Dark Horse Comics and based on the Sci Fi Channel movie, *Man with the Screaming Brain* was a horror-comedy miniseries by Bruce Campbell and David Goodman, with variant covers by Mike Mignola, Eric Powell, Humberto Ramos and Phil Noto.

Based on Rupert Wainwright's remake of the John Carpenter film, *The Fog* from writer Scott Allie and artist Todd Herman chronicled the Chinese curse that set in motion the events in the new movie. Mike Mignola again did the cover.

The Dark Horse Book of the Dead contained nine horror strips by Mignola, Kelley Jones, Pat McEown and others, along with Robert E. Howard's 1933 story "Old Garfield's Heart", illustrated by Gary Gianni.

The Dweller in the Pool and Other Stories, Brothers of the Blade and Other Stories and *Riders of the River-Dragons and Other Stories* were the seventh, eighth and ninth compilations in Dark Horse Books' *The Chronicles of Conan* series. Each volume reprinted more original Marvel strips (including one based on a Gardner F. Fox "Kothar" novel) with remastered colour and more fascinating Afterwords by original writer Roy Thomas.

Inspired by Robert E. Howard's sword-wielding heroine, Dynamite Entertainment launched *Red Sonja: She-Devil with a Sword* with five variant covers by Michael Turner, Paolo Rivera, Joseph Michael Linsner, John Cassaday and Alex Ross. Also from Dynamite, *Re-Animator Returns!* was based on the H. P. Lovecraft-inspired film series.

Del Rey Books brought Richard Corben's *Werewolf* and *Edgar Allan Poe* graphic novels back into print, along with Spanish artist Fernando Fernandez's *Dracula*.

From Heavy Metal came an all-new version of *Dracula*, while dark forces conspired to raise the Count from his unholy slumber in *Castlevania: The Belmont Legacy*, written by Marc Andreyko and illustrated by E. J. Su for IDW Publishing. Jason Henderson's *Sword of Dracula* set the Count up as a target for the military.

Angel: The Curse was a five-part story from IDW, set after the finale of Joss Whedon's now-defunct vampire TV series. *Spike: Old Times* was a one-shot spin-off featuring the undead Brit, released in August, while the three-part *Serenity* filled in the gap between Whedon's cancelled *Firefly* TV show and the movie version he directed.

In June IDW added a comic book of *Shaun of the Dead* to its already busy line-up. The four-issue series was scripted by editor-in-chief Chris Ryall and illustrated by Zach Howard. Titan Books collected the strip as a "director's cut" graphic novel.

Silent Hill: Dead/Alive was a new five-part miniseries from writer Scott Ciencin and artist Nick Stakal featuring an evil eight-year-old attempting to gain power over the eponymous haunted town.

Clive Barker's Thief of Always was a graphic novel compilation of the three comic books scripted by Kris Oprisko and illustrated by Gabriel Hernandez.

Masters of Horror was a new title from IDW Publishing to tie-in with the Showtime anthology series created by Mick Garris. The first issue, based on a Joe R. Lansdale story, featured two variant covers, and the book was also available in an edition signed by director Don Coscarelli.

Steve Niles' *Frankenstein* was the first volume in IDW's *Little Book of Horror* specially-sized hardcovers, with Scott Morse illustrating the prose adaptation. A new translation of Alex Baladi's graphic novel *Frankenstein: Now and Forever*, first published in France in 2001, appeared from Typocrat Press, while *Frankenstein: The Graphic Novel* was adapted by Gary Reed and Frazer Irving from Mary Shelley's novel, from Puffin.

Brian Pulido scripted the first issues of *A Nightmare on Elm Street*, *Friday the 13th*, *Texas Chainsaw Massacre* and *Jason X* from Avatar Press and New Line Cinema's "House of Horror" imprint.

Still trading on his credit as co-creator of *Night of the Living Dead* more than thirty-five years later, John Russo's *Escape of the Living Dead* was a five-issue series from Avatar with artwork by Dheeraj Verma. The book came with regular and wrap covers or terror and gore covers, as did *Species Special #1* written by Brian Pulido.

Titan Books continued its reprints of Peter O'Donnell and Jim Holdaway's black and white newspaper strips with *Modesty Blaise: Bad Suki*, with a new Introduction by artist Walter Simonson. Spanish artist Enric Badia Romero took over the strip in 1970 and the first full volume of his work was collected as *Modesty Blaise: The Green-Eyed Monster*.

From the same imprint, the series of full-colour hardcover reprints of Frank Hampson's *Dan Dare: Pilot of the Future* strips from the 1950s UK comic *Eagle* continued with *Marooned on Mercury*, *Operation Saturn Parts 1* and *2* and *Prisoners of Space*, with Introductions by Queen guitarist Brian May, Philip Pullman, Steve Holland and Sir Tim Rice, respectively.

Titan also began a series of welcome hardcover collections of black and white strips from the classic 1960s British boy's comics, *Lion* and *Valiant. The Spider: King of Crooks* by Jerry Siegel, Ted Cowan and Reg Bunn showcased the first three adventures of the brilliant megalomaniac and his paralysing gas guns, while *The Steel Claw: The Vanishing Man* by SF author Ken Bulmer and Jesús Blasco chronicled the exploits of invisible man Louis Crandell.

Steve Dikto: Space Wars collected various sci-fi strips by the co-creator of Spider-Man in both hardcover and softcover.

Published as an oversized hardcover, David Britton's designed-to-shock *Fuck Off and Die* was illustrated in colour and black and white by Kris Guidio and included digs at Terry Pratchett and James Herbert.

In March, Walt Disney and the Weinstein brothers announced that they would abandon their twelve-year-old Miramax partnership at the end of September. Disney would retain the film library of more than 500 titles, while the Weinsteins would keep the ongoing projects. The Miramax Books imprint was absorbed into Hyperion.

An even bigger upset occurred in December when Viacom's Paramount Pictures agreed to buy DreamWorks SKG for $1.6 billion. Created eleven years earlier by Steven Spielberg, David Geffen and Jeffrey Katzenberg as an alternative to Hollywood's established studios, DreamWorks reportedly could not produce enough movies to become a major distributor.

For much of 2005, Hollywood suffered its worst year at the box-office for twenty years. Despite an increase in ticket prices, takings throughout the year in America were down 10 per cent on 2004. This followed a lacklustre summer in which the top ten box-office gross was down a quarter on the previous year, and many hyped-up blockbusters opened strongly but quickly died following negative word of mouth. Just five films, including *Star Wars Episode III, War of the Worlds* and *Batman Begins*, accounted for one-third of the whole season's profits. In Britain, grosses were only down 4 per cent on the previous year.

However, the box-office was given a late boost at the end of the year with the Christmas release of *The Chronicles of Narnia: The Lion, the Witch and the Wardrobe* and Peter Jackson's three-hour remake of *King Kong*. As it turned out, Disney's family-friendly *Narnia* beat out the over-hyped *Kong*, taking more than $450 million world-wide to the latter's disappointing $222.5 million.

In fact, the year's most successful film in America was George Lucas' *Star Wars Episode III: Revenge of the Sith*, followed by *Harry Potter and the Goblet of Fire* at #2, *War of the Worlds* at #3, *The*

Chronicles of Narnia at #4, *Charlie and the Chocolate Factory* at #6, *Batman Begins* at #7 and *Madagascar* at #8. In the UK, *Harry Potter* (with a world-wide gross of $535 million) just edged out *Star Wars* to take the top slot, and *Wallace & Gromit: The Curse of the Were-Rabbit* and *Nanny McPhee* also both made the top ten (at #4 and #10, respectively).

After twenty-eight years and six films, George Lucas' epic space opera finally came full circle with the third prequel, *Star Wars Episode III: Revenge of the Sith*. Christopher Lee was killed off too early, and it was a pity that Lucas chose not to put Dave Prowse in the Darth Vader suit again or recycle any footage of the late Peter Cushing (a lookalike actor was used), but the special effects were stunning and the script moved along at a cracking pace.

The film opened at #1 on both sides of the Atlantic. It grossed $158.4 million during its first four days in the US (breaking the record held by *The Matrix Reloaded*) and broke more records by taking $303.00 million with simultaneous premieres in 115 countries world-wide. However, with 9,000 prints, *Episode III* was released in 50 per cent more screens than the previous entry, and in its first week accounted for an astonishing 70 per cent of the entire US top ten and two-thirds of business over its first weekend in May. It broke the $250 million barrier after just eleven days, one day faster than *Spider-Man 2* in 2004, and passed the $300 million barrier in seventeen days (one day earlier than the record set by *Shrek 2*).

Mike Newell's *Harry Potter and the Goblet of Fire*, the fourth instalment in the series about the schoolboy wizard, was the fourth-largest opening of all time when it opened at #1 in the US in November with a weekend gross of $102.3 million. The film also took £14.9 million at the British box-office over its first weekend, the highest three-day take in UK cinema history despite being the first *Potter* film to be given a restrictive "12A" rating by the British Board of Film Classification. However, it was also the first of the *Potter* films to actually disappoint, especially Ralph Fiennes' unimpressive Lord Voldemort. The producers needed to learn that sometimes, less *is* more.

Steven Spielberg's lazy remake of *War of the Worlds* starred a dull Tom Cruise as a blue-collar father trying to save his family from an alien invasion. Although H. G. Wells' Victorian novel was relocated to contemporary New Jersey, the film benefited from some great-looking special effects and blink-and-you'll-miss-them cameos by Gene Barry and Ann Robinson, stars of the superior 1953 version.

Based on the classic book series by C.S. Lewis, Andrew Adamson's epic children's fantasy *The Chronicles of Narnia: The Lion, the Witch and the Wardrobe* featured superb CGI effects and Tilda Swinton as a chilling White Witch. Disney hired several Christian marketing groups to promote the film in an attempt to exploit Lewis' religious beliefs. It was endorsed by Focus on the Family, a conservative religious group that claims a membership of two million. The film exceeded industry expectations in the US, where it opened at #1 in December with a $65.6 million gross – the third largest opening of the year, the second highest for a December weekend after the final *Lord of the Rings* film, and the best opening ever for a Disney live-action film. In Britain, *Narnia* took an impressive £8 million in its first three days, the biggest opening ever for a Disney movie in the UK, and it opened at #1 in twelve other countries as well.

Tim Burton's remake of Roald Dahl's *Charlie and the Chocolate Factory* opened in America in July at #1, taking $55.3 million. It was a career-best opening for star Johnny Depp, even beating his 2003 hit *Pirates of the Caribbean: The Curse of the Black Pearl*.

Batman Begins, director Christopher Nolan's oh-so-serious reinvention of the movie franchise starring Christian Bale as the Caped Crusader, didn't break any opening weekend records, but it did open at #1 in both the US and the UK in June.

After being held off the US top slot by *Star Wars Episode III*, DreamWorks' comedy cartoon *Madagascar* eventually went to #1 for a week before going on to gross almost $200 million in the US. A tale of pampered zoo animals shipwrecked on a desert island, it featured the voices of Ben Stiller and Chris Rock.

Released too late in the year to be included in the box-office totals, Peter Jackson's well-intentioned, but overlong and ultimately redundant remake of *King Kong* beautifully recreated the original 1933 setting, but was let down by poor castings choices and variable CGI sequences (a brontosaurus stampede was particularly poor). With special effects shots costing around $100,000 per minute, the film reportedly went an estimated $32 million over its original $175 million budget, with the director apparently covering the extra cost himself in return for a lucrative profit-sharing deal. Andy Serkis created Kong's body movements, but he just looked like a big gorilla.

New York's Times Square was brought to a standstill by the US premier in early December, where a twenty-foot replica of the giant ape was displayed outside the cinema. However, despite all the publicity, *King Kong* opened well below industry expectations.

In John Polson's *Hide and Seek*, a slumming Robert De Niro learned that he'd better take notice of Charlie, the "imaginary" friend of his young daughter Emily (Dakota Fanning) when they moved into a new home. The film went to #1 in the US in January with a gross of just $22 million.

Geoffrey Sax's *White Noise* starred Michael Keaton as a widower attempting to contact his dead wife (Chandra West) through EVP – Electronic Voice Phenomenon.

According to a survey, 59 per cent of the US audience for the "hoodoo" thriller *The Skeleton Key* was female. Kate Hudson found herself looking after a catatonic John Hurt and his complaining wife Gena Rowlands in a haunted Southern plantation house.

A team of experienced spelunkers found themselves trapped in a lost cave system and battling winged "demons" below a 13th-century Carpathian church in Bruce Hunt's high-concept B-movie *The Cave*. Meanwhile, in Neil Marshall's *The Descent*, six British girlfriends on a spelunking holiday in the Appalachian mountains also found themselves trapped in an unexplored cave system and fighting for their survival against flesh-eating albino creatures.

"Based on true events", Scott Derrickson's *The Exorcism of Emily Rose* was inspired by a 1978 case of possession and a priest's subsequent trial for negligent homicide. It became a surprise US box-office #1 in September, with more than half the audience under twenty-five. The film's success was credited to its distributor, Screen Gems, deliberately courting religious conservatives.

And if at first you don't succeed . . . Following the failure of Renny Harlin's underrated *Exorcist: The Beginning* last year, Paul Schrader's $40 million shelved version, *Dominion: Prequel to the Exorcist*, co-scripted by novelist Caleb Carr, received a limited release from Warner Bros./Morgan Creek in May. Stellan Skarsgård starred in both versions as Father Merrin, confronting his own demons in 1940s East Africa.

Based on the cult BBC television series, *The League of Gentlemen's Apocalypse* transported the bizarre characters of Royston Vasey into the "real" world, in search of their creators.

Mark Waters' supernatural romantic comedy *Just Like Heaven*, starring Reese Witherspoon as a dead doctor falling for Mark Ruffalo, opened at #1 in the US. Exit polls revealed that 77 per cent of the audience was female.

In Nora Ephron's post-modern fantasy *Bewitched*, a nose-twitching Nicole Kidman was perfect as the real-life witch cast as Samantha in a revival of the 1960s TV series. But there was no romantic spark between the actress and her hardworking co-star Will Ferrell, and it was left to veterans Shirley MacLaine and Michael Caine to weave any magic.

Ryan Reynolds and Melissa George moved into the Long Island house with a bad history in Andrew Douglas' pointless remake of *The Amityville Horror*. Co-produced by Michael Bay, it was the final major release from MGM, which was sold to Sony.

Having been pushed back from a November 2004 opening, Dark Castle Entertainment's *House of Wax* was directed by "Jaume" (Jaume Collet-Serra), better know for his TV commercials. Although Chad Michael Murray and Elisha Cuthbert were the nominal stars, Paris Hilton had a much-publicised cameo as a victim. A $48.00 limited edition T-shirt emblazoned with the legend "See Paris Die" sold out within three hours of going on sale at a trendy Los Angeles boutique.

John Carpenter co-produced the redundant remake of his own *The Fog*, which starred TV actors Tom Welling and Maggie Grace and opened in the US at #1 with a gross of only $11.8 million.

Walter Salles' *Dark Water* was yet another remake of a hit Japanese horror movie, as separated mother Dahlia (Jennifer Connelly) tried to protect her five-year-old daughter Ceci (newcomer Ariel Gade) from the vengeful ghost in their spooky New York apartment. Pete Postlethwaite, John C. Reilly, Tim Roth and Dougray Scott added some classy support.

Directed by original series creator Hideo Nakata, *The Ring Two* opened to a better box-office than its predecessor did in 2002. It was a no-scares sequel that had investigative reporter Rachel Keller (Naomi Watts) and her creepy-looking son Aidan (David Dorfman) again menaced by the vengeance-seeking videotape. Sissy Spacek had a cameo as a mad mother.

The psychopathic Jigsaw (Tobin Bell) set up another series of lethal booby-traps in *Saw II*, which opened in the US at #1 over Halloween, almost doubling the amount the previous entry took in its first week.

In Larry Guterman's belated comedy sequel *Son of the Mask*, the infant son of aspiring cartoonist Tim Avery (Jamie Kennedy) was transformed by the Mask of Loki, and its manic owner (Alan Cummings) would stop at nothing to reclaim it.

Keanu Reeves gave a brooding performance as the eponymous chain-smoking demon-hunter from Hell in Francis Lawrence's *Constantine*, based on the long-running DC Comics/Vertigo series *Hellblazer*. However, it was Tilda Swinton as the angel Gabriel who stole the film, which opened at #2 in the US before suffering a 64 per cent drop the following week.

Comedy director Tim Story bungled the big-budget origin of the

Marvel comic book *Fantastic Four*. When a scientific experiment in space went wrong, exposure to a cosmic storm caused naïve Dr Reed Richards (a likeable Ioan Gruffudd), sexy Sue Storm (Jessica Alba), reckless Johnny Storm (Chris Evans) and short-tempered Ben Grimm (Michael Chiklis) to develop super-powers. Even Julian McMahon failed to register as metal-skinned villain Dr Victor von Doom.

Rob Bowman's *Daredevil* spin-off *Elektra* starred Jennifer Garner as the high-kicking heroine in red leather. The DVD release included a deleted cameo by Ben Affleck.

Robert Rodriguez's ultra-violent *Sin City* was based on co-director Frank Miller's 1991 graphic novel. A stylized blend of live-action and digital video, Mickey Rourke stood out amongst an all-star cast that included Rosario Dawson, Rutger Hauer, Clive Owen, Bruce Willis and Elijah Wood. Quentin Tarantino was credited as "Special Guest Director".

Rodriguez's other film of the year was the very different children's adventure *The Adventures of Shark Boy & Lava Girl in 3-D*, which was co-written by the director's seven-year-old son.

Although producer Laurie McDonald blamed stars Ewan McGregor and Scarlett Johansson for the box-office failure of Michael Bay's derivative *The Island*, she should perhaps have taken some of the criticism herself for not only hiring them, but also for freely "borrowing" concepts and ideas from Michael Marshall Smith's novel *Spares* and the 1979 movie *Parts: The Clonus Horror*. The film cost almost $150 million to make and grossed an abysmal $12.4 million during its opening weekend.

A computerised jet-fighter with a mind of its own went all *Forbin Project* in Rob Cohen's $124 million high-concept *Stealth*, featuring Josh Lucas, Jessica Biel, Jamie Foxx and Sam Shepard.

Filmed in 2002 and finally given a limited release, Edward Burns and Ben Kingsley starred in *A Sound of Thunder*, Peter Hyams' adaptation of Ray Bradbury's story about a time-travel dinosaur hunt that had repercussions back in the future.

Based on the shoot-them-up video game set on Mars, and starring The Rock as the leader of a group of marines fighting scientifically-created monsters, after opening at #1 in the US, Universal's *Doom* saw takings plummet 73 per cent in its second week.

Nobody wanted to see Joss Whedon's short-lived Fox TV show *Firefly*, so it didn't come as any surprise that equally few people cared about the big-screen version, retitled *Serenity*.

Despite both being nominated for Academy Awards for performances in 2005 films, neither Charlize Theron nor Reese Witherspoon could count their genre appearances from the year amongst their best work. In fact, Karyn Kusama's futuristic action film *Aeon Flux*, set 400 years in the future and starring Theron as the eponymous MTV cartoon assassin, had no previews in America and only managed a disappointing $16 million at the box-office.

Douglas Adams' SF comedy *The Hitchhiker's Guide to the Galaxy* finally reached the screen after twenty-five years in development and went to #1 in both the US and UK.

George A. Romero returned to his roots with *Land of the Dead*, the fourth entry in his "Living Dead" series of zombie movies. Set in the near future, Dennis Hopper played the corrupt owner of an urban apartment complex, defending his investment against a horde of organised walking corpses.

Voodoo snakebites turned people into zombie rednecks in *Venom*, while *Undead* was a low-budget comedy about the inhabitants of a small town being turned into the shambling dead, directed by Australian identical twins Peter and Michael Spierig.

Based on an old script by *Scream* scribe Kevin Williamson, Wes Craven's *Cursed* featured Christina Ricci and Jesse Eisenberg as siblings who found themselves turning into werewolves. Craven had more success with the claustrophobic psycho thriller *Red Eye*, starring Rachel McAdams and Cillian Murphy on a flight from hell.

In John Maybury's box-office flop *The Jacket*, Adrien Brody played an amnesiac Gulf War veteran and convicted murderer whose psychiatric treatment at the hands of Kris Kristofferson's sinister doctor sent him fifteen years into the future, where he encountered Keira Knightley's troubled waitress.

Christian Bale lost sixty-five pounds to play the emaciated lead in Brad Anderson's *The Machinist*, about a man who had gone without sleep for a year, and the ever-busy Ewan McGregor and Ryan Gosling were trapped between reality and fantasy in the confusing *Stay*.

When German girl Kate (an unsympathetic Franka Potente) missed her last train on the London Underground, she found herself pursued by a homicidal mutant cannibal in Christopher Smith's unpleasant debut film *Creep*.

A pre-*Doctor Who* Billie Piper starred in David Smith's *Spirit Trap*, in which five students rented a haunted mansion in North London, and vengeance came to a small town in Sheldon Wilson's low budget *Shallow Ground*.

Room 36, from the creators of *Revenge of Billy the Kid*, was a barely released British horror film that featured veterans Brian Murphy, John Cater and John Forbes-Robertson.

After his father mysteriously vanished, Barry Watson kept peering into dark closets in Stephen T. Kay's "PG-13" horror hit *Boogeyman*, which was "presented" by Sam Raimi and opened at #1 on both sides of the Atlantic in February.

Bill Moseley and Sid Haig starred in *The Devil's Rejects*, Rob Zombie's gory follow-up to *House of 1,000 Corpses*.

A group of students invented their own serial killer on the Internet, who then started hunting them down in Jeff Wadlow's campus slasher *Cry_Wolf*, starring Gary Cole and Jon Bon Jovi.

John Jarratt played the Outback crazy hunting a group of teens in *Wolf Creek*, an Australian slasher "based on true events".

Renny Harlin's *Mindhunters* was shot in 2002 in Holland for less than $40 million. Christian Slater, LL Cool J and a fleeting Val Kilmer starred in the *Ten Little Indians*-inspired plot set during a training session for FBI profiler cadets on a remote island. Uwe Boll's *Alone in the Dark* also headlined Slater who, along with Tara Reid and Stephen Dorff, confronted sharp-toothed monsters that came out at night.

Left on the shelf for two years, Jaume Balagueró's genuinely creepy *Darkness*, starring Anna Paquin and Lena Olin, was set in a Spanish haunted house and involved a group of dead children and a ritual that needed to be completed after forty years during a full eclipse of the sun.

An epic confrontation between Good and Evil was at the heart of Timur Bekmambetov's *Night Watch*, which was a huge hit at the Russian box-office, and Lucile Hadzihalilovic's disturbing *Innocence* was set in a bizarre girl's boarding school.

Made back in 2001, Kiyoshi Kurosawa's J-horror *Pulse* (*Kairo*) involved a sinister website that compelled people to commit suicide.

Emma Thompson both scripted and starred as the Mary Poppins-like *Nanny McPhee* in Kirk Jones' enjoyable children's fantasy set in Victorian times.

Teen star Lindsay Lohan rescued the intelligent VW Beetle from a junkyard in Disney's *Herbie: Fully Loaded*, which also featured Michael Keaton and Matt Dillon.

Jon Favreau's children's SF adventure *Zathura* was a companion piece to *Jumanji* (1995), and both films were based on picture books by Chris Van Allsburg.

Matt Damon and Heath Ledger played the storytelling siblings caught up in one of their own fantasies in Terry Gilliam's long-delayed *The Brothers Grimm*.

Dave McKean's low-budget fairy tale *MirrorMask* was scripted by Neil Gaiman and featured fifteen-year-old circus juggler Helena (a sulky Stephanie Leonidas) waking up in a bizarre fantasy world where the balance between light and darkness had been broken. McKean's unique computer backgrounds were nicely realised, and the film benefited from performances by the excellent Gina McKee and veteran Dora Bryan.

Although under an hour long, Andrew Leman's silent film version of *The Call of Cthulhu*, based on the H. P. Lovecraft story and filmed in "Mythoscope", was an innovative piece of film-making that perfectly captured HLP's nightmare visions.

Produced using stop-motion animation, *Tim Burton's The Corpse Bride* featured the voice of Johnny Depp as the shy Victor Van Dort, who found himself inadvertently married to the blue-skinned Corpse Bride, voiced by Helena Bonham Carter. The actress also contributed her vocal talents to the claymation horror spoof *Wallace & Gromit: The Curse of the Were-Rabbit*, the first feature-length outing for the cheese-loving inventor (voiced by Peter Sallis) and his long-suffering canine companion. It opened at #1 is the US with a gross of $16 million.

Katsuhiro Otomo's *Steamboy* was a steam-punk *anime* from the director of *Akira* (1988), featuring the voices of Anna Paquin, Patrick Stewart and Alfred Molina.

Mark Dindal's *Chicken Little*, Disney's first fully computer-generated film since its split with Pixar Studios, took a healthy $40.1 million over its opening weekend. Featuring the voices of Zach Braff, Joan Cusack and Gary Marshall, it involved the titular character trying to convince his friends that the sky really was falling. The computer-animated SF comedy *Robots* featured the voices of Ewan McGregor, Robin Williams and Greg Kinnear.

The 77th Academy Awards were presented in Los Angeles on February 27th. Amongst a lacklustre bunch, *Spider-Man 2* won the Oscar for Best Visual Effects, *Finding Neverland* won Best Music Score, Best Original Screenplay went to *Eternal Sunshine of the Spotless Mind* and *The Incredibles* was voted Best Animated Feature Film.

Meanwhile, Halle Berry turned up to personally collect her Golden Raspberry Award for Worst Actress for *Catwoman*. The film also won Worst Direction, Worst Screenplay and Flop of the Year at the Razzies' silver anniversary presentation in LA the day before the Oscars.

*   *   *

Probably the most eagerly awaited DVD boxed set of the year was Warner Bros' *The Val Lewton Horror Collection: 9 Tales of Terror from the Legendary Producer* containing double-disc sets of *Cat People/Curse of the Cat People*, *I Walked with a Zombie/The Body Snatcher*, *Isle of the Dead/Bedlam*, *The Leopard Man/The Ghost Ship* and *The Seventh Victim* paired with the original documentary *Shadows in the Dark: The Val Lewton Legacy*, created especially for the DVD set. Commentaries were provided by Greg Mank, Simone Simon, Kim Newman and Stephen Jones, Steve Haberman, Robert Wise, Tom Weaver, and William Friedkin.

The *King Kong* tin collector's box not only included the original 1933 classic, but the sequel *Son of Kong* and the related *Mighty Joe Young*, along with reprints of the original Kong souvenir programme, ten poster postcards (fifteen if you bought from Best Buy) and hours of extras, trailers and documentaries. Although the legendary spider-pit sequence is still missing, in a fascinating but ultimately pointless documentary, Peter Jackson and his New Zealand crew attempted to recreate the footage using stop-motion techniques and original reference material.

King Kong: Peter Jackson's Production Diaries was a two-disc collector's edition of behind-the-scenes video diaries from the 2005 version.

Anchor Bay's *Box of the Banned*, subtitled "The Ultimate Collection of Video Nasties" included such once-banned in the UK movies as *Driller Killer*, *The Last House on the Left*, *Nightmares in a Damaged Brain* and *The Evil Dead*, along with a documentary about the effect that the Obscene Publications Act had on horror films in the 1980s.

Released directly to video the same weekend as Steven Spielberg's multi-million dollar adaptation opened in cinemas, Asylum's low budget *War of the Worlds* had C. Thomas Howell's hero defeating the alien invaders with a rabies vaccine.

Three teenage girls disappeared on their homecoming night in *Urban Legends: Bloody Mary*. This latest entry in the series was released directly to DVD in the UK, where all three films were also available in an "ultimate boxset".

The DVD reissue of Gore Verbinski's *The Ring* remake included the short film *Rings*, directed by Jonathan Liebesman (*Darkness Falls*), that bridged the original film and its 2005 sequel, both starring Naomi Watts.

Universal Studios Home Video released "The Bela Lugosi Collection" in September, containing *Murders in the Rue Morgue*, *The*

Black Cat (1934), *The Raven*, *The Invisible Ray* and *Black Friday*. Bonus features were theatrical trailers for three out of the five films.

The classic Basil Rathbone and Nigel Bruce Sherlock Holmes films *Dressed to Kill* (casually retitled *Prelude to Murder*) and *Terror by Night* were issued by Fox Home Entertainment on DVDs containing both the black white and colorised versions. They did the same for *House on Haunted Hill* as well.

Ray Harryhausen: The Early Years Collection contained the stop-motion wizard's five puppet-animation short films (plus the recently completed *The Tortoise & the Hare*) along with such extras as early dinosaur test footage, conceptual drawings and effusive tributes from other film-makers.

Perhaps the best known of Boris Karloff's final quartet of Mexican films, *Fear Chamber* (1968) was released to DVD with a commentary track by co-director Jack Hill and a deleted nude scene.

Paul Naschy's 1982 film *Panic Beats* (he wrote, directed and starred) was released on the Mondo Macabro label with special features that included an exclusive interview with Naschy and a documentary on Spanish horror cinema. Bruno Gantillon's 1971 French film *Girl Slaves of Morgan Le Fay* was presented on DVD in an uncut version from Mondo Macabro with deleted scenes, bonus short and an interview with the director.

Seduction Cinema's usual line-up of softcore erotica included such titles as *G-String Vampire* starring Barbie Leigh, *The Witches of Breastwick* (produced by Jim Wynorski) and *Lust in Space* (the fourth and final instalment in John Bacchus' *Erotic Witch Project* series). Misty Mundae's *Euro-Vixen Collection* contained European versions of *Satan's School for Lust*, *Vampire Vixens* and *Mummy Raider*, along with numerous special features.

On the companion Shock-O-Rama label, *Prison-a-Go-Go* co-starred cult movie actress Mary Woronov, while *The Devil's Plaything* was the R-rated version of Joseph Sarno's 1974 erotic vampire film *Veil of Blood*. Other Shock-O-Rama releases included Richard Griffin's zombie apocalypse *Feeding the Masses*, Gregory Lamberson's 1989 grindhouse horror *Slime City*, and a double bill of *Criminally Insane/Satan's Black Wedding* from sexploitation director "Nick Philips" (Nick Millard).

Self-styled "Scream Queen" Brinke Stevens scraped the bottom of the barrel with Greg Lewolt's "erotic" *Demon Sex* on Alternative Cinema's budget-priced Video Outlaw label. The DVD release also included Stevens and Johnny Legend in the short *Demon Treasures*. Massachusetts film-maker Brian Paulin's mico-budgeted vampire film *At Dawn They Sleep* was also available from Video Outlaw with director's commentary, out-takes and a behind-the-scenes documentary.

All six seasons of the 1973–76 British TV series *Thriller* were released as a DVD boxed set. Created by Brian Clemens (*The Avengers*), the show comprised forty-three episodes starring such well-known faces as Jenny Agutter and Dennis Waterman.

Star Wars: Clone Wars collected the short cartoons that aired on the Cartoon Network between 2003–04 and filled in the gaps between *Episode II* and *Episode III*.

Although all thirteen episodes of executive producer Tim Minear's wonderfully quirky *Wonderfalls* were screened on British television, American fans of the show finally caught up with the nine unaired episodes in that country with the DVD release of *Wonderfalls: The Complete Viewer Collection*. Caroline Dhavernas' Niagara Falls gift shop slacker found she could communicate with inanimate animal figurines that invariably screwed up her already narcissistic life.

In April, BBC4 broadcast a live on air recreation of Nigel Kneale's 1953 drama *The Quatermass Experiment*. Jason Flemying was miscast as a young Professor Quatermass, but Andy Tiernan gave a fine performance as astronaut Victor Caroon, who returned from a space mission irrevocably changed. Future Doctor Who David Tennant was also in the cast.

Scripted by David Pirie for BBC Scotland, *The Strange Case of Sherlock Holmes and Arthur Conan Doyle* blurred the lines between fact and fiction as the troubled author (the excellent Douglas Henshall) was visited by the mysterious "Mr Selden" (a creepy Tim McInnery), who was not the biographer he claimed to be.

In the Sci Fi Channel's original movie *Path of Destruction*, Danica McKellar's investigative journalist was framed by David Keith's evil industrialist, whose lethal scientific experiment was heading towards Seattle. Meanwhile, Keith and a bunch of zombies also celebrated Day of the Dead in *All Souls Day*.

Dominic Zamprogna and Joe Lando fought futuristic vampires in *Bloodsuckers*, which featured a cameo by Michael Ironside.

Sean Astin invented a ten-minute time machine in *Slipstream*, archaeologist Casper Van Dien uncovered an unholy plot in *The Fallen Ones*, and *Man-Thing* was a cheap adaptation of Marvel Comics' *Swamp Thing* knock-off.

Brad Johnson and Carl Weathers set out to prevent diseased aliens from taking human blood in the Sci Fi Channel's *Alien Siege*, and

Gulf War veteran Lou Diamond Phillips had to stop the double-threat of lizard-like aliens and a suicide bomber on a hijacked train in *Alien Express*.

A group of American soldiers (including Robert Beltran and Heather Donahue) battled a revived half-lion, half-dragon *Manticore* in the Iraq desert, while Dan Cortese led a team attempting to prevent *Locusts: The 8th Plague*. Corin Nemec's clichéd cop tried to stop a mutated *Mansquito* making out with his scientist girlfriend (Musetta Vander), and Greg Evigan's terrorist unleashed the three-headed guardian of Hades in *Cerberus*.

Jeffrey Combs' mad scientist turned his dying son into a shark-human hybrid in the ludicrously inept *Hammerhead: Shark Frenzy*, and director Mark L. Lester's career hit rock bottom with *Ptero-dactyl*, in which a covert US army special forces unit (led by 1990s rapper Coolio) saved a group of students from a nest of flying dinosaurs that had recently hatched in a volcano.

Sam Neill's wealthy shipping magnate sent a team of experts (Eric Stoltz, Catherine Bell, Michael Rodgers and a twitchy Bruce Davison) to investigate disappearances in the Bermuda waters and ended up opening a rift in space and time in the entertaining *The Triangle*, executive produced by Bryan Singer and Dean Devlin. Shown over three nights, it was the Sci Fi Channel's highest-rated miniseries since Steven Spielberg's *Taken* in 2002.

Proving that they could make low-budget B-movies just as well as the Sci Fi Channel, the CBS-TV movie *Locusts* ("If you can hear the buzz, it's already too late") starred Lucy Lawless as a college professor battling against a swarm of bio-engineered insects. The actress returned as the same character saving her campus from mutated bloodsuckers in the Halloween sequel, *Vampire Bats*.

Incredibly, CBS also came up with an even worse sequel to the previous year's risible *Category 6: Day of Destruction*. The two-part *Category 7: The End of the World* upped the disaster quota as Randy Quaid, Shannen Doherty, Gina Gershon, James Brolin, Swoosie Kurtz, Robert Wagner and Tom Skerritt battled mega-storms over Washington DC.

Robert Kubilos' dull supernatural drama *The Scorned* was the result of the E! Entertainment documentary series *Kill Reality*, in which a group of minor reality show losers shared a house. When a group of friends hired a beach house for the summer, a woman in a coma reached out to destroy those cheating on their partners. Forrest J Ackerman appeared in an uncredited cameo.

Patrick Stewart turned up on the Hallmark Channel as an irascible

Captain Nemo in an uninspired adaptation of Jules Verne's *Mysterious Island*, complete with CGI monsters, and astrophysicists Peter Fonda and Luke Perry tried to prevent the Earth burning up in the risible *Supernova*. Meanwhile, Anton Rodgers and Diane Venora co-starred in Hallmark's biography, *C.S. Lewis: Beyond Narnia*.

From producer Robert Halmi, Sr., NBC-TV's *Hercules* starred British actor Paul Telfer battling monsters with the help of Leelee Sobieski, Sean Astin and Timothy Dalton.

Kim Raver starred as identical twins haunted by a dead boy in the Lifetime Halloween movie *Haunting Sara*, and *Chasing Christmas* from ABC Family was yet another reworking of the Charles Dickens classic, with Tom Arnold as a modern-day Scrooge plagued by narcissistic ghosts.

Kermit the Frog, Gonzo and Fozzie Bear helped Ashanti's aspiring singer Dorothy follow the Yellow Brick Road in ABC-TV's "Wonderful World of Disney" movie *The Muppets' Wizard of Oz*, which also featured Jeffrey Tambor as the Wizard, Queen Latifah as Aunt Em, and Quentin Tarantino as himself.

The cowardly canine and pals teamed up with 'N Sync's JC Chasez to investigate couples disappearing from Lovers' Lane in The WB's cartoon special *A Scooby-Doo Valentine*, and those meddling kids were back solving an Egyptian mystery in *Scooby-Doo in Where's My Mummy?* and trying to stop a marauding snowman in *A Scooby-Doo Christmas*.

ABC-TV's network premier of *Harry Potter and the Chamber of Secrets* in May was hosted by teenage stars Daniel Radcliffe, Emma Watson and Rupert Grint and included never-before-seen footage along with an exclusive behind-the-scenes look at *Harry Potter and the Goblet of Fire*.

Showtime Network's unrelentingly grim series *Masters of Horror* lured directors such as Tobe Hooper, Dario Argento, Larry Cohen, Don Coscarelli, John McNaughton, William Malone and Lucky McKee to the small screen, adapting stories by Richard Matheson, Clive Barker, Joe R. Lansdale, David J. Schow and others. The standout episodes included Stuart Gordon's updating of H. P. Lovecraft's "Dreams in the Witch House", John Landis' "Deer Woman", John Carpenter's "Cigarette Burns" and Joe Dante's provocative "Homecoming" (based on a story by Dale Bailey), while series creator Mick Garris scripted and directed a version of one of his own stories. Takashi Miike's episode was apparently considered too strong for even cable television in the US, and was held back for the DVD release.

BBC Three's anthology series *Twisted Tales* featured fourteen contemporary urban horror stories with a comic twist. Homicidal technology, bizarre witchcraft, fake haunted houses, demonic movies, Women's Institute zombies and gay ghosts were all featured, while guest stars included Mary Tamm, Paul Darrow, Adrian Edmondson, Alison Steadman and Jan Francis.

The seventh season of The WB's *Charmed* featured guest stars John De Lancie and Billy Zane, while Julian McMahon returned as the ghost of the evil Cole for the show's 150th episode, which aired in April. In the season finale, the demon Zankou stole the powers of the Charmed Ones so that he could control the mysterious "Nexus". Kaley Cuoco joined the show for its eighth and final season as young witch Billie, who was not averse to using her powers in public while the three Halliwell sisters hid behind their new identities.

A surprise mid-season hit for NBC-TV, *Medium* starred a dour Patricia Arquette as real-life psychic Allison DuBois (the show's consultant) who helped the Phoenix district attorney (the always-excellent Miguel Sandoval) catch killers with the help of dead people. Although the series often appeared more interested in Allison's chaotic family life, it was a hit with American female viewers, who made up more than 60 per cent of the audience. The second season opener picked up the serial killer cliff-hanger, and a special 3-D episode in November cleverly spoofed *The Twilight Zone*, although the 3-D effects were ultimately disappointing. Kelsey Grammer was one of the show's executive producers.

CBS-TV's *Ghost Whisperer* starred the likeable Jennifer Love Hewitt as newlywed Melinda Gordon, who was able to help the spirits of the dead close unresolved issues and cross over. The excellent Lesley Sharp played reluctant clairvoyant Alison Mundy, having a miserable time coming to terms with her powers in the six-part British series *Afterlife*, created by Stephen Volk.

Starring Anthony Michael Hall as psychic Johnny Smith, the apocalyptic fourth season of *The Dead Zone* opened on USA Networks with the conclusion to the previous year's cliff-hanger, and ended with Johnny teaming up with his arch-enemy, scheming senator Greg Stillson (Sean Patrick Flanery), to find a missing woman. A one-off Christmas special reunited Johnny with mischievous psychic Alex Sinclair (Jennifer Finnigan), as they helped a disturbed Santa Claus and a trio of street urchins.

Despite a guest appearance by Hilary Duff and the addition of her older sister Haylie in a recurring role, even God could not save *Joan of Arcadia* from being cancelled by CBS after its second series when viewing figures dropped from an average of ten million to around eight million.

Although Jason Priestley returned as Jack, the antithesis of Eliza Dushku's helping-the-dead morgue attendant, the second season of *Tru Calling* limped through just five episodes before it was abruptly cancelled by Fox. In the UK, the new episodes made their debut on DVD along with a sixth, previously unaired episode.

BBC Scotland's miserable *Sea of Souls* returned for a further three two-part shows in which rumpled university investigator Douglas Monaghan (Bill Paterson) and his team encountered poltergeist activity, precognition, sin-eating and apparent time-travel. As usual, they failed to come up with any proof of the supernatural.

Natasha McElhone's maverick nun teamed up with Bill Pullman's cynical Harvard astrophysicist to investigate the possible birth of the Antichrist and prevent the predicted Apocalypse in David Seltzer's glum limited-run series *Revelations*, which aired on NBC over six weekly episodes. Rock star Fred Durst was featured as a creepy Satanist.

In its two-part opener, simpering Devil-child Christina Nickson (newcomer Elisabeth Harnois) was plucked from the sea off the coast of the eponymous small New Jersey town and cast a Satanic influence over the vacuous inhabitants of *Point Pleasant*, Fox's new teen soap opera created by *Buffy*'s Marti Nixon that played like *Dark Shadows* meets *The O.C.*

Jared Padalecki and Jensen Ackles played Sam and Dean Winchester, two ghost-busting brothers in The WB's *Supernatural*, from *The O.C.*'s ludicrously named executive producer McG. The pair travelled the countryside in a 1967 Chevy Impala investigating local urban legends, such as Bloody Mary, the Hook Man and the Woman in White, while trying to uncover clues to their demon-fighting father's mysterious disappearance.

Irish actor Stuart Townsend gave a pathetic performance in the role of crusading reporter Carl Kolchak, who teamed up with sceptical journalist Perri Reed (Gabrielle Union) to investigate the supernatural and discover what happened to his murdered wife in ABC-TV's ill-conceived revival of the 1970s *Night Stalker*, from *The X Files* executive producer Frank Spotnitz. In America the show was cancelled in the middle of a two-part episode.

It's also hard to imagine why anybody thought it was worth doing a second thirteen-part series of *Hex*, especially when most of the original stars disappeared after the first few episodes. But, having unsuccessfully attempted to terminate fallen angel Azazeal's child that she was carrying, English schoolgirl Cassie (Christina Cole) teamed up again with her lesbian ghost friend Thelma (Jemima Rooper) and Buffy-like demon-hunter Ella (Laura Piper) to destroy the devil-child before its birth lead to the downfall of mankind.

Season two of *The 4400* returned to the USA Network in June with two back-to-back episodes featuring its own devil-child and cameos by genre greats Charles Napier and Jeffrey Combs. In the season finale, Dennis Ryland (Peter Coyote) ordered a widespread quarantine to halt the deadly 4400 plague as government agents Tom (Joel Gretsch) and Diana (Jacqueline McKenzie) uncovered a conspiracy to inhibit the powers of the abductees from the future.

Government contingency analyst Molly Anne Caffrey (Carla Gugino) led a team of experts (including Brent Spiner, Rob Benedict and Peter Dinklage) to come up with a plan to confine a spreading alien infection in the CBS series *Threshold*.

Marine biologist Laura Daughtery (the aptly named Lake Bell), along with an obsessed Louisiana scuba diver (Jay R. Ferguson) and an inquisitive teenager (Carter Jenkins), discovered a new species of sea creature and the usual government cover-up conspiracy in NBC's predictable *Surface*.

Created by former actor Shaun Cassidy, ABC's *Invasion* was about a Florida community invaded by body-snatching aquatic aliens. William Fichtner played enigmatic local sheriff Tom Underlay, who knew more about what was happening than he told his doctor wife Mariel (Kari Matchett) or wildlife ranger Russell Varon (Eddie Cibrian). In the US, viewing figures dropped from a respectable 16.4 million viewers to just 10.1 million, despite a lead-in from the still-popular *Lost*.

Despite its Emmy wins, *Lost* was a major disappointment as the flashback-heavy show kept viewers guessing week after week without any sign of plot resolutions. Two major (and related) characters died, while the survivors of crashed Flight 815 finally attempted to build a raft and escape. The first season finale ran over two nights and ended on a predictable cliff-hanger. At the beginning of season two, Jack discovered Desmond (Henry Ian Cusick), a mysterious figure from his past, living in the hatch; young Walt was kidnapped at sea by the "Others" and some of the "tailies" were revealed to have survived the plane crash, including the trigger-happy Ana Lucia (Michelle Rodriguez).

The second season of HBO's Depression-era limited series *Carnvàle* was more overtly fantastic as the countdown to the Apocalypse grew ever closer. Despite building over twelve episodes to the much-anticipated confrontation between Good's Ben Hawkins (Nick Stahl) and Evil's Justin Crowe (Clancy Brown), the network cancelled the show, even though the cliff-hanger finale had an audience of 2.4 million. Guest stars included John Aylward, Patrick Bauchau, John Savage and Don Swayze.

Doctor Who made a triumphant return to BBC-TV with a new thirteen-part series starring Christopher Eccleston as the eccentric time-traveller and former pop singer Billie Piper as his eighteen-year-old companion Rose Tyler. The best episodes were those *not* scripted by the show's overrated producer Russell T. Davies. These included Mark Gatiss' creepy Victorian ghosts episode (with Simon Callow as Charles Dickens), the discovery of a captured Dalek, an attack by bat-winged "Reapers", and a World War II London over-run by gas-masked zombies. The two-part season finale saw an army of Daleks about to invade the Earth.

DVD compilations of the series were quickly released by the BBC, while Brighton Pier on England's south coast mounted an exhibition of props and costumes from the series under the title *Who's on Brighton Pier*.

The second season of the Sci Fi Channel's revived *Battlestar Galactica* turned out to be just as powerful as the first, with a stand-out two-parter inspired by the original "Living Legend" episode, in which the crew discovered a second surviving battlestar, *Pegasus*, commanded by the obsessed Admiral Cain (Michelle Forbes). With civil war threatening to break out at any moment, Lucy Lawless also joined the cast as an investigative journalist who was more than she appeared.

Ben Bowder joined *Stargate SG-1* as the team's new leader, Lt Colonel Cameron Mitchell. He was joined by his *Farscape* co-star Claudia Black as sexy thief Vala Mal Dorn, Beau Bridges as the new head of Stargate Command and Lou Gossett, Jr as power-hungry Jaffa leader Gerak. The ninth season's two-part opener involved a holographic Merlin and the legendary sword Excalibur. Meanwhile, Mitch Pileggi's spaceship commander Colonel Steven Caldwell arrived in time to prevent a mass attack by the Wraith in *Stargate Atlantis*, and Jason Momoa joined the cast as dreadlocked warrior Ronon Dex.

After a shortened fourth season, UPN's *Star Trek Enterprise* was finally put out of its (and our) misery in May. *Next Generation* cast members Jonathan Frakes and Marina Sirtis looked back 200 years to Captain Archer's final voyage, when Commander Trip Tucker (Connor Trinneer) was killed in an explosion while saving the

Enterprise. Viewing figures had reportedly dropped from thirteen million viewers when the show debuted to just under three million.

Meanwhile, the Sci Fi Channel's *Andromeda* lasted a year longer than *Enterprise*, and the series finale had Kevin Sorbo's Captain Dylan Hunt and his companions preparing for a climactic confrontation with the Abyss.

Despite having to compete against ratings winner *Lost*, The WB's *Smallville* continued its welcome return to its *Twilight Zone*-like roots. The fourth season included Lana Lang (Kristin Kreuk) being possessed by witchy ancestor Isobel Theroux who was burned at the stake, and Lex Luthor (Michael Rosenbaum) being split into two personalities. Jane Seymour, Margot Kidder, and Erica Durance as Lois Lane guest-starred, while Terence Stamp once again supplied the voice of Jor-El in the ninety-minute season finale in which Clark Kent (Tom Welling) finally graduated from high school.

Season five featured former model and *American Idol* contestant Alan Ritchson as visiting student Arthur Curry/the future Aquaman, *Buffy*'s James Masters as artificial super-villain Professor Fine/Braniac, a guest appearance by John Schneider's *Dukes of Hazzard* co-star Tom Wopat, Carrie Fisher playing *Daily Planet* editor Pauline Kahn, Lex having an *It's a Wonderful Life* moment, Clark finally sleeping with Lana, and Lana encountering a vampire sorority girl named Buffy. After losing his super-powers and being shot and killed by a meteor freak, Clark was resurrected by Jor-El, who warned his son that he would lose someone close to him in return for his second chance at life.

Meanwhile, an animated *Krypto the Superdog* series for younger viewers on Cartoon Network teamed Superman's super-powered canine with a boy named Kevin and Batman's Bat-Hound. At least it was closer to the original comic-book character than the golden retriever who was cast as the powerful pooch in *Smallville*.

A new teenage Batgirl made her debut on The WB's *The Batman* animated series, battling classmate Poison Ivy, and Huntress and Black Canary were featured on an episode of the Cartoon Network's *Justice League Unlimited*, scripted by DC Comics' *Birds of Prey* writer Gail Simone.

Over at Fox, *The Simpsons Treehouse of Horror XVI* included a cyborg Bart, a witch's transformation spell, and Homer and friends literally being head-hunted by a crazed Mr Burns.

Pumpkin Moon was a Halloween cartoon for children about a black cat and witches, from the team that produced *The Snowman*.

Warner Bros' *Looney Tunes* characters were given a shameful makeover in the Kids' WB series *Loonatics Unleashed*, which featured the descendants of the original characters in the 28th century. That didn't stop it from becoming the #1 Saturday show for its target audience of boys between six and eleven.

There were also plenty of genre references to be found in more mainstream TV series as well. Secret agent Sydney Bristow (Jennifer Garner) and her extended family/team of spies headed off to Russia to destroy a giant red globe that turned people into homicidal zombies in the delirious season four finale of ABC's *Alias*. Despite a cliff-hanger ending, in which Michael Vartan's character Vaughn was apparently killed in a car crash, not all was what it seemed in the fifth and final season of the show.

In an atypical episode of NBC's *Las Vegas*, set behind-the-scenes in a Nevada casino, a big-spending guest apparently shared all the traits of a traditional vampire, and the third season finale of FX Channel's sexy plastic surgery drama *Nip/Tuck* finally revealed the identity of masked serial killer the Carver.

In its first season, high school sleuth *Veronica Mars* (Kristen Bell) apparently solved the murder of her best friend, Lilly Kane, with a little help from the victim's ghost. With both Alyson Hannigan and Charisma Carpenter in season two, and Joss Whedon making a guest appearance as a testy car-rental manager, UPN's entertaining teen mystery was clearly trying to appeal to the *Buffy* crowd.

George Lucas guest-starred as himself in an episode of *The O.C.*, while actor Vince Chase (Adrian Grenier) was up for the role of Aquaman on the HBO comedy series *Entourage* thanks to his incompetent agent Ari (Jeremy Piven).

The seventh and final season of the BBC's Scottish drama series *Monarch of the Glen* featured the ghost of returning character Hector (Richard Briers), while the ever-more offbeat soap opera *Passions* turned into a cartoon fairy tale for three episodes in mid-November.

In a case of wishful thinking, the ever more ludicrous Paris Hilton portrayed Barbara Eden on the set of *I Dream of Jeannie* in an April episode of NBC's *American Dreams*.

Having moved over from HBO to Bravo, the third season of the hilarious *Project Greenlight* had producers Ben Affleck and Matt Damon (with a little help from Wes Craven) convincing Miramax's Dimension arm to come up with the budget to produce a horror film called *Feast*, directed by shy and insecure first-timer John Gulager (the son of actor Clu).

John Carpenter, Wes Craven, John Landis, Tobe Hooper, Linda

Blair, James Herbert, Robert Englund and Simon Pegg were among the numerous talking heads who contributed to Channel 4's two-hour Halloween special, *The Perfect Scary Movie*, and *The Curse of the Omen* was an hour-long Channel 4 documentary that looked at the jinxes that reputedly plagued the hit 1976 movie.

Also from Channel 4, *Jekyll and Hyde: The True Story* was an hour-long documentary that explored the secret life of 18th century Edinburgh gentleman William Deacon Brodie, who was reputedly the inspiration for Robert Louis Stevenson's 1886 novel.

Dennis Wheatley: A Letter to Posterity and *John Wyndham: The Invisible Man of Science Fiction* were hour-long biographies of the largely forgotten British authors shown on BBC4.

Shown to coincide with the opening of the Roald Dahl Museum and Story Centre in Buckinghamshire, Alan Yentob hosted the BBC's *Imagine . . . Fantastic Mr. Dahl*. It was an intimate hour-long profile of the author's life and work that included an interview with his first wife, actress Patricia Neal.

Alec Baldwin narrated the TCM documentary *I'm King Kong: The Exploits of Merian C. Cooper*, a profile of the co-director of the 1933 movie, while *Watch the Skies!* was a superb look at science fiction films that included contributions from George Lucas, Steven Spielberg and James Cameron.

While Jim Broadbent was no replacement for Vincent Price in the National Theatre's summer production of *Theatre of Blood*, the Grand Guignol-style production had a pantomime exuberance, and the casting of Rachael Stirling was inspired in the role originally played by her mother Diana Rigg in the original 1973 movie.

A musical version of *Lestat*, based on the books by Anne Rice with music by Elton John and lyrics by Bernie Taupin, opened to generally negative reviews in San Francisco. Rice described the show as "The fulfilment of my deepest dreams".

Sam Archer portrayed the sharp-fingered creation in Matthew Bourne's stage version of Tim Burton's *Edward Scissorhands*, which opened at London's Sadler's Wells in November.

Shirley Jackson's *The Haunting of Hill House* was adapted by F. Andrew Leslie and performed by the New Stagers Theatre Club at the New Wimbledon Theatre, while *The League of Extraordinary Gentlemen Are Behind You!* was a dark pantomime based on "Jack and the Beanstalk", featuring the stars of the BBC-TV series.

American-born comedienne Ruby Wax starred in a revival of Roald Dahl's *The Witches* at London's Wyndham's Theatre, while song and dance veteran Tommy Steele returned to the London Palladium in the title role of *Scrooge*.

Susannah York played an ageing actress in a stage adaptation of Wilkie Collins' *The Haunted Hotel*, which toured a number of UK cities, and Anthony Andrews took over the role of Count Fosco in Andrew Lloyd Webber's West End musical of Collins' *The Woman in White*.

A new version of Agatha Christie's classic whodunit *And Then There Were None* at the Gielgud Theatre featured Graham Crowden, Tara Fitzgerald, Richard Johnson and Gemma Jones amongst the cast.

The Royal Opera presented the world premiere of conductor Lorin Mazel's *1984*, with libretto by J. D. McClatchy and Thomas Meehan after George Orwell's classic novel. Simon Keenlyside was the singing Winston Smith.

Jeff Noon's *Dead Code: Ghosts of the Digital Age* was an hour-long drama broadcast as part of the BBC Radio 3 series *The Wire*. Starring Emma Atkins and Paul Simpson, it was set on a dreary futuristic housing estate, where the "ghosts" of past songs haunted the streets.

Trevor Hoyle's ghost story *Haunted Hospital*, set in a hospital in Rochdale, was adapted as an hour-long drama for Radio 3's *The Saturday Play*.

So Long and Thanks for All the Fish and *Mostly Harmless*, the final two books in the late Douglas Adams' "trilogy in five parts", were finally broadcast by BBC Radio 4. Most of the surviving cast members from the original radio productions of *The Hitchhiker's Guide to the Galaxy* were reunited for the series.

In the UK, Neil Gaiman's *Anansi Boys* was issued complete and unabridged by Headline Audiobooks on eight CDs (approximately ten hours' running time) read by comedian Lenny Henry.

Doctor Who: Project WHO? was a two-disc CD set of the BBC Radio 2 documentary featuring Christopher Eccleston and Billie Piper talking about the new TV series.

With the end of the *Lord of the Rings* boom, Games Workshop suffered its first-ever fall in sales, as pre-tax profits to the end of May dropped by almost one-third to £13.5 million on a 10 per cent lower turnover.

In the UK, Microsoft was forced to include parental controls in its new Xbox360 console because of the violence in such electronic games as *Condemned: Criminal Origins*, where players attacked victims with a plank of wood with a nail in it.

The disappointing *Star Wars Episode III: Revenge of the Sith* game for PlayStation 2 and Xbox featured clips from the film as Anakin Skywalker and Obi-Wan battled each other with lightsabres. Meanwhile, *Star Wars: Battlefront II* dropped the player into events from all six movies, and *Lego Star Wars* featured fights between the little square figures.

F.E.A.R. combined an action scenario with Asian horrors as soldiers battled each other and ghostly children with supernatural powers.

For GameCube, *Resident Evil 4* returned to its survival horror roots as a government agent searched for a president's missing daughter, while the online game *Resident Evil Outbreak: File #2* featured more zombies (including an elephant!) and was set in four different milieus.

Bruce Campbell reprised his role as the chainsaw-armed Ash, aided by a Deadite dwarf (voiced by Ted Raimi) in his battle against more zombies in *Evil Dead: Regeneration*.

Constantine was a tie-in to the movie for PlayStation 2 and Xbox that featured the likeness of star Keanu Reeves, and you could stalk your enemies as the Dark Knight in *Batman Begins*, featuring a host of star voices.

Created in association with Nick Park's Aardman Animation, *Wallace & Gromit: The Curse of the Were-Rabbit* was a faithful recreation of the movie, while *The Nightmare Before Christmas: Oogie's Revenge* was set shortly after the original film.

To tie-in with the remake of *King Kong*, the estate of Merian C. Cooper released a hand-numbered fourteen-inch cold cast statue of the 1933 Kong on top of the Empire State Building, sculpted by Joe DeVito.

Meanwhile, New Zealand's Weta Collectibles and Dark Horse Comics created a series of limited edition collectibles, including statues, busts, graphic art and other official merchandise based on *King Kong* and *The Chronicles of Narnia: The Lion, The Witch and the Wardrobe*.

The *Kong* overkill continued with an animatronic figure, light-up snowglobe, drinking flask, stoneware stein, various shooter glasses, lunchbox with thermos, chrome lighter, string of head lights, two types of headknockers, six different kinds of candy dispensers and other tie-in tat.

Imported from Japan by X-Plus USA, "Universal Monster Resin Busts" featured nicely detailed eight-inch pre-painted sculpts of Boris Karloff's *Son of Frankenstein* and Lon Chaney, Jr's *The Mummy's Tomb*. Also available were twelve-inch pre-painted Bust Coin Banks of Karloff's *The Mummy* and Chaney, Jr's *The Wolf Man*.

Available by mail-order only, the "Universal Studios Monsters Halloween Village" contained Dr Frankenstein's Castle, Count Dracula's Castle, The Mummy's Tomb and The Creature's Black Lagoon and featured collectable figurines, spooky sounds, glowing lights and real swirling fog! Somewhat predictably, the same set was a third more expensive in the UK than it was in the US.

"The Munsters Holiday Wreath" was available just in time for Halloween.

A twelve-inch detailed collectible figure of Vincent Price as *The Abominable Dr. Phibes* with interchangeable accessories was available in a window box from Majestic Studios.

Majestic also offered two twelve-inch figures of vampire Barnabas Collins ("1795" and "Present Day") from the cult 1960s TV series *Dark Shadows*, along with a figure of werewolf Quentin Collins from the same show. All three figures came with interchangeable parts and accessories. Reel Toys' second series of "Cult Classics" featured poseabale action figures of Freddy Krueger from *Wes Craven's New Nightmare*, The Tall Man from *Phantasm*, Frank the rabbit from *Donnie Darko* and Leatherface from *The Texas Chainsaw Massacre*.

Meanwhile, Sota Toys' second series of "Now Playing" seven-inch articulated figures featured *Jeepers Creepers 2*, *Killer Klowns from Outer Space* and *The Mummy Returns*, while a *Darkman* mini-bust was limited to 1,500 pieces and featured interchangeable heads and hands. Series 3 included figures from *Dog Soldiers*, *Dune*, John Carpenter's *The Thing* and *Legend*.

Also from Sota, "Nightmares of Lovecraft" featured seven-inch articulated action figures of Dagon, Pickman's Model and, of course, Cthulhu himself. A limited edition six-inch Cthulhu Mini-Santa Plush was also available for the holiday season.

The second series of Mez-Itz's "Cinema of Fear" included new figures of Freddy, Leatherface and Jason in a three-pack.

The "*Friday the 13th* 25th Anniversary Action Figures Boxed Set" featured action figures of Sack-Head Jason, Pamela Voorhees, and Jason's shrine to his dead mother.

For the dedicated serial killer fan, Otis' mask from Rob Zombie's *The Devil's Rejects* sold as a prop replica displayed inside a shadow box, limited to 250 pieces.

A *Buffy the Vampire Slayer* "Buffy vs. Dracula Bust" was limited to 5,000 pieces sculpted by Gentle Giant, while Pablo Viggiano's "D'Hoffryn Bust" from the same show would mostly likely appeal to scorned women. A super-articulate deluxe figure of rival vampire slayer "Faith" was also available.

Mini-paperweights of Jack Skellington and Sally the Patchwork Girl were based on Tim Burton's cult movie *The Nightmare Before Christmas*.

In February, The Hammer House of Horror announced it was producing a line of "Gothic chic" fashion, to be created by bespoke tailor Gresham Blake, and Clive Barker's "Moon Me" T-shirt design was available in black with Barker's signature on the front.

Available in time for Halloween from Artbox Entertainment, the "Universal Frankenstein Trading Cards" set included seventy-two base cards depicting the 1931 movie, along with randomly inserted glow-in-the-dark and sketch cards. The set was also available in a limited edition tin and trading card binder.

A poster for Fritz Lang's 1927 science fiction film *Metropolis* sold in November to a private collector in America for a record $690,000. The previous record, set in 1997, was $453,000 for Universal's *The Mummy*. The sepia-coloured poster designed by German graphic artist Heinz Schulz-Neudamm was one of only four copies known to still exist.

Meanwhile, the Dalek Supreme, from the 1979 *Doctor Who* serial *Destiny of the Daleks*, was purchased for £36,000 in November at a charity auction benefiting London's Great Ormond Street Hospital for Sick Children.

World Horror Convention 2005 was held in New York City over April 7th–10th and boasted an impressive line-up of Special Guests of Honour that included authors Harlan Ellison, Joe R. Lansdale, Tim Lebbon, Jack Ketchum, Tom Piccirilli and Mort Castle, film-maker Mick Garris, artist Allen Koszowski, editors Tom and Elizabeth Monteleone, poet Linda Addison, and Master of Ceremonies Stanley Wiater. Somewhat predictably, *Buffy* actress Amber Benson failed to show up. F. Paul Wilson was the recipient of the 2005 Grand Master Award.

It was the West Coast's turn to host the 2004 Bram Stoker Awards, held in Burbank, California, over June 25th–26th. Among the many people recognised by the members of the Horror Writers Association for Superior Achievement in Writing were Peter Straub for his Novel *In the Night Room*, and John Everson and Lee

Thomas, who tied for First Novel with *Covenant* and *And Stained*, respectively. Kealan-Patrick Burke's *The Turtle Boy* picked up the award for Long Fiction, while Nancy Etchemendy's "Nimitseahpah" (from *The Magazine of Fantasy & Science Fiction*) won for Short Fiction. Thomas F. Monteleone's *Fearful Symmetries* collected the Fiction Collection Award, and the Anthology Award went to *The Year's Best Fantasy and Horror 17th Annual* edited by Ellen Datlow, Kelly Link and Gavin Grant. Judi Rohrig's electronic *Hellnotes* won for Non-fiction and Jai Nitz's *Heaven's Devils* was awarded Illustrated Narrative. The Screenplay Award was a tie between *Eternal Sunshine of the Spotless Mind* and *Shaun of the Dead*, and Clive Barker's *Abarat: Days of Magic, Nights of War* and Steve Burt's *Oddest Yet* tied for Work for Young Readers. *The Women at the Funeral* by Corinne De Winter won for Poetry Collection, and Tom Piccirilli's poetry anthology *The Devil's Wine* received the award for Alternative Forms. Delirium Books picked up the Specialty Press Award, and the Hammer Award for outstanding service to the HWA went to webmaster Steve Dorato. Michael Moorcock was announced as the recipient of the Lifetime Achievement Award.

FantasyCon 2005 was held over the first weekend in October in the West Midlands town of Walsall. Guests of Honour were Mark Chadbourn, Simon Clark and Steven Erikson, with Graham Joyce as Master of Ceremonies.

The 2005 British Fantasy Society Awards were presented at the convention Banquet on October 2nd, and the winner of The August Derleth Award for Best Novel was Stephen King's *The Dark Tower VII: The Dark Tower*, which was accepted by Graham Joyce. Marie O'Regan collected the Best Novella Award for Christopher Fowler's *Breathe*, while Paul Meloy was on hand to accept the Best Short Story Award for his tale "Black Static". Andrew Hook's *The Alsiso Project* was voted Best Anthology and he also collected the Best Small Press Award for Elastic Press. PS publisher Peter Crowther accepted the Best Collection Award on behalf of Stephen Gallagher for *Out of His Mind*, Best Artist went to Les Edwards, and Ramsey Campbell accepted the Karl Edward Wagner Special Award on behalf of Nigel Kneale. The winners were presented with a new-look British Fantasy Award depicting a winged demon perched on a rock, designed and sculpted by Arthur Payn.

The World Fantasy Convention was held November 3rd–6th in Madison, Wisconsin. One of the best World Fantasy Conventions for several years, the eclectic Guest of Honour list included artist Kinuko Y. Craft and writers Graham Joyce, Robert Weinberg and

Terri Windling. Peter Straub was the Toastmaster, and April Derleth and Walden Derleth were the Special Guests from publishing imprint Arkham House.

For the first time, the International Horror Guild Awards recognising outstanding achievement in horror and dark fantasy were announced at a ceremony at the convention. *Lost* won for Television, *Shaun of the Dead* for Film and *The Third Alternative* for Periodical. The Non-fiction Award went to *A Serious Life* by D. M. Mitchell, Anthology went to *Acquainted with the Night* edited by Barbara Roden and Christopher Roden, and Collection went to *The Wavering Knife* by Brian Evenson. Don Tumasonis won the Short Form Award for "A Pace of Change" (from *Acquainted with the Night*), Daniel Abraham was awarded Intermediate Form for "Flat Dance" (from *The Magazine of Fantasy & Science Fiction*), and the Long Form Award went to Lucius Shepard for *Viator*. John Harwood's *The Ghost Writer* picked up the award for First Novel, and Ramsey Campbell's *The Overnight* won the Novel Award. Artist Gahan Wilson was announced as the recipient of the annual Living Legend Award.

As usual, the World Fantasy Awards were presented at the Banquet on the Sunday afternoon. Robert Morgan's Sarob Press won the Special Award, Non-Professional, and the Special Award, Professional went to the ubiquitous S. T. Joshi for his many years of scholarship. John Picacio was presented with the Artist Award in front of his proud parents, and Margo Lanagan's *Black Juice* won for Collection. The award for Anthology was a tie between *Acquainted with the Night* edited by the Rodens, and *Dark Matter: Reading the Bones* edited by Sheree R. Thomas. Margo Lanagan also won the Short Fiction Award for her story "Singing My Sister Down", Michael Shea's "The Growlimb" (from *F&SF*) picked up the Novella Award, and Susanna Clarke's *Jonathan Strange & Mr. Norrell* won for Novel. Life Achievement Awards were presented to Carol Emshwiller and publisher Tom Doherty.

Several months ago I was travelling on a tube train across London when I noticed a young woman reading a book further down the same carriage.

A few years ago, that would have been no big deal. But in these days of cheap iPod downloads and multi-media cellular phones, seeing anybody actually reading a book, anywhere, has to be considered a rarity.

That it just happened to be a copy of the latest volume of *The*

Mammoth Book of Best New Horror merely made the event all the more pleasurable for me. The occasional copy of *The Da Vinci Code* or the latest *Harry Potter* adventure I expect, but to see someone actually reading a horror book – *any* horror book – is unusual these days. The fact that it was also an anthology made the incident akin to discovering that a living Dodo was sharing the same carriage!

The problem is that almost nobody reads books any more – *any* books, let alone horror titles. There are too many distractions in our modern lives for most people to commit their time to sitting down and absorbing two or three-hundred pages of quite often complex prose. Better to wait for the DVD instead.

The problem is that we are producing too many books for an ever-decreasing readership. Last year, according to research firm Bowker, for only the second time in twenty years publishers in Britain produced more English-language books than their American counterparts, despite the US total for 2005 being that country's second-highest on record.

Whereas US output dropped for the first time since 1999, the number of titles churned out in the UK leapt by 28 per cent. With Britain having a population one-fifth the size of America, this is obviously an unsustainable situation. And although horror fiction only accounted for a very small proportion of the 206,000 new titles published in the UK in 2005, it can still be seen as a microcosm of the problems affecting the publishing industry as a whole.

The number of new books being produced has been rising steadily since the mid-1980s, and the amount of books coming from American publishers has jumped by an incredible 51 per cent since 1995.

Meanwhile, in 2005 it was also claimed that if the current rate of decline continued, books would no longer be borrowed from British libraries in just seventeen years' time. With an estimated yearly decline of 2.2 million, borrowings had slumped from 55.2 million in 1997–98 to just 39.7 million for the 2003–04 period. The writing is already on the wall – at least for those who can still be bothered to read it.

With production costs getting increasingly expensive every year, publishers will be forced to squeeze their mid-lists even more than they already have to make their sales figures work – especially for high-discounting outlets such as supermarkets and the Internet. Which means saying goodbye to most first novels, collections and anthologies. Only those titles making the biggest profits – usually reflected in the size of their advances and publicity budgets – will survive.

As for the rest, there's always the small press imprints or print-on-demand publishing, but you can't earn enough money from those markets to survive as a full-time writer or editor. Which means that for future generations, the idea of someone having a career as a writer may be just as esoteric a job as being a gas-lamp lighter or an animal trainer in a circus.

With ever more technological advances flooding the market every day to distract us, and the growth of an apparently sub-literate population, how long can it be before the printed word goes the way of the vinyl record album?

So then, who is actually reading all these books we're currently producing? Somebody must be. I meet a few of them at the conventions I attend each year, and an even smaller number contact me through my website. As for the rest, I can only assume that they are out there happily picking up the occasional title from a chainstore or Amazon.com because they like the cover design or recognize a name whose work they know and enjoy.

Such as that passenger who was reading *The Mammoth Book of Best New Horror* on the London Underground. Of course, I considered approaching her, introducing myself and asking what she thought of the book. And then I thought better of that idea. I didn't want to scare her off buying the next one. So I left the train at the next stop with a self-satisfied grin, and the thought that I had at least one reader out there that I would probably never meet but who would hopefully continue to read horror. Perhaps even seek out more work by some of those authors she first encountered in my anthology.

So if you happen to be that woman who was on the tube, and you are reading this current volume, then all I can say is . . . thank you. This genre needs more people like you – many more – or there may not be a mass-market horror field around in a decade's time. But then again, there may not be such things as books either . . .

The Editor
June, 2006

RAMSEY CAMPBELL

The Decorations

ONE OF THE MOST difficult aspects of compiling *The Mammoth Book of Best New Horror* each year is deciding which story by Ramsey Campbell to reprint.

More than any other author working in the genre, Campbell continues to produce consistently superior short fiction, whether it is for mainstream publishers or obscure small press imprints.

This year it was particularly difficult to choose between all the original short fiction he had published, and in the end I decided that the only way to do his work justice was to reprint the two stories that bookend this current volume.

The Decorations was the first book from Alpenhouse Apparitions, a new imprint of Sutton Hoo Press, dedicated to publishing the best supernatural fiction and other genres in hand-made letterpress editions. A year in the making, *The Decorations* was printed from Joanna types with Perpetua titling on dampened Johannot and Somerset papers. The standard edition was bound in quarter cloth with French marbled paper and foil stamped on the spine. The deluxe edition was bound in a contemporary half-leather and marbled paper binding and housed in a clamshell box.

" 'The Decorations' was written for this special edition," explains the author, "and I thought it might make a good Christmas present – hence the Yuletide theme. Mind you, anyone who has read 'The Chimney' will know that Christmas can be a macabre time in my tales.

"Maybe it's the result of receiving that Rupert Bear annual for Christmas when I was a toddler."

"HERE THEY ARE AT LAST," David's grandmother cried, and her face lit up: green from the luminous plastic holly that bordered the front door and then, as she took a plump step to hug David's mother, red with the glow from the costume of the Santa in the sleigh beneath the window. "Was the traffic that bad, Jane?"

"I still don't drive, Mummy. One of the trains was held up and we missed a connection."

"You want to get yourself another man. Never mind, you'll always have Davy," his grandmother panted as she waddled to embrace him.

Her clasp was even fatter than last time. It smelled of clothes he thought could be as old as she was, and of perfume that didn't quite disguise a further staleness he was afraid was her. His embarrassment was aggravated by a car that slowed outside the house, though the driver was only admiring the Christmas display. When his grandmother abruptly released him he thought she'd noticed his reaction, but she was peering at the sleigh. "Has he got down?" she whispered.

David understood before his mother seemed to. He retreated along the path between the flower-beds full of grass to squint past the lights that flashed MERRY CHRISTMAS above the bedroom windows. The second Santa was still perched on the roof; a wind set the illuminated figure rocking back and forth as if with silent laughter. "He's there," David said.

"I expect he has to be in lots of places at once."

Now that he was nearly eight, David knew that his father had always been Santa. Before he could say as much, his grandmother plodded to gaze at the roof. "Do you like him?"

"I like coming to see all your Christmas things."

"I'm not so fond of him. He looks too empty for my liking." As the figure shifted in another wind she shouted "You stay up there where you belong. Never mind thinking of jumping on us."

David's grandfather hurried out to her, his slippers flapping on his thin feet, his reduced face wincing. "Come inside, Dora. You'll have the neighbours looking."

"I don't care about the fat old thing," she said loud enough to be heard on the roof and tramped into the house. "You can take your mummy's case up, can't you, David? You're a big strong boy now."

He enjoyed hauling the wheeled suitcase on its leash – it was like having a dog he could talk to, sometimes not only in his head – but bumping the luggage upstairs risked snagging the already threadbare carpet, and so his mother supported the burden. "I'll just unpack quickly," she told him. "Go down and see if anyone needs help."

He used the frilly toilet in the equally pink bathroom and lingered until his mother asked if he was all right. He was trying to stay clear of the argument he could just hear through the salmon carpet. As he ventured downstairs his grandmother pounced on some remark so muted it was almost silent. "You do better, then. Let's see you cook."

He could smell the subject of the disagreement. Once he'd finished setting the table from the tray with which his grandfather sent him out of the kitchen, he and his mother saw it too: a casserole encrusted with gravy and containing a shrivelled lump of beef. Potatoes roasted close to impenetrability came with it, and green beans from which someone had tried to scrape the worst of the charring. "It's not as bad as it looks, is it?" David's grandmother said through her first mouthful. "I expect it's like having a barbecue, Davy."

"I don't know," he confessed, never having had one.

"They've no idea, these men, have they, Jane? They don't have to keep dinner waiting for people. I expect your hubby's the same."

"Was, but can we not talk about him?"

"He's learned his lesson, then. No call to make that face at me, Tom. I'm only saying Davy's father – Oh, you've split up, Jane, haven't you. Sorry about my big fat trap. Sorry Davy too."

"Just eat what you want," his grandfather advised him, "and then you'd best be scampering off to bed so Santa can make his deliveries."

"We all want to be tucked up before he's on the move," said his grandmother before remembering to smile.

Santa had gone away like David's father, and David was too old to miss either of them. He managed to breach the carapace of a second potato and chewed several forkfuls of dried-up beef, but the burned remains of beans defeated him. All the same, he thanked his grandmother as he stood up. "There's a good boy," she said rather too loudly, as if interceding with someone on his behalf. "Do your best to go to sleep."

That sounded like an inexplicit warning, and was one of the elements that kept him awake in his bedroom, which was no larger than his room in the flat he'd moved to with his mother. Despite their heaviness, the curtains admitted a repetitive flicker from the letters ERR above the window, and a buzz that suggested an insect was hovering over the bed. He could just hear voices downstairs, which gave him the impression that they didn't want him to know what they were saying. He was most troubled by a hollow creaking that reminded him of someone in a rocking chair, but overhead. The Santa figure must be swaying in the wind, not doing its best to heave itself free. David was too old for stories: while real ones didn't always stay true, that wasn't an excuse to make any up. Still, he was glad to hear his mother and her parents coming upstairs at last, lowering their voices to compensate. He heard doors shutting for the night, and then a nervous question from his grandmother through the wall between their rooms. "What's he doing? Is he loose?"

"If he falls, he falls," his grandfather said barely audibly, "and good riddance to him if he's getting on your nerves. For pity's sake come to bed."

David tried not to find this more disturbing than the notion that his parents had shared one. Rather than hear the mattress sag under the weight his grandmother had put on, he tugged the quilt over his head. His grasp must have slackened when he drifted off to sleep, because he was roused by a voice. It was outside the house but too close to the window.

It was his grandfather's. David was disconcerted by the notion that the old man had clambered onto the roof until he realised his grandfather was calling out of the adjacent window. "What do you think you're doing, Dora? Come in before you catch your death."

"I'm seeing he's stayed where he's meant to be," David's grandmother responded from below. "Yes, you know I'm talking about you, don't you. Never mind pretending you didn't nod."

"Get in for the Lord's sake," his grandfather urged, underlining his words with a rumble of the sash. David heard him pad across the room and as rapidly if more stealthily down the stairs. A bated argument grew increasingly stifled as it ascended to the bedroom. David had refrained from looking out of the window for fear of embarrassing his grandparents, but now he was nervous that his mother would be drawn to find out what was happening. He mustn't go to her; he had to be a man, as she kept telling him, and not one like his father, who ran off to women because there was so little to him. In time the muttering beyond the wall subsided, and David was alone with the insistence of electricity and the restlessness on the roof.

When he opened his eyes the curtains had acquired a hem of daylight. It was Christmas Day. Last year he'd run downstairs to handle all the packages addressed to him under the tree and guess at their contents, but now he was wary of encountering his grandparents by himself in case he betrayed he was concealing their secret. As he lay hoping that his grandmother had slept off her condition, he heard his mother in the kitchen. "Let me make breakfast, Mummy. It can be a little extra present for you."

He didn't venture down until she called him. "Here's the Christmas boy," his grandmother shouted as if he was responsible for the occasion, and dealt him such a hug that he struggled within himself. "Eat up or you won't grow."

Her onslaught had dislodged a taste of last night's food. He did his best to bury it under his breakfast, then volunteered to wash up the plates and utensils and dry them as well. Before he finished she was crying "Hurry up so we can see what Santa's brought. I'm as excited as you, Davy."

He hoped she was only making these remarks on his behalf, not somehow growing younger than he was. In the front room his grandfather distributed the presents while the bulbs on the tree flashed patterns that made David think of secret messages. His grandparents had wrapped him up puzzle books and tales of heroic boys, his mother's gifts to him were games for his home computer. "Thank you," he said, sometimes dutifully.

It was the last computer game that prompted his grandmother to ask "Who are you thanking?" At once, as if she feared she'd spoiled the day for him, she added "I expect he's listening."

"Nobody's listening," his grandfather objected. "Nobody's there."

"Don't say things like that, Tom, not in front of Davy."

"That isn't necessary, Mummy. You know the truth, don't you, David? Tell your grandmother."

"Santa's just a fairy tale," David said, although it felt like robbing a younger child of an illusion. "Really people have to save up to buy presents."

"He had to know when we've so much less coming in this Christmas," said his mother. "You see how good he's being. I believe he's taken it better than I did."

"I'm sorry if I upset you, Davy."

"You didn't," David said, not least because his grandmother's eyes looked dangerously moist. "I'm sorry if I upset you."

Her face was already quivering as if there was too much of it to hold still. When she shook her head her cheeks wobbled like a whitish rubber mask that was about to fall loose. He didn't know whether she meant to answer him or had strayed onto another subject as she peered towards the window. "There's nothing to him at all then, is there? He's just an empty old shell. Can't we get him down now?"

"Better wait till the new year," David's grandfather said, and with sudden bitterness "We don't want any more bad luck."

Her faded sunken armchair creaked with relief as she levered herself to her feet. "Where are you going?" her husband protested and limped after her, out of the front door. He murmured at her while she stared up at the roof. At least she didn't shout, but she began to talk not much less quietly as she returned to the house. "I don't like him moving about with nothing inside him," she said before she appeared to recollect David's presence. "Maybe he's like one of those beans with a worm inside, Davy, that used to jig about all the time."

While David didn't understand and was unsure he wanted to, his mother's hasty intervention wasn't reassuring either. "Shall we play some games? What would you like to play, Mummy?"

"What do you call it, Lollopy. The one with all the little houses. Too little for any big fat things to climb on. Lollopy."

"Monopoly."

"Lollopy," David's grandmother maintained, only to continue "I don't want to play that. Too many sums. What's your favourite, Davy?"

Monopoly was, but he didn't want to add to all the tensions that he sensed rather than comprehended. "Whatever yours is."

"Ludo," she cried and clapped her hands. "I'd play it every Sunday with your granny and grandpa when I was Davy's age, Jane."

He wondered if she wasn't just remembering but behaving as she used to. She pleaded to be allowed to move her counters whenever she failed to throw a six, and kept trying to move more than she threw. David would have let her win, but his grandfather persisted in reminding her that she had to cast the precise amount to guide her counters home. After several games in which his grandmother squinted with increasingly less comical suspicion at her opponents' moves, David's mother said "Who'd like to go out for a walk?"

Apparently everyone did, which meant they couldn't go fast or far. David felt out of place compared with the boys he saw riding their Christmas bicycles or brandishing their Christmas weapons. Beneath a sky frosty with cloud, all the decorations in the duplicated streets looked deadened by the pale sunlight, though they were still among the very few elements that distinguished one squat boxy house from another. "They're not as good as ours, are they?" his grandmother kept remarking when she wasn't frowning at the roofs. "He's not there either," he heard her mutter more than once, and as her house came in sight "See, he didn't follow us. We'd have heard him."

She was saying that nothing had moved or could move, David tried to think, but he was nervous of returning to the house. The preparation of Christmas dinner proved to be reason enough. "Too many women in this kitchen," his mother was told when she offered to help, but his grandmother had to be reminded to turn the oven on, and she made to take the turkey out too soon more than once. Between these incidents she disagreed with her husband and her daughter about various memories of theirs while David tried to stay low in a book of mazes he had to trace with a pencil. At dinner he could tell that his mother was willing him to clean his plate so as not to distress his grandmother. He did his best, and struggled to ignore pangs of indigestion as he washed up, and then as his grandmother kept talking about if not to every television programme her husband put on. "Not very Christmassy," she commented on all of them, and followed the remark with at least a glance towards the curtained window. Waiting for her to say worse, and his impression that his mother and grandfather were too, kept clenching David's stomach well before his mother declared "I think it's time someone was in bed."

As his grandmother's lips searched for an expression he wondered if she assumed that her daughter meant her. "I'm going," he said and had to be called back to be hugged and kissed and wished happy Christmas thrice.

He used the toilet, having pulled the chain to cover up his noises, and huddled in bed. He had a sense of hiding behind the scenes, the way he'd waited offstage at school to perform a line about Jesus last year, when his parents had held hands at the sight of him. The flickers and the buzzing that the bedroom curtains failed to exclude could have been stage effects, while over the mumbling of the television downstairs he heard sounds of imminent drama. At least there was no creaking on the roof. He did his best to remember last Christmas as a sharp stale taste of this one continued its antics inside him, until the memories blurred into the beginnings of a dream and let him sleep.

Movements above his head wakened him. Something soft but determined was groping at the window – a wind so vigorous that its onslaughts made the light from the sign flare like a fire someone was breathing on. The wind must be swinging the bulbs closer to his window. He hadn't time to wonder how dangerous that might be, because the creaking overhead was different: more prolonged, more purposeful. He was mostly nervous that his grandmother would hear, but there was no sign of awareness in the next room, and silence downstairs. He pressed the quilt around his ears, and then he heard sounds too loud for it to fend off – a hollow slithering followed by a thump at the window, and another. Whatever was outside seemed eager to break the glass.

David scrambled onto all fours and backed away until the quilt slipped off his body, but then he had to reach out to part the curtains at arms' length. He might have screamed if a taste hadn't choked him. Two eyes as dead as pebbles were level with his. They didn't blink, but sputtered as if they were trying to come to a kind of life, as did the rest of the swollen face. Worse still, the nose and mouth surrounded by a dirty whitish fungus of beard were above the eyes. The inversion lent the unnecessarily crimson lips a clown's ambiguous grimace.

The mask dealt the window another blundering thump before a savage gust of wind seized the puffed-up figure. As the face sailed away from the glass, it was extinguished as though the wind had blown it out. David heard wires rip loose and saw the shape fly like a greyish vaguely human balloon over the garden wall to land on its back in the road.

It sounded as if someone had thrown away a used plastic bottle or an empty hamburger carton. Was the noise enough to bring his grandmother to her window? He wasn't sure if he would prefer not to be alone to see the grinning object flounder and begin to edge towards the house. As it twitched several inches he regretted ever having tipped an insect over to watch it struggle on its back. Then another squall of wind took possession of the dim figure, sweeping it leftwards out of sight along the middle of the road. David heard a car speed across an intersection, its progress hardly interrupted by a hollow thump and a crunch that made him think of a beetle crushed underfoot.

Once the engine dwindled into silence, nothing moved on the roads except the wind. David let the curtains fall together and slipped under the quilt. The drama had ended, even if some of its lighting effects were still operating outside the window. He didn't dream, and wakened late, remembering at once that there was nothing on the roof to worry his grandmother. Only how would she react to the absence?

He stole to the bathroom and then retreated to his bedroom. The muffled conversations downstairs felt like a pretence that all was well until his grandmother called "What are you doing up there?"

She meant David. He knew that when she warned him that his breakfast would go cold. She sounded untroubled, but for how long? "Eat up all the lovely food your mother's made," she cried, and he complied for fear of letting her suspect he was nervous, even when his stomach threatened to throw his efforts back at him. As he downed the last mouthful she said "I do believe that's the biggest breakfast I've ever had in my life. I think we all need a walk."

David swallowed too soon in order to blurt "I've got to wash up."

"What a good boy he is to his poor old granny. Don't worry, we'll wait for you. We won't run away and leave you," she said and stared at her husband for sighing.

David took all the time he could over each plate and utensil. He was considering feigning illness if that would keep his grandmother inside the house when he saw the door at the end of the back garden start to shake as if someone was fumbling at it. The grass shivered too, and he would have except for seeing why it did. "It'll be too windy to go for a walk," he told his grandmother. "It's like Grandad said, you'll catch cold."

His mouth stayed open as he realised his mistake, but that wasn't the connection she made. "How windy is it?" she said, standing up with a groan to tramp along the hall. "What's it going to do to that empty old thing?"

David couldn't look away from the quivering expanse of grass while he heard her open the front door and step onto the path. His shoulders rose as if he fancied they could block his ears, but even sticking his fingers in mightn't have deafened him to her cry. "He's got down. Where's he hidden himself?"

David turned to find his mother rubbing her forehead as though to erase her thoughts. His grandfather had lifted his hands towards his wife, but they drooped beneath an invisible weight. David's grandmother was pivoting around and around on the path, and David was reminded of ballet classes until he saw her dismayed face. He felt that all the adults were performing, as adults so often seemed compelled to do, and that he ought to stop them if he could. "It fell down," he called. "It blew away."

His grandmother pirouetted to a clumsy halt and peered along the hall at him. "Why didn't you say? What are you trying to do?"

"Don't stand out there, Dora," his grandfather protested. "You can see he only wants—"

"Never mind what Davy wants. It can be what I want for a change. It's meant to be my Christmas too. Where is he, Davy? Show me if you think you know so much."

Her voice was growing louder and more petulant. David felt as if he'd been given the job of rescuing his mother and his grandfather from further embarrassment or argument. He dodged past them and the stranded sleigh to run to the end of the path. "It went along there," he said, pointing. "A car ran it over."

"You didn't say that before. Are you just saying so I won't be frightened?"

Until that moment he hadn't grasped how much she was. He strained his gaze at the intersection, but it looked as deserted as the rest of the street. "Show me where," she urged.

Might there be some trace? David was beginning to wish he hadn't spoken. He couldn't use her pace as an excuse for delay; she was waddling so fast to the intersection that her entire body wobbled. He ran into the middle of the crossroads, but there was no sign of last night's accident. He was even more disconcerted to realise that she was so frightened she hadn't even warned him to be careful on the road. He straightened up and swung around to look for fragments, and saw the remains heaped at the foot of a garden wall.

Someone must have tidied them into the side road. Most of the body was a shattered pile of red and white, but the head and half the left shoulder formed a single item propped on top. David was about to point around the corner when the object shifted. Still grinning, it toppled sideways as if the vanished neck had snapped. The wind was moving it, he told himself, but he wasn't sure that his grandmother ought to see. Before he could think how to prevent her, she followed his gaze. "It is him," she cried. "Someone else mustn't have liked him."

David was reaching to grab her hand and lead her away when the head shifted again. It tilted awry with a slowness that made its grin appear increasingly mocking, and slithered off the rest of the debris to inch along the pavement, scraping like a skull. "He's coming for me," David's grandmother babbled. "There's something inside him. It's the worm."

David's mother was hurrying along the street ahead of his grandfather. Before they could join his grandmother, the grinning object skittered at her. She recoiled a step, and then she lurched to trample her tormentor to bits. "That'll stop you laughing," she cried as the eyes shattered. "It's all right now, Davy. He's gone."

Was the pretence of acting on his behalf aimed at him or at the others? They seemed to accept it when at last she finished stamping and let them usher her back to the house, unless they were pretending as well. Though the adults had reverted to behaving as they were supposed to, it was too sudden. It felt like a performance they were staging to reassure him.

He must be expected to take part. He had to, or he wouldn't be a man. He pretended not to want to go home, and did his best to simulate enjoyment of the television programmes and the games that the others were anxious his grandmother should like. He feigned an appetite when the remnants of Christmas dinner were revived, accompanied by vegetables that his mother succeeded in rescuing from his grandmother's ambitions for them.

While the day had felt far too protracted, he would have preferred it to take more time over growing dark. The wind had dropped, but not so much that he didn't have to struggle to ignore how his grandmother's eyes fluttered whenever a window shook. He made for bed as soon as he thought he wouldn't be drawing attention to his earliness. "That's right, Davy, we all need our sleep," his grand-mother said as if he might be denying them theirs. He suffered another round of happy Christmases and hugs that felt more strenuous than last night's, and then he fled to his room.

The night was still except for the occasional car that slowed outside the house – not, David had to remember, because there was anything on the roof. When he switched off the light the room took on a surreptitious flicker, as if his surroundings were nervous. Surely he had no reason to be, although he could have imagined that the irritable buzz was adding an edge to the voices downstairs. He hid under the quilt and pretended he was about to sleep until the sham overtook him.

A change in the lighting roused him. He was pushing the quilt away from his face so as to greet the day that would take him home when he noticed that the illumination was too fitful to be sunlight. As it glared under the curtains again he heard uncoordinated movement through the window. The wind must have returned to play with the lit sign. He was hoping that it wouldn't awaken his grandmother, or that she would at least know what was really there, when he realised with a shock that paralysed his breath how wrong he was. He hadn't heard the wind. The clumsy noises outside were more solid and more localised. Light stained the wall above his bed, and an object blundered as if it was limbless against the front door.

If this hadn't robbed David of the ability to move, the thought of his grandmother's reaction would have. It was even worse than the prospect of looking himself. He hadn't succeeded in breathing when he heard her say "Who's that? Has he come back?"

David would have blocked his ears if he had been capable of lifting his fists from beside him. He must have breathed, but he was otherwise helpless. The pause in the next room was almost as ominous as the sounds that brought it to an end: the rumble of the window, another series of light but impatient thumps at the front door, his grandmother's loose unsteady voice. "He's here for me. He's all lit up, his eyes are. The worm's put him back together. I should have squashed the worm."

"Stop wandering, for God's sake," said David's grandfather. "I can't take much more of this, I'm telling you."

"Look how he's been put back together," she said with such a mixture of dismay and pleading that David was terrified it would compel him to obey. Instead his panic wakened him.

He was lying inert, his thoughts as tangled as the quilt, when he heard his grandmother insist "He was there."

"Just get back in bed," his grandfather told her.

David didn't know how long he lay waiting for her to shut the window. After that there seemed to be nothing to hear once her bed acknowledged her with an outburst of creaking. He stayed uneasily alert until he managed to think of a way to make sense of events: he'd overheard her in his sleep and had dreamed the rest. Having resolved this let him feel manly enough to regain his slumber.

This time daylight found him. It seemed to render the night irrelevant, at least to him. He wasn't sure about his grandmother, who looked uncertain of something. She insisted on cooking breakfast, rather more than aided by her husband. Once David and his mother had done their duty by their portions it was time to call a taxi. David manhandled the suitcase downstairs by himself and wheeled it to the car, past the decorations that appeared dusty with sunlight. His grandparents hugged him at the gate, and his grandmother repeated the gesture as if she'd already forgotten it. "Come and see us again soon," she said without too much conviction, perhaps because she was distracted by glancing along the street and at the roof.

David thought he saw his chance to demonstrate how much of a man he was. "It wasn't there, Granny. It was just a dream."

Her face quivered, and her eyes. "What was, Davy? What are you talking about?"

He had a sudden awful sense of having miscalculated, but all he could do was answer. "There wasn't anything out here last night."

Her mouth was too nervous to hold onto a smile that might have been triumphant. "You heard him as well."

"No," David protested, but his mother grabbed his arm. "That's enough," she said in a tone he'd never heard her use before. "We'll miss the train. Look after each other," she blurted at her parents, and shoved David into the taxi. All the way through the streets full of lifeless decorations, and for some time on the train, she had no more to say to him than "Just leave me alone for a while."

He thought she blamed him for frightening his grandmother. He remembered that two months later, when his grandmother died. At the funeral he imagined how heavy the box with her inside it must be on the shoulders of the four gloomy men. He succeeded in withholding his guilty tears, since his grandfather left crying to David's mother. When David tried to sprinkle earth on the coffin in the hole, a fierce wind carried off his handful as if his grandmother had blown it away with an angry breath. Eventually all the cars paraded back to the house that was only his grandfather's now, where a crowd of people David hadn't met before ate the sandwiches his mother had made and kept telling him how grown-up he was. He felt required to pretend, and wished his mother hadn't taken two days off from working at the nursery so that they could stay overnight. Once the guests left he felt more isolated still. His grandfather broke one of many silences by saying "You look as if you'd like to ask a question, Davy. Don't be shy."

David wasn't sure he wanted to be heard, but he had to be polite and answer. "What happened to Granny?"

"People change when they get old, son. You'll find that out, well, you have. She was still your grandmother really."

Too much of this was more ominous than reassuring. David was loath to ask how she'd died, and almost to say, "I meant where's she gone."

"I can't tell you that, son. All of us are going to have to wait and see."

Perhaps David's mother sensed this was the opposite of comforting, for she said "I think it's like turning into a butterfly, David. Our body's just the chrysalis we leave behind."

He had to affect to be happy with that, despite the memory it threatened to revive, because he was afraid he might otherwise hear worse. He apparently convinced his mother, who turned to his grandfather. "I wish I'd seen Mummy one last time."

"She looked like a doll."

"No, while she was alive."

"I don't think you'd have liked it, Jane. Try and remember her how she used to be and I will. You will, won't you, Davy?"

David didn't want to imagine the consequences of giving or even thinking the wrong answer. "I'll try," he said.

This appeared to be less than was expected of him. He was

desperate to change the subject, but all he could think of was how bare the house seemed without its Christmas finery. Rather than say so he enquired, "Where do all the decorations go?"

"They've gone as well, son. They were always Dora's."

David was beginning to feel that nothing was safe to ask or say. He could tell that the adults wanted him to leave them alone to talk. At least they oughtn't to be arguing, not like his parents used to as soon as he was out of the way, making him think that the low hostile remarks he could never quite hear were blaming him for the trouble with the marriage. At least he wouldn't be distracted by the buzzing and the insistent light while he tried to sleep or hear. The wind helped blur the voices below him, so that although he gathered that they were agreeing, he only suspected they were discussing him. Were they saying how he'd scared his grandmother to death? "I'm sorry," he kept whispering like a prayer, which belatedly lulled him to sleep.

A siren wakened him – an ambulance. The pair of notes might have been crying "Davy" through the streets. He wondered if an ambulance had carried off his grandmother. The braying faded into the distance, leaving silence except for the wind. His mother and his grandfather must be in their beds, unless they had decided David was sufficiently grown-up to be left by himself in the house. He hoped not, because the wind sounded like a loose voice repeating his name. The noises on the stairs might be doing so as well, except that they were shuffling footsteps or, as he was able to make out before long, rather less than footsteps. Another sound was approaching. It was indeed a version of his name, pronounced by an exhalation that was just about a voice, by no means entirely like his grandmother's but too much so. It and the slow determined unformed paces halted outside his room.

He couldn't cry out for his mother, not because he wouldn't be a man but for fear of drawing attention to himself. He was offstage, he tried to think. He only had to listen, he needn't see more than the lurid light that flared across the carpet. Then his visitor set about opening the door.

It made a good deal of locating the doorknob, and attempting to take hold of it, and fumbling to turn it, so that David had far more time than he wanted to imagine what was there. If his grandmother had gone away, had whatever remained come to find him? Was something of her still inside her to move it, or was that a worm? The door shuddered and edged open, admitting a grotesquely festive glow, and David tried to shut his eyes. But he was even more afraid not to see the shape that floundered into the room.

He saw at once that she'd become what she was afraid of. She was draped with a necklace of fairy lights, and two guttering bulbs had taken the place of her eyes. Dim green light spilled like slimy water down her cheeks. She wore a long white dress, if the vague pale mass wasn't part of her, for her face looked inflated to hollowness, close to bursting. Perhaps that was why her mouth was stretched so wide, but her grin was terrified. He had a sudden dreadful thought that both she and the worm were inside the shape.

It blundered forward and then fell against the door. Either it had very little control of its movements or it intended to trap him in the room. It lurched at him as if it was as helpless as he was, and David sprawled out of bed. He grabbed one of his shoes from the floor and hurled it at the swollen flickering mass. It was only a doll, he thought, because the grin didn't falter. Perhaps it was less than a doll, since it vanished like a bubble. As his shoe struck the door the room went dark.

He might almost have believed that nothing had been there if he hadn't heard more than his shoe drop to the floor. When he tore the curtains open he saw fairy lights strewn across the carpet. They weren't what he was certain he'd heard slithering into some part of the room. All the same, once he'd put on his shoes he trampled the bulbs into fragments, and then he fell to his hands and knees. He was still crawling about the floor when his mother hurried in and peered unhappily at him. "Help me find it," he pleaded. "We've got to kill the worm."

DAVID HERTER

Black and Green and Gold

AS DAVID HERTER EXPLAINS, "'Black and Green and Gold' is an exercise in sinister epistolary narrative, inspired by Robert Aickman, Gene Wolfe and Angelo Rippellino's wonderful *Magic Prague*. It's the first of several projects sparked by my 2004 trip to the Czech Republic."

The author's dark fantasy novella, *On the Overgrown Path*, about the composer Leos Janáček, was released by PS Publishing, and he has recently completed *The Luminous Depths*, a time-slip featuring Karel Capek and an ill-fated production of *Rossum's Universal Robots*. Also forthcoming is *One Who Disappeared*, about expatriate Czechs in Hollywood, circa 1950, which ties all three novellas together.

Herter is nearing completion of two full-length novels: *Dark Carnivals* is an epic horror-fantasy set in 1977 suburbia, USA, while *In the Photon Forests* is a prequel to his first novel, *Ceres Storm*.

D EAR LEV,
    You will find a small package beneath this letter. Do not open it, please, until you finish reading.

This is about Erel, of course. Elizabeth wrote me. Don't blame her for this transgression. She has attempted to maintain the lines of communication, even in these difficult times.

She says her brother hasn't been heard from since March. At the library, I found the May 5 article in your hometown paper with more details. I'm writing for reasons that will soon become apparent.

I too have been to Prague. You may have heard this from Genevieve. (Regrettably, Gen and I have never been as close as Erel and Elizabeth. On the few occasions when she asked me to recount the details, what I told her was not quite the truth).

This was in 1986, three years before the Communists were swept from power. I was working for the University, in the same department where I met Margaret a year later. Visas were more difficult to obtain back then. Pleasure trips, such as Erel's, would have been discouraged. The *Statni Bezpecnost* (StB) scrutinized every visitor, even a dull academic such as myself. Truth be told, I was in the employ, part-time, of a governmental agency, one that routinely took advantage of travelling scholars. The job was low-level, but I expected scrutiny. While leaving Czech customs I was sure I'd spotted the StB agent assigned to keep tabs on me – sloppy black hair, bad teeth, rumpled brown suit. When I joined a queue for the cabs he was right behind me. As I departed, he stubbed his cigarette beneath his shoe and said, with only the slightest of accents, "Enjoy your time in Praha."

I would not see him again until days later, at Sharpshooter Island, but I felt certain he intended to make his presence known that first day.

During the drive into Prague, I remember rolling down the window to cool my face. The city of a hundred spires, it's rightly called. I saw it through a wintry haze, with the cold breeze cutting at my eyes. The green and grey river, and the grey and white snow, out of which rose a forest of cathedral-haunted structures, black and green and gold.

My hotel was in the Smichov district, south of Mala Strana – the Small Quarter – and the castle, southwest of all the well-known sights across the Vltava river.

~~This trip was my~~

That first day, Lev, as I walked to the Institute, I felt eyes upon me. The sensation became so intense I had to stop and look over my shoulder. The snowy sidewalk behind me was clear. The only audience was above-ground, set in stone: gargoyles and placid faces peering down from the lintels.

Even here, the ancient city watches with ancient disinterest.

Lev, this is my first attempt to detail it. I'm having to find my way into the telling.

I should say this was my only excursion into Eastern Europe. Previous trips had been confined to London and Copenhagen. No doubt the exotic surroundings had over-stimulated me: I'd been transported into the realm of a spy novel, causing me, for instance, to believe the man at the airport was StB, something of which I was never entirely certain.

The Institute – its full title is the *Stepan Institute for Historical Studies* – was a mixing pot of European and American scholars. Several were *in the employ*, discreetly. We rarely mingled outside of those dusty stacks of books. I had legitimate research in Prague, in addition to various queries I would make on behalf of the agency. Apart, I tried enjoying the role of tourist.

The second afternoon, after a morning spent with rare holograph manuscripts of Nezval and Seifert, I followed the river north through Mala Strana to the base of Hradcany Castle. Prague is a lure to the walking tourist, but I resisted the urge to climb the ancient steps. I was forty-six, many years past my Army days. This was February; the temperature hovered just above freezing. The smell of soot and sulfur was folded into the frigid air.

Though I was enthralled by St. Vitus Cathedral and its blackened, crenellated spires lifting against the clouds, I worried about catching pneumonia. I had no wish to experience the local health care. So I found a nice vantage on *Karluv most* – the Charles Bridge – from which Hradcany seemed to sit upon a storybook hill, with the quaint red tile roofs of Mala Strana sprawling down to the Vltava. Watching it, I contemplated the legends of the mad Emperor Rudolf II and his ever-changing entourage of astrologers, astronomers, charlatans and crackpots, who had flocked to this city in the 16th century, when Prague was the center of the Holy Roman Empire.

The Charles Bridge is pedestrian-only. That day, I was the only stroller among a bustling crowd, pausing before each of the thirty-two statues. Some were splendorous, some malevolent, blackened with age and soot.

I was standing beside St. John of Nepomuk, and had turned away to look southward at the oncoming currents when I first noticed the island. Not Kampa Island beneath the bridge – which is not quite an island – but that slender, true island to the south called *Strelecky Ostrov*, or Sharpshooter Island; once, it had served as residence for Rudolf's mercenaries.

In winter, bare oak trees fringed the shoreline. The interior was damp parkland, with an Italianesque structure on its south shore.

The Vltava rushed past it, grey and green.

Years later, during the 2002 flood, CNN showed images of the swollen river from nearly this same vantage: the current thundering past, full of broken timber, and Sharpshooter Island lost entirely under the waves.

*   *   *

That crucial day, I behaved as a tourist would – as no doubt Erel did.

Black and green and gold, I wrote above, about my first impression of Prague. As I wandered *Stare Mesto* – the Old Town – I found other vivid colors predominating, the reds of roofs, the pale pinks and blues of the tenement faces, the silvers and grays of cobblestones. I walked north to the Jewish quarter, wandering the crooked, claustrophobic streets. The river was an able marker; it was impossible to get lost for long. South in the Old Town Square, I found the statue of Jan Hus, the Protestant Reformer, holding court amid the Counter-Reformation surroundings. The Old Town Hall's Astrological Clock, such an attraction to tourists today, was mostly unattended as it chimed the afternoon hours and processed its figures of Death and the Apostles. I was drawn past it, to the Church of Our Lady Before Tyn and its pair of grey stone, black-topped towers, whose steeples resembled – somehow – witches' hats. Though many consider Tyn a jewel of Prague buildings, I was struck by its architectural melancholy. History speaks of horrors wrought in its shadow, such as the scores of political prisoners executed in 1437, when the stones near Tyn ran ankle-deep in blood; or the dozen young women hanged for witchcraft (more specifically *aquamancy*) in the summer of 1626, their bodies left out to desiccate, then beheaded, with the heads thrown into the Vltava.

My mother owned a 19th-century folio of Mediaeval and Renaissance paintings by Fra Angelico, Pieter Bruegel the Elder, and Bosch. (She bequeathed it to Genevieve – I remember looking through it with Erel on that winter holiday at your home in 1998.) Staring up at Tyn, I recalled my first views of its pages – how the paintings had sparked a frightening sense of displacement in my child's mind; their grotesque imagery, in faded tempura and oils, depicting a world seemingly at odds with the history books, hinting, however subtly, at some strange underlying reality in the veracity of their nightmarish details.

Tyn is where the astronomer Tycho Brahe is buried. Curious to see the tomb behind the altar, I followed the gallery through the Tyn School (a later construction) to the church door, only to find it locked. I was alone, yet not alone. In a fissure beside the Gothic arch a small stone face, round-cheeked, sullen – remnant of some earlier architecture, perhaps – peered out. Its ancient eyes seemed as unable to believe the sight of me as I of it.

I apologize if this seems a digression. But I thought of Tyn after learning (from the newspaper account) that Erel's last email was traced to the Hasek Café, just down the street from Tyn and the astronomer's tomb.

I had to rest my hand.

Since I'm an able typist, I sometimes forget how important the fourth and fifth fingers are to handwriting.

I trust you can decipher the clarifications printed above that scrawled last sentence.

There is a point to make. I will attempt to reach it now.

On my wandering walk, I found myself at the grand concert hall on the Vltava – the *Narodni Divadlo*, or National Theater. Glittering in green and gold, it projects a grandly linear profile amid all the baroque architecture, its rounded roofline like an elaborate cake festooned (there is no other word) with pickets of gold trim, and fronted with statues. The most prominent is a charioteer ready to launch his steeds into the sky.

A poster advertised Antonin Dvorak's greatest opera, *Rusalka*. Earlier, at the Rudolfium Hall north of the Charles Bridge, I had paused before his statue – Dvorak was a favorite composer of mine. Now, I was pleased to see a performance scheduled – such was my luck – at seven o'clock that evening.

I bought a ticket, and spent the intervening hours at the restaurant across the street, the Kavarna Slavia.

I had been briefed about its reputation as a well-known rendez-vous for both dissidents and State Security, but that afternoon its Art Deco interior was nearly deserted. I took a table by the tall windows overlooking (or actually, *underlooking*) the Divadlo. Nothing re-markable happened, yet I would soon wonder – with staggering ignorance, Lev – if it was there that I piqued the interest of the dissident community.

The National Theatre was as grand inside as out, with three tiers of balconies and boxes, green and gold, over a floor of burgundy-velvet seats. On either side of the stage loomed Grand Boxes decked with full-size statues of Nereids holding back velvet curtains. Overhead, a fresco continued the Grecian theme.

I had secured a perfect seat: sixth row center. The audience was slightly drab and dour, the men in unostentatious dress attire, the women only slightly more glamorous.

The chandeliers dimmed.

Polite applause greeted the conductor.

I will not recount the plot. Genevieve used to mention your

fondness for Mozart and Rossini; perhaps it extends to Dvorak. At any rate, you'll find a synopsis in the Grove Encyclopedia in your library. Rusalka is a water nymph who falls in love with a human, and the opera is a sad one. What opera isn't? The music, however, is plangent and lovely. When the unseen orchestra began to play the tentative, tremulous prelude (however ominous Dvorak intended it) the warm strings seemed to chase the chill from my bones.

Rusalka was sung by Gabriela Berezkova, who was then at the height of her tragically short career. I was close enough to see her Botticellian eyes widen as she sang of her dreamed-for lover. In her first act aria, the famous *Aria to the Moon*, she seemed to be singing to me alone, so perfect was my seat. The performance was sublime. At intermission, when the rest of the audience departed for the lobby, I approached the orchestra pit. I remember placing my hand on the decorous rail, feeling the regard of those gold Nereids on either side, as I looked down.

Below, two musicians – a double bass and a trombone – were chatting in fleet Czech. The pit seemed older than the theater, all the gilt and gold beauty relenting in its depths to drab functionality. Wooden music stands held the scores. Beyond the conductor's podium, empty chairs huddled in the gloom, against a wall whose blackness recalled to me Tyn's towers.

At the opposite end a door led offstage. Its pale light was broken, momentarily, as those last two players exited the pit. Somewhere backstage, a flautist was practicing her lines. Notes drifted up and down, as I leaned further over that gold rail, and caught a sharp scent of – perhaps mildew. As though a pipe had broken from the cold. Nonetheless, it was appropriate to Rusalka's lake.

Leaning forward, my hands tightening on the rail, I felt a sudden wave of dizziness, and a sense of—

To treat it realistically, Lev, I would say it was dizziness brought on by the day's exertions. Yet a *swoon* might be a better term, with all it implies. I experienced a number of heightened sensations. My heart began beating rapidly. I felt light-headed, my skin grew hot, I gained a sudden awkward erection – kindled somehow by that river smell, in the air before me, there by the gold rail. And a sense of movement close by, in my dizziness. Of something very lightly touching my shoulder, my cheek.

I do not speak of ghosts, nor wish to imply their presence. Nor did I think of ghosts then.

I steadied myself, even as my vision became blotchy – as if those dark spots had detached themselves from the *Tynian* shadows of the pit. I straightened, blinked, regaining my composure. Slightly shaken, I returned to my seat. I was able to blame the arduousness of the afternoon's walk: I chided myself for over-exertion.

The remainder of the opera, though no different in quality from before, felt somehow diminished. True, Gabriela Berezkova sang with melancholy sweetness as her human lover died. There was the expected sense of sadness as she returned to her lake. The audience responded with two curtain calls. But I was unmoved. My thoughts were elsewhere.

When the lights came up, I waited for most of the crowd to file out, then followed, more slowly.

Once in the hall, I headed in the opposite direction, surprising myself. I found a door marked *Zakulisi* – Backstage. As I neared it, it was swung wide by a tuxedoed man clutching a violin case. He gave me a distracted glance, and held it open before striding down the hall. Trying to look sure of myself, I stepped through. I wandered a warren of rooms, wondering what I hoped to accomplish. Luckily, everyone was distracted; their duties done, they were heading home.

Was I trying to find Ms Berezkova's dressing room, here to pay foolish compliments to the singer? Even as I asked myself the question, I was descending a stairwell. After a few wrong turns I entered a storeroom of instruments which led, via a tall narrow door, into the pit.

From here, the Tynian blackness had become drab grey.

I stood for a long moment, remembering the strange sensations. I looked up to the gold rail, which seemed a greater height from this angle against the dim, impossibly remote fresco.

The predominant odor was not Rusalka's lake but overused stage lights.

I walked behind the chairs, to the harp, drawn to a grating in the floor.

Leaning close to the black-metal I smelled the sharp, fetid odor, nearly as intense as it had been earlier. Yet easily explainable. Ground water, seepage from the Vltava.

The Theater sat upon its banks, after all.

I remained crouching over the grate, listening to its seashell-like echo. Then, staring down, I had that shivery feeling one gets when, alone in the dark, one imagines a face has been there all along, unseen, looking back.

I rose, put a hand to the harp to steady myself (creating a faint resonance, as though all the strings had just given the slightest of shudders). As I re-entered the store room I nearly collided with a worker come to collect the leftover scores. Startled, I said, in Czech, "Lost. I am lost."

I had to show my passport, then the Institute's card, then I was escorted out.

While crossing the bridge to Smichov, I felt another wave of dizziness. I stumbled to the rail and vomited over the side. Dolorous church bells echoed through *Stare Mesto*. I remember looking over at the glittering *Narodni Divadlo*, waiting for another heave which didn't come. Coughing, I glanced at the opera house, and downward, noticing, level with the river, a stone pier carved into the stone shore, with a portal and a window which looked sealed shut.

By the next morning, the strangeness of those moments in the opera house had receded. I was well rested. I promised myself not to make any more day-long treks through the city.

But I remembered the pier. At the Institute, I asked about it.

A colleague told me it was a remnant of a 17th-century fisherman's port, predating the National Theater and most of the nearby structures.

Eager to feed my curiosity, he pointed me to several excellent volumes.

The Old and New Towns had nearly as vivid a history below ground as above. Prague, like most ancient cities, is built-up with layers of accretion; the earliest catacombs date back to the original settlements that grew a thousand years ago along the Vltava. In the Middle Ages, the pier had connected to alleys and sidestreets that had been subsequently covered.

Krejci's *Praha legend a skutecnosti* (1872) and Heinholz's *Stara Praha* (1906) tell several vivid tales of this underground realm, such as the histories of Charles Square and *Fastuv Dum*.

The Square, three miles south of Tyn Church in Nova Mesto (the New Town) was once called the Cattle Market, built around a mysterious ancient rock topped with a cross. The charlatans who flocked to Prague during Rudolf's reign set up shop there. It became a breeding ground for black deeds and blacker spirits, a place of executions, where corpses were dropped through trap doors into a snarl of underground passages; and those same passages (according to legend) were home to myriad secret and alchemical societies.

Hapless victims, so the legends say, were walled up alive in underground casements.

On the Square's southern edge sits Faustuv Dum – Faust House, dating from the 12th-century.

Edward Kelley, the alchemist, lived there in the late 16th century, conducting experiments at the behest of Rudolf II. During Kelley's diabolical tenure, and after, the legend grew: that the palatial estate had been the last home of Doktor Faust, and the site of his final battle with Mephistopholes. Hence, Faustuv Dum.

My fifth day in Prague, while studying drier texts at the carrels, I heard the bell ringing downstairs. Moments later our German-Irish attendant Jacob whispered that I had a visitor.

Drop-ins were rare; I knew nobody outside the Institute.

In the previous days, Lev, I had discharged my duties to the agency: a series of modest inquiries at local embassies and (surprisingly) a book store. My expectation, as I descended the stairs, was that this visitor was somehow connected to those duties. Or was perhaps my unseen StB agent.

Instead, a derelict waited in the foyer.

"*Dobry den*," he said, barely looking up from his boots. He was bald but for straggles of grey hair, with weak, rheumy eyes and a palsied shake to his hands.

He said my full name, though he pronounced my first as Stefan.

"Yes," I replied. "*Ano*."

He held out a slip of green paper. I took it.

It bore a message, crudely lettered: "*Stephen Madison: Strelechy Ostrov, east shore, 16:00. Hastrman.*"

Hastrman?

Though the name seemed vaguely familiar, it wasn't somebody I'd dealt with in recent duties.

"*Nashela*," he muttered, moving toward the door.

I held up my hand. "Wait. *Prominte*."

He hesitated.

"Who is this Hastrman?"

He shook his head, and looked from me to Jacob. "*Nerozum'm*," he said. *I do not understand*.

Hovering at the door, Jacob translated my question, and quickly asked a follow-up. "He says he wrote the note on behalf of an old gentleman, one he has never seen before, down by Legion Bridge. He was paid a hundred crowns to deliver it."

The derelict shuffled out. With evident relief, Jacob closed the door.

Paul Dawson was my contact at the Institute.

I found him in his attic office, and dropped the note on his desk, beside his tea. He deemed it of slight – but only slight – importance.

"State Security doesn't use bums," he said. "What about those folk you were squeezing at the embassy? Friends of theirs?"

"Perhaps. But I don't think so." I was thinking of that afternoon, days ago, in the Kavarna Slavia, and wondering whether there had been any significant moments there.

Dawson said, "Hastrman – might be a person's name, or might be one of the dissident groups, but this isn't their *modus operandi*. You willing to go?"

I said I was.

There was that thrill, Lev – the excitement of being drawn, seemingly, into a spy novel.

"I'll run the name through our books, see if something comes up." He offered to have a colleague tail me, but I declined. "Keep a record of everything said. You know the drill."

Near the appointed hour, clad in my winter coat, hat and gloves, I trudged down to the Vltava's banks.

Snow had been shoveled from the sidewalks.

There was something spiteful about those cobblestones. They seemed to take pleasure in catching the heel unexpectedly; each step was a slight betrayal of what the eye had expected, reminding me that I was not Prague-born.

As I neared Sharpshooter Island, I realized I didn't know how to reach it. By boat? Could one rent a boat so late on a Saturday – a day when even the coffee houses were closed? With equal swiftness, I noted that the Legion Bridge, which crossed the island, dropped a steep staircase to the surface.

Descending it, I studied the narrow length of somber parkland, as would any good spy. Snowy grass, benches, paths, all deserted. To my left, the sun set over Old Town, casting long shadows.

In the distance, lights shone in the Italianesque structure. Closer, massive oaks shrouding the shore spoke of utter emptiness.

Rain would have been appropriate. There was an underwater ambience to the island, sitting so low beneath the banks of the Vltava.

I crossed the field, passing several baroque-iron lamps, and a lone statue of a nymph with demure down-turned eyes. I approached a bench beside a sprawling oak. A concrete breaker hid the shore, where waves were chortling on stone.

I brushed off the loose snow and sat. Across the river the National Theatre shone in the waning sunlight. I was in view of the stairwell and the surrounding park: My mysterious contact would have to find me.

I took the note from my pocket, and read it once more, pondering those inquiries I'd made at the embassies in Old Town and the book store in the Jewish Quarter – routine questions (*squeezing*, as Dawson called it).

Across the river, church bells tolled the hour.

When I looked up, an old man was standing beside the wall.

He was tall, broad-shouldered, with long grey hair, and had the sharp eyes and nose of a Slav. He wore a green coat over a silvery, high-collared shirt. "*Dobry vecer.*"

I stood. "*Pane* Hastrman?"

"*Ano,*" he replied, bowing stiffly. "I am he." His voice was low, and his English was thickly accented.

I have our conversation now before me, recorded in my little notebook. Though its pages are water-logged, most of the words are legible.

I introduced myself.

With the formality suggestive of a military man (so I wrote, adding "*an acolyte of former President Masaryk?*"), he thanked me for meeting him, bowed once more, then gestured that I should sit down. He sat beside me, folding his long hands on his lap, and after a few more introductory remarks, said, "I represent . . . group, *Pane*. Group of Old Praha. We wish . . . communication." His pale blue eyes peered at me sidelong. "To meet one . . . from your kind."

My kind?

"Someone from the Institute, you mean?" I asked, coyly. "A scholar?"

A spy?

"Yes. We will say . . . *scholar*. Of America." He smiled, baring yellow teeth.

I remember an odor like ginger and shorn wood.

"You chose an interesting method of summoning me, Pane Hastrman." I lifted the note.

"It seemed . . . safe, Sir. Many years, now, and *Strelecky Ostrov* is place most favorite of ours."

How old was he? Deep lines marked his forehead, and accented the base of his nose. One moment I might have said eighty, and the next, sixty.

"How can I help you, *Pane*?"

He seemed to meditate for at least half a minute.

I surveyed the nearby park, looking over my shoulder at the stairs.

"There are . . . *change* happen, Sir." He paused, breathing deeply.

"*Change* to our . . . land. To Praha." The English seemed difficult for him, drawn out of the depths of his chest, articulated curtly.

"Changes? To the *status quo*, you mean?"

He slowly nodded.

I ventured, "Your government, *Pane* – it doesn't follow all the Perestroika ideals. Premier Husak, I mean. Does your group disagree with him?"

A distracted smile. Affable, then sharp, as he gazed at Prague across the river, and a seagull wheeling over the water.

"We . . . not washed by sea."

Confused, I asked him to repeat himself. He did so, adding, "The great sea. They miss." His eyes followed the bird's calligraphic flight. I noted the sleekness of his grey hair. "Even more, those . . . *stranded* . . . here."

"I afraid, Mister Hastrman, I don't understand you." I added, "*Nerozum'm.*"

The smile. Briefly, his eyes shone with some of the vanishing sunlight. "All of us, *Pane. Praha*. Prague. *Ceske*. Our country. Land is locked, and surrounded. A country . . . must to touch the sea, Sir."

Unbidden, the thought came to me of Shakespeare's *Winter's Tale*, where the Bard has a Sicilian ship landing on a Bohemian shore. "It has made difficulties for your people," I said. "What was it, sir, the Battle of the White Mountain, in your history? Ever since that sad defeat . . ."

"The sea . . . it *cleanses*." He might not have heard me. Breathing through his open mouth, he was silent for a moment, then said, "Energies do not . . . leave. We grow ancient. Lakes, rivers, are . . . *dusit* . . . are *choked*. And we forced . . . underground. We need . . . *union* with . . . new worlds." He shook his head, and fell silent, breathing through his open mouth.

"Let us speak of changes, then, *Pane*," I said, awkwardly trying to draw the conversation back to earth. "Your government, under Husak, will continue what they call *normalization*, and grow more harsh, no matter what the Soviets desire. Do you agree?"

With his left hand, he stroked the silvery collar at his throat; the gesture, though casual, seemed anything but. "*Ano*. Country . . . it must change, and . . . embrace West. Even that is no . . . not *solution*."

His eyes took measure of me, as he drew another deep breath through open mouth, and exhaled.

"*Pane* Hastrman, I wish to know more of the group you represent."

His voice was low, almost inaudible. "I bring . . . proposal. For . . . meeting."

I was taken aback. "Another meeting?"

He shook his head. "I . . . I am only messenger."

He reached into his coat, and came out with dim gold between his index finger and thumb.

A ring.

Glancing at me sidelong, he offered it.

And dropped it on my palm.

A heavy ring of greenish-gold – as though it was catching the verdant hue of his coat. It was ornately carved with tiny star-like patterns, entwined with comets and wave-like filigree. It gleamed.

"By this she . . . know you."

"Who, *Pane*?"

He looked upwards, moments before the gull screamed past our heads and soared out over the water.

Clutching the ring in my right hand, I watched it circling. Then I noticed the bridge, the bustling pedestrians, and a single figure among them, walking more slowly. Silhouetted against the clouds were what seemed familiar details, a rumpled suit, and messy dark hair. He seemed to be staring in our direction.

The StB agent. I knew it to be him.

Hastrman was peering at the gull.

I said, "Shall we walk, *Pane*?"

He seemed to understand. Taking another deep breath, he rose to his feet. A moment later, he began following me along the shore.

But only a dozen paces later he slowed, and stopped.

"Do you need to sit?"

"Are we . . . *followed*?"

I dared to glance back, and saw nobody on the nearby bridge, nor on the stairs, or the island.

"I'm not sure."

Hastrman was staring at my hand, and the ring. "There is monastery, *Pane*, in *Nova Mesto. Emauzy*." He spoke the word sharply, and gestured south of the Narodni Divadlo. "Its *kostel* – church – sits over meeting place."

"Emauzy Church."

Straightening, he seemed to gather strength in his shoulders. "There is . . . entrance. In rectory, at northeast corner. A stairwell down. One of us meet you there, *Pane*. And lead you to . . . meeting place, below."

Thinking of my research, I asked, "*Katakomby*?"

He nodded. "Safe, from . . . occupiers, of this city." His voice was nearly lost under the river.

"When?"

"Tomorrow. *Vecer*. Night. Twenty-one *hodin*."

"My superiors at the Institute, *Pane* – they might have more questions. They might refuse to allow me to such a meeting."

"Yet she will wait. Tomorrow. Below. Twenty-one hours."

"Her name, *Pane*?"

He smiled, memorably. "*Milovana*."

I repeated it to myself, noting, in the cold air, the scent of ginger and shorn wood. "If my superiors agree, I'll be there. If not, then I will have to make other arrangements."

Nodding, Hastrman briefly closed his eyes.

"*Dobry den*, Pane Hastrman."

"*Dobry vecer*, Pane."

He gestured, as though to indicate we should walk separately back to the bridge. He remained there in the dusk, visible by the green of his coat and the grey of his hair, bowing to me.

As I walked, I put my hands into my coat pockets. The ring's carved details were as beguiling to touch as they were to see. Quite casually, I caressed the tiny stars and comets, then, using index finger and thumb, I slipped the ring on my fourth finger. When I had climbed the stairs, I found the bridge crowded with cars and pedestrians.

My StB agent was nowhere to be seen.

I spent the next day – Sunday – at the Institute.

Dawson was out, as were most of the scholars.

Jakob was busily cleaning the first floor offices.

In the third-floor stacks, I was able to confirm the outline of Hastrman's story. Catacombs existed beneath Emauzy Monastery Complex, or at least they had eighty years earlier: a 1906 survey by the Habsburgs mentioned a "Romanesque tunnel and the remains of an ancient sellaria, beneath the Church of St John on the Rock," which was the actual name of the church on the complex.

A photograph showed the church's striking baroque-era profile – twin steeples swooping inward like white thorns.

According to the map, the tunnels continued southward, under Charles Square. A similar survey from 1962 made no mention of sellaria or tunnels, but the Soviets had been more concerned with the structures farther north, closer to the subway lines they were building. This discrepancy helped bolster Hastrman's argument that the catacombs served as a perfect meeting place.

Yet troublingly, the account also mentioned that the church, which had been bombed by the Allies in World War II, had never been reopened. The monastery was currently being used by the Academy of Sciences, while the church itself remained gutted.

In the notebook, I dutifully copied down the map. It's nearly illegible now, the ink blurred, the page stained and wrinkled; likewise the notes I made in the hours afterward, regarding the ring.

I should say, Lev, that I had been unable to remove it.

After returning from the island the night before, I had tried tugging it off, and then, using hotel soap and shampoo as lubricant, had tried to finesse it over my second knuckle, but only managed to make my finger raw. By the next morning my knuckle was swollen; ice would not reduce it enough to pull the ring free.

I had resolved to try again later that afternoon.

In the notebook, beneath a description of its patterns, I added a guess as to its origin: "*Holy Roman Empire? Rudolfine?*"

The star-and-comet patterns were key, I felt certain, and so I focused on an encyclopedia dealing with Holy Roman-era jewelry, paging through hundreds upon hundreds of images of gaudy necklaces, bracelets, broaches, rings until, startlingly, I came upon its likeness. A color etching.

I held my hand beside it: identical.

According to the entry, the ring dated from 1590.

Lev, my Czech is adequate to communicate with hotel clerks and taxi drivers. I'm able to parse out the meaning of a sentence when I know the source material in translation, such as the poetry of Jaroslav Seifert. But I wasn't entirely confident with my translation here.

The entry seemed to discuss those star and comet patterns – *vzor* – implying they were symbolic of Rudolf's mania for astrology, while the wave-like crenellations stood for the Vltava. A further mention was perhaps made of "water-based metals."

And there was mention of an inscription – or *napis* – engraved on the inside of the ring.

Z TB znovu a priliv Deceru Temnoty a Zeme.

With the help of a dictionary, I eventually translated: *To TB in time after time Daughter of Earth and Darkness*.

Doubting, I reread the entry, then noticed the small footnote reference.

In the back of the book, I read the note, slowly, unbelieving of what it seemed to say.

The ring, known as the 1590 TB, had apparently been part of the Emperor Rudolf II's *sackomora*.

My mouth went dry. A chill crept down my neck. I clenched and unclenched my right hand.

The *sackomora* was the Emperor's fabled horde of objets d'art, symptomatic of his increasingly unhinged mind. It encompassed gems, paintings, clocks, astronomical instruments, as well as stuffed animals, reptiles, freaks of nature, even the lump of soil said to be that from which Yahweh formed Adam.

Z TB znovu a priliv Deceru Temnoty a Zeme.

Daughter of Earth and Darkness.

And *Z TB*. For TB.

I rose, and went in search of a book specifically detailing the sackomora. I found three in Czech, then one in English, from the late 1960s. I brought it back to the carrel.

I quickly found the listing: *1590 TB*.

Even before I read the entry, I had made the connection – though I refused to believe it.

"1590 TB: This item was a gold and tourmaline ring, exquisitely detailed (see etching). It supposedly belonged to the Danish astronomer Tycho Brahe. Upon Brahe's death in 1601 the ring was added to the Emperor's collection.

"Like most of these other treasures in the sackomora, *1590 TB was presumed lost in the chaos that followed Rudolf's reign.*

"Brahe, in contemporary accounts, was vague as to its origin, though the ring was rumored to be a gift. The astronomer's first biographer, Jaroslav Firkusny, notes that Brahe seemed more protective of it than of his most famous accoutrement – the large silver and gold nose he wore to replace his own, which was sliced off, supposedly, in a duel."

I held my hand close to the library lamp.

Within the tiny swirls of stars, I recognized a familiar pattern – the belt of Orion, and then the rest of the hunter, poised above the gold and silver ripples that represented the Vltava's waves.

She will know you by this, Hastrman had said.

I remember tracing the patterns with my index finger.

What had once been Tycho Brahe's was now in my possession.

This fragment of history – seemingly connected to the tomb at Tyn cathedral.

That evening, in a strange contrary mood, I set out through Smichov in a downpour.

I had decided to walk partway, mostly to clear the fantastic thoughts from my mind.

I carried an umbrella, and was clad in boots, gloves, and heavy coat, notebook in the side pocket. My finger throbbed. With renewed effort – perhaps desperation – I had tried earlier to remove the ring, unsuccessfully.

The snow was melting. The stink of soot and sulfur were more prominent in the cold air. Lamps were haloed by the rain, while the bells of *Stare Mesto* were muted, evasive, as they echoed up the narrow streets, along the empty sidewalks.

There was no sign of my StB agent.

Only the stone faces peering down.

I tried to maintain a brisk pace, but the rain was making slush, and the cobblestones were dangerously slick.

At Zborovska street, along the Vltava, I hailed a taxi.

"Emauzy Kostel, *prosim*," I told the young driver, glancing back at the empty sidewalk.

"Emauzy. *Ano*."

We accelerated sharply.

In the warmth of the back seat (one always remembers the strange detail: the radio was blaring *The Tennessee Waltz*, sung in Czech) I reiterated the rational. That I was meeting a representative of Prague's dissident community, this "Milovana". That I would record our conversation in my notebook. That I was not being followed. That I could cancel the trip at any moment, and would do so if necessary.

Most dangerous, surely, would be the walk through the monastery complex. Here a paranoid thought cropped up again: that if this meeting were a set-up by the StB, meant to entrap a visiting "scholar", to catch him in possession of a priceless Czech artifact – that if the StB truly *had* been following me (I remember looking out the rear window at the rain-swept street) then certainly they would spring the trap as I walked across the monastery complex, or entered the church.

Once below, once in the catacombs, I told myself, the danger would pass.

Rational thoughts, Lev, drawn up from the watery depths, where my thoughts had been circling those last few hours.

I had left a note addressed to Dawson in my hotel room, explaining where I was, and why I'd gone to the meeting. Extra insurance, in case I was in custody by tomorrow morning. (Though the niggling thought returned: what hadn't I called Dawson? Didn't a part of me believe in less rational thoughts, in the mystery of the ring, this fragment of history given to me, to me?)

In *Nove Mesto*, lamplight streamed with the rain onto cobblestone streets. A few hardy pedestrians huddled under umbrellas, coming and going from the local taverns.

Soon, the driver made a gesture, drawing my attention ahead of us.

Coalescing out of the rainy dark were those incurving thorn-like steeples of Emauzy church, grey and misty against the bulk of the church below.

And I felt a twinge of panic, entirely unreasonable, triggered, I knew, by the crookedness of the streets, by the shimmering cobblestones, by the lamp posts seeming to duck against the rain, and by my sudden acute awareness of the Old Town to the North, of the Old Town Square, and of Tyn cathedral.

A sense that these two steeples – witches' hats and thorns, Emauzy and Tyn – were somehow in colloquy in the sky, among the thousand spires of Prague.

The driver began braking.

"No, keep going," I said, in Czech.

The Emauzy grounds seemed empty, but for statues; the only motion that of falling rain.

I told myself: *If Milovana wants to meet me, we'll do it on Sharpshooter Island. Didn't he say that was a favorite haunt of his group?*

By tomorrow, I'll have the ring off my finger. And I'll inform Dawson, according to procedures. Tonight, I'll head back to the hotel. Or the hotel's tavern.

The driver looked back over his shoulder. "*Kde?*" he asked. *Where?*

Again, my mood changed.

I had come this far into *Nove Mesto*.

To meet with a representative of Prague's dissident community. A job I willingly accepted. The work of a good academic spy. Perhaps contributing something to the great democratic changes coming to this part of the world.

Why not risk it?

The only danger is crossing the Emauzy complex.

Then I realized: there is another option. Another means of entry, unseen by any possible agents.

I remembered the map I had copied down. And felt another twinge of panic that somehow pleased me.

Patting my coat pocket and the notebook, I told the driver where to take me.

*   *   *

For all the ominous fables it had collected over the centuries, Faustuv Dum, that day, was an unlikely palace of grey and orange rococo, with rounded windows and a beveled, playful façade. It sat at one end of the long grassy field that had once been the Cattle Market.

Faust House – or the school it had become – appeared closed. Behind the decorative leaded glass of the foyer was a dim hall, sporadically lit. I reached for the swan-wing handle, telling myself that if it were locked, I would return to hotel or tavern. I would drink a toast to rational thoughts and wake the next morning with a slight headache, and a familiar reality.

But it was unlocked.

Furling the umbrella, I stepped inside.

An intruder, I walked along a hall that seemed no older than 1900. I told myself: I'll look down this central hall, past these gilt-framed paintings of Hradcany Castle and St Wenceslas Square; and afterward, I'll return to my hotel, and wait for word to come again from Hastrman.

The hall was silent. The parquet tiles smelled of recent waxing. Doors stood open onto dim halls, where lurked desks and chairs. One was clearly an academic classroom, with steep seating.

All of which conflicted, somewhat eerily, with the history of *Fastuv Dum*. Walking this hall, I was walking through a 12th-century edifice, one which, like most of Prague's historical structures, was untouched by the bombs of World War II.

At the end of the hall, I found, on my right, a narrow door marked with a vivid graphic symbol: a flight of stairs.

And I followed.

Sklepeni, they are called – those vast, barrel-vaulted cellars of old Prague.

I ducked under a stone lintel, into the first of several chambers receding into the dark.

Here was *Fastuv Dum*'s ancient past.

I pulled off my gloves, put them in my right pocket, then took the flashlight from my left. I shone its beam across cracked flagstone, over stacks of boxes, brooms and buckets.

In the corner was a pile of potatoes, sprouting pale tendrils.

Faust, I recalled (to distract myself), had not fought Mephistopheles here in the cellar; rather, the battle had been waged in the attic, and the unfortunate alchemist was snatched up through the ceiling, leaving a hole that had remained for decades afterward, refuting any attempt to patch it.

In the next chamber was an active boiler. I hesitated, feeling the warmth on my face and hands. It woke me, somewhat. I nearly turned around, nearly headed back up the stairs. Instead, thinking of Tyn and Emauzy, of Tycho Brahe and the tomb, I ducked into the next chamber. Tipped in the far corner were dozens of black iron rods, as tall as me or taller, baroquely detailed in golden Rudolfine motifs. Lightning rods.

Smelling the old iron, I hesitated again, drawn by a rod's similar pattern to my ring. Then I continued on, under another vaulted arch, to find an old man seated at a card table, beneath a bare light bulb.

He looked as startled as I. Frozen, wide-eyed, with a spoon halfway to his mouth. He had white brows and a burnished, high-domed forehead. He wore blue overalls and was sparrow-thin.

Striving for a non-threatening tone, I said, "*Dobry vecer*, Pane." I shut off my flashlight. "*Mluvit Anglicky?*"

After a pause, he nodded. "Speak *little*." His voice was faint.

I told him I was an American, and a teacher. This seemed to relax him slightly. He set the spoon back into his soup.

I pointed at him, "You – *custodian?*"

He rose from his chair – the scrape of wood on stone echoed sharply – and gestured in the direction I'd come, back to the stairs. "*Prosim.*"

"No." I shook my head. "*Kde katakomby?*" I pointed at the floor. "*Katakomby?*"

He froze, squinting.

I took out my notebook and flipped to the map I had drawn. His eyes had followed my right hand: the ring.

Lips parted, he stared.

The intensity in his eyes, somehow, gave me strength.

I held it up. "Recognize?"

He licked his lips. "*Ano.*"

I pointed to the map and the sketch of the catacombs.

Nodding, he turned from me, limping further into the chamber, toward the next one. Trading the notebook for the flashlight, I followed, through another chamber of old boxes and barrels, into another with a lower ceiling.

"*Tam jsou,*" he said, pointing. "There."

I shone the flashlight past his shoulder. A lip of grey stone rose from the flagstone, with oaken doors laid in its face.

He pulled a cord overhead: a light bulb shone on silver hinges shaped as stylized spiders. The hasp was a baroque silver eye. A black rod was laid diagonally across.

He hesitated, until I gestured that he should continue.

The hasp, it seemed, was not locked. With both hands, he lifted the lightning rod. Dust stirred as he set it aside.

I had to help him lift the doors. The wood squeaked sharply, echoing behind us, and below. I coughed at the acrid dust. A moment later I smelled the sharp, moist odor rising with it.

A stairway of crumbling stone descended, down and around, out of sight.

I set my umbrella on the ground. I pulled out my wallet, and withdrew a thousand crown note. "Wait." With a slight shake to my hands, I tore the note in half, and handed half to him.

I pointed to the *12* on my wristwatch. "Til midnight."

He seemed to understand.

Lev, such a world exists.

The ancient steps coiled downward, for longer than I expected. I had to crouch under the chill stone, and climb down and around, until the steps ended on slick, algae-stained rock.

In my flashlight's gleam, there were no visible footprints.

How long, I wondered, since someone had come down here?

The air was close, fetid. Treading carefully, I found myself in a barrel-vaulted chamber. Old stone to the right and left. In accordance with the map, the tunnel stretched north, growing more narrow; and southward.

I began to walk southward.

For those first hundred paces, the passage remained narrow enough: with outstretched arms, I could touch the walls on either side. But within another hundred it widened. I felt a moist breeze on my face and hands.

I passed square outlines on either side, and remembered the legends of unlucky folk sealed into casements.

Under my boots, the algae thinned. Soon I was walking on mostly bare stone.

I listened, expecting voices. Emauzy church, after all, was no more than a quarter mile from *Fastuv Dum*; voices should resonate in these acoustics.

The path began to descend, however subtly.

Soon after, my shoe slapped the first puddle. It sparkled in the flashlight's beam. Ahead, an inch of water covered the floor.

The tunnel widened into a vaulted space, remnants of the earliest city, pierced by grey stone columns.

The water was nearly to the top of my boots.

Slogging through, I thought of storm clouds, of lightning striking the Rudolfine spires of loftiest Prague, and the energy surging down here into the dark, dwindling in these primeval spaces, in solitude, the tiniest portions of those distant storms playing over slimed rock and sediment, in spaces lit now by the darting glow of my flashlight. Then, variously, I thought of the stone face peering out of Tyn's doorway, and of Prague's population of gargoyles and statues that must tremble, however slightly, with the thunder, joined to the same ancient stone sunk into the bedrock around me as this space – this space which opened up even further: the underside of the Emauzy church.

And there came a sudden keening sound, tremulous, high-pitched, echoing up and down the chamber, suddenly dropping into the range of a human voice, in imitation of – in parody of – a familiar melody.

Rusalka's *Aria to the Moon.*

Unable to stop myself, I walked toward it.

How to write rationally about what happened next?

Ascribe it to a dream, or a nightmare.

Staggering along the tunnel – being drawn along – by a keening sound that might have been an incantation not unlike music.

My flashlight flickering, dying.

Standing in darkness. A darkness alive with silvery ripples.

Shaking the flashlight. Opening it with trembling fingers, removing the batteries, reinserting them. A faint glow kindling when I turned it on, but quickly fading.

I called out, "Pane Hastrman?" My voice echoing sharply. Then, in the dark, a sudden greenish glow, close by. Stench – burnt ozone, as I lifted my hand to ward off the glow, only to find it was the ring.

I tried – not really thinking, I suppose – to shake it free. Then looked past it, to what the quivering green glow revealed: close to the ground, in the water, something scraping, rattling, as it approached. A vague shape at first, at the edge of green light, and the harsh rattle was its breathing.

Milovana.

Or, as I would later translate it, "*Beloved.*"

She – it – lay in the water, scales glinting, huffing in pained exhalations, her eyes, vertically-irised, widening with something like adulation. As her head lifted, dark-nippled dugs lifted out of the water.

She shuddered there, coiled.

This daughter of Earth and Darkness. No longer quite as beautiful as she'd been in Tycho Brahe's day.

I stepped back – stumbling – tripping. Struck the water with my shoulder, a loud splash, as the chill water invaded my clothes. The ring was lost but for its erratic green glow beneath the surface. The rasp and shudder of her breathing, as she scrabbled closer in the veering light, as I lifted my hand out of the water.

And—

—as I gazed toward the creature – a premonition of Bosch's underworld—

Her teeth, gleaming in the ring's glow, were sharp like a moray eel's. Talons were equally sharp. I shook my head, found my voice, croaking, "No, no," pushing myself up, stumbling backwards – catching my boot in a swirl of green cloth that was a long coat, that was Hastrman's coat, and the silvery weed on the surface of the water his high-collared shirt, just below his pale blue eyes peering up, under the Medusa wreath of his hair.

I tripped, fell backwards. Another anguished cry, an instant before her talons, or teeth, struck.

And the only light – my luminous green – toppled into the water, strangely burdened. Two fingers bobbed on the surface.

Pain was remote. Her wailing cry was all that mattered, as I stumbled backwards. It chased me through the dark as I staggered bleeding, growing fainter, merging with Vltava's thrum, the crazy stutter of my boots on the rock and a painful thud as my knees hit the stairs below *Fastuv Dum*.

"*Vodnici*," the caretaker whispered, eyes wide. He wrapped a cloth around my hand, tightened it, and when the bleeding had slowed he returned to the trapdoor and struggled it shut, then laid the Rudolfine iron atop it.

I tried, in subsequent years, to delude myself.

Dawson – who arranged my swift, confidential medical treatment – never fully accepted the story I had concocted, the same one I would later tell to Genevieve, and, still later, to Margaret. At the Prague airport, I passed easily through Customs. I saw no sign of the StB agent; I doubt there had ever been one.

I'd already begun doubting what I had seen.

It was the beginning of a process. Walling up, covering over those memories, as solidly as the *katakomby* of *Nova Mesto*.

I remember how, during my holiday visit to your house, while showing Erel my mother's Folio of Fra Angelico, Pieter Bruegel the

Elder, and Bosch, I felt a twinge of unease, ascribing it to those childhood nightmares.

In 1994, when the soprano Gabriela Berezkova drowned in the Vltava at the age of thirty-six, I was able to push aside the troubling thoughts. In 1996, when Margaret died in the Elbe river off Saxony, I accepted the official explanation, that the sightseeing boat had struck some rocks, and those same rocks had forced the horrific injuries to my wife's body, alone among the drowned passengers, a hundred miles north of Prague in the Elbe, not far after its junction with the Vltava.

In 2002, when the Vltava flooded its banks, I watched images of Sharpshooter Island on CNN.

That night, I dreamt of its oak-lined paths lost under the roiling waves, and of my Rusalka and her Water Sprite swimming graceful in the cold currents beneath the Legion Bridge, gazing up through the churning rain-struck surface at the human faces peering blindly down.

The next day I dug out my water-logged notebook, and read it with an open mind for the first time in years. And began reconstructing events.

I was the one, Lev – I am now certain – who ignited Erel's interest in Prague.

The stories I told that winter day, of Rusalki and Vodnici, stayed with him, I'm certain, as did the memory of those paintings. In a way similar to my own experience, I'm sure they had an influence, however subtle, in his choosing Medieval History as his major in college.

From the newspaper account, I know that in his last email, which he sent from the café near Tyn, he said he was planning to wander the river bank that day, and explore the New Town as thoroughly as he did the Old Town.

Three weeks ago, only days after Elizabeth wrote of Erel's disappearance, I received a package, circuitously, from Prague.

Perhaps you have already opened the box, unable to wait. If not, do so now.

The ring is more tarnished than I remember.

Lev, research the inscription and the symbolism yourself. Also, have your police forensics test the reddish cast that stains the ring. It looks too recent to be mine.

By the time you receive this, I will not be here.

Milovana is waiting.

You must keep Elizabeth at home: do not let her go in search of her brother.

Milovana is waiting.

I do not expect Genevieve to believe much of this letter. Perhaps neither will you.

You will no doubt have questions.

I will not be there to answer them.

With utmost regret and sadness,
Stephen

CAROL EMSHWILLER

I Live With You
and You Don't Know it

CAROL EMSHWILLER WAS BORN in Ann Arbor, Michigan. She grew up in France, where her father was a professor of linguistics, and she currently lives in New York City, where she teaches writing at New York University School of Continuing Learning.

For many years married to the famous science fiction artist "Emsh", she did not begin writing until she was thirty and her first novel, *Carmen Dog*, was published in 1988. Since then she has followed it with *Venus Rising*, *Ledoyt*, *Leaping Man Hill*, the Nebula Award-nominated *The Mount* and the young adult novel *Mister Boots*. Her acclaimed short fiction has been collected in *Verging on the Pertinent*, the World Fantasy Award-winning *The Start of the End of It All and Other Stories*, *Joy in Our Cause: Short Stories*, *Report to the Men's Club: Stories* and the recent *I Live With You*, which takes its title from the disturbing, Nebula Award-winning tale that follows.

A recipient of the World Fantasy Award for Lifetime Achievement in 2005, since the mid-1960s Emshwiller's stories have appeared in numerous anthologies. However, she admits: "This is the first time I've been in a horror collection. I never thought I would be."

I LIVE IN YOUR HOUSE AND YOU DON'T KNOW IT. I nibble at your food. You wonder where it went . . . where your pencils and pens go . . . What happened to your best blouse. (You're just my size. That's why I'm here.) How did your keys get way over on the bedside table instead of by the front door where you always put them? You *do* always put them there. You're careful.

I leave dirty dishes in the sink. I nap in your bed when you're at work and leave it rumpled. You thought you had made it first thing in the morning and you had.

I saw you first when I was hiding out at the bookstore. By then I was tired of living where there wasn't any food except the muffins in the coffee bar. In some ways it was a good place to be . . . the reading, the music. I never stole. Where would I have taken what I liked? I didn't even steal back when I lived in a department store. I left there forever in my same old clothes though I'd often worn their things at night. When I left, I could see on their faces that they were glad to see such a raggedy person leave. I could see they wondered how I'd gotten in in the first place. To tell the truth, only one person noticed me. I'm hardly ever noticed.

But then, at the bookstore, I saw you: just my size, Just my look. And you're as invisible as I am. I saw that nobody noticed you just as hardly anybody notices me.

I followed you home – a nice house just outside of town. If I wore your clothes, I could go in and out and everybody would think I was you. But I wondered how get in in the first place? I thought it would have to be in the middle of the night and I'd have to climb in a window.

But I don't need a window. I hunch down and walk in right behind you. You'd think somebody that nobody ever notices would notice other people, but you don't.

Once I'm in, right away I duck into the hall closet.

You have a cat. Isn't that just like you? And just like me also. I would have had one were I you.

The first few days are wonderful. Your clothes are to my taste. Your cat likes me (right away better than he likes you). Right away I find a nice place in your attic. More a crawl space but I'm used to hunching over. In fact that's how I walk around most of the time. The space is narrow and long, but it has little windows at each end. Out one, I can look right into a treetop. I think an apple tree. If it was the right season I could reach out and pick an apple. I brought up your quilt. I saw you looking puzzled after I took the hall rug. I laughed to myself when you changed the locks on your doors. Right after that I took a photo from the mantel. Your mother, I presume. I wanted you to notice it was gone, but you didn't.

I bring up a footstool. I bring up cushions, one by one until I have four. I bring up magazines, straight from the mailbox, before you have a chance to read them.

What I do all day? Anything I want to. I dance and sing and play the radio and TV.

When you're home, I come down in the evening, stand in the hall and watch you watch TV.

I wash my hair with your shampoo. Once, when you came home early, I almost got caught in the shower. I hid in the hall closet, huddled in with the sheets, and watched you find the wet towel – the spilled shampoo.

You get upset. You think: I've heard odd thumps for weeks. You think you're in danger, though you try hard to talk yourself out of it. You tell yourself it's the cat, but you know it's not.

You get a lock for your bedroom door – a dead bolt. You have to be inside to push it closed.

I have left a book open on the couch, the print of my head on the couch cushion. I've pulled out a few grey hairs to leave there. I have left a half-full wine glass on the counter. I have left your underwear (which I wore) on the bathroom floor, dirty socks under the bed, a bra hanging on the towel rack. I left a half-eaten pizza on the kitchen counter. (I ordered out and paid with your stash of quarters, though I know where you keep your secret twenties.)

I set all your clocks back fifteen minutes but I set your alarm clock to four in the morning. I hid your reading glasses. I pull buttons off your sweaters and put them where your quarters used to be. Your quarters I put in your button box.

Normally I try not to bump and thump in the night but I'm tired of your little life. At the book store and grocery store at least things happened all day long. You keep watching the same TV programs. You go off to work. You make enough money (I see the bank statements) but what do you do with it? I want to change your life into something worth watching.

I begin to thump, bump, and groan and moan. (I've been feeling like groaning and moaning for a long time, anyway.) Maybe I'll bring you a man.

I'll buy you new clothes and take away the old ones, so you'll *have* to wear the new ones. The new clothes will be red and orange and with stripes and polka dots. When I get through with you, you'll be real . . . or at least realer. People will notice you.

Now you groan and sigh as much as I do. You think: This can't be happening. You think: what about the funny sounds coming from the crawl space? You think: I don't dare go up there by myself, but who could I get to go with me? (You don't have any friends that I know of. You're like me in that.)

Monday you go off to work wearing a fuzzy blue top and red leather pants. You had a hard time finding a combination without stripes or big flowers or dots on it.

I watch you from your kitchen window. I'm heating up your leftover coffee. I'm making toast. (I use up all the butter. You thought there was plenty for the next few days.)

You almost caught me the time I came home late with packages. I had to hide behind the curtains. I could tell that my feet showed out the bottom, but you didn't notice.

Another time you saw me duck into the hall closet but you didn't dare open the door. You hurried upstairs to your bedroom and pushed the deadbolt. That evening you didn't come down at all. You skipped supper. I watched TV . . . any show I wanted.

I put another deadbolt on the *outside* of your bedroom door. Just in case. It's way up high. I don't think you'll notice. It might come in handy.

(Lacy underwear with holes in lewd places. Nudist magazines. Snails and sardines – smoked oysters. Neither one of us like them. All the things I get with your money are for *you*. I don't steal.)

How get through Christmas all by yourself? You're lonely enough for both of us. You wrap empty boxes in Christmas paper just to be festive. You buy a tree, a small one. It's artificial and comes with lights that glimmer on and off. The cat and I come down to sleep near its glow.

But the man. The one I want to bring to you. I look over the personals. I write letters to possibilities but, as I'm taking them to the post office, I see somebody. He limps and wobbles. (The way he lurches sideways looks like sciatica to me. Or maybe arthritis.) He needs a haircut and a shave. He's wearing an old plaid jacket and he's all knees and elbows. There's a countrified look about him. Nobody wears plaid around here.

I limp behind him. Watch him go into one of those little apartments behind a main house and over a garage. It's not far from our house.

It can't be more than one room. I could never creep around in that place and not be noticed.

A country cousin. Country uncle more likely, he's older than we are. Is he capable of what I want him for?

Next day I watch him in the grocery store. Like us, he buys living-alone kind of food, two apples, a tomato, crackers, oatmeal. Poor people's kind of food. I get in line with him at the check out. I bump into him on purpose as he pays and peek into his wallet. That's all he has – just enough for what he buys. He counts out the change a penny at a time and he hardly has a nickel left over. I get ready to give him a bit extra if he needs it.

He's such an ugly, rickety man . . . Perfect.

There's no reason to go into his over-the-garage room, but I want to. This is important. I need to see who he is.

I use our credit card to open his lock.

What a mess. He needs somebody like us to look after him. His bed is piled with blankets. The room isn't very well heated. The bathroom has a curtain instead of a door. There's no tub or even shower. I check the hot water in the sink. It says HOT, but both sides come out cold. All he has is a hot plate. No refrigerator. There're two windows, but no curtains. Isn't that just like a man. I could climb up on the back fence and see right in.

There's nothing of the holidays here. Nothing of any holidays and not a single picture of a relative. And, like our house, nothing of friends. You and he are made for each other.

What to do to show I've been here? But this time I don't feel much like playing tricks. And it's so messy he wouldn't notice, anyway.

It's cold. I haven't taken my coat off all through this. I make myself a cup of tea. (There's no lemons and no milk. Of course.) I sit in his one chair. It's painted ugly green. All his furniture is as if picked up on the curb and his bedside table is one of those fruit boxes. As I sit and sip, I check his magazines. They look as though stolen from somebody's garbage. I'm shivering. (No wonder he's out. I suppose it's not easy to shave. He'd have to heat the water on the hot plate.)

He needs a cat. Something to sleep on his chest to keep him warm like your cat does with me.

I have our groceries in my backpack. I leave two oranges and a doughnut in plain sight beside the hot plate. I leave several of our quarters.

I leave a note: I put in our address. I sign your name. I write: Come for Christmas. Two o'clock. I'll be wearing red leather pants! Your neighbour, Nora.

(I wonder which of us should wear those pants.)

I clean up a little bit but not so much that he'd notice if he's not a noticing person. Besides, people only notice when things are dirty. They never notice when things are cleaned up.

As I walk home, I see you on your way out. We pass each other. You look right at me. I'm wearing your green sweater and your black slacks. We look at each other, my brown eyes to your brown eyes. Only difference is, your hair is pushed back and mine hangs down over my forehead. You go right on by. I turn and look back. You don't. I laugh behind my hand that you had to wear those red leather pants and a black and white striped top.

He's too timid and too self-deprecating to come. He doesn't like to limp in front of people and he's ashamed not to have enough money hardly even for his food, and not to have a chance to shave and take a bath. Though if he's scared by me coming into his room, he might come. He might want to see who Nora is and if the address is real. His pretext will be that he wants to thank you for the food and quarters. He might even want to give them back. He might be one of those rich people who live as if they were poor. I should have looked for money or bankbooks. I will next time.

When the doorbell rings who else could it be?

You open the door.

"Are you Nora?"

"Yes?"

"I want to thank you."

I knew it. I suppose he wants more money.

"But I want to bring your quarters back. That was kind of you but I don't need them."

You don't know what to say. You suspect it's all because of me. That I've, yet again, made your life difficult. You wonder what to do. He doesn't look dangerous but you never can tell. You want to get even with me some way. You suppose, if he *is* dangerous, it would be bad for both of us so it must be all right. You ask him in.

He hobbles into your living room. You say sit down, that you'll get tea. You're stalling for time.

He still holds the handful of quarters. He puts them on the coffee table.

You don't know how those quarters got to him or even if they really are your quarters. "No, no," you say, and, "Where did these come from?"

"They were in my room with a note from you and this address. You said, Come for Christmas."

You wonder what I'll like least. Do I want you to invite him to stay for supper. Unlikely, though, since you only have one TV dinner and you know I know that.

"Somebody is playing a joke on me. But the tea . . ."

You need help getting started so I trip you in the hall as you come back into the room. Everything goes down. Too bad, too, because you'd used your good china in spite of how this man looks.

Of course he pushes himself up and hobbles to you and helps pick up the things and you. You say you could make more but he says, It doesn't matter. Then you both go out to the kitchen. I go, too. Sidling. Slithering. The cat slides in with us. Both yours and his glasses are thick. I'm counting on your blindness. I squat down. He puts the broken cups on a corner of the counter. You get out two more. He says, these are too nice. You say, they're Mother's. He says, "You shouldn't use the Rosenthal, not for me."

There now, are you both rich yet never use your money?

The cat jumps on the table and you swipe him off. No wonder he likes me better then you. I always let him go where he wants and I like him on the table.

You're looking at our man — studying his crooked nose. You see what neither of us has noticed until now. The hand that reaches to help you wears a ring with a large stone. Some sort of school ring. You're thinking: Well, well, and changing your mind. As am I.

He's too good for you. Maybe might be good enough for me.

We are all, all three, the same kind of person. When you leave in the morning, I've seen you look out the door to make sure there's nobody out there you might have to say hello to.

But now you talk. You think. You ask. You wonder out loud if this and that. You look down at your striped shirt and wish you were wearing your usual clothes. I'm under the table wearing your brown blouse with the faint pattern of fall leaves. I look like a wrinkled up paper bag kicked under here and forgotten. The cat is down here with me purring.

It never takes long for two lonely people living in their fantasies to connect — to see all sorts of things in each other that don't exist.

You've waited for each other all your lives. You almost say so. Besides, he'd have a nice place to live if . . . if anything comes of this.

I think about that black lacy underwear. That pink silk nightie. As soon as I have a chance, I'll go get them. I might need them for myself.

But how get you moving? You're both all talk. Or *you* are, he's not talking much. Perhaps one look at the nightie might get things rolling. That'll have to be for later. Or on the other hand . . .

I reach back to the shelf behind me and, when neither he nor you are looking, I bring out the sherry. They'll both think the other one got the bottle out.

(They do.)

You get wineglasses. You even get out your TV dinner and say you'll split it. It's turkey with stuffing. You got it special for Christmas.

Of course he says for you to eat it all, but you say you never do, anyway, so you split it.

I'm getting hungry myself. If it was just you, I would sneak a few bites but there's little enough for the two of you. I'll have to find another way.

You both get tipsy. It doesn't take much. You hardly ever drink and it looks like he doesn't either. And I think you want to get drunk. You want something to happen as much as I do.

Every now and then I take a sip of your drinks. And on an empty stomach it takes even less. With the drone of your talk, talk, talking, I almost go to sleep.

But you're heading upstairs already.

I crawl out from under the table and climb the stairs behind you. I'm as wobbly as you are. Actually I'm wobblier. We, all three, go into your bedroom. And the cat. You push the deadbolt. He wonders why. "Aren't you alone here?"

You say, "Not exactly." And then, "I'll tell you later."

(You're right, this certainly isn't the time for a discussion about me.)

First thing I grab our sexy nightie from the drawer. I get under the bed and put it on. That's not easy, cramped up under there. For a few minutes I lose track of what's happening above me. I comb my hair as you always have it, back away from your face. I have to use my fingers and I don't have a mirror so I'm not sure how it comes out. I pinch my cheeks and bite my lips to make them redder.

The cat purrs.

I lean up to see what's going on.

Nothing much so far. Even though tipsy, he seems shy. Inexperienced. I don't think he's ever been anybody's grandfather.

(We're, all of us, all of a piece. None of us has ever been anybody's relative.)

You look pretty much passed out. Or you're pretending. Either way, it's a good time for me to make an appearance.

I crawl out from under the bed and check myself in the mirror behind them. My hair is a mess but I look good in the silky nightgown. Better than you do in your stripes and red pants. By far.

I do a little sexy dance. I say, "She's not Nora, I'm Nora. I'm the one wrote you that note."

You sit up. You were faking being drunk. You think: Now I see who you are. Now I'll get you. But you won't.

I stroke the cat. Suggestively. He purrs. (The cat, I mean.) I purr. Suggestively.

I see his eyes light up. (The man's, I mean.) Now there'll be some action.

I say, "I don't even know your name."

He says, "Willard."

I'm on his good side because I asked, and you're not because you didn't. All this talk, talk, talk, talk and you didn't.

You slither away, down under the bed. You feel ashamed of yourself and yet curious. You wonder: How did you ever get yourself in this position, and what to do now? But I do know what to do. I give you a kick and hand you the cat.

Willard. Willard is a little confused. But eager. More than before. He likes the nightgown and says so.

I take a good long look at him. Those bushy eyebrows. Lots of white hairs in them. I help him take off his shirt. His is not my favourite kind of chest. He does have a nice flat stomach though. (I liked that about him from the start – back when I first saw him wobbling down the street.) I look into his green/grey/tan eyes.

But what about, I love you?

I say it, "What about I love you?"

That stops him. I didn't mean to do that. I wanted to give Nora a good show. Of course it's much too soon for any sort of thing that might resemble love.

"I take that back," I say.

But it's too late. He's putting on his shirt. (It's a dressy white one. He's even wearing cufflinks engraved with WT.)

Is it really over already?

I pick up the cat, hurry out, slam the door, and push the deadbolt on the outside, then turn back and look through the keyhole. I can see almost the whole bed.

Now look, his hands are . . . all of a sudden . . . on her and on all the right places. He knows. Maybe he actually *is* somebody's grandfather after all. And you . . . you are feeling things that make your back arch.

He tells you he loves you. *Now* he says it. He can't tell us apart. He'll love anything that comes his way.

I have what I thought I wanted . . . a good view of something interesting for a change, except . . .

Actually I can't see much, just his back and then your back and then his back and then yours. (How do they do that, still attached?)

Until we're all, all of us, exhausted.

I go downstairs . . . (I like how this nightgown feels. I'm so slinky and slippery. I bump and grind just for myself.)

I make myself a peanut butter sandwich. I feel better after eating. Things are fine.

I might leave you milk and cookies. Bring it now while you sleep so I can lock you both in again. But I don't suppose that lock will hold against two people who *really* want to get out.

I think about maybe both of you up in my crawl space. He's taller than we are. He'd not like it. I think about your job at the ice cream factory unfolding boxes to put the ice cream in. I wouldn't mind that kind of job. You sit and daydream. I saw you. You hardly talk to anybody.

I think about how you can't prove you're you. You'll go to the police. You'll say you're you, but they'll laugh. Your clothes are all wrong for the you you used to be. They'll say, the person who's lived here all this time dresses in mouse colours. You've lived a claustrophobic life. If you'd had any friends it would be different. Besides, I can do as well as you do, unfolding boxes. I've done the same when I had jobs before I quit for this easier life. I won't be cruel. I'd never be cruel. I'll let you live in the crawl space as long as you want.

Your daydream is Willard. Or most of him, though not all. For sure his eyes. For sure his elegant slim hands and the big gold ring. You'll ask if it's a school ring.

Or one of us will.

Then I hear banging. And not long after that, the crash. They break open the door. It splinters where the deadbolt is. If I'd put it in the middle of the door instead of at the top, it might have held better.

By the time the door goes down I'm right outside it, watching. They run downstairs without seeing me.

I go and look out the window. He's leaving – hurries down the street with only one arm in his coat sleeve and it's the wrong sleeve. Other hand holds up his pants. What did you do to send him off so upset?

I open the window and call out, "Willard!" But he doesn't hear or doesn't want to. Is he trying to get away? From you or me?

What did you do to scare him so? Everything was fine when I came down to eat. But maybe getting locked in scared him. Or maybe you told him to go and never come back and you threw his coat at him as he left. Or he thinks you're me and is in love with me even though he told you he loved you. Or, like most men, he's unwilling to commit to anybody.

But here you go, out the door right behind him. You have your coat on properly and your clothes all straightened up. Now you're the one calling, "Willard."

You'd not have done that before. You've changed. You'll take back your life. Everybody will make way for you now. You'll have an evil look. You'll frown. People will step off the sidewalk to let you go by.

I want for us to live as we did but you'll set traps. I'll trip on trip wires. Fall down the stairs in the middle of the night. There won't be any more quarters lying around. You'll put a deadbolt on the crawl space door. Or better yet you'll barricade it shut with a dresser. Nobody will even know there's a door there.

I made you what you are today, grand and real, but you'll lock me up up here with nothing but your mousy clothes. Your old trunks. Your dust and dark.

I dress in the worn out clothes I wore when I came. I pack the nightgown, the black underwear. I grab a handful of quarters. I don't touch your secret stash of twenties. I pet the cat. I leave your credit cards and keys on the hall table. I don't steal.

PETER ATKINS

The Cubist's Attorney

PETER ATKINS IS A NATIVE of Liverpool, but has lived in Los Angeles for fourteen years now. However, he still prefers his tea made with water that has actually boiled.

He is the author of the novels *Morningstar* and *Big Thunder* and the collection *Wishmaster and Other Stories*. His work has appeared in *Weird Tales*, *The Magazine of Fantasy & Science Fiction*, *Cemetery Dance* and several award-winning anthologies. He has also written for television and the stage, but is probably best known for his work in the cinema, where he has scripted three of the *Hellraiser* movies and created the *Wishmaster* franchise.

Atkins has recently contributed essays to the non-fiction studies *Horror: Another 100 Best Books* and *Cinema Macabre*, and he has just completed a screenplay for Oscar-winning director Errol Morris.

Along with Glen Hirshberg and Dennis Etchison, he co-founded The Rolling Darkness Revue, an annual Halloween reading tour. "The Cubist's Attorney" was written for the Revue's 2005 outing and first appeared in *Darkness Rising*, a chapbook published to accompany the tour by Earthling Publications.

"I've never had a whole story come to me in a dream," recalls Atkins, "but I did get the *title* for this one while sleeping. The dream was very ordinary – but at one point in it I was walking past a pub and looked up at its sign, which read THE CUBIST'S ATTORNEY.

"In the dream the phrase didn't strike me as unusual at all, but when I woke up I found it intriguing enough to lead me to the story."

T HING IS, HE HADN'T EVEN LIKED the guy. Only met him once. Fifteen years ago, and the little prick must have been over eighty then. He'd been one of the other guests at a soiree of Doug Gordon's and, even for Doug's crowd of narcissistic mediacrats, Gabriel Anzullar had seemed to be more than somewhat full of himself.

Demanding attention and delivering aphorisms that sounded not only rehearsed but dusty with long service, he'd monopolized several party conversations – which God knows were dull enough in the first place – with cobwebbed stories of his time in the sun. He'd been a minor painter in a time of giants and, his more talented and more famous colleagues having done him the kindness of dying before him, he could command center stage now simply because he'd survived them all. And that seemed to be a perfectly sufficient reason for many of the other guests at the party to hover around him adoringly. To spend time with him wasn't a brush with greatness exactly, but it was at least a brush with one who had brushed.

Jackson himself, spectacularly uninterested in Anzullar's tales of post-war Paris and nineteen-fifties New York, had exchanged maybe three sentences with the old man. Nothing significant – *Paté's good, huh?*, *Yes, have you tried the squab?*, shit like that – and, after the third, Anzullar had turned to their hostess – Doug's third wife, the anorexic blonde – and asked her, as if teasing out some special secret, "And what does our young friend here do for a living?"

The wife – Margaret, was it? Some piss-elegant version of that anyway. Margaux, that was it – had paused for a second and looked at Jackson as if trying to remember. He took pity on her and answered for himself.

"I'm a lawyer," he said.

"Oh!" Anzullar said, "A *lawyer*."

He'd stressed the word into a ridiculous burlesque of a man overwhelmingly impressed. It was like Jackson had told him he was the guy who'd invented water or gravity or something.

"Do you have a card?" he'd asked as if both the possibility was slim and the audacity of the request breathtaking. Jackson had handed one over and then the tides of the party had taken them both elsewhere.

He hadn't thought about him at all in the decade and a half since then. Hadn't even read past the first paragraph of the *Times* obituary last week.

But now the widow had called and asked him in his capacity as her late husband's attorney to contact the heirs and read the will. Jackson's attempts to tell her that he'd never actually become

Anzullar's lawyer were met with a somewhat offended directness. "Well, he gave me your *card*," she'd said, as if that was that.

And apparently it was, because Jackson had found himself agreeing to take receipt of the will. He wasn't sure exactly what had prompted his why-the-hell-not response. Maybe it was a slow day. Maybe he hadn't wished to upset a recently-bereaved woman, however pissy she was. Maybe he just figured it would make for a fine dinner-party story, one that needed the third act of the actual reading of the will to make its little drama complete. All he knew was that now, with the document actually lying on his desk in front of him, he wished he hadn't been so stupidly amenable. He took another quick glance at it.

Christ, he had to read this shit with a straight face?

It wasn't a will. Not in any sense other than the formal and the clumsy layman's attempt at legalese that opened it. It was more like Anzullar had decided to make this document his last work of art, albeit literary rather than pictorial. Perhaps he thought it was clever. Jackson begged to differ. It was precious and twee and would stand up to any legal challenge about as long as a hard-on in the proximity of a straight razor.

He glanced at his desk-clock.

Three twenty-nine.

The recipients of Anzullar's largesse would be here any moment. He hoped they were bringing their senses of humor.

As if prompted by his very thought of them, the beneficiaries entered his office and sat down. There were three of them and they were absolutely identical.

Jackson had met twins before and knew of course that triplets existed, but there was something really disturbing about staring across his desk at what appeared to be three editions of exactly the same person. It might conceivably have been less disconcerting if the person in question had been – what? An ugly middle-aged guy running to fat and losing his hair? – but what was sitting in triplicate in his room was a stunningly beautiful young woman.

They were the daughters, or so the widow – who was not herself named in the will and was thus not herself present – had told him. Jackson realized now, with a rush of reluctant admiration for the recently departed old bugger, that Anzullar must not only have scored himself quite the hot young chick for his second wife but also have managed to impregnate her sometime in his mid-seventies, because these girls – girl? girl cubed? – couldn't have been more than twenty-one years old.

And gorgeous. Absolutely drop-dead gorgeous.

The three sisters each tipped their head a little to the side in a gesture of inquiry and gentle puzzlement and Jackson realized that he'd been staring at them for several seconds without saying a word.

Gathering his professionalism as best he could, he spoke up, his voice polite and clear and mercifully free of overt lust.

"Thank you all for coming," he said. "My sincere condolences for your loss. I'm Isaac Jackson."

"Chinchilla," said the first daughter.

"Diamante," said the second.

"Sam," said the third.

Hmm. Perhaps Anzullar's copy of *The Poseur's Guide to Naming One's Children* had been missing the entries for "S". Whatever. Jackson gave them all a respectable smile and then picked up their father's will.

A whole page was devoted to the single phrase *Clause the First* written in magenta ink by a spidery hand that was presumably the deceased's own. The following page contained said clause, and Jackson read it aloud just as if it had been written by someone less full of shit.

"To the worms of the earth and other agents of decay I leave all my worldly goods. May their desiccation, liquefaction, ossification, and putrefaction be found sportive to those with eyes to see."

Chinchilla gave a brief musical laugh.

Sam clapped her hands once in delight.

"Oh, Daddy," said Diamante, in that tone of disapproving affection that people use for their mischievous but beloved children or outrageous but adored friends.

Jackson felt an obligation to clarify things for them. "We can assume your father means to let his house and possessions stand and rot," he said. "While that may be his wish, it's certainly something you could seek to overturn on the grounds of—"

Chinchilla interrupted him. "You mean claim his *house*?" she said.

"His *things*?" said Sam. "*I* don't want them. Do *you* want them?" she asked her sisters.

"No," said Diamante, and Chinchilla shook her head.

"All right," said Jackson. "I'll move on."

Clause the Second, equally cavalier in its generous waste of paper, was the first of the bequests to the girls.

"To my precious Diamante," Jackson read aloud, "I give the following observation. May she use it wisely.

"When the philosopher-poet Bob Marley said *Don' worry 'bout a t'ing. Every little t'ing's gwine be a'right*, do you honestly think he was lying?"

That was it. Jackson looked up apologetically at Diamante and was astonished to see that her eyes had misted with tears.

Sam reached her hand over and squeezed her sister's.

"I'm so happy for you," Chinchilla said, as Diamante nodded her thanks.

Jackson did his best to keep his face benignly blank as he looked at them. Jesus Christ. All three of them. Beautiful. Arousing. And as barking mad as their fucking father. He turned his attention back to the will.

"To my adored Sam," he read, "I leave the afternoon of September the seventh, Nineteen-sixty-three, as it appeared in New Brighton, England between the hours of two and five. I also grant her full custody of the adjectives *crepuscular* and *antediluvian*. I trust to her generosity of spirit that she will not unnecessarily withhold their fair usage by others."

Sam seemed as delighted by her inheritance as Diamante had been with hers, whispering her adjectives repeatedly under her breath as Jackson turned to Clause the Third.

"To my beloved Chinchilla, I bequeath the following air:"

Jackson paused there. That single sentence at the top of the page was followed only by a hand-drawn musical staff which contained the notes of a melody spread out over eight measures. The rest of the page was blank.

"I'm afraid I can't read music," Jackson said, and held the page out uncertainly to Chinchilla. She took it eagerly and, holding it to her face, seemed to smell it. No, more than that, really. Seemed almost to breathe it in. After a moment, she held the loose leaf out so that her sisters could see.

"How *generous*!" said Sam, with a pleasure apparently untainted by envy.

"Do you . . . do you know the tune?" Jackson asked, feeling like an idiot.

Chinchilla nodded. "It's a melody from the Italian," she said. "The words tell of how Harlequin came to the shores of a great salt lake and burned the still-beating heart of his lost love."

There was a suitably impressed silence for a moment, which was broken by a braying snort from Diamante. "No it's *not*," she said. "It was written on Daddy's piano by that awful little man from Cedar Rapids. It was a jingle. For a *product*. Metamucil or something equally banal."

"Diamante, you are so fucking *literal*," Chinchilla said. "I'm not sure you're my sister at all. I'm really not."

Chinchilla laid the piece of paper back down on Jackson's desk and looked at him.

"Thank you for your time, Mister Jackson," she said. "Are we done here?"

Jackson hesitated for a second. "Um . . . No. Not quite. This is a little awkward." He glanced down at the final page of the will. "I'll just read the last Clause, shall I?"

"Please," said Sam, encouragingly.

Jackson cleared his throat. "To Isaac Jackson, for services rendered, I leave a gift which will be given to him at a time and place of my daughters' choosing."

The girls were silent for a moment. A look passed between Chinchilla and Sam, and then Chinchilla looked back at Jackson.

"Oh, yes. Yes," she said. "I know about that. I'll be in touch." Her mood seemed to have been ruined a little by her earlier disagreement with Diamante. Not sad or annoyed, really. More distracted. She stood up, gesturing to her sisters to do the same.

Jackson stood too, sweeping the pages of Anzullar's will back together and putting them in a file folder. Sam shook his hand. Diamante did the same. They headed for the door, leaving Chinchilla standing by Jackson's desk. After she too had shaken his hand and repeated her thanks, he nodded down at the file.

"Technically, the page with the melody on it is your inheritance," he said. "Your physical property. If you'll let me Xerox a copy for the files, you could take it now."

"No need," she said.

"Alright," he said. "If you're sure. I should point out, by the way, that if your sister is correct, you own *only* the piece of paper. You can't really do anything with the tune. Commercially, I mean. The copyright remains with the composer or his publisher."

Chinchilla smiled at him.

"You misunderstand," she said. "My father hasn't left me the copyright. Nor that piece of paper. He has left me the melody itself."

She leaned in and whispered in his ear. "And with it I can unlock the world."

Jackson eased the Maserati up to 70 and flicked on the cruise control. The road was so straight and so uncongested that he felt he could probably even prop the *Times* against the steering wheel and take another crack at the crossword but he resisted the temptation. Instead, he pushed the radio pre-sets until he found something he remembered from his college days and then sat back and let Tom Petty explain how American girls were raised on promises.

Over to the west, the sun was setting. Jackson turned off the AC and cracked the windows a little to let in the evening's gathering breeze. The odometer said he'd been traveling thirteen miles since he'd turned off the county road onto the state highway. Shouldn't be far now.

He hadn't expected to ever hear from Chinchilla or her sisters again, and had given little thought to the unspecified gift that he was supposed to receive. What was it likely to be anyway? Custody of all oblique angles found in geometry textbooks published between 1921 and 1934? Part-ownership of the color green? Gimme a fucking break.

But a few days after their first meeting Chinchilla had called. Her voice on the phone had been warm and inviting and Jackson had found himself inevitably wondering while she spoke if there was any possibility at all that the gift she was to give him would involve her being naked and pliant. He was way too old to be led by his pants anymore but he'd nevertheless found himself writing down certain coordinates and travel instructions and agreeing to meet.

And now here he was. On the road. Like a hormone-drenched high-schooler kicked into gear by a kiss and a whisper.

He'd thought he was familiar with this stretch of highway but the lines of strip malls and outlet stores that he'd expected to run all the way to the merge with the Interstate had long since disappeared behind him and all that was visible now on either side of the road was flat grassland, its colors already fading into a uniform deep purple as the sun finally dipped out of sight beyond the low and distant western hills.

A black limousine hurtled past on the other side of the divider line heading back to civilization. Jackson watched its tail-lights disappear in his rear-view and realized it was the only other vehicle he'd seen in either direction for several minutes. He also realized that the breeze coming in through his windows had dropped several degrees once the sun had vanished. He didn't need to put the heater on yet but he rolled up the windows and wondered again why the hell he was doing this.

Chinchilla's instructions, needless to say, had kept up the family tradition. Why use street names or freeway numbers when there was a whole world of latitudes, longitudes, north-by-northwests, and Evening Stars to play with? And the meeting point hadn't been specified so much as poetically alluded to. He'd managed to translate it down to this highway at least and ask her if he'd reach the Interstate. She'd said no and, when he'd asked where he turned off, added that he needn't turn off, that he'd stop when it was appropriate, and that she'd be there. He took that to mean that somewhere between here and the Interstate – theoretically just a mile or so ahead, though he could see no sign of it yet despite the flat ribbon of highway running straight in front of him to the horizon – she'd be parked on the side of the road and would flag him down. Provided it wasn't beneath her dignity to do anything so mundane or rational.

Night had fallen properly now and his headlights were the only illumination on the road. Where the hell *was* everybody? He'd been driving less than an hour but he was as alone as if he were on some back road in the middle of the Mojave. And the road itself, and the land around it, didn't seem to jibe with what Jackson knew to be the geography of the area. This straight? This empty? This dark? It was as if he were driving through a vast flat midnight desert bounded to right and left at the limits of his vision by long low hills scarcely distinct in the darkness from the sky above or the ground below.

Paul Simon had just finished assuring him that, though the day was strange and mournful, the mother and child reunion was only a moment away when the radio cut off completely.

No static, no signal fade, just sudden and instant station loss.

He'd have hit the other pre-sets for an alternative had he not realized at that exact moment that the silence was more profound than merely the absence of music. His engine had stopped too.

"Shit!" he said. His hands flexed instinctively on the wheel. His foot stabbed instinctively in the direction of the brake – but he managed to resist the impulse to slam on and instead tapped at the pedal gently to ease back the momentum that was all that was moving the car.

The lights were still on, thank Christ, so he could guide the car onto the shoulder as it continued to slow down. It took about half a minute for it to coast to a perfectly safe stop. Perfectly safe, but come on – the fuck was up with this? Jackson put the car in park and turned the key back to the off position.

Oh man. It was *really* dark without the lights. Jackson felt a sudden stab of unfocussed anxiety and forced himself to take a breath and let his eyes adjust. All right. That helped. A little.

Through his closed windows, he could hear the chattering of cicadas. He tapped at the plexi-glass of the dash, which was about the extent of his mechanical expertise. None of the dials moved. The car still appeared to have nearly a third of a tank of gas. Already wishing he'd listened when someone had explained to him once how you can tell when you're flooding the engine, he turned the key again.

And again.

Nothing.

The key would click into the first position, powering the lights and electrics, but it simply couldn't make the car start.

He turned it off completely again. It seemed that each time he did, the darkness into which he was plunged was deeper than before but he knew that that was his imagination. He knew that.

He looked out of the windows, ahead and to the sides. Nothing. Alright, fuck it. What did he pay Triple-A for anyway? He pulled out his cell-phone and powered it up. Reassuring tinkle of chimes . . . pretty little screen display . . . and then the message *No Service*. He flung it onto the passenger seat to let it keep searching and turned the key one more time.

His headlights stabbed through the night. Directly ahead, caught in the beams like some vaudeville act who'd been standing waiting for their spotlight, were the three sisters.

They were twelve yards or so down the road from his car and appeared to have arrived here with no vehicle of their own. They were wearing matching white gowns and, from this distance, their expressionless faces seemed almost as white against the darkness of the night.

Jackson opened his door and got out, leaving his headlights on. The sweetly overpowering smell of jasmine hit him as, slowly, he walked towards them. He wasn't sure why he didn't call out a greeting. He wasn't entirely sure that a greeting was what he would have called out anyway.

The sisters were silent too, and remained motionless as he approached them.

When he was just a few feet away, the one in the middle – he assumed it was Chinchilla but who could tell? – stepped forward slightly and the ghost of a welcoming smile slid briefly across her lips.

"Mister Jackson," she said. "How lovely to see you again." There was nothing unpleasant about her voice. Not at all. Perhaps just a hint of mild surprise at this converging of paths.

"I was invited," he said. He didn't know why he said that and he didn't like the way his voice sounded saying it, but it didn't seem to bother Chinchilla.

"Oh yes," she said. "So you were."

"My car. It's . . . stopped. I mean, it won't start."

"That's all right," she said, and her smile grew wider. "You won't be needing it."

She looked as beautiful as ever, but pale. Very pale. She leaned a little towards him to say something more and Jackson had to fight the urge to flinch back from her, though there was nothing threatening or fast about her movement and her voice was a delicate and sweet whisper.

"This is the gift we bring you," she said. "The gift of seeing with one's own eyes."

The car's headlights went out.

The moon must have risen while they'd been talking, or the stars have come out, because Jackson could still see her as she stepped back from him to join her sisters, who moved closer in on either side of her.

There was nothing violent or distressing about the way their flesh melded. It seemed natural and gentle. Like the flow of water into waiting channels or the delicate sweeping application of paint to canvas, the sisters slid into each other effortlessly. Like the sundered images on a stereoscopic photograph marrying themselves to reveal an unsuspected depth, they came together, becoming one.

But not really. Not quite.

There were too many arms. Too many eyes.

The landscape beyond seemed to both thicken and recede, losing definition and light, becoming a backdrop, a setting, a black base against which they . . . she . . . it . . . was foregrounded like a surrealist figure on an abstract canvas.

Jackson could still feel the ground beneath his feet. But his other senses were already protesting their starvation. The sweet heady smell of the night-blooming jasmine had disappeared and the rhythmic chafing of the cicadas gone with it. His eyes were his only passport to the world and what they saw was already reducing itself to these new essentials. The impossible woman and the darkness behind. That was all there was.

From somewhere within the collage of flesh in front of him, what used to be Chinchilla's mouth smiled again.

And then she was vanishing, all of her was vanishing, shrinking in on herself to a point of dazzling white singularity like the last collapsing sun in a voided universe. Impossibly, piercingly bright. Inconceivably distant. Unutterably beautiful.

And then gone.

There was only the darkness now, a darkness from which all definition and distinction was disappearing.

He was not on the road. He was not in the desert. He was just in the dark. All stars a memory now, and the moon forgotten.

He heard Chinchilla's voice whispering the melody of her Italian song.

And the night peeled open like dark petals.

LIZ WILLIAMS

All Fish and Dracula

LIZ WILLIAMS' NOVELS INCLUDE *The Ghost Sister*, *Empire of Bones*, *The Poison Master*, *Nine Layers of Sky*, *Banner of Souls* and *Darkland* (all published by Bantam Spectra/Tor Macmillan), while *Snake Agent* appeared from Night Shade Press.

Forthcoming titles include *Bloodmind* and *Vanish*, while her short fiction was collected in *The Banquet of the Lords of Night*, also from Night Shade. Her more than fifty short stories have appeared in such magazines as *Asimov's*, *Realms of Fantasy* and *Interzone*.

Four of the author's novels have been short-listed for the Philip K. Dick Award. *Banner of Souls* was short-listed for the Arthur C. Clarke Award in 2006, and several have also appeared on the *New York Times* "Best of Year" listings.

As she explains about the tale that follows: "This story was sparked off by a comment overheard in Whitby High Street by my friend, writer Sue Thomason, who subsequently invited me to attend one of the annual Goth weekends in Whitby.

"I remember walking along the fog-bound seafront, seeing a wan-faced Victorian-clad waif drifting out of the sea mist. Then her Nokia rang. It pretty much summed up Goth Weekend for me."

T HE GIRL SLIPPED ACROSS THE COBBLES, black lace trailing over rain-wet stone. The two women were walking a short distance ahead: elderly, bowed down with shopping bags, headscarves keeping out the worst of the October drizzle. In one bag, the girl could see the wet golden skin of an escaping onion. The women were talking together in low voices, the soft Yorkshire accent running the words together.

She shied from the threat of her reflection in a shop window, bouncing back the lights above the rows of jet jewellery. She already knew what she looked like: all lace and velvet beneath the billowing leather coat, lips the colour of what-else, hair slicked back from a high pale forehead. Her hands clicked with silver.

As she drew closer to the two women, she thought: *it would be so easy*. But then she spied the others at the end of the street: her vampire clan. She hurried toward them.

As she passed the old women, she wondered how she must appear: alarming, sinister, a vision out of dark. She smiled to herself, a little. She was a few yards in front of them when one of the women spoke.

"Ee, Mary," she said. "In't it nice to see so many young people taking care of their clothes?"

WHITBY WELCOMES THE GOTHS

The banner was huge, taking up most of an advertising hoarding at the entrance to the main street. Around the letters, someone had painted bats, with little smiling faces.

"Look at that," Lily said, disgusted. But it made Katya smile. Julian twisted around in his seat to look at them, flicking back a black lock of hair.

"What, you were expecting them to meet us with pitchforks and stakes? They love Goth Weekend up here. No one getting pissed and throwing up in their gardens. We're polite. We keep ourselves to ourselves."

"We spend loads of money," Katya murmured. She waved a jet-and-silver decked hand. "What's not to love?"

"Precisely."

But Lily's mouth turned downward, like a child who would not be comforted. Katya sighed. Lily had been in a mood ever since they left Leeds and she was beginning to regret ever accepting Julian's offer of a lift up to Whitby. She didn't know them very well – they were friends of a friend – and even though they were all Goths, she could not help wishing that Lily and Julian were a little less . . . well, Gothic. Lily sulked and pouted, and Julian hadn't stopped talking since they had started, in a superior, educating-the-young kind of way. He was four years older, it was true, twenty-two to Katya's eighteen, but even so . . . She supposed that he did know more about the bands, but she would rather see them for herself and make her own mind up. But she was too polite, or too *something*, to say so.

"Where's the guest house?" she asked, longing now for the journey to be at an end so that she could go and find Damian and the others. As they turned the corner, she saw a huge group of young men, all frock coats and knee boots. She wondered, with an odd stab of disloyalty, how many of them might be called Damian. Or Julian, come to that. Or Katy, with an extra "a".

"Not far now," Julian said, quite kindly, as if reassuring someone very small.

"Oh good."

She spoke more sourly than she had intended, and Lily gave her a glance of surprise, as though she were the one to have a monopoly on sulleness.

"I'll drop you two off and park," Julian said. They were climbing, now, high into the town. Craning back, Katya saw a thin line of estuary through the rainy haze, banked by black harbour walls. The town stepped down to meet it and beyond lay the chilly expanse of the North Sea. A boat, tiny from this height, was setting out from the harbour mouth.

"Herring," Julian said, with authority.

"I'm sorry?"

"That's what they fish for here," Julian amplified. "And cod."

"I thought cod was all fished out?" Katya ventured. She wasn't sure about herring, either. Julian frowned, clearly preferring not to be questioned.

"Is it?"

"Yes. Everything was over-fished up here. There's barely anything left in the North Sea."

"Well, that shouldn't matter much to you, should it? As long as they don't run out of nut roast."

"Don't you even eat fish?" Lily asked.

"No," Katya said. "I'm not that sort of vegetarian. I've never eaten fish or meat. I'm vegan, actually. My mum's a bit of an old hippy. She brought us up that way. It's just the way I am. I don't bang on about it."

She saw Julian's lip curl. "It's natural to eat flesh. We're predators, hunters. We need the protein."

"Beans have protein."

"You can't be a vampire and eat beans."

"I'm not a vampire, am I? I'm just a Goth."

"Anyway," Lily said, suddenly animated. "That's not cod."

Katya peered through the car window in the direction of her pointing finger. Right at the top of the cliff, by the roadside, stood a wishbone gateway: white against the storm-dark sky.

"That's a whale's jawbone," Julian said.

"Big, isn't it?" Katya remarked, and wished she hadn't made such an obvious remark. Of course it was big. It belonged to a whale. She thought of her sister Jess, who had a job in an estate agent and read *Cosmopolitan*.

"*I don't know what you want to go to Whitby for at this time of the year. Whitby's boring. All fish and Dracula. Why don't you book a week in Malaga?*"

"Here we are." Julian pulled up at the kerb.

The guesthouse, set on the wind-driven cliff, had lemon-coloured gables and a garden filled with withered hydrangeas. Wrestling her bags from the car, Katya signed in at the desk, watched by a small, pale woman in a fraying chenille sweater. Then, with relief, she went upstairs and shut the door behind her. She could still hear Julian's voice, lecturing on, and Lily's muttered replies, but they were staying in a room downstairs, well out of earshot, and slowly the sounds faded.

Later, Katya walked down into the town through the October twilight. She had crept through the hallway of the guesthouse and shut the door quietly behind her, in case Lily and Julian overheard and wanted to go with her. She felt a twinge of guilt, but stifled it.

Whitby was crawling with Goths: strolling through the narrow streets in spite of the chill and the rainy air. Anubis Dusk and the Deadmen were playing at the Spa, and Katya slipped into the back after handing over a fiver. And then she was lost for the next hour and twenty minutes, in the shadow-play of music and light.

Coming out, still dazed, into the rain, she had a moment of intense loneliness, just long enough to enjoy, because then she looked up and the others were there. The others, and Damian, thin and nervy and possibly about to become her boyfriend, Katya thought with a rush of hope.

The rest of the evening was snatched up into gossip and chips and pints of snakebite in a nearby pub. Katya was initially too happy to notice what the place was called, but when closing time saw them out on the street once more, she glanced upward and saw that the name of the pub was the *Herring Catch*. Jess's remark floated back into memory and she smiled.

"Walk you back?" Damian asked, and she nodded, overcome with sudden shyness. They set off up the hill together. Halfway up, reminding herself that she was eighteen now, a grown woman, she reached out and took his hand. It was both cold and clammy; Katya did not mind. They did not say very much. At the door of the guesthouse, he kissed her, rather clumsily, and then he was gone. Slowly, Katya made her way through dripping hydrangeas and up the stairs to her room. She was just easing off her boots when there was a sharp tap at the door.

"It's me," Julian's voice said. He sounded younger and strained. "Is Lily with you?"

"Isn't she with you?" Katya did not want to let him in. She wanted to sit down on the bed and think about Damian.

"No. Can I come in?"

Katya stood in indecision for a moment, then opened the door. Julian seemed very pale, but admittedly it was hard to tell.

"We went to the Disappointed gig at the Metropole. I turned round and she was gone. I've been looking for her ever since."

"I haven't seen her since we got here."

"Where did you go, anyway?" He sounded petulant and accusing.

Katya told him. "She'll probably be back in a bit. I wouldn't worry, honestly."

He seemed inclined to linger, but Katya was too tired. She herded him out of the door and fell into bed.

Net morning, to Katya's relief, Julian was not at breakfast. Somewhat guiltily, she ploughed her way through mushrooms and toast, and examined a flyer for the Bat Conservation Raffle, just in case one of the other residents felt the need to talk to her. No one did. She returned to her room to fetch her coat. Beyond the windows, the sky was a deep, lowering grey.

As she reached the front door, however, her mobile rang. The number shown was Julian's. Katya hesitated, then answered it.

"It's me," Julian said, without preamble. "I'm at the police station."

"Why?" Katya asked, blankly. "What have you done?"

"I haven't done anything!" He sounded rattled. The usual slight, superior drawl was absent. "They found Lily last night. She's dead."

"Dead?" Katya turned, to see her own face looking back at her from the hall mirror. In the underwater dimness of the hallway, her face looked pallid and drowned beneath the heavy make-up. She could see each one of the kohl dots around her eyes, in perfect, unnatural clarity.

"Katya? Are you there?"

"Yes?" It sounded more like a question. "What happened?" The

streets had been so slippery, and in high heels . . . Or perhaps a car
. . . "Was she . . . run over, or something?"

"She was killed."

"Someone killed her?" His voice seemed to be coming from a very
long way away.

"They said I can go. I was with people all evening."

She wondered why he was telling her this, then realised that of
course, he would be a suspect, if Lily had been murdered.

"Katya? Can you come to the police station? I don't want to be on
my own."

She had to be strong and decisive. "Tell me where it is," she said.
Her voice sounded more like a squeak.

Under the neon glow of the station reception, Julian looked even
more wan than usual, and scared. He was twisting his long black
scarf between his hands.

"Let's get out of here," Katya said. She took his arm and steered
him through the doors.

"They might want to talk to you, too. I don't know."

"Did you give them my name?" Katya said.

"I had to." He shot her an uneasy look. "They kept asking if there
was anyone else who knew Lily."

"Do they know how she died?" It seemed so unreal, to be having
this conversation. It wasn't like this in books, this floating, shocky
sensation.

"They said there were marks on her neck. But she hadn't been –
you know."

"That means strangling," Katya said in a very small voice.

He glanced at her askance. "Or a bite."

Katya let go of his arm and stared. "A bite? From what?"

He didn't answer. They gaped at one another for a few moments,
then Julian turned, abruptly, and began walking slowly down the
hill.

The police called Katya once they had reached a tea shop. It was
full of Goths and old ladies, mutually ignoring one another save for a
few occasional remarks about the rain. Katya made Julian eat a
scone. When her phone rang, she nearly dropped it.

They wanted her to come in as soon as she could.

"I can't come back with you," Julian said, staring mutinously out
of the window. "I just can't cope with it."

"But I don't want to go on my own," Katya faltered. "And I
waited for *you*."

"Well, sorry, but I can't handle it, okay?"

Angry and scared, she rang Damian and he said he would meet her at the station. He was waiting when she got there.

Katya had always thought that it would be rather cool to be questioned by the police, or involved in a murder, but now that it was happening it seemed merely prosaic, upsetting, and at the same time, strange. The room where they questioned her was dingy and smelled of damp dog. The policewoman was kind, not much older than Katya herself, and she took a painstakingly long time to write down the statement. There was no sense that Katya might be a suspect. They just wanted some details, that was all. Then she was allowed to go. She and Damian traipsed back up the hill to the guesthouse and sat in the lounge, drinking endless cups of tea. Katya had brought mint tea bags, since she did not like black tea, and the thin heat of it revived her a little.

That evening, she found herself determined to have a good time. She tried not to think about Lily. It was a horrible thing, but some small secret voice inside her told her that Lily was hard to miss.

They met up with the others at the *Herring Catch*. It wasn't so busy this early in the evening, and they managed to get a window seat. Katya looked out across the expanse of the harbour. The lights from the high streets of the town glittered across the water, fracturing darkness. She thought she glimpsed something moving, out there toward the harbour mouth, and frowning, she craned her neck to see, but it was gone. Perhaps it had been a fishing boat, though she found it hard to believe that anyone would set out on a night like this.

All the talk was about Lily and how she had managed to choose the most appropriate day of the year to die, really. It was Hallowe'en, after all; Samhain, when the dead come back from the other world and the veil between the realms lies thin.

"It's what she would have wanted," Damian said, in wide-eyed earnest.

"Too right," Amy remarked, sourly. "A great big melodrama."

"That's not very kind," Damian protested.

"No, but it's true." Amy glared around her. "Isn't it?" No one said anything.

The sudden tension, on top of the other events of the day, made Katya uncomfortable.

"Won't be a moment," she muttered, and rose from the table. "Where's the ladies?"

"It's out the back," Amy said, still glaring. Katya made her way through the back door of the pub and found herself in a courtyard: three bare brick walls and a fourth containing a half-open door.

Through it, she glimpsed the black waters of the harbour. And again, there was movement across the water: something gliding. Something big. Katya frowned, trying to make sense of it. She could not help but think of bats. She realised that she was shivering: it was freezing, out here in the courtyard. She wrapped her lace-and-velvet arms around herself and sought refuge in the lavatory, lit by a single bulb.

She was trying to coax some water out of the tap when there was a scream from the courtyard. After a frozen moment, she gathered her wits and rushed outside. A girl was crouching in the middle of the courtyard, clutching her throat.

"God!" Katya rushed to her side. The girl was clearly one of the other participants of Goth Weekend, judging from the clothes. "Are you all right?"

"No." The girl was crying. Her hands were sticky with blood. "Something *bit* me."

Katya helped her to her feet and together they stumbled inside. The landlady took one look and phoned what Katya assumed to be a local doctor, then took charge of the injured girl. Katya made her way back to her seat. The floating sense of unreality was back. Everyone was staring.

"What happened?" Amy was shocked out of her bad temper. She put an arm around Katya and guided her into her seat.

"Something bit her," Katya said, in an unsteady echo. "In the neck."

No one said anything. Then, as though a collective decision had been discussed and made, everyone reached for their coats and bags and left the pub.

"Look, I'll see you back up the hill," Bram said.

"Yeah, okay. Thanks." She had no intention of protesting.

That night, she lay staring sleeplessly into the darkness. She though of vampires, real ones, ones in which, she realised, she did not believe. The Goth scene was no more than role-play, a veneer of dark glamour over the banality of everyday life. But what if some people had started taking it too seriously? She knew that such things happened: there were lifestyle vampires in the States, blood drinkers, people who'd had their teeth filed into fangs. She had never met one. She wondered whether Lily had. And thinking back, the person who had told her about the lifestyle vampires had been Julian . . .

The thunderous knock on the door brought her bolt upright in bed, heart pounding.

"Who is it?"

"It's me."

Warily, Katya opened the door to see Julian standing in the hallway. He looked dishevelled, wide-eyed. He said, "She's going to rise."

"What?"

"Lily. She's going to rise." He made an impatient gesture. "She was bitten last night, and tonight, it's Samhain. She's coming back. I know it."

"Julian, I don't think—"

But he was off, running down the stairs of the guesthouse. Katya hovered in the doorway, wanting desperately to go back to bed. She heard the bang of the front door. But in the end, she could not just leave him. She pulled her clothes over her satin nightdress and followed.

The town was very dark and very quiet. Julian was nowhere to be seen, but as Katya reached the gate, she glimpsed him running along the edge of the cliff in the direction of the whale's jawbone. She thought: *God, if he throws himself off* . . . She might not like Julian much, but it was an awful thought. It was still raining, a thin cold drizzle, and the grass must be as slippery as ice.

"Julian! Wait!"

He did not look back. Katya charged across the road. The rain was getting heavier and a wind was rising, whipping salt into her face. There was a concrete path running along the cliff and she ran down it, spitting wet hair from her mouth. She could hear the crash and boil of the waves against the rocks. Ahead, she saw Julian stumble.

"Wait!" she cried again.

He struggled to his feet and ran on, but when he reached the whale's jawbone, he doubled up, leaning with one hand on the white, spined arch. Katya could feel a cramp of her own, a tight stitch across her gut. The rain was driving in hard and she could barely see the edge of the cliff, now. She slowed and paused, terrified of falling. Above Julian's head, at the joint of the whalebone arch, there was a kind of sparkle of darkness, something that moved and twisted in the air.

"Julian?"

She hurried forward, as quickly as she dared. It came again, darting and swift, and there were more of them now. She reached the top of the cliff. The jawbone towered above her. She saw straight through it, into a churning mass of spray. But the cliff was high, she should not be able to see the sea – yet there were huge silver forms gleaming within it, leaping, hurtling upward in a blur of scales and teeth. There was an amoebic twist of the edge of the shoal and Julian was gone, falling back without a sound into the wall of water beyond the jawbone. A glistening shape sprang from the shoal to hang in the air before Katya's face. She looked into a cold, gleaming eye, alight with gestalt intelligence. The mouth of the great fish opened in a slow gasp to reveal razor teeth, then closed once more. With a flick of its tail it was gone, back into the mass, and the shoal shot through the jawbone and streamed down into the town. In wonder, she watched it go. When it hit the harbour it dispersed; she saw silver flickers in the streets, hunting.

At Samhain, the dead return, she thought, but there is nothing to say which dead, nor which part of the natural world, ravaged and over-plundered, might turn tail on its predators on this one unnatural night of the year. She ran all the way back to the guesthouse and pulled the bedcovers over her head like a child.

In the morning, it was sunny and cold. There was no sign of rain. She dressed in her only pair of jeans, and a red sweater. Avoiding questions from the landlady, she paid her bill with a cheque. This time, she signed it Katy.

CHINA MIÉVILLE, EMMA BIRCHAM AND MAX SCHAEFER

The Ball Room

CHINA MIÉVILLE WAS BORN in Norwich and moved very quickly to London. He has degrees in Social Anthropology and International Relations, and a Ph.D. in the philosophy of International Law.

With influences that include M. John Harrison, Gene Wolfe, Dambudzo Marechera and H. P. Lovecraft, his first novel was *King Rat* in 1998, followed by the Arthur C. Clarke Award and British Fantasy Award-winning *Perdido Street Station*, the British Fantasy Award-winning *The Scar* and the Arthur C. Clarke Award-winning *Iron Council*.

Miéville's novella *The Tain* appeared from PS Publishing, his short fiction is collected in *Looking for Jake*, and his first non-fiction book is *Between Equal Rights*, a study of International Law.

Emma Bircham is fabulous, but a bit tired. She lives in London as well. Max Schaefer was born in London in 1974 and has been intending to do something ever since.

"None of us had ever collaborated on stories before," explain the authors, "but this time it happened very naturally. After a thankless day shopping, one of us came up with the idea, pointing out how creepy certain areas of certain superstores are, another struggled to turn it into a story, and the third fixed it."

I 'M NOT EMPLOYED BY THE STORE. They don't pay my wages. I'm with a security firm, but we've had a contract here for a long time, and I've been here for most of it. This is where I know people. I've been a guard in other places – still am, occasionally, on short notice – and until recently I would have said this was the best place I'd been. It's nice to work somewhere people are happy to go. Until recently, if anyone asked me what I did for a living, I'd just tell them I worked for the store.

It's on the outskirts of town, a huge metal warehouse. Full of a hundred little fake rooms, with a single path running through them, and all the furniture we sell made up and laid out so you can see how it should look. Then the same products, disassembled, packed flat and stacked high in the warehouse for people to buy. They're cheap.

Mostly I know I'm just there for show. I wander around in my uniform, hands behind my back, making people feel safe, making the merchandise feel protected. It's not really the kind of stuff you can shoplift. I almost never have to intervene.

The last time I did was in the ball room.

On weekends this place is just crazy. So full it's hard to walk: all couples and young families. We try to make things easier for people. We have a cheap café and free parking, and most important of all we have a crèche. It's at the top of the stairs when you first come in. And right next to it, opening out from it, is the ball room.

The walls of the ball room are almost all glass, so people in the store can look inside. All the shoppers love watching the children: there are always people outside, staring in with big dumb smiles. I keep an eye on the ones that don't look like parents.

It's not very big, the ball room. Just an annexe really. It's been here for years. There's a climbing frame all knotted up around itself, and a net made of rope to catch you, and a Wendy house, and pictures on the walls. And it's full of colour. The whole room is two feet deep in shiny plastic balls.

When the children fall, the balls cushion them. The balls come up to their waists, so they wade through the room like people in a flood. The children scoop up the balls and splash them all over each other. They're about the size of tennis balls, hollow and light so they can't hurt. They make little pudda-thudda noises bouncing off the walls and the kids' heads, making them laugh.

I don't know why they laugh so hard. I don't know what it is about the balls that makes it so much better than a normal playroom, but they love it in there. Only six of them are allowed at a time, and they queue up for ages to get in. They get twenty minutes inside. You can see they'd give anything to stay longer. Sometimes, when it's time to go, they howl, and the friends they've made cry too, at the sight of them leaving.

I was on my break, reading, when I was called to the ball room.

I could hear shouting and crying from around the corner, and as I turned it I saw a crowd of people outside the big window. A man was clutching his son and yelling at the childcare assistant and the store manager. The little boy was about five, only just old enough to go in. He was clinging to his dad's trouser leg, sobbing.

The assistant, Sandra, was trying not to cry. She's only nineteen herself.

The man was shouting that she couldn't do her bloody job, that there were way too many kids in the place and they were completely out of control. He was very worked up and he was gesticulating exaggeratedly, like in a silent movie. If his son hadn't anchored his leg he would have been pacing around.

The manager was trying to hold her ground without being confrontational. I moved in behind her, in case it got nasty, but she was calming the man down. She's good at her job.

"Sir, as I said, we emptied the room as soon as your son was hurt, and we've had words with the other children . . ."

"You don't even know which one did it. If you'd been keeping an eye on them, which I imagine is your bloody job, then you might be a bit less . . . sodding ineffectual."

That seemed to bring him to a halt and he quieted down down, finally, as did his son, who was looking up at him with a confused kind of respect.

The manager told him how sorry she was, and offered his son an ice-cream. Things were easing down, but as I started to leave I saw Sandra crying. The man looked a bit guilty and tried to apologise to her, but she was too upset to respond.

The boy had been playing behind the climbing frame, in the corner by the Wendy house, Sandra told me later. He was burrowing down into the balls till he was totally covered, the way some children like to. Sandra kept an eye on the boy but she could see the balls bouncing as he moved, so she knew he was okay. Until he came lurching up, screaming.

The store is full of children. The little ones, the toddlers, spend their time in the main crèche. The older ones, eight or nine or ten, they normally walk around the store with their parents, choosing their own bedclothes or curtains, or a little desk with drawers or whatever. But if they're in between, they come back for the ball room.

They're so funny, moving over the climbing frame, concentrating hard. Laughing all the time. They make each other cry, of course, but usually they stop in seconds. It always gets me how they do that: bawling, then suddenly getting distracted and running off happily.

Sometimes they play in groups, but it seems like there's always one who's alone. Quite content, pouring balls onto balls, dropping them through the holes of the climbing frame, dipping into them like a duck. Happy but playing alone.

Sandra left. It was nearly two weeks after that argument, but she was still upset. I couldn't believe it. I started talking to her about it, and I could see her fill up again. I was trying to say that the man had been out of line, that it wasn't her fault, but she wouldn't listen.

"It wasn't him," she said. "You don't understand. I can't be in there any more."

I felt sorry for her, but she was overreacting. It was out of all proportion. She told me that since the day that little boy got upset, she couldn't relax in the ball room at all. She kept trying to watch all the children at once, all the time. She became obsessed with double-checking the numbers.

"It always seems like there's too many," she said. "I count them and there's six, and I count them again and there's six, but it always seems there's too many."

Maybe she could have asked to stay on and only done duty in the main crèche, managing name tags, checking the kids in and out, changing the tapes in the video, but she didn't even want to do that. The children loved that ball room. They went on and on about it, she said. They would never have stopped badgering her to be let in.

They're little kids, and sometimes they have accidents. When that happens, someone has to shovel all the balls aside to clean the floor, then dunk the balls themselves in water with a bit of bleach.

This was a bad time for that. Almost every day, some kid or other seemed to pee themselves. We kept having to empty the room to sort out little puddles.

"I had every bloody one of them over playing with me, every second, just so we'd have no problems," one of the nursery carers told me. "Then after they left . . . you could smell it. Right by the bloody Wendy house, where I'd have sworn none of the little buggers had got to."

His name was Matthew. He left a month after Sandra. I was amazed. I mean, you can see how much they love the children, people like them. Even having to wipe up dribble and sick and all that. Seeing them go was proof of what a tough job it was. Matthew looked really sick by the time he quit, really grey.

I asked him what was up but he couldn't tell me. I'm not sure he even knew.

You have to watch those kids all the time. I couldn't do that job. Couldn't take the stress. The children are so unruly, and so tiny. I'd be terrified all the time, of losing them, of hurting them.

There was a bad mood to the place after that. We'd lost two people. The main store turns over staff like a motor, of course, but the crèche normally does better. You have to be qualified, to work in the crèche, or the ball room. The departures felt like a bad sign.

I was conscious of wanting to look after the kids in the store. When I did my walks I felt like they were all around me. I felt like I had to be ready to leap in and save them any moment. Everywhere I looked, I saw children. And they were as happy as ever, running through the fake rooms and jumping on the bunkbeds, sitting at the desks that had been laid out ready. But now the way they ran around made me wince, and all our furniture, which meets or exceeds the most rigorous international standards for safety, looked like it was lying in wait to injure them. I saw head wounds in every coffee-table corner, burns in every lamp.

I went past the ball room more than usual. Inside was always some harassed looking young woman or man trying to herd the children, and them running through a tide of bright plastic that thudded every way as they dived into the Wendy house and piled up balls on its roof. The children would spin around to make themselves dizzy, laughing.

It wasn't good for them. They loved it when they were in there but they emerged so tired, and crotchety and teary. They did that droning children's cry. They pulled themselves into their parents' jumpers, sobbing, when it was time to go. They didn't want to leave their friends.

Some children were coming back week after week. It seemed to me their parents ran out of things to buy. After a while they'd make some token purchase like tea lights and just sit in the café, drinking tea and staring out of the window at the grey flyovers while their kids got their dose of the room. There didn't look like much that was happy to these visits.

The mood infected us. There wasn't a good feeling in the store. Some people said it was too much trouble, and we should close the ball room. But the management made it clear that wouldn't happen.

You can't avoid nightshifts.

There were three of us on that night, and we took different sections. Periodically we'd each of us wander through our patch, and between times we'd sit together in the staffroom or the unlit café and chat and play cards, with all sorts of rubbish flashing on the mute TV.

My route took me outside, into the front car lot, flashing my torch up and down the tarmac. The giant store behind me, with shrubbery around it black and whispery, and beyond the barriers the roads and night cars, moving away from me.

Inside again and through bedrooms, past all the pine frames and the fake walls. It was dim. Half-lights in all the big chambers full of beds never slept in and sinks without plumbing. I could stand still and there was nothing, no movement and no noise.

One time, I made arrangements with the other guards on duty, and I brought my girlfriend to the store. We wandered hand in hand through all the pretend rooms like stage sets, trailing torchlight. We played house like children, acting out little moments – her stepping out of the shower to my proffered towel, dividing the paper at the breakfast bar. Then we found the biggest and most expensive bed, with a special mattress that you can see nearby cut in cross section.

After a while, she told me to stop. I asked her what the matter was but she seemed angry and wouldn't say. I led her out through the locked doors with my swipe card and walked her to her car, alone in the lot, and I watched her drive away. There's a long one-way system of ramps and roundabouts to leave the store, which she followed, unnecessarily, so it took a long time before she was gone. We don't see each other any more.

In the warehouse, I walked between metal shelf units thirty feet high. My footsteps sounded to me like a prison guard's. I imagined the flat-packed furniture assembling itself around me.

I came back through kitchens, following the path towards the café, up the stairs into the unlit hallway. My mates weren't back: there was no light shining off the big window that fronted the silent ball room.

It was absolutely dark. I put my face up close to the glass and stared at the black shape I knew was the climbing frame; the Wendy house, a little square of paler shadow, adrift in plastic balls. I turned on my torch and shone it into the room. Where the beam touched them, the balls leapt into clown colours, and then the light moved and they went back to being black.

In the main crèche, I sat on the assistant's chair, with a little half-circle of baby chairs in front of me. I sat like that in the dark, and listened to no noise. There was a little bit of lamplight, orangey through the windows, and once every few seconds a car would pass, just audible, way out on the other side of the parking lot.

I picked up the book by the side of the chair and opened it in torchlight. Fairy tales. Sleeping Beauty, and Cinderella.

There was a sound.

A little soft thump.

I heard it again.

Balls in the ball room, falling onto each other.

I was standing instantly, staring through the glass into the darkness of the ball room. Pudda-thudda, it came again. It took me seconds to move, but I came close up to the window with my torch raised. I was holding my breath, and my skin felt much too tight.

My torchbeam swayed over the climbing frame and out the window on the other side, sending shadows into the corridors. I directed it down into those bouncy balls, and just before the beam hit them, while they were still in darkness, they shivered and slid away from each other in a tiny little trail. As if something was burrowing underneath.

My teeth were clenched. The light was on the balls now, and nothing was moving.

I kept that little room lit for a long time, until the torchlight stopped trembling. I moved it carefully up and down the walls, over every part, until I let out a big dumb hiss of relief because I saw that there were balls on the top of the climbing frame, right on its edge, and I realised that one or two of them must have fallen off, bouncing softly among the others.

I shook my head and my hand swung down, the torchlight going with it, and the ball room went back into darkness. And as it did, in the moment when the shadows rushed back in, I felt a brutal cold, and I stared at the little girl in the Wendy house, and she stared up at me.

The other two guys couldn't calm me down.

They found me in the ball room, yelling for help. I'd opened both doors and I was hurling balls out into the crèche and the corridors, where they rolled and bounced in all directions, down the stairs to the entrance, under the tables in the café.

At first I'd forced myself to be slow. I knew that the most important thing was not to scare the girl any more than she must have been already. I'd croaked out some daft, would-be cheerful greeting, come inside, shining the torch gradually towards the Wendy house, so I wouldn't dazzle her, and I'd kept talking, whatever nonsense I could muster.

When I realised she'd sunk down again beneath the balls, I became all jokey, trying to pretend we were playing hide-and-seek. I was horribly aware of how I might seem to her, with my build and my uniform, and my accent.

But when I got to the Wendy house, there was nothing there.

"She's been left behind!" I kept screaming, and when they understood they dived in with me and scooped up handfuls of the balls and threw them aside, but the two of them stopped long before me. When I turned to throw more of the balls away, I realised they were just watching me.

They wouldn't believe she'd been in there, or that she'd got out. They told me they would have seen her, that she'd have had to come past them. They kept telling me I was being crazy, but they didn't try to stop me, and eventually I cleared the room of all the balls, while they stood and waited for the police I'd made them call.

The ball room was empty. There was a damp patch under the Wendy house, which the assistants must have missed.

For a few days, I was in no state to come in to work. I was fevered. I kept thinking about her.

I'd only seen her for a moment, till the darkness covered her. She was five or six years old. She looked washed out, grubby and bleached of colour, and cold, as if I saw her through water. She wore a stained T-shirt, with the picture of a cartoon princess on it.

She'd stared at me with her eyes wide, her face clamped shut. Her grey, fat little fingers had gripped the edge of the Wendy house.

The police had found no one. They'd helped us clear up the balls and put them back in the ball room, and then they'd taken me home.

I can't stop wondering if it would have made any difference to how things turned out, if anyone had believed me. I can't see how it would. When I came back to work, days later, everything had already happened.

After you've been in this job a while, there are two kinds of situation you dread.

The first one is when you arrive to find a mass of people, tense and excited, arguing and yelling and trying to push each other out of the way and calm each other down. You can't see past them, but you know they're reacting ineptly to something bad.

The second one is when there's a crowd of people you can't see past, but they're hardly moving, and nearly silent. That's rarer, and invariably worse.

The woman and her daughter had already been taken away. I saw the whole thing later on security tape.

It had been the little girl's second time in the ball room in a matter of hours. Like the first time, she'd sat alone, perfectly happy, singing and talking to herself. Her minutes were up, her mother had loaded her new garden furniture into the car and come to take her home. She'd knocked on the glass and smiled, and the little girl had waded over happily enough, until she realised what she was being summoned.

On the tape you can see her whole body language change. She starts sulking and moaning, then suddenly turns and runs back to the Wendy house, plonking herself among the balls. Her mother looks fairly patient, standing at the door and calling for her, while the assistant stands with her. You can see them chatting.

The little girl sits by herself, talking into the empty doorway of the Wendy house, with her back to the adults, playing some obstinate, solitary final game. The other kids carry on doing their thing. Some are watching to see what happens.

Eventually, her mother yells at her to come. The girl stands and turns round, facing her across the sea of balls. She has one in each hand, her arms down by her sides, and she brings them up and stares at them, and at her mother. I won't, she's saying, I heard later. I want to stay. We're playing.

She backs into the Wendy house. Her mother strides over to her and bends in the doorway for a moment. She has to get down on all fours to get inside. Her feet stick out.

There's no sound on the tape. It's when you see all the children jerk, and the assistant run, that you know the woman has started to scream.

The assistant later told me that when she tried to rush forward, it seemed as if she couldn't get through the balls, as if they'd become heavy. The children were all getting in her way. It was bizarrely, stupidly difficult to cross the few feet to the Wendy house, with other adults in her wake.

They couldn't get the mother out of the way so between them they lifted the house into the air over her, tearing its toy walls apart.

The child was choking.

Of course, of course the balls are designed to be too big for anything like this to happen, but somehow she had shoved one far inside her mouth. It should have been impossible. It was too far, wedged too hard to prise out. The little girl's eyes were huge and her feet and knees kept turning inward towards each other.

You see her mother lift her up and beat her upon the back, very hard. The children are lined against the wall, watching.

One of the men manages to get the mother aside, and raises the girl for the Heimlich manoeuvre. You can't see her face too clearly on the tape, but you can tell that it is very dark now, the colour of a bruise, and her head is lolling.

Just as he has his arms about her, something happens at the man's feet, and he slips on the balls, still hugging her to him. They sink together.

They got the children into another room. Word went through the store, of course, and all the absent parents came running. When the first arrived she found the man who had intervened screaming at the children while the assistant tried desperately to quiet him. He was demanding they tell him where the other little girl was, who'd come close and chattered to him as he tried to help, who'd been getting in his way.

That's one of the reasons we had to keep going over the tape, to see where this girl had come from, and gone. But there was no sign of her.

Of course, I tried to get transferred, but it wasn't a good time in the industry, or in any industry. It was made pretty clear to me that the best way of holding on to my job was to stay put.

The ball room was closed, initially during the inquest, then for "renovation", and then for longer while discussions went on about its future. The closure became unofficially indefinite, and then officially so.

Those adults who knew what had happened (and it always surprised me, how few did) strode past the room with their toddlers strapped into pushchairs and their eyes grimly on the showroom trail, but their children still missed the room. You could see it when they came up the stairs with their parents. They'd think they were going to the ball room, and they'd start talking about it, and shouting about the climbing frame and the colours, and when they realised it was closed, the big window covered in brown paper, there were always tears.

Like most adults I turned the locked-up room into a blind spot. Even on night shifts when it was still marked on my route I'd turn away. It was sealed up, so why would I check it? Particularly when it still felt so terrible in there, a bad atmosphere as tenacious as stink. There are little card swipe units we have to use to show that we've covered each area, and I'd do the one by the ball room door without looking, staring at the stacks of new catalogues at the top of the stairs. Sometimes I'd imagine I heard could hear noises behind me, a soft little pudda-thudda, but I knew it was impossible so there was no point even checking.

It was strange to think of the ball room closed for good. To think that those were the last kids who'd ever get to play there.

One day I was offered a big bonus to stay on late. The store manager introduced me to Mr Gainsburg from head office. It turned out she didn't just mean the UK operation, but the corporate parent. Mr Gainsburg wanted to work late in the store that night, and he needed someone to look after him.

He didn't reappear until well past eleven, just as I was beginning to assume that he'd given in to jet lag and I was in for an easy night. He was tanned and well dressed. He kept using my Christian name while he lectured me about the company. A couple of times I wanted to tell him what my profession had been where I come from, but I could see he wasn't trying to patronise me. In any case I needed the job.

He asked me to take him to the ball room.

"Got to sort out problems as early as you can," he said. "It's the number one thing I've learned, John, and I've been doing this a while. One problem will always create another. If you leave one little thing, think you can just ride it out, then before you know it you've got two. And so on.

"You've been here a while, right John? You saw this place before it closed. These crazy little rooms are a fantastic hit with kids. We have them in all our stores now. You'd think it would be an extra, right? A nice-to-have. But I tell you John, kids love these places, and kids . . . well, kids are really, really important to this company."

The doors were propped open by now and he had me help him carry a portable desk from the show floor into the ball room.

"Kids make us, John. Nearly forty per cent of our customers have young children, and most of those cite the kid-friendliness of our stores as one of the top two or three reasons they come here. Above quality of product. Above price. You drive here, you eat, it's a day out for the family.

"Okay, so that's one thing. Plus, it turns out that people who are shopping for their kids are much more aware of issues like safety and quality. They spend way more per item, on average, than singles and childless couples, because they want to know they've done the best for their kids. And our margins on the big-ticket items are way healthier than on entry-level product. Even low-income couples, John, the proportion of their income that goes on furniture and household goods just rockets up at pregnancy."

He was looking around him at the balls, bright in the ceiling lights that hadn't been on for months, at the ruined skeleton of the Wendy house.

"So what's the first thing we look at when a store begins to go wrong? The facilities. The crèche, the childcare. Okay, tick. But the results here have been badly off kilter recently. All the stores have shown a dip, of course, but this one, I don't know if you've noticed, it's not just revenues are down, but traffic has sunk in a way that's completely out of line. Usually, traffic is actually surprisingly resilient in a downturn. People buy less, but they keep coming. Sometimes, John, we even see numbers go up.

"But here? Visits are down overall. Proportionally, traffic from couples with children is down even more. And repeat traffic from couples with children has dropped through the floor. That's what's unusual with this store.

"So why aren't they coming back as often? What's different here? What's changed?" He gave a little smile and looked ostentatiously around, then back at me. "Okay? Parents can still leave their kids in the crèche, but the kids aren't asking their parents for repeat visits like they used to. Something's missing. Ergo. Therefore. We need it back."

He laid his briefcase on the desk and gave me a wry smile.

"You know how it is. You tell them and tell them to fix things as they happen, but do they listen? Because it isn't them who have to patch it up, right? So then you end up with not one problem but two. Twice as much trouble to bring under control." He shook his head ruefully. He was looking around the room, into all the corners, narrowing his eyes. He took a couple of deep breaths.

"Okay, John, listen, thanks for all your help. I'm going to need a few minutes here. Why don't you go watch some TV, get yourself a coffee or something? I'll come find you in a while."

I told him I'd be in the staff room. I turned away and heard him open his case. As I left I peered through the glass wall and tried to see what he was laying out on the desk. A candle, a flask, a dark book. A little bell.

Visitor numbers are back up. We're weathering the recession remarkably well. We've dropped some of the deluxe product and introduced a back-to-basic raw pine range. The store has actually taken on more staff recently than it's let go.

The kids are happy again. Their obsession with the ball room refuses to die. There's a little arrow outside it, a bit more than three feet off the ground, which is the maximum height you can be to come in. I've seen children come tearing up the stairs to get in and find out that they've grown in the months since their last visit, that they're too big to come in and play. I've seen them raging that they'll never be allowed in again, that they've had their lot, for ever. You know they'd give anything at all, right then, to go back. And the other children watching them, those who are just a little bit smaller, would do anything to stop and stay as they are.

Something in the way they play makes me think that Mr Gainsburg's intervention may not have had the definitive effect everyone was hoping. Seeing how eager they are to rejoin their friends in the ball room, I wonder sometimes if it was intended to.

To the children, the ball room is the best place in the world. You can see that they think about it when they're not there, that they dream about it. It's where they want to stay. If they ever got lost, it's the place they'd want to find their way back to. To play in the Wendy house and on the climbing frame, and to fall all soft and safe on the plastic balls, to scoop them up over each other, without hurting, to play in the ball room forever, like in a fairy tale, alone, or with a friend.

TIM PRATT

Gulls

TIM PRATT'S STORIES HAVE appeared in *The Year's Best Fantasy and Horror*, *Asimov's*, *Realms of Fantasy*, *Best American Short Stories: 2005* and other titles.

His first collection, *Little Gods*, was published in 2003, and his second, *Hart & Boot & Other Stories* is forthcoming. His first novel, *The Strange Adventures of Rangergirl*, appeared in late 2005.

He has been nominated for the Nebula, the Campbell Award for Best New Writer, and other awards, and he co-edits the literary fanzine *Flytrap* with his wife, Heather Shaw. He lives in Oakland, California, where he works as a senior editor and book reviewer for *Locus*.

"I grew up in North Carolina," reveals the author, "and often in summer several of my relatives would pitch in to rent a house on the beach, two hours east. There were usually various young cousins about, and I spent a lot of time watching chocolate-smeared children running along the waves, beneath the gulls.

"I remember one of my cousins running away, screaming, from a great cloud of gulls that had descended to snatch potato chips from his hands. The birds would swarm anyone foolish enough to offer them food, and something about the open rapacity of the gulls merged in my mind with the equally obvious greed of the tourist traps and tacky souvenir stores along the strip, and my not-entirely-charitable notions about the sort of people who stayed in the *really* fancy resorts, the ones with their own private beaches.

"And, of course, playing with language is part of the point of this story; a gull is a greedy bird, but the word also means 'fool', and to gull someone is to deceive them."

GRADY RAN BOUNCE-BOUNCING down the sidewalk, flip-flops flapping, face smeared with summermelted chocosicle, and Harriet swooped down (like a bandersnatch, she thought, like the poem I read to him) and grabbed him before he could jump off the curb.

He didn't struggle, only goggled with mint-green eyes at Monstrous Miniature Golf across the street. That's where he wanted to go, Harriet thought, to bat balls between Frankenstein's legs, to climb on the papier-mâché tombstones. There were jagged fake trees (coathanger trees, she thought, all twisted and pointed) with rubber bats hanging like rotten bananas from the branches. Harriet clucked and guided Grady along, past the surf-shops and lemonade stands and not-so-discreet stripclubs. They were looking for a public beach access. Harriet's shoulder bag was swollen with towels and sunscreen and grocery-store-checkout romances, and it thumped against her as she walked.

Her nephew, dear Grady, sweet Grady, wanted to swim. That was all he ever wanted to do, swim or chase sandcrabs. He did that all day at the house, the rented house, crammed with relatives pitching in money to make a vacation possible. They slept six to a room in that house but none of them could have afforded it alone, and they were right on the beach. That didn't help now. Harriet had gone shopping with her three sisters and her nephew Grady, and Grady had stomped and been bored and Harriet offered to take him swimming for the afternoon. Her sisters only talked about children and Harriet had no children so she too was bored. She was nearly forty and worry-lined and fifty weeks a year she typed things she didn't understand and fed her cats. Now two weeks of vacation and she was at the beach, unnerved by bikinis and broken glass, surrounded by her squabbling kin who made her nervous, all but Grady, who was almost a son. Once a man had promised to marry her and give her children, but he was gone and no children though they'd done it enough, the thing that makes children, but not enough or well enough to keep him from leaving her, she supposed.

She sweated under her floppy hat and even through tinted glasses everything flashed neon and gleamed metal. She could hardly believe there was an ocean nearby. She could have been in a beach-town theme park, otherwise in the middle of a baking desert. She giggled at the thought and Grady giggled because laughter made him happy. He was already tanned brown despite the pale promise of his yellow hair, just like his mother's and Harriet's (though his mother seldom laughed and never just to make Grady laugh, what sort of mother was that?). Everywhere metal now and no surf sound, only the whoosh of passing cars (too close, even holding his hand it was too close and she moved him away from the street), no salt smell just exhaust and the fried reek of fast food. Nothing to really speak of beach except the wheeling gulls, like Styrofoam gliders overhead, and they flew over other places, inland dumps and sewage treatment plants. The beach is there, she thought, craning her neck to look around buildings and dumpsters; only show me the way.

And then a blue sign, standing up rusty and bullet-holed in a weedy gravel lot, blue with a zigzag diagram of waves and a cartoon picnic table with umbrella. There were no cars in the lot, tiny as it was and jammed between a white hotel and the bar (featuring wet T-shirt contest amateurs only) they'd just passed. "Look, Grady, the beach!" and he streaked but she held his hand and he bounced back like a paddleball. They couldn't really see the beach, but a boardwalk stretched over the grass-covered dune, its steps drifted with fine sand. They crunched over gravel, Grady babbling excitedly about dolphins and mermaids and octopuses and crabs, and clomped over the boardwalk.

Fifty yards of walking before the beach. A high fence of weathered wood ran along the right side, partitioning the beach for the people in the hotel. The fence ran for a distance even into the water before giving up hope of division. Harriet heard happy shouts and laughter from the other side. It was a gleaming white hotel with balconies on the back; she could see the top floors rising over the fence, much better than the ramshackle crammed-in house with rusty shower-heads and sand in the mattresses. Same water, she thought, squelch-ing her envy, they get the same beach we do.

But this was a sad little beach. Grady surged like a live wire, pulling away and eager to be in the grey-green water, but she held on and stepped with distaste around broken beer-bottles and chunks of Styrofoam. The horizon was infinite and curved but the air stank of fish. She saw a dead jellyfish on the line of the lapping water.

"Lookit the boy with the seagulls!" Grady said, and Harriet lifted her hat-shaded eyes to see a boy down the beach. He held his arms open, playing Messiah to the shorebirds who circled around him and dove at his feet. He had a jumbo-bag of potato chips and he scattered them, feeding the devotion of the birds. There was something horribly hungry about the gulls, dirty white feathers drifting and long beaks darting as they squabbled over fragments of food.

"Why they his friends?" Grady demanded, his jealousy an echo of Harriet's when she looked at the fence, screening off a beach without beer bottles and dead things.

"They'll come to anyone who feeds them," she said, "They're not really his friends, not like the animals in cartoons. They're just hungry." Grady nodded, already forgetting and looking at the water. She tenderly ruffled his short gold hair and wished there were time to teach him about friends, about being careful. He wouldn't understand that some people are true friends, but that some people only want to feed on you.

She spread a towel in the long thin rectangle of shade cast by the fence and told Grady to be careful and mind the undertow and stay in the shallows. He nodded, all impatience and eyeing the water, and bolted at her nod. She smiled after him and rummaged through her bag for sunscreen and her current gaudy romance novel; she knew they were foolish, and told herself she read them only because that is what women alone on the beach do, but secretly she loved them and dreamed.

She looked up to check on Grady and he was deep, dog-paddling deeper. "Grady!" She stood and ran but he was swimming, bumping against the hotel's board fence in the water. He didn't hear. She slipped off her sandals and ran, glad she wore shorts now despite her pale thin legs. Her hat fell away and she barely had her feet wet when Grady disappeared around the fence. Harriet hung, a moment of indecision (like a seagull flying against the wind, suspended), then ran back up the beach. There was a gate in the fence, tacked with a sign that said NO ENTRY. She tugged and it opened and she ran through.

An impression of clean sand, beach chairs and sleek dark people in bright swimsuits and trunks, a multitude of children, but her eyes were on Grady, swimming back to shore, grinning impish and in no danger of drowning. Curiosity, she thought, every little boy has to see what's on the other side of the fence, never mind the side they're on.

Grady came out and looked around, face aglow with sun and shiny with water, and Harriet took his hand, scolding until his smile faded and his eyes widened and he nodded, solemn as an owl. Grady never meant to be bad, and if you pointed out bad he seldom did it twice. Harriet was satisfied, even if her heart still pounded in her throat from running and fear, the fear (she imagined) of a mother for her child.

She held his hand and walked from the water to find every eye on her. A dozen adults, all so similar in height and color that they must be a horde of brothers and sisters, all a bit younger than she was. The women were hurrying over, looking concerned, and the men stood in a group around the barbecue grill, the eldest with grey hair holding a spatula. The smell of cooking meat wafted toward her, slightly sweet, she couldn't place it. No smell of dead fish here. She blushed as the women, their oiled bodies firm and cared for beyond the fitness of youth, crowded around. One was older, white-haired, but her face had few lines and her black one-piece swimsuit fit snugly. She was a match for the man at the grill; grandparents to all those children, perhaps? Six wedding rings glittered on six hands, and Harriet supposed these women were married to those men, for all that their husbands looked like blood siblings, too. A similarity of taste, she supposed.

"Is he all right?" white-hair said, smiling a greeting. Grady was looking around them at the gaggle of children, from toddlers to almost-teens, laughing and splashing in the shallows and taking no notice of the interlopers on their beach. Grady was thrumming, wanting to be away with them, but Harriet held on.

"I'm sorry," she said, "I know we shouldn't be here, we'll go." The women exchanged glances with a familiarity that spoke of sisterhood; certainly it was a clan of daughters. But all the men shared the square-jawed features of the grey-haired man (now approaching in a polo shirt, spatula in one hand like a scepter) and they stood nursing beers like brothers.

"You'll do no such thing," white-hair said firmly. The youngest of the others smiled and licked her lips, then looked startled when she met Harriet's eyes. "The boy frightened you, and the beach is awful beyond the fence. Do stay. We'll help you watch the boy."

Grady hooked a finger in his mouth and looked up at the women, who cooed and smiled at him, but Grady seemed only fascinated by the bright colors of their swimsuits.

"We wouldn't want to be trouble," Harriet said, feeling every sag and brittleness of her body, thinking of the broad-shouldered square-faced men and wondering why she'd never found them, why she wasn't oiled and tan and beautiful.

The grey-haired man arrived in time to shake his head and say "No trouble at all, this family makes enough trouble on its own, you won't add to it. You're welcome to stay for dinner. There will be plenty."

He smiled, straight white teeth, and Harriet found herself nodding. Grady sensed the shift and darted toward the children, who greeted him and sucked him into their throng. There must be thirty children, she thought, and glanced at the women again. No sign of stretch-marks, no indications of motherhood, they'd borne perfect children and emerged perfect themselves.

The women hustled her aside giving introductions, establishing relations (though unclearly; three generations of a family on vacation, but which were married, whose children, who belonged to the old couple, and who were in-laws?). The women had long perfect nails and tiny teeth, and Harriet was aware of her own bitten-to-the-quick hands and coffee-stained smile. The women chattered and hardly noticed if Harriet answered. Did they ever ask her name? They certainly never used it. She wondered; why are they being so nice to me? Pity? She thought she heard something, a scream from the children and she turned, but they were only splashing in a knot, playing. She didn't see Grady; his golden hair should have stood out like a beacon in that sea of dark, but there were so many children, he was surely just out of sight, and the women were plucking at her sleeves for attention. The youngest, with her eager eyes, plucked too hard, her fingernails brought a crescent of blood on Harriet's forearm, making her gasp. The girl only licked her lips again and the white-haired woman slapped her daughter (in-law?) hard across the face. She dropped her eyes and murmured and apology. Harriet stared, shocked, but in a moment she was overwhelmed by chattering ministrations, offers of paper towels and exclamations over the small wound.

The white-haired woman smiled graciously, then laughed, looking beyond Harriet to the water. "Those children," she said, "Always snacking when we're about to have dinner."

Harriet turned to look, a tentative smile on her face. The dark children were crouched in a circle, eating something off the sand, reaching down with their hands. One child, very small, sat sullenly away from the rest, tearing at a half-rotted fish with her teeth, shooting glares at her cousins (brothers? sisters?) as she chewed.

"What?" Harriet began, standing, drawing breath to call for Grady. The grey-haired man shouted "These are done! Bring me more meat!" and Harriet smelled the sweet, unidentifiable odor from the grill again.

Why so friendly? She thought. What can they want from me?

The children scattered at the announcement of food, hurrying toward the grill, a flurry of graceful limbs and placid faces. They looked at Harriet as they loped past, wolfish faces and cool dark eyes. What they'd left steamed on the sand, ragged, scattered, wet. She saw a mass of golden hair and a jagged white stick, driftwood or a bone, driven into the sand beside it, but nothing she could call

Grady. The grey-haired man called again for more meat, and his wife and daughters began plucking at Harriet's skin, silent now, no more chatter. Harriet didn't make a sound either, only stood, barely feeling the nips become tugs and wrenchings. She watched a cyclone of white gulls descend to fight over what the children had left.

ELIZABETH MASSIE

Pinkie

ELIZABETH MASSIE IS A TWO-TIME Bram Stoker Award-winning author and World Fantasy Award Finalist whose books include *Sineater*, *Wire Mesh Mothers*, *Power of Persuasion*, *Shadow Dreams*, *The Fear Report*, *A Little Magenta Book of Mean Stories*, *Twisted Branch* (as "Chris Blaine") and many more.

Recent work has been featured in *Outsiders: 22 All-New Stories from the Edge*, *Travel Guide to the Haunted Mid-Atlantic*, *Eulogies*, *Deadly Housewives* and *Lords of the Razor*, while her novella "They Came from the Dark Ride" was published in *The Kolchak Casebook* and an essay on *Harvest Home* appeared in *Horror: Another 100 Best Books*.

She lives in the Shenandoah Valley of Virginia with the illustrator Cortney Skinner.

"Anyone who is familiar with my fiction knows that most often I tend to stick close to home when it comes to story locations," says Massie. "Why go much farther, when so many bizarre, fascinating, and often scary things lurk in the mountains, forests, and fields outside my front door?

"I was raised in the shadow of the Blue Ridge Mountains, surrounded by cattle farms, pig farms, poultry farms. Although, recently, development has been a-chip-chip-chippin' at 200-year-old spreads, knocking down ancient barns and rail fences, there are still a good number of old homesteads tucked away from major roads, beyond the woods or up in the foothills – the kind of farms where you would never stop to ask for directions because doing so would require you to drive up and around into a territory populated by toothless men with guns and axes and pot-bellied women with meat cleavers and gleams in their eyes.

"There is little that terrifies me more than the possibility of something or someone else gaining total power over me, as might happen if I ventured up that rutted driveway.

"Set close-to-home, 'Pinkie' plays with that fear in several different ways."

COME SEPTEMBER, RENNIE DIDN'T LIKE Pinkie so much anymore. The friendship had been going sour throughout the summer, and when it was time to attend the State Fair, Rennie wasn't sure he even wanted to bother. Who wanted to ride two hours to Richmond with a hulking, bristly pig that stared at you, drooled on the passenger's seat, and popped his little red stick in and out, in and out, like an angry, bald prairie dog?

Rennie had few friends besides Pinkie, if you could call the cashier at the Farm Bureau Co-op and the mailman friends, but that never bothered Rennie much. He had a sturdy 110-year-old house on a fifty-two acre mountainside farm, and a television that caught a little NBC and CBS when the night was clear. He had inherited the farm from his father and mother, who'd taken off to explore the country seven years ago and had never come home. Rennie's younger sister, Regina, had left a year after that. She didn't want the farm; she wanted big cities and bright lights and so had moved to DC. Currently, she worked at some museum gift shop selling some sort of educational shit, according to her last Christmas card.

Raising chickens was Rennie's main occupation. Selling eggs, broilers, and nesters didn't bring in a living wage, but he supplemented it with money earned by leasing his pasture acreage to an absentee cattle rancher. Rennie liked his solitude, interrupted by the occasional telemarketer call and visit to the Farm Bureau Co-op when he went for the essentials – chicken feed, canned goods, seeds, new jeans, duct tape.

Pinkie had been with Rennie for two years. The farmer had found the tiny, peach-skinned piglet in the forest, offspring of a neighbor's escaped Hampshire and one of the feral boars that had run the woods ever since Rennie could remember. The sow had been killed and half eaten by the boar after giving birth, and only one piglet was still alive. Rennie had lifted it from the tangle of poison ivy and thistles, wrapped it up in his flannel jacket and carried it home. He fed it cow's milk and oatmeal until it was able to forage the pastures and woods for itself.

Pinkie grew into a very large, very bright, and very amiable pig. He learned to pull the rope to ring the bell beside the front porch at six each morning to keep Rennie from oversleeping. He nosed open the mailbox down by the road to collect whatever the postman had brought that day. He ate at the table, chewing chicken and cabbage delicately with his sharp little teeth then rubbing his nose and lips on a folded paper towel when he was through with his meal. He could light a match, throw clothes into the washer, and punch in channels on the television remote control.

Rennie took Pinkie to the Augusta County Fair when the pig was not quite a year old and entered him into the most talented hog contest. Pinkie won hooves-down, lighting men's cigars, folding newspapers, and tying ropes into knots. Some irritating, scraggly-haired girl with a red, second place 4-H ribbon pinned to her T-shirt took a special liking to Pinkie, and kept coming back to the hog tent to feed Rennie's pig funnel cakes. She called Pinkie "Wilbur," which made no sense to Rennie, and he at last got rid of the kid by telling her that when "Wilbur" got tired of little girls, he bit them and licked their blood. The prize money, twenty-five dollars, went into the truck's gas tank and to burgers for the trip home. The blue ribbon was nailed on the door to Pinkie's shed and looked nice for a couple of weeks, but then rain and sleet chewed it up and took most of the color out.

Pinkie won the most talented pig at the county fair the following July as well, having learned to breathe "Three Blind Mice" into a harmonica, squeeze mustard onto a corndog, and to carve his own name in the dirt with his foot. The other pigs posed no threat to the crown as they rolled balls with their noses and play dead on command. Rennie collected his cash and the ribbon to the cheers of bleachered onlookers. Several pig-raisers approached him afterwards with "How much stud fee you charge for that hog?" Rennie clutched Pinkie's leash and said, "Ain't for stud." Pinkie tilted his head, and gave Rennie a cold look that made him flinch.

Back home, Pinkie started to act obstinate. He would take his time when Rennie called him to dinner, and he took a couple craps on the front porch beneath the swing. While waddling through the living room, he carelessly bumped into the furniture and display cabinets, sending glass trinkets that had belonged to Rennie's mother to the floor. The pig even humped one of the chickens in the chicken yard, squashing the brown-feathered bird to death. Rennie didn't know exactly what to do; he tried bribing the hog into good behavior with special treats of cookies and tomatoes. He made the bed of straw in the pig shed twice as deep. Instead of bathing Pinkie in the aluminum tub out back, Rennie brought the boar inside to his own bathtub, built a little wooden ramp, and let the hog soak in warm, sweet-smelling water instead of cold water from the garden hose. None of it seemed to appease the pig or make a difference in his behavior. Pinkie just took it all in as if warranted, and continued to dump, bump, and hump.

One morning in mid-August Rennie awoke to Pinkie crouching over him in bed, his pointed hooves pressing into Rennie's chest. Rennie squealed and knocked the pig off, then looked over the side of the bed to the floor. His chest felt like two branding irons had been driven into his ribs.

"Damn, that hurts! What the hell you doin' in here?" he squawked. "Ain't six yet! You ain't supposed to come in the house 'til I unlock the door for you."

Pinkie righted himself on the rug, shook his great head, and sniffed.

"What's the matter with you?" insisted Rennie. Then, his chest feeling suddenly more cold than hot: "Wait. I dead bolted the front door last night. How'd you get in?"

The pig sniffed again and licked the slobber from his snout. Then he reached down and licked the skinny dick between his legs. But, of course, he didn't answer because in spite of his many talents, Pinkie couldn't talk.

The day progressed as days did. Meals with Rennie on one side of the kitchen table, Pinkie on the other. Rennie feeding the chickens, sorting through junk mail, writing checks for the heating oil and electricity, and walking the perimeter of the farm to check the security of the fence. But this time, Pinkie didn't walk the whole fence line. Instead, he followed a ways, then disappeared into the woods and returned several times.

"You lookin' for something?" Rennie asked Pinkie on the pig's fourth return. "I don't like it you goin' away from me like that. Am I gonna have to keep you on a leash like I do at the fair?" The pig blinked at Rennie and then turned a rock over with his nose and lapped up the earthworms beneath it.

That afternoon a man came calling, a fellow from the Mid-Atlantic Hog Breeders Association. He had an official car with black lettering that read "MAHBA" and a brown silhouette of a hog rooting the ground. Rennie was collecting eggs in the chicken yard when the car pulled up and the horn honked. The driver was clearly a country-born man; strangers didn't take the chance of coming upon another man's farm unannounced.

"Mr Monroe?" the man called. He came around the side of the house to the chicken yard, hands shoved deep in the pockets of his windbreaker. He wore a tie, tasseled loafers, and an impossibly wide smile. He was young, early thirties, with a head of bushy red hair. "Mr Rennie Monroe? I'm Vernon Via."

"Yep?" replied Rennie as he tossed feed and scraps to the hens wrangling in the dust around his boots.

"Got word you still have that hog you displayed at a couple county fairs. Your postman told me."

"Yep?"

Pinkie appeared from inside the untrimmed tangle of boxwoods against the house. A small ring neck snake dangled between his teeth. He sucked it most of the way in and stared at Rennie.

"Mind I have a look?" asked Vernon Via. "I saw it in July, was mighty impressed. Not sure the breed. You never stated it on your talented hog application."

"Didn't need to. He wasn't in no breed competition."

"Oh, I know that. But your hog is very unusual. May I see it?"

"Him."

"Yes, him. May I?"

"Why?"

"I might like to make an offer to buy him."

Pinkie waddled to the wire fence that separated the chickens from the yard. The tip of the snake's tail wriggled between his lips and then in a quick tip of pig's head, the tail vanished. Rennie looked at Pinkie, then at Mr Vernon Via.

"Oh, here he is," said Vernon Via. He clapped his hands together. Rennie thought that was so prissy, clapping hands like that. "He looks quite healthy."

"Why wouldn't he be?" Rennie frowned. "I feed him good."

"Well, of course you would. But many things can affect an animal that has no proper veterinarian care."

"I . . .," said Rennie, but stopped his tongue. Pinkie had never been to the vet. Had never needed to go to the vet. "He don't need a vet and he ain't for sale."

"I thought you'd say that," said Vernon Via. He tugged a checkbook from his back pocket. "At the last meeting of Mah-Ba, we agreed that we could offer up to," he hesitated, "five hundred dollars for your hog."

Pinkie scraped his hide up and down against one of the chicken pen's splintery fence post, but his little black bean eyes remained fixed on Vernon Via.

"That's a lot of money," admitted Rennie. "But I'm doin' okay. I don't need anything I don't got."

"You could put it in savings. Hold on to it for something you might want later?"

Rennie shook his head. His fingers tightened around the pan of chicken feed.

"But you don't understand," said Vernon Via, smiling and shaking his head as if he were talking to a child. "We plan on breeding your hog. See if we can get a crop of piglets with some of that ability, that talent."

"Pinkie wouldn't want to be away from home."

"He'd be treated royally, I assure you. We'd mate him a couple times a year to a well-selected female, and he'd be given good food, a nice pen, plenty of space. Hog heaven, so to speak." The man winked both eyes as if he thought he was very clever indeed.

"Pinkie don't need nothin' I can't give him. He don't got nothin' to worry about."

"Five hundred dollars and pick of the first litter, then. So you won't be lonely."

"Ain't lonely!" spit Rennie, a flare of anger catching the base of his neck.

"Pardon me, but let's be honest," said Vernon Via, his eyebrows going up. "Out here on this mountain, with nobody to talk to except your pig and a pen full of chickens? Look at it this way. With the money we give you, you could buy yourself a bushel full of piglets to raise and train."

Rennie's anger spread up to his scalp and crawled cross his shoulders. He felt his hog's hot breath on the back of his leg through his jeans. Clearly, Pinkie was pissed, too, pissed someone wanted to take him away.

Vernon Via didn't move. His eyebrows remained up in expectation, like someone had put a staple gun to his forehead.

Then Rennie said evenly through clenched jaws, "Get off my land."

The eyebrows came down. The driver was a country-bred man. He would know how serious that command was.

Rennie went into the house through the back door, carrying the half-empty pan of chicken feed. His ears hummed and his hands were cold. *Damned intruder! Damned outsider!* Rennie slammed the pan on the kitchen table then went into the bathroom under the stairs to wait for Vernon Via to leave. He sat on the wobbly pot, his feet planted apart to keep from rocking. *Damned pig collector!* Rennie clutched his head and saw dark pink in his line of vision, a sickening, oily swirl that made his stomach cramp. He closed his eyes, breathed through his teeth, and listened for the sound of the car's engine.

The sound didn't come.

Rennie came out of the bathroom and went to the front door. He peeked through the glass beside the door. The car was still there.

"Where are you, Mr Pig-Breeder?" Rennie said into the glass, his brows furrowed and his eyes narrowed. "Still here? Tryin' to steal my hog?"

Rennie went back to the kitchen. He looked out the window toward the chicken yard. Vernon Via was not there. Rennie picked up the shotgun he kept beside the door and pushed through the screen. He'd never used it except for scaring off foxes. But it did scare, that was for sure; a solid, ear-shattering blast would clearly say what Rennie didn't want to have to repeat.

He moved out to the back steps. The screen door clapped behind him.

Then he saw Mr Vernon Via. The man was lying up under the boxwoods, with just his legs and shoes sticking out. Rennie almost laughed, because he was reminded of the Wicked Witch of the East who'd been crunched by Dorothy's flying farmhouse, and thought for the barest of seconds how nobody would want Vernon Via's prissy-pants tasseled loafers. But Rennie didn't laugh. There was blood on the shoes.

The heat behind Rennie's eyes went suddenly cold. He put the gun aside and knelt on the damp grass. He grabbed one of the loafers and shook it. "Hey, Vernon Via, you trip?" The man did not answer. He did not move. Rennie grasped the man's ankles and hauled him out from the bushes. The man's face was battered away, leaving little but one eye, a nub of cartilage where the nose had been, and a flap of cheek skin. The rest was a red mangle that looked more hamburger than human.

Rennie squeaked and fell backward on his ass. He dug at his eyes with the heels of his hands, but the ghastly sight remained, unchanged.

There was a wet snuffling beside Rennie, and he look around to see Pinkie licking blood from his lips and jowls.

"Agh," managed Rennie, his tongue a dry and swollen thing in his mouth. "What have you done, Pinkie? What is this you've done to me?"

Rennie cut the man up with his chainsaw and worked the parts into the hills of soil he'd worked up for the late season cabbages and the pumpkins. He put on his winter gloves, lined the seat with a plastic trash bag, and drove the man's car out to the end of the driveway and left it by the side of the road, then hiked the half mile to the house again. Pinkie had wanted to ride along, insisted on it, but Rennie shoved the hog back with a well-aimed foot and then slammed the car door.

It was all Rennie could do to keep from losing his lunch in the hog breeder's car.

Back at the farmhouse, Rennie drank three cups of coffee and paced the floor. He looked at the telephone, willing it not to ring, and it didn't. Pinkie sat at the kitchen table and chewed at burrs between his toes.

Rennie couldn't look at the pig. He had killed Vernon Via. Why had he done that? Did he hate the man that much for wanting to take him away? He was afraid to ask Pinkie, afraid that this time, the pig might actually open up his rubbery lips and give an answer. Pinkie stopped chewing the burrs and starting licking his balls. This made Rennie uncomfortable, so he went into the living room to watch the news.

Bedtime came with a sudden and violent rainstorm. Rennie changed into his sweatshirt and sweatpants and stood at his second floor bedroom window, looking out through the wash of water on the glass, across the darkened side yard to the garden. It was nothing but a black pit until the lightning flashed, then he could see the ribs of the rows. Had he buried Vernon Via deep enough inside the cabbage hills? Would the water wash him out again? Would Pinkie dig the parts up?

The phone rang.

Rennie whipped about and stared at the phone on the nightstand. It rang again. Again. He walked over and picked it up. It nearly shook from his hand.

"Yep?"

"Rennie?" It was his sister. Had she heard about the missing hog breeder already?

"Yep?"

"It's your birthday," said Regina. "Thought I would call to say happy birthday."

"It is?" Rennie squeezed his brain. Yes, it was. He was thirty-seven today. How had he missed that? But again, why would he have remembered? He certainly hadn't taught Pinkie to read a calendar.

"You forgot your own birthday?" Regina had adopted a nasally, northern Virginia accent. She was happy to be free of anything country or farmish. "Are you that busy?"

"Yep." Rennie put one foot on top of the other. "But thanks for calling."

"So you didn't do anything to celebrate? Anything, I don't know, wild and free for once in your life?"

"No." *Well, Pinkie killed a man and ate his face. That's wild and free in a way.*

"When you going to come visit me?" Regina didn't mean it and Rennie knew that. Regina knew Rennie knew that so it was safe to ask. For some reason, she felt it was her sisterly duty to make such moot offers.

"I don't know. I've got the chickens, the fences, crops. You know. And it's a thunderstorm so I better hang up. Don't want to fry through the wire."

"Sure. Well, okay, enjoy the rest of your day. Night."

"Thanks." Rennie hung up and crossed his arms. His fingers picked at the frayed elbows of the soft shirt. A loud thunderclap shook the house. He'd locked Pinkie up in his shed, but the pig had gotten into the farmhouse earlier. Surely he would be able to let himself out of the shed if he got a mind to it.

Rennie went downstairs. He stared out through the kitchen door toward the chicken yard and the pig shed beyond it. The door was still closed, still sealed with the padlock. Rain was coming in sideways, spraying the grass and laying it flat.

Okay, then, okay, Rennie thought. He sat at the kitchen table and spun the salt shaker around. Putting his head down on his arms, he tried not to think of the dead man's body, all in pieces, fertilizing the pumpkins and cabbages.

He woke with a start. It was daylight and the rain was over. His arms ached; his cheek was wrinkled from the fabric of his sweatshirt sleeve. The plastic teapot clock on the wall read 8:47. Rennie rubbed his neck and stood up slowly, working a kink out of his knee. He'd overslept, and Pinkie hadn't rung the morning bell.

But the pig was inside the house. Rennie could hear him in the living room, trying to get up on Rennie's big recliner, rhythmically whacking the coffee table with his spring-loaded tail, grunting with exertion.

"Pinkie?" called Rennie. His throat was dry and his heart picked up an uncomfortably rapid rhythm. He wanted to let the pig know he was coming. He didn't like the idea of coming up on the animal by surprise. Pinkie might not like that.

The pig was on the recliner, the lever flipped back — how could he flip back the lever? – his mouth drawn up in what might have been a smile, revealing the rows of tiny sharp teeth.

"How'd you get out of the shed, Pinkie?" asked Rennie as he pushed the coffee table back into place. "I didn't teach you that. How'd you get out, then get in here?"

Pinkie wriggled himself deeper into the cushion of the seat. His little eyes didn't blink, but focused on Rennie. They reflected light from the window, making them look damp and white.

Rennie swallowed, hard. "What do you want, Pinkie?"

But then Rennie knew. He drew back as the realization hit him, and his jaw opened with a click. "Did you want to go with Vernon Via? Are you mad because I wouldn't let you go?"

The thick, hairy pig tongue flicked out, then back.

"Is that a yes?"

The tongue flicked out again, then back.

"You want to belong to the Mid-Atlantic what-the-hell Association, to be a stud?"

Pinkie's pinkie popped in and out, catching the same wet, white light as his eyes. He grunted with what sounded like expectation, anticipation.

"Oh, Jesus, Pinkie."

Pinkie blinked.

"But you an' me is bachelors. You ain't gettin' any, but neither am I."

The pig stretched his neck and looked at the ceiling. He farted.

The phone rang.

Rennie went back to the kitchen and picked up the receiver from the wall unit. His heart thudded against his ribs. "Yep?" he managed.

"Mr Monroe? This is Marla Via, Vernon Via's wife. Vernon drove out to see you yesterday afternoon. He hasn't come home. Did he make it to your place?"

"Yep." *Goddamn! I should have said no.* "But he left not a half hour after gettin' here."

"Oh." A long pause. She sounded young and scared. "Did he say where he was going after he left your place, maybe?"

"No, sorry."

"Maybe he had car trouble?"

"Maybe."

"He has a cell phone, though. I've called it a bunch of times and couldn't get through. Do you live where there's service?"

"I don't think so."

There was a deep, ragged sigh on the other end of the line. "Okay, thanks. I guess I'll have to call the authorities to find him. I'm scared."

Me, too.

The line went dead. Rennie slowly put the receiver back. He could hear the hog's footsteps and raspy breathing. Rennie whipped around. Pinkie stood just inside the door, his eyes narrowed and his ears up. "What?" asked Rennie. "That was the wife of the dead guy, if you have to know."

Pinkie went to the fridge, tugged the door open, and selected a large piece of fried chicken from an uncovered plate. He dropped it on the floor and began to gnaw at the meat. The cold grease rode up Pinkie's mouth and glistened like frost.

Rennie stomped into his work boots and went outside.

The garden's hills were battered but not gouged; Mr Vernon Via's parts remained buried. Rennie stood in the garden, one foot to either side of a long strip of lumpy soil, leaning on his shovel, wondering how long it would take for a human to literally return to the earth from whence it came, dust to dust, like the Bible said. He didn't know. But when the cabbages and pumpkins pushed up, what might they bring with them? Maybe the garden was a stupid place to hide a body. *Stupid, stupid, stupid!*

A dull pain caught Rennie at the back of the skull and he closed his eyes. Pink and orange sparks pulsed in the darkness. Overhead, there was the honking of Canada geese, arriving for the winter. They would settle in the pond on the southwestern side of the farm. Nest, raise some babies, fly home in March. They didn't have much to worry about, those geese. No planting. No bills. No goddamned smart-ass pigs.

Rennie's eyes jerked open. The geese were gone, the shadows beneath his feet had shortened significantly. His shoulders burned from having leaned on the shovel too long. He thought he heard the phone ringing from inside the house but he wasn't running for it.

He went to the hen house, chased the chickens out, and gathered most of the eggs in the plastic tray he kept in the rafters. Then he took the egg tray across the yard toward the kitchen door. Pinkie was sitting on the step, something floppy and red in his mouth. Rennie stopped.

"What you got there, Pinkie?"

Pinkie rolled his great bulk from the step and trotted happily toward his master, gut swinging. Dangling from his mouth was a set of human fingers. The egg tray flipped from Rennie's hand and landed in the grass. Egg yolk slathered the plastic.

With the pig on his heels, Rennie hurried to the front of the house. In the weedy driveway sat a white sedan, the driver's door hanging open, a thin young woman lying face down on the ground with her feet still in the car. One arm was crumpled beneath her. The other was out, reaching. The hand was missing from the wrist.

God God God God!

Pinkie dropped two of the finger bones at Rennie's feet like a cat offering a dead bird.

"Marla Via?" Rennie said, tapping the woman with his boot. But the woman didn't answer and didn't move.

"You want me in trouble?" Rennie turned to Pinkie, his teeth bared. "You playin' with me, you stupid slob? You want me arrested so you can go fuck some damn sows? Huh?"

Pinkie rubbed his ear on Rennie's leg and Rennie jerked away. "Where I am supposed to bury this one, huh? Tell me? Show me! You don't, and I'll . . . I'll butcher you up for supper tonight, don't think I won't!"

Pinkie bared his own, scarlet-streaked teeth.

Rennie's heart clenched. "Show me a place!"

And Pinkie did. The dry well was deep, and the body small. A couple shovels full of ash, lime, and soil dumped in afterwards would keep Marla Via from probing eyes and noses. Rennie stood back from his work, breathing heavily, his nerves prickling inside his skin.

Then there was the matter of her car.

With Pinkie by his side Rennie returned to the driveway. Marla Via's car was gone.

He caught his breath. It hurt his chest. "What the hell?"

Pinkie laughed. Not a grunt, not a squeal, but a genuine, dark laugh. Then he rolled his head to the side and said, "Didn't think I could drive, did you? I watch. I learn."

Rennie clutched his scalp and wailed. "Where did you put the car?"

"For me to know and you, or the police, to find out."

Rennie's incisors clamped down on his lower lip, piercing the skin and drawing blood. The surface was ragged, salty. It tasted like the calf's liver his mom used to cook. He pulled the tongue back into his head and clapped his jaws so the tongue couldn't snake out again to probe the wound. He didn't want Pinkie to smell the blood.

"Where . . . is . . . the . . . car?" he said slowly.

"You selfish, ignorant, impotent son of a bitch," sneered Pinkie.

"You made your mess, now lie in it!" With that, the pig turned on his heels, strolled up the front porch steps, and let himself in the house.

"I didn't teach you to talk!" Rennie screamed after him. "You're a mutant, a freak, if you ask me!"

Pinkie didn't come out to defend himself. Clearly, he knew he had the upper hand.

Rennie spent the next few hours sweating, cursing, and searching the fields and forest for Marla Via's car. The only things he found were briars and thorns, and they made trash of his jeans, his shirt, his legs. Pinkie would have hid the car somewhere on Rennie's land so the police would locate it and blame Rennie for the woman's death. But wherever the car was, it was well concealed.

It was nearly dark when Rennie returned to the farmhouse. Pinkie had turned on the porch lights for him. Rennie climbed up the steps and dropped onto the porch swing. The rusty chains groaned under his weight. He stared at the cuts on his legs through the flaps of denim. He looked at his hands; they were raked and bruised.

Pinkie came out with a small tray with a glass and a bowl of iced tea clamped in his teeth. Had Rennie taught Pinkie how to make iced tea? Numbly, Rennie picked up the glass and drank it down. It was weak, but cold. Pinkie lapped his from the bowl on the slatted wooden floor, then flopped onto his side and went to sleep.

The sirens came soon thereafter. The police, three cars of them, came rolling up the driveway, bouncing along the ruts, cutting the night air with their blue lights, chasing cicadas from the weeds in whirling clouds. Rennie sat on the swing and waited for them.

They asked Rennie about Mr Vernon Via and Mrs Marla Via. They told him that Mrs Via had said she was on her way out to Rennie's farm to try and retrace Vernon's steps, and had said she'd be in touch. But she never was. Rennie didn't say anything, but looked at Pinkie, hoping the hog would confess. The pig just lay, sleeping, his eyebrow ridges dancing in his dreams.

The officers searched all night and into the mid-morning as Rennie sat on the porch swing and Pinkie flopped back and forth content-edly near his feet, skin twitching beneath a cluster of flies. By ten they had an ambulance in the yard, and another two police cars. By eleven-thirty, they had collected Vernon's remains from the garden, Marla's from the well, two bodies from the cellar, and one from the floor of the hen house.

"Fucking maniac!" swore the cop that snapped the cuffs around Rennie's wrists then slammed Rennie into the back of his cruiser. "The poor Vias, my God, what he did to them."

It wasn't me! It was Pinkie!

"And that helpless little girl, still wearing a second place ribbon from the county fair knitting contest two years ago! Goddamned perverted murderer!"

Little girl? The little Wilbur girl?

"And the couple in the basement," said a second cop with a shake of the head. "Fucked up shit, that. Dead, what, seven-eight years? Hatchet's still buried in the old man's skull. The woman's head was cut off and stuck between her legs."

Couple, what couple?

Rennie sat with his nose pressed to the smudged glass of the cruiser's window. "What couple?" he called out, but the police ignored him. Through the fog of his breath, he could see Pinkie waddling down the porch steps to go sniff at the shrouded bodies on the wheeled stretchers. He then wandered over to poke at one of the police car tires like some regular old pig, like some pig that didn't know a teacup from a chicken pan, a La-Z-Boy from a wallow. "What couple?"

The bodies were loaded onto the ambulance. The ambulance rolled off. One officer jerked open the rear cruiser door and stuck a gold wedding band in Rennie's face. "See the engraving inside there, asshole?" he sneered. "See? Was your dad's. Your dad and mom, dead in the basement. Buried in the dirt floor after you cut them up."

"I what? No! They just went away. They didn't never come back."

"No shit they didn't!" The police's fist drew up then he forced it back down again. He dropped the ring into a small plastic bag and slammed the car door.

"Pinkie did it!" Rennie said, his lips brushing the window. "Pinkie killed them. He doesn't like the way I control his life. He doesn't like living here with me. He wants me in trouble!"

Pinkie wasn't born eight years ago.

Rennie sat straight. He frowned.

Then what. . .?

One of the officers tipped his head in Pinkie's direction. "I hear that thing can do tricks. Hey piggy, piggy, can you write your name for us? Write your name, piggy."

Pinkie wriggled his ass and then clawed the letters "P," "I," "G" in the ground. Then he went back to the porch and lay down in front of the steps.

"Well, that's good for a hog, I think," said the officer. "Can't expect much more for a dumb animal than that. They do what they're taught, that's about it. They sure are more predictable than people. At least with the fucker in the car, he'll be fryin' like bacon in short order."

The other officer chuckled, shook his head, and within minutes he was at the wheel of the cruiser and hauling ass down the drive toward the road, with Rennie in the backseat, forehead against the window, eyes bugged, staring at the trees rushing past.

They didn't let me be with girls. They said sex was nasty and wrong. They said I should never touch myself or anyone else, said I didn't need nothin' they couldn't give me.

They said they fixed it for me so I'd have nothin' to worry about.

Rennie rubbed his crotch, and the empty space where his organs had once been. His vision blurred in pink and orange. He tasted blood.

Pinkie, what have you done to me?

MARK SAMUELS

Glyphotech

MARK SAMUELS IS A WRITER BORN, bred and in thrall to London. Such luminaries in weird fiction as Thomas Ligotti, T. E. D. Klein and Ramsey Campbell hailed his 2003 collection of stories, *The White Hands and Other Weird Tales*, as a major contribution to the literature.

The author's latest book is *The Face of Twilight*, a long novella recently issued by PS Publishing. He has stories scheduled for appearance in *Alone on the Darkside, Terror Tales #3* and *The Year's Best Fantasy and Horror #19*, and is currently working on his first full-length fantasy novel, set in a subterranean city encased by ice.

"A couple of years ago, out of the blue, I was invited to participate in a three-day seminar run by a 'human potential' organization," recalls Samuels. "However, before I decided whether or not to attend, I undertook some research of my own that left me in little doubt that what was really on offer was indoctrination, the handing over of my hard-won lucre and long-term psychological dependency.

"This actual organization has nothing to do with the organization 'Glyphotech', which is entirely imaginary."

FRANKLYN CRISK DID NOT MIND THE JOB or even his colleagues in the office too much. Certainly, both bored him. No, it was the noise and the heat that were becoming intolerable. Outside the Mare Publishing House building, on the crossroads, some men in boiler suits were working on the road. Though the noise they made was more like fingernails clawing across a blackboard rather than the juddering of a pneumatic drill, which is what one would expect to hear. It was the middle of summer but the office workers were forced to close all the windows in order to stifle the sound. Since the company did not regard the comfort of its employees as its concern, there was no air-conditioning and the temperature inside the cramped offices was unbearable. The clean shirt he'd donned this morning was soaked with sweat and his head throbbed painfully.

He wondered how he'd wound up being employed in this company, housed in a whitewashed four-storey structure on the corner of Fytton Square. It was obvious to him now that he had spent too long overseas. Twenty years in Kyoto, Japan, had rendered him almost unemployable back in his home country. He had (without being particularly aware of it) picked up the Japanese obsession with ritual and social custom to the degree that even his speech patterns betrayed a clipped formality that set him apart.

This job at the Mare firm was the only vacancy that had been offered to him, despite several other fruitless positions he'd applied for and which he felt he was more qualified. His work was drudgery; inputting book royalties onto a computer system, printing them out and then mailing the statements to authors. It meant eight hours staring at a dim monitor screen. The computers utilised by the firm for the tasks were almost obsolete. Their lack of modernity meant that there was no spare memory capacity for any other programs that might serve as a welcome distraction. There was no access to the Internet, or even an email facility to connect him with the world outside.

And now this ceaseless noise and heat! The worst of it was that the labourers always worked behind a tall screen that they'd erected and no one could see just what it was they were up to. The junction looked like a patchwork quilt, with different shades of grey indicating the age of the tarmac that had been overlaid there.

The men were only glimpsed when they emerged from behind their screens, walking to or from their dirty green van. Strangely, one never seemed to see them carrying shovels or pickaxes. Invariably clad in their nondescript black boiler suits, despite the heat, the operatives were not of the type that one would willingly approach directly in order to ask their business. They had none of the raucous bonhomie common to labourers, but were silent, unsmiling individuals with pale white faces, mouths like a slash and eyes like huge inkblots. Their abnormally long hands and fingernails were caked with dirt and one of Crisk's office colleagues joked that perhaps they dug with their bare hands.

The name on the side of the vehicle read "Glyphotech Reconstruction Co.". But when one of the Mare staff dialled the telephone number that was also blazoned across the side of the van, he said he obtained a connection that rang without ever being answered. After a few days, however, the screens were taken away and merciful quiet reigned again. Strangely enough this happened to coincide with the onset of thunderstorms after the intense heat. A double relief, since as well as the irritating noise being gone, the temperature dropped.

"Sir," said Crisk in that clipped Japanese manner that he could not shake off since his return to the West, "please be good enough to explain. You say that I should go. But why you have not made clear. Respectfully I ask, of course."

"I am just," James O'Hara responded, wincing as he listened to Crisk's strangled English, "making a suggestion that may improve your quality of life. I've been watching you for a while and it seems to me that you're down in the dumps a lot of the time. What Glyphotech can provide is a focus in your life: a way of realising possibilities that you yourself might not have thought of."

Crisk stared at O'Hara for a brief moment, considering what response he should give. His superior merely stood there smiling with his hands folded behind his back. Crisk remembered the name "Glyphotech": it had been written on the side of the van of the workers who'd been digging up the crossroads weeks before. But he could not fathom just what they had to do with this other venture. As if picking up on his thoughts, O'Hara interjected.

"Yes, yes," he said, "Glyphotech is a diverse company. As well as undertaking the reconstruction of buildings and roads, their course of psychological transformation is one of the other aspects of their enterprise. I really would recommend that you take the course, Crisk. Bear in mind that several of your colleagues have already signed up and not to do so might appear, well . . ."

He had to say no more in order to convince Crisk. Here was his office superior telling him that it was best to conform. The idea of falling out of favour was not pleasant to Crisk. He needed the job, even though he was bored by it. He had a duty, after all, to Mare Publishing Company.

"Sir," he replied, stifling the slight bow he wanted to make by force of habit, "Of course, I agree. Further discussion not necessary. Let me know time and meeting place. Gladly I will take part."

When Crisk got back to his desk after the meeting with O'Hara, he discreetly asked his office colleagues whether they too had been asked to attend the course run by Glyphotech. All had been requested to do so, some, they said, with the clear implication that not to accept O'Hara's suggestion would be severely frowned upon. From what Crisk could gather most of his co-workers viewed it as some kind of motivational seminar that would improve efficiency in the workplace and raise staff morale.

Later that same day one of the office juniors came around the various departments to hand out flyers. The heading bore the logo of "Glyphotech Reconstruction Co.", with the same design that Crisk had seen blazoned across the side of the workmen's van. In bold capitals, underneath the logo, were the words:

"*Do not underestimate the effect our process can have on* YOUR *life!*"

In smaller characters beneath this was the following short text:

"Do you feel drained, hopeless or adrift? At the mercy of what life throws at you instead of in control of events? We guarantee to provide empowerment and a sense of purpose you might never think you could achieve! Using our proven mental technology you will overcome all obstacles without fear, you will enjoy a renewed sense of purpose and success in both your private life and in your work-place environment. Attend our introductory seminar in the spirit of openness and friendship. Your life is too urgent to waste! Join us!"

The flyer provided details of where and when the seminar was to be held; at the Grantham Hall Hotel, only a few minutes walk from the Mare Publishing House's offices. When Crisk saw the hours involved, however, his spirits sank. It was a two-day affair, lasting from 10 a.m. in the morning until 10pm and repeated the next day. Moreover, it was to take place this coming weekend.

There were stifled groans around the office as each individual got to this part of the text and realised they'd been duped into giving up not company time but their own personal time, and on an ostensibly voluntary basis.

In the days leading up to the weekend a dull sense of resentment permeated the offices of the Mare Publishing House, though nothing was actually said aloud. This was undoubtedly due to the fact that the only one of those duped who had been brave enough to confront O'Hara about the deception was instantly dismissed from his job. The person, called David Hogg, found his desk cleared within five minutes of his speaking to O'Hara. He was forcibly escorted off the premises by the security guards moments before his personal belong-ings were flung out onto the street after him.

Crisk had been standing beside the doorway from which Hogg was ejected. The company had a strict no-smoking policy and Crisk would, at a quarter past every hour, enjoy a crafty cigarette at that spot. After helping the bewildered ex-employee collect together the various odds and ends not connected with work now strewn around him, they had a brief conversation.

"I am sorry . . ." said Crisk, "but if it is okay for me to ask, why did Mare Publishing so harshly treat with you?"

Hogg groaned.

"I know all about those Glyphotech seminars," he finally replied, "I told O'Hara there was no way I'd go along with it, I'd warn the others to stay away. We had a hell of a row and he told me to get out. I could tell you things about Glyphotech that . . ."

Crisk trembled inwardly at Hogg's audacity. To upset O'Hara was to challenge the Mare Publishing Co. itself. He looked around him, horrified at the prospect of being seen even talking with the ex-employee. To give up one weekend in order to curry favour was something Crisk was more than prepared to do. Backing away from Hogg, as if the man were contaminated, Crisk made his apologies, mumbled a word or two of consolation and scurried back inside the building. Crisk knew that O'Hara would find it easy to justify Hogg's immediate dismissal, for he had only very recently been hired by the company and was often drunk at his workstation.

When Crisk was back and seated at his desk, he again looked over the Glyphotech flyer that had been handed out to everyone. Surely it was a wild over-reaction to make so much of a fuss over what seemed to be nothing more than a motivational seminar.

At 10 a.m. sharp (O'Hara had warned everybody that being late for the seminar would not be looked upon kindly) on Saturday morning Crisk was seated amongst about a hundred other people in a ball-room within the Grantham Hall Hotel. There were the usual mur-murings and muted conversations one would expect amongst a crowd of that size. As he looked around he spotted a number of his work colleagues and nodded at them in recognition. Seated right at the front, he noticed, was O'Hara.

At the end of the room was a stage, a raised dais and behind it a screen on which slides could be projected.

Someone at the front of the room made a signal to a person at the back and the heavy panelled doors opened to admit a figure. The man, immaculately dressed in an expensive tailored suit, walked confidently down the aisle between the rows of seats towards the dais. His bearing was impressive; he seemed to exude an aura of unshakeable confidence. And yet, at least to Crisk, there was also something of the arrogant mixed in with it.

The man mounted the platform behind the dais and smiled dazzlingly. He was in his mid-forties and his well-groomed black hair was swept back high over his forehead.

"Welcome to all you strangers, soon to be friends!" He said in a voice that rang out across the hall with clarity and purpose. Here was a man well used to public speaking.

"I want," he continued, "to congratulate each and every one of you for deciding to come along to the seminar. You've made a decision that I know none of you will ever have cause to regret. Let me introduce myself. I'm Hastane Ebbon. Now I know . . ."

Again he flashed that dazzling smile, looking around the room with a mock-comical expression.

". . . that some of you may be wondering just what you've signed up for. I want to say one thing right now. You're free to leave. Really. But if you do you're going to miss out on the rest of your life. What will happen to you over the next few days is that you'll experience a personal revolution."

Someone in a row towards the back tittered. Crisk looked over his shoulder and saw that it was a very overweight woman in her early thirties, wearing glasses and dressed all in black.

"Hey, that lady out there is only expressing what a lot of you are thinking. I mean, come on, these things are simply a moneymaking exercise, right? Wrong, my friends. If you take what we can offer, I mean, if you're really *open* to it: believe me, things will never be the same for you again."

He paused.

"Anybody want to leave?"

Ebbon was staring and smiling at the overweight lady. She lowered her head, and looked a little sheepish.

"NO?"

There was a ripple of tension in the ballroom. At that moment, thought Crisk, it would have taken someone with a degree of self-assurance equal to Ebbon's to have stood up and walked out. And no one did so.

Crisk was suddenly very uncomfortable. This wasn't like any motivational seminar he'd been to before. And he'd been forced to attend a number whilst employed by agencies over in Japan. This was something quite different. For perhaps the first time, he began to wonder whether his sense of company loyalty was not misplaced.

Ebbon grinned.

"Well this is unusual, let me tell you. You're obviously a lot more intelligent than the last crowd of seminar attendees we had. But then they came from the south of the city . . ."

A number of people in the audience laughed and the tension dissipated.

What Crisk realised after a couple of hours was that a significant number of persons attending the seminar had actually done the course previously. They were there to guide the newcomers and instruct them in the correct protocols that Glyphotech wished them to follow. For example, asking questions without permission was just not done. Daydreaming was not allowed. And in what few breaks there were, for meals or coffee, newcomers were encouraged only to mingle with those who were there for their guidance. Talk centred around discussions and explanations of Glyphotech's "technology" and a series of terms such as "eureka moments" and "routines" were frequently employed. The first referred to, apparently, a juncture in one's life where the possibility of happiness was within grasp. Whilst the second referred to an individual's habits; the displacement activities he would use to justify avoiding doing something he knew he had to do.

There were many more such terms, but Crisk lost interest in hearing about them. It seemed to him that this was simply some junk mixture of psychology, counselling, with elements of Zen-Buddhism tagged on to give it an ethereal sheen.

What came next turned his stomach. Back in the ballroom persons were encouraged to come up to the microphone on the dais and expose their weaknesses, traumas and failings before the rest of the attendees. By the time the tenth had gone up (she seemed to be well versed in this form of communal confession) Crisk actually suspected that many welcomed the opportunity to bare their souls again in public. He wondered whether they had not become addicted to the experience. For what it brought in its wake, after the tears and sobbing, was a round of thunderous clapping from the audience. The first one or two confessions had been greeted with hesitant applause, but once things really got going tears dribbled down the cheeks of most participants. Such was the wave of warmth and mass acceptance generated it was with great difficulty that Crisk restrained himself from joining in with the process, and advancing up to the dais himself.

He could not help noticing throughout this part of the seminar that

O'Hara kept glancing back at him from the front of the hall. Crisk was the only one of the Mare Publishing employees who had not yet succumbed to the hysterical atmosphere in the room.

Ebbon returned to make periodic appearances on the stage, one of which was to explain the concept of "monologues" Glyphotech had developed.

"Monologues," Ebbon said cheerfully, his teeth flashing with that fake smile, "are the way we come to interpret what's happening to us, and of dealing with things that make us uncomfortable. Now let's take an example. Say your boss shouts at you because you're late for work. What's your reaction? You're angry, you're annoyed, YOU MAKE EXCUSES TO YOURSELF! And then you convince yourself he's a bad person, just because he's made you upset. You're using your monologue to avoid dealing with the real issue. Now here's the deal: don't get upset. He's not the problem. YOU'RE THE PROBLEM. Yes, get that and get it good. You see what I mean now? A monologue is when someone is talking to himself and not listening to someone else because he's angry or afraid. Aren't some of you doing that right now – EVEN WHEN I'M TALKING?"

Crisk squirmed uncomfortably in his seat. All the people around him were now nodding enthusiastically as if light bulbs had been turned on inside their minds. They were hanging on Ebbon's every word. A horrible kind of blind faith and exultation spread palpably throughout the ballroom.

After Ebbon stopped speaking he invited people to share their own examples of "monologues" with the rest of the group. There was almost a stampede to the dais, and a queue had to be formed.

One after the other people poured out their stories of how they'd neglected their mothers, their children, even their work, because they'd shifted the blame unreasonably instead of taking responsibility themselves. Yet what was worrying, at least to Crisk, was that he felt that some of these people had, by any reasonable and objective standard, been right in feeling resentment. One person told how he came to detest his dying mother who had been bedridden for four years. He'd cleaned up after her, fed her and the only thanks he'd got was to be told that she hated him and wanted to see her daughter who could not bear to see her in that state. Why shouldn't this person have had the right to resent such ingratitude? It was clear that he loved his mother, but to deny him access to a quite natural response, where was the logic in that? Another person told of being raped and was encouraged to forgive her attacker, to declare that she bore some complicity in his attack. And this plainly was not the case except through an almost deranged reading of the facts.

Rather than the light that had illuminated all those other minds in the hall, a cool and comforting darkness, like shade in the summer sun, entered Crisk's own mind.

I don't want my pain blanked out, he thought to himself; I need to keep my pain. It is a part of who I am, every bit as integral as the joy I've felt. It is not a mental cancer.

And, to his own astonishment, and that of all the others in the ballroom, he calmly rose to his feet, ignored the cold glare of O'Hara and walked out.

"Please excuse," he muttered in his strange English to anyone who might listen, "but this is no more than simple brainwashing exercise."

Outside the ballroom, in the corridor, a man whom Crisk didn't recognise accosted him. He was flanked by two boiler-suited operatives, the kind Crisk had seen emerging from the Glyphotech van that had been parked outside the Mare Publishing Co.

"Are you leaving?" the man said in a tone that was firm yet offered the prospect of reconciliation, "I'd advise you not to. The very fact that you desire to quit now is the strongest indication of how much you are in need of our assistance."

He didn't acknowledge the presence of the two menacing figures either side of him though their unspoken participation in this blatant attempt at coercion was clear.

Crisk saw that the workers of Glyphotech looked even weirder close up than from a distance. For some bizarre reason the sleeves of their black boiler suits were too long and flopped over at the ends, totally concealing their hands. Their deathly white faces were absolutely expressionless, so much so that their features, the slash-like mouths and inkblot eyes, looked uncannily as if they'd been worked into soft white putty rather than flesh.

"I made stupid mistake," said Crisk, "absolutely the blame is mine. Further explanation not necessary. Now I will go."

The other man just stood there silently, as if weighing up his options. Crisk became uneasy. His eyes flickered to the name badge the man wore (no one was permitted to remove them whilst the seminar was in progress) and to the indistinct faces of the Glyphotech operatives. He addressed the man personally.

"Mr Collins, I will have you let me pass," said Crisk, his voice admirably level and betraying no sense of the fear gnawing at his innards, "have told friends that if I do not call them at 5 p.m. they are to come here and collect me. If necessary, with police. Reason being, pre-warned by colleague against attendance at Glyphotech reconstruction seminar. Such precaution unfortunate but necessary, I felt."

"Not in the least necessary, I assure you Mr Crisk. We are not in the business of press-ganging people into our circle of friends. If you feel that you must leave, then do so. You are free to make whatever choice you wish." Collins replied. There was an edge in his voice though, and the last few words were almost a hiss.

Crisk brushed past the three men, through the lobby and out of the Grantham Hall Hotel. He was already beginning to dread the reception he would receive from O'Hara when he turned up for work on Monday morning, if that is, he still had a job at the Mare Publishing Co.

But on Monday morning it was as if his conduct were forgotten. O'Hara greeted him with a pleasant smile (though Crisk admitted to himself that the sight of O'Hara grinning was horrible in its own way) and Crisk began his computer inputting as usual. He did detect a new furtiveness in his office colleagues however, but it was hardly sinister, more like they felt somewhat sorry for him. He could not help noticing that they now employed Glyphotech terminology in a lot of their talk, and went about their duties much more assiduously than before.

It was only after he got home to his flat that same evening that he was made aware there were, after all, certain consequences resulting from his having failed to complete the seminar. The phone rang at 7.30pm, just as he was preparing some sushi for dinner.

"Hello, Mr Crisk, it's John Collins here, from Glyphotech. I hope you don't mind me calling but I wanted to go over the conversation we had when last we met, at the seminar, you remember."

Inwardly, Crisk groaned. He felt the urge to slam down the telephone but his sense of gentility prevented him from doing so.

"To speak the truth nothing more to say," Crisk responded, "now busy preparing food. Cannot talk, even prefer not to . . ."

"This won't take long, I assure you." Collins said, cutting in, "I just wanted to let you know that there's another course beginning at the end of this week and that we'd be happy to welcome you along. Forget what happened before, and make a fresh start. Many of our best friends took their time coming around to total acceptance of the benefits Glyphotech can provide."

"Sorry, but I have no interest," Crisk said sharply.

"Please reconsider. No need to be hasty. Think about it. I'll call you back tomorrow or whenever is convenient. You see it's not possible for you to phone us, it's against protocol."

"Do not call again. How did you obtain my number at home? Intrusion of privacy: will advise telephone company of this outrage . . ."

"Let me be frank with you, Mr Crisk. We checked. We know that what you said about your friends coming to take you from the seminar was just a monologue you'd created. You see we have lists of your calls; the Phone Company understood it was for your own good. Their managers and employees found a recent Glyphotech seminar of great use in reconstructing their . . ."

Crisk hung up. Then he dialled the operator's number.

"Hello operator?" He said. "I am Franklyn Crisk, calling from phone 456 67304. I wish to report unwelcome intrusion of privacy by Glyphotech Recon . . ."

"Of course, Sir," a dull voice cut in; "I'll transfer you to the appropriate department."

But the number he was transferred to just rang and rang without ever being answered. And when he spoke to the operator for a second time all that happened was that he was transferred nearly immediately to the unanswered line again, without even being given the opportunity to finish uttering a complete sentence. After the seventh attempt he gave up.

A scant two days later Crisk realised that what he had at first taken for amused condescension on the part of O'Hara and his office colleagues was the primary stage of tactical psychological warfare. Crisk suspected that he had initially been given the benefit of the doubt. Their self-belief in the validity of Glyphotech's reconstruction seminar made them think that he would eventually come to embrace its tenets, despite his faltering start and refusal to co-operate. But as the days passed and he was still clearly as antagonistic to the idea as he had been when he'd walked out of the seminar in front of everyone, their attitude changed slightly. Although never outwardly hostile it became obtrusive. Scarcely an hour would pass without some employee making a remark about how Glyphotech's technology had improved their lives beyond recognition, how much happier they were in their work, or how much they were looking forward to socialising with their fellow seminar attendees. These comments were made deliberately within Crisk's earshot, presumably with the intention of making him feel left out, peculiar or downright freakish in not having realised its benefits.

John Collins, or some other Glyphotech devotee, still telephoned him at his flat, sometimes three or four times an evening, but Crisk would cut the conversation short by slamming down the receiver the moment he recognised the voice. That they had resorted to using a rota of individuals so that he was off-guard when he answered almost drove him to distraction. And Crisk's attempts to contact the Phone Company and have the matter dealt with proved as futile as before. He was beginning to believe it really was just another branch of the Glyphotech phenomenon.

Although these developments were unnerving enough in themselves, they were not as unnerving as the fact that Crisk discovered he was being watched. A Glyphotech Reconstruction Company van had parked itself on the street directly opposite the building in which his flat was situated. In the evenings, when Crisk glanced out of his window, it was always there, a dirty green vehicle with white-faced operatives clearly visible through the windscreen, who peered up at him with eyes like dark smudges.

Another week passed. Crisk had given the Mare Publishing Company no excuse to terminate his employment, since he ensured that his work and time keeping were beyond reproach. O'Hara and his colleagues became increasingly resentful of his intransigence and their former cheerfulness seemed somehow brittle, as if his own presence was a factor in their discomfort. Whether this was the case or not, he was sure they would never dare admit to it. He began to suspect that the persons who had completed the seminar and who claimed to have got the most from it harboured a real sense of dread at letting Glyphotech down by admitting any tiny doubt as to the success of their psychological reconstruction. All of them were now paying considerable amounts of money in order to attend advanced courses. The Mare Publishing Company gave interest-free loans to those who could not afford to pay so that their continued participation was ensured.

The effect the stress had upon Crisk was that he suffered episodes of insomnia. Still, he felt some comfort, at least, from the fact that the Glyphotech rota of phone callers had finally ceased their campaign to persuade him to change his mind. However, when at work, and when walking home to his flat from the office, he thought he detected unusually intense and hate-filled stares from passers-by. Moreover, he could not rid himself of the persistent notion that he saw alarming physiognomic alterations in large numbers of the people whom he encountered. Those who stared at him for too long seemed to be developing black smudged eyes that were sinking back into their sockets, whilst their hands, digits and fingernails were of a horribly abnormal length.

An open-top lorry carrying scaffolding equipment had recently joined the van parked outside Crisk's flat. The lorry also bore the Glyphotech logo emblazoned across both its sides. Crisk had noticed that the company had recently added scaffolding to its ever-growing list of enterprises. It made some vague sense, seeing as they had, he'd read in a newspaper, secured contracts to refurbish a large number of buildings throughout the city. The latticed scaffolding structures and plastic-sheeted fronts with their logo were becoming evident almost everywhere one looked.

Although Crisk hoped that this new activity might, at least, divert some of their energies away from their bogus psychological reprogramming of the populace, he tried to avoid passing buildings fronted by the Glyphotech scaffolding as much as possible. From behind the sheets of opaque white plastic attached to the poles and clamps, he clearly heard the sound of scratching, as if dozens of long fingernails were clawing over and over again at glass, brick and concrete.

In order to calm his nerves after his fractious working day, Crisk would often pass a couple of hours drinking in a bar in a back street close to the Mare Publishing Company's offices. None of the other employees spent time at this bar anymore; teetotalism being Glyphotech protocol. It was a quiet, dark place, and good for quiet reflection.

As he sat there sipping a pint of beer, a man whose head was wrapped in bandages entered. Crisk tried not to stare but couldn't help pity the fellow. He must have been involved in quite a nasty accident. Instead of going up to the counter, however, the stranger made straight for Crisk and slumped in the seat directly opposite him.

"How are you, Crisk?" he said in a voice that, though croaky, Crisk recognised as belonging to the former Mare employee David Hogg.

"I have troubles," Crisk replied, "but none to compare to your own, I think. You have met with an accident, I suppose. It is very unfortunate, especially coming after your dismissal."

Hogg's eyes, staring out through holes in the bandages, were watery. Beneath the wrappings there seemed to be neither a nose nor cheeks, only deep hollows. He spoke again:

"I thought that those at Mare who didn't succumb to the Glyphotech brainwashing might come in here now and again for a drink. The converts hate the stuff of course. But I admit that I didn't think you personally would reject the seminar, seeing as you were such a loyal company man."

Crisk wasn't certain whether Hogg was complimenting or denigrating him, perhaps a mixture of both.

"Glyphotech repulsive organisation," Crisk said, "attack free thought, harasses ones who speak against it. Any honourable man who understands duty would do as I did."

"Could you buy me a drink, Crisk? I'm sorry to ask. But I have no money, and I need one rather badly. In return I'll give you some advice. It's a small price to pay in exchange, believe me."

"Advice? Explain please."

"After the drink." Hogg responded.

Crisk returned to the table with another beer for himself and a double Scotch and soda for Hogg. He guzzled the amber fluid rapidly through the mouth-slit in his wrappings, spilling a few drops onto the bandage around his chin.

"How far into the seminar did you get?" Hogg asked, putting the half-empty glass down.

"First day, about five hours. Left when . . ."

"I did the whole day," Hogg cut in, "and most of the next. They nearly got me. That was back before I joined Mare. I left my previous job because I saw what the Glyphotech seminar did to the company. But Glyphotech wouldn't let me reject what it was offering. They kept phoning me at home, and then my office colleagues ostracised me for not enrolling, since they themselves had all done so. By now, you must be experiencing something similar."

Crisk nodded. He felt a deep sense of shame at having badly misjudged Hogg.

"They no longer ring me," Crisk responded.

Hogg seemed to be agitated rather than soothed by the news.

"You realise they don't actually have a working centre of operations, don't you?" Hogg continued. "I mean, they say they do. But it's just an empty old office somewhere with a desk and a telephone and no one around to answer it. The calls they harass you with don't come from there. I don't even know if that swine Ebbon has ever been to the office. It's against protocol to ask about the place."

The bandaged man reached for the remains of his Scotch and soda and downed it with a single gulp.

"Another, how about?" Crisk asked him.

"Get the bottle," Hogg replied; coughing a little as the alcohol made his throat tighten.

The two men drank heavily.

"You know," Hogg said, his voice slightly slurred by the booze, "what happens on day two? They tell you about the core of their mental technology. The bastards repeat their propaganda over and over again, until it begins to make sense, until, as they say – you reach the understanding. It's called the suicide-resolution. Funny isn't it, in a grim way? The suicide-resolution. When you accept that final piece of the jigsaw, you belong to them, utterly and totally. I didn't. What they tell attendees is that the suicide-resolution is the secret of extracting the maximum joy from life, living each day like your last: because soon it really will be. And everyone, by then, is so brainwashed they believe it."

"Too fantastic: ask people to kill themselves?" Crisk responded, "such things cannot be, except in trashy horror tales of the worst type. Why not inform the police?"

"You don't understand, they RUN everything." Hogg spluttered, "Anyway, you didn't get as far into it as I did. By day two you'll swallow all they say. Brainwashing only works when the victims refuse to accept they've been brainwashed. The suicide-resolution is bad enough, but it's what comes after that's even worse. Things don't end there; suicide's just the beginning. The technology somehow works on parts of the brain we don't normally use. It ensures you come back afterwards so that they can carry on with the reconstruction process, carry on with it even after you're dead. Glyphotech never let go. Never, ever."

Crisk suspected Hogg had gone mad. He was pointing to the bandages in which his head was swathed.

"I'm telling you, they nearly had me, Crisk! Leave while you still can. Don't hang around like I did. Those ghouls managed to get to my face before I . . ."

Crisk stumbled to his feet. He didn't care whether Hogg was telling the truth or not: he could take no more, and left the bar without looking back.

". . . get out of the city, Crisk," Hogg cried behind him. "When they stop calling you it means they'll take more drastic measures."

The next day Crisk left the Mare Publishing Company for good. What Hogg had told him the previous night made a horrible kind of sense, even if he could not accept every word of it as literal truth.

He had, however, noted the same physiognomic mutations occur-

ring in his office colleagues that he'd observed develop in the people
on the streets. Perhaps it was some disease, but he was baffled at the
fact no one had commented upon its having been allowed to spread
unchecked.

He would quit his job without giving notice, go home, pack some
of his belongings in a couple of suitcases and leave the city by the first
available train out. Unless he took this decisive action he felt he might
well trip over the edge of reason and go completely insane, as Hogg
had done. He told no one of his plans and walked out of the Mare
Publishing Company at 6pm as usual.

Only O'Hara saw him depart and, to Crisk's horror, his boss
raised a hand with abnormally long digits and nails and gave him a
mock-ironic farewell wave. There was a horrible knowing smile
beneath his smudgy eyes.

It was a 10-minute walk, at a leisurely pace, from the office to Crisk's
flat. But he covered the distance in half that time, breaking into a trot
as often as he could and only slowing to a normal pace when
breathless. Already he was going over in his mind what he would
take with him: the bare essentials, cash he'd saved for an emergency,
some clothing, toiletries and perhaps one or two treasured items he'd
brought back from Kyoto; his tea-set and sake bowls. Yes, they had
"wabi" and could not be left behind.

Crisk tried to avoid looking at the people he passed in the street
and at the buildings. He knew the way almost by instinct in any case.
When, however, he finally reached his flat he saw, with a jolt of
panic, that Glyphotech scaffolding covered the front of the building
all the way to the top. On the other side of the street the truck with
the poles was no longer there, though the other vehicle, the dirty
green van, remained. However there didn't seem to be any Glyphotech operatives inside.

Had he not needed the cash he'd put away in the drawer of his
bureau for the train-fare, he would have abandoned any notion of
going up to his flat, deeming the risk too great. Instead, he stood out
on the street and then cautiously moved towards the sheets and
poles, straining his ears to detect noise from within the structure. He
waited for several minutes, but heard nothing. Perhaps, if he were
quick, he might get in and out without being noticed. Crisk always
bolted his windows from the inside and was confident that any
break-in would have aroused too much attention, so he doubted that
intruders were lying in wait for him within the flat itself.

He let himself in through the front door, passed along the hallway and ascended the stairs. The light bulbs had blown on the second floor, so he had to pass through a pool of darkness before reaching the third where his own flat was situated. Unlocking it quietly, he opened the door halfway, reached in and turned on the light switch just to the right of the entrance. Then he entered.

Everything was as he'd left it that morning and he saw, with relief, that the windows were still bolted and closed. The scaffold platform and its opaque plastic sheeting closed off the usual view. But there was no one out there. He left the door slightly ajar behind him for a quick exit should it prove necessary.

After removing the cash from his bureau and transferring it to his wallet, he took two suitcases from underneath his bed and began packing them as swiftly as he was able. The tea-set and sake bowls were the most troublesome, as they were quite delicate and required careful wrapping in layers of newspaper.

Then he heard loud scuffling noises. Several people seemed to be frantically climbing the ladders that led from one platform of the scaffolding to the next. They were headed in his direction; there could be no doubt about it. Crisk spun around to the door, his only escape route, and saw a horribly long hand snaking around the edge, as if someone were about to push it open and enter his flat. He dashed across the room in and tried to jam the door shut, trapping the hand. It was attenuated and spider-like, and the fingers twitched convulsively as Crisk put all his weight into his shoulder, ultimately succeeding in forcing the door shut. As it closed tight, the digits on the hand squashed and broke off as if made from damp putty.

Directly behind him Crisk heard the sound of fingernails scratching upon the window-pane. He turned and saw half a dozen deathly-white faces leering through the glass. The things were all clawing idiotically at the surface.

Crisk picked up the telephone and frantically dialled the operator. He was transferred to another line at once, without saying a word, and heard the familiar ringing tone begin. Perhaps if he could get through to Glyphotech, he hoped, if he could persuade them he'd changed his mind, there might still be a chance.

"Answer it," he mumbled to himself, "answer it, answer it . . ."

Just before the window shattered and the things crawled over the sill towards him, raking their hellish fingernails across everything they touched, Crisk thought of the dusty and empty office, long disused, where an unattended telephone rang and rang.

HOLLY PHILLIPS

One of the Hungry Ones

HOLLY PHILLIPS LIVES AND WRITES in a crooked little house overlooking the Columbia River in the mountains of western Canada.

She is the author of the critically acclaimed story collection *In the Palace of Repose* and the dark fantasy novel *The Burning Girl*, both published by Prime Books, as well as many stories and poems which have been appeared in such diverse magazines as *The New Quarterly* and *Asimov's*. This is her first appearance in print outside the North American continent.

The author is currently revising a fantasy novel called *The Engine's Child* whilst simultaneously researching her next book, a slipstream novel entitled *Before the Age of Miracles*.

"I wrote 'One of the Hungry Ones' over a couple of grey and rainy days in June 2002," recalls Phillips. "My dear cat Calypso, who had shared my home for seven years, had disappeared, and although the people and events in the story are wholly imaginary, I think the sense of loneliness was very real to me that summer. As was the idea of hunting and being hunted, perhaps, since I have always supposed that Calypso, a talented mouser, became a larger predator's prey. Although we seldom saw the coyotes, bobcats and cougars prowling the hills behind the house, we always knew they were there."

W HEN SHE ENTERED THE UNDERPASS between the Avenue and the park, she found Raz and a couple of his boys hanging out there, at one with the mould-and-urine smell and the insomniac sodium light. Raz, who somehow knew her name.

"Sexy Sadie," the pimp sang, a line from an old song. "Sex-y Sa-die."

She fixed her eyes on the tunnel end, where a flight of stairs led to the dusk of grass and autumn trees, and walked, her face stiff with a mask of no-fear.

"Hey, Sadie, are you hungry yet?" one of Raz's boys whispered at her back. The tunnel magnified his voice, her footsteps, the growl of traffic overhead. "Are you hungry yet?"

"Sex-y Sa-die."

As much as she hated the tunnel, she loved emerging into the freedom of the park. A dangerous place after dark, people said, haunted by rapists and crazies who treated insanity with alcohol and crack. Night was the time street kids came together to canvass the restaurant diners and movie crowd, and to share their scores in the cold of an abandoned store. Safety in numbers. But Sadie hated the press of dirty bodies, the mumble of drugged voices, the grope of unwanted hands – hated the pack and hated the fear that dragged them all together – so when the whisper had come her way, Mullein's Park on Friday night, she had determined to come, Raz or no, shadows or no.

Under the trees the air smelled of burning leaves.

It was Rayne who had whispered in her ear. (How did Sadie come to meet them, Rayne and Leo and Tom? They must have spoken to her first, she was too shy, too wary to talk freely to strangers. But she had watched them since her arrival on the Avenue, spent weeks yearning after their cleanliness, their fierce swagger, their mysterious affairs. They were bright as firelit knives, shining as jewels.) Rayne, slip-thin and blond, had sauntered over to Sadie panhandling on the corner and whispered, promise or tease, *Mullein's Park on Friday night*, and it was the smell of her, soap and new leather, that had conjured Sadie's need. Need, not courage. Courage is a flame that requires fuel, and Sadie was too hungry to sustain that kind of fire.

Too hungry for that, not hungry enough for . . . *Sex-y Sa-die* . . .

A breeze scattered frost-dried leaves from the trees. The rustle made a screen for footsteps or voices. Sadie doubled her oversized cardigan around her and started down the gravel path. Mullein's Park covered a whole block. There were a lot of tall lamps casting pools of light, a lot of trees shedding black skirts of shade. The three could be anywhere, if they were here at all, if Sadie wasn't too early, or too late, or otherwise entirely wrong. She couldn't think what she had done to earn this invitation.

Someone was running towards her, dashing from shadow to man

back to shadow as he passed through a lighted space. Sadie caught a flash of his face – beard and weathered skin, eyes wet with fear – then he was in the dark and past her, and all there was left of him, all there was left of any human thing in the night, was the stink of aged sweat and the phut-phut of newspaper shoes retreating to the tunnel stairs.

Then a woman laughed. The sound was a bright echo to Sadie's fear, a spark to warm her hollow gut: relief as the three of them walked towards her into the round of light. Rayne, tall catling with a tuft of pale hair and a silver ring in the curve of her smile. Tom, like his name, big, soft-walking, ruddy and cool of eye. Leo, with wind-tossed straw for hair and the loose-limbed, big-handed grace of an athlete. The warmth in Sadie's middle grew, tentative, but strong enough to light a smile.

"Sadie!" Rayne cried.

"Sadie," Tom murmured.

"Sadie," Leo said, smiling and reaching out a friendly hand.

And she was among them. Rayne laughed and slipped an arm around her shoulders. "A true name three times spoken," she said. "You're ours, now, Sadie."

Sadie didn't know what she meant, but it sounded like a joke, so she laughed.

They took her to a house on the other side of the park. It was a neighbourhood she hardly knew. Old houses, some indifferently kept, some fixed up like new, most guarded this month by a candlelit pumpkin scowl: a welcome for children, but not for the homeless or the lost. Even in company she shrank a little in her thrift-store clothes. Be invisible, instinct whispered. Make yourself too small to see. She dragged her feet through harsh leaves when the trio turned off the pavement and onto the front walk of a house.

But Rayne tugged at her sleeve, her silvered grin bright in the streetlight dusk. "Come on, Sadie, don't be shy. We'll get you all dressed up and you won't have a thing to fear."

"But I don't have any clothes?"

Rayne laughed. She had an easy laugh, a tripping chuckle that sounded happy and true. "Trust Sister Rayne," she said. "We'll find everything you need."

"Don't worry," Leo added, more sensibly. "The owner's a friend. He lets us keep our things here."

"And he'll lend you a mask," Tom finished.

"A mask?" This brought Sadie to a stop. "But it isn't Hallowe'en for . . ." But she wasn't sure what day it was, maybe the month's end was closer than she thought.

" 'Tis the season," Leo said, smiling. "Hallowe'en all October, just like when we were kids."

"Only more fun." Rayne hummed it in her ear, and somehow she was moving again, along the walk and up the stairs. There was a glass panel in the door, stained glass that flashed as the door opened, something red, something green, and a creature's snarling or laughing face, white fangs and cat-languid eyes – just a colourful glance as the door swung open and she passed through, and then she was inside.

The hall was dark save for the glow that came through a doorway on the right. The air was warm and smelled of honey, beeswax, maybe, for the banister on the stairs caught a yellow gleam. The place was so alien to her after a summer of living city rough, Sadie felt disoriented, almost dizzy. She looked at smiling Leo, at Tom's watchful eye.

"Come on." Rayne slipped her arm through Sadie's. "We still have to wash and change before everyone else arrives."

Shower? Clean clothes? Sadie let Rayne pull her up the stairs, still dizzy, but now it was luck that spun her head, and warmth, and the sweet welcoming smell of the house. Trick? Or treat? She did not have to ask.

Thick candles that slumped under their own heat. Deep tub, hot water, vanilla foam. Oval mirror in a swivel frame. Sadie stroked the wet cloth up and down her skin and watched while Rayne came in to try her costumes in the mirror. Every passage made the candle flames jump and flicker; Rayne's reflection shimmered with mystery. Sadie was fascinated to see the same gamin face and pale shock of hair become twenties flapper wearing a sheath of blue-green beads, renaissance lady in an embroidered bodice, fantastic pirate in tight leather and parrot scarves.

Sadie wrung out the cloth and draped it on the rim of the tub before soberly clapping her hands.

"Yes?" Pirate Rayne cocked her head in the mirror, studying Sadie's face rather than her own form.

Sadie twisted her hair into a knot on her neck and reached for the towel rack. "Yes."

Rayne quit posing long enough to hand her the towel, then turned back to the mirror. For a moment her face was still, almost numb, all the life in her searching eyes. Then, as Sadie stood in the tub, dripping foam, and steam swirled through the candle light,

Rayne planted her fists on her hips and threw back her head, arrogant and laughing.

"Yes!"

There was a bottle of wine in the next room. Glasses, too, but Rayne-the-pirate drank from the neck of the bottle, and Sadie did the same, when she wasn't burrowing in the deep closet full of clothes. The smell was strangely delicious: rich fabrics, faded perfumes, and the dim hint of strangers' skin.

"Your friend must have a lot of parties," Sadie said as she emerged with an armful.

"He loves them," the pirate said, swigging. "He lives for this time of year."

Sadie spread her choices on the bed. A double bed with a brass frame and wine-dark spread, it was the only furniture in the room. The window, uncurtained, looked out on the back yard. Sadie was wary of the naked glass, suspecting eyes in the night beyond, but Rayne was careless, so she pretended she was as well.

"Here," she said, holding a gown against her towelled body. It was Ginger Rogers elegant, with a fringe of fluffy feathers at hem and shoulders.

Rayne made a face and shook her head. The feathers felt good on Sadie's skin, but she put the dress aside. "How about this?" Another flapper dress, peacock-beaded with a fringe.

"No," Rayne said, reaching over her shoulder. "This."

In the mirror she looked surprised. The silk frock coat, blue-white-gold, was a little too long in the sleeves, the matching breeches a little tight in the ass, but the ruffled collar and buckled shoes made her, even with her damp brown hair tangled on her shoulders, a youth from one of the French Louis' courts. Blinking her surprise away, she tossed her head and tweaked the lace of her sleeve. Rayne, just a scarved head at her shoulder, grinned and nudged her elbow with the bottle, now mostly empty of wine.

The boys were waiting at the top of the stairs, Tom in a Chinese robe of crimson silk and dragons, Leo a cheerful Hamlet in black doublet and hose. The hall below was still dark, but through the lighted doorway came the murmur of voices and the melancholy dance of a gypsy guitar. Leo clapped as Sadie and Rayne came up. Tom padded round them, nodding his approval. Enjoying their scrutiny, Rayne struck a pose, and Sadie bowed, a little drunk, a little happy, and trying not to wonder . . . *why me?*

Another pair of hands joined Leo's applause. Sadie, who'd almost forgotten the host she had yet to meet, straightened with a flush. He was tall, taller than Leo, and like Leo dressed in black, but the blackness of his clothes, the straight simple cut of them, made Leo seem like the imitator, himself the original. He wore a tight cap of black hair and, making Sadie stare, a mask, skin-tight black velvet with eye-holes rimmed in black sequins, and mouth outlined in red.

"This is Sadie," Rayne said, nudging her in the back.

"Sadie." The masked man's clapping hands drifted apart, white against the black of his coat. "Sadie." His voice was musing. His teeth were white as he smiled. "Sadie, you are welcome."

"Thank you," she said, remembering the manners of another life. "It's nice of you to have me."

"Any friend of Rayne's." Her host's laugh was dark and velvet as his mask. "Any friend of Rayne's is a friend of mine."

She knew, then, that there was something wrong here. Knew it in the way Rayne went stiff and still at her back, in the way Tom's eyes drifted to a far distance and Leo's smile grew wide and false. Knew it, most of all, in the way her own skin shivered down her spine. Instinct sang a warning. But it's Rayne, Sadie thought and, seeing the slant of the masked man's look, she was sure. Rayne, not her. Relief, a buoyant burst of defensive anger for her friend (Rayne became her friend in that instant), even a dark slink of curiosity, they all crowded out the twinge of fear. The wine probably helped as well.

"Thanks," she said again.

Then their host took them aside to choose their masks.

Leo: a black domino, diamond slits for his nervous eyes.

Tom: a snarling dragon, red and gold to cover his own stiff calm.

Rayne (hesitated, started a hand for this one, fiddled another's ribbons, bit her lip over a third): finally: a spangled cat drawn in crazy lines that made her eyes seem not fearful but wild.

And then Sadie. The room was all masks, on tables, on stands, on hooks on the walls. A crowd of eyeless orbits and breathless mouths awaited life. It was strange, so strange, and then the others' faces were hidden, and she was the only one exposed.

"Here," said their host, though he had stood silent in the corner shadows while the rest had made their choices. His white hand offered Sadie a pale mask formed in wicked, laughing lines, an imp's face, a cheerful demon's. It was not quite ugly, but not what she

would have chosen. She wanted something to suit her costume,
something gilded from the Sun King's court.

But, "Take it," their host said. "I insist." As if she hesitated
because she thought the honour too great for her to accept.

So she took it, and she put it on.

A mask's eyes are brighter than the eyes in a naked face. They are
livelier, more intelligent, more eloquent of meaning: doorways onto
being, windows on the soul. Eyes. And mouths, lips taut or smooth,
humorous creases, lascivious tongues. And the voices that spill forth.
The laugh that, by a twisted lip, is proved a lie. The word that, by the
witness of the shining eyes, is proven true.

And the touch of her own mask, at first cool and clammy leather,
but quickly like a second skin, and the play it gives her, herself a
stage, her every breath a performance, and yet (herein lies the magic)
also and entirely true. Every game, every lie flirting and cruel – and
the house is full of them, games and lies – is real as knives, for the
masquerade has come to define the night. The false face of everyday,
that hides reality beneath flesh and skin, is itself hidden beneath the
fantasy that, because it is a product and reflection of the mind, is an
honest facade. Sadie has lived a wary, defensive life, always urged by
that self-preserving instinct to stay small, hidden, safe. She did not
know she had an imp inside her until she wore it on her face.

Of course it lived inside her, somewhere deep within. What else
drew her to Rayne and Leo and Tom to begin with? What else
carried her through risk to their meeting place, and from there, here,
to this stranger's house?

The imp, who knew where freedom waited.

And now it's free, indeed. Sadie-imp, frock-coated and masked,
has become the perfect androgyne, and therein lies the heart of her
game. A broad man with a grizzled braid and the mask of a weary
angel feeds her tiny pastries (cheese and herbs, she's greedy for them,
and bites the tips of his fingers to catch the crumbs) and then stands
confounded while from a bare-breasted Kali she teases sips of wine,
importunate youth from her tangled hair to her buckled shoes. And
that's only one game, there are a dozen more, until she's bored and
so:

she dances to campfire music of guitars and drums, as like to the
mechanical rhythm of a rave as the giddy wine is to the chemical
sterility of the pills she's swallowed there. No, here, *here* is life, here is
the blood leaping wine-bright in her veins. She dances, imp-Sadie,
with men, with women, with no one – once in the arms of dragon-

Tom, who moves softly on his feet – once (or did she only glimpse his mask in the whirl?) with their host all in black, his red-sequined mouth smiling, white teeth agleam – once with Rayne, whose laughter sounds like wine in the neck of a bottle, like water cascading down a drain—

then, though the music comes tangled behind them, they are not dancing but running through the wild-tree moonlit-lawn park, the park grown to woodland, an autumn forest all in a city block, running, no, hunting (but still dancing, too, perhaps this is a dream?) imp dragon cat and leaping Hamlet chasing after their quarry

poor shambling bear, shaggy and lost in the forever city-block wood, weeping when they bring him down

and then there is wine again, poured from a weeping bottle opened by imp's needle teeth and passed all around

bright wine in all their veins

Or perhaps this is a dream?

Sadie sat on the park bench in the morning drizzle, elbows on her knees, head in her hands. She sat for what seemed like a long time, watching a dirty trickle of water run between her feet toward the middle of the path, nothing much in her mind. Then someone sat down beside her and said in a half-familiar voice, "Hangover?"

She straightened and turned. Leo, in jean jacket, sweater, jeans. She, also, was in her usual clothes, though she couldn't quite remember changing, or how she came to be sitting here. Too much wine. Leo looked tired, incipient lines running from nose to chin, his eyes a little sunken into shadow. Half-familiar, half a friend.

She remembered his question and said, "Not yet."

He smiled, but she hadn't meant it as a joke. She felt odd, not sick, not hurting, but weirdly, ominously full. Not just in her belly, but under her skin as well, as if she'd been inflated like an inner tube. She glanced at the backs of her hands, but the bones were as prominent as ever, the veins like faint blue worms.

"Have a good time last night?" Leo asked.

She looked at him again, but he was watching a puddle form. The rain was cold in her hair, heavy on her shoulders. She'd been sitting there a while, then. "Yes," she said. "Yes, it was amazing."

He nodded, then swallowed as if he didn't feel too well himself. "Good." He passed his hands over his hair, making it stand out in all directions, then turned with a smile and a nudge to her arm. "C'mon. Let's go find some breakfast."

"I'm not really all that hungry."

He laughed. "Coffee, at least. Yes? Coffee? My treat."

As if the word conjured the reality, she could smell the possibilities, dark roast, hot steam . . . "Coffee. Yes."

When they were sitting in the café, immersed in the Saturday morning crowd, Sadie asked Leo, "Why did you guys ask me to go with you?"

Leo lifted his brows. "Why wouldn't we?"

"You hardly know me."

He carefully tore the corner off a packet of sugar and poured it into his cup.

"We know you better now."

Somehow she thought things would change. Maybe she thought she would be included in the trio's mysterious business, maybe she just thought her luck had turned. But after Leo said goodbye that noon, she did not see them for days. Days of *Please can you spare some change?* in the October rain. Days of grocery store alleys at closing time, waiting for the bruised fruit and stale bread to be thrown away. Nights huddled with others as cold as herself, wondering if it would be the cops or the suburban punks who would roust them next. Wondering if she'd been forgotten. Wondering if she shouldn't, herself, forget.

It would be easy to forget such a night, its passages so like a dream's. Yes, she'd gone to the house, had a bath, drunk wine with Rayne. The clothes, all right, she remembered the feel of silk on her skin. But the masks? The black, white-handed figure of the nameless host? Yet she also remembered the feel of cool leather on her face. Indeed, sometimes when the rain touched her cheek she started, surprised even after so long to find her face exposed. But the chase in the park-that-was-a-forest – the bear hunt in the trees – that had to be a dream. So where did the real night end, and the dream night begin? That was what troubled Sadie.

That, and why her new friends had decided she was not one of them after all.

One night, cold and hungry and numb, she passed Raz on the street.

"Sex-y Sa-die."

"Leave me alone."

"C'mon, Sadie-girl. Let me buy you a hot meal. A nice hot meal, and then maybe you and me can party, after. You like to party, don't you, Sadie-girl? Sexy Sadie. Aren't you hungry yet?"

"Not enough," she said, and he let her pass.

But, "You will be," the pimp said to her back, and she went on sick with the realization that it might, it just might be true.

Then Friday night came around again, the month creeping farther into the hunting season, and because she couldn't help herself, she went to Mullein's Park. No Raz in the underpass this time, just a couple of winos sharing a bottle.

"Nice night," one said as she passed. "Nice night to stay in out of the rain."

His voice reverberated in the tunnel. Like his own echo, he mumbled the phrase over again, as if he couldn't figure out how it worked. *In out of the rain. In out of the rain.* Sadie climbed the stairs to the sharp bonfire smell of the park, the treed darkness run through by the lighted paths, and felt the week's misery cut loose by hope. Maybe . . . Maybe . . .

Rayne, with a whoop, grabbed her in a hug, big-handed Leo ruffled her hair, and even cool Tom was grinning. She was home free.

Only the second time, and already it had the feeling of a ritual: the bath, the wine, the clothes.

This time Rayne was a spacewoman in white zipper boots and a skin-slick jumpsuit of green. She wet her hands in Sadie's bath water and smoothed back her pale hair, becoming sleek and cold, while Sadie, already feeling the wine, slithered into silk pantaloons and flowing robe and became a Persian prince. Like an older sister, Rayne pulled the tangles out of her hair and wrapped it up in a black fringed scarf. Ready, they stood for a moment at the mirror, Rayne a long cool pillar at Sadie's back.

Sadie, stupid with pleasure, said, "I thought you'd forgotten about me."

Rayne ducked to prop her chin on Sadie's shoulder. Now they were two faces on one body. "Nope."

"I never saw you all week."

"Places to go, people to see." Rayne tipped her head against Sadie's. "You shouldn't have worried, Sadie-girl. Didn't we say you were ours?"

Sadie flinched at the echo of Raz.

"What?"

"Nothing. Just don't call me that. Okay?"

Rayne looked in her eyes, reflection-wise. "Somebody giving you a hard time?"

Sadie shrugged, making Rayne's head nod. Rayne wrapped her arms around her.

"Don't worry. We take good care of our own."

She smiled, and Sadie smiled back, but she was thinking, *Like you did all this week?*

But the hug felt good.

Leo was a medieval alchemist with a skull cap and spangled robe. Tom was a British huntsman, red coat, tall boots, riding crop and all. Spacewoman, magician, huntsman and prince, they stood at the top of the stairs and watched as people came through the glass-panelled door, into the dark hall and the lighted room beyond.

"They all have their own masks," Sadie said.

Tom put a heavy hand on her shoulder. "It's only special guests who are granted access to Mr Nero's private collection."

A warm buzz of excitement grew in Sadie's belly, fed by the touch, by the pleasure of watching unseen from above, by the anticipation of the revels to come. She was glad, too, to finally know their host's name.

"Nero," she said. "Wasn't he an emperor or something?"

They all laughed.

"Probably," Tom said.

"Or something," Rayne said.

"The question is," Leo murmured, "what is he now?"

Sadie turned to look at him and saw a ghost at his back. She yelped, jumped a little. Tom's hand held her fast. The ghost stepped forward and she saw it was their host, Mr Nero all in white, his mask of clinging feathers white as swans save for the corners of his mouth that were splashed with macaw scarlet. Only his hair and his eyes were still black.

He bowed. "My friends. Another night, another dance." He looked at Sadie and held out his hands. "And you have come back again."

Guided by the pressure of Tom's grip, she stepped forward and put her hands in Mr Nero's. Slender and strong, they closed about her fingers. His eyes were bright as a bird's. "Sadie, lovely Sadie. Welcome."

"Thank you," she said, breathless.

He did not let go. "I hope this means you enjoyed yourself a sennight ago?"

"Last week," Tom murmured in her ear.

"Yes, thank you. It was. . . It was. . ."

"Yes." Mr Nero squeezed her hands, his teeth bright in his smile . . . and her blood seemed to ebb and draw strangely through her veins . . . and then everyone was laughing, and he let her go. "Yes," he said, "it always is."

The mask touched her face damply, like a kiss.

Imp-Sadie dances with the red-coated hunter who wears the fox's face, with the magician who has a bat's visage, with the tall all-in-white birdman. The spacewoman with the fractured-glass ice-mask eludes her.

"Have you seen Rayne?" she asks the satyr while his hands burrow like moles beneath her robe.

"I'm looking for Rayne," she tells the Egyptian slave who bows his jackal head against her thigh.

"Do you know Rayne?" she asks the King's Fool, who capers and howls, "Not well enough to come out from in!"

Come out from in. In out of the rain. Rayne? It's raining, it's pouring, the old man is snoring . . .

There is a game. Everyone is looking, everyone has a clue to give, no one knows the object of the search. There is much hilarity. The imp finds a button lost from someone's costume and yells, she has the prize! Then spins off and away through the crowd leaving a tangle of would-be captors behind her. Hide it again, hide it again! Shivering with silent laughter, the imp slips through a door into a darkened hall and is hunting out a corner when she comes upon the fox-faced hunter and the alchemist-bat conferring beneath the stairs.

The bat says, "It's wrong."

The fox says, "I agree that if she's going to go through with it, she should at least be here."

The bat says, "You know what I mean. The whole thing is wrong."

The fox says, "And losing Rayne would be right? The girl is—"

"Right as rain!" the imp cries. "Come on, you guys, shouldn't we be dancing?"

So the white-bird man calls for music, and so the musicians play.

A princely imp goes dancing, she-prince, Persian djinn, fire-dervish of the Eastern sands. Dancing, dancing, the Eastern night hot as blazes and lit by lampshade stars. Her court is a wild place, rowdy randy and raucous, and a white bird hangs over all, black eyes bright with reflected glory. Greedy white bird with a red beak wet with the juice of the Persian fruits, berries plucked from burning coals. Dancing, dancing, huntsman-fox and squeaking bat and ice-cool spacewoman who melts in the heat of the star-lamps, dancing, dancing, caught in the whirl spun by the dervish-prince and the white bird's fanning wings, dancing, dancing, until the fever races them out of doors into the cold, the dark, the giddy giddy night where the fox blows his horn and the sweet bat sings and the ice-woman runs into rain and the princely imp wins the game, a button, a bottle, a bear!

And pours them all a glass of the red, of the red, of the blood-red wine.

With the end of the month and the beginning of winter in sight, Sadie was not willing to be ignored.

She waited two days, three days, though not patiently. She was so restless in the daytime she could not settle on any corner but walked and walked, listening for three bright voices and gleaning no money at all. Night time, too hungry to sleep, she haunted lit sidewalks, ignored by the roaming police cars (no need to hide from the indifferent) and almost too angry to hide from the scavengers who preyed on the abandoned.

Almost.

Though angry was perhaps the wrong word. Wounded? Yes, but fiercely so. Everything was fierce, her hunger, her hurt, even her fear. Perhaps the imp inside her, twice released, was less content to hide beneath her weekday face. Finally, midweek, she gave up the pretence of survival and on the Wednesday dusk dropped down to the tunnel to Mullein's Park.

There was a crowd in the sodium-lit underpass. A conclave of bums. Like dead leaves washed into the gutter by rain, the homeless littered both of the tunnel's curved walls, leaving a narrow alley down the middle. Some stood, some sprawled, most hunkered down. The stink was of old sweat and older piss, of wood smoke and booze, and the sound was a growl of low voices and ruined lungs.

The weird thing was, it wasn't even raining.

Sadie walked by the bleary, crazed, grieving eyes, startled a little way out of her mission, though not much afraid. These men and women were far more likely to be victims than perpetrators – more likely even than she was. Towards the park end, one man in a burn-scarred army coat raised a bottle to her in a toast and said, "Nice night."

"Nice night to be in out of the rain," she said impishly.

He peered at her, then slowly pulled his bottle close to his chest, eyes widening with – what? – shock, fear – recognition – something that shocked Sadie in her turn.

Taking this exchange for encouragement, the woman crouched beside him held out a cupped palm. "Pardon me, ma'am—"

But the man in the burned coat pulled at her arm and whispered in her ear, and she clasped both hands beneath her chin, staring at Sadie with the same wide look.

"Sorry," she said. "Sorry, sorry, sorry. . ." echoing down the tunnel as Sadie hurried to the stairs and climbed into the park.

Not her, the crazy man in the burned coat had said, his voice magnified by the steel walls. *She's one of the hungry ones.*

The sun had shone for a while that afternoon, and now the evening sky was deep and blue above the waking streetlights, the air sharp with the coming frost. People lingered, ordinary folks taking advantage of the fine weather and the unusual absence of beggars. Sadie got a few wary looks (street kid, watch your purse), but nothing to match the tunnel people's eyes. *She's one of the hungry ones.* An after-work jogger pounded along the path, his sweatshirt going from grey to blue to grey again as he passed beneath a lamp, and Sadie felt a surge of dizziness.

The runner goes from grey to blue to grey.
from shadow to man back to shadow
Not her. She's one of the hungry ones.
beard and weathered skin, eyes wet with fear
a button, a bottle, a bear!

Flicker, flicker, like flames catching a draft, just enough seen to make up a dream. What did it mean?
the blood-red wine

Sadie bent double on the path and retched. Too long since she'd eaten, too long since she'd slept. The park was darker now, and emptier. When she spat out the taste of bile and straightened, no one was watching. There was no one near enough to watch. She wiped her mouth, her sweating face. Ran her tongue over her scummy teeth.
She's one of the—

She shook her head, chasing out the lunatic's words and the dizzy delirium they had conjured. Just a crazy bum. Just a street kid too long without food. Too long without friends. She followed the path to a water fountain and drank, filling her belly with a water ballast to keep her steady. Then paced back to where she'd met them before, under the street lamp, gravel gritting under her feet, thread of breeze pattering through the last of the leaves. The park was hemmed in by traffic, yet somehow the trees' bare limbs invoked a kind of silence, a listening quiet, an expectant hush. No peace, though, no tranquillity. Sadie paced the diameter of the circle of light. Traced the circumference. Measured out the geometry of waiting and found it added up to nothing. Nothing.

The imp was jumping inside her skin.

Brisk and sure, as if she knew what she were doing, she left the park. Not through the underpass. Across the street on the other side.

Heading for Mr Nero's house.

There were children everywhere. Innocent witches, monsters, heroes, ghosts, small and colourful, with treasure sacks in their hands. Party guests, Sadie thought, and then she shivered with hot and cold: not children, not in Mr Nero's house. She was confused, she hadn't noticed, or had forgotten, what day it was. What night it was. She tried to remember the taste of chocolate melting on her tongue, and could only conjure the dusky warmth of wine, the scent of honey candles and vanilla foam, sweeter than candy, warmer than the pumpkin lanterns grinning at her from every step. A guardian parent herded his clutch of movie stars and thieves around her, protective as a sheepdog in wolf country, and she realized she was standing in the middle of the sidewalk. Before her, the gate, the narrow walk, the door with the stained glass panel faintly lighted from within. She looked away from the father-shepherd's eyes and headed for the stairs.

Knock? Ring the bell? There was no bell that she could see. Her fist hovered over the half-visible face of the creature in the glass, then touched, knuckle to cool, too softly to make a noise. She stepped close and pressed her ear to the panel. The glass seemed to hum, but to traffic or music or voices inside? Children were shouting up and down the street. Sadie couldn't tell. Her hand closed around the doorknob. She let it turn. The door was open, and she was in.

The party, if there was to be a party tonight (but of course there was) had not started yet.

Halfway up the stairs, she heard voices and paused. Her heart was beating hard, and yet the familiar dark, the scent of beeswax and wine, reassured her. She was even strangely elated. This was not survival, she realized. This was an adventure!

Then a door slammed upstairs and feet clattered in the hall – she was frozen, caught – and Leo was running down the stairs.

"Sadie!" He rocked to a stop one step above her.

She craned her neck to look up at him, unsure if she should laugh or run. "The door was open."

"Christ!" He wiped the back of his hand across his mouth, his eyes staring at someone, something, else. "What the hell are you doing here?"

"Looking for you," she said. Then, hearing how that might sound: "Looking for Rayne."

His eyes did see her then. He rubbed his knuckles against his palm, then reached to put his fingers against her cheek. He was so much taller, and she was a step down. She might have been a child next to him. "Listen, Sadie," he began, very sober.

A man was speaking, coming towards them from the back of the house.

"Shit," said Leo. "Come on." He grabbed her arm and pulled her up the stairs. But in the upper hall they heard a door shut, and footsteps, and Leo, quick as reflex, opened the nearest door and shoved Sadie inside.

"Don't move until I come for you. Don't!"

Then he pulled the door shut and she was standing alone in the dark, listening to what happened on the other side.

Rayne's voice: "You weren't in there, were you?"

Leo's: "No. Well, yes. I do, sometimes, just to look. Don't you?"

Rayne: "Not anymore."

Brief pause.

Leo: "They're waiting."

Rayne: "Leo. . ."

Pause.

Rayne: "I know you're angry at me."

Leo: "I'm not."

Rayne: "I don't blame you. I don't like it either. You don't think I wanted this to happen, do you?"

Leo, sighing: "No."

Rayne: "It was Tom that brought us here."

Leo: "Don't blame Tom! We all wanted to be here. We all wanted. . ."

Rayne: "Yes. We all wanted. And we still do, don't we?"

Long pause.

Rayne: "Don't we?"

Leo: "Yes."

Rayne: "Then Sadie can wear the mask the third time and I—"

Leo, interrupting: "Come on. We're already late."

Footsteps retreating.

*   *   *

Sadie put her back against the door and slid to the floor. I can wear the mask the third time and she. . .what? What?

Light from a street lamp came through the bare window. As her eyes adjusted she began to see the eyes and mouths crowding the room. The mask room. Staring eyes and gaping mouths, mindless, breathless, lifeless. Sadie shuddered, folded her arms around her knees.

They all wanted. . .what?

The masks seemed to hoard what little light there was. Beak, horn, scale, howl, laugh, scream – the night wore all the faces, watching and waiting for someone, for Sadie, to put it on. Put on the night, dancing prince, courtly youth. Sadie, imp, put on the night and run.

Not her. She's one of the hungry ones.

Hungry. Well, she was, as hungry as anyone, as empty. Empty eyes, empty mouths, empty, empty . . . except . . . one? On the table beneath the window, propped on a stand so that it could peer down at Sadie sitting huddled on the floor. Slant-laughing eyes gleamed with lamp-shine, shifted, looked her up and down as a car on the street drove by, headlights shining. Crooked grinning mouth ghost-gleamed with teeth and lapping tongue. A wind tilted through the tree outside and the left eye winked. Sadie, imp, put on the night and run.

Sadie leapt to her feet and slapped at the wall by the door. One mask flew, another, a tick-patter of broken beads. Then her hand found the light switch, and lamps on the walls blinked on.

When Leo came back, she was at the window, watching the groups of children that still prowled the street, although it was getting late. The imp mask was on its face beneath the table.

He slipped through the door and said, "You shouldn't have turned the light on."

"It was dark."

"You don't know what kind of trouble you'd be in if he caught you here. Especially in here." His eyes pointed out the faces on the walls, as if she might have missed them.

"You opened the door."

"I didn't want Rayne to see you. You shouldn't be here!"

"You mean, I shouldn't be here *yet*. Or aren't I supposed to be invited tonight?"

Leo said nothing.

"Why shouldn't Rayne see me? Isn't she my friend?"

It was a challenge. He hissed at her to keep her voice down.

"Well, isn't she?"

Leo pressed his hands to his eyes. His mouth twisted as if he were crying. "Shit. Shit. Shit."

"Leo." Sadie waited for a response, then picked up the imp mask by its ribbon ties and held it out between them. "Leo, what happens when I wear this the third time?"

He pulled his hands away from his face and looked bleakly at the mask. It swivelled on its ties, glaring at the populated walls. He said, "The same thing that happened the first two times."

"And what," her voice was husky, she coughed, "what happened? The first two times?"

"You – we – you led the dance. And the hunt."

The mask was still, staring now at Leo's feet.

"The hunt," Sadie said. "The bear. Only the bear isn't a bear. Is it? Leo?"

He looked old and bitter, his shoulders slumped against the door.

"The third time isn't the same, not really, is it?"

"The same." He licked his lips. "Except after. . .there is no after. You can't take it off. You lead the dance, and the hunt, forever."

"Forever?"

"Until it kills – until something – someone—"

"Until one of you kills me."

"To be free," Leo whispered. "If we ever want to be free again."

They stared at each other. The masks, silent audience, watched. The imp danced, impatient on the end of its ties, as Sadie's hand sank to her side.

"Why?" she said. "Why me?"

"Because Rayne wore it." Leo took a ragged breath, leaned his head against the door and closed his eyes. "Rayne wore it twice. We love it, the dance, the hunt." He sighed. "But you know how it is."

Sadie bit her lips. She knew.

"He loves it too. Mr Nero. He lives for it. Tom realized he was waiting for Rayne to wear it again, to keep it always hunting season, and we – Christ! – we love it but we love her more."

"So you found someone expendable. Someone you didn't care about, who would wear it for her," her voice shrank, "for all of you."

Leo squeezed his eyes tighter, then opened them to meet her gaze. "Yes." He said it simply. "Yes."

Her hand shook, throwing the imp into a giddy spin. "So that's how it is."

"That's how it is."

Silence spilled from the mouths on the walls, loud enough to fill her ears. She began to wonder if she would ever hear, ever speak again. What was there left to say?

Leo said it, pushing himself away from the door. "We're supposed to be going to meet you, but I'll get them into the kitchen. Give me a couple of minutes, then get down the stairs as quietly as you can and out the door." He reached for the handle. "Two minutes. Got it?"

"But," Sadie said. "But."

"Just do me a favour." He looked at her, and his eyes were narrowed, his teeth showing, it was so hard for him to say. "Take that thing with you. Burn it and wash the ashes down the drain. Can you do that for me, Sadie?"

She took a long, stuttering breath. The imp's ties were tangled in her fingers. Its chin nuzzled against her leg.

"Sadie?"

"Yes."

He nodded and opened the door. "Two minutes."

Then he was gone.

Down the stairs, out the door, running light-footed into the street. The night air was sharp and cold. There was a moon cruising white among remnant clouds, only a few children's voices crying the sweet seasonal choice. Trick or treat? Sadie ran, the imp gyrating on the end of its ribbons, ran because she could, because her blood was on fire and she needed to gulp the cooling air. Free again.

Leo! she wanted to shout. Rayne! Tom!

Free!

Across the street and into the park. There were no children here. Folded into darkness, she slowed to a jog, to a walk. To a halt. For a moment she'd forgotten how hungry she was. Her head whirled. The imp mask nudged her leg.

Burn it and wash the ashes down the drain. Fine. All she needed was something to light it with, something to help it burn. And then . . .

And then?

"Sex-y Sa-die."

That damn stupid bit of song.

"Sex-y Sa-die."

The call of the hunter who stalks his game through the dark. She flinches, deep inside. But the imp, ah, the imp does so love to dance – to hunt. The mask's ribbons still tangled in her fingers, she turns, slow and graceful as a line of music, gravel biting under her heel.

BRIAN HODGE

If I Should Wake Before I Die

BRIAN HODGE LIVES IN Boulder, Colorado. He is the author of ten novels and close to 100 short stories and novellas – all told, roughly two million words and counting.

His recent works include *Hellboy: On Earth As It is in Hell* (Pocket Books) and the short novel *World of Hurt* (Earthling Publications). Forthcoming titles include his next crime novel, *Mad Dogs*, and his fourth story collection, *A Loving Look of Agony*, both from Cemetery Dance Publications.

An avid home studio rat, he was also the first musical guest on a recent CD-ROM version of *Dark Recesses* magazine. For this, he worked up two new extended tracks of industrial and atmospheric music and sound design, interests that influenced the story that follows.

"I'd promised a story to Nancy Holder and Nancy Kilpatrick for their *Outsiders* anthology," Hodge explains, "but with a month to go before the deadline, didn't have anything yet.

"So I did what I sometimes do: took off one day with no fixed agenda, just trusting that I would blunder into the right story. I was wandering around Denver on a chilly, rainy, early spring morning and saw some balloons snagged in the top of a tree next to a cathedral bell tower. That did it. I headed for a coffee house and got to work."

M Y WRITING THIS CAN ONLY BE REGARDED as a tremendous act of faith. That I believe you will not only live to be born and see the world outside my belly, but that you'll reach an age when you

can read this cumulative letter and understand what a miracle all of
that will have been.

And I don't use the word *miracle* lightly. Used to, I was the type to
roll my eyes whenever I heard prospective parents talk of their
fertilized egg as being something miraculous. Cause for rejoicing,
sure. But a miracle? It just didn't seem to qualify. It's the most natural
thing in the world, something that happens somewhere every moment of the day. But then, that goes back to something said by Albert
Einstein (and you'd better have studied him in school by now!): that
we can live as if nothing is a miracle, or as if everything is. Okay, so
you got me there. Still, I don't think I felt any different about
pregnancy-as-miracle even after the doctor confirmed what the
pharmacy test kit and I already knew.

But times change, my little one. In ways we can't possibly foresee.

We'll have to continue this later. It's morning, and I have to get
things together for school, and don't take this personally, because I
thought we were past all of this months ago, but you're making me
sick.

Today was bad. But maybe now you'll better understand why I'm
frightened enough to need this ongoing show of faith that soon I will
see your beautiful squalling face.

Like most people, I've made a habit of not looking up. Sure, the
sky could fall – but in my experience most of the things you really
have to worry about live at ground level, so that's where you keep
your eyes. Just by being watchful, I've thwarted two muggings in the
past year alone, me and my trusty canister of pepper spray.

But this afternoon I looked up . . . had to, my attention drawn by
the sight of deflated balloons high in some oaks, a splash of color
against the slate sky and stark branches, their tiny buds struggling
against the ice after a false spring. Helium-filled runaways, let go by
the careless hands of children during some function or other on the
grounds of St Mark's. I walk past the place twice each weekday, to
and from school. It's the most peaceful route I can find, keeps me
away from the busier streets and the incessant traffic noise that seems
impossible to escape when you just want to think. So the balloons
caught my eye, hanging before twin belltowers that, if you must
know, preside over the crack dealers and prostitutes two streets over.
Hanging up there, they made me think of souls lost halfway to
heaven.

And they were the only reason I saw the girl before she jumped.
She stood in one of the high, narrow openings near the top of the

closer tower, portals through which the bells peal each Sunday to call whatever flock remains. All I saw was a pale face and an indistinct body framed by rough grey stone. When she nudged one foot into empty space, at first I thought she was only reckless.

Our eyes met then, I think – she did seem to look down in my direction. So was this her cue to jump? To do it before anyone could try talking her out of it? I took it that way, but then (not to speak ill of your grandparents) I was born and raised for guilt.

No scream, from either of us. It was a remarkably quiet death. I stared at her all the way down, past seventy-odd feet of stone. She didn't thrash, and even seemed to fall in slow motion. I barely heard the impact over the traffic two streets over.

Maybe she lived for a moment, or maybe not. Certainly there was no life left by the time I reached her. Kneeling beside her hip, I tried to ignore the blood seeping from the back of her skull onto the walkway. Her face, fragile and too young, looked oddly peaceful and resolved, her eyes half-open.

I put one hand on her belly – flat, definitely flatter than mine right now, but the skin felt slack and loose, as recently deflated as one of those balloons overhead. For me, it was as good as a signed suicide note. There was no baby in a crib somewhere. It lay like wax in a fresh little grave. Or worse, if she'd miscarried early enough, it became hospital waste, incinerated with wrappings and tumors.

"I'm so sorry for you," I told her. "I felt like doing this too, after I lost mine."

So few of you seem to make it out of the third trimester these days.

The hand I held must have been cold even before death, and didn't squeeze back.

And to be totally honest with you, I still can't say whether or not I would've given in to my despair had it not been for you. You and I may have lost your twin, but because you'd hung in there and survived, I knew there was something yet to live for.

I told about the jumper at group tonight, to a rapt and silent audience. At group, it goes without saying: we've *all* been up in that bell tower. If only for a few moments, we've all looked down and stuck a foot into empty space. All of the women, and maybe a few of the men, too, the guys who haven't been too stoic to admit they need the support of strangers after their hopes for fatherhood came unexpectedly slithering out in an ill-formed mass from between the thighs of their wives and girlfriends.

I'm very aware that I'm sometimes describing things in a way that no mom should describe them to her child, at any age . . . but why sugarcoat it? Along with love and care, I owe you truth: You're struggling for life in a perilous time, just as I'm struggling to maintain hope.

About the jumper, a woman named Danika said, "Ain't nobody should die alone that way. Did you get to her in time?" Danika's been coming to group for a month. "Did she say anything at the end?"

"Just barely," I told her, and in the silence of our borrowed classroom you could hear the slightest creak. "She asked me to forgive her. Because she knew it was wrong. I know I don't look anything like a nun, but maybe she thought I was from the church."

We'd all stood in the balance and wavered, then chosen life.

But for some, I suspect that the debate still isn't entirely settled.

Group – ah, yes. What seems so thoroughly a part of my life right now will, I hope, by the time you're reading this, be just a distant memory.

Citywide, these past months, support groups have become a way of life, a spontaneous network arising to meet a growing need. They meet in church basements, in classrooms, in fraternal halls and civic centers. Their attendees drink lots of coffee and smoke lots of cigarettes, because now, for them, there's no reason not to. They find themselves in the heartbreaking position of suddenly having no unborn to think of.

Except for me. Even in groups bound together to survive losses that we don't understand, I don't entirely fit in. If any other woman out there is in my position, lucky enough to still be carrying a surviving twin, I haven't heard of her.

How else to describe what's going on but as a wave of spontaneous abortions? Pregnancies failing first by the handful, then by the dozens, an epidemic that cuts across all ethnic groups, all income levels, that reaches into urban and suburban wombs alike. It continues to stymie the Department of Public Health as much today as after that first spike in the miscarriage rate . . . which I was part of, dismally enough. The Centers for Disease Control is here, but has yet to find any evidence of one. Nothing in the water, nothing in the air, nothing in the tissues scraped for tests. No genetic abnormalities in a thousand sperm samples; no toxins contaminating the food supply. Or, should I say, nothing worse than usual, still within the "safe" levels allowed by law – but I *am* thinking of you, trying to eat organic whenever I can afford it.

I started attending group on the north side while staying with my parents after the miscarriage that robbed us of your brother. At the time, it was a way to get out of the house for a couple hours to escape my parents' habit of tiptoeing around me as if I were china poised to shatter.

Except that first group was just as bad, in its own way. Yes, they all knew how I felt. I knew how all of them felt. We understood one another . . . to a point. But I wasn't one of them, not anymore, if ever, and they knew it. Knew it in my clothes, my hair. I imagine they thought I'd just strayed into the wrong neighborhood, with no idea that I remembered what it was like to grow up among them.

You'd think that a thing like a plague of miscarriages would be enough to tear down the walls of pretense, to let us at least see eye to eye on our shared tragedies. You'd think our differences wouldn't matter, but they did. Oh, the others were polite enough. They're often polite. But as we traded tales of sorrow and struggle, I couldn't help but notice an undercurrent of judgment, so many of these inwardly sneering women seeming to believe that they had lost so much more. *My child would have had potential*, they might as well have said. *What would your child have been but an eventual burden on the rest of us?*

I hadn't told them about you, you see. I wasn't showing as much then as I am now. So I'm glad I hadn't said anything about you, because while they could pass judgment on me all they wanted, how dare they judge you. How dare they think they know you, your future, your dreams and your determination. By the time you're reading these pages, I hope I've told you this so often it's running out of your ears, but here it is for the very first time: *You can be anything you want to be.* Me, I'm working on it. I know there are plenty of people who'd say that if all I am at this stage in my life is an underpaid teacher and unwed mother, then I haven't exactly set the world on fire.

To that, I'd just say that it seems to burn quite well on its own.

So. While I didn't like this particular group, I found the idea of a support group in general to be very therapeutic, and found the fit much better much closer to home. Where we meet isn't nearly as nice – of course not; it's a classroom in a public school, one district over from where I teach. The paint may peel and the ceiling tiles may have huge brown water stains, but from the moment I walked in, I could tell that nobody was going to care if in my off-hours I still had a stubborn streak or two about totally outgrowing the aesthetics of my malcontented youth.

Please don't take that as a license to make my life miserable someday. I prefer to delude myself into thinking that with me as your mother, you won't have anything to rebel against.

You're giving me a terribly restless night, I hope you know. We should be asleep right now. I'm game. But you, at two a.m., are evidently competing in a swimming meet. Let's blame it on the neighbors, shall we? Somebody fired off a gunshot and you mistook it for a starter pistol.

But I don't begrudge you your recreational activities one bit, for reasons that should be obvious.

You know something . . .? The strangest thing for me about this letter is that I'm writing to someone who doesn't have a name yet. For that matter, your gender is a mystery as well. I haven't wanted to know, and the few who do are under strict orders to not say a word. I want surprises, the kind of good old-fashioned surprises that went out of style after doctors gained the ability to peek inside and see what I've been growing all these months.

Odds are, you're a boy. But maybe not. If you and the brother we'll sadly never know were identical twins, of course you're a boy. But if you were fraternal twins, well, we're back to a toss-up again, aren't we?

So for now, I just think of you as the Tadpole.

What your non-amphibian name should be fills me with constant soul-searching. I half suspect that our destinies are intrinsically tied into our names, as if these are templates imposed for us to fill. If my parents hadn't named me Melody, would I still have gone into music? Who knows, and maybe I overstate the case – those who can't do, teach, right? Well, all I have to say to that is: *you* try making a living off talent alone when your repertoire rarely extends much past 1790.

So I'm sure there will come a point when you find it thoroughly humiliating that your mom's great sustaining passion, besides her brilliant and talented child of course, is a batch of instruments with names like recorder and schreierpfeif and crumhorn.

Say, that reminds me of an Early Music joke: what's the difference between a crumhorn and a lawn mower? You can tune a lawn mower.

Someday you'll appreciate just how funny that really is.

Who knows if we'll still be doing it when you're old enough to humiliate, but for now, I'm with a group of like-minded women who specialize in the hits of the late medieval era and beyond. The Hedgewaifs, we call ourselves, and our performances have begun to attract a devoted little following, although there's endless debate about whether that's because of the music or what we wear to perform in. Well, we do make quite a fetching quintet, in our lace and corsets and dark lipstick.

Whenever we play or practice, I'm sure that in each of us it scratches different itches. For my friend Heather (she plays the viola da gamba, and can't wait to meet you), it's the best way to shut out the rest of the world. She grew up in a factory town, where even her dreams were filled with the sounds of machinery, so taking up a horsehair bow was her way of driving them back.

For myself, our music recalls a different age, in which I can at least imagine there was more civility than today. That's important, civility. You wouldn't think I could miss it so badly, an age I never even knew. Oh, but I do. Especially on days like today, after encounters like the one this afternoon.

After school, I went to my favorite used record/CD shop to see if I could find a few things I wanted for class. Buried treasures always seem to await there, which makes it worth straying into the block it's in. A few doors away, I walked past this guy who wasn't doing much of anything, just leaning against a grimy brick wall and smelling of whatever he'd been drinking during the day. He noticed me, I could tell. If you live here, you can't help but develop this radar; you *know* when somebody's just decided to include you in his day, in all the wrong ways. He looked at me – looked down at *you*, actually – and here's what he said:

"So. Haven't lost it yet, have you?"

I had no idea what to say to that. Not that it deserved a response. He went on: "Maybe later. Looks like there's still time."

The thing that got me is that he didn't even say this with any particular scorn. It was so flat and without affect, as if all the losses going on around him were complete trivialities. What kind of deadness is at the heart of a person when he thinks that's an acceptable thing to say to someone?

He's far from alone, too. This may have been the most face-to-face it's been, but I've been encountering these kinds of sentiments for months. They're in homemade signs, in graffiti, even in new music from local artists . . . an undercurrent that seems to regard this death-of-innocents as some answer to a prayer for population control. I've seen the most terrible clinical pictures reproduced on flyers, with the most terrible slogans, actually celebrating what's going on.

We're getting it from both sides by now, too. Let one woman

miscarry, and she's treated with sympathy. Let it happen to a thousand, and we're often shunned as defective, or contagious. Or those who claim to have a direct link to God's brain shout at the top of their lungs that we're undergoing the cleansing of his latest judgmental wrath, one final warning before he toasts the rest of us from the face of the earth.

Awfully considerate of him, don't you think?

I've just now taken enough of a breather to realize what I'm saying and who I'm saying it to. Shame on me. I shouldn't be venting to you before you're even born. So if you're reading this someday and wonder what the black marker scratch-outs are all about, trust me, the letter has been censored to protect you from wondering what the hell was wrong with Mom back then.

Hi, Tadpole. My little miracle worker.

I've heard of people becoming addicted to support groups, and have been hoping that that isn't what impels me to go as often as I do, but I've finally realized the appeal. Out in the world, I'm just another one of the growing number of defectives. But at group, because I have you, I'm a beacon of hope. It doesn't matter what I've lost. I'm the glass that's still half-full, rather than half-empty.

I just thought you should know how deeply you've touched a couple dozen lives already, before you've even drawn your first breath.

And if there's anything that's needed now, it's hope. Group wasn't especially supportive tonight. It's nobody's fault. We were just preoccupied with the news that the miscarriages are spreading. At first it was local. Now we're the epicenter, the red dot on the map surrounded by concentric rings.

A thousand times a day I wrap my arms around the bulge you've made of my belly, trying to hold you inside me. There are even times I think I'd rather keep you there forever, where it's safe and warm and snug, away from what's waiting for you on this side. This machine out here that only wants you to be one more tooth in its grinding gears.

I wish I could play now, for both of us, to take our minds off what's going on, but it's too late at night. I know the reaction it would bring: hostile pounding on the ceiling over our heads from, yes, the very same upstairs neighbor who thinks nothing of blasting his TV six hours at a stretch, so loud I can sometimes tell what he's watching. He has a name, I'm sure, but I just like to refer to him by a word you're not allowed to speak until you're twenty-five.

Goodnight, Tadpole. Feel free to dogpaddle around tonight, a little. You and I are as close right now as two people can be, which makes it all the more difficult to explain how alone I feel sometimes.

It's my free period at school, so we don't have much time, but I'm wondering:

Just what do you *hear* inside there?

In one sense you're a world away, yet I also have to remember that there's only a few layers of me between you and the world that's waiting. All in all, that's much less insulation than what's protecting us from the neighbors.

I remember the doctor telling me that you – not just you, but all of your short, damp, wrinkly kind – hear a constant soft rush of the blood as it's pumped through my body. But you wouldn't just hear it, would you . . . you'd be enveloped by it.

So I wonder what else you hear. Everything, I imagine, as long as it's loud enough. Maybe it sounds muffled and watery, like hearing something going on beside a swimming pool while you were sunk a foot or two under. But you'd hear it.

This is really starting to concern me lately. Like, I'll walk by a construction site near my school, and the earthmovers will be scraping away, or some worker will have a jackhammer going, and I'll wonder, "Oh, what must Tadpole think of that?"

Because you have no context for these things. You've never seen them. You've never had them explained to you. You just know what they sound like, somewhere on the other side of the wall.

If it seems like I'm fixated on this, we can thank Danika for it. Remember her, one of the women at group? The other night she got to talking about the day before her loss, something I hadn't heard about before. She lives in the flight path near the airport, and on the day in question, a commuter plane crashed two blocks away. So for hours, her neighborhood was this ungodly riot of sirens and fire trucks and ambulances and wreckage equipment, and all the screaming and shouting that goes along with them.

Danika blamed her miscarriage on the stress of that day.

Sometimes, when I think of everything you must hear, I think that all of us out here have so much to apologize for.

Like I said, support group is a way of life these days.

But now you attend at your peril.

I told you how the miscarriages were spreading beyond? Well, they just keep going. The way they've spread, you'd suspect there was something viral about it, except nobody has managed to find a single thing to indicate that. Which hasn't stopped some people from jumping to the conclusion anyway. They come in from miles away and they look at us here, the first ones affected, as having caused it. They want someone to blame for their own losses, and we're the most convenient Typhoid Marys.

They firebombed the locations of two groups earlier tonight. Not mine, and nobody was hurt, but the ignorance and hatefulness in such an act is beyond my comprehension. I've been watching it on the news and wondering if this is the way of the future for us now . . . we've lost our babies so now we're pariahs, and the only response is to drive us away, into hiding or extinction.

I don't know what's worse: trying to get this all out of my system by telling you about it, or sitting here dwelling on it. Either way, it feels like I'm putting you at risk, that it will seep into you.

We can't have that. You keep me going, you know?

You're much too little to lean on, but you still keep me going.

Do you dream, Tadpole? Do you *dream* in there?

If we can watch cats and dogs while they're asleep, with their paws twitching and their mouths smacking, and accept that they must be dreaming, then why not unborn babies? You just wouldn't dream like the rest of us, would you? You couldn't dream about things you could see, because you haven't seen anything yet. You haven't smelled or tasted anything, either, so you couldn't dream about those. You can only feel and hear. That's all your developing mind has to work with.

Maybe now I know what it's like, a little, because last night I had a dream like that. I dreamed of what it must be like to be you, in the only place you've ever known, curled up all warm and wet, in the complete absence of light. I was *inside* myself, I guess . . . literally. And it felt wonderful, until the noise began and it all started to get oppressive, as if everything was shrinking around me . . . like I was in a duffel bag and someone had cinched the opening and was twisting it around and around, squeezing me into a smaller and smaller space. And the whole time there was no getting away from the noise, this huge screeching roar that revved and pulsated and just went on and on and on . . .

Did *you* dream that, Tadpole? Was that *your* dream in there?

We share things all the time. Oxygen, nutrition, blood, going back and forth between us. With so intimate an exchange going on, why not a dream?

I woke up and you were kicking, but it wasn't quite like any kicking that I can remember. It wasn't . . . strong. More like you were flailing weakly about in there, or just trembling. In five seconds I went from being sound asleep to being absolutely terrified, so I did the only thing I could think to do: got my mellowest recorder, a tenor made of maple wood, and tried to serenade you, tell you somehow that everything was all right . . . and who cares if Mr A **hole upstairs hears and thinks it's after-hours.

It seemed to work and you quieted down, so we could go back to sleep. Except by then the damage was done. Not to you, to *me*. Next it was my turn to come up with bad dreams. Should I tell you? You'll think I'm silly if I tell you. You'll be disappointed if I don't.

Very well . . .

I was in the classroom where we have group, okay, but it was obvious nobody had been in the room for a very long time. Nobody came here to learn, nobody came here to mourn. Nobody came here at all anymore. All that was left was a lot of dust and a couple empty chairs. I was sitting at a desk in the very center of the room, both feet on the floor and facing forward, the way we rigid teachers expect you to sit. And then *you* came in . . . crawled in, actually. You couldn't have been more than several months old. I watched you crawl across the front of the room, then turn the corner and crawl down the length of the room at my left side. The whole time, you were moving along the baseboard, stopping to eat the paint chips flaking from the walls. Do they even use lead-based paint anymore? I don't think so, but it didn't matter, because the place was so old. I kept trying to tell you not to put them in your mouth, but you never seemed to hear me. You just kept going until you moved out of sight, behind me, into the back half of the room. I could see the trail you'd left in the dust, and every now and then I'd hear you eat something else, so I waited for you to come around into view again, on the right side of the room. Except you never did. And I couldn't turn around to see where you were and what had become of you . . . because nobody had given me permission.

If we're sharing dreams, I hope it's a one-way connection, that *that* one didn't seep through to you, along with the soy milk I had before bedtime.

And you're probably wondering again, aren't you: What the hell *was* wrong with Mom back then?

Don't judge her too harshly. I think she was afraid she was poisoning you, just by being alive.

*   *   *

If anyone knew how many support groups I've attended lately, they'd think there was something wrong with me. That I'm developing an unhealthy obsession, unable to function without them. True, that's about all my life is lately – school and group.

But I call it something else: research.

I started out by asking the question at my own group. Then, night after night, I've been going to another, and another, and another. I'll walk up and be sure to thank the cop or security guard on duty, assigned to look after the place and protect it from attacks. They don't seem to have them covered 100%, except on the north side, but it's better than nothing.

It isn't just loss groups anymore, either. Now there are meetings for pregnant women who still have their babies, praying they won't have to change groups.

I can go to either one, and belong.

I'm quiet at first, the way newcomers are. Even within tiny, temporary societies founded on grief and fear, there are unwritten rules, taboos you don't break. I listen to their heartbreaking stories, their outpouring of anguish. The voices may be new, but I've heard their stories already. There can be only so many variations.

After a while, they make room for me, ready to accept me because I've been respectful, so I tell my own version . . . or part of it. Whether or not I say much about you depends on the group. Sometimes I get the feeling that they'd think I was gloating, so I say as little as possible. Other times I know how much hope you'll bring, so you're front and center in more ways than one. I've gotten good at judging the moods of these groups.

And finally, when I sense that I can, I'll ask the question: "Do you/ did you ever get the feeling that your babies are/were dreaming?"

Some of them look at me like they think I'm crazy. Others, it's obviously the first time they've considered this, but they don't necessarily dismiss it. And others . . . I can tell just by looking into their eyes that they've felt it too. They know exactly what I'm talking about, each woman thinking it was something unique to her, or that it was her imagination, and that nobody has quite brought it up before.

So we talk about the experiences that everyone's had, and, in fewer instances, whatever impressions we felt were shared between our babies and ourselves. There are variations; I'd expect this. But compared to the dream of yours that I felt I tapped into, they're all much more alike than not.

My God, all of you, you tiny things, you're in there, and you've grown terrified at what you hear waiting for you, haven't you?

"So they've been letting go," a woman said tonight, the conclusion she'd drawn. This was the first I've heard it spoken aloud, but maybe it's something that many of us, deep down, have intuited. Because for all the tests, all the theories, nobody has come up with an explanation for this plague, much less a way to stop it.

And I think that's about as far as anyone was willing to go tonight. But what I want to know is: If it's true you're letting go by the dozens, by the hundreds, *who told you how*? Who told you all that you *could*? Who gave you *permission*?

So now I keep wondering what would've happened if I hadn't awakened the other night, if I'd remained asleep and so had you, without me to serenade and reassure you, knowing what you were dreaming in there: the noise and the compression, squeezed before your time . . . like garbage in a truck. In such a dark place, experiencing the first dreams you've ever had, how could you possibly distinguish between what's real and what isn't?

And from all the way out here, how can I possibly protect you every moment?

No school today. For me, that is. For everyone else it's education as usual.

I did get halfway there. Walking, like normal. I've always maintained it's good for us . . . me and my Tadpole, out for a stroll. Ever since the jumper, though, I've been detouring from the usual route. My mistake. Keep going by the bell towers, and all I would have had to contend with is a daily reminder of what that poor girl did in front of me.

The block I was in is kind of run-down, but then, close to home, they all are; it's just that this one wears its age in a more picturesque way. There's a deli that's been in the same family for four generations, and a flower shop run by a woman old enough to have diapered at least three of those generations from the deli. I wasn't even there yet, just crossing the street, when I started to hear someone crying. I wasn't quite sure where it was coming from, just that it was getting louder, and seeming to echo off the bricks.

Before I saw even saw her, I knew where she must've been, because by then a little crowd had gathered, so as I came up, I was thinking, "Well, surely somebody's with her, somebody must be taking care of this . . ."

Except nobody was.

She sat at the bottom of a stairwell leading up to some second-floor apartments, half-in and half-out of the doorway, one leg tucked underneath her as she sat beneath a row of mailboxes, one hand hanging onto the doorknob. And the other . . .

The main thing I remember is the bright red stain seeping through the yellow fabric bunched around her waist.

Somebody pointed and laughed, I recall that much. Everyone else, once they had the idea, they went on their way. Conversations resumed, footsteps quickened to be away from her. I wanted to help, I really did, and I know that I would have if she could've just *shut up* for a minute, but instead she kept crying, and crying, and . . .

I didn't want you exposed to it, I guess. So I did an about-face, turning around to go home. I looked over my shoulder once, at the end of the block, and could see her arm still reaching out of the doorway.

All in all, not one of my prouder moments.

So it's just you and me today. Maybe all the rest of this week. The way I feel right now, maybe until after you're born.

The thing that gets me, though, is that no matter how hard I try, when I think back to that final glance I had of the woman in the doorway, with just her arm visible, I can't quite remember if she was still beckoning for help . . . or pointing. At us.

Which probably wouldn't be a big deal at all, if it weren't for that stupid dream I had last night, about you whispering something in your brother's ear. Just before . . . well, you know.

That's just me being silly, right? First-time pregnancy jitters and everything?

All I want is to keep clinging to the same reassuring hopes that every woman has for her baby: That you can be anything you want to be. That instead of being forced to bend to the world's will, you can make it bend to yours. That you can plant your ideas like seeds, and they'll take root and spread like wildfire. That you'll discover your own way to make things better.

Except right now I can't help but wonder: have you started that already?

Come on, Tadpole . . . tell me I'm just being neurotic. Because the more I think about this morning, the clearer it seems to me that the woman in the doorway really was pointing at us. In accusation. I mean, for a moment there, I saw her eyes. But why would she do that? What did we ever do to her?

So come on, Tadpole. Tell me I'm just stressed out. That you didn't talk your brother into letting go. Not with a whisper, but with a dream. Tell me that if I check with the doctors and demand to know, they won't tell me he wasn't merely *one* of the first to be lost . . . but *the* first. That you haven't dreamed a dream so dreadful it echoes on and on.

Tell me nothing went wrong in there. I only want you to be normal.

Okay, all this is destined for the black marker. But I feel so much better getting it off my chest.

Remember our Einstein: "There are only two ways to live your life: as though nothing is a miracle, or as though everything is a miracle."

To me, in this world, every day that you and I have together is a miracle. When you're born, I promise to celebrate you as one. No matter what.

Until then, I promise to keep serenading you, to tell you how much you're loved and that everything will be all right . . . or I'll try to, at least. Lately there seems to be something terribly wrong, either with my playing or with my instruments. I never knew they could make these kinds of ghastly noises.

But you seem to like it anyway.

It perks you right up, and you dance until I'm sick.

ROBERTA LANNES

The Other Family

ROBERTA LANNES IS A NATIVE of Southern California, where she has been teaching high school English, along with fine and digital art, for thirty-three years.

Her first horror story was written and sold in Dennis Etchison's UCLA extension course in "Writing Horror Fiction" and appeared his anthology *The Cutting Edge* in 1985. Since then she has been widely published in the science fiction, fantasy and horror genres. She also has every intention of finally finishing her novels as retirement from teaching approaches.

In 1994, film-maker Ian Kerkhof made an award-winning "docu-drama" entitled *Ten Monologues from the Lives of Serial Killers*, using the writings of William S. Burroughs, Roberta Lannes, Charles Manson and Henry Rollins.

As the author explains: "'The Other Family' grew out of my absolute greatest supernatural fear – being trapped in an alternate or parallel universe, able to observe but not interact with the universe from whence I came.

"As a child with the same fears as most children (the boogie man, the creature under the bed), I was curious as to where these monsters originated. It was an innocent comment by someone, I don't recall who, that these things came from a parallel universe; that they could cross over and take you into their world and you were lost forever.

"During a trip when I was nine-years-old with my family to a beach resort in Oregon, with its foggy days and string of cottages lining the shore, a child went missing from a neighbouring cottage. She was found before we left, but I believed for that time she'd been taken by the thing under the bed.

"It all came together after a visit with my husband to his former home in Cumbria – seeing the cottages line the sand where the ocean had receded far into the distance. I knew this story belonged in England."

S IXTEEN SEASHELLS RATTLED and sloshed in Madeline's bucket as she wobbled over the sand from the shoreline. The shovel in her little hand was a yellow flag she waved at her parents sitting on the veranda. Her mother set her book down in her lap and stretched. Her father pushed his glasses up his nose and went back to making one of his driftwood sculptures. Madeline put the bucket and shovel down at the bottom of the steps.

"Mum, I saw a crab! It walked sideways!"

Her mother put her thumb and forefinger to her forehead and shielded her eyes as she went down the steps. She scanned the beach in front of their cottage for Nicholas, Madeline's older brother. Her pale shirt and shorts waffled in the breeze.

"Mum, look, I've got lots of shells!" Madeline held the bucket up, the blue plastic handle straining from the weight of shells, sand and water.

"Yes, my, look at all of those. You can clean them up and sell them at the street fair the week after we get home on Sunday."

"Can I? Oh, yes, please, Mum."

"Where's your brother, Maddie?"

Madeline looked up at her Mum, then to the beach. Nicholas had been wading in the cold water, periodically scooping up froth and flinging it at Madeline. He'd tortured her with seaweed dangled over her back and slapped wet sand on her head when they were wading. No one scolded him from the cottage veranda; no one tramped down to the water and hauled Nicholas back to his room. Madeline wasn't at all happy he was getting away with his mischief. And now Mum wanted to know where he was! He'd been there when she'd turned to take her shells to Mum and Dad.

"I don't see him, Mummy. Is he swimming very far? You said no swimming because we've just had lunch."

The shoreline was dotted with the occasional child and parent, but few people were out on the beach in a hazy day like this one. They went for drives in the nearby countryside instead. The townsfolk who lived in the cottages and rented them for summer had gone to Italy or Spain. The families on holiday were beginning to leave at the end of the season, so many of the houses were standing empty, awaiting their owners.

"Frank, I'm going to look for Nicholas. He's not in the water and I can't see him on the beach. He might have sneaked up the beach to one of the vacant houses. It's like him."

"Right, then, Hildy, I'll watch Maddie." Madeline's father smiled down at her then turned back to his artwork.

"Mum, can't I come with you?"

Her mother wrung her hands, looked back and forth along the shoreline. "I think it's best you stay here. I don't want two lost children."

That made no sense to Madeline. If she was with her Mum, how could she be lost? She watched her mother amble off down the wooden planked walkway that strung together the steps to each of the cottages along the strand. Her mother's short, cropped hair spiked into the air as she walked into the breeze. She held herself, as if she was cold.

"Maddie, come up on the veranda and show me your shells."

Madeline jammed the shovel into the sand and stood up. She lugged her bucket up the steps and padded over the wooden veranda to her father's worktable. She set the bucket down and peeked over the tabletop.

"Is it a bird?" She fiddled with her hair.

He grinned. "Yes, it's an egret. If I'm lucky, I find driftwood that already looks like something. This one looked like a bird right off."

Madeline picked up some gnarled bits of wood. "This one looks like a snail. And that one looks like an angel."

Her father pointed to her tanned face. "You are going to be an artist like your father, Maddie. You have a good eye."

Madeline touched one eye. "Is it this one?" Her father laughed heartily. "What's so funny?"

"You are."

Maddie watched him whittling and sanding his piece, pleased she might grow up and be like her father with a good eye. After a few minutes, she forgot about Nicholas and her mum.

Nicholas was still quiet from all the shouting his father did before supper. Madeline crawled into the bed next to him. He was moping. He didn't like being told off, especially in front of his little sister. He always said she was the good one, always got away with stuff. She knew how wrong he was. She was sent to her room for touching Nicholas's things, for going into his room without permission, for watching television when she was supposed to be doing schoolwork. No one ever swatted his bottom for using Mum's make-up or letting the dog chew on her moccasins. And then there were the days following their arrival to the cottage. Mum and Dad hadn't seemed to care one way or the other who did what to whom, until someone disappeared.

"Where did you go, Nic?"

"Go to sleep, you little twit." He rolled away from her.

"I'm just curious. Mum looked scared and Dad was really angry." Nicholas made mocking whining noises, then went quiet again.

Their Mum came to the door. "Are you two going to need a blanket?"

Madeline rose up on her elbow, looked at Nic, then sighed. "Nic's upset. But, I'm all right. Would you read me a story?"

"Nicholas, you and I will be on the bus home tomorrow if you keep this up. You ran off and scared us silly, and you're going to stay *in* this house until Saturday." Then her tone changed completely. "Maddie, sweetheart, Mummy is tired. I'll read to you another night, all right?"

Nicholas breathed deeply and sighed, but said nothing.

"Okay." Madeline was petulant. Mum and Dad were just not as fun as they usually were on their holiday. They barely talked to each other. Nicholas acted as though he knew something she didn't, but Madeline didn't know what question to ask to find out what it was. This time, Mum was always reading or cooking or staring at the sea, and Daddy did his sculptures, went for a swim without them, and grumbled about the fog when it came in. She could recall the last time they holidayed at one of the cottages listening to her parents laughing and playing cards after she and Nic had been put to bed, the sound of the bedsprings above them and howling from tickle fights. They went into town as a family and shopped and had ice cream with Flakes. This holiday was boring and endlessly long.

Mum closed the door and the hall light went off. The sky was still light and cast the room in an amber glow. Madeline lay back and stared at the ceiling. There were shadows and streaks of light that moved with the sheer curtains. They made her think of fairies and sprites.

This was the third year coming to the seaside. Madeline liked this cottage. It was cleaner and had nice new furniture. Now that she was eight, she could appreciate it. She was allowed to swim without a rubber ring, and collect things and even though Nicholas was supposed to be watching her, she could wander off when he was distracted. Not like last time when her mother stuck to their sides like cockles. Some kids had disappeared so all the parents were playing with their children, not allowing them out of their sight. Nicholas was miserable then. But he was miserable now, too. He was twelve; too old to have to take care of a "baby".

She must have fallen asleep, because when she looked up to the ceiling next, it was dark. The curtains were still. Madeline put her hand out on the bed where Nic slept beside her. He was gone. Slipping out of bed, she crept to the hall and went to the kitchen and living area. She was afraid to call out for him. Her parents would wake and he'd be in trouble again.

The light was eerie, undulating; a full moon bristling off the ocean was cast on the walls. Madeline went to the window by the front door and peered out. The beach was barren, the water bright beneath the moon. Her tummy tightened and she swallowed hard. If Nicholas wasn't in the bedroom, the kitchen or living area, he had to be in the bathroom upstairs. She waited at the bottom of the stairs. But Nicholas didn't come down.

Madeline had to find him, bring him back. The trouble he would be in, well, she could just imagine how much worse the holiday would get. She went to the front door and out. The air was faintly musty and moist, bright with moonlight. A bank of fog that threatened far off on the horizon glowed like a string of lights in a mist. The T-shirt she'd worn to sleep clung to her thighs as she went down the steps to the boardwalk. She glanced up to the bedroom window where her parents slept. She had to find Nic before morning so that they were both found waking in their bed.

Which direction would Nicholas go, she wondered. Towards town or away? She chose away and stepped gingerly over the splintered wood walkway in her bare feet. She whispered his name as she went. She stared at the dark faces of each cottage, not knowing if there were people inside or the place was hollow.

A huge Victorian mansion stood at the end of the wooden path. There were lights on in the highest tower room. Madeline stared up at it, willing Nicholas to appear, see her there and wave, happy to see her. Instead, the lights went out. The house was the only one on the strand with an ironwork fence around it. Nicholas wouldn't have found a way in, and besides, it was a scary-looking thing.

She turned back, walking quickly, more afraid. The air seemed very still. A splinter from a wooden plank caught her big toe and Madeline stopped. She pulled her foot up, but her own shadow kept the splinter from clear sight. She felt for it, started to yank it out, and toppled onto the sand. Her mouth closed around the grit as she yelped.

"Ow, ow, ow." She spat sand as the splinter came out between her fingers. She squeezed to make the wound bleed, remembering her Mum's advice about punctures. She wiped her toe on her T-shirt.

As she stood, she looked at the cottage across the boardwalk and glimpsed someone standing on the veranda. She squinted to see if it was Nic, but the figure was too far away. She limped over the walkway to the low wooden gate and pushed it open. The person remained still before the front door, a darker shadowy form.

"Nicholas?" She strained to see. As she got closer she saw it was a girl, about her size, her age, similar long curly brown hair, but wearing a long dress to her ankles.

"Are you lost?" Madeline approached the girl cautiously.

The girl shook her head "no".

"Is your cottage?"

Again the girl shook her head.

"Where do you live? Why are you out so late?"

The girl pointed towards the end of the boardwalk where the Victorian mansion loomed up like an ornate peg holding down the ribbon of boardwalk.

"You live in the big house?"

The girl nodded. When she spoke, Madeline felt her voice as much as heard it. It was light and young, yet sharp and steely. "I cannot get back inside. My brother has locked me out. Everyone is asleep now."

Madeline thought of Nicholas. "I can't find my brother. I think he's gone exploring. If I help you get home, will you help me find my brother?"

The girl came to the edge of the veranda at the top of the stairs. She glided more than stepped. "Yes, please." She came down the steps and stood before Madeline, the moonlight turning her skin a pale waxen yellow. "I know where the boys like to hide. There is a conservatory behind my house. It is huge and full of plants and places to hide. The gate is broken at the side. Come. Let us look there."

"I'm Maddie." Madeline reached to take the girl's outstretched hand. When their hands touched, Madeline pulled hers away. The girl's hand was so cold it hurt.

"Sorry." The girl wiped her hands on her dress. "I'm called Celine. My mother is French."

"My name is French, too, but my Mum is from Coventry."

"Maddie doesn't sound French." The girl straightened imperiously.

Madeline frowned. She didn't like know-it-all girls one bit. "Maddie is short for Madeline. Madeline is French. My Mum said so."

"Well, then, let us go, Madeline, whose name is French."

Celine walked past her to the boardwalk and continued towards the mansion. Madeline scurried after her, her toe throbbing a bit. They came to the side gate Celine mentioned. Celine stopped, looking at the gate as if it was on fire.

"Go on, Maddie. It is broken. Just push it open."

Madeline reached for the latch, which hung limply against the ivy that was entwined in the ironwork. A mere nudge was all it took for the gate to swing wide. The path from the gate was in the shadow of tall junipers, but once they were inside, Celine walked ahead of her, sure of the way.

It seemed a long way to the conservatory. The path wound around trees circled in brick and manicured patches of flowers and lawn. Celine was a radiant figure moving smoothly through the garden, as if lit from inside by moonlight.

"Here we are."

"Oh!" Madeline thought the huge glass building must have risen up from the earth when she blinked because it hadn't been there before.

The double doors were open and faint tiny lights illuminated a central area with a table and chairs. Celine went to the centre and turned to Madeline.

"He is here, hiding. Call out. When he comes, send him home. Then you can help me get back into the house."

"But Nicholas could help you better. He's twelve years old!"

"Only *you*." Celine put her hands on her hips, insistent.

Madeline looked about the conservatory. It smelled of peat and flowers and ripe greenery. There were many paths leading from the centre. Nicholas would like it here, she thought. Yes, he's here.

"Nic! Nic, come out! You're going to be in big trouble if you don't!"

"That is well and good. Call louder now. I will wait outside." Celine moved past her.

"Nicholas Charles Bennett, you come out right now!" Madeline mimicked Celine's insistence.

The tiny lights winked off and on a few times, then Nic stepped out from behind a potted palm. His face was dirty, his hair pushed about as if he had sleepwalked straight out of bed, and his shorts were dark with fingerprints. He looked down at his knees and Madeline noticed they were scraped. He was embarrassed, she thought. He likes to be so tough.

"What are you doing here?" His voice was a high whisper.

"Looking for you, silly. I woke up and you were gone. If Mum and Dad find us gone, we'll both be locked in that room until Saturday!" Madeline's little fists pushed the air beside her.

"Don't you dare tell or you'll be sorry!" Nic walked towards her, his words menacing but his voice and posture that of someone caught out.

"I'm smart enough to know I'll get into trouble if I tell, too, twit. Go back to the cottage."

"What? You can't tell me what to do." He started to walk back into the shadows of the trees.

"Fine, get in trouble. See if I care." Madeline turned and went back outside. She expected to see Celine, but instead was met by darkness. "Celine?" she whispered.

Nicholas stormed out past her, then stopped a few yards away. "I'm going back because I want to. We're done playing around anyway." He turned back to Madeline for moment, his eyes fierce. "You better come back, too, or I'm telling Mum and Dad it was me out looking for *you*." With that, he ran out down the path and was gone.

"He is so like Paul." Celine was behind her. Madeline jumped.

"You scared me!" The gravel under her feet hurt and she began to shift from foot to foot. "Who's Paul?"

"My awful brother. He is twelve, too. My parents allow him to do whatever he chooses. He never gets scolded and always gets a sweet after supper no matter what he has done. If I look at him the wrong way, he locks me out. I cannot call to my parents or the servants. They will simply believe I was naughty and went outside on my own and I will be punished. It is just not fair."

"That's terrible. Same with me."

Celine stepped over the edge of the path onto the lawn. "Come. You will help me get in by the window on the back veranda. It is the only way."

Madeline nodded, then followed Celine over the lawn towards the manse. They met a path as it ran to the servant's entrance. They went up the steps to a landing that turned at the top to the back veranda. A bank of low windows book-ended a large set of double glass doors. Celine went to one window furthest from the door, nearest the servant's entrance.

The girls cupped their hands around the sides of their eyes and peered in. It was too dark to see detail, but Madeline could see a white lace runner on a sideboard and the contrast of two framed paintings against a lighter wall. It wasn't a modern house at all. More like a museum room she'd seen in London.

"This is a back dining room. The servants use it because it is off the kitchen. They leave the window unlatched sometimes. They are not very good. The servants we have in the country house are very good, indeed." Celine shook her head at Madeline's blank look. "The window is too big and heavy for me to push up on my own." Celine stepped back. "Will you try it with me?"

Madeline felt suddenly brave, and curious. "Can I come inside with you?"

"No!" Celine's voice was a harsh whisper, almost a shriek. "It is not acceptable!"

"Then I won't help you." Madeline turned to go.

Celine grabbed onto Madeline's T-shirt and pulled. She nearly landed on her backside, but Celine held her up. She was very strong, Madeline thought, swerving out of her grasp.

"Please." Celine stretched out her arms and made a sad face. "Help me get back inside. You may come back tomorrow."

That was good enough, Madeline decided. "Okay." It was what she was angling for all along.

They put their hands flat against the glass and both pushed up with all their might. The sound of wood moaning against wood told them the window was unlatched and up it came. Celine stepped over the window sill into the house.

"Will you find your way back to your cottage?"

Madeline nodded. "See you tomorrow."

Celine seemed to fade out of sight as she waved goodbye.

After dusting the sand off her face and feet and out of her hair on the veranda, Madeline quietly padded down the hall to the bedroom. The door was ajar. She pushed it open and saw Nicholas in bed. By the sound of his breathing, he was deep asleep. The room was dark now that the moon had moved away and dawn would come too soon. Madeline hurried to bed, did a last minute check she was sand-free, and climbed in beside her brother.

The day came hot and windless. Nicholas and Madeline awoke at the same time, turning to see the other.

Nic frowned at his sister. "Where were you? I waited around. Mum and Dad could've have checked in on us."

"I just helped Celine get back into her house. Her brother locked her out. Then I came back." She saw how scared he was. She added, "Sorry."

"I didn't see any girl." He wiped sleep from his eyes.

"Well, who were you playing with in the conservatory?" She sat up. The blood from her toe was dark on her shirt.

"Paul. He lives in that big house."

"That's Celine's brother. He's a bully. Celine said so."

"He's cool! He wears stupid stuff, but . . . what do you know. You're just a baby."

"I am not." Madeline folded her arms. "What are you going to tell Dad about your knees? I saw them last night. He'll know you were up to something."

Nic sat up, flung the eiderdown off his legs. Both knees were badly scuffed. There was green around them as if he'd skidded across the lawn. "Oh, shit!" He popped out of bed, went to the door and waited. Satisfied there was no one there, he hurried up the stairs to the bathroom.

Madeline took off her T-shirt and went to the chest of drawers to find a pair of shorts and a clean top to put on for the day. She hoped Nic would be quick cleaning up; she had to use the toilet. As she sat down in the stuffed chair, she looked at her toe. It was red and swelling. She should have just gone back to the cottage as soon as she hurt herself. She pulled on the shorts and top and brushed her hair.

Nic dashed in and shut the door. "Have they come down yet?"

Madeline shook her head. "I can't even hear them. Maybe they're still asleep. I have to go." She then rushed out and up the stairs to the toilet.

She bandaged her toe after putting on some antiseptic. Sitting on the toilet, her mind wandered to her seashells and selling them when they got home. She could use the money to buy some doll's clothes her mother was refusing to get for her. Then she thought about how hungry she was and wondered why she didn't smell her father's coffee. He couldn't start the day without his coffee. She washed and went to the door of her parents' bedroom.

Tapping lightly, her heart was pounding. What if she woke them and they were still upset with Nic? But the sun was out brightly, it had to be late morning. She tapped harder. Then she tried the door. Locked.

"Mum? Mum. Dad?"

Suddenly Nic was there at the bottom of the stairs. "Maddie! Where are they? No one's been in the kitchen or anything." He sounded frantic.

"It's locked, Nic. Look!" She tried the door loudly so he could hear.

He took the stairs two at a time and stood beside her. They shouted and Madeline began crying. Nic pounded on the door.

"Do something, Nic!" Madeline wailed.

Nicholas turned to the side and bashed at the door with his sturdy frame. It took seven tries before the lock gave and he fell into the room. It was empty.

Madeline wiped at her eyes, but she couldn't stop crying. The bed was messed from her parents having gone to bed and slept, and their clothes were laid out for the day. The window was open and the heat in the room made her perspire. She continued looking about as if they would suddenly walk out of the wallpaper, or peek out from under the bed frame and say "Surprise!".

Nicholas wasn't much more composed. He went to the window, back to the bed, his face ashen, his eyes wet. "Where are they?"

Madeline offered a tearful suggestion. "Maybe they're on the veranda? Outside?"

Nic turned, his face colouring. "Don't you think I looked out there? Stop crying. We have to find them!" Just then, a tear rolled down his cheek and he nearly punched himself trying to wipe it away before Maddie saw. But she did.

"I want Mum!" Madeline ran out, down the stairs, out the front door onto the veranda and forgetting her sore toe, stomped down the stairs to the wooden walkway.

She kept going toward town, scanning the beach and the cottages, determined behind her fear. Twice she saw women with the similar short hair and long legs, but they were older or younger, neither her Mum. When she came to the steps onto the high street, she turned back. She could see Nicholas walking on the sand to the water and back to the boardwalk, head whipping side to side like a light on top of a police car.

He rushed to her. "Did you see them?"

"No, did you?"

He shook his head. "What are we going to do?"

"I don't know. I'm just a baby." Madeline began weeping again.

Nic stared at her for a moment, then grabbed her hand and led her back to the cottage.

Nicholas poured cornflakes and milk into bowls for them, but they both sat and looked at it as if it was creamed spinach. Their bellies growled. Madeline stopped crying, but her face remained red.

By the afternoon, Madeline wanted Nic to call the police. He tried to reassure her. "They'll be back. They're just giving me a taste of my own medicine." But he well understood now how his mum must have felt when he'd gone off with Paul; the panic, the grief setting in even without proof anyone had died. *Enough*, he thought, *you can come out now*. He folded his arms over his chest and went quiet.

At suppertime, famished, they threw away the congealed cereal and ate half a chocolate cake that Mum had made for the evening before they were to go home two days hence. They finished the milk and put the leftover cake back in the refrigerator. Three quarters of an hour later, Madeline vomited hers up. Nic washed her face and hugged her, but said nothing.

As the sun set, they sat on chairs pulled up to the windows, watching the wooden path crossing in front of them. Finally, Nicholas spoke.

"It's no joke, Maddie. Something's happened to Mum and Dad. I've got to take care of us now." He stared out at the water.

"I'm scared."

"Yeah, me, too."

"I feel cold inside my chest. I might be ill." Madeline pressed her hands on her ribs.

"You're not ill. I feel the same way. I think it's because this is the worst thing that's ever happened to us."

"How can we not be scared any more?"

Nicholas looked at her. "We have to get help. Paul. I can ask him to help."

Madeline smiled grimly. "Celine's brother? I forgot about them."

"You helped her, maybe they'll help us. Let's go to their house."

Madeline looked at her toe. Nic had rewashed it and bandaged it with too much gauze and tape, but if she put on sandals, she thought she could make it over the wooden walkway. Nic slipped into a pair of trainers and put Madeline's sandals on the floor for her to step into.

They left a light on in case their parents came back and set out to the end of the strand. Nic held Maddie's hand and made sure she could walk. There were still people awake in the cottages along the way, oblivious to the two children and their troubles. Nicholas told Madeline he was so sorry for running off, as if she was her Mum.

"We can go in the side gate, its broken," Madeline offered as they stood in front of the mansion, its tall, foreboding gate shut tight.

"Right." Nicholas lead her around the side. They noticed some lights on in the house, dim, flickering strangely. The moon was behind clouds this evening and it made finding the gate difficult. Vines wound around the fence all along the side path. Nic felt for it more than looked. "Here." He stopped.

"What?" Madeline clung to him.

"The lock's been fixed. It's firm." He shook the gate but it made no sound. "Never mind, I know where there is a bent fence railing near the conservatory, we'll get in there."

It wasn't much further along the fence that the gaping space allowed them entry. The gravel path from Madeline's memory was nowhere to be found. The ground was brambles, thistle and nettles, stinging them as they went, but they hardly noticed. This was not a part of the garden she'd been through.

"I think we're lost. Last night there was a path and lawns and flowers."

"Look, we're not far from the house. Do you want me to carry you?"

Madeline looked up at Nic, maybe six inches taller than she, and doubted his strength. She nodded hesitantly. He swooped her up and kept going.

Madeline pointed to stairs going up to the veranda, grander stairs than the ones she and Celine had used by the servant's entry. Nicholas carried her up, the wood creaking and snoring as their weight went over them. Once on the veranda, they saw a large hole in front of the double door where something heavy had fallen through the floor. The long low windows around the double doors were broken and dirty.

"It didn't look like this last night." She shivered.

"I know. Paul let me look in on the back parlour and I could see the edge of a big staircase. It was cool. Fancy and sparkly. Now it looks like nobody has been here for years." He set Madeline down.

Madeline saw a glow deep inside the house emanating from a hallway. She gasped when she saw someone pass through.

"There's somebody inside!"

"What. Where? I didn't see anything." They edged closer to the windows. "Let's go inside."

"No. No, Nic. I don't want to. Celine told me I couldn't."

"She's not here now, so let's go in." He grabbed her hand and she pulled away.

"No! Let's go back to the cottage. My legs hurt from the nettles. I want to go back."

"Don't be a wimp, Maddie. We came here for help. Don't you want Mum and Dad?"

"I won't go inside. Let's go around to the front and ring the doorbell. Sneaking in is bad." She pouted and began walking back on her own to the stairs. She kept going hoping he would follow and he did. This time, there was a path to follow, right around to the front garden.

The smells of the sea were masked by the scent of honeysuckle and roses. As they went up the steps to the front door, Nic took Madeline's hand. The long front veranda stretched completely across the length of the mansion. He gently pulled Madeline along to the largest window. The heavy draperies were tied back and they could see into the dimly lit sitting room.

There, sitting on the floor with an embroidery hoop stitching away was Celine. A boy sat putting a paper house together at a table with a man whose back was to them. Madeline saw that Nic was going to tap on the window and she slapped his hand.

"Don't," she whispered harshly. "Just look. Something's wrong."

"What?"

"I don't know. It's not real."

"Stop it. Look. It's Paul. He'll help us. Look, he has parents. They can call the police if we can't find Mum and Dad." Nicholas's eyes were pleading with her.

"But look how they're dressed. Look at the lights." Gaslights glowed against the walls. "They're all wrong."

Out of the corner of Madeline's eye she caught a woman coming into the room. Her dress was dark and long and tight at the middle, her hair tightly wound into a chignon. They both then saw the woman's face. Nic's jaw dropped, but Madeline shrieked. The four people inside turned to the sound. Then Nic screamed.

Sitting at the table with Paul was their Dad, and their Mum stood by Celine, a basket of sewing in her hands. They seemed cosy together. A real family. Celine set down her embroidery and got up.

Madeline wanted to run away but her feet wouldn't move. Nicholas seemed equally paralysed. Celine went to the window beside them and waited. Nic threw his arms around his sister and they buried their heads in their arms. Madeline felt her brother shaking, or maybe it was her. She lifted her head a little and saw Celine standing on the veranda a few feet away. The sound that came out of Madeline was like a wounded animal. It made Nicholas look behind him.

"Wha . . ." His words wouldn't come. He started to back away with Madeline clinging to him.

"It's a bad dream, Nic. Please. Say this is a bad dream!" Madeline was crying now.

Nic stopped shaking. "It's a bad dream, Maddie." He sounded
sure, but took a hold of her hand and pulled her with him as he
rushed past Celine down the steps to the path leading to the front
gate. They ran with arms out, pushed at the gates which fought them,
creaking and yawing. Madeline glanced behind them. Celine was
coming down the steps. They threw their weight into the wrought
iron and it opened with a metal grumble, just enough for them to
squeeze through. Once they were out, past the boardwalk onto the
sand, they stopped, huffing, shaking, and crying.

They stood holding each other, staring at the mansion, seeing the
faintly lit scene inside, the happy family. *Their mum and dad* with
two other children.

The young couple in the cottage were kind to Madeline and Nicholas. The light in the front window was left on, just as when they'd left
to find Paul and Celine. The man and woman hadn't minded being
woken up, no, and they wanted to help. At first Madeline and
Nicholas refused to speak to these strangers in the cottage where they
had been staying for nearly two weeks. What had happened to their
mum and dad? Why were these people there? But there was no one
else, not now. The man and woman listened as the woman tended to
their scrapes and nettle stings while the man made them tea as if they
had lived in the cottage all along. The couple exchanged glances.
They thought the children had wild imaginations. Surely there would
be an explanation to satisfy everyone.

Nicholas and Madeline exchanged glances of their own. Nicholas
thought the man spoke in a stilted, old-fashioned manner, with silly
words. Madeline felt the woman was too proper, and that she
smelled musty and dirty like an old house; not like their cool
mum who spiked her hair and wore exotic perfumes. The cottage
looked the same as when they were last there, but sheets covered
most of the furniture, just as they would leave it when they went
home. Madeline couldn't tell if it was the same furniture as before.

As Nic and Maddie sat at the table staring into the cups of tea, the
young couple told them it might be better if they stay with them for
the night. Just until they could sort things out in the morning. They
had a bed made up in the front room. Really, it would be just fine.

Lying in bed, the same one they had woken from in the morning,
they couldn't sleep. So very tired they were, too. Madeline sniffed at
the sheets to see if they still smelled of Nicholas's sandy feet and her
sweaty head on the pillow. But it smelled foreign, like damp and
disuse. They listened for the couple's footsteps going upstairs to the

bedroom above, but there were no sounds except whispers that could have been a wind going through the reeds on the beach.

Madeline rolled close to Nicholas, and he clung to her. Somehow she knew they were thinking the same thing. They must not fall asleep. They had to think of things to keep them awake, anything.

Madeline imagined herself sitting behind a small table, Mum beside her, at the fair. Lined up on a sheet of Hessian were many beautiful clean seashells, ten pence a piece. She'd made the little sign all by herself with a marker. There was nearly a pound in coins in her pocket. If she just closed her eyes, she could see Nic racing through the stands with his friends, upsetting displays and hear the shouting of the vendors.

When she woke, the day was grey and cloudy. Madeline turned to see Nicholas, but she wasn't in the bed she'd fallen asleep in. This one was higher off the floor with curly iron feet and head boards. The room was different, too. Old fashioned and flowery with three kinds of wallpaper and heavy draperies. She threw her feet over the edge of the bed and saw she was wearing a long thin cotton gown. She grabbed her foot and looked at her toe. It was perfectly healed!

She stepped onto the wood floor and headed to the door. For a moment she feared it would be locked, but it opened with a soft whine. She could hear people moving about, no one speaking, though. She looked to the end of the hall and saw an inlet where the cold light of morning from a curved bank of bay windows touched heavy white wicker furniture. She hurried to it.

At the windows, she looked out and down. The familiar front garden three floors below her stretched to the ironwork gate to the boardwalk. A wooden pier met the wood planks of the boardwalk. At the end was a large yacht, and huge rocks formed a small harbour from the rolling of the sea.

The sound of footsteps made her turn.

"Maddie!" Nicholas ran to her, nearly knocking her over. "Maddie." He hugged her so tight, she struggled to breath. His wool shirt made her arms itch.

The sound of more footsteps made them both turn.

The light made them pale and their fear was etched like death their faces, but there they were, Mum and Dad. Mum wore the dark restricting dress, her short hair gone. Dad wore a suit. He hated suits and ties with a passion. They came forward and embraced Nicholas and Madeline. They mumbled "sorry" and Mum wept.

Madeline wanted to shout, "What's happened? Why are we here? What is this?" Somehow, she knew they all wondered and was quiet.

"Look." Her father went to the windows and pointed out to the beach. The family huddled around him, no one letting go an arm or hand. And they looked.

Down on the beach, a boy and a girl splashed at the edge of the ocean while a mum and dad stood on the beach, arms around each other's waists. They wore familiar clothing; the mum in pale shirt and shorts, the dad in khaki cargo trousers and faded work shirt. Suddenly, they all stopped and twisted to look back at the huge old house on the beachhead. They stared up, their faces unreadable. Then they looked at each other and smiled self-satisfied smiles.

The sun broke through the grey and cast the beach in a hot light, though the grey still shrouded the house. Nicholas recognized Paul wearing his surfer trunks, and Madeline knew Celine, ghostly pale, in Maddie's bright orange and yellow bikini. And there on the beach was the yellow shovel and blue bucket, just brimming with shells to sell.

GAHAN WILSON

The Outermost Borough

GAHAN WILSON WILL ALWAYS BE best known for his macabre cartoons in *Playboy* and *The New Yorker*. His artwork has also appeared in publications as diverse as *Punch*, *Paris Match*, *New York Times*, *Newsweek*, *National Lampoon* during its glory days and *Gourmet*.

His cartoons have been collected in *Gahan Wilson's Graveside Manner*, *The Man in the Cannibal Pot*, *I Paint What I See*, *Is Nothing Sacred?*, *... And Then We'll Get Him*, *The Weird World of Gahan Wilson*, *Gahan Wilson's Cracked Cosmos*, *Still Weird*, *Even Weirder*, *Gahan Wilson's Gravedigger's Party* and *Gahan Wilson's Monster Party*.

An anthology of his work, *The Best of Gahan Wilson*, was published by Underwood Books, and he recently completed a new children's book, *Didn't*.

Gahan Wilson's Diner was a cartoon short for Twentieth Century Fox, while *Gahan Wilson's Kid* was an animated special from the Showtime Network. A number of other film projects are currently in development and some may actually happen.

Wilson has also written a number of short stories for magazines and anthologies, some of which were collected in *The Cleft and Other Odd Tales*. He has also published a number of children's books, including the *Harry the Fat Bear Spy* series, written two unusual mystery novels (*Eddy Deco's Last Caper* and *Everybody's Favourite Duck*), and edited the anthologies *First World Fantasy Awards* and *Gahan Wilson's Favorite Tales of Horror*.

He relates the following true anecdote regarding "The Outermost Borough": "Writing this story stirred up memories of way back when starving artists such as I was could rent a dinky perch in a

254
GAHAN WILSON

Greenwich Village tenement for very little money and didn't have to move to an outer borough, but they were pretty grim.

"I remember a wonderful comment made by a highly talented Japanese painter friend of mine one night after the two of us had just heard a dreadful fight between a wretched couple in the horrible lair next to his horrible lair terminate with a shocking thud on the wall followed by an awful, long-lasting silence.

"'It must be terrible,' he said, and paused. 'To live like this,' he said, and paused again. 'If you are ordinary people.'

"I've never heard a better summing up of what you need if you hope to successfully survive bohemian life."

ONCE AGAIN, WITH A GESTURE which had turned into a sort of nervous tic during this morning's long waiting, Barstow pressed his face against the dirty glass of his studio's wide central window in order to peer anxiously down the crowded city street below, westward towards Manhattan.

At first his body began to sag in disappointment yet again but then he suddenly straightened and his sharp little eyes brightened in their darkish sockets at the sight of a shiny black speck making its way smoothly as a shark through the otherwise dingy traffic.

Barstow clenched his hands into small triumphant fists as he saw the speck draw nearer to the ancient building his loft perched atop and gleefully observed it shape itself into a long, sleek limousine gliding with regal incongruity amidst graffiti-laden delivery trucks and unwashed second hand cars scarred with multitudes of dents and dings.

Without any doubt he knew it was the vehicle of Max Ratch, Barstow's long-time associate and the owner of one of New York's most prestigious galleries. He had come as he had promised!

Barstow turned for one last burning survey of the works of art he had spent the whole of last week arranging for Ratch's inspection. He was pleased to see that the thickly textured strokes of oil paint he had spread upon the canvases gave out satisfactorily ominous gleams in the gray light seeping into the studio and delighted to observe that the portraits and cityscapes lurking like muggers in the studio's darker corners created exactly the dangerous and intimidating effect he had striven so carefully to achieve.

Suddenly struck by a disturbing notion, the artist whirled and darted back to the windows just in time to see the large chauffeur open the rear passenger door of the limo and be suddenly diminished by the emergence of Ratch's long, bulky body. The art dealer had barely got both feet on the sidewalk when the very much smaller form of his ever-present assistant, Ernestine, darted out after him with the scuttling alacrity of a pet rat.

Barstow peered nervously up and down the street and spat a strangled curse as he spotted Mrs Fengi and her son, Maurice, swaying rhythmically like inverted pendulums as they waddled unevenly but directly towards his approaching visitors. He could see Mrs Fengi's enormous, toad-like eyes bulge eagerly while, with considerable difficulty, she accelerated her froggish shuffle.

It was obvious the weird old creature was desperate to buttonhole these exotic strangers to the neighborhood and to gossip with them and Barstow knew that would never do!

He glared intently down, unbreathing, his teeth clenched, his heart throbbing hurtfully in his chest and desperately prayed that the dealer and his aide would not turn and observe the approaching duo.

But then a huge wave of grateful relief rushed through his thin body as he saw Ratch and Ernestine purposefully make their way from the limo to the stoop of Barstow's building and glide efficiently up its old worn steps without having made any contact with – or even so much as taken a sideways glance at – the approaching Fengis.

The doorbell rang and Barstow rushed through his studio to push the button releasing the lock downstairs. He shouted instructions to his guests via the entrance intercom as to how they could locate and use the freight elevator, then hurried to the door of his studio and threw it open.

He stood on the landing, rubbing his hands and gloating at the sound of the ancient lift whining and rattling five stories upwards, then reached forward so he could haul its squeaking door open the moment it arrived.

Ratch strode majestically out with Ernestine behind him and gazed down at Barstow with his large blue eyes.

"Well, well," he said in his usual reverberating basso, "When you said you'd moved from Manhattan to an outer borough, dear boy, you truly meant an *outer* borough!"

"It's almost as long a trip as that ghastly drive to the Hamptons!" snapped Ernestine behind him.

"I wasn't all that crazy about being this far away from everything myself, at first," Barstow admitted apologetically, "But then I got used to it, really began to see the place, and finally I realized it had turned out to be an inspiration!"

"That is very interesting," murmured Ratch gazing speculatively at Barstow, and then he turned to his assistant. "Besides, Ernestine, we must not chide poor Barstow for living in such a far-off place. The rents in Manhattan have forced all artists save for the most outrageously successful to shelter in odd and obscure locations such as this."

He turned to gaze down benignly at the artist and then bent to firmly grasp both of Barstow's narrow shoulders possessively in his huge, gloved hands.

"But let us leave all that aside, shall we? I have a feeling that what we are about to see here will be well worth the ordeal of the journey!"

He increased his stately downward inclination further until his wide, pink face almost touched Barstow and stared closely at the artist with an odd look of crafty affection.

"Am I right, Kevin?" he whispered. "Do I really smell a breakthrough? Dare I hope that the potential I have always sensed in you has finally started to flower?"

The skin of Barstow's face skin gave little mouse-like quivers under the impact of Ratch's breath and he smiled up at Ratch as a frightened child might smile at a Santa Claus who had actually, terrifyingly, climbed out of the family fireplace.

"I think so!" he whispered back. "I really do!"

Ratch regarded him for a long moment before letting go of the artist and then pointed to the open door of the studio with a flourish.

"Then lead on!" he said.

Without any further discussion the three of them immediately absorbed themselves into the business at hand with Barstow gently and unobtrusively guiding Ratch and Ernestine from one work to the next, always moving quietly, always keeping just a glance or two ahead of the art dealer as the large man stepped thoughtfully and elegantly from painting to painting.

Skillfully, like a sort of acolyte, Barstow unobtrusively carried the works to a back wall once they had been observed by Ratch and then gently moved forward the ones he wanted him to look at next.

A clammy – he hoped not very noticeable – sheen of sweat now covered Barstow's face and hands and occasionally a tremor ran the length of both his arms as he leaned a painting against the leg of an easel or delicately adjusted the positioning of several connected works in a row. It took him an enormous effort to keep his breathing steady and inaudible.

So far he could not determine exactly how positively Ratch was reacting to these new works, but he found himself becoming increasingly hopeful. Though he had made no spoken comment since starting his slow march through Barstow's domain the artist was encouraged to observe the obvious depth of the dealer's absorption in the paintings.

It was an enormously good sign that Ratch sometimes paused silently before one or another of them for long, thoughtful moments but when he stripped off his gloves and stuffed them into a pocket of his Astrakhan coat so that he could reach upwards with his thick but sensitive fingers and tug delicately at the sensuous pout of his full lips a great beat of triumph throbbed through Barstow for he knew, from long years of experience, that this was always a foolproof sign of great approval.

After a full hour that seemed to last at least a century Ratch came to a halt before the grand finale, an enormous painting of a gigantic female nude gazing through what was recognizably the studio's main window at pigeons milling on its sill.

He stood absolutely motionless and expressionless for a very lengthy time and then a satisfied smirk curled his lips and slowly spread into a smile which grew broader and wider and more open until Ratch turned toward Barstow with a full display of his famously fearsome toothiness and violently broke the long silence with an enthusiastic clapping of his hands.

"Bravo, Kevin, Bravo!" he cried, spreading his arms like the ringmaster of a three ring circus and gazing happily at the multitude of paintings about him. Ernestine, who up to now had tagged along behind her employer in quiet watchfulness, vouchsafed the first sure indication that the project would successfully advance by drawing a notebook from her carrying case and from that moment on jotting down in shorthand every word said which might be of historical or legal import.

"Thank you, Max," said Barstow, "Thank you so much!"

"Ah, no, Kevin, ah, no – thank *you*!" said Ratch, waving a huge paw in an elegant sweep around the room. "Not only have you assuredly made both yourself and my gallery a very large amount of money, I am convinced you have guaranteed yourself everlasting fame and glory."

The blood rushed to Barstow's head and for a moment or two he was terrified that he would actually faint for joy. The art dealer had always been supportive, occasionally even highly encouraging, but this was a level of praise dazzlingly higher than any which had ever been granted before.

In a giddy daze he watched Ratch almost waltz from one of the paintings to another, gently patting their tops or stroking the sides of their stretchers and sometimes even stopping to inhale the perfume of their paint.

"This is the work you were born to do, my friend," he said. "Everything you have done before has only been a promise of what was to come – merely the tiniest hint!"

He paused at the painting of a hunched, grotesque news dealer peering out bleakly from the small, dark pit of his shoddy sidewalk stand kiosk plastered with newspapers bannered with headlines of war and plague and tabloid magazines displaying gaudy photos of mutilated freaks and sobbing celebrities and smiled benignly at the way the grotesque creature's fearful, pockmarked face stared out at the viewer with eyes slitted like a lurking crocodile's.

"The totally convincing way you have depicted the reptilian quality of this wretched fellow, the believability of his actually not being altogether human, is simply astounding," he gently whispered while stroking the heads of the tacks which pinned the canvas to its frame.

He stood back and continued to survey the painting.

"Forget Bacon, my dear boy," he said, "forget even Goya."

"Even Goya?" Barstow gasped, then gulped and made his way to a paint splotched stool lest he indeed fall to the floor. "You say even *Goya*?"

Ratch grinned down at him and for the first time in his whole long association with this legendary entrepreneur of art it seemed to Barstow that the broad white curve of his gleaming teeth seemed to have an almost motherly gentleness.

"Even Goya," whispered Ratch, gently patting the artist on his pale, sweat-bedewed forehead, "And all form within this odd little skull of yours. Ah – the sublime mystery of creative talent!"

He stepped to a painting of extraordinary ominousness depicting a neighborhood butcher store window filled to bursting with glistening red fragments of dismembered animals artfully displayed in order to promote their consumption and with a sly expression began to archly mimic the speech of a museum guide.

"Here you see that the artist has delicately implied, but somehow not directly revealed, that the meat on display may be even more horribly varied than that put on view in the usual butcher's window. Has this steak with a largish round bone, for instance, come from a lamb's hindquarters or was it chopped from a neighborhood school girl's pale and tender thigh? Eh? *Eh*?"

He chuckled in a sinister, highly theatrical fashion and moved on to a night scene showing a dim and lonely street lamp only barely illuminating a hunched and frightened old woman in black mourning making her way along a cracked sidewalk and staring anxiously into the almost impenetrable darkness of the ancient city street beyond.

"I marvel at the way you've suggested . . . *something* . . . on the glistening tarmac of the narrow street approaching the woman from the direction of the other sidewalk!" whispered Ratch in genuine awe. "It is brilliant how the viewer sometimes reads it this way, sometimes that – it is genuine painterly magic, my dear boy! Wizardry! You can rest assured the critics will never be finished writing competitive essays attempting to explain *that* one."

He then pointed at a painting of a gaping policeman, his gun still drawn, kneeling in hard, bright sunlight over a man he'd clearly just shot and staring in horror, along with a small surrounding crowd, at the thing which was bloodily tearing its way out of the dead man's chest and glaring furiously up at the officer.

"But the true underlying miracle of all these new works is their universal *convincingness*!" he said, patting gently, even lovingly, the glistening face of the entity scrabbling its way out of the corpse. "In spite of myself I find I suspect that this horrible thing may actually exist, that it *may even be alive today* in a hidden chamber of some prison hospital!"

He turned to study Barstow intently and tapped the artist at the exact same spot where the gruesomely productive wound had been painted on the slain man's chest.

"Somehow, Kevin, you have suddenly developed the ability to present fictitious images which are simultaneously entirely fantastic and totally realistic," the art dealer intoned with great solemnity. "Never in my whole career as a dealer have I seen such a world of grotesquely macabre impossibilities more believably presented. I am both frightened and thrilled."

He paused to once again study the gory thing depicted in the painting with undisguised affection and then murmured softly, almost inaudibly, but with enormous pleasure: "We shall become unbelievably rich."

Then, almost reverently, he returned to the largest and most centrally located painting of all: the one of the pale, elephantine female nude staring out through the studio's window. The dead-looking flesh of the huge creature's back was turned to the viewer as she idly observed a crowd of subtly bizarre pigeons milling on the widow's ledge and the fire escape beyond.

"This, as I am sure you are well aware, is the supreme work of the exposition," said Ratch with great solemnity, and then he turned to look at the artist curiously. "Have you given this painting a name?"

Barstow nodded.

"I call it 'Louise'," he said.

Ratch nodded sagely.

"As though it was the name of an actual model," he said approvingly. "And so enhanced the ghastly notion it might actually be the depiction of a living monster."

Ernestine, on the other hand, had begun to show signs she had at least momentarily lost something of her customary professional detachment and was regarding the painting with undisguised repulsion.

"My God," she whispered, "Look at the thing's hands! Look at its *claws*!"

Ratch gazed at the unmistakable fear in his assistant's eyes with enormous satisfaction.

"You see?" he crowed, "Even my cool Ernestine is very seriously disturbed by our monster."

A sudden spasm crossed Barstow's face at Ratch's second use of this description.

"I do not think of her as a monster," he said.

Ratch regarded the little artist first with some surprise and then with dawning understanding.

"Of course you don't," he said, and then he waved in an oddly gentle sort of way at the paintings grouped around them. "Nor do you regard any of the creatures depicted in these other works as monsters. As in the work of Goya, one can tell that they are sympathetically, even affectionately observed. That is the secret of their beauty."

Then, after a thoughtful pause, Ratch turned back to the paintings and began to walk among them as he softly dictated observations and instructions to the now partially recovered Ernestine. Barstow stood by and watched them at it until he caught a flickering to his side. He turned and his eyes widened when he saw that a great crowd of pigeons had assembled on the window's outside sills and the old iron work fire escape beyond.

Quietly, unobtrusively, he made his way over to the windows and though some of the birds flopped clumsily off at his approach most of the creatures ignored him.

They were a much more varied group of pigeons than those one would ordinarily observe in, say, Manhattan. Not only were their markings extraordinarily colorful and individual – ranging from playful Matisse-like patterns of stars and spiralings to blurry Monet style shadings to stern geometric blockings of black and gray and sooty white highly reminiscent of Mondrian's abstractions – their bodies were also quite remarkably unlike one another.

The pigeon pecking at the sill just to Barstow's left, for example, was almost as big as a cat and sported a spectacular hunch on its back; the one next to it was extremely narrow and so thin that the rest of its body seemed an almost snakish extension of its neck and the one next to that appeared to be little more than a feathered pulsating blob with wings and an oddly skewed beak.

Barstow stole a quick look behind him to make sure both Ratch and Ernestine were absorbed in their cataloguing and calculations and when he looked back outside he was alarmed to see that one of the pigeons had wandered off from the sill and begun to march awkwardly but casually up the dirty pane of window with its fat, gummy feet clinging to the dirty glass and that another, after alternately extending and shrinking the length of its body in a series of odd, painful-looking little heaves, was working its way along the underside of the railing of the fire escape for all the world like a beaked, glittery eyed worm.

Barstow hastily threw another glance back at his guests to make absolutely certain they still hadn't noticed any of these goings-on and then he executed a series of violent and abrupt gestures which, much to his relief, successfully startled all the pigeons into clumsily flying away from the sills and fire escape and out of sight.

Eventually, after what seemed to be aeons of discussion and plan-making, Ratch and Ernestine and their summoned chauffeur descended in the creaking elevator along with a very sizable selection of paintings leaving Barstow with his triumph and a great exhaustion.

He made his way to the stool by his easel and sagged onto it with an enormous sigh. It would be a while before he'd have the energy to stir.

He heard the soft opening of a door behind him and smiled as the studio's floorboards groaned nearer and nearer under Louise's enormous weight. When she leaned over him Barstow gratefully and deeply breathed in the spicy, slightly moldy air that wafted out from her body.

He felt the hugeness of her breasts resting on his shoulders and shuddered with pleasure when she cooed something not quite words and stroked the top of his head with a sweet tenderness which was truly remarkable considering the potential brutality of her huge paws.

"He liked them," murmured Barstow, relaxing back against her vast belly. "He'll buy all the work I do from now on. We'll be rich, Louise, you and I. And millions will adore your painting. Millions. And they will see how beautiful you are."

She cooed again, carefully retracted her talons, and began to knead the tension from his narrow shoulders.

GLEN HIRSHBERG

American Morons

"AMERICAN MORONS" IS THE TITLE STORY for Glen Hirshberg's latest collection, recently out from Earthling Publications. His first collection, *The Two Sams*, was published by Carroll & Graf, won the International Horror Guild Award, and was selected by *Publishers' Weekly* and *Locus* as one of the best books of 2003.

Hirshberg is also the author of *The Snowman's Children* (also from Carroll & Graf) and a forthcoming novel, *Sisters of Baikal*. With Dennis Etchison and Peter Atkins, he co-founded The Rolling Darkness Revue, a travelling ghost story performance troupe that tours the West Coast of the United States each October.

His fiction has appeared in numerous magazines and anthologies, including multiple appearances in *The Mammoth Book of Best New Horror* and *The Year's Best Fantasy and Horror*, *Dark Terrors 6*, *Trampoline*, *Acquainted with the Dead*, *Cemetery Dance* and *The Dark*.

He lives in the Los Angeles area with his wife and children.

About the following story, the author notes: "A couple of summers ago, on our way back to Rome from a cousin's wedding, my brother poured gasoline into a car gas tank marked with a cap reading DIESEL, and we spent four scorching hours broken down beside the *superstrade* before eventually receiving a tow into a neighbourhood overrun with peacocks (most, but not all of them, living).

"My brother scrawled the titular phrase in the filthy passenger-side window before we abandoned the car, as per our instructions from the rental company. Most of the good, self-mocking lines at the beginning of the story are his. I had the whole piece sketched long before we finally staggered into a hotel room in the middle of the night."

Omnibus umbra locis adero: dabis, improbe, poenas."
("My angry ghost, arising from the deep
Shall haunt thee waking, and disturb thy sleep.")
                                                    —Virgil

IN THE END, THE CAR MADE IT MORE THAN A MILE after leaving the gas station, all the way to the toll gate that marked the outskirts of Rome. Ignoring the horns behind them and the ominous, hacking rattle of the engine, the two Americans dug together through the coins they'd dumped in the dashboard ash tray. Twice, Kellen felt Jamie's sweat-streaked fingers brush his. The horn blasts got more insistent, and Jamie laughed, so Kellen did, too.

When they'd finally assembled the correct change, he threw the coins into the bin, where they clattered to the bottom except for one ten-cent piece that seemed to stick in the mesh. Ruefully, Kellen imagined turning, trying to motion everyone behind him back so he could reverse far enough out of the toll island to open his door and climb out. Then the coin dropped and disappeared into the bottom of the basket.

Green light flashed. The gate rose. Kellen punched the accelerator and felt it plunge straight down. There was not even a rattle, now.

"Uh, Kel?" Jamie said.

As though they'd heard her, or could see his foot on the dead pedal, every car in the queue let loose with an all-out sonic barrage. Then – since this was Italy, where blasting horns at fellow drivers was like showering rice on newlyweds – most of the cars in the queues to either side joined in.

Expressionlessly, Kellen turned in his seat, his skin unsticking from the rental's cracked, roasted vinyl with a pop. The setting sun blazed through the windshield into his eyes. "At least," he said, "it's not like you warned me the car might only take diesel."

"Yes I –" Jamie started, caught the irony, and stopped. She'd been in the midst of retying her maple syrup hair on the back of her neck. Kellen found himself watching her tank top spaghetti strap slide in the slickness on her shoulder as she spoke again. "At least it doesn't say the word *DIESEL* in big green letters on the gas cap."

He looked up, blinking. "Does it really?"

"Saw it lying on the trunk while that attendant dude was trying whatever he was trying to fix it. What'd he pour in there, anyway?"

Goddamnit, Kellen snarled inside his own head for perhaps the thousandth time in the past week. Jamie and he had been a couple all the way through high school. Three years into their separate college lives, he still considered them one. She said she did, too. *And she wasn't lying, exactly.* But he'd felt the change all summer long. He'd thought this trip might save them.

A particularly vicious horn blast from the car behind almost dislodged his gaze. Almost. "At least *diesel* isn't the same word in Italian as it is in English," he said, and Jamie burst out laughing.

"Time to meet more friendly Romans."

Too late, Kellen started issuing his by now familiar warning, cobbled from their parents' pre-trip admonishments about European attitudes toward Americans at the moment, plus the words that had swirled around them all week, blaring from radios, the front pages of newspapers they couldn't read, TV sets in the lobbies of youth hostels they'd stayed in just for the adventure, since their respective parents had supplied plenty of hotel money. *Cadavere. Sesto Americano. George Bush. Pavone.* Not that Jamie would have listened, anyway. He watched her prop her door open and stick out one tanned, denim-skirted leg.

Instantly, the horns shut off. Doors in every direction popped like champagne corks, and within seconds, half a dozen Italian men of wildly variant ages and decisions about chest hair display fizzed around the Americans' car.

"Stuck," Jamie said through her rolled down window. "Um. *Kaput.*"

"I'm pretty sure that's not Ital –" Kellen started, but before he could finish, his door was ripped open. Startled, he twisted in his seat. The man pouring himself into the car wore no shirt whatsoever, and was already gripping the wheel. The rest of the men fanned into formation, and then the car was half-floating, half-rolling through the toll gate into traffic that made no move to slow, but honked gleefully as it funneled around them. Seconds later, they glided to a stop on the gravel shoulder.

Jamie leaned back in her seat, folding her arms and making a great show of sighing like a queen in a palanquin. Whether her grin was for him or the guy who'd grabbed the steering wheel, Kellen had no idea. The guy hadn't let go, and Kellen remained pinned in place.

What was it about Italian men that made him want to sprout horns and butt something? "I say again," he murmured to Jamie. "*Kaput?*"

"It's one of those universal words, ol' pal. Like diesel." Then she was lifted out of the car.

Even Jamie seemed taken aback, and made a sort of chirping sound as the throng enveloped her. "*Bella,*" Kellen heard one guy coo, and something that sounded like "*Assistere*," and some tongue-clucking that could have been regret over the car or wolfish slavering over Jamie or neither. Kellen didn't like that he could no longer see her, and he didn't like the forearm stretched across his chest.

Abruptly, it lifted, and he wriggled out fast and stood. The man before him looked maybe forty, with black and grey curly hair, a muscular chest, and Euro-sandals with those straps that pulled the big toes too far from their companions. He said nothing to Kellen, and instead watched Jamie slide sunglasses over her eyes, whirling amid her circle of admirers with her skirt lifting above her knee every time she turned. Back home, Jamie was borderline pretty – slim, athletic, a little horse-faced – at least until she laughed. But in Italy, judging from the response of the entire male population during their week in Rome and Tuscany, she was a goddess. Or else all women were.

Ol' pal. That's what he was, now.

Almost seven o'clock, and still the blazing summer heat poured down. Two more miles, Kellen thought, and he and Jamie could at least have stood in one of Rome's freezing fountains while they waited for the tow truck. Jamie would have left her loafers on the pavement, her feet bare.

"It's okay, thanks guys," he said abruptly, and started around the car. Digging into his shorts pocket for his cell phone, he waved it at the group like a wand that might make them disappear. "*Grazie*." His accent sounded pathetic, even to him.

Not a single Italian turned. One of them, he noticed, had his hand low on Jamie's back, and another had stepped in close alongside, and Kellen stopped feeling like butting anything and got nervous. And more sad.

"All set, guys. Thanks a lot." His hand was in his pocket again, lifting out his wallet and opening it to withdraw a fistful of five-Euro notes. Jamie glanced at him, and her mouth turned down hard as her eyes narrowed. The guy with the sandals made that clucking sound again and stepped up right behind Kellen.

For a second, Kellen went on waving the money, knowing he shouldn't, not sure why he felt like such an asshole. Only after he stopped moving did he realize no one but Jamie was looking at him.

In fact, no one was anywhere near them anymore. All together, the men who'd encircled Jamie and the sandal guy were retreating toward the toll gate. Catching Kellen's glance, sandal guy lifted one long, hairy arm. *Was that a wave?*

Then they were alone. Just he, Jamie, the cars revving past each other as they reentered the laneless *superstrade*, and the other car, parked maybe fifty feet ahead of them. Yellow, encased in grit, distinctly European-box. The windows were so grimy that Kellen couldn't tell whether anyone was in there. But someone had to be, because the single, sharp honk that had apparently scattered their rescuers had come from there.

"What was that bullshit with the money?" Jamie snapped. "They're not waiters. They were help—"

The scream silenced her. Audible even above the traffic, it soared over the retaining wall beyond the shoulder and seemed to unfurl in the air before dissipating. In the first instant, Kellen mistook it for a siren.

Glancing at Jamie, then the retaining wall, then the sun squatting on the horizon, he stepped closer. He felt panicky, for all sorts of reasons. He also didn't want this trip to end, ever. "Got another one of those universal words for you, James. Been in the papers all week. Ready? *Cadaver*."

"*Cadavere*," Jamie said, her head twisted around toward the origin of the scream.

"Right."

Together, they collapsed into leaning positions against their rented two-seater. It had been filthy when they got it – cleanliness apparently not the business necessity here that it was back home – and now sported a crust as thick as Tuscan bread.

"Well, you got that thing out." She was gesturing at the cell phone in his hands, and still sounded pissed. "Might as well use it."

Kellen held it up, feeling profoundly stupid. "Forgot to charge."

Instantly, Jamie was smiling again, bending forward to kiss him on the forehead, which was where she always kissed him these days.

"Sorry about the money thing," Kellen said, clinging to her smile. "I didn't mean anything bad, I was just . . ."

"Establishing dominance. Very George Bush."

"Dominance? I was about as dominant as . . . I was being nice. I was showing appreciation. Sincere appreciation. If not for those guys, we'd still be—"

The passenger door of the yellow car swung open, and Kellen stopped talking.

His first thought, as the guy unfolded onto the gravel, was that he shouldn't have been able to fit in there. This was easily the tallest Italian Kellen had seen all week. And the thinnest, and lightest-skinned. The hair on his head shone lustrous and long and black. For a few seconds, he stood swaying with his back to them, like some roadside reed that had sprung up from nowhere. Then he turned.

Just a boy, really. Silvery blue eyes that sparkled even from fifteen feet away, and long-fingered hands that spread over his bare, spindly legs like stick-bugs clinging to a branch. The driver's side door opened, and a second figure tumbled out.

This one was a virtual opposite of his companion, short and stumpy, with curly, dirty hair that bounced on the shoulders of his striped red rugby shirt. He wore red laceless canvas shoes. Black stubble stuck out of his cheeks like porcupine quills and all but obscured his goofy, ear-to-ear smile. He stopped one step behind the reedy kid. All Kellen could think of was *prince* and *troll*.

"*Ciao,*" said the troll, his smile somehow broadening as he bounded forward. Unlike everyone else they'd met here, he looked at Kellen at least as much Jamie. "*Ciao.*" He ran both hands over the hood of the rental car, then seemed to hold his breath, as though checking for a heartbeat.

"*Parla Inglese?*" Jamie tried.

"*Americano?*"

"Ye—" Kellen started, and Jamie overrode him.

"Canadian."

"*Si. Americano.*" Bouncing up and down on his heels, the troll grinned his prickly grin. "George Bush. Bang bang."

"John Kerry," Jamie said, rummaging in her purse and pulling out one of the campaign buttons her mother had demanded she keep there, as though it were mace. She waved it at the troll, who merely raised his bushy eyebrows and stared a question at them.

"What?" Kellen said. "*Non parlo l'Italiano.*"

"He didn't say anything, idiot," Jamie said, then gasped and stumbled forward.

Whirling, Kellen found the reedy boy directly behind them, staring down. He really was tall. And his eyes were deep-water blue. *Nothing frightening about him*, Kellen thought, wondering why his heart was juddering like that.

"*Mi dispiace.*" This one's voice rang, sonorous and way too big for its frame, like a bell-peal. From over the retaining wall, another one of those screams bloomed in the air, followed by a second and third in rapid succession.

"Howler monkeys?" Kellen said softly to Jamie. "What the hell is that?"

But Jamie was casting her eyes back and forth between the two

Italians. The troll pointed at the hood of their car, then raised his hands again.

"Oh," Jamie said. "The gas. My friend put in . . ."

The troll cocked his head and smiled uncomprehendingly.

Abruptly, Jamie started around to the gas tank and came back with the cap. She pointed it toward the troll. "See? Diesel."

"Diesel. *Si*."

"No diesel." Forming her fingers into a sort of gun, Jamie mimed putting a pump into the tank. "Gas."

For one more moment, the troll just stood. Then his hands flew to his cheeks. "Ohhh. Gas. No diesel. Ohhh." Still grinning, he drew one of his fingers slowly across his own throat. Then he let loose a stream of Italian.

After a minute or so of that, Kellen held up his cell phone. "You have one?" He was trying to control his embarrassment. And his ridiculous unease.

"Ohhh," the troll said, glancing at his companion.

Reedy boy's smile was regal and slow. He said nothing at all.

"Ohhh." Now, the troll seemed to be dancing as he moved around the front of the car. Instinctively, Kellen stepped a half pace back toward the retaining wall, just to feel a little less like he and Jamie were being maneuvered in between these two. "In America, auto break, call. Someone come." He snapped his fingers. "But *a l'Italia* . . . *Ohhh*." He smacked his palm to his forehead and made a Jerry Lewis grimace.

The troll's grunting laugh – unlike reedy boy's voice – simply annoyed Kellen. "They'll come. You have?" He waved the cell phone again.

"Why are you talking like that?" Jamie snapped.

"You have one? This one's . . ." He waved the phone some more, looking helplessly at his girlfriend. *Friend*, she'd said. "*Kaput*."

"Ah!" said prickly guy. "*Si. Si*." With another glance toward his companion, he raced back to the yellow car and stuck his head and hands inside the window. From the way his body worked, he was still yammering and gesturing as he rummaged around in there. Then he was back, waving a slim, black phone. He flipped open the face plate, put it to his ears, then raised the other hand in the questioning gesture again.

"I'll do it," Kellen said, reached out, and reedy boy seemed to lean forward. But he made no blocking movement as his companion handed over the phone.

"Thanks. *Grazie*," Kellen said, while Jamie beamed her brightest naïve, Kerry-loving smile at both Italians. Kellen's father said all Kerry supporters smiled like that. Jamie was quite possibly the only Democrat Kellen's father loved.

He had his fingers on the keypad before he realized the problem. "Shit," he barked.

The troll grinned. "Ohhh."

"What?" Jamie asked, stepping nearer. "Just call someone. Call American Express."

"You know the number?"

"I thought you did."

"It's on speed dial on my phone. My dad programmed it in. I've never even looked at it."

"Get your card."

"They didn't give me that card. They gave me the Visa."

"*Mi scusi,*" said the troll, stepping close as yet another of those long, shrieking cries erupted from behind the retaining wall. Reedy boy just looked briefly over his shoulder at the yellow car before returning his attention to Jamie and Kellen. Neither of the Italians seemed even to have heard the screams.

Tapping his red-striped chest, the troll reached out and chattered more Italian. Kellen had no idea what he was saying, but handed him the phone. Nodding, the troll punched in numbers. For a good minute, he stood with the phone at his ear, grinning. Then he started speaking fast into the mouthpiece, turning away and walking off down the shoulder.

"We're pretty lucky these guys are here to help," Jamie said against his ear.

Kellen glanced at her. She had her arms tucked in tight to her chest, her bottom lip curled against her teeth. For the first time, he realized she might be even more on edge than he was. She'd seen the same stories he had, after all. Same photos. The couple left dangling upside down from a flagpole outside the Colosseum, tarred and feathered and wrapped in the Stars and Stripes. The whole Tennessee family discovered laid out on a Coca-Cola blanket inside the ruins of a recently excavated 2000 year-old catacomb near the Forum, all of them naked, gutted from genitalia to xiphoid, stuffed with feathers. The couple on the flagpole had reminded Jamie of a paper she'd written on Ancient Rome, something about a festival where puppets got hung in trees. The puppets took the place of the little boys once sacrificed on whatever holiday that was.

The troll had walked all the way back to his yellow car, now, and he was talking animatedly, waving his free arm around and sometimes holding the cell phone in front of his face and shouting into it. Reedy boy simply stood, still as a sentry, gazing placidly over Kellen and Jamie's head toward the toll gate.

Overhead, the sun sank toward the retaining wall, and the air didn't cool, exactly, but thinned. Despite the unending honks and tire squeals from the A1, Kellen found something almost soothing about the traffic. There was a cheerfulness to it that rendered it completely different from the American variety. The horns reminded him mostly of squawking birds.

On impulse, he slid his arm around Jamie's shoulders. Her skin felt hot but dry, now. Her flip-flopped foot tapped in the dirt. She neither leaned into him nor away. Years from now, he knew, they'd be telling this story. To their respective children, not the children he'd always thought they'd have together. As an excuse to tell it, just once more, to each other.

At least, that's how it would be for him. "Diesel," he muttered. "Who uses diesel anymore?"

"People who care about the air. Diesel's a million times cleaner than regular gas."

"But it stinks." He tried putting a playful arm around her shoulders, but she shook him off.

"You smell anything?"

Kellen realized that he didn't.

"They fixed the smell problem ages ago. You're just brainwashed."

"Brainwashed?"

"Oil company puppet. George Bush puppet. Say W, little puppet."

"W," said Kellen, tried a smile though he still felt unsettled and dumb, and Jamie smiled weakly back, without taking her eyes off the placid face of the thin boy.

"Okay!" called the troll, waving. He stuck his head into the yellow car, continuing to gesture even though no one could see him, then reemerged. "*Arrivo. Si?* Coming."

Jamie smiled her thanks. Reedy boy turned his head enough to watch the sun as it vanished. Shadows poured over the retaining wall onto the freeway, and with them came a chorus of shrieks that flooded the air and took a long time evaporating.

Squeezing Jamie once on the elbow in what he hoped was a reassuring manner, Kellen made his way around their dead rental, climbed the dirt incline that rimmed the *superstrade*, and reached the retaining wall, which was taller than it looked. Even standing at its base, Kellen couldn't see over the top. The wall was made of the same chipped, ancient-looking stone that dotted excavation sites all over Italy. What, Kellen wondered, had this originally been built to retain?

Standing on tiptoe, he dropped his elbows on top of the stone, wedged a foot into the grit between rocks, and hoisted himself up. There he hung, elbows grinding into the wall, mouth wide open.

Without letting go, he turned his head after a few seconds. "Jamie," he said quietly, hoping somehow to attract her and not the reedy boy. But his voice didn't carry over the traffic, and Jamie didn't turn around. Against the yellow car, the troll leaned, smoking a thin, brownish cigarette. "*Jamie*," Kellen barked, and she glanced up, and the reedy boy, too, slowly. "Jamie, come here."

She came. Right as she reached the base of the wall, the screeching started once more. Knowing the source, as he now did, should have reassured Kellen. Instead, he closed his eyes and clutched the stone.

"Kel?" Jamie said, her voice so small, suddenly, that Kellen could barely hear it. "Kellen, what's up there?"

He opened his eyes, staring over the wall again. "Peacock Auschwitz."

"Will you stop saying shit like that? You sound like your stupid president, except he probably thinks Auschwitz is a beer."

"He's your president, too."

She was struggling to get her feet wedged into the chinks in the wall. He could have helped, or told her to stay where she was, but did neither.

"Oh, God," she said, as soon as she'd climbed up beside him. Then she went silent, too.

The neighborhood looked more like a gypsy camp than a slum. The tiny, collapsing houses seemed less decayed than pieced together out of discarded tires, chicken wire, and old stones. The shadows streaming over everything now had already pooled down there, so that the olive trees scattered everywhere looked like hunched old people, white haired, slouching through the ruins like mourners in a graveyard.

Attached to every single structure – even the ones where roofs had caved in, walls given way – was a cage, as tall as the houses, lined with some kind of razor wire with the sharp points twisted inward. Inside the cages were birds.

Peacocks. Three, maybe four to a house, including the ones that were already dead. The live ones paced skittishly, great tails dragging in the dust, through the spilled innards and chopped bird feet lining the cage bottoms. There was no mistaking any of it, and even if there were, the reek that rose from down there was a clincher. Shit and death. Unmistakable.

In the cage nearest them, right at the bottom of the wall, one bird glanced up, lifted its tail as though considering throwing it open, then tilted its head back and screamed.

"You know," said the reedy boy, right beneath them, in perfect though faintly accented English, and Kellen and Jamie jerked. Then they just hung, clinging to the wall. "The Ancient Romans sacrificed the *pavone* – the peacock, *si?* – to honor their emperors. They symbolized immortality. And their tails were the thousand eyes of God, watching over our civilization. Of course they also sacrificed humans, to the *Larvae*".

Very slowly, still clutching the top of the wall, Kellen turned his head. The boy was so close that Kellen could feel the exhalation of his breath on the sweat still streaming down his back. Even if Kellen had tried a kick, he wouldn't have been able to get anything on it. Jamie had gone rigid, and when he glanced that way, he saw that her eyes had teared up, though they remained fixed unblinkingly on the birds below.

"Larvae?" he asked, just to be talking. He couldn't think what else to do. "Like worms?"

"Dead men. Demons, really. Demons made of dead, bad men."

"Why?"

"Yes!" The boy nodded enthusiastically, folding his hands in that contemplative, regal way. "You are right. To invoke the *Larvae* and set them upon the enemies of Rome? Or to pacify them, and so drive away ill fortune? Which is the correct course? I would guess even they did not always know. What is your guess?"

That I'm about to die, Kellen thought crazily, closed his eyes, and bit his lip to keep from crying out like the peacocks beneath him. "So Romans cherished their dead bad men?"

"And their sacrifices. And their executioners. Like all human civilizations do."

Carefully, expecting a dagger to his ribs at any moment, Kellen eased his elbows off the stone, let one leg drop, then the other. The birds had gone silent. He stood a second, face to the stone. Then he turned.

The reedy boy was fifteen feet away, head aimed down the road as he walked slowly to his car.

"Jamie," Kellen hissed, and Jamie skidded down the wall to land next to him.

"Ow," she murmured, crooking her elbow to reveal an ugly red scrape.

"Jamie. Are we in trouble?"

She looked at him. He'd never seen the expression on her face before. But he recognized it instantly, and it chilled him almost as much as the reedy boy's murmur. *Contempt.* He'd always been terrified she'd show him that, sooner or later. And also certain that someday she would.

Without a word, she walked down the dirt incline, holding her elbow against her chest. When she reached the car, she stuck out a forefinger and began trailing it through the dirt on the driver's side window.

Okay, Kellen urged himself. *Think.* They had no phone. And who would they call? What was 911 in Italian? Maybe they could just walk fast toward the toll gate. Run out in traffic. People would honk. But they'd also see them. Nothing could happen as long as someone was looking, right?

Then he remembered the way the men who'd helped them to the shoulder had vanished. His mind veered into a skid. *They all know. The whole country. An agreement they've come to. They knew the yellow car, the location. The birds. They knew. They left us here. Put us here. Even the guy at the gas station, just what had he poured in the tank to supposedly save them?*

Peacock screams. A whole chorus of them, as the last light went out of the day. Kellen scrambled fast down the dirt toward the car, toward Jamie, who was crouched on the gravel now, head down and shaking back and forth on her long, tanned neck.

At the same moment, he saw both what Jamie had scrawled in the window grime and the two men by the yellow car starting toward them again. They came side by side, the reedy boy with one long-fingered hand on the stumpy one's shoulders.

AMERICAN MORONS. That's what she'd written.

"I love you," Kellen blurted. She didn't even look up.

The men from the yellow car were twenty feet away, now, ignoring the cars, the bird-screams, everything but their quarry.

Hop the wall, Kellen thought. But the idea of hiding in that neighborhood – of just setting foot in it – seemed even worse than facing down these two. Also, weirdly, like sacrilege. *Like parading with camera bags and iPods and cell phones through places where people had prayed, played with, and killed each other.*

This was what he was thinking, as the two Romans ambled ever nearer, when the truck loomed up, let loose a gloriously throaty, brain-clearing honk, and settled with a sigh right beside them.

"We're saved," he whispered, then dropped to his knees as the first and only girl he'd loved finally looked up. "Jamie, the tow truck's here. We're saved."

In no time at all, the driver was out, surveying the ruined rental, shoving pieces of puffy, cold pizza into their hands. He didn't speak English either, just gestured with emphatic Italian clarity. The cab of his truck was for him and his pizza. Jamie and Kellen could ride in their car. They climbed back in, and as the driver attached a chain and winch to the bumper, began to drag them onto the long, high bed of the truck, Kellen thought about blasting his horn, giving a chin-flick to the yellow car guys.

Except that that was ridiculous. The yellow car guys had called the tow truck. There'd never been any danger at all.

He started to laugh, put his hand on Jamie's. She was shivering, though it was still a long way from cold. The tow truck driver chained them into place, climbed back into his cab. Only then did it occur to Kellen that now they were really trapped.

With a lurch, the truck edged two wheels onto the *superstrade*, answering a volley of horn blares with a bazooka blast of its own. Perched there, eight feet off the ground, chained in the car in the tow truck bed, Kellen had a perfect view of the blue Mercedes coupe as it swerved onto the shoulder directly behind the yellow car. He saw the driver climb out of the blue car, wearing a black poncho that made no sense in the heat.

Stepping away from his own door, this new arrival simply watched as the reedy guy pointed a command and the troll dragged a little boy, bound in rusty wire, kicking and hurling his gagged head from side to side, out of the back seat of the yellow car. All too clearly, Kellen saw the boy's face. So distinctly American he could practically picture it on a milk carton already. Wheat-blond hair, freckles like crayon dots all over his cheeks, Yankees cap still somehow wedged over his ears.

Except it would never wind up on a milk carton, Kellen realized, grabbing at the useless steering wheel. *When he'd called home to tell his father about the murders, his father had snorted and said, "Thus proving there are ungrateful malcontents in Italy just like here." No one else they'd called had even heard the news. This boy would simply evaporate into the new American history, like the dead soldiers lined up in their coffins in that smuggled photograph from the second Gulf War.*

Shuddering himself now, still holding the wheel, Kellen wondered where the boy's face would appear in its Italian newspaper photo. *Drowned in a fountain atop the Spanish Steps? Wedged into one of the slits in the underground walls of Nero's Crptoporticus? Strewn amid the refuse and scraps of fast-food wrappers and discarded homeless-person shoes along the banks of the Tiber?*

Just as the truck rumbled forward, plowing a space for itself in the traffic, the guy in the poncho closed the door of his Mercedes on his new passenger, and both the troll and the reedy boy looked up and caught Kellen's eyes.

The troll waved. The reedy boy smiled.

ADAM L. G. NEVILL

Where Angels Come In

ADAM L. G. NEVILL LIVES IN LONDON, England. He is the author of *Banquet for the Damned* from PS Publishing – an original novel of the occult and supernatural, and homage to M. R. James and the great age of the British weird tale.

His recent anthology appearances include *Gathering the Bones*, *Poe's Progeny*, *Bernie Hermann's Manic Sextet* and *Cinema Macabre*.

"Knowing of my admiration for the stories of M. R. James, Gary Fry of Gray Friar Press invited me to submit a short story to his anthology *Poe's Progeny*. Not a pastiche, nor imitation, but something original that captured the spirit of the master. It was a challenge that I relished.

"As the spectres of M. R. James haunted my own childhood with a 'pleasing terror' (to this day little has frightened me more than 'Wailing Well') I decided to write a story incorporating not dissimilar spectres from that ghastly well, but told directly from a child's point of view. Something James never did.

"I also wanted to strip the style down to a childlike simplicity – minus Jamesian scholars and erudition – while still maintaining his suggestive and restrained approach when handling the supernatural element. Curiously, I realised that young narrators are far more receptive to, and accepting of, the uncanny, and their psychic terror is probably greater than that of an adult character.

"For fans of James, see if you can spot the three references to his stories in the sculpture garden. And I can only hope the master would approve of my tribute. Thus far, nothing has visited to inform me otherwise (touch wood)."

O NE SIDE OF MY BODY IS FULL OF TOOTH-ACHE. Right in the middle of the bones. While the skin and muscles have a chilly pins-and-needles tingle that won't ever turn back into the warmth of a healthy arm and leg. Which is why Nanna Alice is here; sitting on the chair at the foot of my bed, her crumpled face in shadow. But the milky light that comes through the net curtains finds a sparkle in her quick eyes and gleams on the yellowish grin that hasn't changed since my mother let her into the house, made her a cup of tea and showed her into my room. Nanna Alice smells like the inside of overflow pipes at the back of the council houses.

"Least you still got one 'alf," she says. She has a metal brace on her thin leg. The foot at the end of the calliper is inside a baby's shoe. Even though it's rude, I can't stop staring. Her normal leg is fat. "They took me leg and one arm." Using her normal fingers, she picks the dead hand from a pocket in her cardigan and plops it on to her lap. Small and grey, it reminds me of a doll's hand. I don't look for long.

She leans forward in her chair so I can smell the tea on her breath. "Show me where you was touched, luv."

I unbutton my pyjama top and roll on to my good side. Podgy fingertips press around the shrivelled skin at the top of my arm, but she doesn't touch the see-through parts where the fingertips and thumb once held me. Her eyes go big and her lips pull back to show gums more black than purple. Against her thigh, the doll hand shakes. She coughs, sits back in her chair. Cradles the tiny hand and rubs it with living fingers. When I cover my shoulder, she watches that part of me without blinking. Seems disappointed to see it covered so soon. Wets her lips. "Tell us what 'appened, luv."

Propping myself up in the pillows, I peer out the window and swallow the big lump in my throat. Dizzy and a bit sickish, I don't want to remember what happened. Not ever.

Across the street inside the spiky metal fence built around the park, I can see the usual circle of mothers. Huddled into their coats and sitting on benches beside pushchairs, or holding the leads of tugging dogs, they watch the children play. Upon the climbing frames and on the wet grass, the kids race about and shriek and laugh and fall and cry. Wrapped up in scarves and padded coats, they swarm among hungry pigeons and seagulls; thousands of small white and grey shapes, pecking around the little stamping feet. Sometimes the birds panic and rise in curving squadrons, trying to get their plump bodies into the air with flap-cracky wings. And the children are blind with their own fear and excitement in brief tornadoes of dusty feathers, red feet, cruel beaks and startled eyes. But they are safe here – the children and the birds – closely watched by tense mothers and kept inside the stockade of iron railings: the only place outdoors the children are allowed to play since I came back, alone.

A lot of things go missing in our town: cats, dogs, children. And they never come back. Except for me and Nanna Alice. We came home, or at least half of us did.

Lying in my sick bed, pale in the face and weak in the heart, I drink medicines, read books and watch the children play from my bedroom window. Sometimes I sleep. But only when I have to. Because when I sink away from the safety of home and a watching parent, I go back to the white house on the hill.

For the Nanna Alice, the time she went inside the big white place as a little girl, is a special occasion; like she's grateful. Our dad calls her a "silly old fool" and doesn't want her in our house. He doesn't know she's here today. But when a child vanishes, or someone dies, lots of the mothers ask the Nanna to visit them. "She can see things and feel things the rest of us don't," my mom says. Like the two police ladies, and the mothers of the two girls who went missing last winter, and Pickering's parents, my mom just wants to know what happened to me.

At least when I'm awake, I can read, watch television, and listen to my mom and sisters downstairs. But in dreams I have no choice: I go back to the white house on the hill, where old things with skipping feet circle me, then rush in close to show their faces.

"Tell us, luv. Tell us about the 'ouse," Nanna Alice says. Can't think why she's smiling like that. No adult likes to talk about the beautiful, tall house on the hill. Even our dads who come home from the industry, smelling of plastic and beer, look uncomfortable if their kids say they can hear the ladies crying again: above their heads, but deep inside their ears at the same time, calling from the distance, from the hill, from inside us. Our parents can't hear it anymore, but they remember the sound from when they were small. It's like people are trapped and calling out for help. And when no one comes, they get real angry. "Foxes," the parents tell us, but don't look you in the eye when they say it.

For a long time after what people call "my accident" I was unconscious in the hospital. After I woke up, I was so weak I stayed there for another three months. Gradually, one half of my body got stronger and I was allowed home. That's when the questions began. Not just about my injuries, but about my mate Pickering, who they never found. And now crazy Nanna Alice wants to know every single thing I can remember and all of the dreams too. Only I never know what is real and what came out of the coma with me.

For years, we talked about going up there. All the kids do. Pickering, Ritchie and me wanted to be the bravest boys in our school. We wanted to break in there and come out with treasure to use as proof that we'd been inside, and not just looked in through the gate like all the others we knew.

Some people say the house and its grounds was once a place where old, rich people lived after they retired from owning the industry, the land, the laws, our houses, our town, us. Others say it was built on an old well and the ground is contaminated. A teacher told us it used to be a hospital and is still full of germs. Our dad said it was an asylum for lunatics that closed down over a hundred years ago and has stayed empty ever since because it's falling to pieces and is too expensive to repair. That's why kids should never go there: you could be crushed by bricks or fall through a floor. Nanna Alice says it's a place "where angels come in". But we all know it's the place where the missing things are. Every street in the miles of our town has lost a pet or knows a family who's lost a child. And every time the police search the big house, they find nothing. No one remembers the big gate being open.

So on a Friday morning when all the kids in our area were walking to school, me, Ritchie and Pickering sneaked off, the other way. Through the allotments, where me and Pickering were once caught smashing deck chairs and bean poles; through the woods full of broken glass and dog shit; over the canal bridge; across the potato fields with our heads down so the farmer wouldn't see us; and over the railway tracks until we couldn't even see the roofs of the last houses in our town. Talking about the hidden treasure, we stopped by the old ice-cream van with four flat tyres, to throw rocks and stare at the faded menu on the little counter, our mouths watering as we made selections that would never be served. On the other side of the woods that surround the estate, we could see the chimneys of the big, white mansion above the trees.

Although Pickering had been walking out front the whole time telling us he wasn't scared of security guards or watch dogs, or even ghosts – "cus you can just put your hand froo 'em" – when we reached the bottom of the wooded hill, no one said anything or even looked at each other. Part of me always believed we would turn back at the black gate, because the fun part was telling stories about the house and planning the expedition and imagining terrible things.

Going inside was different because lots of the missing kids had talked about the house before they disappeared. And some of the young men who broke in there for a laugh always came away a bit funny in the head, but our dad said that was because of drugs.

Even the trees around the estate were different, like they were too still and silent and the air between them real cold. But we still went up through the trees and found the high brick wall that surrounds the grounds. There was barbed wire and broken glass set into concrete on top of it. We followed the wall until we reached the black iron gate. Seeing the PRIVATE PROPERTY: TRESPASSERS WILL BE PROSECUTED sign made shivers go up my neck and under my hair. The gate is higher than a house with a curved top made from iron spikes, set between two pillars with big stone balls on top.

"I heard them balls roll off and kill trespassers," Ritchie said. I'd heard the same thing, but when Ritchie said that I just knew he wasn't going in with us.

We wrapped our hands around the cold black bars of the gate and peered through at the long flagstone path that goes up the hill, between avenues of trees and old statues hidden by branches and weeds. All the uncut grass of the lawns was as high as my waist and the old flower beds were wild with colour. At the summit was the tall, white house with big windows. Sunlight glinted off the glass. Above all the chimneys, the sky was blue. "Princesses lived there," Pickering whispered.

"Can you see anyone?" Ritchie asked. He was shivering with excitement and had to take a pee. He tried to rush it over some nettles – we were fighting a war against nettles and wasps that summer – but got half of it down his legs.

"It's empty," Pickering whispered. "'Cept for 'idden treasure. Darren's brother got this owl inside a big glass. I seen it. Looks like it's still alive. At night, it moves its 'ead."

Ritchie and I looked at each other; everyone knows the stories about the animals or birds inside the glass that people find up there. There's one about a lamb with no fur, inside a tank of green water that someone's uncle found when he was a boy. It still blinks its little black eyes. And someone said they found skeletons of children all dressed up in old clothes, holding hands.

All rubbish; because I know what's really inside there. Pickering had seen nothing, but if we challenged him he'd start yelling, "Have so! Have so!" and me and Ritchie weren't happy with anything but whispering near the gate.

"Let's just watch and see what happens. We can go in another day," Ritchie couldn't help himself saying.

"You're chickening out," Pickering said, kicking at Ritchie's legs. "I'll tell everyone Ritchie pissed his pants."

Ritchie's face went white, his bottom lip quivered. Like me, he was imagining crowds of swooping kids shouting, "Piss pot. Piss pot." Once the crowds find a coward, they'll hunt him every day until he's pushed out to the edges of the playground where the failures stand and watch. Every kid in town knows this place takes away brothers, sisters, cats and dogs, but when we hear the cries from the hill, it's our duty to force one another out here. It's a part of our town and always has been. Pickering is one of the toughest kids in school; he had to go.

"I'm going in first," Pick said, standing back and sizing up the gate. "Watch where I put my hands and feet." And it didn't take him long to get over. There was a little wobble at the top when he swung a leg between two spikes, but not long after he was standing on the other side, grinning at us. To me, it now looked like there was a little ladder built into the gate – where the metal vines and thorns curved between the long poles, you could see the pattern of steps for small hands and feet. I'd heard that little girls always found a secret wooden door in the brick wall that no one else can find when they look for it. But that might just be another story.

If I didn't go over and the raid was a success, I didn't want to spend the rest of my life being a piss pot and wishing I'd gone with Pick. We could be heroes together. And I was full of the same crazy feeling that makes me climb oak trees to the very top branches, stare up at the sky and let go with my hands for a few seconds knowing that if I fall I will die.

When I climbed away from whispering Ritchie on the ground, the squeaks and groans of the gate were so loud I was sure I could be heard all the way up the hill and inside the house. When I got to the top and was getting ready to swing a leg over, Pick said, "Don't cut your balls off." But I couldn't smile, or even breathe. My arms and legs started to shake. It was much higher up there than it looked from the ground. With one leg over, between the spikes, panic came up my throat. If one hand slipped off the worn metal I imagined my whole weight forcing the spike through my thigh, and how I would hang there, dripping. Then I looked up toward the house and I felt there was a face behind every window, watching me.

Many of the stories about the white place on the hill suddenly filled my head: how you only see the red eyes of the thing that drains your blood; how it's kiddy-fiddlers that hide in there and torture captives for days before burying them alive, which is why no one ever finds the missing children; and some say the thing that makes the crying noise might look like a beautiful lady when you first see her, but she soon changes once she's holding you.

"Hurry up. It's easy," Pick said from way down below. Ever so slowly, I lifted my second leg over, then lowered myself down the other side. He was right; it wasn't a hard climb at all; kids could do it.

I stood in hot sunshine on the other side of the gate, smiling. The light was brighter over there too; glinting off all the white stone and glass up on the hill. And the air seemed weird – real thick and warm. When I looked back through the gate, the world around Ritchie – who stood alone biting his bottom lip – looked grey and dull like it was November or something. Around us, the overgrown grass was so glossy it hurt your eyes to look at it. Reds, yellows, purples, oranges and lemons of the flowers flowed inside my head and I could taste hot summer in my mouth. Around the trees, statues and flagstone path, the air was a bit wavy and my skin felt so good and warm I shivered. Closed my eyes. "Beautiful," I said; a word I wouldn't usually use around Pick. "This is where I want to live," he said, his eyes and face one big smile. Then we both started to laugh. We hugged each other, which we'd never done before. Anything I ever worried about seemed silly now. I felt taller. Could go anywhere, do anything I liked. I know Pick felt the same.

Protected by the overhanging tree branches and long grasses, we kept to the side of the path and began walking up the hill. But after a while, I started to feel a bit nervous as we got closer to the top. The house looked bigger than I thought it was down by the gate. Even though we could see no one and hear nothing, I also felt like I'd walked into this big, crowded, but silent place where lots of eyes were watching me. Following me.

We stopped walking by the first statue that wasn't totally covered in green moss and dead leaves. Through the low branches of a tree, we could still see the two naked children, standing together on the stone block. One boy and one girl. They were both smiling, but not in a nice way, because we could see too much of their teeth. "They's all open on the chest," Pickering said. And he was right; their dry stone skin was peeled back on the breastbone and in their outstretched hands they held small lumps of stone with veins carved into them – their own little hearts. The good feeling I had down by the gate was completely gone now.

Sunlight shone through the trees and striped us with shadows and bright slashes. Eyes big and mouths dry, we walked on and checked some of the other statues we passed. You couldn't help it; it's like they made you stare at them to work out what was sticking through the leaves and branches and ivy. There was one horrible cloth thing that seemed too real to be made from stone. Its face was so nasty, I couldn't look for long. Standing under it gave me the queer feeling that it was swaying from side to side, ready to jump off the stone block and come at us.

Pick walked ahead of me a little bit, but soon stopped to see another. He shrunk in its shadow, then peered at his shoes. I caught up with him but didn't look too long either. Beside the statue of the ugly man in a cloak and big hat, was a smaller shape covered in a robe and hood, with something coming out of a sleeve that reminded me of snakes.

I didn't want to go any further and knew I'd be seeing these statues in my sleep for a long time. Looking down the hill at the gate, I was surprised to see how far away it was now. "Think I'm going back," I said to Pick.

Pickering looked at me, but never called me a chicken; he didn't want to start a fight and be on his own in here. "Let's just go into the house quick," he said. "And get something. Otherwise no one will believe us."

But being just a bit closer to the white house with all the staring windows made me sick with nerves. It was four storeys high and must have had hundreds of rooms inside. All the windows upstairs were dark so we couldn't see beyond the glass. Downstairs, they were all boarded up against trespassers. "They's all empty, I bet," Pickering said to try and make us feel better. But it didn't do much for me; he didn't seem so smart or hard now; just a stupid kid who hadn't got a clue.

"Nah," I said.

He walked away from me. "Well I am. I'll say you waited outside." His voice was too soft to carry the usual threat. But all the same, I suddenly couldn't stand the thought of his grinning, triumphant face while Ritchie and I were considered piss pots, especially after I'd climbed the gate and come this far. My part would mean nothing if he went further than me.

We never looked at any more of the statues. If we had, I don't think we'd have ever got to the wide stone steps that went up to the big iron doors of the house. Didn't seem to take us long to reach the house either. Even taking small, slow, reluctant steps got us there real quick. On legs full of warm water I followed Pickering up to the doors.

"Why is they made of metal?" he asked me. I never had an answer.

He pressed both hands against the doors. One of them creaked but never opened. "They's locked," he said.

Secretly relieved, I took a step away from the doors. As all the ground floor windows were boarded over too, it looked like we could go home. Then, as Pickering shoved at the creaky door again, this time with his shoulder and his body at an angle, I'm sure I saw movement in a window on the second floor. Something whitish. Behind the glass, it was like a shape appeared out of the darkness and then sank back into it, quick but graceful. I thought of a carp surfacing in a cloudy pond before vanishing the same moment you saw its pale back. "Pick!" I hissed at him.

There was a clunk inside the door Pickering was straining his body against. "It's open," he cried out, and stared into the narrow gap between the two iron doors. But I couldn't help thinking the door had been opened from inside.

"I wouldn't," I said to him. He just smiled and waved at me to come over and help as he pushed to make a bigger space. I stood still and watched the windows upstairs. The widening door made a grinding sound against the floor. Without another word, he walked inside the big white house.

Silence hummed in my ears. Sweat trickled down my face. I wanted to run down to the gate.

After a few seconds, Pickering's face appeared in the doorway. "Quick. Come an' look at all the birds." He was breathless with excitement.

I peered through the gap at a big, empty hallway and could see a staircase going up to the next floor. Pickering was standing in the middle of the hall, not moving. He was looking at the ground. At all the dried-up birds on the wooden floorboards. Hundreds of dead pigeons. I went in.

No carpets, or curtains, or light bulbs, just bare floorboards, white walls, and two closed doors on either side of the hall. On the floor, most of the birds still had feathers but looked real thin. Some were just bones. Others were dust. "They get in and they got nuffin' to eat," Pickering said. "We should collect all the skulls." He crunched across the floor and tried the doors at either side of the hall, yanking the handles up and down. "Locked," he said. "Both of 'em locked. Let's go up them stairs. See if there's summat in the rooms."

I flinched at every creak caused by our feet on the stairs. I told him to walk at the sides like me. He wasn't listening, just going up fast on his plumpish legs. I caught up with him at the first turn in the stairs and began to feel real strange again. The air was weird; hot and thin like we were in a tiny space. We were both all sweaty under our school uniforms from just walking up one flight of stairs. I had to lean against a wall while he shone his torch up at the next floor. All we could see were the plain walls of a dusty corridor. A bit of sunlight was getting in from somewhere upstairs, but not much. "Come on," he said, without turning his head to look at me.

"I'm going outside," I said. "I can't breathe." But as I moved to go back down the first flight of stairs, I heard a door creak open and then close, below us. I stopped still and heard my heart banging against my eardrums from the inside. The sweat turned to frost on my face and neck and under my hair. Real quick, and sideways, something moved across the shaft of light falling through the open front door. My eyeballs went cold and I felt dizzy. Out the corner of my eye, I could see Pickering's white face, watching me from above on the next flight of stairs. He turned the torch off with a loud click.

It moved again, back the way it had come, but paused this time at the edge of the long rectangle of white light on the hall floor. And started to sniff at the dirty ground. It was the way she moved down there that made me feel light as a feather and ready to faint. Least I think it was a *she*. But when people get that old you can't always tell. There wasn't much hair on the head and the skin was yellow. She looked more like a puppet made of bones and dressed in a grubby nighty than an old lady. And could old ladies move so fast? Sideways like a crab, looking backwards at the open door, so I couldn't see the face properly, which I was glad of.

If I moved too quick, I'm sure it would look up and see me. I took two slow side-steps to get behind the wall of the next staircase where Pickering was hiding. He looked like he was about to cry. Like me, I knew all he could hear was his own heartbeat.

Then we heard the sound of another door open from somewhere downstairs, out of sight. We knelt down, trembling against each other and peered around the corner of the staircase to make sure the old thing wasn't coming up the stairs, sideways. But a second figure had now appeared down there. I nearly cried when I saw it skittering around by the door. It moved quicker than the first one with the help of two black sticks. Bent right over with a hump for a back, it was covered in a dusty black dress that swished over the floor. What I could see of the face through the veil was all pinched and as sickly-white as grubs under wet bark. When she made the whistling sound, it hurt my ears deep inside and made my bones feel cold.

Pickering's face was wild with fear. I was seeing too much of his eyes. "Is they old ladies?" he said in a voice that sounded all broken.

I grabbed his arm. "We got to get out. Maybe there's a window, or another door 'round the back." Which meant we had to go up these stairs, run through the building to find another way down to the ground-floor, before breaking our way out.

I took another peek down the stairs to see what they were doing, but wished I hadn't. There were two more of them. A tall man with legs like sticks was looking up at us with a face that never changed because it had no lips or eyelids or nose. He wore a creased suit with a gold watch chain on the waistcoat, and was standing behind a wicker chair. In the chair was a bundle wrapped in tartan blankets. Above the coverings I could see a small head inside a cloth cap. The face was yellow as corn in a tin. The first two were standing by the open door so we couldn't get out.

Running up the stairs into an even hotter darkness on the next floor, my whole body felt baggy and clumsy and my knees chipped together. Pickering went first with the torch and used his elbows so I couldn't overtake. I bumped into his back and kicked his heels. Inside his fast breathing, I could hear him sniffing at tears. "Is they comin'?" he kept saying. I didn't have the breath to answer and kept running through the long corridor, between dozens of closed doors, to get to the end. I looked straight ahead and was sure I would freeze-up if one of the doors suddenly opened. And with our feet making such a bumping on the floorboards, I can't say I was surprised when I heard the click of a lock behind us. We both made the mistake of looking back.

At first we thought it was waving at us, but then realised the skinny figure in the dirty night-dress was moving its long arms through the air to attract the attention of the others that had followed us up the stairwell. We could hear the scuffle and swish as they came through the dark behind us. But how could this one see us, I thought, with all those rusty bandages around its head? Then we heard another of those horrible whistles, followed by more doors opening real quick like things were in a hurry to get out of the rooms.

At the end of the corridor, there was another stairwell with more light in it that fell from a high window three floors up. But the glass must have been dirty and greenish, because everything around us on the stairs looked like it was underwater. When he turned to bolt down them stairs, I saw Pick's face was all shiny with tears and the front of his trousers had a dark patch spreading down one leg.

It was real hard to get down them stairs and back to the ground. It was like we had no strength left in our bodies, as if the fear was draining it through the slappy, tripping soles of our feet. But it was more than the terror slowing us down; the air was so thin and dry it was hard to get our breath in and out of our lungs fast enough. My shirt was stuck to my back and I was dripping under the arms. Pick's hair was wet and he was slowing right down, so I overtook him.

At the bottom of the stairs I ran into another long, empty corridor of closed doors and greyish light, that ran through the back of the building. Just looking all the way down it, made me bend over with my hands on my knees to rest. But Pickering just ploughed right into me from behind and knocked me over. He ran across my body and stamped on my hand. "They's comin'," he whined in a tearful voice and went stumbling down the passage. I got back to my feet and started down the corridor after him. Which never felt like a good idea to me; if some of them things were waiting in the hall by the front doors, while others were coming up fast behind us, we'd get ourselves trapped. I thought about opening a door and trying to kick out the boards over a window in one of the ground-floor rooms. Plenty of them old things seemed to come out of rooms when we ran past them, like we were waking them up, but they never came out of every room. So we would just have to take a chance. I called out to Pick to stop. I was wheezing like Billy Skid at school who's got asthma, so maybe Pickering never heard me, because he kept on running toward the end. I looked back at the stairwell we'd just come out of, then looked about at the doors in the passage. As I was wondering which one to pick, a little voice said, "Do you want to hide in here!"

I jumped into the air and cried out like I'd trod on a snake. Stared at where the voice came from. I could see a crack between this big brownish door and the doorframe. Part of a little girl's face peeked out. "They won't see you. We can play with my dolls." She smiled and opened the door wider. She had a really white face inside a black bonnet all covered in ribbons. The rims of her dark eyes were bright red like she'd been crying for a long time.

My chest was hurting and my eyes were stinging with sweat. Pickering was too far ahead of me to catch him up. I could hear his feet banging away on loose floorboards, way off in the darkness and I didn't think I could run any further. I nodded at the girl. She stood aside and opened the door wider. The bottom of her black dress swept through the dust. "Quickly," she said with an excited smile, and then looked down the corridor, to see if anything was coming. "Most of them are blind, but they can hear things."

I moved through the doorway. Brushed past her. Smelled something gone bad. Put a picture in my head of the dead cat, squashed flat in the woods, that I found one time on a hot day. But over that smell was something like the bottom of my granny's old wardrobe, with the one broken door and little iron keys in the locks that don't work any more.

Softly, the little girl closed the door behind us, and walked off across the wooden floor with her head held high, like a "little Madam" my dad would say. Light was getting into this room from some red and green windows up near the high ceiling. Two big chains hung down holding lights with no bulbs, and there was a stage at one end with a thick greenish curtain pulled across the front. Little footlights stuck up at the front of the stage. It must have been a ballroom once.

Looking for a way out – behind me, to the side, up ahead, everywhere – I followed the little girl in the black bonnet over to the stage and up the stairs at the side. She disappeared through the curtains without making a sound, and I followed because I could think of nowhere else to go and I wanted a friend in here. The long curtains smelled so bad around my face, I put a hand over my mouth.

She asked my name and where I lived. I told her like I was talking to a teacher who's just caught me doing something wrong, even giving her my house number. "We didn't mean to trespass," I said. "We never stole nothing." She cocked her head to one side and frowned like she was trying to remember something. Then she smiled and said, "All of these are mine. I found them." She drew my attention to the dolls on the floor; little shapes of people I couldn't see properly in the dark. She sat down among them and started to pick them up one at a time to show me, but I was too nervous to pay much attention and I didn't like the look of the cloth animal with its fur worn down to the grubby material. It had stitched up eyes and no ears; the arms and legs were too long for its body. And I didn't like the way the little, dirty head was stiff and upright like it was watching me.

Behind us, the rest of the stage was in darkness with a faint glow of white wall in the distance. Peering from the stage at the boarded-up windows down the right side of the dance floor, I could see some bright daylight around the edge of two big hardboard sheets nailed over patio doors. There was a breeze coming through. Must have been a place where someone got in before. "I got to go," I said to the girl behind me, who was whispering to her animals and dolls. I was about to step through the curtains and head for the daylight when I heard the rushing of a crowd in the corridor that me and Pickering had just run through – feet shuffling, canes tapping, wheels squeaking and two hooting sounds. It all seemed to go on for ages. A long parade I didn't want to see.

As it went past, the main door clicked open and something glided into the ballroom. I pulled back from the curtains and held my breath. The little girl kept mumbling to the nasty toys. I wanted to cover my ears. Another crazy part of me wanted it all to end; wanted me to step out from behind the curtains and offer myself to the tall figure down there on the dance-floor, holding the tatty parasol over its head. It spun around quickly like it was moving on tiny, silent wheels under its long musty skirts. Sniffing at the air. For me. Under the white net attached to the brim of the rotten hat and tucked into the high collars of the dress, I saw a bit of face that looked like skin on a rice pudding. I would have screamed but there was no air inside me.

I looked down, where the little girl had been sitting. She had gone, but something was moving on the floor. Squirming. I blinked my eyes fast. For a moment, it looked like all her toys were trembling, but when I squinted at the Golly with bits of curly white hair on its head, it was lying perfectly still where she had dropped it. The little girl may have hidden me, but I was glad she had gone.

Way off in the stifling distance of the big house, I then heard a scream; full of all the panic and terror and woe in the whole world. The figure with the little umbrella spun right around on the dance-floor and then rushed out of the ballroom toward the sound.

I slipped out from behind the curtains. A busy chattering sound came from the distance. It got louder until it echoed through the corridor and ballroom and almost covered the sounds of the wailing boy. It sounded like his cries were swirling round and round, bouncing off walls and closed doors, like he was running somewhere far off inside the house, in a circle that he couldn't get out of.

I crept down the stairs at the side of the stage and ran across to the long strip of burning sunlight I could see shining through one side of the patio doors. I pulled at the big rectangle of wood until it splintered and I could see broken glass in a doorframe and lots of thick grass outside.

For the first time since I'd seen the first figure scratching about the front entrance, I truly believed I could escape. I could climb through the gap I was making, run around the outside of the house and then go down the hill to the gate, while they were all busy inside with the crying boy. But just as my breathing went all quick and shaky with the glee of escape, I heard a whump sound on the floor behind me, like something had just dropped to the floor from the stage. Teeny vibrations tickled the soles of my feet. Then I heard something coming across the floor toward me – a shuffle, like a body dragging itself real quick.

Couldn't bear to look behind me and see another one close up. I snatched at the board and pulled with all my strength at the bit not nailed down, so the whole thing bent and made a gap. Sideways, I squeezed a leg, hip, arm and shoulder out. Then my head was suddenly bathed in warm sunlight and fresh air.

It must have reached out then and grabbed my left arm under the shoulder. The fingers and thumb were so cold they burned my skin. And even though my face was in daylight, everything went dark in my eyes except for little white flashes, like when you stand up too quick. I wanted to be sick. Tried to pull away, but one side of my body was all slow and heavy and full of pins and needles.

I let go off the hardboard sheet. It slapped shut like a mouse trap. The wood knocked me through the gap and into the grass outside. Behind my head, I heard a sound like celery snapping. Something shrieked into my ear which made me go deafish for a week.

Sitting down in the grass outside, I was sick down my jumper. Mucus and bits of spaghetti hoops that looked all white and smelled real bad. I looked at the door I had fallen out of. Through my bleary eyes I saw an arm that was mostly bone, stuck between the wood and door-frame. I made myself roll away and then get to my feet on the grass that was flattened down.

Moving around the outside of the house, back toward the front of the building and the path that would take me down to the gate, I wondered if I'd bashed my left side. The shoulder and hip were achy and cold and stiff. It was hard to move. I wondered if that's what broken bones felt like. All my skin was wet with sweat too, but I was shivery and cold. I just wanted to lie down in the long grass. Twice I stopped to be sick. Only spit came out with burping sounds.

Near the front of the house, I got down on my good side and started to crawl, real slow, through the long grass, down the hill, making sure the path was on my left so I didn't get lost in the meadow. I only took one look back at the house and will wish forever that I never did.

One side of the front door was still open from where we went in. I could see a crowd, bustling in the sunlight that fell on their raggedy clothes. They were making a hooting sound and fighting over

something; a small shape that looked dark and wet. It was all limp.
Between the thin, snatching hands, it came apart, piece by piece.

In my room, at the end of my bed, Nanna Alice has closed her eyes.
But she's not sleeping. She's just sitting quietly and rubbing her doll
hand like she's polishing treasure.

TERRY LAMSLEY

Sickhouse Hospitality

TERRY LAMSLEY WAS BORN in the south of England but lived in the north for most of his life. He currently resides in Amsterdam, Holland.

His first collection of supernatural stories, *Under the Crust*, was initially published in a small paperback edition in 1993. Originally intended to only appeal to the tourist market in Lamsley's home town of Buxton in Derbyshire (the volume's six tales are all set in or around the area), its reputation quickly grew, helped when stories from the book were included in two of the annual "Year's Best" horror anthologies.

The book was subsequently nominated for three prestigious World Fantasy Awards, with the title story winning the award for Best Novella. Ramsey Campbell accepted it on the author's behalf, and Lamsley's reputation as a writer of supernatural fiction was assured.

In 1997, Canada's Ash-Tree Press reissued *Under the Crust* as a handsome hardcover, limited to just five hundred copies and now as sought-after as the long out-of-print first edition. A year earlier, Ash-Tree had published a second, equally remarkable collection of Lamsley's short stories, *Conference with the Dead: Tales of Supernatural Terror*, and it was followed in 2000 by a third collection, *Dark Matters*.

More recently, Night Shade Books has reprinted *Conference with the Dead*, with the limited edition containing a previously-uncollected story. Edited by Peter Crowther, *Fourbodings: A Quartet of Uneasy Tales from Four Members of the Macabre* showcases the fiction of Lamsley, Simon Clark, Tim Lebbon and Mark Morris, while *Made Ready & Cupboard Love* is a collection of two original novellas from Subterranean Press, illustrated by Glenn Chadborne.

About the following story, the author reveals: "Having worked in a number of hospitals, I have had plenty of opportunity to observe how, when, due to disease or accident people are abruptly removed from their familiar circumstances and taken into care, they are forced to develop strategies to help them deal with their state of dependency.

"They find themselves surrounded by people involved in complex, inexplicable activities. Isolated in their own beds, they have to put their trust in expert strangers whose motives they must assume are well-meaning and benign.

"Recently, however, I have detected signs that this is not now always the case."

"COULD I HAVE the name again?"
    "Jasper Jonette."
The receptionist took a second look through some sheets of paper on her desk then turned her attention to a computer screen. As her fingers fluttered above the keyboard her face settled into a mask of bemused concentration.

"I don't suppose you know when he was admitted?"

She turned her head and glanced at Erik over the top of her tiny spectacles. A small scar on the right corner of her mouth gave her lower lip a downturn that made her look mildly sceptical.

"I last saw him a month ago. It could have been any time since."

"Sorry to keep you waiting. I've been off sick and the system has been changed while I was away. I'm not quite with it yet." She pushed more keys then said, "Here he is, up on the fourth floor. The man you're looking for is in D12 in the Samuel Taylor Unit."

"Is that the new building? The one they just opened, with the dome? I saw something about it on TV. It looked impressive."

"Very up-to-date I believe," the woman confirmed, "though I haven't had the opportunity to take a look round there yet." She sank back in her chair and allowed her shoulders to sag, as though her efforts to locate Jasper Jonette had tired her.

"Okay if I just go on up?" Erik said.

"You'd better hurry. Visiting time ends at three and it's a quarter past two now."

"Is it far?"

The woman nodded. "Quite a distance. Take the lift to the fourth floor then follow the signs to the Exotology Department. When you get there you should see indicators pointing to the Samuel Taylor

Unit. Then you'd better ask someone for D12. I'm not sure exactly how to get there."

"I see. And the lift is . . .?"

The receptionist pointed to a sign above Erik's head. "That way," she said, and gave a welcoming smile to the first of the queue of people standing behind him.

Erik walked off at a smart pace. After three or four minutes he'd failed to find an elevator and a man pushing a trolley loaded with medical supplies was not able to help him. "You're in the wrong part. As far as I know, there isn't a visitor's lift at this end any more," he said, "and you can't use our porter's one. You'd better get up them stairs."

The first flight was easy enough and Erik took it at a run, but the original Victorian section of the hospital had high ceilings and the ascent soon took the breath out of him. He was panting when he reached the fourth floor but was relieved to see, amongst a cluster of a dozen or more similarly brash signs, one, clearly arrowed in bright blue, pointing to Exotology.

As it happened, there was no shortage of such signs; a new one appeared every time he turned a corner, and he turned many of them. Following their prompting, he covered a lot of ground, and was pleased when he was able to exchange them for a smaller, more discreet, and less obviously situated set of cards marked SAMUEL TAYLOR. These led him into a much quieter and less populated part of the hospital.

He had passed many large wards on his way to Exotology, and all of them had been fully occupied by patients sitting or repining on or in closely packed beds. Groups of mostly uneasy-looking guests stood around a large proportion of the beds and the air along the corridors was made pleasant by the scents of the flowers they had brought. Nursing staff, though few and far between, stood ready to receive the questions, compliments and complaints of the visitors, or hastened about, dutifully providing bedpans for the relief of the patients and water-filled vases for the garlands of flowers.

But once Erik had got Exotology behind him he entered a different, more orderly, world where the ward spaces were much smaller and none of them contained more than two or three beds, a surprising number of which were empty. Some attempt had been made to brighten up the corridors in the old building with posters and bright paint, but the walls in the most modern part of the hospital complex were unadorned with decoration of any kind, beyond a thin coat of mousy grey matt emulsion. The place had an unfinished look.

When he came to a SAMUEL TAYLOR UNIT sign that did not have an arrow pointing away from it, Erik assumed he had arrived at his destination, or close to it. He found himself standing on a broad corridor that curved away from him on either side, with many doors off it. Remembering the receptionist's advice, he looked around for someone to ask about the location of D12. There was no sign or sound of any member of staff: the area seemed deserted. To make sure it wasn't, Erik went and looked through a glass panel in one of the doors on the assumption that it led into yet another ward. On the nearest of two beds an elderly man with a close-cropped head and dull eyes, lying on his side, dressed, in spite of the cool air, only in what might have been a large nappy, stared back at Erik. Or it could have been through him. He made no sign that he was aware that he was being observed. A number of colour-coded lines and tubes connected him to a bank of machinery above his bed. His legs were tightly bent, but his back was unnaturally straight and his position did not look comfortable. In fact, he must have been making an effort to maintain the posture. The other bed contained the stretched-out form of somebody sleeping, presumably, face down.

Erik pushed the door experimentally. When it was open wide enough, he stuck his head around the edge of it and said, "Excuse me. I'm looking for D12. Am I close?"

The man reposing on his side didn't respond; gave no sign that he was aware of Erik's presence. Erik was just about to withdraw when a voice from under the blankets on the other bed said, "You've a way to go yet. This is D24."

"Thanks. Which way do I go now, though? Left or right?"

"I don't know, but it doesn't matter," said the prone man. "We're on the circle outside of the dome."

Erik considered this for a moment. "So, either way, I'm bound to come to D12?"

"Sooner or later. Shut the door behind you. There's a draught."

Erik did as he was told then turned from right to left, then right again, and walked on. It was annoying that there were no numbers on the doors, and it must be very confusing for the staff. He assumed the building had opened on schedule, even though it had not been finished.

As he walked he started counting, "Twenty-six, twenty-eight, thirty," since there were wards on both sides of the curving corridor, and it made some sort of sense to him to do so. After making a rough calculation, he decided he couldn't believe there were more than thirty of the little wards on the circle suggested by the curve of the corridor ahead of him, so he stopped when he reached that number and started to count from two. When he reached twelve he stopped and stared through the ward door in front of him. The room was empty, so he went on and looked into the next one.

Inside, Jasper Jonette, who was sitting up in bed fumbling with both hands at some apparatus attached to throat and chest, started at the sight of Erik. He held up his hands and shook his head in what could have been a gesture of disbelief or a warning to keep out.

"Is it contagious?" Erik said as he entered the ward and sat down on a chair near the bottom end of Jasper's bed.

"What the hell are you doing here? How did you find me?"

"Applied guess work."

"I was sure no one knew where I was."

Jasper's voice was so weak Erik had to move the chair closer to hear him clearly.

"People were saying they'd not seen you around so, since you've been off-colour for a while, I went to your flat to look you up. As I was going, your landlady ran after me to tell me someone had told her he'd seen you getting into an ambulance some time ago."

"The rent's not been paid," Jasper said.

"So she said. She was okay about that. She knows you're not short of cash. But she was worried about you. Is there something going on between you and her?"

Jasper said. "Not recently, since I started seeing Carol."

"I was going to ask about her, Jasper. Have you two fallen out? I saw her the other day in the Waldorf and she didn't mention you once. When I did, she pretended she hadn't heard me, insisted on talking about something else, and left as soon as she decently could. She had a peculiar expression on her face. I couldn't describe it."

"I don't want to talk about her, either."

"Please yourself. But does she know where you are? Would you like me to tell her so she can come and see you?"

"Christ, no!" Jasper lurched forward, then flopped back down in agitation. Staring up at the ceiling he said, "Don't meddle in my affairs, Erik. I warn you; keep your nose out."

"Okay. That's fine. Just as you like. But let's get back to your landlady. Mrs Pollit, isn't it? What a nice woman. We had a long talk. Anyway, because she was so concerned about you – we both were, of course – I said I'd dig about, see if I could track you down. She'll be pleased when I tell her I've found you."

"You keep away from there, Erik."

Erik tipped the contents of a bag he'd been carrying onto the bed.

"I've been lugging these around for a couple of days," he said. "They're a bit battered, but they're still edible."

Jasper gave the pile of bruised fruit by his knees a dismal look and said, "Good of you. Thanks. But *how* did you find me?"

"Simple. Both local hospitals are close to where I live. I did the Royal Free yesterday and this one today."

"I'm surprised you've nothing better to do."

"I've got time on my hands."

"And they just sent you up?"

"No problem at all."

"We're not supposed to have visitors. The doctors promised me there wouldn't be any."

"The woman at the reception desk didn't seem to know quite what she was doing. Maybe she made a mistake."

Jasper pulled a face that revealed his slightly protuberant front teeth and made him look like a cartoon fox. He said, "I was under the impression this place was supposed to provide state-of-the-art health care *and* privacy and security."

"That's what I heard, Jasper. It must have cost you plenty to get in here, eh? Samuel Taylor is mostly private, isn't it?"

"It would appear not, if people like you can come strolling in whenever you like."

Erik stretched out his legs and made himself more comfortable in his seat. "You know that's not what I mean," he said. "Some people say Sam Taylor is a cuckoo in the nest: the private sector infiltrating the public health service. They see it as a threat. There are a couple of people outside the main entrance with banners demanding its closure."

"Name something innovative that some fool won't protest about nowadays. Waving placards has the same significance to them as waving a holy book has to religious fundamentalists."

"Well, if the organisation here is as inefficient as you seem to think it is, they may have a point."

Jasper Jonette made a snuffling noise, moved onto his side, and contracted his legs. Somewhere under his bed a switch clicked softly and a machine came to life. There were gurgling sounds in a tube attached to the apparatus fastened to his chest. Jasper's whole body twitched from head to foot a couple of times. A louder, dreadful sound came from under the blankets covering his lower trunk. He glared defiantly at Erik as the device below the bed gave out a low whine, like a vacuum cleaner.

"I'll wait outside for a couple of minutes," Erik said.

When he returned Jasper looked more comfortable. Enfeebled perhaps by his recent violent spasms, he was lying on his back now with his head propped up on two pillows. In this position, with his long prematurely grey hair parted in the middle and hanging over his ears, he resembled a figure in a Victorian painting of a Great Man of the Age on his deathbed.

"What *are* you in here for, Jasper?" Erik said solicitously, dropping his jaunty bedside manner. "If you're doing a stretch in a place like this it must be something serious, I suppose?"

At first Jasper seemed modestly reluctant to discuss his condition but, after pausing for consideration, he said, somewhat testily, "The truth is, as yet, no one can tell me. I'm still at the 'exploration and observation' stage. After sixteen days! Obviously, a lot of me is not functioning correctly, but why that should be is still a mystery to everyone. But I believe I'm not the only person in this unit with the same symptoms. They keep us apart for obvious reasons – they don't want us cross-infecting each other. But the few people I have been able to snatch a conversation with, on the occasions I've been moved to and from the various departments, described the same – complaints – if that's the word, that I have, or something like them."

"So I suppose I'm taking a risk being here at all?"

Jasper nodded. "Almost certainly. For your own good, you'd better go. Now." He turned away from Erik, reached out an arm, and jerked down a cord with a large red bead on the bottom of it. "Someone will be along in a moment and I'll ask them to escort you back to the main hospital. It was kind of you to think of me and make the effort to find me, but I'd rather you didn't come again. If and when I make a recovery, I'll get in touch. If you feel you have to tell Mrs Pollit where I am, you could also tell her I'll get a cheque for the rent owing plus six months in advance to her soon. I don't want her or anyone else bothering me. In fact, after your intrusion, I'll get the people here to tighten up security around me."

"Well, it's been a pleasure speaking to you, Jasper," Erik said. "I'm glad I took the time and trouble to look you up." He picked up an apple from the selection of fruit on the bed. "Since you've shown no enthusiasm for my presents, I might as well eat this myself. I've had no lunch."

"I'm on a strict diet," Jasper said, worming his feet further down under the blankets. "Take what you like."

"I don't think I'm going to wait to be shown the way out," Erik said. "I'll have a look around before I go."

"You'd be unwise to do that, Erik."

"Oh, would I? Why? I'm beginning to find this place interesting."

"In what way?"

"All that money spent and nothing much seems to be going on, for instance. And that at a time when there's supposed to be a desperate shortage of hospital beds in the county."

"But it's none of your business, Erik'" Jasper said, his weak voice strained with emotion. "Who do you think you are? Some kind of whistle-blower?"

"And then there's you, Jasper. You interest me. You always have done."

"I wish I could return the compliment, if that's what it is."

"Professionally speaking, of course, your interests interest me."

"Oh, that's it, is it?"

"What are you doing for reading matter in here? I don't see any books around, and I don't imagine they'd have much of your sort of thing in the hospital library. Though maybe they do. Anyway, I came upon a couple of well-illustrated titles I know you've been searching for the other day. Would you like me to bring them in?"

"So, it's money you're after."

"There's no hurry for payment. Any time soon will do."

"Let me tell you, once more and for all time, Erik, I have no further use for you or your – merchandise. I thought I'd explained that before."

"It's no wonder people are worried about you, Jasper."

"Nonsense. I don't believe you. Why should anyone be concerned about me?"

"You've cut yourself off from everyone you knew recently, all your old friends, including Carol, who must be heartbroken—"

"That's the result of a misunderstanding between us. She was assuming too much."

"— and now you've somehow managed to get yourself incarcerated in this place, where you can indulge, in solitary splendour, in the pleasure of your illness and your voyeuristic obsession with surgical implements and procedures to your heart's content."

"Don't be ridiculous."

"And don't you forget it was me who kept you supplied with those – well, let's say dubious books down the years."

"Very much to your profit."

"Anyway, I can't see any sign that your stay here has done you any good at all," Erik said as he got up and moved to the door. "In fact, you look a lot worse than you ever did."

"I'll tell whoever comes to answer my call that you're on the loose out there. There are cameras everywhere, so you won't get far."

Erik looked at his watch. Almost three already.

"Get well soon, Jasper," he said. "That's not just from me, it's from everyone who ever cared about you."

"You bastard."

Erik took a last look around the bleak, blank-walled little room, then walked quickly out into the corridor. He could hear distant footsteps approaching from the right so he turned left, the way he'd come. On his way to Jasper's ward he'd noticed a couple of arched passages leading inwards towards the dome. When he reached the first of them he crossed over and stepped along it.

The atmosphere became a little warmer as he approached the dome, and once again there was an odour of vegetation in the air which grew heavier and more pungent as he advanced. The origin of this became apparent as soon as he walked out onto the floor of the dome. The central area was full of dark green exotic plants with huge uplifted leaves and numerous tendrils that hung down from the main stems and over the sides of the black-glazed stoneware jars they were potted in. Many of these tendrils had already crawled some distance across the floor around the jars and had reached out for and embraced each other in a grip that looked tight and relentless. Most of the plants were topped with fat buds, a few of which had started to burst open to permit the violet and orange flowers within to partially unfurl. A light cloud hung around the lower halves of the plants like an early morning mist.

A board on a little easel by the pots announced that:

These
Oroborelium Plants
are a gift to the
SAMUEL TAYLOR TRUST
from
THE PORLOCK FOUNDATION

Under the last words were printed the date of a day about three weeks earlier.

In among the nearest of the roots Erik could see a number of small, dark, sausage-shaped pellets with slightly pointed ends. At first he thought they must be seeds from the plants above, but the plants were in flower and seeds formed after blossoms died. Since the plants had only been in position such a short time the pellets could not be seeds remaining from the previous season. Erik dropped a few of them into his pocket for consideration later and walked on.

He took a bite out of the apple he was carrying, that he had purloined from Jasper's sickbed. It tasted foul – there was no juice in it, and the piece he had bitten off sat in his mouth and resisted the action of his teeth, like a tiny over-stuffed cushion. He spat the fragment out into his hand and hurled the apple into the thicket of potted plants where it landed with a noise like a hardball hitting concrete. The sound echoed and amplified in a most peculiar way, as though someone was thwacking a large muffled drum inside a much bigger one, and the beat of this continued to roll around the sides of the dome for a surprising length of time. As it subsided, a man in a long white coat appeared from somewhere on the far side of the thicket of plants. He was wearing white plimsolls so his feet made no din as he approached. He stopped and, with one hand on his hip and the other plucking at his chin, stood and stared speculatively at Erik.

"You are Mr Frank?" he said, loudly enough for his voice to set off another round of echoes in the freakish acoustical confusion of the dome's interior.

Erik shook his head. "The name's Condon."

"You've come to be interviewed?"

"Definitely not."

While the room was still ringing with reverberations from this conversation, the man took a few steps to the side, to where Erik's apple had come to rest, and briefly gave the remains of the fruit his full attention. "Is this yours?" he said.

"It was."

"It's not from our kitchen. It has a strange label on it. Has it been brought in from outside this establishment?"

Erik agreed that it had.

After hunkering carefully down, the man pulled a roll of small plastic bags from his trouser pocket, tore one off, tucked his hand inside it, drew the apple up into it, then turned the bag inside out. "What are you doing here?" he said, as he tied a knot in the top of his little package and dropped it into a nearby bin.

"I called in to visit a patient and got lost trying to find my way out."

"Lost? You don't look lost to me. I saw you come in. You appeared to be finding your way about in a confident way."

"Okay, not exactly lost then, but taking a look around. I've heard so much about this place I couldn't resist checking it out a little, while I was here."

"I see."

"There's no problem, is there?"

"I very much regret that publicity. We all do here."

"But this is a public building after all, built with public money. Or some of it was, anyway. I'm a member of the public, so . . ."

"Did you manage to locate the person you had come to visit?"

"With some difficulty, yes."

"And *where*, exactly, did you find him or her?"

Something in the man's voice and the way he looked as he asked for this information made it a question too far for Erik. He decided it was time to prevaricate.

"I'm not sure. It must have been quite a way from here. I've forgotten the number of the ward."

"It doesn't matter. We can easily trace your movements since you entered the unit."

Erik had had enough of the man. "That's fine then, isn't it? I'll leave you to get on with doing that. Right now, if you'll move aside."

Even though Erik was free to move in all directions but forward, that was the one way he wanted to go, because the man in the white jacket had stepped purposely in front of him, apparently to stop him doing so. It was a threatening and slightly ridiculous gesture that Erik, already irritated by the man's persistent and, he considered, impertinent questioning, felt he could not ignore.

He said, "Get out of my way."

The man shook his head. "I'm afraid you're not free to leave. We can't allow it."

Erik was on the point of saying something foolishly melodramatic like, "Try and stop me," when he became aware, too late, that somebody was standing close behind him. Two people were, in fact. Each of them grabbed one of his arms and jerked them backwards. Then both his knees were bent by pressure from behind and, still partly supported by the hands of his assailants, he slumped like an unstrung puppet to the floor. After a few moments one of the men standing above him leaned down to take measure of his condition and said, "You're not in any pain, I hope?"

Erik thought about it. "None at all. You're obviously expert at what you do. I feel fine."

"You can get up now, sir, if you want to," said the other man who had floored him. Both of them were a good few inches taller and wider than Erik. They were dressed in long, loosely-buttoned drab overalls. Hospital porters with special qualifications in protection and security, Erik guessed. There was probably a well-equipped gym in the building where they were encouraged to work out.

As Erik climbed to his feet, a phone bleeped in the breast pocket of the white coat worn by the man who had earlier interrogated him. Whatever the message for him was, it must have been urgent because, after a few quietly spoken words of instruction to the two in overalls, the first man stalked off and away down one of the corridors leading out of the dome.

"What now?" Erik said, giving the porters a dog-like and he hoped beguiling smile. He'd decided that though they certainly were not on his side, it would be as well to try to give the impression he was on theirs. Though built like brick buildings, they were polite enough and seemed to have whatever aggressive tendencies they might have – that may have caused them to choose their potentially violent line of employment – well under control. There could be no harm in trying to befriend them, and no point in antagonising them.

"We're going to escort you to the labs," one of them said.

"Labs? What labs?"

"Them. There." The man pointed to a floor above the one they were on. Its inner walls, Erik realised, supported the weight of the many huge sheets of curved glass that formed the vast bubble of the dome that stretched above them. He had not been aware of the existence of a fifth floor before, and had seen no stairs leading up to it.

"And what sort of labs would those be?"

"All kinds."

"Why do I have to go there, do you think?"

"I expect you're going to have some tests done."

"Tests?"

While Erik was absorbing the possible implications of this prediction, the two men decided it was time to leave. One of them walked ahead of him and the other behind until, after a short distance, they were on the curving corridor on the outer rim of the building, where Erik had earlier called on Jasper Jonette. The leading man came to a stop, motioned to Erik to do the same. Then, after fumbling about clumsily with his thumb, he managed to make contact with an almost invisible button on the wall in front of him.

"In you get," he said, when the lift door slid back.

Erik hesitated. The man behind pushed him firmly forward.

As he entered the lift, Erik saw that in the corridor behind him a number of patients, still in their beds, were being wheeled out of their wards by spick-looking female orderlies. They were all moving towards the passages that led to the dome.

Erik thought he might have spotted Jasper's head on one of the beds but didn't have time, before the lift doors closed, to be certain.

Erik had been staring at the ceiling for a long time and wanted to look at something, anything, else. But he couldn't move his head to either side more than a fraction of an inch because it felt as though it had been set in a vice. In fact, the only parts of his body he could change the position of were his arms, or that part of them below the elbows. If he lifted his hands, he'd discovered, he could just about see the tips of his fingers up in the air in front of him, and he waggled them every few minutes to demonstrate to himself that he had control over something, if not very much.

The rest of his body was restricted, when he tried to move, as though it was weighed down from above rather than held in position from below. Pressure on his chest made breathing uncomfortable. He found that if he made himself relax this didn't give him much trouble, his lungs just took in a little less air than they would like to have done, but it's not easy to relax physically when you are in a state of extreme mental confusion. Erik was lost and alone, and he had no idea how he'd got that way. There was a blank in his life.

One moment he'd been sitting in a chair in a small room with an EMERGENCY sign over the door, close to the exit of the lift that had taken him and his captors to the fifth floor, submitting himself to the taking of a blood sample from his arm by another man in a white coat. He'd been told it was a precautionary measure, for his own protection, and he had removed his jacket, rolled up his sleeve readily enough, and offered his arm for the needle. The next thing he knew, here he was, locked in position somehow on a hard high bed, with his nose a couple of feet from the ceiling. Because of this elevation he could only see a small area of the ceiling, so he had no idea how big or small was the room he was in.

He had no idea what space of time separated those two moments that had taken him in and out of consciousness, but he felt very hungry so assumed he'd missed a few meal times. There were tubes hanging around him that he guessed were probably plugged into him, but none of them could have been drip-feeding him. His stomach told him that as it whined and growled in protest at his dereliction of it.

Apart from the complaints of his gut and the catch of his own breathing, there was nothing else to listen to. All was quiet on every front. Erik was certain he was on his own in whatever space he occupied. And he'd been in his present predicament how long, since he'd regained consciousness? Hours, and many of them, or so it seemed.

Later, when he was trying unsuccessfully to consume time by sleeping, he heard footsteps approaching his bed. Very quiet footsteps made by rubber-soled shoes like those the man who had confronted him in the dome had been wearing.

They drew close and stopped. A woman said, "Dr Mallory is of the opinion we might have problems with this one. We need to be a lot more careful. I don't want any more like him turning up."

Erik thought her mouth must be very close – a few inches down from his left ear.

A man said, "None of us were aware that those signs had been put up this morning. Some overzealous meddler in the main body of the hospital took it upon themselves to do it."

"They've been removed now, though?"

"Of course. I told Administration *emphatically* that we won't be ready to open to the public for some time."

"A long time. Tell them that."

"I also suggested there might be a problem with some mild form of infection here in the Unit, something we had pretty well under control but that we don't want to talk too much about. Mustn't put the public at risk, etc. Best to keep the place in purdah for a while, without imposing an actual quarantine. I thought a few brightly coloured tapes in strategic positions across the corridors would do the trick. The Hospital Manager saw the sense of that at once. He's well aware if any suggestion that the slightest thing was wrong here got out, there could be more trouble with the sort of people we had waving banners out front. A lot more. They understood that in Administration. Apologised, even, about the direction signs, and promised that whoever put them up will be disciplined. They're scared stiff of the slightest whiff of scandal."

"I'm glad to hear it," the woman said.

"What the fuck have you done to me?" Erik tried to shout but his voice was not much louder than a whisper.

The man said, "Do you want to take a look at him?"

The woman, as though her mind was on other things, who sounded as though she might be chewing gum, said, "No, I don't think so. Not particularly."

"Better give him a quick check out. Tick his card so those who care about these things know you've done your duty."

"You're right, of course."

"Won't take you a moment."

The bed and Erik descended slowly and smoothly with a hydraulic sigh. The top of two heads became visible, one on each side of him. They bent down together and he caught the briefest glimpse of their faces. He raised his hands to their highest extent and, to say hello, waved his fingers like a woman drying her newly polished nails.

The man, who had an amber moustache and a bald scalp, said, "He was fairly healthy when he came in but, as you can see from his chart, we've done most of the preliminary work on him already. Who knows, perhaps we'll find a use for him?"

"Okay. We'll leave it at that then," said the woman, who was far more attractive than Erik thought she deserved to be. "What's next on the agenda?"

Some paperwork rustled as the bed elevated to its former position. After a short pause the man said, "We'd need to take a look in D12."

"Surely there's not a problem there?"

"Seems to be. Mr Jonette, one of our first red card self-referrals, wants access to his bank account."

"Oh, *does* he," the woman said. "We'll see about that."

"He is on your list, isn't he?"

"And on Dr Mallory's. We share him."

"That must be highly satisfactory for you both," the man said.

Erik tried again. "What about me?" he attempted to shout, but it came out as a whimper. His tongue felt shrivelled and dry, and his mouth huge. "I want food. Water. Please."

"I believe he might be hungry, Dr Stranghaver. We might allow him a little nourishment," the man suggested.

"I'll permit that, since you say he's worth preserving. But put something in whatever you give to keep him placid. Let's have some peace and quiet in here."

The pair of them left Erik's bedside. From some way off Dr Stranghaver said, "This Jonette person. I haven't been able to get to see him for some days. What's your assessment? How is he progressing?"

"He's coming along very nicely," the man said. "As you know, his case is extraordinarily complicated. Delightfully so. A prize patient. He's something of a prodigy, in my opinion."

"There's no danger that he might be making any kind of limited recovery, then? I was somewhat concerned. He was looking a little better on my last visit, and I couldn't account for it."

"No. You'll see for yourself. That was just a passing phase."

"Ah," said Dr Stranghaver, well satisfied.

Erik tried once more to give voice to a plea for assistance, but merely managed a sound like a dying crow's last croak as their footsteps faded away.

The bed descended again some time later. A young lady in a pale green uniform presented herself to Erik by bending towards him and offering him half a smile. Her mouth was in it but not her eyes which were troubled, possibly deranged.

"I'm Christabel from C and C, the Care and Comfort Department," she said. "You're going to be fed, you lucky man."

Her plump arms and hands moved around him, making adjustments to equipment and parts of himself he couldn't see. Again he tried to speak, and this time made such an alarming noise he scared himself and startled the girl from C and C.

"Was that a cough? Are you choking?"

Erik was able to shake his head from side to side just a little. He opened his mouth wide and manoeuvred his right hand up and back so he was able to point a finger down towards his throat. He poked out his bone-dry tongue.

Christabel raised her eyebrows in incomprehension and shook her head back at him.

"Ghhhhhaaa." Erik snatched at one of her hands that was hovering above his chest and took firm hold of the wrist. He glared at the girl in what was intended to be his most appealing way, but that was probably terrifying. He struggled in the back of his throat and made a final effort to make noises that sounded something like one word:

"*Wah-er*."

"Ah, so that's it," Christabel said, making no attempt to release her hand. "I don't know about that. I was authorised to feed and sedate you, but no mention was made of any kind of liquid refreshment." She reached with her free hand for a clipboard attached to the end of his bed, glanced at it, held it up above his face and said, "See for yourself. That box where it says, NO LIQUIDS – it's been ticked."

It seemed to Erik that the girl was losing her solidity or had become enveloped in a light mist, and he realised there were tears in his eyes. He shut them and let go of her wrist.

The envoy from the C and C Dept. turned and walked away from him and out of sight. Immediately after she'd gone, Erik felt the seeds of a warm feeling deep inside him that seemed, literally, to be putting out roots in his guts and spreading repletion and well-being throughout his body. Before long the inside of his mouth started to dampen.

Greedily he began to pump away under his tongue until his mouth filled with saliva, whereupon he subsided, relaxed and drifted away until he fell over the edge of something and stumbled into oblivion, or oblivion tumbled into him.

A familiar face stared down at him – that of the man who had first apprehended him in the dome.

"So what do we know about him, Hendrix?" said Dr Stranghaver, invisible to Erik because she was standing behind the head-end of his bed. He tipped his neck back, but a pillow prevented him from moving far so he still couldn't catch sight of her. What he could see, under the roof of the great dome, was the tops of the tall plants that took up the central space of the floor. Many more of them had burst into garish blossom since he had last seen them, which could have been days ago. A sweet, sweaty, but not thoroughly unpleasant smell, that was probably their scent, hung heavy as a mist in the otherwise clear, warm air.

"Enough," the man called Hendrix said. Peculiarly muffled echoes of the Doctor's loud voice and his own higher-pitched one rattled and clattered round the dome. "Erik John Condon is no one of any importance. Runs a second-hand book business from home, mostly through the Internet. Some of the stuff he specialises in is at the seedy end of the market, but not illegal. He and his customers prefer to remain anonymous. PO box numbers, that sort of thing. He's capable of setting up some ingeniously unorthodox financial dealings. Otherwise he's harmless enough."

"So, no close outside contacts there. What about family? Friends?"

"A few old friends, mostly rackety types like himself, scattered about the country. Loners, all of them. One of them is a patient here, of course. Not sure what's going on there. I suspect that Jonette in D12 could better be described as a customer. As to family, Condon's mother died years ago and his demented father is embedded in a council-run home in Solihull. Our subject was married but there were no children. His wife left him to move in with a building contractor in Brisbane, Australia, which is about as far away from England as you can get, so she won't miss him."

The gorgeous Dr Stranghaver moved around the bed to a position where the dumbfounded Erik could observe the front of her from the waist up. He could see, hear, and even smell her, and perceived everything else he normally could, but remained incapable of reacting to any stimuli. Speechless, immobile and thoroughly sedate, he lay on his back and watched the play of the world around him. He felt he was in a dream, but was fairly sure he wasn't.

Dr Stranghaver was holding against her breasts a young leaf, like those sprouting from the nearby plants. From time to time, in a thoughtless, distracted way, she tore small pieces off the leaf, rolled them between her fingers, pressed them in to her mouth, and chewed them slowly.

"No women in his life now, then?" she said.

She offered the leaf to her companion but he shook his head, having already produced the remains of one like it from his pocket. He set about tearing off a strip for his own consumption.

"None have turned up so far in our investigations," he said, "which is peculiar because he had a reputation as a small town Casanova in the past and he's a good-looking man."

"You think so, Hendrix?"

"Was before we got to him, I mean. I've seen photographs."

"Before he got to us," Dr Stranghaver corrected. "What about money?"

Hendrix pushed a plug of green leaf into his mouth. "There must be some somewhere," he said as he munched. "His business was successful as these things go. Not much to show in his bank accounts, though."

"We have the keys to his house, don't we?"

"That's being taken care of. There's the building itself, of course, and its contents, including some valuable-looking books, though dealing with that will all take time and a lot of work from our legal department. But there were no money bags hidden under the mattress, if that's what you mean."

"How disappointing. Perhaps we ought to hold him upside down and shake him. See what falls out."

Hendrix considered for a moment then said, "The sort of drugs you're thinking of, administered as an effective dose, would almost certainly be fatal in his condition."

"I'm aware of that, Hendrix. Maybe we should allow him to get a little better, then. He needs to pay his way and get his name up on our Plaque of Patrons if he is to stay around, and we can't let him go. After all, he's well on the way to becoming incurable now and the kind of treatment he's receiving here doesn't come cheap. Our team of outreach workers are telling us to expect an influx of new and highly promising and rewarding patients during the next weeks. Bed space will be at a premium before we know it and there'll be no room for slackers. There is no contingency plan for creatures like this who drift in off the street."

"Perhaps we should devise one?"

Dr Stranghaver tore off another, larger section of leaf. "I'm shocked by your defeatist attitude, Hendrix. I'm no longer sure you're the right person to liaise with Administration over the handling of security on the Unit. Perhaps, coming on top of your many medical duties, the responsibility is over-stretching you."

"I think it's time I sampled some of the petals from those newly opened buds," Hendrix said, gazing wistfully up at the highest parts of the spreading jungle of potted herbage. "One or two of them may be just about ready."

"I'll join you," the doctor said. "My shift is over in five minutes."

"I see the ladder we ordered has arrived at last."

"Yes, but I've no head for heights." Stranghaver giggled and the dome giggled back at her. "I'll hold the steps so you can get to the blooms at the top."

Hendrix nodded enthusiastically. "Okay, let's do it," he said and clapped his hands, sending out round the walls of the dome a cascade of echoes that slowly drowned in wave after wave of echoes of themselves. "Today's inspection is completed," he called to someone nearby. "Get the Establishment patients back to their designated sites. The couple without coloured cards are for disposal, of course. Remove them first." He tapped Erik on the chest with a finger and looked across the bed at Dr Stranghaver. "What about this one, though?"

"A green card for him. Have him taken to one of the wards. Reduce his medication by half. We'll put him under a bit of pressure."

Erik saw her wink at Hendrix, who drew in his lips, nodded to her in a mock-solemn way and said, "I know just what you mean, Dr Stranghaver."

"Good morning, Mr Condon. How are you today?"

Christabel from C and C. He remembered she had come for him while he had been watching the doctor and her companion harvesting petals high overhead in the dome, and had sped away with him down measureless corridors to a featureless ward where, after connecting him up to God-knows-what, she had left him. Though he still retained some vague and dim recollection of the general purport of the conversation between Dr Stranghaver and her assistant, with the exception of a few scattered sentence fragments the rest had vanished like reflections on a lake into which someone had tossed a rock.

Erik was seriously thinking about providing an answer to Christabel's enquiry about his condition, but he soon realised she wasn't waiting for one and anyway, he couldn't speak, could he? Had he been able to do so, he would have told her he felt, well – different. For a start he felt scared now; fear sat on his chest, stared into his eyes, and told him nothing was right with him and everything was wrong. And, whereas he'd been drifting in a not too uncomfortable dream since he'd been escorted up to the fifth floor by the two burly porters, he now felt bruised, full of sharp aches and pains and wide awake. Too wide awake, in fact – so very wide awake he suddenly felt like screaming.

"Ahhhhhh," he said, and flipped the top half of his body up into the sitting position. Tubes were snatched out of his arms by the sudden movement and blood began to flow from the entry wounds they had vacated. A grey warm liquid poured down from one tube fixed to a steel stand next to his bed and soaked the mattress beneath him as it swung back and forth in the air.

Here was work for Christabel from C and C and she threw herself efficiently at it. She got Erik in some kind of arm lock and forced him back into the horizontal position while at the same time sliding the needles at the ends of the tubes back into place in his body with her free hand. Erik struggled against her attempts to hook him up to the machines again, and because he had been forced to lie in a pool of the warm, sticky liquid that was now pouring down over his face. But she was too much for him and easily held him down. It seemed that all members of staff in the Samuel Taylor Unit were highly trained in restraint techniques.

Something Erik had done had set off an alarm bell. A few minutes passed and no one had come to the woman from C and C's assistance, but by that time she didn't need any. She had Erik under control.

"Now don't go giving me any more trouble," she said, wagging a finger in front of his nose. "Cut up rough again and I'll put you down and out. You're only a green grade card. You're not high priority."

"So I gather," Erik said. "Sorry. But you gave me a rude awakening." His voice seemed to be coming from deeper down in his chest than usual.

"That's how we do things in the ST Unit."

"How long have I been in this place?"

"So, you're talking again," Christabel said. "Not heard a word from you before. You've got a weird voice."

"It's not normally like that."

"They've done something to your chest. Can't you feel the stitches?"

"I feel as though I've been beaten all over."

"That's what they all say first thing, when they come out of it."

"How long?" Erik repeated.

"I don't know if I can tell you."

"Oh, come on. What harm can it do?"

"That's not the point."

"Look on that clip-board on the end of the bed. Show me where it says I can't be told how long I've been here."

To Erik's surprise she picked up the board and studied it. "This is the eighth day," she said. "They kept you in Probation for longer than most new patients."

"Probation?"

Christabel disappeared and returned minutes later pushing a bed like the one Erik was stretched out on. "I'm going to switch you over, get you out of that mess you've made," she said. "I don't have to, so co-operate."

"Kind of you," Erik said, as she edged him sideways. When he emerged from the soiled bedding and was being given a perfunctory bed bath, he discovered he was naked except for areas of his chest and stomach that were covered in heavy dressings and bandages, and that his body from the neck down was completely hairless.

"I've lost weight," he observed.

Christabel, pulling clean sheets up over Erik on the clean bed, looked mildly embarrassed at this. "Well, yes, you've lost a few things. You're not the man you were when you came in here."

"I'm not?"

"No, you've been stripped down to basics."

This remark sent Erik's fear and anxiety levels up to record levels.

"I want my belongings," he said. "My clothes, my wallet, my *mobile*. I need to make a call."

"Your personal effects are being kept safe in the Property Department," Christabel said. "I'm off now. If there's *anything else* you need just pull that cord and wait. And you're not alone here, you know. There're gentlemen in both the other beds. I expect they'll introduce themselves when they feel like it."

Erik looked from one of these beds to the other. The nearest of them was somewhat shorter and narrower than the other. The body of the "gentleman" under the blankets could have been that of an undernourished child of about twelve, with a large white, hairless head that was turned away from Erik. The other bed was an untidy sprawl of blankets with two long scraggy feet sticking out at the bottom. A pillow rested on the spot Erik calculated the head of the occupant might be, held in place by a bent arm and tightly grasping hand, also long and bony.

As Christabel left, she switched off the ward's main light so the room was only illuminated by tiny, low wattage lamps at the rear of each bed. The grey blank walls crept in a little closer and Erik was certain the ceiling had descended a foot or two. The heavy silence he'd experienced in other places he'd been held in the Unit, outside of the dome, returned, broken only by disquieting noises from the smaller of his two companions, whose quick, laborious breathing sounded like paper being crumpled in a plastic cup. Five minutes later, after Erik had established that there was no television or radio headphones attached to his bed; no aids to the passing of time at all, in fact; he started to experimentally move about. This was, as he anticipated, painful, particularly when he leaned forward and compressed his stomach and chest, but he found if he kept his spine straight and humped and bumped his torso carefully about he could swing his legs over the side of the bed and almost touch the floor with his feet. The tubes in his arms held him back at first, but he discovered that if he reached out on both sides with his arms there was enough give in the tubes for him to edge himself down a little further, which he did, until he was standing, arms outstretched, with his feet almost flat on the ground.

"Christ Almighty!" someone said. "What the hell do you think you're doing?"

The man in the messed-up bed had taken the pillow away from his head and was resting on his side with his chin on his bent arm staring goggle-eyed at Erik.

Even in the dim light of the ward Erik was instantly certain he'd seen the man's face before, and recently, too, though it was now much changed. Erik stared bleakly back. After a few seconds he remembered where and when he'd seen the person on the opposite bed. Now he was much thinner than he had been: his flattened bruiser's nose and the scar tissue on his forehead were even more noticeable.

"I was thinking of getting out of here," Erik said.

The man gave a sardonic snort. "They won't let you walk out, that's for sure."

"You've tried, then?"

"No. No chance. They've done too much work on my legs."

Erik looked down at himself. "Mine seem okay."

"By the look of it they're the only parts of you that are. Get back in bed before you fall down."

"If I do, and I can't get up, I'll pull the alarm cord."

"No one will come. You're not worth their trouble."

"How do you know?"

"There's a green card on the clip-board at the end of your bed."

"Ah, yes. I know about that. Low priority."

"No priority," the man said. "I'm in the same category. We're both on the slippery end of the shit list. If they think you might still be – useful – to them in some way they'll keep you alive, just, if you behave, but they won't if you don't."

Slowly and cautiously Erik manoeuvred himself back onto the bed. "You certainly were right to protest about this place," he said.

"You saw me, did you?"

"As I was coming in. You and a woman were by the main entry waving banners. She asked me to sign a petition."

"That was my wife. She's in here somewhere too."

"Did they just grab you off the street?"

"They're not that stupid. Unfortunately they're not stupid at all. They invited us in to discuss our objections with Dr Stranghaver, one of the people in charge round here."

"Had you any idea what this place was really like?"

"Of course not. How could we?"

Erik was silent for a while then said, "Do you belong to some kind of official protest group?"

"One that might send people out looking for us, you mean? That was one of the first questions Stranghaver asked. But no, Jenny and I were on our own. We don't even have any official party political affiliations. When Stranghaver heard that, she asked us if we'd like some coffee. We'd been standing out front for hours, so we said yes. It tasted all right. That was three weeks ago, and I haven't seen Jenny since, but told me she's here and I have no reason not to believe them."

"Three weeks! That can't be right. I've only been here eight days myself, and you must have come in after me."

"Is that what they told you, eight days?"

"The woman from C and C said that."

"I guess they like to keep us guessing," the man with the boxer's nose said. He flopped heavily back on his bed and shut his eyes. Not long after that he started snoring.

Perhaps the sound of this disturbed the man in the other bed because, without turning his head, he began to thrash about and punch the air feebly with one of his little fists, as though he was fending off some invisible invader hanging in the air above him. His arm was wrapped in bandages that had become loose and were starting to unfurl to reveal sections of pale flesh speckled with splotches the colour of a boiled lobster beneath. After a few moments he settled down and tugged the blanket back over his shoulder, but it continued to move urgently from time to time as though he were compulsively scratching himself. Since there was nothing else of the slightest interest to occupy his mind in the ward, Erik sat back and watched as the man with the large head and small body tackled his itch, causing the blanket up around his neck to edge, in fits and starts, back down in the direction of his chest. It had subsided two or three inches when Erik, who was beginning to doze, sat up suddenly because, for a second, something revealed itself from out of the edge of the blanket that could not have been part of the person under it, unless that person had previously kept hidden one grey, very hairy hand.

Whoever was in the bed grabbed at the blanket and pulled it hard down around his neck. There followed a brief burst of a soft but urgent chittering sound from the bed. The scratching motions intensified then stopped altogether, and a small dark, pointed head emerged a little way from under the bedding close to its occupant's one visible ear, and took a look around. Erik felt, because it turned its lightly whiskered snout in his direction, it was looking at him with its beady, dull ebony eyes but it was impossible to tell from the blankness of its gaze what, if anything, it had focused its attention upon.

Erik shouted a curse and tugged at the large red bead on the end of his alarm cord.

The man he had been talking to earlier stopped snoring, spluttered, woke up and rasped out something incomprehensible. Then, composing himself, he said, "What's the matter with you now? If you're in pain, there's nothing I can do about it."

"It's not that. It's him." Erik pointed to the third bed. "There's something in there with him."

The man made no answer to this but stared quizzically at Erik who, he appeared to think, was acting in an over-excited manner.

"An animal of some kind," Erik insisted. "A rat – I'm sure it was a rat."

"Oh, another one of them. They come up from underneath the Victorian sections of the hospital. Ten years ago the Council shut the whole place down for a week and sent in an extermination team to try to scourge the building and get rid of them, but when they reopened, the pests were back in days. They breed in the cellars down below the hospital and it would cost a fortune to properly do anything about *them* nowadays: they've been used as warehouses for storing all kinds of junk for a hundred and fifty years. The Hospital Authorities occasionally make some pretence of making an effort to keep the rats down, or, more often, try to hush things up as best they can, but you know how the things breed. If whoever spent the money they wasted on the Samuel Taylor Unit had used it to replace those cellars with a modern storage system, the rats would have been driven out. That was one of the things my wife and I felt so strongly about. Why we were protesting."

He spoke with swiftly rising anger that subsided as soon his final sentence ended.

Erik remembered the dark brown "seeds" he had discovered among the plants in the dome and put in the pocket of his jacket. Rat shit! The creatures must have developed a taste for the vegetation.

"But don't the staff here poison them or lay traps?" he said.

The man seemed to find this amusing but he didn't laugh. "You've been here long enough not to ask such foolish questions," he said. "I doubt if the medical staff are aware that they're there. You must have noticed they are all a bit . . . preoccupied."

As he spoke, Erik noticed the rat, that had drawn its head back under the blanket when he had shouted, was re-emerging, this time with more confidence. It lifted its head, scuttled nonchalantly forward over the pillow at the end of the bed and, taking a route along the frame beneath that it was obviously familiar with, descended to the floor. Then, apparently in no hurry, lewdly rolling its fat rump from side to side as it stretched its back legs, it made its way across the shiny floor and made an exit by squeezing through a tiny gap at the bottom of the ward doors.

"Must have bones like rubber," Erik's companion observed. "Clever buggers too. They'll get in anywhere."

"I don't want them in with me."

"They won't bother you yet. You're too lively. So am I, just about, whereas him," he pointed across at the figure concealed in the third bed, "he's hardly moved for days, except when he panics in his sleep when they're having a go at him. The rats can do anything they like with that poor sod. Anyone can, in fact. But you should be okay."

Nevertheless, Erik spent the next few hours on high alert, with his eyes wide open.

* * *

Dr Stranghaver's voice was different; more husky and less mono-
tonous and mechanically correct. From the sound of it she had
allowed herself to become somewhat excited about something.

She had been talking very quietly to someone on her mobile but
now that call was over, she obviously felt impelled to give vent to
some strong feelings.

"Everything changed," she said, gripping her colleague – another
man in a white coat, but much taller than the one that had previously
accompanied her – by the shoulder and squeezing him hard with her
crimsoned fingertips.

"Why?"

"I can't go into details. No time for that. But something very
serious has come up and a decision has been made by our sponsors.
We're going to be pulling in all of the successful self-referrals much
sooner than we anticipated. Today, in fact."

"Not every one of them, surely?"

"Well, obviously we'll start with the red and blue categories."

"The richest pickings."

"Right. Get them established, then we'll know how many of the
yellows we can accommodate. The official prediction is there will be
far too many of them, so we'll select the best. Our Files and Statistics
Department is running a cull on them now. But that's not important
at the moment. What matters is that we do everything we can to
make ourselves available to welcome today's intake."

"Get them safely stashed away."

"That's the priority."

"So there must be something very big in the air."

"There has been for a long time, Professor Morgan, but now
whatever has been hanging fire above us is going to drop and hit the
ground. Today, according to the Intelligence Department."

"It's time to make our move."

"Exactly. And we'll be safe here, shut away as we will be with our
hand-picked patients and with ample provisions for a long siege."

"If it comes to that."

Stranghaver pulled a rolled-up leaf from one of the plants in the
dome from her pocket and took a few hungry bites.

"Oh, Professor Morgan," she said, her voice ecstatic now, "if
only you knew how much I hope it does. I would have unlimited
scope to pursue my researches. It would be the culmination of my
career."

Erik had closed his eyes when she had come into the ward five
minutes earlier, confident that no rodents would dare show their

faces or take advantage of him while she was around. He was pretending to be asleep to discourage her attention, but that was not really necessary since, after taking her phone call, the doctor had obviously lost touch with her immediate surroundings and had gone off into a future world of her own imagining.

"Come along with me, Morgan," she said flirtatiously. "I need you. All members of staff are to assemble in the dome at once. I'm going to give everyone their orders."

As her voice faded, Erik opened his eyes. She was pulling the Professor along by the hand through the doors with an air of triumph, as though she were dragging him through the shallows after rescuing him from a sinking ship.

As soon as they were out of hearing, the former protestor on the other bed said, "Did you notice they mentioned red, blue and yellow cards, but said nothing about green ones?"

"That struck me too," Erik said.

Neither of them found cause to continue their conversation after that for at least a couple of hours.

It was Erik who finally broke the silence. "What the hell is going on over there, do you suppose?" He pointed towards the third bed, where some violent activity was taking place under the section of blanket covering the bottom edge of the mattress.

"Rat again," the man said.

"Must be a bloody big one."

"You're right," the old protester agreed. "I didn't think they got that big. What are you doing?"

Erik had swung his legs out of bed and started detaching the tubes and needles that had been stuck into him. "I'm going to take a look at that rat, if that's what it is. Then I'll see if I can do something for the poor bugger in there with it."

"He's past helping, believe me, and if you remove that equipment, you'll soon end up in the same state. They're keeping you alive, those tubes."

Erik, unencumbered, stood up and walked unsteadily away from his bed. "Maybe, maybe not," he said, "but I'm pretty convinced that Stranghaver will be ordering somebody to shut down our support machines anyway, and sooner rather than later."

"The green cards, eh? That possibility crossed my mind."

"It's more than a possibility. You heard what she said. It's inevitable."

Erik reached the third bed without as much difficulty as he had anticipated and sat down on the end of it near where the commotion continued. He untucked a corner of the blanket from under the mattress and slowly peeled it back.

There were two rats under there; one on top of the other. The lower rodent was quite still and had what seemed to Erik to be a contemplative look of nun-like resignation on its face. The top one, that was doing all the furious humping and bumping bore, behind its whiskers, an expression that was very different. It stared up at Erik, opened its jaws, snarled once, then ignored him and got on with its work.

"There's a pair of them," he reported. "Both of them big. You can guess what they're doing."

"How is *he*, though?"

Erik pulled the blankets back further and peered down and under.

"Ah, Christ," he said, his voice muffled by his left hand that had shot up involuntarily to clutch his mouth. He threw the blanket violently back down, scaring the rats off and away at last, and staggered to his feet.

"Not good?" said the protester.

"If he's not dead he ought to be."

After walking around the bed to the side its occupant was facing, Erik bent painfully down – it hurt a lot when he bent his torso forward – and stared at what was visible of the unfortunate man's face.

"How does he look?"

Erik, speechless for the moment, shook his head.

"As bad as that, eh?"

"I thought he might be someone I know."

"And is he?"

"I can't be sure," Erik said. "Probably not."

He went and sat down on that part of his own bed that was not yet soaked in liquid draining from one of the pipes. He looked down at his body, naked except for the dressings on his chest and belly, and saw that the smaller holes that had been punched into him in various places were not bleeding as much as he had expected. A couple of them already appeared to be congealing. So far he didn't feel too bad at all. Physically weak, yes, but his brain was clearer than it had been for a long time.

Almost unnoticed by Erik until now, an increasing amount of movement had been going on in the corridor outside the ward during the last half-hour, causing a rising clatter of noise and conversation. He was about to open one of the doors to take a look outside to assess just what was causing the hubbub, when both of them burst open in front of him and a porter's trolley, loaded with large items of expensive-looking luggage, was hastily shoved in through the gap towards him. The man behind it, stooping low to get behind the weight of it, was unaware of his surroundings until he looked up to steer it into the place he'd chosen for it, against the wall and alongside Erik's bed. The path the trolley took forced Erik to scamper awkwardly and uncomfortably back into a corner of the ward, but the porter couldn't see him because he was a small man and the luggage was piled high. Fortunately, the trolley came to a stop a foot or so short of the wall. Erik had feared, if he'd been crushed by it, his stitched up wounds would have split open and he would literally have burst apart.

The porter retreated out onto the corridor, but returned at once with another similar load. As he barged through the door he shouted at someone on the corridor behind him, "There's room for more in here."

"That's the idea," a woman replied. "You can come back for them later, when we get round to impounding the possessions. Your most urgent task is to keep a way open along the corridor so we can keep the red cards moving through to the E wards." It was Dr Stranghaver's voice and she sounded as though she was enjoying herself.

Erik remained where he was for five minutes until the porter had crammed the ward full of over-laden trolleys then, when the doors finally swung shut, he wormed his way up on to his bed.

The luggage heaped beside him showed every sign of having been packed in a hurry. Much of it had not been properly closed and locked, and a number of over-stuffed cases had sprung open in transit. Erik dipped into one of the nearest of these and found it contained the clothing of a large elderly woman. He pushed it aside and searched others at random. Most were full of more of the same, but he was astonished to find one of them – a leather case that had been merely zipped shut – was half-full of bank notes of high denominations in rubber-banded rolls. He was tempted but, reflecting that they were no use to him in his present position, he turned his attention to opening bags on one of the other trolleys.

His companion on the adjacent bed watched him for a while then said, "What are you up to? Thieving? You seem to know what you're doing. Professional, are you?"

Erik didn't bother to answer because he'd found what appeared to be just what he was looking for, a solution to his nudity problem: a case full of men's clothing. He pulled out a pair of needle-cord trousers and laid them out along the length of his legs. They were an

inch or so too long, but he decided to try them on. This proved to be
an extremely difficult and painful operation. As soon as he bent his
spine forward to draw them up, everything inside him howled with
hurt and he shouted aloud. When the pain ebbed away he realised
that the task was impossible in the position he was in. So he turned
on his back, pulled his knees towards his belly and tucked his feet
into the tops of the trousers. Then he stuck his feet into the air and
moved them in such a way as to encourage the garment to descend
towards him down the length of his legs.

When he had zipped himself in, the man on the next bed clapped
his hands quietly and said, "That was well done. Bloody marvellous.
You're going to try to get out."

"Now is the time, with all that confusion in the corridor."

Erik had wriggled into a shirt, buttoned it partially, and pulled a
jacket on over it. He gave up the idea of socks, but dropped some
slip-on shoes onto the floor and forced his feet down into them as he
stood up. He said, "It shouldn't take too long for me to get to the old
hospital. I'll raise the alarm when I get there."

"Do you think anyone will listen?"

"Why shouldn't they?"

"Because of the way you look. Like a dangerously crazy person.
Unshaven chin, flashing eyes, floating hair, blood stains on your shirt
already, and that jacket is so tight you have to walk with your elbows
sticking out."

Erik shrugged his shoulders as best he could under their present
restrictions and slipped out through the ward doors.

He was cheered to see the extent of the chaos around him.
Members of staff in different uniforms everywhere mingled with
dozens of well-heeled civilians. Although at first sight the scene was
one of apparent disorder, Erik soon got the impression that most of
the individuals milling around him knew where they were going and
what they were doing. Porters and sundry other helpers struggled
through the crowds with quantities of luggage, their minds set on
reaching their destinations and getting the job done. There was
something of the atmosphere of a railway station or the check-in
desks at a busy airport about the Unit now. Indeed, those individuals
not in uniform looked from happy to downright gleeful, as though
they were setting off on the holiday of their dreams. Even the
seriously handicapped on crutches or in wheelchairs – and there
were plenty of them – looked eagerly about them at the pallid grey
walls and seemed transfixed with joy at the sight of their new home.

As Erik passed one of the corridors leading to the dome, he saw it was less crowded, so he turned down it, thinking it would be quicker to go straight on across the dome and out through the opposite exit. There, his sense of direction told him, he might find his way out of the Samuel Taylor Unit. He was convinced he had come in from that side.

In the dome, facing half-a-dozen desks, were queues of people that stretched right across the floor. They surrounded the now somewhat-battered and much less luxuriously leafed collection of plants, and effectively blocked off the whole of the inner floor area of the dome. Erik had to circumnavigate them. The countless echoes of their voices were disturbing and disorientating. Baffling sounds bounced around Erik like dancing bones and soft rubber balls and caused an extra interior echoing, as though his brain was clanging like a muffled bell inside his skull. This didn't stop even when he put his hands over his ears. Also, he found he had to walk with a stoop to avoid stretching his wounds, and two or three times his legs had failed to do what he had expected and he had staggered a few steps sideways. As yet nobody had taken any undue notice of him, so far as he could tell, but he knew if he fell over it would not be easy or perhaps possible for him to get up again.

It must have been night-time, because the roof of the dome was dark and there was insufficient artificial lighting provided. Erik made his way around the dome by keeping close to the wall and staying in touch with it with the back of his left hand, like a blind man. When he found he was no longer in contact with anything, he knew he had reached the passage he was seeking on the far side, and thankfully turned into it.

When he emerged onto the circular corridor again, he faced a scene of even greater confusion than before, and it took him some time to realise that, in itself, this was good news, because most of the people in front of him were coming towards him and turning left and right. They were part of the new intake being met by hospital staff who inspected the red and blue cards the visitors were carrying and directed them where to go, in one direction or the other. If these people were coming in, then forward, for Erik, had to be the way out.

He launched himself into the approaching crowd who, for the most part, were reluctant or unable to step aside for him, so he had to dodge around most of the individuals pressing towards him. This was hard to achieve, as he felt he needed to keep moving as fast as he could. The constant stepping from side to side made him dizzy, and he began to find it difficult to focus his eyes. When he had gone just a few yards, he banged into someone pushing a wheelchair and only managed to keep upright by grabbing the arm of the next nearest person, a tall grey-bearded man, who slapped his face. Behind him someone shouted, and Erik guessed the call was an order for him to stop.

He had realised that in going against the flow he would mark himself out for the attention of those representatives of the Unit who were receiving the new patients, but they were being kept busy and he'd good reason to hope they might not notice him. Now, due to his clumsiness, it seemed they had. He daren't look around to confirm this speculation because he feared if he did, he'd lose his balance, fall, and get swept along or trampled by the crowd. He kept going, trying to press on faster than ever, aware that someone much fitter could be in pursuit.

Having made some unimpeded progress, he got to a turning in the corridor he thought he could remember taking, widdershins, on his way in. As he changed direction, the crowd ahead of him appeared to be somewhat thinner than that which he'd left behind. Since no one had grabbed him so far, he assumed that if anyone had been chasing him they had given up.

He was attempting to calculate how much further he might have to get to the borderline of the Samuel Taylor Unit – it couldn't be far now, he was sure – when, somewhere in the distance, certainly outside the hospital, there was a burst of sound that shook the foundations of the building. The floor beneath Erik's feet became, for some seconds, unsteady. Ahead of him he could hear glass shattering and something heavy crashed to the ground. There was a second louder, because nearer, explosion. Some of the people around him faltered in their steps and looked indignantly at each other with expressions on their faces that said they demanded an explanation for this violation of peace and order. Others hurried forward faster, while those more feeble looked nervously back the way they had come and called for help.

None of this had any impact on Erik. He staggered on, but at a deliberately slower pace, to spare himself a little and preserve his remaining stock of energy and determination as much as he felt he safely could. Anyway, there were no more eruptions from without or interruptions from within, and the noises-off had given all those heading towards the Unit something more alarming to worry about than the oddly-dressed, bloody, possibly lunatic figure lurching towards them in the opposite direction.

Erik was not much aware of his surroundings, but he realised that the people he was passing must be the tail-end of the new intake when he came to a point where there was hardly anyone approaching him in the corridor ahead. He was, therefore, running out of indicators to show him the way to go. The significance of this was just beginning to sink in, causing an extra dimension of despair to rise up in Erik's addled and shook-up brain, when he noticed a kaleidoscopic spread of bright colours in front of him that seemed to be hovering and vibrating in the otherwise empty air. Fearing he'd reached exhaustion and was hallucinating, he wiped his eyes with the sleeve of his ill-fitting jacket, then looked again towards the way ahead.

The last decorations he had passed on the walls of the old hospital on the way in, he remembered, had been posters advertising reduced-rate holiday weekends in Ireland. They featured a selection of luridly colourful photographs of gardens and beaches a tourist taking advantage of those offers could hope to enjoy. They had remained in Erik's memory because he'd stayed at one of the hotels illustrated himself within the last year.

He was looking at the posters now. They were just a couple of yards away. Their colours had shocked his eyes because for so long his surroundings had been uniformly grey.

A few paces more and he had put the Samuel Taylor Unit behind him. He stopped running, propped himself against the wall alongside the posters, and reached out to touch the nearest of them fondly, with an unsteady hand.

His first thought then was to get help for the protestor and any one else like him who might still be left alive in the Unit. Once he had discharged that duty, he could get medical assistance for himself then do the one simple thing he wanted to do more than anything else – sleep.

He pushed himself away from the wall and continued his progress into the hospital. He had not gone many paces when all the lights in the building flickered, went off for perhaps half a minute, then flashed on again. During the period of darkness, cries of consternation sounded from the nearby wards.

Erik had blundered on without stopping, with his arms outstretched, feeling his way through the darkness. When the electric power came on again, he found he was standing next to the open door of a Children's Ward that was full of frantic activity. It took him a few seconds to work out that the place was being evacuated. Nurses were attempting to push the obviously frightened children in their beds towards the door. The first of these was emerging into the corridor close to him when Erik saw the cause of the commotion.

Rats. There were perhaps half-a-dozen of them running helter-skelter across the floor, over the beds, and anywhere else they pleased. The nurses were trying to stamp on the creatures when they got the chance but, as far as Erik could make out, there had only been one casualty so far, and that was not quite dead.

A tall, hawk-faced woman appeared in front of him, running. As she passed him, she shouted to the nurses in the Children's Ward that there had been yet another change of plan. "The patients are to be kept where they are," she added.

The nurses angrily protested at this.

"Of course I know about the rats," the obviously managerial woman said, almost shouting, "but it's a case of the least of two evils. Things are happening outside. Nobody seems to know what yet, but there's serious trouble of some kind so your orders are to keep the children here. You know the emergency procedures. Close the doors and windows and keep them shut until you're told to do otherwise." She started pushing the bed of the one child who had been brought out back in to the ward.

Erik decided there was nothing he could do to help and that the nurses were in no position to help him. So, following the exit signs that had begun to appear, he walked on.

There was an increasing amount of noise and movement on either side and up ahead, and it wasn't long before he found himself in a situation similar to the one he had put behind him in the Samuel Taylor Unit, if not worse. It must have been the evening visitors' hour, because the wards he passed were again full of the families and friends of the bed-bound patients, but the atmosphere was very different now. The shaking floors and flickering lights minutes earlier had caused general consternation and alarm among the guests who had, in some cases, deserted the people they had come to see to discuss with each other the possible cause of the disturbances. Some, drawn by the screeches of many sirens, had come out into the corridor and were staring out of the windows into the darkness beyond and reporting the hyperactivity of police cars and ambulances in the streets outside. The upper floors of the hospital had a good view of a large section of the city.

"There're fire engines going by, but there's no smoke anywhere," one woman said, "and I can't smell anything burning."

"The street lights are off in some parts," her partner observed. "Other than that, I can't see much to worry about."

Erik walked into one of the wards and asked a nurse for help. He held his jacket open so she could see the blood that had seeped out of his wounds and onto his shirt. The sight of this did not produce the reaction he had anticipated. She gave him a glare of suspicion and anger. "Who are you?" she demanded. "How did you get like that?"

Erik began to tell her, but soon realised he was wasting words and the nurse's time. What he was saying didn't sound to make much sense, even to him, and he could see in the nurse's eyes that she was becoming increasingly irritated. She waved a hand to shut him up and snapped, "That's enough. You'll have to go away, please. I don't want you on my ward. People are upset enough. Having someone who looks the way you do here can only make things worse."

Erik glanced down at himself. He hadn't given a thought to his appearance for some time.

"I can see you're hurt," the nurse said, with some slight note of apology, "but there's no help for you here. We can't treat you. You need to go to Accident and Emergency on the ground floor." She put a hand on his shoulder and urged him towards the door, then turned back to the task of keeping order.

Erik left the ward and stumbled on until he came to a lift close to some stairs leading down. A nervous-looking porter stood in front of the lift. Erik asked him what was going on.

"No idea," the man said. "I've to keep people out of the elevator in case they get trapped if there's another power cut."

Erik said, "I don't think I can make it down the stairs."

"You're in a bad way, I can see that."

"If the lift is working, I'd like to risk it."

"Going down, you mean? I can't let you do that."

"I'm going to fall down soon, and I know I won't be able to get up again." Erik opened his jacket again. "I have to get to A and E."

The porter took a look at Erik's chest, hissed and said, "Fuck that!"

Erik nodded. "I know," he said.

The porter looked from side to side, then made up his mind and pressed the call button of the lift. The doors opened at once.

"It's on the ground floor."

"The A and E?"

"Yep. There'll be someone like me waiting when you get out," the porter said. "Tell him Kev Naylor said it's okay to let you go."

"Thanks."

"Right in front of you, it will be, the A and E."

Erik thought about the porter's last words as the lift sank. Poetry! There was a rat in the lift with him: an old, scabby, skinny one with a kink in its tail where it must once have been injured. It didn't take any notice of Erik, but stuck its twitchy nose up a couple of times to sniff the air. Erik thought it could probably smell his blood. It waited by the edge of the door, and when the door opened it was first out.

The rat and Erik passed an astonished porter, who looked as though he was going to try and stop Erik's progress until Erik told him what Kev Naylor had said about it being okay. The porter rubbed the back of his neck in consternation but let Erik pass.

"Dirty bloody things," he said, as the creature scuttled away. "Don't know what's got into them. Used to see one or two sometimes, cowardly buggers, slinking about in the shadows, but in the last few weeks they're everywhere and they don't seem to give a toss about anyone."

"Maybe it's something they've eaten," Erik said.

"And they'll go for you," the porter said. "They're as brave as lions."

Seconds after the lift doors slid shut the overhead lights flickered again, then dimmed and stayed that way.

Through the resulting gloom, Erik could see that the reception area of the A and E Department in front of him was crowded with a clutter of stretcher trolleys that had been left at all angles, like derailed carriages after a train wreck. On each of them was a fully-clothed body with arms and legs thrust out as though each person had been caught and frozen in the middle of some strenuous activity. The expressions on the faces Erik could see were similarly grotesque, expressing various degrees of mental and bodily excruciation. Among the trolleys a number of bewildered, stranded people stood twisting and stumbling on the spot, searching around for familiar faces. Most of the outstretched people were silent and, Erik assumed, dead, though some occasionally coughed in soft, painful spasms. The area stank of vomit and something else that Erik could not identify, a stench he had never come across before.

The stretcher trolleys were packed so closely together it would have been impossible for a fit person to push through them to the treatment rooms of the A and E, and Erik knew that in his condition there was no hope that he could do so. He was near the end of his strength. His legs felt boneless, and when he moved he swayed from side to side like an elastic man.

Aware that he would soon tumble, and for the last time too, almost certainly, unless he received some medical attention, Erik sought a place to sit down and rest for a while. All the chairs around the sides of the A and E waiting room were full of slumped bodies, so he made his way back out past the lift door towards the deserted reception desk near the Main Entrance. It was a long way, but Erik thought if there was no hope for him in the building, he might as well try to seek help outside of it. Though there was no panic, there were many bewildered people milling apparently aimlessly about and nobody seemed to be in charge of any part of the establishment. Erik made his way through the chaos until he came to a stop by a radiator under a large window. He judged that the top of the heater was about the right height for him to rest his backside on.

A number of people were pressed against the window, looking out. Erik joined them and leaned over the radiator to lay claim to some part of it. After pushing aside a couple of small potted plants similar to those he'd seen in the dome – cuttings, presumably – he supported his sagging weight by resting his elbows on the window ledge. Beyond the window, the stabbing lights of stationary police cars and ambulances, dancing in stroboscopic staccato, made it impossible to make out exactly what, if anything, was happening on the approach to the A and E and the main entry to the Admission Section of the hospital. The vehicles drawn up outside remained where they were, and nobody came or went in or out of them.

Someone near Erik said, "I tried to get out of the main door but couldn't. It's locked."

"And sealed," a woman said, sounding almost pleased. "It's an emergency. A nurse told me the hospital is on Red Alert."

Another woman said. "But I need to get home to my kids. Where's the danger? What is it? Does anybody know?"

"Terrorists."

The common opinion seemed to be that bombs had been detonated close by.

Erik felt something brush against his sockless ankles, then a sharp pain at the top of his left foot. He turned away from the window, kicked out at the rat with his other foot and hit it, but it did him no good because he lost his balance along with the last vestige of his strength and found himself sinking. He reached out to grasp something to stop himself falling, but only managed to grab hold of one of the small potted plants that he pulled down with him as he descended.

He sank slowly. His collision with the floor was a soft landing. He bounced gently off the radiator then found himself grounded, lolling forward in a sitting position clutching the plant to his chest with his left hand. There were dozens of short but sharp spikes on the stalks of the plant that had penetrated his palm and fingers and caused him some mild discomfort. He tried to get rid of them with his free hand, but just got more ensnared, so he left them in place.

A woman standing near him squealed in a way that suggested rats to Erik, rather than anything directly life-threatening. This was confirmed when she said, "Christ, there's something running up my arm," then stepped back and tripped over Erik's legs. She landed on top of him, but he hardly felt a thing. A numbness that had started in his hand soon after he'd clutched the plant cutting was spreading through his chest and out into his limbs. He closed his eyes, and for a moment he was under the illusion that he was back in the ward, plugged into painkillers again. The thought made him feel nostalgic. He wondered if he'd made a big mistake getting out of that bed.

The woman said, "Sorry," then clambered up off him and started calling for someone called John.

A man said, "Ann, I'm over here, at the far end of the window. Come and see this." His voice was hushed. From his calm tone he must have been unaware of much that had occurred in the main body of the hospital. He sounded like an ornithologist trying to draw attention to a rare finch he'd spotted without disturbing it.

The woman hurried away from Erik and joined her companion.

"Look there," the man said, "I thought everyone had gone off somewhere, but something's happening down by the gates. Can you see?"

"No, I can't," Ann said. "I just fell. My glasses must have dropped off."

John gave a grunt of sympathy then said, "Yes, no doubt about it, there's definitely something going on out there"

A second man said, "What's this then? What have we got here, then? There's a vehicle of some kind coming up the driveway towards us. A huge thing. I never saw anything like that before."

"Me neither," John said. "Looks military. There are people moving up behind it. A lot of them. Wearing some kind of protective clothing."

The second man said, "I reckon there's been a poison gas or biological weapons attack. They've got masks on under their helmets."

"Must be police or the army. I expect they'll soon have things under control."

Ann squeaked nervously again and said, "There are more and more rats coming in here all the time, John. I can hear them moving all around us. I think they must be coming up from underground."

"Ann," John said paternalistically, all his attention now on the events outside. "Don't worry about them. They won't eat you."

The man John had been talking to said, "That bloody great truck, or whatever it is, is getting very close."

"No, I think it's stopping now."

"You're right. And someone's getting out."

No one spoke for some time until John said, "Can you make out what's written on the side of that vehicle? My eyesight is not much better than Ann's. There are two words, and I believe the first one starts with 'P' but I don't think it is 'Police'."

"'Porlock', that's what it is," the second man said. "Porlock Foundation. Don't know who they are."

"Me neither," John said. "How about you, Ann?"

"No idea. Never heard of them."

"Must be some kind of private security firm."

"I don't care who they are as long as they get us out of here."

"From the way those men are spreading out and lining up," the un-named man said, "you'd think they were getting ready to attack the place."

"I expect they're well trained and know what they're doing," John said. "They look well-equipped and very professional."

"If they do come in hard," the second man said, "through the windows, for instance, there's going to be a lot of glass flying about."

"He's right, Ann," John said, for the first time sounding slightly alarmed. "They do look rather – determined – as though they might do something rash. Do you think we'd better stand back a bit?"

Erik, merely bemused by the conversation he'd been overhearing, waited for an answer. But if one came, he didn't hear it.

Someone outside, at the front of the hospital, blew a whistle.

During the next few moments Erik was vaguely aware that the men and women who had been standing nearby were hurrying away in some confusion, but he didn't mind being left behind. It was a relief not to have to listen to their chatter. For a short while everything went quiet and that pleased him very much.

He sat clutching, cuddling really, his little plant in complete contentment. The rats bustling busily around him weren't playing games, but they couldn't trouble Erik any more. They couldn't reach him. He'd given them the slip. He was off on a voyage, sailing away all on his own.

When all the lights in the hospital went out and did not come back on again, Erik fell into a doze, but one that did not last long.

At first, as the uniformed figures smashed their way in and woke him up, he assumed they were coming to rescue him, but soon realised he was wrong.

They didn't have any interest in him or anyone else in the building. Their orders were to release the rats.

JOE HILL

Best New Horror

JOE HILL'S TALE "20th Century Ghost" appeared in the fourteenth volume of *The Mammoth Book of Best New Horror* and later became the title story of his first book, an acclaimed collection released by PS Publishing last year.

He was awarded the William Crawford Award for outstanding new fantasy writer in 2006 and his first novel, *Heart-Shaped Box*, is due is early 2007.

The author had a number of excellent stories published last year, but when it came to making a decision, how could I *not* include a tale with this particular title? It justifiably won the 2006 Bram Stoker Award for Long Fiction.

"Most of my short stories contain some element of fantasy or surrealism or supernatural horror," explains Hill. "When I began to gather them together, with the idea of trying to sell them as a collection, I began to get this terrible urge to explain myself, to say why *these* tales, instead of Carveresque narratives about emotionally isolated bird-watchers, or stories of morally vacuous teens engaged in titillating acts of self-destruction.

"I knew the urge – that desire to explain – had to be strangled in its crib, needed to be killed and chucked in a dumpster, before it could grow-up and make me do things I would regret. I did away with it.

"The ghost of the urge, though, haunted me. I often woke to find it sitting on the end of my bed, a weeping homunculus, wrapped in death shrouds, giving me accusing looks. At last, it drove me to write this story, which is, I guess, not an explanation at all, but an argument for a certain kind of fiction: the depraved kind.

"Also, as I've said elsewhere, I felt like my collection needed a story with a chainsaw in it. 'Best New Horror' was the inevitable result."

A MONTH BEFORE HIS DEADLINE, Eddie Carroll ripped open a manila envelope, and a magazine called *The True North Literary Review* slipped out into his hands. Carroll was used to getting magazines in the mail, although most of them had titles like *Cemetery Dance* and specialized in horror fiction. People sent him their books, too. Piles of them cluttered his Brookline townhouse, a heap on the couch in his office, a stack by the coffee maker. Books of horror stories, all of them.

No one had time to read them all, although once – when he was in his early thirties and just starting out as the editor of America's Best New Horror – he had made a conscientious effort to try. Carroll had guided sixteen volumes of *Best New Horror* to press, had been working on the series for over a third of his life now. It added up to thousands of hours of reading and proofing and letter-writing, thousands of hours he could never have back. He had come to hate the magazines especially. So many of them used the cheapest ink, and he had learned to loathe the way it came off on his fingers, the harsh stink of it.

He didn't finish most of the stories he started any more, couldn't bear to. He felt weak at the thought of reading another story about vampires having sex with other vampires. He tried to struggle through Lovecraft pastiches, but at the first painfully serious reference to the Elder Gods, he felt some important part of him going numb inside, the way a foot or a hand will go to sleep when the circulation is cut off. He feared the part of him being numbed was his soul.

At some point following his divorce, his duties as the editor of *Best New Horror* had become a tiresome and joyless chore. He thought sometimes, hopefully almost, of stepping down, but he never indulged the idea for long. It was twelve thousand dollars a year in the bank, the cornerstone of an income patched together from other anthologies, his speaking engagements and his classes. Without that twelve grand, his personal worst-case scenario would become inevitable: he would have to find an actual job.

The True North Literary Review was unfamiliar to him, a journal with a cover of rough-grained paper, an ink print on it of leaning pines. A stamp on the back reported that it was a publication of Kathadan University in upstate New York. When he flipped it open, two stapled pages fell out, a letter from the editor, an English professor named Harold Noonan.

The winter before, Noonan had been approached by a part-time man with the university grounds crew, a Peter Kilrue. He had heard

Noonan had been named the editor of *True North*, and was taking open submissions, and asked him to look at a short story. Noonan promised he would, more to be polite than anything else. But when he finally read the manuscript, "Buttonboy: A Love Story", he was taken aback by both the supple force of its prose and the appalling nature of its subject matter. Noonan was new in the job, replacing the just-retired editor of twenty years, Frank McDane, and wanted to take the journal in a new direction, to publish fiction that would "rattle a few cages".

"In that I was perhaps too successful," Noonan wrote. Shortly after "Buttonboy" appeared in print, the head of the English department held a private meeting with Noonan to verbally assail him for using *True North* as a showcase for "juvenile literary practical jokes". Nearly fifty people cancelled their subscriptions – no laughing matter for a journal with a circulation of just a thousand copies – and the alumnus who provided most of *True North*'s funding withdrew her financial support in outrage. Noonan himself was removed as editor, and Frank McDane agreed to oversee the magazine from retirement, in response to the popular outcry for his return.

Noonan's letter finished:

> I remain of the opinion that (whatever its flaws), 'Buttonboy' is a remarkable, if genuinely distressing work of fiction, and I hope you'll give it your time. I admit I would find it personally vindicating if you decided to include it in your next anthology of the year's best horror fiction.
>
> I would tell you to enjoy, but I'm not sure that's the word.
> Best,
> Harold Noonan

Eddie Carroll had just come in from outside, and read Noonan's letter standing in the mudroom. He flipped to the beginning of the story. He stood reading for almost five minutes before noticing he was uncomfortably warm. He tossed his jacket at a hook and wandered into the kitchen.

He sat for a while on the stairs to the second floor, turning through the pages. Then he was stretched on the couch in his office, head on a pile of books, reading in a slant of late October light, with no memory of how he had got there.

He rushed through to the ending, then sat up, in the grip of a strange, bounding exuberance. He thought it was possibly the rudest, most awful thing he had ever read, and in his case that was saying something. He had waded through the rude and awful for most of his professional life, and in those fly-blown and diseased literary swamps had discovered flowers of unspeakable beauty, of which he was sure this was one. It was cruel and perverse and he had to have it. He turned to the beginning and started reading again.

It was about a girl named Cate – an introspective seventeen-year-old at the story's beginning – who one day is pulled into a car by a giant with jaundiced eyeballs and teeth in tin braces. He ties her hands behind her back and shoves her onto the backseat floor of his station wagon . . . where she discovers a boy about her age, who she at first takes for dead and who has suffered an unspeakable disfiguration. His eyes are hidden behind a pair of round, yellow, smiley-face buttons. They've been pinned right through his eyelids – which have also been stitched shut with steel wire – and the eyeballs beneath.

As the car begins to move, though, so does the boy. He touches her hip and Cate bites back a startled scream. He moves his hand over her body, touching her face last. He whispers his name is Jim, and that he's been traveling with the giant for a week, ever since the big man killed his parents.

"He made holes in my eyes and he said after he did it he saw my soul rush out. He said it made a sound like when you blow on an empty Coke bottle, real pretty. Then he put these over my eyes to keep my life trapped inside." As he speaks, Jim touches the smiley-face buttons. "He wants to see how long I can live without a soul inside me."

The giant drives them both to a desolate campground, in a nearby state park, where he forces Cate and Jim to fondle one another sexually. When he feels Cate is failing to kiss Jim with convincing passion, he slashes her face, and removes her tongue. In the ensuing chaos – Jim shrieking in alarm, staggering about blindly, blood everywhere – Cate is able to escape into the trees. Three hours later she staggers out onto a highway, hysterical, drenched in blood.

Her kidnapper is never apprehended. He and Jim drive out of the national park and off the edge of the world. Investigators are unable to determine a single useful fact about the two. They don't know who Jim is or where he's from, and know even less about the giant.

Two weeks after her release from the hospital, a single clue turns up by US Post. Cate receives an envelope, containing a pair of smiley-face buttons – steel pins caked with dry blood – and a Polaroid of a bridge in Kentucky. The next morning a diver finds a boy there, on the river bottom, horribly decomposed, fish darting in and out of his empty eye sockets.

Cate, who was once attractive and well-liked, finds herself the object of pity and horror among those who know her. She understands the way other people feel. The sight of her own face in the mirror repels her as well. She attends a special school for a time and learns sign language, but she doesn't stay long. The other cripples – the deaf, the lame, the disfigured – disgust her, with their neediness, their dependencies.

Cate tries, without much luck, to assume a normal life. She has no close friends, no employable skills, and is self-conscious about her looks, her inability to speak. In one particularly painful scene, Cate drinks her way into courage, and makes a pass at a man in a bar, only to be ridiculed by him and his friends.

Her sleep is troubled by regular nightmares, in which she relives unlikely and dreadful variations on her abduction. In some, Jim is not a fellow victim, but in on the kidnapping, and rapes her with vigor. The buttons stuck through his eyes are mirrored discs that show a distorted image of her own screaming face, which, with perfect dream logic, has already been hacked into a grotesque mask. Infrequently, these dreams leave her aroused. Her therapist says this is common. She fires the therapist when she discovers he's doodled a horrid caricature of her in his notebook.

Cate tries different things to help her sleep: gin, painkillers, heroin. She needs money for drugs and goes looking for it in her father's dresser. He catches her at it and chases her out. That night her mother calls to tell her Dad is in the hospital – he had a minor stroke – and please don't come to see him. Not long after, at a day care for disabled children, where Cate is part-timing, one child pokes a pencil into another child's eye, blinding him. The incident clearly isn't Cate's fault, but in the aftermath, her assorted addictions become public knowledge. She loses her job and, even after kicking her habit, finds herself nearly unemployable.

Then, one cool Fall day, she comes out of a local supermarket, and walks past a police car parked out back. The hood is up. A policeman in mirrored sunglasses is studying an overheated radiator. She happens to glance in the backseat – and there, with his hands cuffed behind his back, is her giant, ten years older and fifty pounds heavier.

She struggles to stay calm. She approaches the trooper, working under the hood, writes him a note, asks him if he knows who he has in the backseat.

He says a guy who was arrested at a hardware store on Pleasant

Street, trying to shoplift a hunting knife and a roll of heavy-duty duct tape.

Cate knows the hardware store in question. She lives around the corner from it. The officer takes her arm before her legs can give out on her.

She begins to write frantic notes, tries to explain what the giant did to her when she was seventeen. Her pen can't keep pace with her thoughts, and the notes she writes hardly make sense, even to her, but the officer gets the gist. He guides her around to the passenger seat, and opens the door. The thought of getting in the same car with her abductor makes her dizzy with fear – she begins to shiver uncontrollably – but the police officer reminds her the giant is handcuffed in the back, unable to hurt her, and that it's important for her to come with them to the precinct house.

At last she settles into the passenger seat. At her feet is a winter jacket. The police officer says it's his coat, and she should put it on, it'll keep her warm, help with her shivering. She looks up at him, prepares to scribble a thank you on her notepad – then goes still, finds herself unable to write. Something about the sight of her own face, reflected in his sunglasses, causes her to freeze up.

He closes the door and goes around to the front of the car to shut the hood. With numb fingers she reaches down to get his coat. Pinned to the front, one on each breast, are two smiley-face buttons. She reaches for the door but it won't unlock. The window won't roll down. The hood slams. The man behind the sunglasses who is not a police officer is grinning a hideous grin. Buttonboy continues around the car, past the driver's side door, to let the giant out of the back. After all, a person needs eyes to drive.

In thick forest, it's easy for a person to get lost and walk around in circles, and for the first time, Cate can see this is what happened to her. She escaped Buttonboy and the giant by running into the woods, but she never made her way out – not really – has been stumbling around in the dark and the brush ever since, traveling in a great and pointless circle back to them. She's arrived where she was always headed, at last, and this thought, rather than terrifying her, is oddly soothing. It seems to her she belongs with them and there is a kind of relief in that; in belonging somewhere. Cate relaxes into her seat, unconsciously pulling Buttonboy's coat around her against the cold.

It didn't surprise Eddie Carroll to hear Noonan had been excoriated for publishing "Buttonboy". The story lingered on images of female degradation, and the heroine had been written as a somewhat willing accomplice to her own emotional, sexual and spiritual mistreatment. This was bad . . . but Joyce Carol Oates wrote stories just like it for journals no different than *The True North Review*, and won awards for them. The really unforgivable literary sin was the shock ending.

Carroll had seen it coming – after reading almost ten thousand stories of horror and the supernatural, it was hard to sneak up on him – but he had enjoyed it nonetheless. Among the literary cognoscenti, though, a surprise ending (no matter how well executed) was the mark of childish, commercial fiction and bad TV. The readers of *The True North Review* were, he imagined, middle-aged academics, people who taught Grendel and Ezra Pound and who dreamed heartbreaking dreams about someday selling a poem to *The New Yorker*. For them, coming across a shock ending in a short story was akin to hearing a ballerina rip a noisy fart during a performance of *Swan Lake* – a *faux pas* so awful it bordered on the hilarious. Professor Harold Noonan had either not been rooming in the ivory tower for long, or was subconsciously hoping someone would hand him his walking papers.

Although the ending was more John Carpenter than John Updike, Carroll hadn't come across anything like it in any of the horror magazines, either, not lately. It was, for twenty-five pages, the almost completely naturalistic story of a woman being destroyed a little at a time by the steady wear of survivor's guilt. It concerned itself with tortured family relationships, shitty jobs, the struggle for money. Carroll had forgotten what it was like to come across the bread of everyday life in a short story. Most horror fiction didn't bother with anything except rare bleeding meat.

He found himself pacing his office, too excited to settle, "Buttonboy" folded open in one hand. He caught a glimpse of his reflection in the window behind the couch, and saw himself grinning in a way that was almost indecent, as if he had just heard a particularly good dirty joke.

Carroll was eleven years old when he saw *The Haunting* in The Oregon Theater. He had gone with his cousins, but when the lights went down, his companions were swallowed by the dark and Carroll found himself essentially alone, shut tight into his own suffocating cabinet of shadows. At times, it required all his will not to hide his eyes, yet his insides churned with a nervous-sick frission of pleasure. When the lights finally came up, his nerve-endings were ringing, as if he had for a moment grabbed a copper wire with live current in it. It was a sensation he developed a compulsion for.

Later, after he was a professional, and it was his business, his feelings were more muted – not gone, but felt distantly, more like the memory of an emotion than the thing itself. More recently, even the memory had fled, and in its place was a deadening amnesia, a numb disinterest when he looked at the piles of magazines on his coffee table. Or no – he was overcome with dread, but the wrong kind of dread.

This, though, here in his office, fresh from the depredations of "Buttonboy" . . . this was the authentic fix. It had clanged that inner bell and left him vibrating. He couldn't settle, wasn't used to exuberance. He tried to think when, if ever, he had last published a story he liked as much as "Buttonboy". He went to the shelf and pulled down the first volume of *Best New Horror* (still his favorite), curious to see what he had been excited about then. But, looking for the table of contents, he flipped it open to the dedication, which was to his then-wife, Elizabeth. "Who helps me find my way in the dark," he had written, in a dizzy fit of affection. Looking at it now caused the skin on his arms to crawl.

Elizabeth had left him after he discovered she had been sleeping with their investment banker for over a year. She went to stay with her mother, and took Tracy with her.

"In a way I'm almost glad you caught us," she said, talking to him on the phone, a few weeks after her flight from his life. "To have it over with."

"The affair?" he asked, wondering if she was about to tell him she had broken it off.

"No," Lizzie said. "I mean all your horror shit, and all those people who are always coming to see you, the horror people. Sweaty little grubs who get hard over corpses. That's the best part of this. Thinking maybe now Tracy can have a normal childhood. Thinking I'm finally going to get to have a life with healthy, ordinary grown-ups."

It was bad enough she had fucked around like she had, but that she would throw Tracy in his face that way made him short of breath with hatred, even now. He flung the book back at the shelf and slouched away for the kitchen and lunch, his restless excitement extinguished at last. He had been looking to use up all that useless distracting energy. Good old Lizzie – still doing him favors, even from forty miles away and another man's bed.

That afternoon he e-mailed Harold Noonan, asking for Kilrue's contact information. Noonan got back to him less than an hour later, pleased to hear Carroll wanted "Buttonboy" for *Best New Horror*.

He didn't have an e-mail address for Peter Kilrue, but he did have an address of the more ordinary variety, and a phone number.

But the letter Carroll wrote came back to him, stamped RETURN TO SENDER, and when he rang the phone number, he got a recording, this line has been disconnected. Carroll called Harold Noonan at Kathadin University.

"I can't say I'm shocked," Noonan said, voice rapid and soft, hitching with shyness. "I got the impression he's something of a transient. I think he patches together part-time jobs to pay his bills. Probably the best thing would be to call Morton Boyd in the grounds department. I imagine they have a file on him."

"When's the last time you saw him?"

"I dropped in on him last March. I went by his apartment just after 'Buttonboy' was published, when the outrage was running at full boil. People saying his story was misogynistic hate speech, saying there should be a published apology and such nonsense. I wanted to let him know what was happening. I guess I was hoping he'd want to fire back in some way, write a defense of his story for the student paper or something . . . although he didn't. Said it would be weak. Actually it was a strange kind of visit. He's a strange kind of guy. It isn't just his stories. It's him."

"What do you mean?"

Noonan laughed. "I'm not sure. What am I saying? You know how when you're running a fever, you'll look at something totally normal – like the lamp on your desk – and it'll seem somehow unnatural? Like it's melting or getting ready to waddle away? Encounters with Peter Kilrue can be kind of like that. I don't know why. Maybe because he's so intense about such troubling things."

Carroll hadn't even got in touch with him yet, and liked him all ready. "What do you mean? Tell me."

"When I went to see him, his older brother answered the door. Half-dressed. I guess he was staying with him. And this guy was – I don't want to be insensitive – but I would say disturbingly fat. And tattooed. Disturbingly tattooed. On his stomach there was a wind-mill, with rotted corpses hanging from it. On his back, there was a fetus with – scribbled over eyes. And a scalpel in one fist. And fangs."

Carroll laughed, but he wasn't sure it was funny.

Noonan went on, "But he was a good guy. Friendly as all get out. Led me in, got me a can of soda, we all sat on the couch in front of the TV. And – this is very amusing – while we were talking, and I was catching them up on the outcry, the older brother sat on the floor, while Peter gave him a homemade piercing."

"He what?"

"Oh God, yes. Right in the middle of the conversation he forces a hot needle through the upper part of his brother's ear. Blood like you wouldn't believe. When the fat guy got up, it looked like he had been shot in the side of the head. His head is pouring blood, it's like the end of *Carrie*, like he just took a bath in it, and he asks if he can get me another Coke."

This time they laughed together, and after, for a moment, a friendly silence passed between them.

"Also they were watching about Jonestown," Noonan said suddenly – blurted it really.

"Hm?"

"On the TV. With the sound off. While we talked and Peter stuck holes in his brother. In a way that was really the thing, the final weird touch that made it all seem so absolutely unreal. It was footage of the bodies in French Guyana. After they drank the Kool-Aide. Streets littered with corpses and all the birds, you know . . . the birds picking at them." Noonan swallowed thickly. "I think it was a loop, because it seems like they watched the same footage more than once. They were watching like . . . like in a trance."

Another silence passed between them. On Noonan's part, it seemed to be an uncomfortable one. Research, Carroll thought – with a certain measure of approval.

"Didn't you think it was a remarkable piece of American fiction?" Noonan asked.

"I did. I do."

"I don't know how he'll feel about getting in your collection, but speaking for myself, I'm delighted. I hope I haven't creeped you out about him."

Carroll smiled. "I don't creep easy."

Boyd in the grounds department wasn't sure where he was either. "He told me he had a brother with public works in Poughkeepsie. Either Poughkeepsie or Newburgh. He wanted to get in on that. Those town jobs are good money, and the best thing, once you're in, they can't fire you, it doesn't matter if you're a homicidal maniac."

Mention of Poughkeepsie stirred Carroll's interest. There was a small fantasy convention running there at the end of the month – Dark Wonder-con, or Dark Dreaming-con, or something. Dark Masturbati-con. He had been invited to attend, but had been ignoring their letters, didn't bother with the little cons anymore, and besides, the timing was all wrong, coming just before his deadline.

He went to the World Fantasy Awards, every year, though, and Camp NeCon, and a few of the other more interesting get-togethers. The conventions were one part of the job he had not come entirely to loathe. His friends were there. And also, a part of him still liked the stuff, and the memories the stuff sometimes kicked loose.

Such as one time, when he had come across a bookseller offering a first edition of *I Love Galesburg in the Springtime*. He had not seen or thought of *Galesburg* in years, but as he stood turning through its browned and brittle pages, with their glorious smell of dust and attics, a whole vertiginous flood of memory poured over him. He had read it when he was thirteen, and it had held him rapt for two weeks. He had climbed out of his bedroom window onto the roof to read; it was the only place he could go to get away from the sounds of his parents fighting. He remembered the sandpaper texture of the roof shingles, the rubbery smell of them baking in the sun, the distant razz of a lawnmower, and most of all, his own blissful sense of wonder, as he read about Jack Finney's impossible Woodrow Wilson dime.

Carroll rang public works in Poughkeepsie, was transferred to Personnel.

"Kilrue? Arnold Kilrue? He got the ax six months ago," said a man with a thin and wheezy voice. "You know how hard it is to get fired from a town job? First person I let go in years. Lied about his criminal record."

"No, not Arnold Kilrue. Peter. Arnold is maybe his brother. Was he overweight, lot of tattoos?"

"Not at all. Thin. Wiry. Only one hand. His left hand got ate up by a baler, said he."

"Oh," Carroll said, thinking this still somehow sounded like one of Peter Kilrue's relations. "What kind of trouble was he in?"

"Violatin' his restraining order."

"Oh," Carroll said. "Marital dispute?" He had sympathy for men who had suffered at the hands of their wives' lawyers.

"Hell no," Personnel replied. "Try his own mother. How the fuck do you like that?"

"Do you know if he's related to Peter Kilrue, and how to get in touch with him?"

"I ain't his personal secretary, buddy. Are we all through talking?"

They were all through talking.

*   *   *

He tried information, started calling people named Kilrue in the greater Poughkeepsie area, but no one he spoke to would admit to knowing a Peter, and finally he gave up. Carroll cleaned his office in a fury, jamming papers into the trash basket without looking at them, picking up stacks of books in one place, and slamming them down in another, out of ideas and out of patience.

In the late afternoon, he flung himself on the couch to think, and fell into a furious doze. Even dreaming, he was angry, chasing a little boy who had stolen his car keys through an empty movie theater. The boy was black and white and flickered like a ghost, or a character in an old movie, and having himself a hell of a time, shaking the keys in the air and laughing hysterically. Carroll lurched awake, feeling a touch of feverish heat in his temples, thinking Poughkeepsie.

Peter Kilrue lived somewhere in that part of New York and on Saturday he would be at the Dark FutureCon in Poughkeepsie, would not be able to resist such an event. Someone there would know him. Someone would point him out. All Carroll needed was to be there, and they would find each other.

He wasn't going to stay overnight – it was a four-hour drive, he could go and come back late – and by 6:00 a.m. he was doing 80 in the left-hand lane on I-90. The sun rose behind him, filling his rear view mirror with blinding light. It felt good to squeeze the pedal to the floor, to feel the car rushing west, chasing the long thin line of its own shadow. Then he had the thought that his little girl belonged beside him, and his foot eased up on the pedal, his excitement for the road draining out of him.

Tracy loved the conventions, any kid would. They offered the spectacle of grown-ups making fools of themselves, dressed up as Pinhead or Elvira. And what child could resist the inevitable market, that great maze of tables and macabre exhibits to get lost in, a place where a kid could buy a rubber severed hand for a dollar. Tracy had once spent half an hour playing pinball with Neil Gaiman, at the World Fantasy Convention in Washington D.C. They still wrote each other.

It was just noon when he found the Mid-Hudson Civic Center and made his way in. The marketplace was packed into a concert hall, and the floor was densely crowded, the concrete walls echoing with laughter and the steady hollow roar of overlapping conversations. He hadn't let anyone know he was coming, but it didn't matter, one of the organizers found him anyway, a chubby woman with frizzy red hair, in a pinstripe suit-jacket with tails.

"I had no idea – " she said, and, "We didn't hear from you!" and, "Can I get you a drink?"

Then there was a rum-and-coke in one hand, and a little knot of the curious around him, chattering about movies and writers and *Best New Horror* and he wondered why he had ever thought of not coming. Someone was missing for the 1:30 panel on the state of short horror fiction and wouldn't that be perfect –? Wouldn't it, he said.

He was led to a conference room, rows of folding chairs, a long table at one end with a pitcher of ice water on it. He took a seat behind it, with the rest of the panel: a teacher who had written a book about Poe, the editor of an online horror magazine, a local writer of fantasy-themed children's books. The redhead introduced them to the two dozen people or so who filed in, and then everyone at the table had a chance to make some opening remarks. Carroll was the last to speak.

First he said that every fictional world was a work of fantasy, and whenever a writer introduces a threat or a conflict into his story, they create the possibility of horror. He had been drawn to horror fiction, he said, because it took the most basic elements of literature and pushed them to their extremes. All fiction was make-believe, which made fantasy more valid (and honest) than realism.

He said that most horror and fantasy was worse than awful: exhausted, creatively bankrupt imitations of what was shit to begin with. He said sometimes he went for months without coming across a single fresh idea, a single memorable character, a single striking sentence.

Then he told them it had never been any different. It was probably true of any endeavor – artistic or otherwise – that it took a lot of people creating a lot of bad work to produce even a few successes. Everyone was welcome to struggle, get it wrong, learn from their mistakes, try again. And always there were rubies in the sand. He talked about Clive Barker and Kelly Link and Stephen Gallagher and Peter Kilrue, told them about "Buttonboy". He said for himself, anyway, nothing beat the high of discovering something thrilling and fresh, he would always love it, the happy horrible shock of it. As he spoke he realized it was true. When he was done talking, a few in the back row began clapping, and the sound spread outward, a ripple in a pool, and as it moved across the room, people began to stand.

He was sweating as he came out from behind the table to shake a few hands, after the panel discussion was over. He took off his glasses to wipe his shirt-tail across his face, and before he had put them back on, he had taken the hand of someone else, a thin, diminutive figure. As he settled his glasses on his nose, he found he was shaking hands with someone he was not entirely pleased to recognize, a slender man with a mouthful of crooked, nicotine-stained teeth, and a mustache so small and tidy it looked penciled on.

His name was Matthew Graham and he edited an odious horror fanzine titled *Rancid Fantasies*. Carroll had heard Graham had been arrested for sexually abusing his underage stepdaughter, although apparently the case had never gone to court. He tried not to hold that against the writers Graham published, but had still never found anything in *Rancid Fantasies* even remotely worth reprinting in *Best New Horror*. Fiction about drug-addled morticians raping the corpses in their care, moronic hicks giving birth to shit-demons in outhouses located on ancient Indian burial grounds, work riddled with misspellings and grievous offenses to grammar.

"Isn't Peter Kilrue just something else?" Graham asked. "I published his first story. Didn't you read it? I sent you a copy, dear."

"Must've missed it," said Carroll. He had not bothered to look at *Rancid Fantasies* in over a year, although he had recently used an issue to line his catbox.

"You'd like him," Graham said, showing another flash of his few teeth. "He's one of us."

Carroll tried not to visibly shudder. "You've talked with him?"

"Talked with him? I had drinks with him over lunch. He was here this morning. You only just missed him." Graham opened his mouth in a broad grin. His breath stank. "If you want, I can tell you where he lives. He isn't far, you know."

Over a brief late lunch, he read Peter Kilrue's first short story, in a copy of *Rancid Fantasies* that Matthew Graham was able to produce. It was titled "Piggies", and it was about an emotionally disturbed woman who gives birth to a litter of piglets. The pigs learn to talk, walk on their back legs, and wear clothes, à la the swine in *Animal Farm*, but at the end of the story revert to savagery. They use their tusks to slash their mother to ribbons and penetrate her sexually, and as the story comes to a close they are locked in mortal combat to see who will get to eat the tastiest pieces of her corpse.

It was a corrosive, angry piece, and while it was far and away the best thing *Rancid Fantasies* had ever published – written with care and psychological realism – Carroll didn't like it much. One passage, in which the piggies all fight to suckle at their mother's breasts, read like an unusually horrid and grotesque bit of pornography.

Matthew Graham had folded a blank piece of typing paper into the back of the magazine. On it he had drawn a crude map to Kilrue's house, twenty miles north of Poughkeepsie, in a little town called Piecliff. It was on Carroll's way home, up a scenic parkway, the Taconic, which would take him naturally back to I-90. There was no phone number. Graham had mentioned that Kilrue was having money troubles, and the phone company had shut him off.

By the time Carroll was on the Taconic, it was already getting dark, gloom gathering beneath the great oaks and tall firs that crowded the side of the road. He seemed to be the only person on the parkway, which wound higher and higher into hills and wood. Sometimes, in the headlights, he saw families of deer standing at the edge of the road, their eyes pink in the darkness, watching him pass with a mixture of fear and alien curiosity.

Piecliff wasn't much: a strip mall, a church, a graveyard, a Texaco, a single blinking yellow light. Then he was through it and following a narrow state highway through piney woods. By then it was full night and cold enough so he needed to switch on the heat. He turned off onto Tarheel Road, and his Civic labored through a series of switchbacks, up a hill so steep, the engine whined with effort. He closed his eyes for a moment, and almost missed a hairpin turn, had to yank at the wheel to keep from crashing through brush and plunging down the side of the slope.

A half a mile later the asphalt turned to gravel and he trolled through the dark, tires raising a luminescent cloud of chalky dust. His headlights rose over a fat man in a bright orange knit cap, shoving a hand into a mailbox. On the side of the mailbox, letters printed on reflective decals spelled KIL U. Carroll slowed.

The fat man held up a hand to shield his eyes, peering at Carroll's car. Then he grinned, tipped his head in the direction of the house, in a follow-me gesture, as if Carroll were an expected visitor. He started up the driveway, and Carroll rolled along behind him. Hemlocks leaned over the narrow dirt track. Branches swatted at the windshield, raked at the sides of his Civic.

At last the drive opened into a dusty dooryard before a great yellow farmhouse, with a turret and a sagging porch that wrapped around two sides. A plywood sheet had been nailed into a broken window. A toilet bowl lay in the weeds. At the sight of the place, Carroll felt the hairs stirring on his forearms. Journeys end in lovers meeting, he thought, and grinned at his own uneasy imagination. He parked next to an ancient tractor with wild stalks of Indian corn growing up through its open hood.

He shoved his car keys in his coat pocket and climbed out, started toward the porch, where the fat man waited. His walk took him past a brightly lit carriage house. The double doors were pulled shut, but from within he heard the shriek of a bandsaw. He glanced up at the house, and saw a black, backlit figure staring down at him from one of the second floor windows.

Eddie Carroll said he was looking for Peter Kilrue. The fat man inclined his head toward the door, the same follow-me gesture he had used to invite Carroll up the driveway. Then he turned and let him in.

The front hall was dim, the walls lined with picture frames that hung askew. A narrow staircase climbed to the second floor. There was a smell in the air, a humid, oddly male scent . . . like sweat, but also like pancake batter. Carroll immediately identified it, and just as immediately decided to pretend he hadn't noticed anything.

"Bunch of shit in this hall," the fat man said. "Let me hang up your coat. Never be seen again." His voice was cheerful and piping. As Carroll handed him his coat, the fat man turned and hollered up the stairs, "Pete! Someone here!" The sudden shift from a conversational voice to a furious scream gave Carroll a bad jolt.

A floorboard creaked above them, and then a thin man, in corduroy jacket and glasses with square, black plastic frames, appeared at the top of the steps.

"What can I do for you?" he asked.

"My name is Edward Carroll. I edit a series of books, America's *Best New Horror*?" He looked for some reaction on the thin man's face, but Kilrue remained impassive. "I read one of your stories, 'Buttonboy,' in *True North* and I liked it quite a bit. I was hoping to use it in this year's collection." He paused, then added, "You haven't been so easy to get in touch with."

"Come up," Kilrue said, and stepped back from the top of the stairs.

Carroll started up the steps. Below, the fat brother began to wander down the hall, Carroll's coat in one hand, the Kilrue family mail in the other. Then, abruptly, the fat man stopped, looked up the stairwell, waggled a manila envelope.

"Hey, Pete! Mom's social security came!" His voice wavering with pleasure.

By the time Carroll reached the top of the staircase, Peter Kilrue was already walking down the hall, to an open door at the end. The corridor itself seemed crooked somehow. The floor felt tilted underfoot, so much so that once Carroll had to touch the wall to steady himself. Floorboards were missing. A chandelier hung with crystal pendants floated above the stairwell, furred with lint and cobwebs.

In some distant, echoing room of Carroll's mind, a hunchback played the opening bars of *The Addams Family* on a glockenspiel.

Kilrue had a small bedroom located under the pitch of the roof. A card table with a chipped wooden surface stood against one wall, a humming Selectra typewriter set upon it, and a sheet of paper rolled into the platen.

"Were you working?" Carroll asked.

"I can't stop," Kilrue said.

"Good."

Kilrue sat on the cot. Carroll came a step inside the door, couldn't go any further without ducking his head. Peter Kilrue had oddly colorless eyes, the lids red-rimmed as if irritated, and he regarded Carroll without blinking.

Carroll told him about the collection. He said he could pay two hundred dollars, plus a percentage of shared royalties. Kilrue nodded, seemed neither surprised nor curious about the details. His voice was breathy and girlish. He said thank you.

"What did you think of my ending?" Kilrue asked, without forewarning.

"Of 'Buttonboy'? I liked it. If I didn't, I wouldn't want to reprint it."

"They hated it down at Kathadin University. All those co-eds with their pleated skirts and rich daddies. They hated a lot of stuff about the story, but especially my ending."

Carroll nodded. "Because they didn't see it coming. It probably gave a few of them a nasty jolt. The shock ending is out of fashion in mainstream literature."

Kilrue said, "The way I wrote it at first, the giant is strangling her, and just as she's passing out, she can feel the other one using buttons to pin her twat shut. But I lost my nerve and cut it out. Didn't think Noonan would publish it that way."

"In horror, it's often what you leave out that gives a story its power," Carroll said, but it was just something to say. He felt a cool tingle of sweat on his forehead. "I'll go get a permissions form from my car." He wasn't sure why he said that either. He didn't have a permissions form in the car, just felt a sudden intense desire to catch a breath of cold fresh air.

He ducked back through the door into the hall. He found it took an effort to keep from breaking into a trot.

At the bottom of the staircase, Carroll hesitated in the hall, wondering where Kilrue's obese older brother had gone with his jacket. He started down the corridor. The way grew darker the further he went.

There was a small door beneath the stairs, but when he tugged on the brass handle it wouldn't open. He proceeded down the hall, looking for a closet. From somewhere nearby he heard grease sizzling, smelled onions, and heard the whack of a knife. He pushed open a door to his right and looked into a formal dining room, the heads of animals mounted on the walls. An oblong shaft of wan light fell across the table. The tablecloth was red and had a swastika in the center.

Carroll eased the door shut. Another door, just down the hall and to the left, was open, and offered a view of the kitchen. The fat man stood behind a counter, bare-chested and tattooed, chopping what looked like liver with a meat cleaver. He had iron rings through his nipples. Carroll was about to call to him, when the fat Kilrue boy came around the counter and walked to the gas range, to stir what was in the pan. He wore only a jock strap now, and his surprisingly scrawny, pale buttocks trembled with each step. Carroll shifted further back into the darkness of the hall, and after a moment continued on, treading silently.

The corridor was even more crooked than the one upstairs, visibly knocked out of true, as if the house had been jarred by some seismic event, and the front end no longer lined up with the back. He didn't know why he didn't turn back; it made no sense just wandering deeper and deeper into a strange house. Still his feet carried him on.

Carroll opened a door to the left, close to the end of the hall. He flinched from the stink and the furious humming of flies. An unpleasant human warmth spilled out and over him. It was the darkest room yet, a spare bedroom, and he was about to close the door when he heard something shifting under the sheets of the bed. He covered his mouth and nose with one hand and willed himself to take a step forward, and to wait for his eyes to adjust to the light.

A frail old woman was in the bed, the sheet tangled at her waist. She was naked, and he seemed to have caught her in the act of stretching, her skeletal arms raised over her head.

"Sorry," Carroll muttered, looking away. "So sorry."

Once more he began to push the door shut, then stopped, looked back into the room. The old woman stirred again beneath the sheets. Her arms were still stretched over her head. It was the smell, the human reek of her, that made him hold up, staring at her.

As his eyes adjusted to the gloom, he saw the wire around her wrists, holding her arms to the headstand. Her eyes were slitted and her breath rattled. Beneath the wrinkled, small sacks of her breasts he could see her ribs. The flies whirred. Her tongue popped out of her mouth and moved across her dry lips but she didn't speak.

Then he was moving down the hall, going at a fast walk on stiff legs. As he passed the kitchen, he thought the fat brother looked up and saw him, but Carroll didn't slow down. At the edge of his vision he saw Peter Kilrue standing at the top of the stairs, looking down at him, head cocked at a questioning angle.

"Be right back with that thing," Carroll called up to him, without missing a step. His voice was surprisingly casual.

He hit the front door, banged through it. He didn't leap the stairs, but took them one at a time. When you were running from someone, you never jumped the stairs, that was how you twisted an ankle. He had seen it happen in a hundred horror movies. The air was so frosty it burned his lungs.

One of the carriage house doors was open now. He had a look into it on his way past. He saw a smooth dirt floor, rusted chains and hooks dangling from the beams, a chainsaw hanging from the wall. Behind a table-saw, stood a tall, angular man with one hand. The other was a stump, the tormented skin shiny with scar tissue. He regarded Carroll without speaking, his colorless eyes judging and unfriendly. Carroll smiled and nodded.

He opened the door of his Civic and heaved himself in behind the wheel . . . and in the next moment felt a spoke of panic pierce him through the chest. His keys were in his coat. His coat was inside. He almost cried out at the awful shock of it, but when he opened his mouth what came out was a frightened sob of laughter instead. He had seen this in a hundred horror movies too, had read this moment in three hundred stories. They never had the keys, or the car wouldn't start, or—

The brother with one hand appeared at the door of the carriage house, and stared across the drive at him. Carroll waved. His other hand was disconnecting his cell phone from the charger. He glanced at it. There was no reception up here. Somehow he wasn't surprised. He laughed again, a choked, nerve-jangling sound.

When he looked up, the front door of the house was open, and two figures stood in it, staring down at him. All the brothers were staring at him now. He climbed out of the car and started walking swiftly down the driveway. He didn't start to run until he heard one of them shout.

At the bottom of the driveway, he did not turn to follow the road, but went straight across it and crashed through the brush, into the trees. Whip-thin branches lashed at his face. He tripped and tore the knee of his pants, got up, kept going.

The night was clear and cloudless, the sky filled to its limitless depth with stars. He paused, on the side of a steep slope, crouching among rocks, to catch his breath, a stitch in one side. He heard voices up the hill from him, branches breaking. He heard someone pull the ripcord on a small engine, once, twice, then the noisy unmuffled scream-and-roar of a chainsaw coming to life.

He got up and ran on, pitching himself down the hill, flying through the branches of the firs, leaping roots and rocks without seeing them. As he went, the hill got steeper and steeper, until it was really like falling. He was going too fast and he knew when he came to a stop, it would involve crashing into something, and shattering pain.

Only as he went on, picking up speed all the time, until with each leap he seemed to sail through yards of darkness, he felt a giddy surge of emotion, a sensation that might have been panic but felt strangely like exhilaration. He felt as if at any moment his feet might leave the ground and never come back down. He knew this forest, this darkness, this night. He knew his chances: not good. He knew what was after him. It had been after him all his life. He knew where he was – in a story about to unfold an ending. He knew how these stories went better than anyone, and if anyone could find their way out of these woods, it was him.

CAITLÍN R. KIERNAN

La Peau Verte

CAITLÍN R. KIERNAN WAS BORN in Ireland and now lives in Atlanta, Georgia. She has published six novels, including *Silk*, *Threshold*, *Low Red Moon*, *The Five of Cups* and *Murder of Angels*. Her seventh, *Daughter of Hounds*, will be released early in 2007.

Her short fiction has been collected in *Tales of Pain and Wonder*, *From Weird and Distant Shores*, *Wrong Things* (with Poppy Z. Brite), *To Charles Fort, With Love* and *Alabaster*.

"I am a great aficionado of absinthe," reveals Kiernan. "I first tasted it in 1999 and have been in love ever since. 'La Peau Verte' was originally written for an absinthe-themed anthology which, unfortunately, never materialised.

"The worst part about the book not being published, for me, was that I never received the bottle of Mari Mayans I'd been promised as part of my payment, nor the *second* bottle that Poppy Z. Brite had promised to pass along to me, since she doesn't like the stuff.

"However, the absinthe anthology's still-birth did provide me with a previously unpublished story to include in *To Charles Fort, With Love*. To date, 'La Peau Verte' pleases me more than any other piece of fiction I've written, and it stands as evidence that I can do my best work in the arms of the Green Fairy, as it was written entirely under the influence of absinthe."

I

IN A DUSTY, ANTIQUE-LITTERED back room of the loft on St Mark's Place, room with walls the color of ripe cranberries, Hannah stands naked in front of the towering, mahogany-framed mirror and stares at herself. No – not *her* self any longer, but the new thing that

the man and woman have made of her. Three long hours busy with
their airbrushes and latex prosthetics, grease paints and powders and
spirit gum, their four hands moving as one, roaming excitedly and
certainly across her body, hands sure of their purpose. She doesn't
remember their names, if, in fact, they ever told their names to her.
Maybe they did, and the two glasses of brandy have set the names
somewhere just beyond recall. Him tall and thin, her thin but not so
very tall, and now they've both gone, leaving Hannah alone. Perhaps
their part in this finished; perhaps the man and woman are being
paid, and she'll never see either of them again, and she feels a sudden,
unexpected pang at the thought, never one for casual intimacies, and
they have been both casual and intimate with her body.

The door opens, and the music from the party grows suddenly
louder. Nothing she would ever recognize, probably nothing that has
a name, even; wild impromptu of drumming hands and flutes, violins
and cellos, an incongruent music that is both primitive and drawing-
room practiced. The old woman with the mask of peacock feathers
and gown of iridescent satin stands in the doorway, watching
Hannah. After a moment, she smiles and nods her head slowly,
appreciatively.

"Very pretty," she says. "How does it feel?"

"A little strange," Hannah replies and looks at the mirror again.
"I've never done anything like this before."

"Haven't you?" the old woman asks her, and Hannah remembers
her name, then – Jackie, Jackie something that sounds like Shady or
Sadie but isn't either. A sculptor from England, someone said. When
she was very young, she knew Picasso, and someone said that, too.

"No," Hannah replies. "I haven't. Are they ready for me now?"

"Fifteen more minutes, give or take. I'll be back to bring you in.
Relax. Would you like another brandy?"

Would I? Hannah thinks and glances down at the crystal snifter
sitting atop an old secretary next to the mirror. It's almost empty
now, maybe one last warm amber sip standing between it and empty.
She wants another drink, something to burn away the last, lingering
dregs of her inhibition and self-doubt, but, "No," she tells the
woman. "I'm fine."

"Then chill, and I'll see you in fifteen," Jackie Whomever says,
smiles again, her disarming, inviting smile of perfect white teeth, and
she closes the door, leaving Hannah alone with the green thing
watching her from the mirror.

The old Tiffany lamps scattered around the room shed candy
puddles of stained-glass light, light as warm as the brandy, warm as

the dark chocolate tones of the intricately carved frame holding the tall mirror. She takes one tentative step nearer the glass, and the green thing takes an equally tentative step nearer her. *I'm in there somewhere*, she thinks. *Aren't I?*

Her skin painted too many competing, complementary shades of green to possibly count, one shade bleeding into the next, an infinity of greens that seem to roil and flow around her bare legs, her flat, hard stomach, her breasts. No patch of skin left uncovered, her flesh become a rain-forest canopy, waves on the deepest sea, the shells of beetles and leaves from a thousand gardens, moss and emeralds, jade statues and the brilliant scales of posionous tropical serpents. Her nails polished a green so deep it might almost be black, instead. The uncomfortable scleral contacts to turn her eyes into the blaze of twin chartreuse stars, and Hannah leans a little closer to the mirror, blinking at those eyes, *with* those eyes, the windows to a soul she doesn't have. A soul of everything vegetable and living, everything growing, soul of sage and pond scum, malachite and verdigris. The fragile translucent wings sprouting from her shoulder blades – at least another thousand greens to consider in those wings alone – and all the many places where they've been painstakingly attached to her skin are hidden so expertly she's no longer sure where the wings end and she begins.

The one, and the other.

"I definitely should have asked for another brandy," Hannah says out loud, spilling the words nervously from her ocher, olive, turquoise lips.

Her hair – not *her* hair, but the wig *hiding* her hair – like something parasitic, something growing from the bark of a rotting tree, epiphyte curls across her painted shoulders, spilling down her back between and around the base of the wings. The long tips the man and woman added to her ears so dark that they almost match her nails, and her nipples airbrushed the same lightless, bottomless green, as well. She smiles, and even her teeth have been tinted a matte pea green.

There is a single teardrop of green glass glued firmly between her lichen eyebrows.

I could get lost in here, she thinks and immediately wishes she'd thought something else instead.

Perhaps I am already.

And then Hannah forces herself to look away from the mirror, reaches for the brandy snifter and the last swallow of her drink. Too much of the night still ahead of her to get freaked out over a costume, too much left to do and way too much money for her to risk getting cold feet now. She finishes the brandy, and the new warmth spreading through her belly is reassuring.

Hannah sets the empty glass back down on the secretary and then looks at herself again. And this time it *is* her self, after all, the familiar lines of her face still visible just beneath the make-up. But it's a damn good illusion. *Whoever the hell's paying for this is certainly getting his money's worth,* she thinks.

Beyond the back room, the music seems to be rising, swelling quickly towards crescendo, the strings racing the flutes, the drums hammering along underneath. The old woman named Jackie will be back for her soon. Hannah takes a deep breath, filling her lungs with air that smells and tastes like dust and old furniture, like the paint on her skin, more faintly of the summer rain falling on the roof of the building. She exhales slowly and stares longingly at the empty snifter.

"Better to keep a clear head," she reminds herself.

Is that what I have here? and she laughs, but something about the room or her reflection in the tall mirror turns the sound into little more than a cheerless cough.

And then Hannah stares at the beautiful, impossible green woman staring back at her and waits.

II

"Anything forbidden becomes mysterious," Peter says and picks up his remaining bishop, then sets it back down on the board without making a move. "And mysterious things always become attractive to us, sooner or later. Usually sooner."

"What is that? Some sort of unwritten social law?" Hannah asks him, distracted by the Beethoven that he always insists on whenever they play chess. *Die Geschöpfe des Prometheus* at the moment, and she's pretty sure he only does it to break her concentration.

"No, dear. Just a statement of the fucking obvious."

Peter picks up the black bishop again, and this time he almost uses it to take one of her rooks, then thinks better of it. More than thirty years her senior and the first friend she made after coming to Manhattan, his salt-and-pepper beard and mustache that's mostly salt, his eyes as grey as a winter sky.

"Oh," she says, wishing he'd just take the damn rook and be done with it. Two moves from checkmate, barring an act of divine intervention, and that's another of his games, Delaying the Inevitable. She thinks he probably has a couple of trophies for it stashed away somewhere in his cluttered apartment, chintzy *faux* golden loving cups for his Skill and Excellence in Procrastination.

"Taboo breeds desire. Gluttony breeds disinterest."

"Jesus, I ought to write these things down," she says, and he smirks at her, dangling the bishop teasingly only an inch or so above the chessboard.

"Yes, you really should. My agent could probably sell them to someone or another. *Peter Mulligan's Big Book of Tiresome Truths.* I'm sure it would be more popular than my last novel. It certainly couldn't be *less* –"

"Will you stop it and *move* already? Take the damned rook, and get it over with."

"But it *might* be a mistake," he says and leans back in his chair, mock suspicion on his face, one eyebrow cocked, and he points towards her queen. "It could be a trap. You might be one of those predators that fakes out its quarry by playing dead."

"You have no idea what you're talking about."

"Yes I do. You know what I mean. Those animals, the ones that only *pretend* to be dead. You might be one of those."

"I *might* just get tired of this and go the hell home," she sighs, because he knows that she won't, so she can say whatever she wants.

"Anyway," he says, "it's work, if you want it. It's just a party. Sounds like an easy gig to me."

"I have that thing on Tuesday morning though, and I don't want to be up all night."

"Another shoot with Kellerman?" asks Peter and frowns at her, taking his eyes off the board, tapping at his chin with the bishop's mitre.

"Is there something wrong with that?"

"You hear things, that's all. Well, *I* hear things. I don't think you ever hear anything at all."

"I need the work, Pete. The last time I sold a piece, I think Lincoln was still President. I'll never make as much money painting as I do posing for *other* people's art."

"Poor Hannah," Peter says. He sets the bishop back down beside his king and lights a cigarette. She almost asks him for one, but he thinks she quit three months ago, and it's nice having at least that one thing to lord over him; sometimes it's even useful. "At least you *have* a fallback," he mutters and exhales; the smoke lingers above the board like fog on a battlefield.

"Do you even know who these people are?" she asks and looks impatiently at the clock above his kitchen sink.

"Not first-hand, no. But then they're not exactly my sort. Entirely too, well . . ." and Peter pauses, searching for a word that never comes, so he continues without it. "But the Frenchman who owns the place on St Mark's, Mr Ordinaire – excuse me, *Monsieur* Ordinaire – I heard he used to be some sort of anthropologist. I think he might have written a book once."

"Maybe Kellerman would reschedule for the afternoon," Hannah says, talking half to herself.

"You've actually never tasted it?" he asks, picking up the bishop again and waving it ominously towards her side of the board.

"No," she replies, too busy now wondering if the photographer will rearrange his Tuesday schedule on her behalf to be annoyed at Peter's cat and mouse with her rook.

"Dreadful stuff," he says and makes a face like a kid tasting brussels sprouts or Pepto-Bismol for the first time. "Might as well have a big glass of black jelly beans and cheap vodka, if you ask me. *La Fée Verte* my fat ass."

"Your ass isn't fat, you skinny old queen," Hannah scowls playfully, reaching quickly across the table and snatching the bishop from Peter's hand. He doesn't resist. This isn't the first time she's grown too tired of waiting for him to move to wait any longer. She takes her white rook off the board and sets the black bishop in its place.

"That's suicide, dear," Peter says, shaking his head and frowning. "You know that, don't you?"

"You know those animals that *bore* their prey into submission?"

"No, I don't believe I've ever heard of them before."

"Then maybe you should get out more often."

"Maybe I should," he replies, setting the captured rook down with all the other prisoners he's taken. "So, are you going to do the party? It's a quick grand, you ask me."

"That's easy for you say. You're not the one who'll be getting naked for a bunch of drunken strangers."

"A fact for which we should *all* be forevermore and eternally grateful."

"You have his number?" she asks, giving in, because that's almost a whole month's rent in one night and, after her last show, beggars can't be choosers.

"There's a smart girl," Peter says and takes another drag off his cigarette. "The number's on my desk somewhere. Remind me again before you leave. Your move."

III

"How old were you when that happened, when your sister died?" the psychologist asks, Dr Edith Valloton and her smartly-cut hair so black it always makes Hannah think of fresh tar, or old tar gone deadly soft again beneath a summer sun to lay a trap for unwary, crawling things. Someone she sees when the nightmares get bad, which is whenever the painting isn't going well or the modeling jobs aren't coming in or both. Someone she can tell her secrets to who has to *keep* them secret, someone who listens as long as she pays by the hour, the place to turn when faith runs out and priests are just another bad memory to be confessed.

"Almost twelve," Hannah tells her and watches while Edith Valloton scribbles a note on her yellow legal pad.

"Do you remember if you'd begun menstruating yet?"

"Yeah. My periods started right after my eleventh birthday."

"And these dreams, and the stones, this is something you've never told anyone?"

"I tried to tell my mother once."

"She didn't believe you?"

Hannah coughs into her hand and tries not to smile, that bitter, wry smile to give away things she didn't come here to show.

"She didn't even *hear* me," she says.

"Did you try more than once to tell her about the fairies?"

"I don't think so. Mom was always pretty good at letting us know whenever she didn't want to hear what was being said. You learned not to waste your breath."

"Your sister's death, you've said before that it's something she was never able to come to terms with."

"She never tried. Whenever my father tried, or I tried, she treated us like traitors. Like we were the ones who put Judith in her grave. Or like we were the ones *keeping* her there."

"If she couldn't face it, Hannah, then I'm sure it did seem that way to her."

"So, no," Hannah says, annoyed that she's actually paying someone to sympathize with her mother. "No. I guess never really told anyone about it."

"But you think you want to tell me now?" the psychologist asks and sips her bottled water, never taking her eyes off Hannah.

"You said to talk about all the nightmares, all the things I think are nightmares. It's the only one that I'm not sure about."

"Not sure if it's a nightmare, or not sure if it's even a dream?"

"Well, I always thought I was awake. For years, it never once occurred to me I might have only been dreaming."

Edith Valloton watches her silently for a moment, her cat-calm, cat-smirk face, unreadable, too well-trained to let whatever's behind those dark eyes slip and show. Too detached to be smug, too concerned to be indifferent. Sometimes Hannah thinks she might be a dyke, but maybe that's only because the friend who recommended her is a lesbian.

"Do you still have the stones?" the psychologist asks, finally, and Hannah shrugs out of habit.

"Somewhere, probably. I never throw anything away. They might be up at Dad's place, for all I know. A bunch of my shit's still up there, stuff from when I was a kid."

"But you haven't tried to find them?"

"I'm not sure I *want* to."

"When is the last time you saw them, the last time you can remember having seen them?"

And Hannah has to stop and think, chews intently at a stubby thumbnail and watches the clock on the psychologist's desk, the second hand traveling round and round and round. Seconds gone for pennies, nickels, dimes, and *Hannah, this is the sort of thing you really ought to try to get straight ahead of time,* she thinks in a voice that sounds more like Dr Valloton's than her own thought-voice. *A waste of money, a waste of time . . .*

"You can't remember?" the psychologist asks and leans a little closer to Hannah.

"I kept them all in an old cigar box. I think my grandfather gave me the box. No, he didn't. No, he gave it to Judith, and then I took it after the accident. I didn't think she'd mind."

"I'd like to see them someday, if you ever come across them again. Wouldn't that help you to know whether it was a dream or not, if the stones are real?"

"Maybe," Hannah mumbles around her thumb. "And maybe not."

"Why do you say that?"

"A thing like that, words scratched onto a handful of stones, it'd be easy for a kid to fake. I might have made them all myself. Or someone else might have made them, someone playing a trick on me. Anyone could have left them there."

"Did people do that often? Play tricks on you?"

"Not that I can recall. No more than usual."

Edith Valloton writes something else on her yellow pad and then checks the clock.

"You said that there were always stones after the dreams. Never before?"

"No, never before. Always after. They were always there the next day, always in the same place."

"At the old well," the psychologist says, like Hannah might have forgotten and needs reminding.

"Yeah, at the old well. Dad was always talking about doing something about it, before the accident, you know. Something besides a couple of old sheets of tin to hide the hole. Afterwards, of course, the county ordered him to have the damned thing filled in."

"Did your mother blame him for the accident, because he never did anything about the well?"

"My mother blamed *everyone*. She blamed him. She blamed me. She blamed whoever had dug that hole in the first goddamn place. She blamed God for putting water underground so people would dig wells to get at it. Believe me, Mom had blame down to an art."

And again, the long pause, the psychologist's measured consideration, quiet moments she plants like seeds to grow ever deeper revelations.

"Hannah, I want you to try to remember the word that was on the first stone you found. Can you do that?"

"That's easy. It was 'follow'."

"And do you also know what was written on the last one, the very last one that you found?"

And this time she has to think, but only for a moment.

" 'Fall'," she says. "The last one said 'fall'."

IV

Half a bottle of Mari Mayans borrowed from a friend of Peter's, a goth chick who DJs at a club that Hannah's never been to because Hannah doesn't go to clubs. Doesn't dance and has always been more or less indifferent to both music and fashion. The goth chick works days at Trash And Vaudeville on St Mark's, selling Doc Martens and blue hair dye only a couple of blocks from the address on the card that Peter gave her. The place where the party will be. *La Fête de la Fée Verte*, according to the small white card, the card with the phone number. She's already made the call, has already agreed to be there, seven sharp, seven on the dot, and everything that's expected of her has been explained in detail, twice.

Hannah's sitting on the floor beside her bed, a couple of vanilla-scented candles burning because she feels obligated to make at least half a half-hearted effort at atmosphere. Obligatory show of respect for mystique that doesn't interest her, but she's gone to the trouble to borrow the bottle of liqueur; the bottle passed to her in a brown paper bag at the boutique, anything but inconspicuous, and the girl glared out at her, cautious from beneath lids so heavy with shades of black and purple that Hannah was amazed the girl could open her eyes.

"You're a friend of Peter's?" the girl asked suspiciously.

"Yeah," Hannah replied, accepting the package, feeling vaguely, almost pleasurably illicit. "We're chess buddies."

"A painter," the girl said.

"Most of the time."

"Peter's a cool old guy. He made bail for my boyfriend once, couple of years back."

"Really? Yeah, he's wonderful," and Hannah glanced nervously at the customers browsing the racks of leather handbags and corsets, then at the door and the bright daylight outside.

"You don't have to be so jumpy. It's not illegal to have absinthe. It's not even illegal to drink it. It's only illegal to import it, which you didn't do. So don't sweat it."

Hannah nodded, wondering if the girl was telling the truth, if she knew what she was talking about. "What do I owe you?" she asked.

"Oh, nothing," the girl replied. "You're a friend of Peter's, and, besides, I get it cheap from someone over in Jersey. Just bring back whatever you don't drink."

And now Hannah twists the cap off the bottle, and the smell of anise is so strong, so immediate, she can smell it before she even raises the bottle to her nose. *Black jelly beans*, she thinks, just like Peter said, and that's something else she never cared for. As a little girl, she'd set the black ones aside, and the pink ones, too, saving them for her sister. Her sister had liked the black ones.

She has a wine glass, one from an incomplete set she bought last Christmas, secondhand, and a box of sugar cubes, a decanter filled with filtered tap water, a spoon from her mother's mismatched antique silverware. She pours the absinthe, letting it drip slowly from the bottle until the fluorescent yellow-green liquid has filled the bottom of the glass. Then Hannah balances the spoon over the mouth of the goblet and places one of the sugar cubes in the tarnished bowl of the spoon. She remembers watching Gary Oldman and Winona Ryder doing this in *Dracula*, remembers seeing the movie with a boyfriend who eventually left her for another man, and the memory and all its associations are enough to make her stop and sit staring at the glass for a moment.

"This is so fucking silly," she says, but part of her, the part that feels guilty for taking jobs that pay the bills but have nothing to do with painting, the part that's always busy rationalizing and justifying the way she spends her time, assures her it's a sort of research. A new experience, horizon-broadening something to expand her mind's eye, and, for all she knows, it might lead her art somewhere it needs to go.

"Bullshit," she whispers, frowning down at the entirely uninviting glass of Spanish absinthe. She's been reading, *Absinthe: History in a Bottle* and *Artists and Absinthe*, accounts of Van Gogh and Rimbaud, Oscar Wilde and Paul Marie Verlaine and their various relationships with this foul-smelling liqueur. She's never had much respect for artists who use this or that drug as a crutch and then call it their muse; heroin, cocaine, pot, booze, what-the-hell-ever, all the same shit as far as she's concerned. An excuse, an inability in the artist to hold himself accountable for his *own* art, a lazy cop-out, as useless as the idea of the muse itself. And *this* drug, this drug in particular, so tied up with art and inspiration there's even a Renoir painting decorating the Mari Mayans label, or at least it's something that's supposed to *look* like a Renoir.

But you've gone to all this trouble, hell, you may as well taste it, at least. Just a taste, *to satisfy curiosity, to see what all the fuss is about.*

Hannah sets the bottle down and picks up the decanter, pouring water over the spoon, over the sugar cube, and the absinthe louches quickly to an opalescent, milky white-green. Then she puts the decanter back on the floor and stirs the half-dissolved sugar into the glass, sets the spoon aside on a china saucer.

"Enjoy the ride," the goth girl said as Hannah walked out of the shop. "She's a blast."

Hannah raises the glass to her lips, sniffs at it, wrinkling her nose, and the first, hesitant sip is even sweeter and more piquant than she expected, sugar-soft fire when she swallows, a seventy-proof flower blooming warm in her belly. But the taste not nearly as disagreeable as she'd thought it would be, the sudden licorice and alcohol sting, a faint bitterness underneath that she guesses might be the wormwood. The second sip is less of a shock, especially since her tongue seems to have gone slightly numb.

She opens *Absinthe: History in a Bottle* again, opening the book at random, and there's a full-page reproduction of Albert Maignan's

The Green Muse. Blonde woman with marble skin, golden hair, wrapped in diaphanous folds of olive, her feet hovering weightless above bare floorboards, her hands caressing the forehead of an intoxicated poet. The man is gaunt and seems lost in some ecstasy or revelry or simple delirium, his right hand clawing at his face, the other hand open in what might have been meant as a feeble attempt to ward off the attentions of his unearthly companion. *Or*, Hannah thinks, *perhaps he's reaching for something*. There's a shattered green bottle on the floor at his feet, a full glass of absinthe on his writing desk.

She takes another sip and turns the page.

A photograph, Verlaine drinking absinthe in the Café Procope.

Another, bolder swallow, and the taste is becoming familiar now, almost, *almost* pleasant.

Another page. Jean Béraud's *Le Boulevard, La Nuit*.

When the glass is empty, and the buzz in her head and eyes so gentle, buzz like a stinging insect wrapped in spider silk and honey, Hannah takes another sugar cube from the box and pours another glass.

V

"Fairies.

'Fairy crosses.'

Harper's Weekly, 50–715:

That, near the point where the Blue Ridge and the Allegheny Mountains unite, north of Patrick County, Virginia, many little stone crosses have been found.

A race of tiny beings.

They crucified cockroaches.

Exquisite beings – out the cruelty of the exquisite. In their diminutive way they were human beings. They crucified.

The 'fairy crosses', we are told in *Harper's Weekly*, range in weight from one-quarter of an ounce to an ounce: but it is said, in the *Scientific American*, 79–395, that some of them are no larger than the head of a pin.

They have been found in two other states, but all in Virginia are strictly localized on and along Bull Mountain . . .

. . I suppose they fell there."

Charles Fort, *The Book of the Damned* (1919)

VI

In the dream, which is never the same thing twice, not precisely, Hannah is twelve years old and standing at her bedroom window watching the backyard. It's almost dark, the last rays of twilight, and there are chartreuse fireflies dappling the shadows, already a few stars twinkling in the high, indigo sky, the call of a whippoorwill from the woods nearby.

Another whippoorwill replies.

And the grass is moving. The grass grown so tall because her father never bothers to mow it anymore. It could be wind, only there is no wind; the leaves in the trees are all perfectly, silently still, and no limb swaying, no twig, no leaves rustling in even the stingiest breeze. Only the grass, and *It's probably just a cat*, she thinks, *a cat or a skunk or a raccoon.*

The bedroom has grown very dark, and she wants to turn on a lamp, afraid of the restless grass even though she knows it's only some small animal, awake for the night and hunting, taking a short cut across their backyard. She looks over her shoulder, meaning to ask Judith to please turn on a lamp, but there's only the dark room, Judith's empty bunk, and she remembers it all again. It's always like the very first time she heard, the surprise and disbelief and pain always that fresh, the numbness that follows that absolute.

"Have you seen your sister?" her mother asks from the open bedroom door. There's so much night pooled there that she can't make out anything but her mother's softly glowing eyes the soothing color of amber beads, two cat-slit pupils swollen wide against the gloom.

"No, Mom," Hannah tells her, and there's a smell in the room then like burning leaves.

"She shouldn't be out so late on a school night."

"No, Mom, she shouldn't," and the eleven-year-old Hannah is amazed at the thirty-five-year-old's voice coming from her mouth; the thirty-five-year-old Hannah remembers how clear, how unburdened by time and sorrow, the eleven-year-old Hannah's voice could be.

"You should look for her," her mother says.

"I always do. That comes later."

"Hannah, have you seen your sister?"

Outside, the grass has begun to swirl, rippling round and round upon itself, and there's the faintest green glow dancing a few inches above the ground.

The fireflies, she thinks, though she knows it's not the fireflies, the way she knows it's not a cat, or a skunk, or a raccoon making the grass move.

"Your father should have seen to that damned well," her mother mutters, and the burning leaves smell grows a little stronger. "He should have done something about that years ago."

"Yes, Mom, he should have. You should have made him."

"No," her mother replies angrily. "This is not my fault. None of it's my fault."

"No, of course it's not."

"When we bought this place, I told him to see to that well. I *told* him it was dangerous."

"You were right," Hannah says, watching the grass, the softly-pulsing cloud of green light hanging above it. The light is still only about as big as a basketball. Later, it'll get a lot bigger. She can hear the music now, pipes and drums and fiddles, like a song from one of her father's albums of folk music.

"Hannah, have you seen your sister?"

Hannah turns and stares defiantly back at her mother's glowing, accusing eyes.

"That makes three, Mom. Now you have to leave. Sorry, but them's the rules," and her mother does leave, obedient phantom fading slowly away with a sigh, a flicker, a half-second when the darkness seems to bend back upon itself, and she takes the burning leaves smell with her.

The light floating above the backyard grows brighter, reflecting dully off the windowpane, off Hannah's skin and the room's white walls. The music rises to meet its challenge.

Peter's standing beside her now, and she wants to hold his hand, but doesn't, because she's never quite sure if he's supposed to be in this dream.

"I am the Green Fairy," he says, sounding tired and older than he is, sounding sad. "My robe is the color of despair."

"No," she says. "You're only Peter Mulligan. You write books about places you've never been and people who will never be born."

"You shouldn't keep coming here," he whispers, the light from the backyard shining in his grey eyes, tinting them to moss and ivy.

"Nobody else does. Nobody else ever could."

"That doesn't mean –"

But he stops and stares speechlessly at the backyard.

"I should try to find Judith," Hannah says. "She shouldn't be out so late on a school night."

"That painting you did last winter," Peter mumbles, mumbling like he's drunk or only half awake. "The pigeons on your windowsill, looking in."

"That wasn't me. You're thinking of someone else."

"I hated that damned painting. I was glad when you sold it."

"So was I," Hannah says. "I should try to find her now, Peter. It's almost time for dinner."

"I am ruin and sorrow," he whispers.

And now the green light is spinning very fast, throwing off gleaming flecks of itself to take up the dance, to swirl about their mother star, little worlds newborn, universes, and she could hold them all in the palm of her right hand.

"What I need," Peter says, "is blood, red and hot, the palpitating flesh of my victims."

"Jesus, Peter, that's purple even for you," and Hannah reaches out and lets her fingers brush the glass. It's warm, like the spring evening, like her mother's glowing eyes.

"I didn't write it," he says.

"And I never painted pigeons."

She presses her fingers against the glass and isn't surprised when it shatters, explodes, and the sparkling diamond blast is blown inward, tearing her apart, shredding the dream until it's only unconscious, fitful sleep.

VII

"I wasn't in the mood for this," Hannah says and sets the paper saucer with three greasy, uneaten cubes of orange cheese and a couple of Ritz crackers down on one corner of a convenient table. The table is crowded with fliers about other shows, other openings at other galleries. She glances at Peter and then at the long white room and the canvases on the walls.

"I thought it would do you good to get out. You never go anywhere anymore."

"I come to see you."

"My point exactly, dear."

Hannah sips at her plastic cup of warm merlot, wishing she had a cold beer instead.

"And you said that you liked Perrault's work."

"Yeah," she says. "I'm just not sure I'm up for it tonight. I've been feeling pretty morbid lately, all on my own."

"That's generally what happens to people who swear off sex."

"Peter, I didn't *swear off* anything."

And she follows him on their first slow circuit around the room, small talk with people that she hardly knows or doesn't want to know at all, people who know Peter better than they know her, people whose opinions matter and people whom she wishes she'd never met. She smiles and nods her head, sips her wine, and tries not to look too long at any of the huge, dark canvases spaced out like oil and acrylic windows on a train.

"He's trying to bring us down, down to the very core of those old stories," a woman named Rose tells Peter. She owns a gallery somewhere uptown, the sort of place where Hannah's paintings will never hang. " 'Little Red Riding Hood,' 'Snow White,' 'Hansel and Gretel,' all those old fairy tales," Rose says. "It's a very post-Freudian approach."

"Indeed," Peter says. *As if he agrees*, Hannah thinks, *as if he even cares*, when she knows damn well he doesn't.

"How's the new novel coming along?" Rose asks him.

"Like a mouthful of salted thumbtacks," he replies, and she laughs.

Hannah turns and looks at the nearest painting, because it's easier than listening to the woman and Peter pretend to enjoy one another's company. A somber storm of blacks and reds and greys, dappled chaos struggling to resolve itself into images, images stalled at the very edge of perception; she thinks she remembers having seen a photo of this canvas in *Artforum*.

A small beige card on the wall to the right of the painting identifies it as *Night in the Forest*. There isn't a price because none of Perrault's paintings are ever for sale. She's heard rumors that he's turned down millions, tens of millions, but suspects that's all exaggeration and PR. Urban legends for modern artists, and from the other things that she's heard he doesn't need the money, anyway.

Rose says something about the exploration of possibility and fairy tales and children using them to avoid any *real* danger, something that Hannah's pretty sure she's lifted directly from Bruno Bettelheim.

"Me, I was always rooting for the wolf," Peter says, "or the wicked witch or the three bears or whatever. I never much saw the point in rooting for silly girls too thick not to go wandering about alone in the woods."

Hannah laughs softly, laughing to herself, and takes a step back from the painting, squinting at it. A moonless sky pressing cruelly down upon a tangled, writhing forest, a path and something waiting in the shadows, stooped shoulders, ribsy, a calculated smudge of scarlet that could be its eyes. There's no one on the path, but the implication is clear – there will be, soon enough, and the thing crouched beneath the trees is patient.

"Have you seen the stones yet?" Rose asks and no, Peter replies, no we haven't.

"They're a new direction for him," she says. "This is only the second time they've been exhibited."

If I could paint like that, Hannah thinks, *I could tell Dr. Valloton to kiss my ass. If I could paint like that, it would be an exorcism.*

And then Rose leads them both to a poorly-lit corner of the gallery, to a series of rusted wire cages, and inside each one is a single stone. Large pebbles or small cobbles, stream-worn slate and granite, and each stone has been crudely engraved with a single word.

The first one reads "follow."

"Peter, I need to go now," Hannah says, unable to look away from the yellow-brown stone, the word tattooed on it, and she doesn't dare let her eyes wander ahead to the next one.

"Are you sick?"

"I need to go, that's all. I need to go *now*."

"If you're not feeling well," the woman named Rose says, trying too hard to be helpful, "there's a rest room in the back."

"No, I'm fine. Really. I just need some air."

And Peter puts an arm protectively around her, reciting his hurried, polite goodbyes to Rose. But Hannah still can't look away from the stone, sitting there behind the wire like a small and vicious animal at the zoo.

"Good luck with the book," Rose says and smiles, and Hannah's beginning to think she *is* going to be sick, that she will have to make a dash for the toilet, after all. A taste like foil in her mouth, and her heart like a mallet on dead and frozen beef, adrenaline, the first eager tug of vertigo.

"It was good to meet you, Hannah," the woman says, and Hannah manages to smile, manages to nod her head.

And then Peter leads her quickly back through the crowded gallery, out onto the sidewalk and the warm night spread out along Mercer Street.

VIII

"Would you like to talk about that day at the well?" Dr. Valloton asks, and Hannah bites at her chapped lower lip.

"No. Not now," she says. "Not again."

"Are you sure?"

"I've already told you everything I can remember."

"If they'd found her body," the psychologist says, "perhaps you and your mother and father would have been able to move on. There could have at least been some sort of closure. There wouldn't have been that lingering hope that maybe someone would find her, that maybe she was alive."

Hannah sighs loudly, looking at the clock for release, but there's still almost half an hour to go.

"Judith fell down the well and drowned," she says.

"But they never found the body."

"No, but they found enough, enough to be sure. She fell down the well. She drowned. It was very deep."

"You said you heard her calling you—"

"I'm not sure," Hannah says, interrupting the psychologist before she can say the things she was going to say next, before she can use Hannah's own words against her. "I've never been absolutely sure. I told you that."

"I'm sorry if it seems like I'm pushing," Dr Valloton says.

"I just don't see any reason to talk about it again."

"Then let's talk about the dreams, Hannah. Let's talk about the day you saw the fairies."

IX

The dreams, or the day from which the dreams would arise and, half-forgotten, seek always to return. The dreams or the day itself, the one or the other, it makes very little difference. The mind exists only in a moment, always, a single flickering moment, remembered or actual, dreaming or awake or something between the two, the precious, treacherous illusion of Present floundering in the crack between Past and Future.

The dream of the day – or the day – and the sun is high and small and white, a dazzling July sun coming down in shafts through the tall trees in the woods behind Hannah's house. She's running to catch up with Judith, her sister two years older and her legs grown longer, always leaving Hannah behind. *You can't catch me, slowpoke. You can't even keep up.* Hannah almost trips in a tangle of creeper vines and has to stop long enough to free her left foot.

"Wait up!" she shouts, and Judith doesn't answer. "I want to see. Wait for me!"

The vines try to pull one of Hannah's tennis shoes off and leave bright beads of blood on her ankle. But she's loose again in only a moment, running down the narrow path to catch up, running through the summer sun and the oak-leaf shadows.

"I found something," Judith said to her that morning after breakfast. The two of them sitting on the back porch steps, and "Down in the clearing by the old well," she said.

"What? What did you find?"

"Oh, I don't think I should tell you. No, I *definitely* shouldn't tell you. You might go and tell Mom and Dad. You might spoil everything."

"No, I wouldn't. I wouldn't tell them anything. I wouldn't tell anyone."

"Yes, you would, big mouth."

And, finally, she gave Hannah half her allowance to tell, half to show whatever there was to see. Her sister dug deep down into the pockets of her jeans, and her hand came back up with a shiny black pebble.

"I just gave you a whole dollar to show me a *rock*?"

"No, stupid. *Look* at it," and Hannah held out her hand.

The letters scratched deep into the stone – JVDTH – five crooked letters that almost spelled her sister's name, and Hannah didn't have to pretend not to be impressed.

"Wait for me!" she shouts again, angry now, her voice echoing around the trunks of the old trees and dead leaves crunching beneath her shoes. Starting to guess that the whole thing is a trick after all, just one of Judith's stunts, and her sister's probably watching her from a hiding place right this very second, snickering quietly to herself. Hannah stops running and stands in the centre of the path, listening to the murmuring forest sounds around her.

And something faint and lilting that might be music.

"That's not all," Judith said. "But you have to *swear* you won't tell Mom and Dad –"

"I swear."

"If you do tell, well, I *promise* I'll make you wish you hadn't."

"I won't tell anyone *anything*."

"Give it back," Judith said, and Hannah immediately handed the black stone back to her. "If you *do* tell –"

"I already said I won't. How many times do I have to say I won't tell?"

"Well then," Judith said and led her around to the back of the little tool shed where their father kept his hedge clippers and bags of fertilizer and the old lawnmowers he liked to take apart and try to put back together again.

"This better be *worth* a dollar," Hannah said.

She stands very, very still and listens to the music, growing louder; she thinks it's coming from the clearing up ahead.

"I'm going back home, Judith!" she shouts, not a bluff because suddenly she doesn't care whether or not the thing in the jar was real, and the sun doesn't seem as warm as it did only a moment ago.

And the music keeps getting louder.

And louder.

And Judith took an empty mayonnaise jar out of the empty rabbit hutch behind the tool shed. She held it up to the sun, smiling at whatever was inside.

"Let me see," Hannah said.

"Maybe I should make you give me another dollar first," her sister replied, smirking, not looking away from the jar.

"No way," Hannah said indignantly. "Not a snowball's chance in hell," and she grabbed for the jar, then, but Judith was faster, and her hand closed around nothing at all.

In the woods, Hannah turns and looks back towards home, then turns back towards the clearing again, waiting for her just beyond the trees.

"Judith! This isn't funny! I'm going home right this second!"

Her heart is almost as loud as the music now. Almost. Not quite, but close enough.

Pipes and fiddles, drums and a jingle like tambourines.

And Hannah takes another step towards the clearing, because it's nothing at all but her sister trying to scare her, stupid because it's broad daylight, and Hannah knows these woods like the back of her hand.

Judith unscrewed the lid of the mayonnaise jar and held it out so Hannah could see the small, dry thing curled in a lump at the bottom. Tiny mummy husk of a thing, grey and crumbling in the morning light.

"It's just a damn dead mouse," Hannah said disgustedly. "I gave you a whole dollar to see a rock and a dead mouse in a jar?"

"It's *not* a mouse, stupid. Look closer."

And so she did, bending close enough that she could see the perfect dragonfly wings on its back, transparent, iridescent wings to glimmer faintly in the sun. Hannah squinted and realized that she could see its face, realized that it *had* a face.

"Oh," she said, looking quickly up at her sister, who was grinning triumphantly. "Oh, Judith. Oh my God. What is it?"

"Don't you know?" Judith asked her. "Do I have to tell you everything?"

Hannah picks her way over the deadfall just before the clearing, the place where the path through the woods disappears beneath a jumble of fallen, rotting logs. There was a house back here, her father said, a long, long time ago. Nothing left but a big pile of rocks where the chimney once stood and the well covered over with sheets of rusted corrugated tin. There was a fire, her father said, and everyone in the house died.

On the other side of the deadfall, Hannah takes a deep breath and steps out into the daylight, leaving the tree shadows behind, forfeiting her last chance not to see.

"Isn't it cool," Judith said. "Isn't it the coolest thing you ever seen?"

Someone's pushed aside the sheets of tin, and the well is so dark that even the sun won't go there. And then Hannah sees the wide ring of mushrooms, the perfect circle of toadstools and red caps and spongy brown morels growing round the well. The heat shimmers off the tin, dancing mirage shimmer like the air here is turning to water, and the music is very loud now.

"I found it," Judith whispered, screwing the top back onto the jar as tightly as she could. "I found it, and I'm going to keep it. And you'll keep your mouth shut about it, or I'll never, *ever* show you anything else again."

Hannah looks up from the mushrooms, from the open well, and there are a thousand eyes watching her from the edges of the clearing. Eyes like indigo berries and rubies and drops of honey, gold and silver coins, eyes like fire and ice, eyes like seething dabs of midnight. Eyes filled with hunger beyond imagining, neither good nor evil, neither real nor impossible.

Something the size of a bear, squatting in the shade of a poplar tree, raises its shaggy charcoal head and smiles.

"That's another pretty one," it growls.

And Hannah turns and runs.

X

"But you *know*, in your soul, what you must have really seen that day," Dr. Valloton says and taps the eraser end of her pencil lightly against her front teeth. There's something almost obscenely earnest in her expression, Hannah thinks, in the steady *tap tap tap* of the pencil against her perfectly-spaced, perfectly white incisors. "You saw your sister fall into the well, or you realised that she just had. You may have heard her calling out for help."

"Maybe I pushed her in," Hannah whispers.

"Is that what you *think* happened?"

"No," Hannah says and rubs at her temples, trying to massage away the first dim throb of an approaching headache. "But, most of the time, I'd rather believe that's what happened."

"Because you *think* it would be easier than what you remember."

"Isn't it? Isn't easier to believe she pissed me off that day, and so I shoved her in? That I made up these crazy stories so I'd never have to feel guilty for what I'd done? Maybe that's what the nightmares are, my conscience trying to fucking force me to come clean."

"And what are the stones, then?"

"Maybe I put them all there myself. Maybe I scratched those words on them myself and hid them there for me to find, because I knew that would make it easier for me to believe. If there was something that real, that tangible, something solid to remind me of the story, that the story is supposed to be the truth."

A long moment of something that's almost silence, just the clock on the desk ticking and the pencil tapping against the psychologist's teeth. Hannah rubs harder at her temples, the real pain almost within sight now, waiting for her just a little ways past this moment or the next, vast and absolute, deep purple shot through with veins of red and black. Finally, Dr Valloton lays her pencil down and takes a deep breath.

"Is this a confession, Hannah?" she asks, and the obscene earnestness is dissolving into something that may be eager anticipation or simple clinical curiosity or only dread. "Did you kill your sister?"

And Hannah shakes her head and shuts her eyes tight.

"Judith fell into the well," she says calmly. "She moved the tin and got too close to the edge. The sheriff showed my parents where a little bit of the ground had collapsed under her weight. She fell into the well, and she drowned."

"Who are you trying so hard to convince? Me or yourself?"

"Do you really think it matters?" Hannah replies, matching a question with a question, tit for tat, and "Yes," Dr Valloton says. "Yes, I do. You need to know the truth."

"Which one?" Hannah asks, smiling against the pain swelling behind her eyes, and this time the psychologist doesn't bother answering, lets her sit silently with her eyes shut until the clock decides her hour's up.

XI

Peter Mulligan picks up a black pawn and moves it ahead two squares; Hannah removes it from the board with a white knight. He isn't even trying today, and that always annoys her.

Peter pretends to be surprised that's he's lost another piece, then pretends to frown and think about his next move while he talks.

"In Russian," he says, " 'chernobyl' is the word for wormwood. Did Kellerman give you a hard time?"

"No," Hannah says. "No, he didn't. In fact, he said he'd actually rather do the shoot in the afternoon. So everything's jake, I guess."

"Small miracles," Peter sighs, picking up a rook and setting it back down again. "So you're doing the anthropologist's party?"

"Yeah," she replies. "I'm doing the anthropologist's party."

"*Monsieur* Ordinaire. You think he was born with that name?"

"I think I couldn't give a damn, as long as his check doesn't bounce. A thousand dollars to play dress-up for a few hours. I'd be a fool not to do the damned party."

Peter picks the rook up again and dangles it in the air above the board, teasing her. "Oh, his book," he says. "I remembered the title the other day. But then I forgot it all over again. Anyway, it was something on shamanism and shape-shifters, werewolves and masks, that sort of thing. It sold a lot of copies in '68, then vanished from the face of the earth. You could probably find out something about it online."

Peter sets the rook down and starts to take his hand away.

"Don't," she says. "That'll be checkmate."

"You could at least let me *lose* on my own, dear," he scowls, pretending to be insulted.

"Yeah, well, I'm not ready to go home yet," Hannah replies, and Peter Mulligan goes back to dithering over the chessboard and talking about Monsieur Ordinaire's forgotten book. In a little while, she gets up to refill both their coffee cups, and there's a single black and grey pigeon perched on the kitchen windowsill, staring in at her with its beady piss-yellow eyes. It almost reminds her of something she doesn't want to be reminded of, and so she raps on the glass with her knuckles and frightens it away.

XII

The old woman named Jackie never comes for her. There's a young boy, instead, fourteen or fifteen, sixteen at the most, his nails polished poppy red to match his rouged lips, and he's dressed in peacock feathers and silk. He opens the door and stands there, very still, watching her, waiting wordlessly. Something like awe on his smooth face, and for the first time Hannah doesn't just feel nude, she feels *naked*.

"Are they ready for me now?" she asks him, trying to sound no more than half as nervous as she is, and then turns her head to steal a last glance at the green fairy in the tall mahogany mirror. But the mirror is empty. There's no one there at all, neither her nor the green woman, nothing but the dusty back room full of antiques, the pretty hard-candy lamps, the peeling cranberry wallpaper.

"My Lady," the boy says in a voice like broken crystal shards, and then he curtsies. "The Court is waiting to receive you, at your ready." He steps to one side, to let her pass, and the music from the party grows suddenly very loud, changing tempo, the rhythm assuming a furious speed as a thousand notes and drumbeats tumble and boom and chase one another's tails.

"The mirror," Hannah whispers, pointing at it, at the place where her reflection should be, and when she turns back to the boy there's a young girl standing there, instead, dressed in his feathers and make-up. She could be his twin.

"It's a small thing, My Lady," she says with the boy's sparkling, shattered tongue.

"What's happening?"

"The Court is assembled," the girl child says. "They are all waiting. Don't be afraid, My Lady. I will show you the way."

The path, the path through the woods to the well, the path down the well . . .

"Do you have a name?" Hannah asks, surprised at the calm in her voice; all the embarrassment and unease at standing naked before this child, and the one before, the fear at what she didn't see gazing back at her in the looking glass, all of that gone now.

"My name? I'm not such a fool as that, My Lady."

"No, of course not," Hannah replies. "I'm sorry."

"I will show you the way," the child says again. "Never harm, nor spell, nor charm, come our Lady nigh."

"That's very kind of you," Hannah replies. "I was beginning to think that I was lost. But I'm not lost, am I?"

"No, My Lady. You are here."

"Yes. Yes, I *am* here, aren't I?" and the child smiles for her, showing off its sharp crystal teeth. Hannah smiles back, and then she leaves the dusty back room and the mahogany mirror, following the child down a short hallway; the music has filled in all the vacant corners of her skull, the music and the heavy living-dying smells of wildflowers and fallen leaves, rotting stumps and fresh-turned earth. A riotous hothouse cacophony of odors – spring to fall, summer to winter – and she's never tasted air so violently sweet.

. . . the path down the well, and the still black water at the bottom. Hannah, can you hear me? Hannah?

It's so cold down here. I can't see . . .

At the end of the hall, just past the stairs leading back down to St Mark's, there's a green door, and the girl opens it.

And all the things in the wide, wide room – the unlikely room that stretches so far away in every direction that it could never be contained in any building, not in a thousand buildings – the scampering, hopping, dancing, spinning, flying, skulking things, each and every one of them stops and stares at her. And Hannah knows that they should frighten her, that she should turn and run from this place. But it's really nothing she hasn't seen before, a long, long time ago, and she steps past the child (who is a boy again) as the wings on her back begin to thrum like the frantic, iridescent wings of bumblebees and hummingbirds, red wasps and hungry dragonflies. Her mouth tastes of anise and wormwood, sugar and hyssop and melissa, and sticky verdant light spills from her skin and pools in the grass and moss at her bare feet.

Sink or swim, and so easy to imagine the icy black well water closing thickly over her sister's face, filling her mouth, slipping up her nostrils, flooding her belly, as clawed hands dragged her down.

And down.

And down.

And sometimes, Dr Valloton says, sometimes we spend our entire lives just trying to answer one simple question.

The music is a hurricane, swallowing her.

My Lady. Lady of the Bottle. *Artemisia absinthium*, Chernobyl, *absinthion*, Lady of Waking Dreaming, Green Lady of Elation and Melancholy.

I am ruin and sorrow.

My robe is the color of despair.

They bow, *all* of them, and Hannah finally sees the thing waiting for her on its prickling throne of woven branches and bird's nests, the hulking antlered thing with blazing eyes, wolf-jawed hart, the man and the stag, and she bows, in her turn.

DAVID MORRELL

Time Was

DAVID MORRELL IS THE AUTHOR of *First Blood*, the award-winning novel in which the character of Rambo was created. He holds a Ph.D. in American literature from the Pennsylvania State University and was a professor in the English department at the University of Iowa until he gave up his tenure to devote himself to a full-time writing career.

"The mild-mannered professor with the bloody-minded visions," as one reviewer called him, Morrell has written numerous best-selling thrillers that include *The Brotherhood of the Rose* (the basis for a highly rated NBC-TV mini-series), *The Fifth Profession* and *Extreme Denial* (the latter set in Santa Fe, New Mexico, where he lives).

His short stories have appeared in many of the major horror/fantasy anthologies, including the *Whispers*, *Shadows*, *Night Visions* and the *Masters of Darkness* series, as well as *The Twilight Zone Magazine*, *The Dodd Mead Gallery of Horror*, *Psycho Paths*, *Prime Evil*, *Dark at Heart*, *MetaHorror*, *Revelations*, *999* and *Redshift*.

Two of his novellas received Bram Stoker Awards from the Horror Writers Association. He has also received Bram Stoker and World Fantasy Award nominations a total of four times for other stories. His non-supernatural horror novel *The Totem*, which reinvented the werewolf myth, was covered in *Horror: 100 Best Books*.

Morrell's latest novel, the award-winning *Creepers*, has been called "genre defining" because of its unusual combination of thriller and horror elements.

"A lot of my fiction deals with struggling to keep one's identity," the author explains, "about the fear of walking down the wrong corridor and entering the wrong room, only to discover a dangerously different version of reality.

"Often, these themes are dramatised against large landscapes. In 'Time Was', the landscape is the American Southwest. I live in New Mexico and often drive through Arizona. I'm struck by how vast the country is, and how forbidding it can be.

"On one occasion, I travelled from Tucson, Arizona, to Phoenix, and I wondered what would happen if a blocked highway forced a motorist to take a detour through the desert. What might he find out there? And what if the thing he found caused him to lose everything he held dear?"

"**D**EBBIE, I'M GOING TO BE LATE," Sam Wentworth said into his cell phone.

"*Late?*" In the shimmering desert, the weak connection made his wife's voice hard to hear, but the strength of her inflection compensated.

"Maybe not till after dark."

"You promised Lori you'd be at her birthday party."

"I know, but—"

"You missed her birthday *last* year, too."

"Traffic's backed up for miles. The radio says a big motor home flipped over and burst into flames. The reporter says it's going to take hours before the police clear the wreck and get traffic moving again. I'll try to make it up to her. Look, I realize I haven't been home a lot lately, but—"

"*Lately?*"

"You think I enjoy working this hard?" As the Ford Explorer's temperature gauge drifted toward the red zone, Sam turned off the engine and the air conditioning. He opened the window. Despite the desert's dry heat, sweat trickled off his chin.

"I don't mean to sound complaining." Debbie's voice was fainter. "It's just . . . Never mind. Where *are* you?"

"On I-Ten. The hell of it is, I planned ahead, finished my appointments, and left Tucson an hour ago. If everything had gone smoothly, I've have been home in time for Lori's party."

Static crackled.

"Debbie?"

"If we hadn't bought the new house, maybe you wouldn't have to—"

The static got louder.

"Debbie?"

"Don't rush and maybe get in an accident just because—"

Something broke the connection. Now Sam didn't even hear static. He almost called back but then thought better. The conversation hadn't turned into an argument. Leave it at that. Besides, the car ahead of him budged forward a little.

Maybe traffic's starting to move sooner than the radio predicted, Sam hoped. Then he realized that the car ahead was only filling a gap created when a vehicle pulled off the highway and followed the shoulder to an exit ahead. A handful of other vehicles did the same. So what? he thought. Maybe those drivers live in whatever town that exit leads to. But *I* need to get back to Phoenix.

Traffic inched forward, filling the other gaps. He started his SUV, noted that the heat gauge had fallen to normal, and followed the slow line of vehicles. Now he saw that the exit led to a gas station, a convenience store, and about twenty sun-faded adobe houses whose cracked stucco indicated their losing battle with the desert. Something else caught his attention: A few of the cars that had taken the exit were now throwing up dust as they continued along a sandy road that paralleled the highway.

What do *they* know that *I* don't? he wondered. When traffic stopped again, he opened the glove compartment and pulled out a map, spreading it across the steering wheel.

A faint broken line went from a town called Gila Gulch – the name on the exit sign – to a town farther along called Stage Stop. Must be from when stage coaches came through here, Sam thought. The distance looked to be about twenty miles and would bring him back onto I–10 past the mile marker where the radio news had said the motor home was blocking the highway. He looked at the dashboard clock. 5:25. I've got a chance to get home in time, he realized.

The next thing, he steered onto the highway's shoulder, reached the exit ramp, drove into Gila Gulch, and stopped at the gas station. His fuel gauge showed between a quarter and a half tank. Enough to get home. But why take chances? Fill it up. As the sun's heat squeezed him, he also bought a jug of radiator fluid and added some to the Explorer's reservoir, which looked slightly low, accounting for the increase he'd noticed on the temperature gauge. He always kept plenty of bottled water in the car. No problem there. Time to hit the road.

"Hit" was almost the word. As Sam headed along the road, which had looked smooth from the highway, he was surprised by its bumps, but if he kept his speed at forty, they were tolerable. Nothing that the Explorer, built for rough terrain, couldn't handle. At this speed, he'd finish the twenty miles in a half-hour. A hell of a lot better than sitting in traffic for *three* hours, as the radio had predicted. Pleased that the temperature gauge remained at normal, he closed the window, turned the air conditioner back on, and put a Jimmie Dale Gilmore CD into the car's player. Humming to Jimmie's definitive version of "I'm So Lonesome I Could Cry", he glanced at the traffic jam he passed on his left and smiled. Imagine the look on Lori's face when I show up, he thought. The look on *Debbie's* face will be even better.

What Sam hadn't told her was that the trip to Tucson had been pointless, that the land his boss thought might be worth developing – Grand Valley Vistas – turned out to have once been a toxic dump site. Lawsuits about it could go on forever. Another waste of my time, he thought. If Sheperton – Sam's boss – had done his homework, the site never would have seemed tempting in the first place. It took a lot of investigating to discover the liabilities. But that's why Joe pays me the bucks. To keep him from screwing up. If I had his money, I could make Sheperton Enterprises (Wentworth Enterprises, Sam fantasized) ten times as successful as it is.

He glanced to his left and wondered if he was imagining that the traffic jam on the highway seemed a little farther away. There seemed more rocks and saguaro cactuses than there'd been before. An optical illusion. But peering ahead, he was forced to admit that the road did seem to be shifting to the right. No big deal. When they built this road a long time ago, they probably needed to adjust for going around obstacles like that hill ahead. Dust clouds beyond it indicated the progress of the handful of cars preceding him. In the rearview mirror, another plume of dust showed a vehicle following. I'm surprised a lot more drivers haven't realized how to save time, he thought. Or maybe they don't have what it takes to try something different. Or they don't have a good enough reason.

As Jimmie Dale sang another mournful song, Sam's attention drifted to the tall, sentry-like cactuses that now stuck up everywhere around him. Many looked sick, with drooping arms and black spots that might have been rot. That's supposed to be from global warming, he thought. From the thinning ozone layer and unfiltered ultraviolet rays. From air pollution and car exhaust. He could actually see haze over the blocked traffic on the highway farther to the left.

The hill got bigger. As the road veered to the right around it, noises startled him. *Shots.* He stomped the breaks and gaped at what confronted him. An old-fashioned western town had board sidewalks, mule-drawn wagons, and one of the stage coaches he'd earlier thought about. Horses were tied to wooden railings. Unlike the adobe buildings in Gila Gulch, these structures were wooden, most painted a white that had paled in the sun and the blowing sand. Most had only one level. Men in Stetsons and women in gingham dresses walked the dirt street he'd been about to enter. The noises he'd heard came from cowboys shooting at each other outside a corral. A man with a rifle fired from a roof. One of the cowboys turned, aimed upward, and shot him, sending him falling onto the street.

The gunfight might have continued to alarm Sam if anybody else in the town had paid attention. But the men in Stetsons and the women in gingham dresses went on about their business, never once looking in the direction of the shots, making Sam quickly conclude that this was a tourist attraction. He'd heard of a similar western-town replica called Old Tucson, where tourists paid to see chuck-wagon races and staged gunfights. A lot of western movies had been made there also, including one of Sam's favorites, John Wayne's *Rio Bravo*. He'd also heard that Old Tucson had been destroyed in a fire. Perhaps it had never been rebuilt. Perhaps *this* town was its replacement. If so, it was situated awfully far from Tucson to be a success. The lack of cars and tourists made *that* clear. Back at the highway, a couple of signs would have helped.

Maybe they're not open for business yet, Sam thought as the gunfight ended and the survivors carried the bodies away. Maybe this is a kind of dress rehearsal. Noticing a sign that read MERIDIAN, he eased his foot onto the accelerator and passed a livery stable, a blacksmith shop, and a general store. They looked as if they'd been recently built and then cleverly made to seem aged. A muscular man came out of the general store, carrying a heavy burlap sack of what might have been flour toward a buckboard wagon.

Impressed by the realism, Sam continued past a restaurant where a sign in the lace-curtained window indicated that a steak dinner could be obtained for fifty cents. A boy rode past on a mule. I've got to bring Lori and Debbie to see this, Sam thought. They won't believe their eyes. I won't tell them where we're going. I'll make it a surprise.

Swinging doors led into a saloon. A large sign boasted about whiskey you could trust, beer that was cold, and (in less bold letters) the best sarsaparilla anybody ever tasted. Sam had heard sarsaparilla referred to in the westerns he enjoyed watching. A rancher was always buying a bottle for his son, or a gunfighter trying to mend his ways was always being told that he wasn't man enough to drink whiskey anymore, that he needed to stick with milk or sarsaparilla. In the movies, they always called it "sasparilla", though. Sam had no idea the word was actually spelled the way the sign indicated.

And what on earth was sarsaparilla anyhow? Sam had always assumed it was a carbonated drink. But what did it taste like? Root beer? He suddenly had an idea. Why not buy a case and take it home for the party? "Have some sarsaparilla," he'd tell Lori and her friends. "What's sarsaparilla?" they'd ask, tripping over the word. "Oh, you've got to try some," he'd say. "It's just out of this world."

And Debbie would give him a smile.

He stopped the car. When he got out, the heat was overwhelming, literally like an oven. How the hell does anybody think tourists will tolerate coming here? he thought. There weren't any poles for electricity or phones. The lines must have been underground. Even so, doors and windows were open in every building, indicating that they didn't have air conditioning. A slight breeze did nothing to cool him but did blow dust on his lips.

Well-trained, none of the actors gave him a second look (or a first look for that matter) as he approached the saloon's swinging doors. In western movies, that type of door – with open space at the top and the bottom – always seemed fake, as if in the old days people hadn't cared about dirt blowing in. He pushed through, leaving the searing daylight for smoke-filled shadows that felt no cooler than the outside. Then he noticed that, on each side, solid doors had been shoved back. So the entrance *could* be closed if the weather necessitated, he thought, and was reassured by the realistic detail. He heard a tinny, somewhat out-of-tune piano playing a song that he didn't recognize but that sounded very old. The piano was in the far left corner. No one sat at it as the keys rose and fell and its mechanized music drifted through the saloon. On the far right, stairs led up to rooms on an indoor balcony. In the old days, that's where the prostitutes would have taken their customers, Sam thought. On the left, cowboys sat at circular tables, drinking and silently playing cards. Their cigarette smoke thickened, almost making Sam cough. They'll never get families in here, he thought.

On the right was a room-length bar, its wood darkened with age and grime. Cowboys leaned against it, silently drinking from beer mugs or shot glasses that probably contained tea or ginger ale. A barkeep wore a white shirt and vest and stood guard, arms crossed, next to the cash register.

Sam went over. "Is that sign outside accurate? Do you sell sasparilla?" Realizing that he mispronounced it the way actors in movies did, he hurriedly said, "I mean sarsaparilla." The word felt strange in his mouth.

The barkeep didn't answer. None of the cowboys looked at him.

Part of the show, Sam thought. We're supposed to feel like we're back in the 1800s and can't be seen.

"How much for a case?" Sam asked.

Again no answer.

Sam glanced to the right along the bar and noticed generic-looking soda bottles on a shelf behind it, near the front window. They were made of clear glass that showed dark liquid in them – like root beer. They were labeled sarsaparilla. Corks were held in place with spring devices that he'd occasionally seen on pressurized bottles, indicating that the contents of *these* bottles were probably carbonated. Like root beer.

Sam counted ten bottles. "I'll take them all. How much?"

No answer. The actors maintained the illusion that he wasn't there.

Sam went over to the bottles and saw a price tag on each. Five cents.

"This can't be true," he said. "What's the real price?"

The only sound came from the tinny piano.

"Okay then, if that's how you want it. I'll give you a bonus and take the whole lot for a dollar."

Sam put a dollar on the counter and moved to pick up the bottles.

No one bothered to stop him.

"I don't know how you're going to stay in business," he said.

Then he started wondering about what he was buying. Suppose these bottles were merely stage props, or suppose this was the worst-tasting stuff imaginable. Suppose he took it home and gave it to Lori and her friends, only to watch them spit it out.

"Is there anything *wrong* with this stuff?"

No answer.

"Well, if there is, you're about to be involved in a lawsuit." Sam picked up a bottle, freed the spring device, and tugged on the cork, needing a couple of tries to yank it out. Dark fluid fizzed, running over the bottle's mouth.

He sniffed it. Smells like root beer, he thought.

"I'm going to drink this now. If it's gone bad and makes me sick or something, you're all going to be out of jobs."

The piano kept tinkling. No one turned.

Hell, they're not going to let me poison myself, Sam thought.

"You had your chance."

He sipped.

*   *   *

A tickle roused him. On his hand. As the tickle persisted, he forced his heavy eyelids open and found himself lying face down in the sand, his head angled sideways toward his outstretched right arm. The last rays of sunset showed a scorpion on the back of that hand. The creature was about two-and-a-half inches long. Despite the crimson of the dying sun, its yellow was vivid. Its pincers, its eight legs, its curved tail, stinger poised, made him want to scream.

Don't move, he thought. No matter what, pretend you're paralyzed. If you startle this thing, it'll jab you. You could die out here.

Here? Sam's mind was so fogged, his head aching so bad, that it took him several moments to remember walking into the saloon and drinking the saspa . . . sarsa . . . His mind couldn't form the word.

But that had been around six o'clock. The sun had still been strong. So how the hell did it get to be sunset so fast? he wondered in a panic. And what are you doing on the ground?

The scorpion remained poised on his hand. A terrible taste in Sam's mouth made him start to retch. No! Don't move! Don't scare it!

The heat of the sunset was against his back. As the blood-tinted light dimmed, he stifled the urge to be sick and stared breathlessly at the scorpion's stinger, which wavered, rose, and seemed about to dart toward his skin. But instead of jabbing him, the scorpion eased forward. One by one, its tickling legs shifted toward the sand.

The instant it was gone, Sam rolled violently in the opposite direction, came to his knees, vomited, and frantically realized that there might be other scorpions around him. Scrambling to his feet, he swatted at his clothes and felt something hard fly off him. Jesus, did it sting you? He stared at his hands but saw no swelling and felt no fire. Trembling, he wiped mucus from his lips but couldn't free the terrible taste from his mouth. Like rotten potatoes. He vomited again, rubbed more mucus from his mouth, and stared around in frightened confusion.

The town had vanished. *No, not completely*, he realized. In the swiftly paling sunset, he saw a few charred boards projecting from the sand. Part of a wagon wheel lay among rocks. The ribcage of what might have been a horse was partially exposed next to a mound that could have been collapsed mud-and-straw bricks from a chimney.

What the hell happened? he thought. Continuing to turn, scanning his surroundings, he whimpered with relief when he saw his Explorer. Then the air became grey, and he stumbled toward his car, desperately hurrying despite stiff legs, lest he lose his way if darkness suddenly overcame him.

When he opened the driver's door, the heat in the car shoved him, prompting another attack of dry heaves. He grabbed a bottle of water from next to his briefcase, rinsed his mouth, spat, couldn't get rid of the taste of rotten potatoes, waited for the spasms to stop, and sipped. Abruptly, he was so thirsty that he finished the bottle before he knew what he'd done. Apprehensive, he waited for his stomach to spew it out. Seconds passed. Slowly, he relaxed.

After he managed to buckle his seat belt, he had an irrational fear that the car wouldn't start. But a twist of the ignition key instantly engaged the engine. He turned on the headlights. Ahead, he saw sand, rocks, and diseased cactuses, their limbs drooping. But only the tips of charred boards, along with the few other things he'd noticed, gave any indication of where the town had been.

Damn it, what *happened*? he thought. Immediately, he grasped at a possible answer. Maybe this isn't the same place. Maybe you collapsed, and somebody moved you.

But that didn't make sense, either. Why would anybody have moved him? He stared out the windshield toward the shadowy outline of a hill that resembled the hill behind which the town had been situated. On each side of the hill, in the distance, tiny lights drifted through the darkness. In pairs. Headlights. The highway. More evidence that this was the same place where the town had been.

But it couldn't be. His head pounded. Nothing made sense. Having wondered if someone had moved him, he now recalled the solitary dust cloud that had followed him along the road. Surely, whoever was in the car would have found him. After all, the road went directly past where the Explorer was parked. Anyone following couldn't possibly have failed to notice it and the town.

At once, Sam shivered as he realized that, among the rocks, sand, diseased cactuses, and occasional tips of charred boards, the one thing his headlights didn't show was the road. That's impossible! he thought, shivering so hard now that he worried he might have a fever. It wasn't much of a road, but you couldn't miss it. Damn it, the road was here!

Debbie, he thought. Lori. They expect you to be home soon. He pulled his cell phone from its case on his belt, pressed the "start" button, and moaned when it failed to respond. He tried again. Nothing happened. That's all you need, he thought. You left it on too long. The battery's dead.

Debbie, he thought. He put the car in gear. As his headlights pierced the darkness, he navigated around rocks and cactuses.

Passing the hill, he lurched over bumps toward the headlights of smoothly moving traffic on I–10. Then he stopped and felt sick again as he came to a dirt road that ran parallel to the highway. It had to be the same road he'd followed. Heading in this direction, he'd seen only one. The map had indicated there was only one. But how in God's name could the road now be in front of the hill instead of veering behind it?

The house was dark when he got there. Good, Sam thought. They didn't stay up, waiting for you. He'd done his best to get home quickly, but several times, he felt sick again and pulled to the side of the highway until he felt better. Now the time was shortly after midnight. His head pounding worse, he reached to press the garage-door opener but quickly changed his mind. The garage was under Lori's bedroom. The rumble might waken her. Then Lori might waken Debbie, and he didn't know how to tell them what had happened. Hell, if *he* didn't understand it, how could *they*? Feeling hungover, straining to think clearly, he parked in the driveway, remembered to take his briefcase, walked past murky bushes, and fumbled to unlock the front door.

Shadows revealed stairs leading up to the bedroom area. On the right was the large living room that they hardly ever used. On the left was the family area with a big-screen TV. In back was the kitchen. Sam made his way in that direction, setting his briefcase on a counter. He turned on the lights, poured a glass of water, finished it in three gulps, and noticed the dried vomit on his shirt. In fact, he smelled it. Jesus, if Debbie saw him like this . . .

He yanked off his shirt and hurried into the bathroom next to the kitchen. There wasn't a tub or a shower. But at least he could fill the sink and wipe a soapy washcloth over his face, then rinse his mouth and cheeks with warm water. Toweling himself, feeling almost human, he returned to the kitchen and faltered when he saw Lori.

Her hair was in pig tails. She wore her Winnie the Pooh pajamas and her fuzzy, bunny slippers. She rubbed her sleepy eyes.

"Hi, sweetheart," he said. "Sorry if I woke you. Are you thirsty? I'll get you a glass of water while you tell me about the party."

She screamed and raced into the family room.

"Lori?"

Screaming louder, she scrambled up the stairs.

"Lori, it's me." He ran after her. "It's Dad. What's wrong? There's nothing to be afraid of."

A door banged open, followed by loud voices and urgent foot-steps.

"Lori?"

Stair lights came on. A muscular man in boxer shorts lunged into view at the top of the stairs.

"Who the hell are *you*?" Sam asked.

"No," the man growled, charging down the stairs. "Who the hell are *you*? What are you doing here? How'd you get in?"

Behind the man, Debbie appeared. She wore a hastily put-on housecoat open at the middle, showing the panties and tee-shirt she liked to sleep in. Her red hair was silhouetted by the light up there as she held Lori.

"Debbie?" Sam asked. "Is this some kind of joke?"

"Call the police!" the man yelled.

"Debbie, what's —"

The man reached the bottom of the stairs and punched Sam's stomach, knocking him to the floor.

Landing hard, Sam groaned and fought to catch his breath. He tried to explain, but the man kicked his side, making him roll against an end table that crashed in the shadows. At once, the man stumbled back, hopping, holding a bare foot that he'd injured when he'd kicked Sam. The man knocked a lamp over.

"Hurry!" Debbie blurted into a phone. "He's trying to kill my husband!"

Lori screamed again.

Sam struggled to his feet. He saw the man lower his injured foot and pick up the broken lamp to throw at him. He saw Debbie pleading into the phone and Lori screaming. He yanked the front door open and raced into the darkness.

What the hell is . . .

Although the confusion of Sam's emotions made him sweat, his shirtless back felt cold against the driver's seat. Speeding from the neighborhood, he heard approaching sirens. He tried to judge the direction from which they came, but no matter which street he took, the sirens wailed nearer, prompting him to steer into a driveway, turn off the engine and the headlights, and slide down out of sight. Fifteen seconds later, flashing lights sped past.

The moment he couldn't see them, he restarted the car and backed onto the street, moving in the opposite direction. Jesus, you're losing your mind, he thought.

"Debbie, it's Sam," he said anxiously into the pay phone.

"*Who*?"

"Quit kidding around. Who *is* that guy? Why did you and Lori pretend you don't know me?"

"We *don't*! We've never seen you before! For God's sake, stop this! Leave us alone!"

"I'm serious. Are you punishing me for missing Lori's party, for not being home enough, is that it? If you're trying to scare me—"

The phone made bumping noises. A gruff voice came on the line. "This is Sgt Malone of the Phoenix police department. The penalty for stalking—"

Sam broke the connection.

"No non-smoking rooms," the motel clerk said.

Sam's stomach ached where he'd been punched. Nauseous again, too exhausted to try anywhere else, he murmured, "Whatever you've got." His sport coat had been in the Explorer. He wore it buttoned and held the lapels together, concealing his bare chest.

"Fill out this form. All I need is your credit card."

Sam gave it to him, then finished the form. But when he glanced up, the clerk was frowning.

"Something wrong?" Sam asked.

"The credit-card company won't accept this card."

"What?"

"I tried twice."

"Try again. There's got to be a mistake. Maybe your scanning machine's broken."

"Worked ten minutes ago." The clerk slid the card through the scanner and studied an indicator on the machine. "Nope. Still won't take it."

"But that's impossible."

"If you say so, but I can't rent you a room without a card."

"Cash. You still take cash, don't you?"

"As long as you don't use the phone or charge incidentals. Eighty-five dollars."

Sam reached into his pocket and came out with two fives.

SHEPERTON ENTERPRISES.

The Explorer's headlights blazed across the large, empty parking lot. At two in the morning, most of the windows in the two-story glass-and-metal building were dark. Exterior lights compensated, so harsh that they aggravated Sam's headache. Barely able to keep his eyes open, he almost parked in the executive area, but then he realized that this was the first place the police would look.

Trembling, he drove from the building and stopped at an apartment complex a block away. Staying in shadows as much as possible, he walked back to Sheperton Enterprises, where he couldn't avoid the lights as he unlocked the side door and entered the building. Before closing the door, he glanced behind him. No flashing lights sped across the parking lot. No one had seen him.

On his left, an intrusion detector gave off a warning beep that stopped as he tapped in the security code. He headed up echoing stairs toward the executive offices and their view of a nearby golf course. He unlocked his office, went inside, and kept the lights off as he relocked the door. Huge windows had blinds that he shut. He always kept a shaving kit and a change of clothes here. Tomorrow morning, he could make himself presentable in the washroom down the hall. For now, all he cared about was lying down, trying to understand, trying to make his head stop pounding.

Feeling his way to the couch, he told himself, Sleep. That's all you need. If you can get some sleep, you'll be able to figure this out.

Voices woke him. He struggled to rouse himself from the darkest sleep he'd ever known. As the voices grew louder, he jerked his eyes open, bolted up from the couch, and found two security guards scowling at him while several men and women stood behind them.

"Buddy, how'd you get in here?" a guard asked.

"How'd I . . .? I *work* here. This is my office."

"Not likely, friend," the other guard said. "Not when it belongs to Ms Taylor." He pointed over his shoulder toward a slender, blond woman.

"Ms Taylor? Who on earth is . . .? Look, I'm Sam Wentworth and—"

"Never heard of you." The second guard turned toward the people behind him. "Anybody here heard of somebody named Sam Wentworth?"

Puzzled murmurs of "no". Several people shook their head from side to side.

"*Never heard of me?*"

"Take it easy, buddy."

"What are you talking about? I've worked here nine years! I've been Joe's vice-president since he started the business! Who the hell *are* those people?"

"I said, take it easy, buddy. Don't make this worse. The police'll be here soon. You can sort this out at the police station."

"*If I didn't work here, how did I get in? How did I get the keys to this building and my office?*"

"*You* tell *me*," the first guard said. "What did you do, steal them and have copies made? Hand them over."

"*Where's Joe?* Ask Joe! He'll tell you I work for him! He'll tell you I'm his vice-president!"

"We would, except that if you're as close to him as you claim, you'd know he's in Europe."

"On my desk! There's a photo of me and my wife and little girl!" Sam hurried over to show them. But what he saw was a photo of the slender, blond woman behind the guards. She had a geeky-looking man on her right and two children – twin girls – on her left.

He screamed.

"Your name's Sam Wentworth," the detective said.

"Yes."

"Your wife's name is Debbie, and your daughter's name is Lori, both of whom live in the house your broke into last night."

"I didn't break in! I had a key!"

"And how did you get the key?"

"I've always had the key!"

"The same as you always had the keys to Sheperton Enterprises."

"Yes! As long as I've worked there! For the past nine years! And the house is new for us! We've only owned it eight months! That's how long I've had the key! Look, I can prove I work for Sheperton Enterprises! Check the documents in the briefcase I left at my house!"

"We'll get to the briefcase in a second. For now, apart from the unlawful entry charges, the ID you gave us is fake."

"*What*?"

"Your social security number belongs to a man named Walter Barry."

"*WHAT?*"

"Who lives in Seattle. The birth place and date you gave us don't pan out, either."

"My briefcase! Look in my briefcase!"

"I already did. It's empty."

". . . name's Sam Wentworth."

"Debbie. I've been married eleven years. My daughter's name is . . ."

*   *   *

"Joe Sheperton. I've been his vice-president for . . ."

Mystery Man Still Not Identified

PHOENIX, AZ (*May 14*)—*Authorities continue to be baffled about the identity of a man who broke into a home a year ago and was subsequently discovered sleeping in an office in the real-estate development firm of Sheperton Enterprises.*

"*He claims to be my vice-president, but I've never laid eyes on the guy*," *Joe Sheperton said.*

"*He says he's my husband*," *Debbie Bolan told reporters, "but I've been happily married to my husband Ward for the past eleven years. To the best of my knowledge, I've never met this Sam Wentworth. I have no idea why he's fixated on me and my daughter. He scares me. I don't know what I'm going to do if they let him go.*"

"*I've never encountered a situation like this*," *Dr Philip Kincaid, chief of staff for the Maricopa Mental Health Facility, explained. "After a year, we still haven't been able to identify the man who calls himself Sam Wentworth. The FBI has no record of his fingerprints. Neither do any branches of the US military. There haven't been any DNA matches. The social security number he insists on using doesn't belong to him. There's no record that he was born when and where he claims. Nor is there any record of the man and woman he insists are his parents. He claims he has a business degree from UCLA. There's no record of that, either. It's as if he spontaneously appeared with no ties to the past. But of course that's not possible. At first, we classified him as an amnesiac. But he keeps insisting that something happened to him in a town in the desert, a town that doesn't exist we found out, so we're now treating him as delusional, as a schizophrenic with catatonic tendencies. All he does is murmur to himself and read history books.*"

. . . *which brings us to one of the least known and most fascinating puzzles of southern Arizona in the nineteenth century: the fate of the town of Meridian. Located along the old stage-coach route between Tucson and Phoenix, Meridian was founded in 1882 by the religious zealot Ebenezer Cartwright, who led a band of pilgrims from Rhode Island in search of what he called the Land of Salvation. After two years of wandering, Cartwright finally settled in the Arizona desert because, as he told a passing stage-coach driver, "its heat will perpetually remind us of the flames and peril of everlasting Hell." His statement turned out to be prophetic inasmuch as, exactly one*

year after Meridian came into existence, it was destroyed in a fire.
Cartwright chose the town's name, he said, to describe "the highest
point of the burning sun, which encourages us to strive for the highest
points of human endeavor." Whatever his intentions, the reverse
turned out to be the case, for during Meridian's brief existence,
stage-coach drivers reached Tucson and Phoenix with rumors about
a hell town in the desert in which debauchery and drunkenness knew
no bounds. Since no one survived the fire, we can only conjecture
about Meridian's fate. Perhaps Ebenezer Cartwright's only purpose
was to isolate his devoted followers in the middle of nowhere and use
them for his own twisted ends. Or perhaps the relentless heat of the
desert drove the community insane. After a stage-coach driver reached
Phoenix, claiming a false name as well as a home, a wife, and a son
that weren't his (delusions that were no doubt the consequence of heat
stroke), other drivers avoided the ruins. "Old Cartwright's still out
there, trying to suck out our souls," one of them said. Only the desert,
which shows a few scorched boards and remnants of wagons and
walls of the ghost town, knows the truth.

"Now that you've met the committee, do you understand the
seriousness of this interview?" Dr Kincaid asked.

"Yes."

"Do you have a wife named Debbie and a daughter named Lori?"

"No."

"Do you own a home at forty-eight Arroyo Road?"

"No."

"Are you a vice-president at Sheperton Enterprises?"

"No."

"What's your name?"

"I don't remember. I know it isn't Sam Wentworth, even though
that's the name I thought was mine when I came here."

"And which we've decided is convenient for you to use inasmuch
as we don't know what your real name is."

"Yes."

"Perhaps one day, you'll remember your actual name or your
actual social security number, and we'll be able to connect you with
your past. But for now, the best we can do is prepare you to be a
productive member of society. We've arranged for you to have a
valid social-security number. We've tried to get you employment in
the area you claim to be expert in, real-estate development, but your
condition and lack of qualifications made our efforts unsuccessful.
However, since you enjoy spending most of your time with books,

we've obtained employment for you as a custodian at a branch of the Phoenix public library. We've also obtained a room for you at a boarding house near that facility. You'll be obligated, of course, to pay the rent and to keep taking your medication."

"Of course."

"Do you understand that you'll be arrested if you go anywhere near Debbie and Lori Bolan or their home on forty-seven Arroyo Road? Do you also understand that you'll be arrested if you go anywhere near Joe Sheperton or Sheperton Enterprises?"

"I do."

"Have you any questions?"

"One."

"Yes?"

"What happened to my Ford Explorer?"

"Since the license plate and VIN numbers were invalid, the car was impounded and sold at public auction."

"I see."

"How does that make you feel?"

"If the Explorer wasn't mine, I don't have a right to it."

"Exactly. I commend you on your progress."

"Thank you."

Careful, Sam thought as he stepped from the car. He thanked the driver, a male nurse at the mental-health facility. Squinting from the sun, he watched the vehicle proceed along the shimmering street. Then he turned toward the two-story, Spanish-style boarding house. A stern man stared from the front door. Picking up the cheap suitcase a social worker had given him, Sam approached. For the past two years he had thought only about his lost life, about Debbie and Lori, about the family he'd taken for granted, about hugs and kisses and not being able to see his daughter grow, about family meals and Lori's piano recitals and all the things he'd never made time for. Now they were the most precious things imaginable. With all his heart, he wanted to rush to Debbie and Lori and beg them to help him understand. Free at last, he needed to . . .

Careful, he warned himself again. The police and Dr Kincaid will keep an eye on you. The guy who runs this place will report everything you do. Remember what the police said about the penalties for stalking. You'll never learn the truth if you end up in jail or back at the nut house.

The motorcycle, which had taken him a month to make a down

payment on, transferred every punishing jolt as he followed the primitive road next to I–10. Replicating the route that had destroyed his life, he'd left the highway at Gila Gulch and now headed toward the hill behind which he'd found Meridian. The arms on the human-shaped cactuses looked even more droopy, black-specked, and diseased than two years earlier. Heat waves radiated off the rocks and the sand. The bleak hill loomed closer. Staring along the road, he noted in distress that it didn't curve to the right of the hill as it had that evening. Instead, it went to the left, remaining parallel with I–10.

Leaving the road, veering to the right, he felt increasingly torturous bumps as he rounded the hill and came to more black-specked cactuses. Beneath the goggles that protected his eyes from blowing sand, tears welled. It was a mark of his desperation that he'd managed to convince himself that Meridian would be here when he returned. Maybe you *are* insane, he told himself. Isn't thinking of yourself as "you", as someone apart from you, isn't that one of the signs of schizophrenia? Maybe you're as crazy as everybody thinks you are. Admit it – whatever happened to you out here, it had nothing to do with a place from 1882 that appears and disappears like a literal ghost town, like some kind of evil version of Brigadoon. If you believe that, you *are* crazy.

He stopped the motorcycle where he estimated he'd parked the Explorer that evening. Amid rocks and sand, he recalled where the livery stable, blacksmith shop, and general store had been. Where you *imagined* they were, he thought. And stop calling yourself "you".

The restaurant with the fifty-cent steak dinner had been farther along the street, and the saloon with its swinging doors and its sign for whiskey, beer, and sarsaparilla (he still had trouble with the word) had been even farther along. He could see it in his mind so vividly.

But obviously, it hadn't been here. Heartsick, he got off the motorcycle and propped it on its kick stand. He took off his helmet and felt a dry hot wind on his sweat-matted hair. For a time, after his release from the mental-health facility, he'd followed orders and taken his medication. But it had made him feel so groggy, so out of touch with things, that whatever cure it was supposed to be seemed worse than what Dr Kincaid had said was wrong with him. Each day, he had taken less and less, his consciousness regaining focus, his senses becoming more alert. And each day, he had felt more certain that he was in fact Sam Wentworth, that he did have a wife and daughter, that he worked for Sheperton Enterprises. The only problem was, nobody else in the world agreed with him.

How could it seem so real? he inwardly shouted. Is that what schizophrenia's like? Do you become convinced that a false world's true?

Damn it, stop thinking of yourself as "you".

Sick at heart, he shuffled along the non-existent street that he could see so vividly in his memory. Here and there, he noticed charred tips of boards poking from the sand, just as he'd noticed them the evening he'd wakened here. He paused and pulled one of the boards free, studying the scorch marks on it. He stared at the partially exposed bones of a large animal. He had a mental image of the cowboys shooting at each other, of the muscular man carrying the sack of flour. He plodded farther along the non-existent street.

Here, he thought. The saloon had been just about here. The swinging doors with the gaps at the top and bottom. The tinkly music from the player piano. He stepped through where he imagined the doors had been. He glanced to the left where cowboys had smoked and silently played cards. He looked to the right where other cowboys had leaned against the bar and drank. The saspa . . . sarsaparilla bottles had been just about . . .

Here. This is where you woke up, he thought, staring down at the sand. Something small moved among rocks. A scorpion? So real. So false. You shouldn't have come back. All you're doing is making yourself worse. With a palpable sense of horror, he backed away, as if retreating through the swinging doors, and stopped when a glint in the sand caught his attention. Sunlight reflected off something. A shiny piece of stone, he told himself. Fool's gold or whatever. The reflection seemed to pierce his eye. Before he realized what he was doing, he walked toward it and kicked his shoe in the sand. He expected a glinting pebble to roll free. Instead, his shoe dislodged something bigger, something solid enough to resist his shoe.

A circular tip of glass beckoned. He stooped, gripped it, and pulled a bottle from the sand. The bottle was empty. It was the same kind of bottle that had contained the liquid he'd drunk. Despite the sun's heat, he shivered. How could you have imagined something that you never saw, something that was buried under the sand? he thought.

That's when he knew he was truly in Hell.

The next day, he pulled a collapsed tent from the back of the motorcycle and quickly set it up, using a rock to drive the extra-long stakes deep into the sand. The tent had a reflective exterior that made it an excellent shield against the desert sun, he'd been assured. He zipped the entrance shut so scorpions and snakes couldn't get inside. Then he unstrapped a fold-down camp shovel from the motorcycle, opened it, and thrust it into the sand where he'd found the bottle. That was all the equipment he'd been able to fit on the bike. The next time, he'd bring more. If he was going to live out here when he wasn't working at the library, he had to make himself as comfortable as possible. A sleeping bag. A Coleman lantern and stove. A cooler. A portable radio. Maybe a sun umbrella. His janitor's salary didn't allow him to afford all that and, given his lack of history, no bank would give him a loan, but his junk mail (the only mail he received, all of it addressed to "current occupant") brought a never-ending stream of invitations to apply for credit cards, and credit-card companies, he'd discovered, would give a card to everybody, no matter how broke or crazy they were.

Frenzied, he dug the shovel into the sand.

"Sir, you can't stay here," a voice said.

Sam dug harder. After two months, he'd excavated almost the entire length and breadth of where the saloon had been. Mounds of sand marked its perimeter. Stacks of burnt wood rose next to a huge scorched section of the bar. Piles of glasses and bottles lay to one side.

"You can't do this, sir. This is private property. You're trespassing."

A special hoard lay near Sam's tent: the generic-looking soft-drink bottles, from one of which he'd sipped two years ago. He'd been praying that he'd find one that had fluid in it. Maybe, if he drank from it, he could make Meridian return. Maybe he could reverse what had happened. Maybe he could get his soul back. But to his dismay, enough to cause him to whimper each time he made a discovery, most of the bottles had been broken, and the few intact ones had been empty. He dug faster.

"*Sir,*" the deep voice insisted.

A hand touched his shoulder.

Trance broken, Sam whirled.

"Don't do anything stupid," a hard-faced man said. He raised his callused hands protectively in case Sam tried to use the shovel as a weapon. He wore a metal hat, a faded denim shirt, jeans, and construction worker's boots.

To Sam's astonishment, trucks, bulldozers, back-hoes, and other earth-moving equipment raised dust, rumbling into view from the side of the hill. He'd been so focused on digging that he hadn't been aware of anything else. Construction workers got out of numerous vans. An SUV jounced across the bumpy terrain and stopped,

SHEPERTON ENTERPRISES stenciled on its side. A man in a dress shirt and loosened tie, his sleeves rolled up, got out, put on a metal hat, and barked orders at some of the men. His stomach was more ample than it had used to be, his chin more jowly, his dark hair a little thinner, but there was no mistaking him.

Joe, Sam thought.

After yelling more orders, Joe stared in Sam's direction. "What's going on over there?" he shouted to the worker. "Who the hell's that guy? What's he doing here?"

"Digging," the worker shouted back.

"Don't you think I can see that!" Joe stormed over.

"Looks like he lives here." The worker pointed at the tent. "Homeless. He's scavenging glass and stuff."

"Jesus."

"Joe," Sam murmured.

"Tear down the tent, and get him out of here," Joe told the worker, then turned to leave.

"Joe," Sam managed to say louder.

"What?" Joe looked back and scowled. "Do I know you?"

"Don't you recognize me?" Immediately, Sam realized how much his sun-leathered skin and two months of beard had changed his appearance. "It's Sam. Sam Wentworth."

"Sam?" Joe asked blankly. Apprehension crossed his beefy face. "That nutcase? Sam *Wentworth*? The guy who thinks he's my vice-president, for crissake? Call the cops," Joe told the worker. "Tell them he's a stalker. When I come back from Grand Valley, I want this crazy son of a bitch out of here."

"Grand Valley?" Sam asked.

Joe marched through the dust toward a group of workers.

"Did you say *Grand Valley?* Joe! My God, don't tell me you're talking about Grand Valley Vistas outside Tucson?"

Joe scowled back harder. "How come you know about Grand Valley?"

"You went ahead and bought it?"

Joe straightened cockily. "In two hours, just about the time the police lock you in a cell, I'll be signing the papers."

"Carson talked you into it?"

"Carson? What do you know about Carson? And nobody talks me into *anything*!"

"Yeah, right, like that Hidden Estates deal you so regretted getting tricked into that you hired me to double-check the deals you were tempted to make."

"Hidden Estates?" Joe stormed back to him. "Have you been breaking into my building again? Reading my files?"

"I can save you ten million dollars."

"That's exactly what Carson wants for the land! How did you know? You have been reading my files!"

"And I can save you *another* ten million in lawsuits."

"Jesus, you're crazier than I thought."

"It's not going to cost you anything to wait another day, but it'll cost you at least twenty million if you sign those papers."

"Okay, you know so much about my business? Prove it."

"What?"

"Prove I'll be making a mistake."

"And if I can?"

"You poor dumb . . . The fact is, you *can't* prove it. But maybe that'll make you realize how deluded you are. Maybe you'll finally leave me alone."

"But if I *can?*"

"You mean, will that convince me you used to be my vice-president? No damned way."

"It doesn't matter. That's not what I want. I don't care about that anymore."

"Then what *do* you want?"

"One of the lots here."

"What?"

"*This* lot." Sam pointed toward his excavation. "If I prove buying Grand Valley Vistas would be a disaster, giving me this lot will be the best investment you ever made."

"Fat chance of *that* happening." Joe looked amused. "Fine. Prove I shouldn't buy Grand Valley Vistas, and the lot's yours."

Sam held out his hand. "Shake on it."

"Yeah, sure, right." Joe smirked as he shook Sam's hand.

"You've got your faults, Joe, but breaking your word didn't used to be one of them."

"And it sure as hell isn't now. This man's our witness to the deal. Where's your proof?"

"In the fifties, Grand Valley Vistas used to be a toxic dump site."

"*What?*"

"From a chemical plant that used to be there. It's got enough poisons buried there to cause multiple birth defects and give anybody who lives there cancer."

"And you can *prove* this?" Joe's normally florid face paled.

"I can tell you how to contact a man who was on the crew that dumped the chemicals, and a man who quit working at the plant because of the dumping. They're old now, but their memories are excellent. I can also tell you how to get your hands on the company's records, the ones that authorized the dumping before the plant shut down."

For the first time in Sam's experience, Joe had trouble speaking. "If you're right . . ."

"You save twenty million, and I get this lot."

Sam's shovel clinked against another bottle. In the sweltering sun, he raised the glass container, heartsick that it too was empty. One day, he thought. *One day*, you'll find a bottle with dark liquid in it, and when you drink from it, you'll have your wife and daughter back.

Around him, saws whined, and hammers pounded as homes went up with the speed Joe Sheperton was famous for. Here and there, portable radios played golden oldies or frenzied conversations on political call-in shows. Sam barely noticed them. The saloon was all that mattered. Meridian. Getting his soul back. Impressed with the accuracy of Sam's information, Joe had offered him a position in the company ("Maybe you're a natural."), but Sam had meant what he said. He no longer cared about his former job. Hell, if it hadn't been for that job, he thought, you never would have lost your family.

What he needed was to retrieve the life he'd taken for granted. One day, you'll find a bottle filled with liquid in it, he kept telling himself. One day, you'll be able to return to Debbie and Lori. You'll hug and kiss them. Overjoyed to see you, they'll wonder what kept you all these years. They'll stare in amazement as you explain. In the meantime, maybe the town'll reappear, just as it reappeared two years ago. Maybe that'll be another way to get your soul back. But how can that happen – a sudden panic seized him – if a new town's here to take its place and keep it from reappearing? Not much time. You don't have much time. As the searing sun reached its meridian, he dug with a greater frenzy.

CLIVE BARKER

Haeckel's Tale

CLIVE BARKER WAS BORN in Liverpool, England, where he went to all the same schools as John Lennon before attending Liverpool University. He now lives in California with his partner, photographer David Armstrong, and their daughter Nicole.

The author of more than twenty books, including the *Books of Blood*, *The Damnation Game*, *Weaveworld*, *Cabal*, *The Great and Secret Show*, *Imajica*, *The Thief of Always*, *Everville*, *Sacrament*, *Galilee*, *Coldheart Canyon: A Hollywood Ghost Story* and the *New York Times* bestselling *Arabat* series, he is one of the leading authors of contemporary horror and fantasy, as well as being an acclaimed artist, playwright, film producer and director.

Barker is currently working on a new collection, *The Scarlet Gospels*, the title story of which centres around his two most famous characters, the demonic Pinhead and occult detective Harry D'Amour.

Recently, IDW published a three-issue comic book adaptation of Barker's children's fantasy novel *The Thief of Always*, written and painted by Kris Oprisko and Gabriel Hernandez, and *The Great and Secret Show* is set to be a twelve-issue series from the same publisher.

As a film-maker, he created the hugely influential *Hellraiser* franchise in 1987 and went on to direct *Nightbreed* and *Lord of Illusions*. Barker also executive produced the Oscar-winning *Gods and Monsters*, while the *Candyman* series, along with *Underworld*, *Rawhead Rex*, *Quicksilver Highway* and *Saint Sinner*, are all based on his concepts.

The following story was adapted for the Showtime cable series *Masters of Horror* by Mick Garris and directed by John McNaugh-

ton (*Henry: Portrait of a Serial Killer*) after original director Roger
Corman had to pull out because of a back injury.

As Corman observed at the time: "Clive Barker's provocative
short story suggests an opportunity to go one step further than Mary
Shelley's nightmare masterpiece, *Frankenstein*, in suggesting how
closely the erotic drive and the obsession with death are linked."

P URRUCKER DIED LAST WEEK, after a long illness. I never much
liked the man, but the news of his passing still saddened me.
With him gone I am now the last of our little group; there's no one
left with whom to talk over the old times. Not that I ever did; at least
not with him. We followed such different paths, after Hamburg. He
became a physicist, and lived mostly, I think, in Paris. I stayed here in
Germany, and worked with Herman Helmholtz, mainly working in
the area of mathematics, but occasionally offering my contribution
to other disciplines. I do not think I will be remembered when I go.
Herman was touched by greatness; I never was. But I found comfort
in the cool shadow of his theories. He had a clear mind, a precise
mind. He refused to let sentiment or superstition into his view of the
world. I learned a good deal from that.

And yet now, as I think back over my life to my early twenties (I'm
two years younger than the century, which turns in a month), it is not
the times of intellectual triumph that I find myself remembering; it is
not Helmholtz's analytical skills, or his gentle detachment.

In truth, it is little more than the slip of a story that's on my mind
right now. But it refuses to go away, so I am setting it down here, as a
way of clearing it from my mind.

In 1822, I was – along with Purrucker and another eight or so bright
young men – the member of an informal club of aspirant intellectuals
in Hamburg. We were all of us in that circle learning to be scientists,
and being young had great ambition, both for ourselves and for the
future of scientific endeavor. Every Sunday we gathered at a coffee-
house on the Reeperbahn, and in a back room which we hired for the
purpose, fell to debate on any subject that suited us, as long as we felt
the exchanges in some manner advanced our comprehension of the
world. We were pompous, no doubt, and very full of ourselves; but
our ardour was quite genuine. It was an exciting time. Every week, it
seemed, one of us would come to a meeting with some new idea.

It was an evening during the summer – which was, that year,

oppressively hot, even at night – when Ernst Haeckel told us all the
story I am about to relate. I remember the circumstances well. At
least I think I do. Memory is less exact than it believes itself to be,
yes? Well, it scarcely matters. What I remember may as well *be* the
truth. After all, there's nobody left to disprove it. What happened
was this: towards the end of the evening, when everyone had drunk
enough beer to float the German fleet, and the keen edge of
intellectual debate had been dulled somewhat (to be honest we were
descending into gossip, as we inevitably did after midnight), Eisentrout, who later became a great surgeon, made casual mention of a
man called Montesquino. The fellow's name was familiar to us all,
though none of us had met him. He had come into the city a month
before, and attracted a good deal of attention in society, because he
claimed to be a necromancer. He could speak with and even raise the
dead, he claimed, and was holding seances in the houses of the rich.
He was charging the ladies of the city a small fortune for his services.

The mention of Montesquino's name brought a chorus of slurred
opinions from around the room, every one of them unflattering. He
was a contemptuous cheat and a sham. He should be sent back to
France – from whence he'd come – but not before the skin had been
flogged off his back for his impertinence.

The only voice in the room that was not raised against him was
that of Ernst Haeckel, who in my opinion was the finest mind
amongst us. He sat by the open window – hoping perhaps for some
stir of a breeze off the Elbe on this smothering night – with his chin
laid against his hand.

"What do you think of all this, Ernst?" I asked him.

"You don't want to know," he said softly.

"Yes, we do. Of course we do."

Haeckel looked back at us. "Very well then," he said. "I'll tell
you."

His face looked sickly in the candlelight, and I remember thinking
– distinctly thinking – that I'd never seen such a look in his eyes as he
had at that moment. Whatever thoughts had ventured into his head,
they had muddied the clarity of his gaze. He looked fretful.

"Here's what I think," he said. "That we should be careful when
we talk about necromancers."

"Careful?" said Purrucker, who was an argumentative man at the
best of times, and even more volatile when drunk. "Why should we
be *careful* of a little French prick who preys on our women? Good
Lord, he's practically stealing from their purses!"

"How so?"

"Because he's telling them he can raise the dead!" Purrucker yelled, banging the table for emphasis.

"And how do we know he cannot?"

"Oh now Haeckel," I said, "you don't believe –"

"I believe the evidence of my eyes, Theodor," Haeckel said to me. "And I saw – once in my life – what I take to be proof that such crafts as this Montesquino professes are real."

The room erupted with laughter and protests. Haeckel sat them out, unmoving. At last, when all our din had subsided, he said: "Do you want to hear what I have to say or don't you?"

"Of *course* we want to hear," said Julius Linneman, who doted on Haeckel; almost girlishly, we used to think.

"Then listen," Haeckel said. "What I'm about to tell you is absolutely true, though by the time I get to the end of it you may not welcome me back into this room, because you may think I am a little crazy. More than a little perhaps."

The softness of his voice, and the haunted look in his eyes, had quieted everyone, even the volatile Purrucker. We all took seats, or lounged against the mantelpiece, and listened. After a moment of introspection, Haeckel began to tell his tale. And as best I remember it, this is what he told us.

"Ten years ago I was at Wittenberg, studying philosophy under Wilhem Hauser. He was a metaphysician, of course; monkish in his ways. He didn't care for the physical world; it didn't touch him, really. And he urged his students to live with the same asceticism as he himself practiced. This was of course hard for us. We were very young, and full of appetite. But while I was in Wittenberg, and under his watchful eye, I really tried to live as close to his precepts as I could.

"In the spring of my second year under Hauser, I got word that my father – who lived in Luneburg – was seriously ill, and I had to leave my studies and return home. I was a student. I'd spent all my money on books and bread. I couldn't afford the carriage fare. So I had to walk. It was several day's journey, of course, across the empty heath, but I had my meditations to accompany me, and I was happy enough. At least for the first half of the journey. Then, out of nowhere there came a terrible rainstorm. I was soaked to the skin, and despite my valiant attempts to put my concern for physical comfort out of my mind, I could not. I was cold and unhappy, and the rarifications of the metaphysical life were very far from my mind.

"On the fourth or fifth evening, sniffling and cursing, I gathered some twigs and made a fire against a little stone wall, hoping to dry myself out before I slept. While I was gathering moss to make a pillow for my head an old man, his face the very portrait of melancholy, appeared out of the gloom, and spoke to me like a prophet.

" 'It would not be wise for you to sleep here tonight,' he said to me.

"I was in no mood to debate the issue with him. I was too fed up. 'I'm not going to move an inch,' I told him. 'This is an open road. I have every right to sleep here if I wish to.'

" 'Of course you do,' the old man said to me. 'I didn't say the right was not yours. I simply said it wasn't wise.'

"I was a little ashamed of my sharpness, to be honest. 'I'm sorry,' I said to him. 'I'm cold and I'm tired and I'm hungry. I meant no insult.'

"The old man said that none was taken. His name, he said, was Walter Wolfram.

"I told him my name, and my situation. He listened, then offered to bring me back to his house, which he said was close by. There I might enjoy a proper fire and some hot potato soup. I did not refuse him, of course. But I did ask him, when I'd risen, why he thought it was unwise for me to sleep in that place.

"He gave me such a sorrowful look. A heart-breaking look, the meaning of which I did not comprehend. Then he said: 'You are a young man, and no doubt you do not fear the workings of the world. But please believe me when I tell you there are nights when it's not good to sleep next to a place where the dead are laid.'

" 'The dead?' I replied, and looked back. In my exhausted state I had not seen what lay on the other side of the stone wall. Now, with the rain-clouds cleared and the moon climbing, I could see a large number of graves there, old and new intermingled. Usually such a sight would not have much disturbed me. Hauser had taught us to look coldly on death. It should not, he said, move a man more than the prospect of sunrise, for it is just as certain, and just as unremarkable. It was good advice when heard on a warm afternoon in a classroom in Wittenberg. But here – out in the middle of nowhere, with an old man murmuring his superstitions at my side – I was not so certain it made sense.

"Anyway, Wolfram took me home to his little house, which lay no more than half a mile from the necropolis. There was the fire, as he'd promised. And the soup, as he'd promised. But there also, much to my surprise and delight, was his wife, Elise.

"She could not have been more than twenty-two, and easily the most beautiful woman I had ever seen. Wittenberg had its share of beauties, of course. But I don't believe its streets ever boasted a woman as perfect as this. Chestnut hair, all the way down to her tiny waist. Full lips, full hips, full breasts. And such eyes! When they met mine they seemed to consume me.

"I did my best, for decency's sake, to conceal my admiration, but it was hard to do. I wanted to fall down on my knees and declare my undying devotion to her, there and then.

"If Walter noticed any of this, he made no sign. He was anxious about something, I began to realize. He constantly glanced up at the clock on the mantel, and looked towards the door.

"I was glad of his distraction, in truth. It allowed me to talk to Elise, who – though she was reticent at first – grew more animated as the evening proceeded. She kept plying me with wine, and I kept drinking it, until sometime before midnight I fell asleep, right there amongst the dishes I'd eaten from."

At this juncture, somebody in our little assembly – I think it may have been Purrucker – remarked that he hoped this wasn't going to be a story about disappointed love, because he really wasn't in the mood. To which Haeckel replied that the story had absolutely nothing to do with love in any shape or form. It was a simple enough reply, but it did the job: it silenced the man who'd interrupted, and it deepened our sense of foreboding.

The noise from the café had by now died almost completely; as had the sounds from the street outside. Hamburg had retired to bed. But we were held there, by the story, and by the look in Ernst Haeckel's eyes.

"I awoke a little while later," he went on, "but I was so weary and so heavy with wine, I barely opened my eyes. The door was ajar, and on the threshold stood a man in a dark cloak. He was having a whispered conversation with Walter. There was, I thought, an exchange of money; though I couldn't see clearly. Then the man departed. I got only the merest glimpse of his face, by the light thrown from the fire. It was not the face of a man I would like to quarrel with, I thought. Nor indeed even meet. Narrow eyes, sunk deep in fretful flesh. I was glad he was gone. As Walter closed the door I lay my head back down and almost closed my eyes, preferring that he not know I was awake. I can't tell you exactly why. I just knew that something was going on I was better not becoming involved with.

"Then, as I lay there, listening, I hear a baby crying. Walter called for Elise, instructing her to calm the infant down. I didn't hear her response. Rather, I heard it, I just couldn't make any sense of it. Her voice, which had been soft and sweet when I'd talked with her, now sounded strange. Through the slits of my eyes I could see that she'd gone to the window, and was staring out, her palms pressed flat against the glass.

"Again, Walter told her to attend to the child. Again, she gave him some guttural reply. This time she turned to him, and I saw that she was by no means the same woman as I'd conversed with. She seemed to be in the early stages of some kind of fit. Her colour was high, her eyes wild, her lips drawn back from her teeth.

"So much that had seemed, earlier, evidence of her beauty and vitality now looked more like a glimpse of the sickness that was consuming her. She'd glowed too brightly; like someone consumed by a fever, who in that hour when all is at risk seems to burn with a terrible vividness.

"One of her hands went down between her legs and she began to rub herself there, in a most disturbing manner. If you've ever been to a mad-house you've maybe seen some of the kind of behavior she was exhibiting.

"'Patience,' Walter said to her, 'everything's being taken care of. Now go and look after the child.'

"Finally she conceded to his request, and off she went into the next room. Until I'd heard the infant crying I hadn't even realized they had a child, and it seemed odd to me that Elise had not made mention of it. Lying there, feigning sleep, I tried to work out what I should do next. Should I perhaps pretend to wake, and announce to my host that I would not after all be accepting his hospitality? I decided against this course. I would stay where I was. As long as they thought I was asleep they'd ignore me. Or so I hoped.

"The baby's crying had now subsided. Elise's presence had soothed it.

"'Make sure he's had enough before you put him down,' I heard Walter say to her. 'I don't want him waking and crying for you when you're gone.'

"From this I gathered that she was breast-feeding the child; which fact explained the lovely generosity of her breasts. They were plump with milk. And I must admit, even after the way Elise had looked when she was at the window, I felt a little spasm of envy for the child, suckling at those lovely breasts.

"Then I returned my thoughts to the business of trying to understand what was happening here. Who was the man who'd come to the front door? Elise's lover, perhaps? If so, why was Walter *paying* him? Was it possible that the old man had hired this fellow to satisfy his wife, because he was incapable of doing the job himself? Was Elise's twitching at the window simply erotic anticipation?

"At last, she came out of the infant's room, and very carefully closed the door. There was a whispered exchange between the husband and wife, which I caught no part of, but which set off a new round of questions in my head. Suppose they were conspiring to kill me? I will tell you, my neck felt very naked at that moment . . .

"But I needn't have worried. After a minute they finished their whispering and Elise left the house. Walter, for his part, went to sit by the fire. I heard him pour himself a drink, and down it noisily; then pour himself another. Plainly he was drowning his sorrows; or doing his best. He kept drinking, and muttering to himself while he drank. Presently, the muttering became tearful. Soon he was sobbing.

"I couldn't bear this any longer. I raised my head off the table, and I turned to him.

"'Herr Wolfram,' I said, '. . . what's going on here?'

"He had tears pouring down his face, running into his beard.

"'Oh my friend,' he said, shaking his head, 'I could not begin to explain. This is a night of unutterable sadness.'

"'Would you prefer that I left you to your tears?' I asked him.

"'No,' he said. 'No, I don't want you to go out there right now.'

"I wanted to know why, of course. Was there something he was afraid I'd see?

"I had risen from the table, and now went to him. 'The man who came to the door –'

"Walter's lip curled at my mention of him. 'Who is he?' I asked.

"'His name is Doctor Skal. He's an Englishman of my acquaintance.'

"I waited for further explanation. But when none was forthcoming, I said: 'And a friend of your wife's.'

"'No,' Walter said. 'It's not what you think it is.' He poured himself some more brandy, and drank again. 'You're supposing they're lovers. But they're not. Elise has not the slightest interest in the company of Doctor Skal, believe me. Nor indeed in any visitor to this house.'

"I assumed this remark was a little barb directed at me, and I began to defend myself, but Walter waved my protestations away.

"'Don't concern yourself,' he said, 'I took no offence at the looks you gave my wife. How could you not? She's a very beautiful woman, and I'd be surprised if a young man such as yourself *didn't* try to seduce her. At least in his heart. But let me tell you, my friend: you could never satisfy her.' He let this remark lie for a moment.

Then he added: 'Neither, of course, could I. When I married her I was already too old to be a husband to her in the truest sense.'

" 'But you have a baby,' I said to him.

" 'The boy isn't mine,' Walter replied.

" 'So you're raising this infant, even though he isn't yours?'

" 'Yes.'

" 'Where's the father?'

" 'I'm afraid he's dead.'

" 'Ah.' This all began to seem very tragic. Elise pregnant, the father dead, and Walter coming to the rescue, saving her from dishonour. That was the story constructed in my head. The only part I could not yet fit into this neat scheme was Doctor Skal, whose cloaked presence at the door had so unsettled me.

" 'I know none of this is my business –' I said to Walter.

" 'And better keep it that way,' he replied.

" 'But I have one more question.'

" 'Ask it.'

" 'What kind of Doctor is this man Skal?'

" 'Ah.' Walter set his glass down, and stared into the fire. It had not been fed in a while, and now was little more than a heap of glowing embers. 'The esteemed Doctor Skal is a necromancer. He deals in a science which I do not profess to understand.' He leaned a little closer to the fire, as though talking of the mysterious man had chilled him to the marrow. I felt something similar. I knew very little about the work of a necromancer, but I knew that they dealt with the dead.

"I thought of the graveyard, and of Walter's first words to me:

" '*It would not be wise for you to sleep here tonight.*'

"Suddenly, I understood. I got to my feet, my barely sobered head throbbing. 'I know what's going on here,' I announced. 'You paid Skal so that Elise could speak to the dead! To the man who fathered her baby.' Walter continued to stare into the fire. I came close to him. 'That's it, isn't it? And now Skal's going to play some miserable trick on poor Elise to make her believe she's talking to a spirit.'

" 'It's *not* a trick,' Walter said. For the first time during this grim exchange he looked up at me. 'What Skal does is real, I'm afraid to say. Which is why you should stay in here until it's over and done with. It's nothing you need ever—'

"He broke off at that moment, his thought unfinished, because we heard Elise's voice. It wasn't a word she uttered, it was a sob; and then another, and another, I knew whence they came, of course. Elise was at the graveyard with Skal. In the stillness of the night her voice carried easily.

" 'Listen to her,' I said.

" 'Better not,' Walter said.

"I ignored him, and went to the door, driven by a kind of morbid fascination. I didn't for a moment believe what Walter had said about the necromancer. Though much else that Hauser had taught me had become hard to believe tonight, I still believed in his teachings on the matter of life and death. The soul, he'd taught us, was certainly immortal. But once it was released from the constraints of flesh and blood, the body had no more significance than a piece of rotted meat. The man or woman who had animated it was gone, to be with those who had already left this life. There was, he insisted, no way to call that spirit back. And nor therefore – though Hauser had never extrapolated this far – was there any validity in the claims of those who said that they could commune with the dead.

"In short, Doctor Skal was a fake: this was my certain belief. And poor distracted Elise was his dupe. God knows what demands he was making of her, to have her sobbing that way! My imagination – having first dwelt on the woman's charms shamelessly, and then decided she was mad – now reinvented her a third time, as Skal's hapless victim. I knew from stories I'd heard in Hamburg what power charlatans like this wielded over vulnerable women. I'd heard of some necromancers who demanded that their seances be held with everyone as naked as Adam, for purity's sake! Others who had so battered the tender hearts of their victims with their ghoulishness that the women had swooned, and been violated in their swoon. I pictured all this happening to Elise. And the louder her sobs and cries became the more certain I was that my worst imaginings were true.

"At last I couldn't bear it any longer, and I stepped out into the darkness to get her.

"Herr Wolfram came after me, and caught hold of my arm. 'Come back into the house!' he demanded. 'For pity's sake, leave this alone *and come back into the house!*'

"Elise was shrieking now. I couldn't have gone back in if my life had depended upon it. I shook myself free of Wolfram's grip and started out for the graveyard. At first I thought he was going to leave me alone, but when I glanced back I saw that though he'd returned into the house he was now emerging again, cradling a musket in his arms. I thought at first he intended to threaten me with it, but instead he said:

" 'Take it!' offering the weapon to me.

" 'I don't intend to kill anybody!' I said, feeling very heroic and self-righteous now that I was on my way. 'I just want to get Elise out of this damn Englishman's hands.'

"'She won't come, believe me,' Walter said. 'Please take the musket! You're a good fellow. I don't want to see any harm come to you.'

"I ignored him and strode on. Though Walter's age made him wheeze, he did his best to keep up with me. He even managed to talk, though what he said – between my agitated state and his panting – wasn't always easy to grasp.

"'She has a sickness . . . she's had it all her life . . . what did I know? . . . I loved her . . . wanted her to be happy . . .'

"'She doesn't sound very happy right now,' I remarked.

"'It's not what you think . . . it is and it isn't . . . oh, God, please come back to the house!'

"'I said no! I don't want her being molested by that man!'

"'You don't understand. We couldn't begin to please her. Neither of us.'

"'So you hire Skal to service her? Jesus!'

"I turned and pushed him hard in the chest, then I picked up my pace. Any last doubts I might have entertained about what was going on in the graveyard were forgotten. All this talk of necromancy was just a morbid veil drawn over the filthy truth of the matter. Poor Elise! Stuck with a broken-down husband, who knew no better way to please than to give her over to an Englishman for an occasional pleasuring. Of all things, an Englishman! As if the English knew anything about making love.

"As I ran, I envisaged what I'd do when I reached the graveyard. I imagined myself hopping over the wall and with a shout racing at Skal, and plucking him off my poor Elise. Then I'd beat him senseless. And when he was laid low, and I'd proved just how heroic a fellow I was, I'd go to the girl, take her in my arms, and show her what a good German does when he wants to make a woman happy.

"Oh, my head was spinning with ideas, right up until the moment that I emerged from the corner of the trees and came in sight of the necropolis . . ."

Here, after several minutes of headlong narration, Haeckel ceased speaking. It was not for dramatic effect, I think. He was simply preparing himself, mentally, for the final stretch of his story. I'm sure that none of us in that room doubted that what lay ahead would not be pleasant. From the beginning this had been a tale overshadowed by the prospect of some horror. None of us spoke; that I do remember. We sat there, in thrall to the persuasions of Haeckel's tale, waiting for him to begin again. We were like children.

After a minute or so, during which time he stared out of the window at the night sky (though seeing, I think, nothing of its beauty) he turned back to us and rewarded our patience.

"The moon was full and white," he said. "It showed me every detail. There were no great, noble tombs in this place, such as you'd see at the Ohlsdorf Cemetery; just coarsely carved headstones and wooden crosses. And in their midst, a kind of ceremony was going on. There were candles set in the grass, their flames steady in the still air. I suppose they made some kind of circle – perhaps ten feet across – in which the necromancer had performed his rituals. Now, however, with his work done, he had retired some distance from this place. He was sitting on a tombstone, smoking a long, Turkish pipe, and watching.

"The subject of his study, of course, was Elise. When I had first laid eyes on her I had guiltily imagined what she would look like stripped of her clothes. Now I had my answer. There she was, lit by the gold of the candle flames and the silver of the moon. Available to my eyes in all her glory.

"But oh, God! What she was doing turned every single drop of pleasure I might have taken in her beauty to the bitterest gall.

"Those cries I'd heard – those sobs that had made my heart go out to her – they weren't provoked by the pawings of Doctor Skal, but by the touch of the dead. The dead, raised out of their dirt to pleasure her! She was squatting, and there between her legs was a face, pushed up out of the earth. A man recently buried, to judge by his condition, the flesh still moist on the bone, and the tongue – Jesus, the tongue! – still flicking between his bared teeth.

"If this had been all it would have been enough. But it was not all. The same grotesque genius that had inspired the cadaver between her legs into this resemblance of life, had also brought forth a crop of smaller parts – pieces of the whole, which had wormed their way out of the grave by some means or other. Bony pieces, held together with leathery sinew. A rib-cage, crawling around on its elbows; a head, propelled by a whiplash length of stripped spine; several hands, with some fleshless lengths of bone attached. There was a morbid bestiary of these things And they were all upon her, or waiting their turn to be upon her.

"Nor did she for a moment protest their attentions. Quite the contrary. Having climbed off the corpse that was pleasuring her from below, she rolled over onto her back and invited a dozen of these pieces upon her, like a whore in a fever, and they came, oh, God, they came, as though they might have out of her the juices that would return them to wholesomeness.

"Walter, by now, had caught up with me.

" 'I warned you,' he said.

" 'You knew this was happening?'

" 'Of course I knew. I'm afraid it's the only way she's satisfied.'

" 'What is she?' I said to him.

" 'A woman,' Walter replied.

" 'No natural woman would endure *that*,' I said. 'Jesus! Jesus!'

"The sight before me was getting worse by the moment. Elise was up on her knees in the grave dirt now, and a second corpse – stripped of whatever garments he had been buried in – was coupling with her, his motion vigorous, his pleasure intense, to judge by the way he threw back his putrefying head. As for Elise, she was kneading her full tits, directing arcs of milk into the air so that it rained down on the vile menagerie cavorting before her. Her lovers were in ecstasy. They clattered and scampered around in the torrents, as though they were being blessed.

"I took the musket from Walter.

" 'Don't hurt her!' he begged. 'She's not to blame.'

"I ignored him, and made my way towards the yard, calling to the necromancer as I did so.

" 'Skal! *Skal!*'

"He looked up from his meditations, whatever they were, and seeing the musket I was brandishing, immediately began to protest his innocence. His German wasn't good, but I didn't have any difficulty catching his general drift. He was just doing what he'd been paid to do, he said. He wasn't to blame.

"I clambered over the wall and approached him through the graves, instructing him to get to his feet. He got up, his hands raised in surrender. Plainly he was terrified that I was going to shoot him. But that wasn't my intention. I just wanted to stop this obscenity.

" 'Whatever you did to start this, *undo it*!' I told him.

"He shook his head, his eyes wild. I thought perhaps he didn't understand so I repeated the instruction.

"Again, he shook his head. All his composure was gone. He looked like a shabby little cut-purse who'd just been caught in the act. I was right in front of him, and I jabbed the musket in his belly. If he didn't stop this, I told him, I'd shoot him.

"I might have done it too, but for Herr Wolfram, who had clambered over the wall and was approaching his wife, calling her name.

"'Elise . . . please, Elise . . . you should come home.'

"I've never in my life heard anything as absurd or as sad as that man calling to his wife. '*You should come home . . .*'

"Of course she didn't listen to him. Didn't *hear* him, probably, in the heat of what she was doing, and what was being done to her.

"But her *lovers* heard. One of the men who'd been raised up whole, and was waiting his turn at the woman, started shambling towards Walter, waving him away. It was a curious thing to see. The corpse trying to shoo the old man off. But Walter wouldn't go. He kept calling to Elise, the tears pouring down his face. Calling to her, calling to her —

"I yelled to him to stay away. He didn't listen to me. I suppose he thought if he got close enough he could maybe catch hold of her arm. But the corpse came at him, still waving its hands, still shooing, and when Walter wouldn't be shooed the thing simply knocked him down. I saw him flail for a moment, and then try to get back up. But the dead – or pieces of the dead – were everywhere in the grass around his feet. And once he was down, they were upon him.

"I told the Englishman to come with me, and I started off across the yard to help Walter. There was only one ball in the musket, so I didn't want to waste it firing from a distance, and maybe missing my target. Besides I wasn't sure what I was going to fire at. The closer I got to the circle in which Elise was crawling around – still being clawed and petted – the more of Skal's unholy handiwork I saw. Whatever spells he'd cast here, they seemed to have raised every last dead thing in the place. The ground was crawling with bits of this and that; fingers, pieces of dried up flesh with locks of hair attached; wormy fragments that were beyond recognition.

"By the time we reached Walter, he'd already lost the fight. The horrors he'd paid to have resurrected – ungrateful things – had torn him open in a hundred places. One of his eyes had been thumbed out, there was a gaping hole in his chest.

"His murderers were still working on him. I batted a few limbs off him with the musket, but there were so many it was only a matter of time, I knew, before they came after me. I turned around to Skal, intending to order him again to bring this abomination to a halt, but he was springing off between the graves. In a sudden surge of rage, I raised the musket and I fired. The felon went down, howling in the grass. I went to him. He was badly wounded, and in great pain, but I was in no mood to help him. He was responsible for all this. Wolfram dead, and Elise still crouching amongst her rotted admirers; all of this was Skal's fault. I had no sympathy for the man.

" 'What does it take to make this stop?' I asked him. '*What are the words?*'

"His teeth were chattering. It was hard to make out what he was saying. Finally I understood.

" 'When . . . the . . . sun . . . comes up . . .' he said to me.

" 'You can't stop it any other way?'

" 'No,' he said. 'No . . . other . . . way . . .'

"Then he died. You can imagine my despair. I could do nothing. There was no way to get to Elise without suffering the same fate as Walter. And anyway, she wouldn't have come. It was an hour from dawn, at least. All I could do was what I did: climb over the wall, and wait. The sounds were horrible. In some ways, worse than the sight. She must have been exhausted by now, but she kept going. Sighing sometimes, sobbing sometimes, moaning sometimes. Not – let me make it perfectly clear – the despairing moan of a woman who understands that she is in the grip of the dead. This was the moan of a deeply pleasured woman; a woman in bliss.

"Just a few minutes before dawn, the sounds subsided. Only when they had died away completely did I look back over the wall. Elise had gone. Her lovers lay around in the ground, exhausted as perhaps only the dead can be. The clouds were lightening in the East. I suppose resurrected flesh has a fear of the light, because as the last stars crept away so did the dead. They crawled back into the earth, and covered themselves with the dirt that had been shovelled down upon their coffins . . ."

Haeckel's voice had become a whisper in these last minutes, and now it trailed away completely. We sat around not looking at one another, each of us deep in thought. If any of us had entertained the notion that Haeckel's tale was some invention, the force of his telling – the whiteness of his skin, the tears that had now and then appeared in his eyes – had thrust such doubts from us, at least for now.

It was Purrucker who spoke first, inevitably. "So you killed a man," he said. "I'm impressed."

Haeckel looked up at him. "I haven't finished my story," he said.

"Jesus . . ." I murmured, ". . . what else is there to tell?"

"If you remember, I'd left all my books, and some gifts I'd brought from Wittenberg for my father, at Herr Wolfram's house. So I made my way back there. I was in a kind of terrified trance, my mind still barely able to grasp what I'd seen.

"When I got to the house I heard somebody singing. A sweet lilting voice it was. I went to the door. My belongings were sitting there on the table where I'd left them. The room was empty. Praying that I'd go unheard, I entered. As I picked up my philosophy books and my father's gift the singing stopped.

"I retreated to the door but before I could reach the threshold Elise appeared, with her infant in her arms. The woman looked the worse for her philanderings, no question about that. There were scratches all over her face, and her arms, and on the plump breast at which the baby now sucked. But marked as she was, there was nothing but happiness in her eyes. She was sweetly content with her life at that moment.

"I thought perhaps she had no memory of what had happened to her. Maybe the necromancer had put her into some kind of trance, I reasoned; and now she'd woken from it the past was all forgotten.

"I started to explain to her. 'Walter . . .' I said.

" 'Yes, I know –' she replied. 'He's dead.' She smiled at me; a May morning smile. 'He was old,' she said, matter-of-factly. 'But he was always kind to me. Old men are the best husbands. As long as you don't want children.'

"My gaze must have gone from her radiant face to the baby at her nipple, because she said:

" 'Oh, this isn't Walter's boy.'

"As she spoke she tenderly teased the infant from her breast, and it looked my way. There it was: life-in-death, perfected. Its face was shiny pink, and its limbs fat from its mother's milk, but its sockets were deep as the grave, and its mouth wide, so that its teeth, which were not an infant's teeth, were bared in a perpetual grimace.

"The dead, it seemed, had given her more than pleasure.

"I dropped the books, and the gift for my father there on the doorstep. I stumbled back out into the daylight, and I ran – oh, God in Heaven, I ran! – afraid to the very depths of my soul. I kept on running until I reached the road. Though I had no desire to venture past the graveyard again, I had no choice: it was the only route I knew, and I did not want to get lost, I wanted to be home. I wanted a church, an altar, piety, prayers.

"It was not a busy thoroughfare by any means, and if anyone had passed along it since day-break they'd decided to leave the necromancer's body where it lay beside the wall. But the crows were at his face, and foxes at his hands and feet. I crept by without disturbing their feast."

Again, Haeckel halted. This time, he expelled a long, long sigh. "And that, gentlemen, is why I advise you to be careful in your judgments of this man Montesquino."

He rose as he spoke, and went to the door. Of course we all had questions, but none of us spoke then, not then. We let him go. And for my part, gladly. I'd enough of these horrors for one night.

Make of all this what you will. I don't know to this day whether I believe the story or not (though I can't see any reason why Haeckel would have *invented* it. Just as he'd predicted, he was treated very differently after that night; kept at arm's length). The point is that the thing still haunts me; in part, I suppose, *because* I never made up my mind whether I thought it was a falsehood or not. I've sometimes wondered what part it played in the shaping of my life: if perhaps my cleaving to empiricism – my devotion to Helmholtz's methodologies – was not in some way the consequence of this hour spent in the company of Haeckel's account.

Nor do I think I was alone in my preoccupation with what I heard. Though I saw less and less of the other members of the group as the years went by, on those occasions when we did meet up the conversation would often drift round to that story, and our voices would drop to near-whispers, as though we were embarrassed to be confessing that we even remembered what Haeckel had said.

A couple of members of the group went to some lengths to pluck holes in what they'd heard, I remember; to expose it as nonsense. I think Eisentrout actually claimed he'd retraced Haeckel's journey from Wittenberg to Luneburg, and claimed there was no necropolis along the route. As for Haeckel himself, he treated these attacks upon his veracity with indifference. We had asked him to tell us what he thought of necromancers, and he'd told us. There was nothing more to say on the matter.

And in a way he was right. It was just a story told on a hot night, long ago, when I was still dreaming of what I would become.

And yet now, sitting here at the window, knowing I will never again be strong enough to step outside, and that soon I must join Purrucker and the others in the earth, I find the terror coming back to me; the terror of some convulsive place where death has a beautiful woman in its teeth, and she gives voice to bliss. I have, if you will, fled Haeckel's story over the years; hidden my head under the covers of reason. But here, at the end, I see that there is no asylum to be had from it; or rather, from the terrible suspicion that it contains a clue to the ruling principle of the world.

BRIAN LUMLEY

The Taint

A WIDELY TRAVELLED MAN, Brian Lumley has visited or lived in the US, France, Italy, Cyprus, Germany and Malta, not to mention at least a dozen or more Greek islands. His hobbies have included hang-gliding in Scotland and spear-fishing and octopus-hunting in the Greek islands. He still makes regular visits to the Mediterranean, indulging his passion for moussaka, retsina, just a little ouzo . . . and Metaxa, of course!

When not travelling, Brian and his American wife Barbara Ann keep house in Devon, England.

With the recent publication of *Harry Keogh: Necroscope, & Others*, the author has completed his epic "Necroscope" saga in an amazing fourteen volumes. Thirteen countries (and counting) have now published or are in the process of publishing these books, which in the US alone have sold well over 2,000,000 copies.

Lumley's list of titles now runs to fifty and counting. A prolific if not compulsive writer, the bulk of his work has seen print in the last twenty-three years, this following a full span of twenty-two years of military service.

Although he had long been an acknowledged master of the "Cthulhu Mythos" sub-genre inspired by H. P. Lovecraft's fiction, it wasn't until 1986, with his military career behind him, that the UK saw first publication of his ground-breaking horror novel *Necro-scope*, featuring Harry Keogh, the man who talks to dead people.

Twenty years later, the book has been reissued in a deluxe edition by Subterranean Press, profusely illustrated by Bob Eggleton.

Lumley received the prestigious Grand Master Award in recogni-tion of his work at the World Horror Convention in Phoenix, Arizona, in 1998.

"It would be impossible to deny HPL's influence on 'The Taint' even if I wanted to, which I don't," reveals the author. "Because H. P. Lovecraft's Deep Ones, those 'batrachian dwellers of fathomless ocean', which he employed so effectively in his story 'The Shadow Over Innsmouth', and hinted at in others of his stories, have always fascinated me. And not only me, but an entire generation of authors most of whom weren't even born until long after Lovecraft's tragically early death.

"As for the novella that follows: much like 'Dagon's Bell' and 'The Return of the Deep Ones', it's the result of my wondering – what if certain members of the Esoteric Order of Dagon somehow escaped or emigrated from degenerate old Innsmouth to resurface elsewhere? For instance, in England. But more than that I mustn't say . . ."

J AMES JAMIESON LOOKED THROUGH BINOCULARS at the lone figure on the beach – a male figure, at the rim of the sea – and said, "That's pretty much what I would have wanted to do, when I was his age. Beachcombing, or writing books; maybe poetry? Or just bumming my way around the world. But my folks had other ideas. Just as well, I suppose. 'No future in poetry, son. Or in daydreaming or beachcombing.' That was my father, a doctor in his own right. Like father like son, right?" Lowering his binoculars, he smiled at the others with him. "Still, I think I would have enjoyed it."

"Beachcombing, in the summer? Oh, I could understand that well enough!" John Tremain, the middle-aged headmaster at the technical college in St Austell, answered him. "The smell of the sea, the curved horizon way out there, sea breezes in your hair, and the wailing of the gulls? Better than the yelping of brats any time – oh yes! The sun's sparkle on the sea and warm sand between your toes – it's very seductive. But this late in the season, *and* in my career?" He shook his head. "Thanks, but no thanks. You won't find me with my hands in my pockets, sauntering along the tidemark and picking over the seaweed."

He paused, shrugged, and continued, "Not now, anyway. But on the other hand, when I was a young fellow teaching arts and crafts: carpentry and joinery, woodcraft in general – I mean, working *with* woods as opposed to surviving in them – now would have been the ideal time for a stroll on the beach. And I used to do quite a bit of it. Yes, indeed. For it's autumn when the best pieces get washed ashore."

"Pieces?" Jilly White came back from wherever her thoughts had momentarily wandered, blinked her pretty but clouded green eyes at Tremain, then glanced from face to face in search of a hint, a clue. "I'm sorry, John, but I wasn't quite . . .?"

"Driftwood," the teacher smiled. "All those twisted, sand-papered roots that get tumbled in with the tide when the wind's off the sea. Those bleached, knotted, gargoyle branches. It's a long time ago now, but—" He almost sighed, gave another shrug, and finished off, "But searching for driftwood was as close as I ever got to being a beachcomber."

And Doreen, his tall, slender, haughty but not unattractive wife, said, "You've visited with us often enough, Jilly. Surely you must have noticed John's carvings? They were all driftwood originally, washed up on the beach there."

And now they all looked at Jilly . . .

There were four of them, five if you included Jilly White's daughter, Anne, curled up with a book in the lee of a sand-dune some twenty-five yards down the beach and out of earshot. Above her, a crest of crabgrass like some buried sand-giant's eyebrow framed the girl where her curled body described a malformed eye in the dune's hollow. And that was where Jilly White's mind had been: on her fifteen-year-old daughter, there in the lee of the dune; and on the muffled, shuffling beachcomber on the far side of the dunes, near the water's edge where the waves frothed and the sand was dark and damp.

All of them were well wrapped against a breeze off the sea that wasn't so much harsh as constant, unremitting. Only endure it long enough, it would cool your ears and start to find a way through your clothes. It was getting like that now; not yet the end of September, but the breeze made it feel a lot later.

"John's carvings?" said Jilly, who was still a little distant despite that she was right there with the others on Doctor (or ex-Doctor) James Jamieson's verandah overlooking the beach. But now, suddenly, she snapped to. "Oh, his *carvings!* The driftwood! Why, yes, of course I've noticed them – and admired them, honestly – John's driftwood carvings. Silly of me, really. I'm sorry, John, but when you said 'pieces' I must have been thinking of something broken. Broken in pieces, you know?"

And Jamieson thought: *She looks rather fragile herself. Not yet broken but certainly brittle . . . as if she might snap quite easily.* And taking some of the attention, the weight off Jilly, he said, "Scrimshaw, eh? How interesting. I'd enjoy to see your work some time."

"Any time at all," Tremain answered. "But, er, while it's a bit rude of me to correct you, er, James, it isn't scrimshaw."

"Oh?" The old man looked taken aback. "It isn't?"

The headmaster opened his mouth to explain, but before he could utter another word his wife, Doreen, cut in with, "Scrimshaw is the art or handicraft of old-time sailors, Doctor." She could be a little stiff with first names. "Well, art of a *sort*, anyway." And tut-tutting – apparently annoyed by the breeze – she paused to brush back some ruffled, dowdy-looking strands of hair from her fore-head before explaining further. "Scrimshaw is the name they've given to those odd designs that they carve on shells and old whalebones and such."

"Ah!" Jamieson exclaimed. "But of course it is!" And glancing at Jilly, now huddling to herself, shivering a little and looking pale, he smiled warmly and said, "So you see, Jilly my dear, you're not alone in mixing things up this afternoon. What with driftwood and scrimshaw and the wind – which is picking up I think, and blowing our brains about – why, it's easy to lose track of things and fall our with the facts. Maybe we should go inside, eh? A glass of cognac will do us the world of good, and I'll treat you to something I've newly discovered: a nice slice of homemade game pie from that bakery in the village. Then I'll be satisfied that I've at least fed and watered you, and warmed your bones, before I let you go off home."

But as his visitors trooped indoors, the ex-Doctor quickly took up his binoculars to scan the beach again. In this off-the beaten-track sort of place, one wouldn't really expect to see a great many people on the shore; none, at this time of year. The beachcomber was still there, however; hunched over and with his head down, he shambled slowly along. And it appeared that Anne, Jilly's bookish, reserved if not exactly retiring daughter, had finally noticed him. What's more, she had stood up and was making her way down the beach toward him.

Jamieson gave a start as Jilly touched his arm. And: "It's all right," she said quietly, (perhaps even confidentially, the doctor thought). "It's nothing you should feel concerned about. Young Geoff and Anne, they're just friends. They went to school together . . . well, for a while anyway. The infants, you know?"

"Oh dear!" Jamieson blinked his slightly rheumy old eyes at her. "I do hope you don't think I was spying on them – I mean, on your daughter. And as for this, er, Geoff?"

"It's all right," she said again, tugging him inside. "It's quite all right. You've probably bumped into him in the village and he may

well have sparked some professional interest in you. That's only
natural, after all. But he's really quite harmless, I assure you . . ."

Eating slowly, perhaps to avoid conversation, Jilly wasn't done with
her food when the Tremains were ready to go. "Anyway," she said,
"I'll have to wait for Anne. She won't be long . . . knows better than
to be out when the light starts failing."

"You don't mind her walking with the village idiot?" John's words
sounded much too harsh; he was probably biting his lip as he turned
his face away and Doreen helped him on with his coat.

"Ignore my husband," Doreen twisted her face into something that
didn't quite equal a smile. "According to him *all* children are idiots. It
seems that's what being a teacher does to you."

Jilly said, "Personally, I prefer to think of the boy as an unfortunate. And of course in a small seaside village he stands out like a sore
thumb. I'm glad he has a . . . a friend in Anne."

And John half relented. "You're right, of course. And maybe I'm in
the wrong profession. But it's much like Doreen says. If you work all
day with kids, especially bolshy teenagers, and in this day and age
when you daren't even frown at the little sods let alone slap their
backsides—"

At the door, Doreen lifted her chin. "I don't recall saying anything
like that. Nothing as rude as that, anyway."

"Oh, you know what I mean!" John said testily, trailing her
outside, and colliding with her where she'd paused on the front
doorstep. Then – in unison but almost as an afterthought – they stuck
their heads back inside to thank Jamieson for his hospitality.

"Not at all," their host answered. "And I'll be dropping in on you
soon, to have a look at those carvings."

"Please do," John told him.

And Doreen added, "Evenings or weekends, you'll be welcome.
We're so glad that you've settled in here, Doctor."

"Oh, call me James, for goodness sake!" Jamieson waved them
goodbye, closed the door, turned to Jilly and raised an enquiring,
bushy grey eyebrow.

She shrugged. "A bit pompous maybe, but they're neighbours.
And it does get lonely out here."

They went to the bay window in the end wall and watched the
Tremains drive off down the road to their home less than a mile
away. Jilly lived half a mile beyond that, and the tiny village – a
huddle of old fishermen's houses, really – stood some four or five
hundred yards farther yet, just out of sight behind the rising, rocky

promontory called South Point. On the far side of the village, a twin promontory, North Point, formed a bay, with the harbour lying sheltered in the bight.

For a moment more Jamieson watched the Tremains' car speed into the distance, then turned a glance of covert admiration on Jilly. She noticed it, however, cocked her head on one side and said, "Oh? Is there something . . .?"

Caught out and feeling just a little uncomfortable now, the old man said, "My dear, I hope you won't mind me saying so, but you're a very attractive woman. And even though I'm a comparative stranger here, a newcomer, I can't say I've come across too many eligible bachelors in the village."

Now Jilly frowned. Her lips began to frame a question – or perhaps a sharp retort, an angry outburst – but he beat her to it:

"I'm sorry, I'm so sorry!" He held up his hands. "It's none of my business, I know. And I keep forgetting that your husband . . . that he—"

"— Died less than eighteen months ago, yes," Jilly said.

The old man sighed. "My bedside manner hasn't improved any with age," he said. "I retired here for what I thought would be solitude – an absence of everything that's gone before – only to find that I can't seem to leave my practice behind me! To my patients I was a healer, a father confessor, a friend, a champion. I didn't realize it would be so hard not to continue being those things."

She shook her pretty head, smiled wanly and said, "James, I don't mind your compliments, your concern, or your curiosity. I find it refreshing that there are still people who . . . who care about anyone. Or anything for that matter!"

"But you frowned."

"Not at what you said," she answered, "but the way you said it. Your accent, really."

"My accent?"

"Very similar to my husband's. He was an American, too, you know."

"No, I didn't know that. And he had a similar accent? A New England accent, you say?" Suddenly there was a new, a different note of concern in Jamieson's voice, unlike the fatherly interest he'd taken in Jilly earlier. "And may I ask where he hailed from, your husband? His home town?"

"George was from Massachusetts, a town on or near the coast – pretty much like this place, I suppose – called, er, Ipswich? Or maybe Arkham or Innsmouth. He would talk about all three, so I can't be certain. And I admit to being a dunce where American geography is concerned. But I'm sure I have his birth certificate somewhere in the house, if you're that interested?

Sitting down, the old man bade Jilly do the same. "Interested?" he said. "Well, perhaps not. Let sleeping dogs lie, eh?"

"Sleeping dogs?" Now she was frowning again.

And he sighed before answering. "Well, I did practice for a few months – *just* a few months – in Innsmouth. A very strange place, Jilly, even for this day and age. But no, you don't want to know about that."

"But now you've got *me* interested," she said. "I mean, what was so strange about the place?"

"Well, if you must know, it was mainly the people – degenerate, inbred, often retarded – in fact much like young Geoff. I have bumped into him, yes, and there's that about the boy . . . there's a certain look to him . . ." But there the old man paused, probably because he'd seen how Jilly's hands fluttered, trembling on the arms of her chair. Seeing where he was looking, she put her hands in her lap, clasping them until her fingers went white. It was obvious that something he had said had disturbed her considerably. And so:

"Let's change the subject," he said, sitting up straighter. "And let me apologise again for being so personal. But a woman like you – still young and attractive, in a place like this – surely you should be looking to the future now, realizing that it's time to go, time to get out of here. Because while you're here there are always going to be memories. But there's an old saying that goes 'out of sight—'"

"'— Out of mind?'" She finished it for him.

"Something like that." He nodded. "A chance to start again, in a place, some town or city, that *does* have its fair share of eligible bachelors . . ." And then he smiled, however wryly. "But there I go, being personal again!"

Jilly didn't return his smile but told him, "I do intend to get away, I have intended it, but there are several things that stop me. For one, it's such a short time since George . . . well, since he . . ."

"I understand." Jamieson nodded. "You haven't yet found the time or the energy to get around to it."

"And two, it's not going to be easy to sell up – not for a decent price, anyway. I mean, look how cheaply you were able to secure this place."

Again the old man nodded. "When people die or move away, no one moves in, right? Well, except for old cheapskates like me."

"And all perfectly understandable," said Jilly. "There's no school in the village, and no work; the fishing has been unproductive for years now, though of late it has seemed to pick up just a little. As for amenities: the nearest supermarket is in St Austell! And when the weather gets bad the old road out of the village is like a death trap; it's always getting potholed or washed out. So there's no real reason why anyone would want to come here. A few holidaymakers, maybe, in the summer season, and the very rare occasion when someone like you might want to retire here. But apart from that . . ."

"Yes?" He prompted her, slyly. "But apart from that? Jilly, almost everything you've said seems to me contradictory. You've given some very excellent reasons why you *shouldn't* stay, and a few pretty bad ones why you *should*. Or haven't I heard them all yet?"

She shrank down into herself a little, and Jamieson saw her hands go back to the arms of her chair, fluttering there like a pair of nervous birds . . .

"It's my daughter," she said after a while. "It's Anne. I think we'll have to stay here a little longer, if only for her sake."

"Oh?"

"Yes. She's . . . she's doing piano with Miss Harding in the village, and twice a week she studies languages at night school in St Austell. She loves it; she's quite a little interpreter, you know, and I feel I have to let her continue."

"Languages, you say?" The old man's eyebrows went up. "Well, she'll find plenty of work as an interpreter – or as a teacher, for that matter."

"Yes, I think so, too!" said Jilly, more energetically now. "It's her future, and she has a very real talent. Why, she even reads sign!"

"I'm sorry?"

"Sign language, as used by the deaf and dumb."

"Oh, yes, of course. But no, er, higher education?"

"She had the grades," said Jilly, protectively. "She would have no trouble getting into university. But what some desire, others put aside. And to be totally honest . . . well, she's not the communal type. She wouldn't be happy away from home."

Again Jamieson's nod of understanding. "A bit of a loner," he said.

"She's a young girl," Jilly quickly replied, "and so was I, once upon a time. And I know that we all go through our phases. She's unsettled enough – I mean, what with her father's death, and all – so any move will just have to wait. And that's that."

Now, having firmly indicated that she no longer desired to talk about her daughter, it was Jilly's turn to change the subject. And in doing so she returned to a previous topic.

"You know," she said, after a moment, "despite that you'll probably think it's a morbid sort of fascination, I can't help being interested in what you were saying about Innsmouth – the way its denizens were, well, strange."

Denizens, Jamieson repeated her, but silently, to himself. *Yes, I suppose you could describe them that way.*

He might have answered her. But a moment earlier, as Jilly had spoken the last few words, so the verandah door had glided open to admit Anne. There she stood framed against the evening, her hair blowing in the unrelenting sea breeze, her huge green eyes gazing enquiringly into the room. But her face was oh-so-pale, and her gaze cold and unsmiling. Maybe she'd been out in the wind too long and the chill had finally got to her.

Sliding the door shut behind her, and going to the fire to warm herself, she said, "What was that you were saying, Mother? Something about strange denizens?"

But Jilly shrugged it off. "Mr Jamieson and I were engaged in a private conversation, dear, and you shouldn't be so nosy."

That was that; Anne's return had called a halt to any more talk. But when Jamieson drew the verandah curtains he couldn't help noticing that hulking, shambling, head-down figure silhouetted against the sand dunes; the shape of Geoff, casting long ugly shadows as he headed back toward the village.

Following which it was time to drive Anne and Jilly home . . .

There was a week of bad weather. James Jamieson would sit in a chair by his sliding patio window and gaze out across the decking of the verandah, across the dunes and beach, at the roaring, rearing ocean. But no matter the driving rain and pounding surf, the roiling sky split by flashes of lightning and shuddering to drum rolls of thunder, sooner or later there would be a hulking figure on the sands: "Young Geoff," as Jilly White had seen fit to call him, the "unfortunate" youth from the village.

Sometimes the boy – or young man, whatever – would be seen shambling along the tidemark; at others he'd walk too close to the turbulent water, and end up sloshing through the foam when waves cast their spume across his route. Jamieson made a point of watching him through his expensive high-resolution binoculars, and now and then he would bring Geoff's face into sharper focus.

The sloping forehead and almost bald head; the wide, fleshy

mouth, bulging eyes and scaly bump of a chin, with the bristles of a stubby beard poking through; the youth's skin – its roughness in general, with those odd folds or wattles – especially the loose flaps between his ears and his collar . . .

One afternoon toward the end of the week, when the weather was calmer, Jamieson also spied John Tremain on the beach. The link road must have washed out again, relieving the headmaster of his duties for a day or so and allowing him time to indulge his hobby. And sure enough as he walked the tidemark, he would stoop now and then to examine this or that piece of old driftwood. But at the same time "the village idiot" was also on the beach, and their paths crossed. Jamieson watched it all unfold in the cross hairs of his binoculars:

Tremain, crouching over a dark patch of seaweed, and Geoff coming over the dunes on a collision course. Then the meeting; the headmaster seeing the youth and jerking upright, lurching backward from the advancing figure and apparently threatening him with the knobby end of a stripped branch! The other coming to an awkward halt, and standing there with his arms and hands flapping uselessly, his flabby mouth opening and closing as if in silent protest.

But was it revulsion, hatred, or stark terror on Tremain's part? Or simply shock? Jamieson couldn't make up his mind. But whichever, it appeared that Tremain's dislike of "bolshy" teenagers went twice for those who weren't so much bolshy as, well, unfortunate.

That, however, was all there was to it; hardly a confrontation as such, and over and done with as quickly as that. Then Tremain scuttling for home, and Geoff standing there, watching him go. The end. But at least it had served to remind Jamieson of his promise to go and see John's driftwood carvings – which was one reason at least why he should pay a return visit . . .

At the weekend Jamieson called the Tremains on the telephone to check that the invitation was still open, and on Sunday evening he drove the solitary mile to his neighbour's place, parking by the side of the road. Since he, the Whites and the Tremains had the only properties on this stretch of potholed road, it wasn't likely that he'd be causing any traffic problems.

"Saw you on the beach the other day," he told John when he was seated and had a drink in his hand. "Beachcomnbing, hey?"

The other nodded. "It seems our talking about it must have sparked me off again. I found one or two rather nice pieces."

"You certainly have an eye for it," the old man commented, his flattery very deliberate. "Why, I can see you have several 'nice pieces' – expertly finished pieces, that is – right here. But if you'll forgive my saying so, it seems to me these aren't so much carvings as wind-, sea-, and sand-sculptures really . . . which you have somehow managed to revitalize with sandpaper and varnish, imagination and infinite skill. So much so that you've returned them to a new, dramatic life of their own!"

"Really?" Tremain was taken aback; he didn't see Jamieson's flattery for what it really was, as a means to an end, a way to ingratiate himself into the Tremains' confidence. For Jamieson found himself in such a close-knit microcosm of isolated community society that he felt sure the headmaster and his wife would have knowledge of almost everything that had gone on here; they would have the answers to questions he couldn't possibly put to Jilly, not in her condition.

For the old man suspected – indeed, he more than suspected – that Jilly White's circumstances had brought her to the verge of nervous exhaustion. But what exactly were her circumstances? As yet there were loose ends here, which Jamieson must at least attempt to tie up before making any firm decision or taking any definite course of action.

Which was why the ex-Doctor was here at the Tremains' this evening. They were after all his and Jilly's closest neighbours, and closest in status, too. Whereas the people of the village – while they might well be the salt of the earth – were of a very different order indeed. And close-mouthed? Oh, he'd get nothing out of them.

And so back to the driftwood:

"Yes, really," the old man finally answered John Tremain's pleased if surprised inquiry. "I mean, this table we're sitting at, drinking from: a table of driftwood – but see how the grain stands out, the fine polish!" In fact the table was quite ugly. Jamieson pointed across the room. "And who could fail to admire your plant stand there, so black it looks lacquered."

"Yacht varnish," Tremain was all puffed up now. "As for why it's so black, it's ebony."

"*Diospyros*," said Doreen Tremain, entering from the kitchen with a tray of food. "A very heavy wood, and tropical. Goodness only knows how long it was in the sea, to finally get washed up here."

"Amazing!" Jamieson declared. "And not just the stand. Your knowledge of woods – and indeed of most things, as I've noted – does both of you great credit."

And now she preened and fussed no less than her husband. "I do so hope you like turbot, er, James?"

"*Psetta maxima,*" said Jamieson, not to be outdone. "If it's fish, dear lady, then you need have no fear. I'm not the one to turn my nose up at a good piece of fish."

"I got it from Tom Foster in the village," she answered. "I like his fish, if not his company." And she wrinkled her nose.

"Tom Foster?" Jamieson repeated her, shaking his head. "No, I don't think I know him."

"And you don't want to," said John, helping the old man up, and showing him to the dining table. "Tom might be a good fisherman, but that's all he's good for. Him and his Gypsy wife."

Sitting down, Jamieson blinked his rheumy eyes at the other and enquired, "His Gypsy wife?"

"She's not a Gypsy," Doreen shook her head. "No, not Romany at all, despite her looks. It seems her great grandmother was a Polynesian woman. Oh, there are plenty such throwbacks in Devon and Cornwall, descendants of women brought back from the Indies and South Pacific when the old sailing ships plied their trade. Anyway, the Fosters are the ones who have charge of that young Geoff person. But there again, I suppose we should be thankful that someone is taking care of him."

"*Huh!*" John Tremain grunted. "Surely his mother is the one who should be taking care of him. Or better far his father . . . except we all know that's no longer possible."

"And never would have been," Doreen added. "Well, not without all sorts of complications, accusations, and difficulties in general."

Watching the fish being served, Jamieson said, "I'm afraid you've quite lost me. Do you think you could . . . I mean, would you mind explaining?"

The Tremains looked at each other, then at the old man.

"Oh?" he said. "Do I sense some dark secret here, one from which I'm excluded? But that's okay – if I don't need to know, then I don't need to know. After all, I am new around here."

"No," said Doreen, "it's not that. It's just that—"

"It's sort of delicate," her husband said. "Or not exactly delicate, not any longer, but not the kind of thing people like to talk about. Especially when it's your neighbour, or your ex-neighbour, who is concerned."

"My *ex*-neighbour?" Jamieson frowned. "George White? He was your neighbour, yes, but never mine. So, what's the mystery?"

"You've not 'sensed anything?" This was Doreen again. "With

poor Jilly? You've not wondered why she and Anne always seem to be sticking up for—"

"For that damned idiot in the village?" John saw his opportunity to jump in and finish it for her.

And the old man slowly nodded. "I think I begin to see," he said. "There's some connection between George White, Jilly and Anne, and—"

"And Geoff, yes," said Doreen. "But do you think we should finish eating first? I see no reason why we can't tell you all about it. You are or were a doctor, after all – and we're sure you've heard of similar or worse cases – but I'd hate the food to spoil."

And so they ate in relative silence. Doreen Tremain's cooking couldn't be faulted, and her choice of white wine was of a similar high quality . . .

"It was fifteen, sixteen years ago," John Tremain began, "and we were relative newcomers here, just as you are now. In those days this was a prosperous little place; the fish were plentiful and the village booming; in the summer there were people on the beaches and in the shops. Nowadays – there's only the post office, the pub, and the bakery. The post office doubles as a general store and does most of the business, and you can still buy a few fresh fish on the quayside before what's left gets shipped inland. And that's about it right now. But back then:

"They were even building a few new homes here, extending the village, as it were. This house and yours, they were the result. That's why they're newish places. But the road got no further than your place and hasn't been repaired to any great extent since. Jilly and George's place was maybe twenty years older; standing closer to the village, it wasn't as isolated. As for the other houses they'd planned to build on this road, they just didn't happen. Prices of raw materials were rocketing, the summers weren't much good any more, and fish stocks had begun a rapid decline.

"The Whites had been here for a year or two. They had met and married in Newquay, and moved here for the same reason we did: the housing was cheaper than in the towns. George didn't seem to have a job. He'd inherited some fabulous art items in gold and was gradually selling them off to a dealer in Truro. And Jilly was doing some freelance editing for local publishers."

Now Doreen took over. "As for George's gold: it was jewellery, and quite remarkable. I had a brooch off him that I wear now and then. It's unique, I think. Beautiful but very strange. Perhaps you'd like to see it?"

"Certainly," said the old man. "Indeed I would." While she went to fetch it, John continued the story.

"Anyway, Jilly was heavy with Anne at the time, but George wasn't a home body. They had a car – the same wreck she's got now, more off the road than on it – which he used to get into St Austell, Truro, Newquay, and goodness knows where else. He would be away for two or three days at a time, often for whole weekends. Which wasn't fair on Jilly who was very close to her time. But look, let me cut a long story short.

"Apparently George had been a bit of a louse for quite some time. In fact as soon as Jilly had declared her pregnancy, that was when he'd commenced his . . . well, his—

"– Womanizing?" The old man sat up straighter in his chair. "Are you saying he was something of a rake?"

By now Doreen had returned with a small jewellery box. "Oh, George White was much more than *something* of a rake," she said. "He was a great deal of a rake, in fact a roué! And all through poor Jilly's pregnancy he'd been, you know, doing it in most of the towns around."

"Really?" said Jamieson. "But you can't know that for sure, now can you?"

"Ah, but we can," said John, "for he was seen! Some of the locals had seen him going into . . . well, 'houses of ill repute', shall we put it that way? And a handful of the village's single men, whose morals also weren't all they might be, learned about George's reputation in those same, er, houses. But you'll know, James – and I'm sure that in your capacity as a doctor you *will* know – it's a sad but true fact that you do actually reap what you sow. And in George White's case, that was true in more ways than one."

"Which is where this becomes even more indelicate," Doreen got to her feet. "And I have things to do in the kitchen. So if you'll excuse me . . ." And leaving her jewellery box on the table she left the room and closed the door behind her. Then:

"George caught something," said John, quietly.

"He what?"

"Well, that's the only way I can explain it. He caught this bloody awful disease, presumably from some woman with whom he'd er, associated. But that wasn't all."

"There's more?" Jamieson shook his head. "Poor Jilly."

"Poor Jilly, indeed! For little Anne was only a few months old when this slut from Newquay arrived in the village with her loathsome child – a baby she blamed on George White."

"Ah!" Jamieson nodded knowingly. "And the child was Geoff, right?"

"Of course. That same cretin, adopted by the Fosters, who shambles around the village even now. A retarded youth of some fifteen years – but who looks like and has the strength of an eighteen-year-old – who in fact is George White's illegitimate son and young Anne's half-brother. And because I'm quite fond of Jilly, I find that . . . that *creature* perfectly unbearable!"

"Not to mention dangerous," said Jamieson.

"Eh? What's that?" The other looked startled.

"I was out on my verandah," said the old man. "It was just the other day, and I saw you with . . . with that young man. You seemed to be engaged in some sort of confrontation."

"But that's it exactly!" said Tremain. "He's suddenly there – he comes upon you, out of nowhere – and God only knows what goes on in that misshapen head of his. Enough to scare the life out of a man, coming over the dunes like that, and blowing like a stranded fish! A damn great fish, yes, that's what he reminds me of. *Ugh!* And it's how Tom Foster uses him, too!"

"What? Foster uses him?" Jamieson seemed totally engrossed. "In what way? Are we talking about physical abuse?"

"No, no, nothing that bad!" Tremain held up his hands. "No, but have you seen that retard swim? My God, if he had more than half a brain he'd be training for the Olympics! What? Why, he's like a porpoise in the water! *That's* how Foster uses him."

"I'm afraid I'm still not with you," Jamieson admitted, his expression one of complete bafflement. "You're saying that this Foster somehow uses the boy to catch fish?"

"Yes." The other nodded. "And if the weather hadn't been so bad recently you wouldn't have seen nearly so much of the idiot on the beach. No, for he'd have been out with Tom Foster in his boat. The lad swims – in all weathers, apparently – to bring in the fish for that degenerate who looks after him."

Jamieson laughed out loud, then stopped abruptly and asked, "But . . . do you actually believe that? That a man can herd fish? I mean, that's quite incredible!"

"Oh?" Tremain answered. "You think so? Then don't just take my word for it but the next time you're in town go have a drink in the Sailor's Rest. Get talking with any of the local fishermen and ask them how come Foster always gets the best catches."

"But herding fish—" the old man began to protest.

And Tremain cut him off: "Now, I didn't say that. I said he brings them in – somehow attracts them." Then he offered a weak grin. "Yes, I'm well aware that sounds almost as silly. But –" He pursed his lips, shrugged and fell silent.

"So," said Jamieson. "Some truths, some rumours. But as far as I'm concerned, I still don't know it all. For instance, what was this awful disease you say George White contracted? What do you mean by 'awful'? All venereal diseases are pretty awful."

"Well, I suppose they are," Tremain answered. "But not like this one. There's awful and awful, but this was hideous. And he passed it down to his idiot child, too."

"He did what?"

"The way 'young Geoff' looks now, that was how George White looked in the months before he—"

"Died?"

"No." The other shook his head, grimly. "It's not as simple as that. George didn't just die, he took his own life."

"Ah!" said the old man. "So it was suicide."

Tremain nodded. "And I know this is a dreadful thing to say, but with a man like that – with his sexual appetites – surely it's just as well. A disease like that . . . why, he was a walking time bomb!"

"My goodness!" Jamieson exclaimed. "Was it never diagnosed? Can we put a name to it? Who was his doctor?"

"He wouldn't see a doctor. The more Jilly pressed him to do so, the more he retreated into himself. And only she could tell you what life must have been like with him, during his last few weeks. But since she'd already stuck it out for fifteen or more years, watching it gradually come out in him during all of that time . . . God, how strong she must have been!"

"Terrible, terrible!" said Jamieson – and then he frowned. "Yet Jilly and *her* child, I mean Anne – apparently they didn't come down with anything."

"No, and we can thank God for that!" said Tremain. "I think we'll have to assume that as soon as Jilly knew how sick George was, she – or they – stopped . . . well, you know what I mean."

"Yes." Jamieson nodded. "I do know: they were man and wife in name only. But if both Anne and Geoff were born within a few months of each other – and if young Geoff was, well, *defective* from birth – then Anne is a very fortunate young woman indeed."

"Exactly," said Tremain. "And is it any wonder her mother's nerves are so bad? My wife and I, we've known the Whites a lot longer than you, James, and I can assure you that there's never been a woman more watchful of her child than Jilly is of Anne."

"Watchful?"

Doreen had come back in, and she said, "Oh, yes. That girl, she can't cough or catch a cold, or even develop a pimple without having her mother fussing all over her. Why, Anne's skin is flawless, but if you should see them on the beach together next summer – and if Anne's skin gets a little red or rough from the sun and the sand – you watch Jilly's reaction."

And Tremain concurred. "It's a wonder Jilly so much as lets that kid out of the house . . ."

The subject changed; the conversation moved on; half an hour or so later Jamieson looked at his watch. "Almost time I was on my way," he said. "There are some programmes I want to watch on TV tonight." He turned to Doreen. "Before I go, however, you might like to show me that brooch of yours. You were, er, busy in the kitchen for a while when we were talking and I didn't much like to open the box in your absence."

"Yes," she said. "It was very thoughtful of you to wait for me." She opened the small velvet-lined box and passed it across to him. The brooch was pinned to a pad in the bottom of the box and the old man let it lie there, simply turning the box in his hand and looking at the brooch from all angles.

"You're absolutely right." He nodded after a moment or two. "Without a doubt it has a certain beauty, but it's also a very odd piece. And it's not the first time I've seen gold worked in this style. But you know . . ." Here he paused and frowned, apparently uncertain how best to continue.

"Oh?" she said. "Is something wrong?"

"Well—" he began to answer, then paused again and bit his lip. "Well, it's just that . . . I don't know. Perhaps I shouldn't mention it."

Doreen took back the box and brooch, and said, "But now you really *must* mention it! You have to! Do you think there's something wrong with the brooch? But then, what could be wrong with it? Some kind of fake, maybe? Poor quality gold? Or not gold at all!" Her voice was more strident, more high-pitched, moment by moment. "Is that it, James? Have I been cheated?"

"At the price, whatever it was you paid? Probably not. It's the meaning of the thing. It's what it stands for. Doreen, this isn't a lucky item."

"It's unlucky? In what way?"

"Well, anthropology was a hobby of mine no less than driftwood

art is your husband's. And as for the odd style and native workmanship we see here . . . I believe you'll find this brooch is from the
South Seas, where it was probably crafted by a tribal witchdoctor."

"What? A witchdoctor?" Doreen's hand went to her throat.

"Oh, yes." Jamieson nodded. "And having fashioned it from an
alloy of local gold and some other lustrous metal, the idea would
have been to lay a curse upon it, then to ensure it fell into the hands of
an enemy. A kind of sympathetic magic – or in the poor victim's case,
quite *un*sympathetic."

Now Doreen took the box back, and staring hard at its contents
said, "To be honest, I've never much liked this thing. I only bought it
out of some misguided sense of loyalty to Jilly, so that I could tell
myself that at least some money was finding its way into that
household. What with George's philandering and all, they couldn't
have been very well off."

Her husband took the box off her, peered at the brooch for a few
moments, and said, "I think you must be right, James. It isn't a very
pleasant sort of thing at all. It's quite unearthly, really. These weird
arabesques, not of any terrestrial foliage but more of . . . what?
Interwoven seaweeds, kelp, suckered tentacles? And these scalloped
edges you see in certain shells. I mean, it's undeniably striking in its
looks – well, until you look closer. And then, why, you're absolutely
right! It's somehow crude, as if crafted by some primitive islander."

He handed the box back to his wife who said, "I'll sell it at once! I
believe I know the jewellers where George White got rid of those
other pieces." And glancing at the old man: "It's not that I'm
superstitious, you understand, but better not to risk it. You never
know where this thing's been."

"Dear lady, you're so right," Jamieson said. "But myself, having
an interest in this sort of thing – and being a doctor of an entirely
different stamp – I find the piece fascinating. So if you do decide to
sell it, don't take it to a dealer but offer it to me first. And whatever
you paid for it, I think we can safely say you won't be the worse off."

"Why, that's so very kind of you!" she said, seeing him to the door.
"But are you sure?"

"Absolutely," the old man answered. "Give me a ring in the
morning when you've had time to think it over, and let me know
what I owe you."

With which the Tremains walked him to his car . . .

The winter came in quickly and savagely, keeping almost everyone in
the village to their houses. With the fishermen's boats sheltering

within the harbour wall, only the old Sailor's Rest was doing anything like good business.

Driving his car to work at the college in St Austell over frequently
washed-out and ever potholed roads, headmaster John Tremain
cursed the day he'd bought his place (a) for its cheapness and (b)
for its "seclusion and wild dramatic beauty". The seclusion was fine
and dandy but he could do without the wildness of winters like this
one, and of drama he'd had more than enough. Come spring and the
first half-decent offer he got, he and Doreen would be out of here for
a more convenient place in St Austell. It would be more expensive,
but what the hell . . . he'd sell the car, cycle to work, and save money
on petrol and repairs.

As for the Whites: Jilly and Anne were more or less housebound,
but they did have a regular visitor in the old American gentleman.
James Jamieson had seemed to take to them almost as family, and
never turned up on their doorstep without bringing some gift or
other with him. Often as not it was food: a fresh pie from the bakery,
a loaf of bread and slab of cheese, maybe a bottle of good wine. All to
the good, for Jilly's old car was well past reliable, and Anne had to
attend her piano and language lessons. Jamieson would drive the girl
to and fro without complaint, and wouldn't accept a penny for all his
kindness.

Also, when Anne went down with a sore throat, which served to
drive her mother frantic with worry, Jamieson gave the girl a
thorough examination and diagnosed a mild case of laryngitis.
His remedy – one aspirin three times daily, and between times a
good gargle with a spoonful of salt in water – worked wonders, for
mother and daughter both! But his ministrations didn't stop there.
For having now seen Jilly on several occasions when her nervous
condition was at its worst, the old man had in fact prescribed for her,
too; though not without protesting that in fact he shouldn't for he'd
retired from all that. Nevertheless, the pills he made up for her did the
trick, calming her nerves like nothing she'd tried before. They
couldn't entirely relieve her obsession or anxieties with regard to
Anne, however, though now when she felt compelled to fuss and fret
her hands wouldn't shake so badly, and her at best fluffy mind would
stay focussed for longer. Moreover, now that certain repetitive
nightmares of long-standing no longer visited her quite so frequently,
Jilly was pleased to declare that she was sleeping better . . .

Occasionally, when the weather was a little kinder, Anne would walk
to her piano lesson at Miss Harding's thatched cottage on the far side

of the village. Jilly would usually accompany her daughter part way, and use the occasion to visit the bakery or collect groceries at the post office. The winter being a hard one, such times were rare; more often than not, James Jamieson would arrive in his car in time to give Anne a lift. It got so that Jilly even expected him, and Anne – normally so retiring – had come to regard him as some kind of father or grand-father figure.

One day in mid-January, when the wind drove the waves high up the beach, and stinging hail came sleeting almost horizontally off the sea, the old man and his young passenger arrived at Miss Harding's place to find an agitated Tom Foster waiting for them – in fact waiting for Jamieson.

The old man had bumped into Foster once or twice before in the Sailor's Rest, and had found him a surely, bearded, weather-beaten brute with a gravelly voice and a habit of slamming his empty mug on the bar by way of catching the barman's attention and ordering another drink. He had few friends among the other fishermen and was as much a loner as any man Jamieson had ever known. Yet now, today, he was in need of a friend – or rather, in need of a doctor.

The village spinster, Miss Julia Harding, had kept Foster waiting in the small conservatory that fronted her cottage; he wasn't the sort of person she would allow in the house proper. But Foster, still shaking rain from his lank hair, and pacing to and fro – a few paces each way, which was all the conservatory allowed – pounced on Jamieson as soon as the old man was ushered into view by Miss Harding.

"It's the boy," he rasped, grabbing Jamieson's arm. "Can't get no sleep, the way um itches. I know'd you'd be comin' with the lass fer the teachin', and so I waited. But I do wish you'd come see the boy. I'd consider it a real favour, and Tom Foster dun't forget um that does um a favour. But it's more fer young Geoff'n fer me. Um's skin be raw from scatchin', so it be. And I got no car fer gettin' um inter the city . . . beside which, um dun't want no big city doctor. But um won't fuss any with you, if you'll come see um."

"I don't any longer practise . . ." The old man appeared at a loss what to do or say.

But Anne took his other arm. "Please go," she said. "Oh do *please* go and see Geoff! And I'll go with you."

Miss Harding wagged her finger at Anne, and said, "Oh? And what of your lesson, young lady?" But then, looking for support from Tom Foster and Jamieson, and seeing none, she immediately shook her head in self denial. "No, no – whatever was I thinking? If something ails that poor lad, it's surely more important than a piano lesson. It must be, for Mr Foster here, well, he's hardly one to get himself all stirred up on a mere whim – nor for anything much else, except maybe his fishing – and not even that on a bad day!"

"That I'm not," growled Foster, either ignoring or failing to recognize the spinster's jibe for what it really was. And to Jamieson: "Will you come?"

"Well," the old man sighed, "I don't suppose it can do any harm to see the boy, and I always carry my old medicine bag in the back of the car . . . not that there's a lot of medicine in it these days. But –" He threw up his hands, took Anne and Foster back out to his car, and drove them to the latter's house where it stood facing the sea across the harbour wall in Fore Street.

Tom Foster's wife, a small, black-haired, dark-complexioned woman, but not nearly as gnarled or surly as her husband, wiped her hands on her apron to clasp Jamieson's hand as she let them into the house. She said nothing but simply indicated a bedroom door where it stood ajar.

Geoff was inside, a bulky shape under a coarse blanket, and the room bore the unmistakable odour of fish – but then, so did the entire house. Wrinkling his nose, Jamieson glanced at Anne, but she didn't seem to have noticed the fish stink; all she was interested in was Geoff's welfare. As she approached the bed so its occupant seemed to sense her presence; the youth's bulbous, ugly head came out from under the blanket, and he stared at her with luminous green eyes. But:

"No, no, lass!" Tom Foster grunted. "I knows you be friends but you can't be in 'ere. Um's naked under that blanket, and um ain't nice ter look at what wi' um's scratchin' and all. So out you goes and Ma Foster'll see ter you in the front." And coarse brute of a man that he was, he gentled her out of the room.

As Foster closed the door behind her, so Jamieson drew up a chair close to the bed, and said, "Now then, young man, try not to be alarmed. I'm here to see what the trouble is." With which he began to turn back the blanket. A squat hand, short-fingered and thickly webbed, at once grasped the top edge of the blanket and held it fast. The old man saw blood under the sharp fingernails, the trembling of the unfortunate's entire body under the blanket, and the terror in his huge, moist, oh-so-deep eyes.

Foster immediately stepped forward. "Now, dun't you take on so, lad," he said. "This un's a doctor, um be. A friend ter the lass and 'er Ma. If you let um, um'll see ter your scratchin'."

The thing called Geoff (for close up he was scarcely human) opened his mouth and Jamieson saw his teeth, small but as sharp as needles. There was no threat in it, however – just a popping of those pouty lips, a soundless pleading almost – as the hand slowly relaxed its grip, allowing the old man to turn back the cover without further hindrance.

Despite that Foster was hovering over the old man, watching him closely, he saw no evidence of shock at what was uncovered: that scaly body – which even five years ago a specialist in St Austell had called the worst case of ichthyosis he'd ever seen, now twice as bad at least – that body under a heavily wattled neck and sloping but powerful shoulders, and the raw, red areas on the forearms and under the ribcage where the rough grey skin had been torn. And as the old man opened his bag and called for hot water and a clean towel, Foster nodded his satisfaction. He had done the right thing sure enough, and Jamieson was a doctor good and true who would care for a life even if it were such as this one under the blanket.

But as Foster turned away to answer Jamieson's request, the old man took his arm and said, "Tom, do you care for him?"

"Eh?" Foster grunted. "Why, me and my old girl, we've cared fer um fer fifteen years! And in fifteen years you can get used ter things, even them things that never gets no better but only worse. And as fer folks – even poorly made 'uns such as the boy – why, in time you can even get fond of 'em, so you can!"

Jamieson nodded and said, "Then look after him better." And he let Foster go . . .

Anne saw the wet, pink-splotched towels when Mrs Foster brought them out of Geoff's room. And then Tom Foster allowed her in.

The old man was putting his things back into his bag as she hurried to the bedside. There was a clean white sheet under the blanket now, and it was tucked up under Geoff's blob of a chin. The youth's neck was bandaged to hold a dressing under his left ear; his right arm lay on top of the blanket, the forearm bandaged where a red stain was evidence of some small seepage.

"What was it?" Anne snatched a breath, touching her hand to her lips and staring at Jamieson wide-eyed, her face drawn and pale, even paler than usual. "Oh, what was it?"

"A skin disorder," he told her. "Something parasitic – like lice or scabies – but I think I got all of it. No need to worry about it, however. It must have been uncomfortable for him, but it certainly wasn't deadly. Geoff will recover, I assure you."

And Tom Foster said, "Anythin' I can do fer you, Mr Jamieson, sir, jus' you ask. I dun't forget um who's done me or mine a favour – no, not never."

"Well, Tom," Jamieson answered, "I might come to you for a nice piece of fish some time, and that would be payment enough for what little I've done here. Right now, though, we've other things to talk about." He turned to the girl. "Anne, if you'll wait in the car?"

Anne had sat down in the chair by the bed. She was holding Geoff's hand and they were looking at each other, and Jamieson couldn't help noticing a striking similarity in the deep green colour of their eyes . . . but *only* in their colour. It was true that Anne's eyes were slightly, almost unnoticeably protruberant, but as for the other's . . .

. . . In his current physical condition, and despite that his eyes were huge and bulging, even more so than was usual, still the old man had to grant them the dubious distinction of being Geoff's most human feature!

And now the youth had taken his hand from the girl's, and his stubby fingers were moving rapidly, urgently, making signs which she appeared to understand and began answering in a like fashion. This "conversation" lasted only a moment or so longer, until Geoff turned his watery gaze on Jamieson and twisted his face into what had to be his version of a smile. At which Anne said:

"He says I'm to thank you for him. So thank you." Then she stood up and left the room and the house . . .

Inside the front door, Jamieson spoke to Tom Foster in lowered tones. "Do you know what I dug out and scraped off him?"

"How'd I know that?" the other protested. "You be the doctor."

"Oh?" said the old man. "And you be the fisherman, but you tell me you've never seen such as that before? Very well, then I'll tell you: they were fish-lice, Tom. Copepods, small crustaceans that live on fish as parasites. Now then, Mr Fisherman – tell me you've never seen fish-lice before."

The other looked away, then slowly nodded. "I've seen 'em, sure enough. Usually on plaice or flounder, flatties or bottom-feeders. But on a man? In the flesh of a man?" And now he shook his head. "I jus' din't want ter believe it, that's all."

"Well, now you can believe it," said Jamieson. "And the only way he could have got them was by frequent periods of immersion in the sea. They got under his skin where it's especially scaly and fed there like ticks on a dog. They were dug in quite deep, so I know he's had them for a long time."

"Oh? And are you sayin' I ain't looked after um, then?" Tom was angry now. "Well, I'm tellin' you as how I din't see 'em on um afore! And anyways, you answer me this – if um's had 'em so long, why'd they wait ter flare up now, eh?"

The old man nodded. "Oh, I think I can tell you that, Tom. It's because his skin was all dried out. And because they need it damp, they started digging in for the moisture in his blood. So all of a sudden the boy was itching and hurting. And when he scratched, the hurt only got worse. That's what happened here. So now then, you can tell me something: when were you last out at sea, Tom? *Not recently*, I'll wager!"

"Ah-*hah!*" The other narrowed his eyes, thrust his chin out. "So then, Mr Jamieson. You've been alistenin' ter rumours, eh? And what did them waggin' village tongues tell you . . . that Tom Foster makes um's poor dumb freak swim fer um? And that um gets um ter chase up the fish fer um? *Hah!*" He shook his head. "Well it ain't so! That 'un swims 'cos um *likes* ter swim, and 'cos um *wants* ter swim – and in all weathers if I dun't be watchin' um! That's all there be ter such tall stories. But if you be askin' does um know where the best fish can be found? Then you're damn right um do, and that's why I gets the best catch – always! So then, what else can I tell you?"

"Nothing, Tom," said Jamieson. "But there is something you can do for that youth. If he wants to swim, let him – you don't need to let the village see it. And if he gets . . . well, infested again, you saw me working and know what to do. But whatever you do, you mustn't let him dry out like that again. No, for it seems to me his skin needs that salt water . . ."

It had stopped hailing, and protected by the building Anne was waiting just outside the door. Since the door had been standing ajar, she must have heard the old man's and Foster's conversation. But she said nothing until they were in the car. Then:

"He had fish-lice?" It wasn't a shocked exclamation, just a simple enquiry.

And starting up the car Jamieson answered, "Oh, people are prone to all kinds of strange infections and infestations. I've heard it said that AIDS – a disease caused by immune deficiency – came from monkeys; and there's that terrible CJD that you can get from eating contaminated or incorrectly processed beef. And how about psittacosis? From parrots, of all things! As for that poor boy: well, what can I say? He likes to swim."

"It's very strange," she said, as Jamieson drove out of the village, "but my father . . . he didn't like the sea. Not at all. He had those books about it – about the sea and other things – and yet was afraid of it. He used to say it lured him. They say he killed himself, suicide, and perhaps he did; but at least he did it his way. I remember he once said to me, 'If a time comes when I must go, it won't take me alive.' Toward the end he used to say all sorts of things that didn't make a lot of sense, but I think he was talking about the sea."

"And what makes you think that?" Jamieson asked her, glancing at her out of the corner of his eye, and aware that she was watching him, probably to gauge his reaction.

"Well, because of the way he did it . . . jumped off the cliff at South Point, down onto the rocks. He washed up on the beach, all broken up."

"How awful!" The old man swung the car onto the lonely road to Jilly White's house. "And yet you and your mother, you continue to live right here, almost on the beach itself."

"I think that's because she needs to be sure about certain things," the girl answered. "Needs to be sure of me, perhaps?"

Jamieson saw Jilly standing on the doorstep and stopped the car outside the house. He would have liked to carry on talking, to have the girl clarify her last cryptic remark, or learn more about the books she'd mentioned – her father's books, about the sea. But Jilly was already coming forward. And now Anne touched the old man's arm and said, "It's best she doesn't know we were at the Fosters'. If she knew about Geoff's fish-lice, it might only set her off again."

Then, lifting her voice a little as she got out of the car, she said, "Thank's again for the ride." And in a whisper added, "And for what you did for Geoff . . ."

The winter dragged on. Jamieson spent some of the time driving, visiting the local towns, even going as far afield as Falmouth and Penzance. And to break the boredom a little, usually there would be a weekly "social evening" alternating between Jilly's, the Tremains', and Jamieson's place. The old man even managed to inveigle Jilly into joining him and the Tremains in a visit to the dilapidated Sailor's Rest one night.

On that occasion Anne went with them. She was under age for drinking – even for being in the pub – but the proprietor knew her, of course, and served her orange juice; and in any case it wasn't as if the place was about to be raided.

Their table was close to a great open fireplace where logs popped and hissed, and the pub being mainly empty, the service couldn't be faulted. In an atmosphere that was quietly mellow, the country food bought fresh from the village bakery was very good. Even Jilly appeared clear-headed and in good spirits for once, and as for the Tremains: putting their customary, frequently unwarranted snobbery aside, they were on their very best behaviour.

That was the up-side, but the down-side was on its way. It came as the evening drew to a close in the forms of the fisherman Tom Foster, and that of his ward the shambling Geoff, when the pair came in from the cold and took gloomy corner seats at a small table. It was doubtful that they had noticed the party seated near the fire on the far side of the room, but Foster's narrowed eyes had certainly scanned the bar area before he ushered his ward and companion to their more discreet seats.

And as suddenly as that the evening turned sour. "Checking that his enemies aren't in," said Tremain under his breath. "I can understand that. He's probably afraid they'll report him."

"His enemies?" said Jamieson. "The other village fishermen, you mean? Report him for what?"

"See for yourself," said the other, indicating the barman, who was on his way to Foster's corner with a tray. "A pint for Tom, and a half for that . . . for young Geoff. He lets that boy drink here – alcohol, mind – and him no older than Anne here. I mean, it's one thing to have that . . . well, that poor unfortunate in the village, but quite another to deliberately addle what few brains he's got with strong drink!"

Anne, visibly stiffening in her chair, at once spoke up in the youth's defence. "Geoff isn't stupid," she said. "He can't speak very well, and he's different, but he isn't stupid." And, staring pointedly at Tremain, "He isn't ignorant, either."

The headmaster's mouth fell open. "Well, I . . .!" But before he could say more:

"John, you asked for that," Doreen told him. "You're aware that Anne is that youth's friend. Why, she's probably the only friend he's got! You should mind what you say."

"But I . . ." Tremain began to protest, only to have Jamieson step in with:

"Oh, come, come! Let's not ruin the pleasant evening we're having. Surely our opinions can differ without that we have to fight over them? If Tom Foster does wrong, then he does wrong. But I say let that youth have whatever pleasures he can find."

"And I agree," said Doreen, glowering at her husband. "God only knows he'll find few enough!"

With which they fell silent, and that was that. Things had been said that couldn't be retracted, and as for the evening's cosy atmosphere and light-hearted conversation: suddenly everything had fallen flat. They tried to hang on to it but were too late. John Tremain took on a haughty, defensive attitude, while his wife turned cold and distant. Jilly retreated quietly into herself again, and young Anne's presence continued to register only by virtue of her physically being there – but as for her thoughts, they could be anywhere . . .

After that, such get-togethers were few and far between. Their friendship – the fact that the Tremains, Whites, and Jamieson stuck together at all – continued on a far less intimate level, surviving mainly out of necessity; being of the village's self-appointed upper crust, they couldn't bring themselves to mingle too freely with those on the lower rungs of the social ladder.

The old man was the odd man out – or rather the pig in the middle; while he maintained contact with the Tremains, Jamieson never failed to assist Jilly and Anne White whenever the opportunity presented itself. Moreover, he visited the Sailor's Rest from time to time, building at least tentative friendships with several of the normally taciturn locals. The Tremains reckoned him either a fool or a saint, while the Whites – both of them – saw him as a godsend.

One evening in early March Jilly called the old man, ostensibly to tell him she was running low on medication, the pills which he'd prescribed and made up for her. But Jamieson sensed there was more than that to her call. The woman's voice hinted of loneliness, and the old man's intuition was that she wanted someone to talk to . . . or someone to talk to her.

He at once drove to her house.

Waiting for his knock, Jilly made him welcome with a glass of sherry. And after he had handed over a month's supply of her pills, and she had offered him a chair, she said, "I feel such an idiot calling you so late when I've had all day to remember my medication was getting low. I hope you don't mind?"

"Not at all, my dear," the old man answered. "If anything, I'm just a little concerned that you may be taking too many of those things. I mean, by my calculations you should still have a fortnight's supply at least. Of course, I could be wrong. My memory's not as keen as it used to be. But . . .?"

Oh!" she said. And then, quickly recovering: "Ah! No – not at all – your memory's fine. I'm the one at fault. For like a fool I . . . well, I *spilled* some pills the other day, and didn't like to use them after they'd been on the floor."

"Very sensible, too!" he answered. "And anyway, I've let it go too long without asking you how you've been feeling. But you see, Jilly, I'm not getting any younger, and what used to be my bedside manner is all shot to pieces. I certainly wouldn't like to think those pills of mine were doing you any harm."

"Doing me harm? On the contrary," she replied. "I think I'm feeling better. I'm calmer – perhaps a little easier in my mind – but . . . Well, just a moment ago, James, you were complaining about your memory. *Huh!* I should be so lucky! No, I don't think it's your pills – though it could be a side effect – but I do seem to stumble a lot. And I don't just mean in my speech or my memory, but also physically. My balance is off, and I sometimes feel quite weak. You may have noticed?"

"Side effects, yes." He nodded. "You could be right. But in a remote place like this it's easy to get all vague and forgetful. I mean, who do you talk to? You see me occasionally – and of course there's Anne – but that's about it." He looked around the room, frowning. "Talking about Anne, where is she?"

"Sleeping." Jilly held a finger to her lips. "What with the weather improving and all, she's been doing a lot of walking on the beach. Walking and reading, and so intelligent! Haven't you ever wondered why she isn't at school? They had nothing more to teach her, that's why. She left school early, shortly after her father . . . after George . . . after he . . ." She paused, touched her hand to her brow, looked suddenly vague.

"Yes, I understand," said the old man, and waited.

In another moment Jilly blinked; and shaking her head as if to clear it, she said, "I'm sorry, what were you saying?"

"I was just wondering if there was anything else I could do for you," Jamieson answered. "Apart from delivering your pills, that is. Did you want to talk, perhaps? For after all, we could all of us use a little company, some friendly conversation from time to time."

"Talk?" she said – and then the cloud lifted from her brow. "Ah, *talk!* Now I remember! It was something you were telling me one time, but we were somehow interrupted. I think it was Anne. Yes, she came on the scene just as you were going to talk about . . . about . . .

wasn't it that coastal town in America, the place that George came from, that you were telling me about?"

"Innsmouth?" said the old man. "Yes, I believe I recall the occasion. But I also recall how nervous you were. And Jilly, in my opinion – from what I've observed of you, er, in my capacity as a doctor or ex-doctor – it seems to me that odd or peculiar subjects have a very unsettling effect on you. Are you sure you want to hear about Innsmouth?"

"While it's true that certain subjects have a bad affect on me," she began slowly, "at the same time I'm fascinated by anything concerning my husband's history or his people. Especially the latter, his genealogy." She speeded up a little. "After all what do we really know of genetics – those traits we carry down the generations with us – traits passed on by our forbears? And I think to myself, perhaps I've been avoiding George's past for far too long. Things have happened here, James . . ." She clutched his arm. "Weird alterations, alienations, and I need to be sure they can't ever happen again, not to me or mine!" She was going full tilt now. "Or if they do happen, that I'll know what to do – what to do about – do about . . ."

But there Jilly stopped dead, with her mouth still open, as if she suddenly realized that she'd said too much, too quickly, and even too desperately.

And after a long moment's silence the old man quietly said, "Maybe I'd better ask you again, my dear: are you sure you want me to tell you about Innsmouth?"

She took a deep breath, deliberately stilled the twitching of her slender hands on the arms of her chair, and said "Yes, I really would like to know all about that place and its people."

"And after I've gone, leaving you on your own here tonight? What of your dreams, Jilly? For I feel I must warn you: you may well be courting nightmares."

"I want to know," she answered at once. "As for nightmares: you're right, I can do without them. But still I *have* to know."

"Anne has told me there are some books that belonged to her father." Jamieson tried to reason with her. "Perhaps the answer you're seeking can be found in their pages?"

"George's books?" She shuddered. "Those ugly books! He used to bury himself in them. But when they were heaping the seaweed and burning it last summer, I asked Anne to throw them into the flames!" She offered a nervous, perhaps apologetic shrug. "What odds? I couldn't have read them anyway, for they weren't in English; they weren't in any easily recognizable language. But the worst thing was the way they felt. Why, just touching them made me feel queasy!"

The old man narrowed his eyes, nodded and said, "And do you really expect me to talk about Innsmouth, when the very thought of a few mouldy old books makes you look ill? And you asked the girl to burn them, without even knowing their value or what was in them? You know, it's probably a very good thing I came along when I did, Jilly. For it's fairly obvious that you're obsessed about something, and obsessions can all too easily turn to psychoses. Wherefore—"

"— You're done with me," she finished it for him, and fell back in her chair. "I'm ill with worry – or with my own, well, 'obsession' if you like – and you're not going to help me with it."

The old man took her hand, squeezed it, and shook his head. "Oh, Jilly!" he said. "You've got me all wrong. Psychology may be one of our more recently accepted medical sciences, but I'm not so ancient that I predate it in its entirety! Yes, I know a thing or two about the human psyche; more than enough to assure you that there's not much wrong with yours."

She looked bewildered, and so Jamieson continued, "You see, my dear, you're finally opening up, deliberately exposing yourself to whatever your problem is, taking your first major step toward getting rid of it. So of course I'm going to help you."

She sighed her relief, then checked herself and said, "But, if that involves telling me about Innsmouth—?"

"Then so be it," said the old man. "But I would ask you not to interrupt me once I start, for I'm very easily sidetracked." And after Jilly nodded her eager assent, he began . . .

"During my time at my practice in Innsmouth, I saw some strange sad cases. Many locals are inbred, to such an extent that their blood is tainted. I would very much like to be able to put that some other way, but no other way says it so succinctly. And the 'Innsmouth look' – a name given to the very weird, almost alien appearance of some of the town's inhabitants – is the principal symptom of that taint.

"However, among the many myths and legends I've heard about that place and those with 'the look', some of the more fanciful have it the other way round; they insist that it wasn't so much inbreeding that caused the taint as miscegenation . . . the *mixed* breeding between the town's old-time sea captains and the women of certain South Sea island tribes with which they often traded during their voyages. And what's more, the same legends have it that it wasn't only the native *women* with whom these degenerate old sea dogs associated, but . . . but I think it's best to leave that be for now, for tittle-tattle of that nature can so easily descend into sheer fantasy.

"Very well, but whatever the origin or source of the town's problems – the *real* source, that is – it's still possible that it may at least have some *connection* with those old sea-traders and the things they brought back with them from their ventures. Certainly some of them married and brought home native women – which in this day and age mightn't cause much of a stir, but in the mid-nineteenth century was very much frowned upon – and in their turn these women must surely have brought some of their personal belongings and customs with them: a few native gewgaws, some items of clothing, their 'cuisine', of course . . . possibly even something of their, er, religions? Or perhaps 'religion' is too strong a word for what we should more properly accept as primitive native beliefs.

"In any case, that's as far back as I was able to trace the blood taint – if such it is, – but as for the 'Innsmouth look' itself, and the horrible way it manifested itself in the town's inhabitants . . . well, I think the best way to describe that is as a disease; yes, and perhaps more than one disease at that.

"As to the form or forms this affliction takes," (now Jamieson began to lie, or at least to step aside from the truth) "well, if I didn't know any better, I might say that there's a fairly representative example or specimen, as it were, right here in our own backyard: that poor unfortunate youth who lives with the Fosters, Anne's friend, young Geoff. Of course, I don't know of any connection – and can't see how there could possibly be one – but that youth would seem to have something much akin to the Innsmouth stigma, if not the selfsame affliction. Just take a look at his condition:

"The unwholesome scaliness of the skin, far worse than any mere ichthyosis; the strange, shambling gait; the eyes, larger than normal and increasingly difficult to close; the speech – where such exists at all – or the guttural gruntings that pass for speech; and those gross anomalies or distortions of facial arrangement giving rise to fishy or froggy looks . . . and all of these features present in young Geoff. Why, John Tremain tells me that the youth reminds him of nothing so much as a stranded fish! And if somehow there is something of the Innsmouth taint in him . . . well then, is it any wonder that such dreadful fantasies came into being in the first place? I think not . . ."

Pausing, the old man stared hard at Jilly. During his discourse she had turned very pale, sunk down into her chair, and gripped its arms with white-knuckled hands. And for the first time he noticed grey in her hair, at the temples. She had not, however, given way to those twitches and jerks normally associated with her nervous condition, and all of her attention was still rapt upon him.

Now Jamieson waited for Jilly's reaction to what he'd told her so far, and in a little while she found her voice and said, "You mentioned certain gewgaws that the native women might have brought with them from those South Sea islands. Did you perhaps mean jewellery, and if so have you ever seen any of it? I mean, what *kind* of gewgaws, exactly? Can you describe them for me?"

For a moment the old man frowned, then said, "Ah!" and nodded his understanding. "But I think we may be talking at cross purposes, Jilly. For where those native women are concerned – in connection with their belongings – I actually *meant* gewgaws: bangles and necklaces made from seashells, and ornaments carved out of coconut shells . . . that sort of thing. But it's entirely possible I know what *you* mean by gewgaws . . . for of course I've seen that brooch that Mrs Tremain purchased from your husband. Oh yes; and since I have a special interest in such items, I bought it back from her! But in fact the only genuine 'gewgaws' in the tales I've heard were the cheap trinkets which those old sea captains offered the islanders in so-called 'trade'. Trade? Daylight robbery, more like! While the gewgaws that *you* seem to be interested in have to be what those poor savages parted with in exchange for those worthless beads and all that useless frippery – by which I mean the quaintly-worked jewellery, but *real jewellery*, in precious golden alloy, that Innsmouth's seafarers as good as stole from the natives! And you ask have I actually seen such? Indeed I have, and not just the piece I bought from Doreen Tremain . . ."

The old man had seemed to be growing more and more excited, carried away by his subject, apparently. But now, calming down, he paused to collect his thoughts and settled himself deeper in his chair before continuing. And:

"There now," he finally said. "Didn't I warn you that I was easily sidetracked? And wouldn't you know it, but now I've completely lost the thread!"

"I had asked you about that native jewellery," she reminded him. "I thought maybe you could describe it for me, or at least tell me where you saw it. And there was something else you said – something about the old sea captains and . . . and *things* they associated with other than the natives? – that I somehow found, well, interesting."

"Ah!" the old man answered. "But I can assure you, my dear, that last was sheer fantasy. And as for the jewellery . . . where did I see it? Why, in Innsmouth itself, where else? In a museum there – well, a *sort* of museum – but more properly a shrine, or a site of remembrance, really. I suppose I could tell you about it if you still wish it? And if you're sure none of this is too troubling for you?" The way he looked at her, his gaze was very penetrating. But having come this far, Jilly wasn't about to be put off.

"I do wish it," she nodded. "And I promise you I'll try not . . . not to be troubled. So do please go on."

The old man nodded and stroked his chin, and after a while carried on with his story.

"Anthropology, the study of man's origins and ways of life, was always something of a hobby of mine," he began. "And crumbling old Innsmouth, despite its many drawbacks, was not without its sources – its own often fascinating history and background – which as yet I've so poorly delineated.

"Some of the women – I can't really call them ladies – who attended my practice were of the blood. Not necessarily tainted blood but native blood, certainly. Despite the many generations separating them from their dusky forebears, still there was that of the South Sea islands in them. And it was a handful of these patients of mine, my clients, so to speak, that led to my enquiries after the jewellery they wore . . . the odd clasp or brooch, a wrist bangle or necklace. I saw quite a few, all displaying a uniform, somehow rude style of workmanship, and all very similarly adorned or embellished.

"But as for a detailed description, that's rather difficult. Floral? No, not really. Arabesque? That would more properly fit the picture; weird foliage and other plant forms, curiously and intricately intertwined . . . but *not* foliage of the land. It was oceanic: seaweeds and sea grasses, with rare conches and fishes hidden in the design – particularly fishes – forming what may only be described as an unearthly piscine or perhaps batrachian depiction. And occasionally, as a backdrop to the seaweeds and grasses, there were hinted buildings: strange, squat pyramids, and oddly-angled towers. It was as if the unknown craftsman – who or whatever – had attempted to convey the lost Atlantis or some other watery civilization . . ."

The old man paused again, then said, "There. As a description, however inadequate, that will have to suffice. Of course, I was never so close to the Innsmouth women that I was able to study their clasps and brooches in any great detail, but I did enquire of them as to their origin. Ah, but they were a close-mouthed lot and would say very little . . . well, except for one, who was younger and less typical of her kind; and she directed me to the museum.

"In its heyday it had been a church – that was before the tainted blood had moved in and the more orthodox religions out, – a squat-towered stone church, yes, but long since desanctified. It stood close to another once-grand building; a pillared hall of considerable size, still bearing upon its pediment the faded legend, 'Esoteric Order of Dagon'.

"Dagon, eh? But here a point of great interest:

"Many years ago, this great hall, too, had been a place of worship . . . or obeisance of some sort, certainly. And how was this for an anthropological puzzle? For of course the fish-god Dagon – half man, half fish – had been a deity of the Philistines, later to be adopted by the Phoenicians who called him Oannes. And yet these Polynesian islanders, thousands of miles away around the world, had offered up their sacrifices – or at least their prayers – to the selfsame god. And in the Innsmouth of the 1820s their descendants were carrying on that same tradition! But you know, my dear, and silly as it may seem, I can't help wondering if perhaps they're doing it still . . . I mean today, even now . . .

"But there you go, I've sidetracked myself again! So where was I? Ah, yes! The old church, or rather the museum.

"The place was gothic in its looks, with shuttered windows and a disproportionately high basement. And it was there in the half-sunken basement – the museum proper – that the 'exhibits' were housed. There under dusty glass in unlocked boxwood cases, I saw such a fabulous collection of golden jewellery and ornaments . . . why, it amazed me that there were no labels to describe the treasure, and more so that there was no curator to guard it against thieves or to enlighten casual visitors with its story! Not that there were many visitors. Indeed, on such occasions as I was there I saw no one – not even a church mouse.

"But that jewellery, made of those strange golden alloys . . . oh, it was truly fascinating! As was a small, apparently specialized library of some hundreds of books; all of them antiques, and all quietly rotting away on damp, easily accessible shelves. Apart from one or two titles of particularly unpleasant connotation, I recognized nothing that I saw; and, since most of those titles were in any case beyond me, I never so much as paused to turn a page. But as with the exotic, alien jewellery – and *if* I had been a thief, of course – I'm sure I might have walked out of there with a fortune in rare and forbidden volumes under my coat, and no one to stop, accuse or search me. In fact, searching my memory, I believe I've heard mention that certain books and a quantity of jewellery were indeed stolen from the museum some twenty-odd years ago. Not that gold was ever of any great rarity in Innsmouth, for those old sea captains had brought it home in such large amounts that back in the 1800s one of them had even opened up a refinery in order to purify his holdings! I tried to visit the refinery, too, only to find it in a state of total dereliction . . . as was much of the old town itself in the wake of a . . . well, of a rumoured epidemic, and subsequent government raids in 1927–8. But there, that's another story."

And fidgeting a very little – seeming suddenly reticent – Jamieson brought his narrative to an abrupt halt, saying, "And there you have it, my dear. With regard to your question about the strange jewellery . . . well, I've tried to answer it as best possible. So, er, what else can I tell you? Nothing, I fear . . ."

But now it was Jilly White's eyes searching the old man's face, and not the other way about. For she had noticed several vague allusions and some major omissions in his narrative, for which she required explanations.

"About the jewellery . . . yes, I believe I understand," she said. "But you've said some other things that aren't nearly so clear. In fact you seemed to be avoiding certain subjects. And I w-w-want . . . I *wan-w-w* . . .!" She slammed her arms down on the arms of her chair, chair, trying to control her stammering. "I *want* to know! About – how did you put it? – the *associations* of those old sea captains with something other than the island women, which you said was sheer fantasy. But fantasy or not, I want to know. And about . . . about their beliefs . . . their religion and d-d-*dedication* to Dagon. Also, w-w-with regard to that foreign jewellery, you said something about its craftsman, '*who or whatever!*' Now what did you mean by that? And that epidemic you mentioned: what was all that about? What, an epidemic that warranted government raids? James – if you're my friend at all – surely you m-m-*must* see that I have to know!"

"I can see that I've upset you," he answered, reaching out and touching her hand. "And I believe I know what it is that's so unsettling for you. You're trying to connect all of this to George, aren't you? You think that his blood, too, was tainted. Jilly, it may be so, but it's not your fault. And if the taint is in fact a disease, it probably wasn't his fault either. You can't blame yourself that your husband may have been some kind of . . . of carrier. And even if he was, surely his influence is at an end now? You mustn't go on believing that it . . . that it isn't over yet."

"Then convince me otherwise," she answered, a little calmer now that she could speak openly of what was on her mind. "Tell me about these things, so that I'll better understand them and be able to make up my own mind."

Jamieson nodded. "Oh, I can tell you," he said, "if only by repeating old wives tales – myths and rumours – and fishermen's stories of mermaids and the like. But the state of your nerves, I'd really rather not."

"My nerves, yes," she said. "Wait." And she fetched a glass of water and took two of her pills. "There, and now you can see that I'm following doctor's orders. Now *you* must follow my orders and tell me." And leaning forward in her chair, she gripped his forearms. "Please. If not for my sake . . . for Anne's?"

And knowing her meaning, how could he refuse her?

"Very well," the old man answered. "But my dear, this thing you're worrying about, it is – it – it *has* to be – a horrible disease, and nothing more. So don't go mixing fantasy and reality, for that way lies madness."

And after a moment's thought he told her the rest of it . . .

"The stories I've heard . . . well, they were incredible. Legends born of primitive innocence and native ignorance both. You see, with regard to Dagon, those islanders had their own myths which had been handed down from generation to generation. Their blood and looks being so debased, and the taint having such a hold on them – probably since time immemorial – they reasoned that they had been created in the image of their maker, the fish-god himself, Dagon.

"Indeed they told those old sea captains just such stories, and also that in return for worshipping Dagon they'd been given all the wealth of the oceans in the abundance of fish they were able to catch, and in the strange golden alloy, which was probably washed out of their mountains in rainy-season streams. It would be the native priests, of course – their witch doctors, priests of Dagon or his 'esoteric order' – who secretly worked the gold into the jewellery whose remnants we occasionally see today.

"But the *modern* legend – the one you'll hear in Innsmouth and its environs – is that in return for the good fishing and the gold, the natives gave of their children to the sea, or to man-like beings who lived in the sea: the so-called 'Deep Ones', servitors of Dagon and other alleged, er, 'deities' of the deep, such as Great Cthulhu and Mother Hydra. And the same legend has it that Innsmouth's sea captains, in their lust for alien gold, the favours of mainly forgotten gods out of doubtful myths, and the promise of life everlasting, followed suit in the sacrifice of *their* young to Dagon and the Deep Ones. Except they were not sacrifices as such but matings! Thus in *both* legends, it became possible to blame the 'Innsmouth look' or taint on this miscegenation: the mingling of Deep One and clean human blood. But of course no such matings took place because there's no such thing as a merman! Nor was there ever, but that didn't stop a handful of the more degenerate Innsmouth people from adopting the cult, as witness that weathered, white-pillared hall dedicated to the Esoteric Order of Dagon.

"Which leaves only the so-called 'epidemic' of 1927–28 . . .

"Well, seventy years ago our society was far less tolerant. And sad to say that when stories leaked out of Innsmouth of the sheer scale of the taint – the numbers of inbred, diseased and malformed people living there – the federal government's reaction was excessive in the extreme. But there's little doubt that it would have been the same if AIDS had been found there in the same period: panic, and a knee-jerk reaction, yes. And so there followed a vast series of raids and many arrests, and a burning and dynamiting of large numbers of rotting old houses along the waterfront. But no criminal charges were brought and no one was committed for trial; just vague statements about malignant diseases, and the covert dispersal of a great many detainees into various naval and military prisons.

"Thus old Innsmouth was depopulated, and these seventy-odd years later its recovery is still only very sluggish. There is, however, a modern laboratory there now, where pathologists and other scientists – some of them Innsmouth people themselves – continue to study the taint and to offer what help they may to the descendants of survivors of those frenzied federal raids. I worked there myself, however briefly, but it was disheartening work to say the least. I saw sufferers in every stage of degeneration, and could only offer the most basic assistance to any of them. For among the doctors and other specialists there . . . well, the general consensus is that there's no hope for a cure as yet for those with the Innsmouth blood. And until or unless the taint is allowed to die out by gradual dispersion or depletion of that diseased foreign gene pool, there shall always be those with the Innsmouth look . . ."

Jilly was as calm as Jamieson had ever seen her now – too calm, he thought – like the calm before a storm. Her eyes were unblinking and had a distant quality, but her look was reflective rather than vague or vacant. And finally, after a few long moments of silence, the old man prompted her, "What now, Jilly? Is something still bothering you?"

Her gaze focussed on him and she said, "Yes. I think there is one more thing. You said something about everlasting life – that the Innsmouth seafarers had been promised everlasting life if they embraced the worship of Dagon and these other cult figures. But

. . . what if they reneged on the cult, turned back from such worship? You see, toward the end George frequently rambled in his sleep, and I'd often hear him say that he didn't *want* to live forever, not like that. He meant his condition, of course. But I can't believe – no, no, I *can!* I *do!* – that *he* believed in s-s-such things. So, do you think – I mean, is it p-p-possible – that my husband was once a m-member of that old Innsmouth c-c-cult? And could there be anything of t-truth in it? I mean, anything at all?"

Jamieson shook his head. "Anything to it? Only in his mind, my dear. For you see, as George's condition worsened, it would have been more than a merely physical thing. He would have been doing what you are doing: looking for an explanation where none exists. And having had to do with those cultists – and knowing the legends – he might have come to believe that certain things were true. But as for you, you mustn't. You simply mustn't!"

"B-b-but that tainted blood," she said, her voice a whisper now, as if from far away. "His blood, and Geoff's blood, and . . . and w-w-what of Anne's?"

"Jilly, now I want you to listen." The old man took hold of her arms, grasping her very firmly. And of all the lies or half truths he had told her in the past half hour, the next would be his biggest deceit of all. "Jilly, I have known you and Anne – especially Anne – for quite a while now, and from my knowledge of the Innsmouth taint, and also from what I know and have seen of your daughter, I would be glad to stake my reputation on the fact that she is as normal as you or I."

At which she sighed, relaxing a little in her chair . . .

And taking that as his signal to depart, Jamieson stood up. "I must be off," he said. "It's late and I've some things to do before bed." Then, as he made his way to the door, he said: "Do give my regards to Anne, won't you? It's a shame I missed her – or perhaps not, since we needed to have our talk."

Jilly had followed him – rather stumblingly, he thought – and at the door said, "I really d-d-don't know how to thank you. My mind feels so much more at ease now. But then it always does after I-I-I've spoken with you." She waited until he'd got into his car, and waved him a shaky goodbye before closing the door.

Pulling away from the house, the old man noticed an almost furtive flicker of movement in the drapes of an upstairs window. It was Anne's bedroom; and very briefly he saw her face – those huge eyes of hers – in the gap of partly drawn-aside curtains.

At which he wondered how long she had been awake; even

wondered if she had been asleep! And if not, how much she'd overheard. Or had she perhaps already known it all . . .?

The long winter with its various ailments – Anne White's laryngitis, and Doreen Tremain's flu – merged slowly into spring; green shoots became flowers in village gardens or window boxes; lowering skies brightened, becoming bluer day to day.

But among these changes were others, not nearly so natural and far less benign, and old Jamieson was witness to them all.

He would see the beachcomber – "young Geoff", indeed, as if he were just another village youth – shambling along the tidemark. But he wasn't like other youths, and he was ailing.

Jamieson watched him in his binoculars, that tired shambler on the shore: his slow lurching, feet flip-flopping, shoulders sloping, head down and collar up. And despite that the weather was much improved, he no longer went out to sea. Oh, he *looked* at the sea – constantly pausing to lift his ugly head and gaze out across that wide wet horizon – gaze longingly, the old man thought, as he attempted to read something of emotion into the near-distant visage – but the youth's great former ability in the water, and his untried but suspected strength on dry land, these seemed absent now. Plainly put, he was in decline.

The old man had heard rumours in the village pub. The fishing was much improved but Tom Foster wasn't doing as well as in previous years; he'd lost his good luck charm, the backward boy who guided his boat to the best fishing grounds. At least, that was how they saw it, the other fishermen, but it was Tom Foster himself who had told the old man the truth of it one evening in the Sailor's Rest.

"It's the boy," he said, concernedly. "Um's not umself. Um says the sea lures um, and um's afeared of it. Oh, um walks the shore and watches all the whitecaps, the seahorses come rollin' in, but um ain't about ter go aridin' on 'em. I dun't know what um means, but um keeps complainin' as how um 'ain't ready', and doubts um ever will be, but if um 'goes now' it'll be the end of um. Lord only knows where um's thinkin' of goin'! And truth is, um sickens. So while I knows um'd come out with me if I was ter ask um, I won't fer um's sake. The only good thing: um lies in the bath a lot, keeps umself well soaked in fresh water so um's skin dun't suffer much and there be no more of them fish-lice."

And the leathery old seaman had shrugged – though in no way negligently – as he finished his pint, and then his ruminations with the words, "No more sea swimmin', no more fish-lice – it's as simple as that. But as fer the rest of it . . . I worries about um, that I do."

"Answer me one question," the old man had begged of Foster then. "Tell me, why did you take him in? You had no obligation in that respect. I mean, it wasn't as if the youth – the child – was of your blood. He was a foundling, and there were, well, complications right from the start."

Foster had nodded. "It were my woman, the missus, who took ter um. Her great-granny had told of just such young 'uns when um were a little 'un out in the islands. And Ma Foster felt fer um, um did. Me too, 'ventually, seein' as how we've had um all this time. But we always knew who um's dad were. No big secret that, fer um were here plain ter see. Gone now, though, but um did used ter pay um's share."

"George White gave you money?"

"Fer Geoff's upkeep, yes." Foster had readily admitted it. "That's a fact. The poor bugger were sellin' off bits of precious stuff – jewell'ry and such – in all the towns around. Fer the lad, true enough, but also fer um's own pleasure . . . or so I've heard it said. But that's none of my business . . ."

Then there was poor Jilly White. She, too – her health, – was very obviously in decline. Her nightmares were of constant concern, having grown repetitive and increasingly weird to the point of grotesque. Also, her speech and mobility were suffering badly; she stuttered, often repeated herself, occasionally fell while negotiating the most simple routines both in and out of doors. Indeed, she had become something of a prisoner in her own home; she only rarely ventured down onto the beach, to sit with her daughter in the weak but welcome spring sunshine.

As to her dreams:

It had been a long-drawn-out process, but Jamieson had been patient; he had managed to extract something of the nightmarish contents of Jilly's dreams from the lady herself, the rest from Anne during the return journey from a language lesson trip into St Austell. Unsurprisingly, all of the worst dreams were centered upon George White, Jilly's ex-husband; not on his suicide, as might at least in some part be expected, but on his disease: its progression and acceleration toward the end.

In particular she dreamed of frogs or the batrachia in general, and of fish . . . but *not* as creatures of Nature. The horror of these visitations was that they were completely alien, gross mutations or hybrids of man and monster. And the man was George White, his human face and something of his form transposed upon those of the amphibia and fishes alike – and all too often upon beings who had the physical components of both genera *and more!* In short, Jilly dreamed of Deep Ones, where George was a member of that aquatic society!

And Anne White told of how her mother mumbled and gibbered, gasping her horror of "great wet eyes that wouldn't or couldn't close"; or "scales as sharp and rough as a file"; or "the flaps in George's neck, going right through to the inside and pulsing like . . . like *gills* when he snorted or choked in his sleep!" But these things with regard to her mother's nightmares weren't all that Anne had spoken of on the occasion of that revealing drive home from her language lesson. For she had also been perfectly open in telling Jamieson:

"I know you saw me at my window that time when you brought her pills and spoke to my mother at length, the night you told her about Innsmouth. I heard you start to talk, got out of bed, and sat listening at the head of the stairs. I was as quiet as could be and must have heard almost everything you said."

And Jamieson had nodded. "Things she probably wouldn't have spoken of if she'd known you were awake? Did it . . . bother you, our conversation?"

"Perhaps a little . . . but no, not really," she had answered. "I know more than my mother gives me credit for. But about what you told her, in connection with my father and what she dreamed about him, well, there is something I'd like to know – without that you need to repeat it to her."

"Oh?"

"Yes. You said that you'd seen those sick Innsmouth people, 'in every stage of degeneration'. And I wondered . . ."

". . . You wondered just what those stages were?" The old man had prompted her, and then gone on: "Well, there are stages and there are states. It usually depends on how they start out. The taint might occur from birth, or it might come much later. Some scarcely develop the Innsmouth look at all . . . while others are born with it."

"Like Geoff?"

"Like him, yes." Again Jamieson nodded. "It rather depends on the strength of the Innsmouth blood in the parents . . . or in at least one of them, obviously. Or in the ancestral blood line in general."

And then, out of the blue and without any hesitation, she'd said, "I know that Geoff is my half-brother. It's why my mother let's us be friends. She feels guilty for my father's sake – in his place, I mean. And so she thinks of Geoff as 'family'. Well, of a sort."

"And you? How do you think of him?"

"As my brother, do you mean?" She had offered an indecisive shake of her head. "I'm not really sure. In a way, I suppose. I don't find him horrible, if that's what you mean."

"No, of course not, and neither do I!" The old man had been quick to answer. "As a doctor, I've grown used to accepting too many abnormalities in people to be repulsed by any of them."

"Abnormalities?" Anne had cocked her head a little, favouring Jamieson with a curious, perhaps challenging look. And:

"Differences, then," he had told her.

And after a moment's silence she'd said, "Go on, then. Tell me about them: these states or stages."

"There are those born with the look, as I've mentioned," he had answered, "and those who gradually develop it, some of whom stay mostly, well, *normal*-looking. There are plenty of those in Innsmouth right now. Also, there is always a handful who retain their, er, agreeable – their acceptably, well, *human* – features for a great many years, changing only towards the end, when the metamorphosis occurs very rapidly indeed. At the hospital where I worked, some of the geneticists – Innsmouth people themselves – were trying to alter certain genes in their patients; if not to kill off the process entirely, at least to prolong the human looks of those who were likely to suffer the change."

" 'Human-looking', and 'metamorphosis', and 'geneticists'." Anne had nodded, thoughtfully. "But with those words – and the way you explained it – it doesn't sound so much a disease as a, well, a 'metamorphosis', yes; and that *is* your own word! Like a pupa into a butterfly, or rather a tadpole into a frog. Except, instead of a tadpole . . ."

But there she'd frowned, broken off and sat back musing in her seat. "It's all very puzzling, but I think the answers are coming and that I'm beginning to understand." Then, sitting up straight again until she strained against her safety belt, she had said. "But look – we're almost home!" And urgently turning to stare at Jamieson's profile: "We're through the village and there are still some things I wanted to ask – just one or two more, that's all."

At which the old man had slowed down, allowing her time to speak, and prompting her, "Go on then, ask away."

"This cult of Dagon," she had said then. "This religion or 'Esoteric Order' in Innsmouth – does it still exist? I mean, do they still worship? And if so, what if someone with the look or the blood – what if he doesn't want to be one of them – what if he reneges and . . . and runs away? My mother asked you much the same question, I know. But you didn't quite answer her."

"I think," Jamieson had said then, bringing his vehicle to a halt outside the Whites' house, "I think that would be quite bad for this hypothetical person. What would he do, if or when the change came upon him? With no one to help him; none of his own kind, that is."

Anne's mother had come to the door of the house, and stood there all pale and uncertain. But Anne, getting out of the car, had looked at the old man with her penetrating gaze, and he had seen that it was all coming together for her – and that indeed she knew more than her mother had given her credit for . . .

In the second week of May things came to a head.

The first handful of tourists and early holidaymakers were in the village, staying at two or three cheap bed-and-breakfast places; and these city folk were making their way down onto the beaches each day, albeit muffled against the still occasionally brisk weather.

And in the lenses of Jamieson's binoculars, the gnarled Tom Foster and his malformed ward had also been seen – as often as not arguing, apparently – the younger one pulling himself away, and the elder dragging after him, shaking his head and pointing back imploringly the way they'd come. And despite that the ill-favoured youth was failing, he yet retained enough strength to power him stumblingly, stubbornly on, leaving his foster-father panting and cursing in his wake. But when the youth was alone – fluttering there like a stumpy scarecrow on the sands, with his few wisps of coarse hair blowing back from his head in the wind off the ocean – then as always he would be seen gazing out over the troubled waters, as if transfixed by their vast expanse . . .

It happened on a reasonably warm Sunday afternoon that the Tremains, Jamieson, and Anne White were on the beach together, or rather at the same time. And so was young Geoff.

For ease of walking the old man held to firmer ground set back from the dunes, on a heading that would take him past the Tremains' house as he visited Jilly White's place. Doreen and John Tremain were taking the air maybe two hundred yards ahead of Jamieson; with their backs to him, they hadn't as yet observed him. And Anne was a small dot in the distance, huddled with a book in the lee of a grass-crested dune, a favourite location of hers, just one hundred or so yards this side of her mother's house. Today she stayed close to home out of necessity, for the simple reason that Jilly had taken to her bed four days ago as the result of some sort of physical or mental collapse, if not a complete nervous breakdown.

There were a very few holidaymakers on the beach . . . fewer still in bathing costumes, daring the water for the first time. But closer to the sea than the rest – coming from the direction of the village and avoiding the small family groups – there was young Geoff. Jamieson had his binoculars with him; he paused to focus on the youth, finding himself mildly concerned on noting his poor condition.

He was stumbling very badly now; his flabby mouth had fallen fully open, and his bulbous chin wobbled on his chest. Even at this distance, the youth's eyes seemed filmed over, and the scaly skin of his face was grey. He seemed to be gasping at the air, and his broad, rounded shoulders went up and down with the heaving of his chest.

As the old man watched, so that strange figure tore off its shapeless jacket and threw it aside, then angled its route even closer to the band of damp sand at the sea's rim. Some children paddling and splashing there, laughing as they jumped the small waves in six inches of water, noticed Geoff's approach. They at once quit their play and fell silent, backed away from him, and finally turned to run up the beach.

And sensing that something was about to happen here, Jamieson put on a little more speed. Likewise the Tremains; they too were walking faster, cresting the dunes, heading for the softer sands of the beach proper. Being that much closer to the youth, they had obviously witnessed his antics and noted his poor condition, and like the old man they'd sensed something strange in the air.

Anne, on the other hand, remained seated, reading in the scoop of her dune, as yet unaware of the drama taking shape close by.

Jamieson, no longer showing any sign of his age or possible infirmity, put on yet more speed; he was anxious to be as close as possible to whatever was happening here. He only paused when he heard a weird cry – a strange, ululant howling – following which he hurried on and crested the dunes in the prints left by the Tremains. Then, from that slightly higher elevation, and at a distance of less than one hundred and fifty yards, he scanned the scene ahead.

Having heard the weird howling, Anne was on her feet now at the crest of her dune, looking down across the beach. And there was her half-brother, up to his knees in the water, tearing off his shirt and dropping his ragged trousers, making these nerve-jangling noises as he howled, hissed, and shrieked at the sea!

Anne ran down across the beach; the Tremains hurried after, and Jamieson raced to catch up. He was vaguely aware that Jilly White had appeared on the decking at the back of her house, and was standing or staggering there in her dressing-gown. White as a ghost, clutching at the handrail with one shaking hand, Jilly held the other to her mouth.

Anne was into the water now, wading out toward the demented – or tormented – youth. John Tremain had kicked off his
shoes; he tested the water, hoisted the cuffs of his trousers
uselessly, and went splashing toward the pair. And meanwhile
Jamieson, puffing and panting with the effort, had closed in on
the scene as a whole.

Geoff had stopped hissing and howling; he grasped at Anne's
hand, held it tight, pointed urgently out to sea. Then, releasing her,
he made signs: *Come with me, sister, for I have to go! I am not ready,
but still I must go! It calls to me . . . the sea is calling and I can no
longer resist . . . I must go!*

Then he saw her uncertainty, her denial, stopped making his signs,
and began dragging her deeper into the water. But it was now clear
that he was deranged, unhinged, and his teeth gleamed the yellowy-
white of fish-bone as he recommenced his gibbering, his howling, his
awful cries of supplication . . . his liturgy to the unknown lords of the
sea.

Jamieson was much closer now, and Tremain closer still. The
headmaster grabbed at Anne, tried to fight the youth off. Geoff
released Anne's hand and turned on Tremain, fastening his sharp
teeth on the other's shoulder and biting through his thin shirt.
Tremain gave a cry of pain! Lurching backwards, he stumbled
and fell into the water, which momentarily covered his head.

But the youth saw what he had done – knew he'd done wrong –
and with Tremain's blood staining his face, and streaming from his
gaping circle of a mouth, he appeared to regain his senses . . . at least
partly. And shaking his head, Geoff signalled his farewell to Anne,
waddled a foot deeper into the water's surge, let himself fall forward
and began to swim.

He swam, and it was at once apparent that this was his natural
element. And seeing him go, Jamieson thought, *Alas that he isn't
equipped for it . . .*

Tremain had dragged himself to the beach; Anne had returned to
where the water reached her knees, and watched Geoff's progress as
his form diminished with distance. Jamieson helped John Tremain up
out of the shallows, dampened a handkerchief in salt water, applied
it to the raw, bleeding area between the other's neck and shoulder.
Doreen Tremain hurried forward, wringing her hands and asking
what she should do.

"Take him home," said the old man. "Keep my handkerchief on
the wound to staunch the bleeding. Treat it with an antiseptic, then
pad and bandage it. When John recovers from the shock take him

into St Austell for shots: anti-tetanus, and whatever else is prescribed. But don't delay. Do you understand?"

She nodded, helped her husband up the beach and away.

Anne was at the water's rim. Soaked from the waist down and shocked to her core – panting and gasping – she stared at the old man with her mouth wide open. And turning her head, looking out to sea, she said, "Geoff . . . Geoff!"

"Let's get you home," said Jamieson, taking her hand.

"But Geoff . . . what of Geoff?"

"We'll call the coastguard." The old man nodded reassuringly, and threw his jacket round her shoulders.

"He said . . . said he wasn't ready." She allowed him to lead her from the water.

"None of us were," Jamieson muttered under his breath. "Not for this."

Half-way up the beach toward the house, they heard a gurgling cry. It was Jilly White, staggering on the decking of her ocean-facing patio, one hand on the rail, the other pointing at the sky, the horizon, the sea, the beach . . . and finally at her daughter and Jamieson. Her drawn face went through a variety of changes; vacant one moment, it showed total horror in the next, and finally nothing as her eyes rolled up like white marbles.

Then, as her knees gave way beneath her, Jilly crumpled to the decking and lay there jerking, drooling, and mouthing incoherently . . .

The coastguard found no sign of Geoff, despite that their boat could be seen slicing through the off-shore water all that day, and then on Monday from dawn till dark. A doctor – a specialist from St Austell – gave Jilly White a thorough examination, and during a quiet, private discussion with Jamieson out of earshot of Anne, readily agreed with the old man's diagnosis. Of course Anne asked about it after the specialist had left, but Jamieson told her it could wait until all had settled down somewhat; and in any case things being as they were, for the moment incapable of improvement, Jilly's best interests lay in resting. He, Jamieson himself, would remain in attendance, and with Anne's help he would care for her mother until other decisions were made if such should become necessary.

In the event, however, the old man didn't expect or receive too much help from Anne; no, for she was out on the beach, walking its length mile upon mile, watching the sea and only coming home to eat and sleep when she was exhausted. This remained her routine for four days, until Geoff's bloated body was washed up on a shingle beach some miles down the coast.

Then Anne slept, and slept, a day and a night.

And the next morning – after visiting her mother's bedside and finding her sleeping, however fitfully – Anne went to the old man in the hollow of her dune, and sat down with him in the sand on the first truly warm day of the year.

He was in shirt-sleeves, grey slacks, canvas shoes; dressed for the fine weather. And he had her book in his lap, unopened. Handing it over, he said, "I found it right here where you left it the other day. I was going to return it to you. You're lucky no one else stumbled on it, and that it hasn't rained."

She took the heavy old book and put it down away from him, asking, "Did you look at it?"

He shook his head. "It's your property. For all I know you might have written in it. I believe in privacy, both for myself and for others."

She took his hand and leaned against him, letting him know that come what may they were friends. "Thank you for everything that you've done, especially for my mother," she said. "I mean, I'm so glad you came here, to the village. Even knowing you *had* to come—" (a sly sideways glance at him,) "—still I'm glad. You've been here just a few months, yet I feel like I've known you, oh, for a very long time."

"I'll take that as a compliment," Jamieson answered her.

"I feel I can talk to you," she quickly went on. "I've felt that way since the first time I saw you. And after you treated Geoff when he was sick . . . well, then I knew it was so."

"And indeed we do talk," said the old man. "Nothing really deep, or not *too* deep, not yet – or until now? – but we talk. Perhaps it's a question of trust, of a sort of kinship?"

"Yes." She nodded. "I know I can tell you things, secrets. I've needed to tell someone things. I'd like to have been able to tell my mother, but she wouldn't have listened. Her nerves. She used to get worried, shake her head, walk away. Or rather, she would stumble away. Which has been getting worse every day. But you . . . you're very different."

He smiled. "Ah, well, but that's always been my lot. As I believe I once told Jilly, sometimes I'm seen as a father confessor. Sort of odd, really, because I'm not a Catholic."

"Then what are you?" Anne tilted her head on one side. "I mean, what's your religion? Are you an atheist?"

"Something like that." Jamieson shrugged. "Actually, I do have certain beliefs. But I'm not one to believe in a conventional god, if that's what you're asking. And you? What do you believe in?"

"I believe in the things my father told me," she answered dreamily. "Some beautiful things, some ugly, and some strange as the strangest myths and fables in the strangest books. But of course *you* know what I mean, even if I'm not sure myself." As she spoke, she took up her book and hugged it to her chest. Bound in antique leather, dark as old oak and glossy with age, the book's title, glimpsed between Anne's spread fingers, consisted of just three ornately tooled letters: E.O.D.

"Well," said Jamieson, "and here you are with just such a book. One of your strange books, perhaps? Certainly its title is very odd. Your mother once told me she gave you such books to burn . . ."

She looked at the book in her hands and said "My father's books? There were some she wanted rid of, yes. But I couldn't just burn them. This is one of them. I've read them a lot and tried to make sense of them. Sometimes I thought I understood them; at others I was at a loss. But I knew they were important and now I know why." And then, suddenly galvanized, gripping his arm below the elbow. "Can we please stop pretending? I know almost everything now . . . so won't you please tell me the rest? And I swear to you – whatever you tell me – it will be safe with me. I think you must know that by now."

The old man nodded and gently disengaged himself. "I think I can do that, yes. That is, as long as you're not going to be frightened by it, and provided you won't run away . . . like your father."

"He was very afraid, wasn't he?" she said. "But I'll never understand why he stole the books and the Innsmouth jewellery. If he hadn't taken them, maybe they'd have just let him go."

"I think that perhaps he planned to sell those books," the old man answered. "In order to support himself, naturally. For of course he would have known that they were very rare and valuable. But after he fled Innsmouth, changed his name, got back a little self-confidence and started to think clearly, he must also have realized that wherever the books surfaced they would be a sure link – a clue, a pointer – to his whereabouts. And so he kept them."

"And yet he sold the jewellery." She frowned.

"Because gold is different to books." Jamieson smiled. "It becomes very personal; the people who buy jewellery wear it, of course, but they also guard it very closely and they don't keep it on library shelves or places where others might wonder about it. Also, your father was careful not to spread it too thickly. Some here, some there;

never too much in any one place. Perhaps at one time he'd reasoned that just like the books he shouldn't sell the jewellery – but then came the time when he had to."

"Yet the people of the Esoteric Order weren't any too careful with it," she said, questioningly.

"Because they consider Innsmouth their town and safe," Jamieson answered. "And also because their members rarely betray a trust. Which in turn is because there are penalties for any who do."

"Penalties?"

"There are laws, Anne. Doesn't every society have laws?"

Her huge eyes studied his, and Jamieson felt the trust they conveyed . . . a mutual trust, passing in both directions. And he said, "So is there anything else I should tell you right now?"

"A great many things," Anne answered, musingly. "It's just that I'm not quite sure how to ask about them. I have to think things through." But in the next moment she was alert again:

"You say my father changed his name?"

"Oh yes, as part of the merry chase he's led us – led me – all these years. But the jewellery did in the end let him down. All winter long, when I've been out and about, I've been buying it back in the towns around. I have most of it now. As for your father's name: actually, he wasn't a White but a Waite, from a long line – a very, *very* long line – of Innsmouth Waites. One of his ancestors, and mine, sailed with Obed Marsh on the Polynesian trade routes. But as for myself . . . well, chronologically I'm a lot closer to those old seafarers than poor George was."

She blinked, shook her head in bewilderment; the first time the old man had seen her caught unawares, which made him smile. And: "You're a Waite, too?" she said. "But . . . Jamieson?"

"Well, actually it's Jamie's son." He corrected her. "Jamie Waite's son, out of old Innsmouth. Have I shocked you? Is it so awful to discover that the kinship you've felt is real?"

And after the briefest pause, while once again she studied his face: "No," she answered, and shook her head. "I think I've probably guessed it – some of it – all along. And Geoff, poor Geoff . . . Why, it would also make you kin to him, and I think he knew it, too! It was in his eyes when he looked at you."

"Geoff?" The old man's face fell and he gave a sad shake of his head. "What a pity. But he was a hopeless case who couldn't ever have developed fully. His gills were rudimentary, useless, unformed, atrophied. Atavisms, throwbacks in bloodlines that we hoped had been successfully conditioned out, still occur occasionally. That poor boy was in one such 'state', trapped between his ancestral heritage and his – or his father's – scientifically engineered or altered genes. And instead of cojoining, the two facets fought."

"A throwback," she said, softly. "What a horrible description!"

And the old man shrugged, sighed, and said, "Yes. Yet what else can we call him, the way Geoff was, and the way he looked? But one day, my dear, our ambassadors – our agents – will walk among people and look no different from them, and be completely accepted by them. Until eventually we Deep Ones will be the one race, the true amphibious race which nature always intended. We were the first . . . why, we *came* from the sea, the cradle of life itself! Given time, and the land and sea both shall be ours."

"Ambassadors . . ." Anne repeated him, letting it all sink in. "But in actual fact agents. Spies and fifth columnists."

"Our advance guard." He nodded. "And who knows – you may be one of them? Indeed, that's my intention."

She stroked her throat, looked suddenly alarmed. "But Geoff and me, we were of an age, of a blood. And if his – his gills? – those flaps were gills? But . . ." Again she stroked her throat, searchingly now. Until he caught at her hand.

"Yours are on the inside, like mine. A genetic modification which reproduced itself perfectly in you, just as in me. That's why your father's desertion was so disappointing to us, and one of the reasons why I had to track him down: to see how he would spawn, and if he'd spawn true. In your case he did. In Geoff's, he didn't."

"My gills?" Yet again she stroked her throat, and then remembered something. "Ah! My *laryngitis!* When my throat hurt last December, and you examined me! Two or three aspirins a day was your advice to my mother, and I should gargle four or five times daily with a spoonful of salt dissolved in warm water."

"You wouldn't let anyone else see you." The old man reminded her. "And why was that, I wonder? Why me?"

"Because I didn't *want* any other doctor looking at me," she replied. "I didn't want anyone else examining me. Just you."

"Kinship," he said. "And you made the right choice. But you needn't worry. Your gills – at present the merest of pink slits at the base of your windpipe – are as perfect as in any foetal or infant land-born Deep One. And they'll stay that way for . . . oh, a long time – as long or even longer than mine have stayed that way, and will until I'm ready – when they'll wear through. For a month or so then they'll feel tender as their development progresses, with fleshy canals like empty veins that will carry air to your land lungs. At which time you'll be as much at home in the sea as you are now on dry land. And that will be *wonderful*, my dear!"

"You want me to . . . to come with you? To be a . . . a . . .?"

"But you already are! There's a certain faint but distinct odour about you, Anne. Yes, and I have it, too, and so did your half-brother. But you can dilute it with pills we've developed, and then dispel it utterly with a dab of special cologne."

A much longer silence, and again she took his bare forearms in her hands, stroking down from the elbow. His skin felt quite smooth in that direction. But when she stroked upwards from the wrist . . .

"Yes," she said, "I suppose I am. My skin is like yours . . . the scales don't show. They're fine and pink and golden. But if I'm to come with you, what of my mother? You still haven't told me what's wrong with her."

And now, finally, after all these truths, the old man must tell a lie. He must, because the truth was one she'd never accept – or rather she would – and all faith gone. But there had been no other way. And so:

"Your mother," the old man hung his head, averted his gaze, started again. "Your mother, your own dear Jilly . . . I'm afraid she won't last much longer." That much at least was the truth.

But Anne's hand had flown to her mouth, and so he hurriedly continued. "She has CJD, Anne – Creutzfeldt-Jacob disease – the so-called mad cow disease, at a very advanced stage." (That was another truth, but not the whole truth.)

Anne's mouth had fallen open. "Does she know?"

"But how can I tell her? And how can you? She may never be herself again. And if or when she were herself, she would only worry about what will become of you. And there's no way we can tell her about . . . well, you know what I mean. But Anne, don't look at me like that, for there's nothing that can be done for her. There's no known cure, no hospital can help her. I wanted her to have her time here, with you. And of course I'm here to help in the final stages. That specialist from St. Austell, he agrees with me."

Finally the girl found her voice. "Then your pills were of no use to her."

"A placebo." *Now* Jamieson lied. "They were sugar pills, to give her some relief by making her *think* I was helping her."

No, not so . . . and no help for Jilly, who would never have let her daughter go; whose daughter never *would* have gone while her mother lived. And those pills filled with synthetic prions – rogue proteins indistinguishable from the human form of the insidious bovine disease, developed in a laboratory in shadowy old Innsmouth – eating away at Jilly's brain even now, faster and faster.

Anne's hand fell from her face. "How long?"

He shook his head. "Not long. After witnessing what happened the other day, not long at all. Days, maybe? No more than a month at best. But we shall be here, you and I. And Anne, we can make up for what she'll miss. Your years, like mine . . . oh, you shall have years without number!"

"It's true, then?" Anne looked at him, and Jamieson looked back but saw no sign of tears in her eyes, which was perfectly normal. "It's true that we go on – that our lives go on – for a long time? But not everlasting, surely?"

He shook his head. "Not everlasting, no – though it sometimes feels that way! I often lose count of my years. But I am your ancestor, yes."

Anne sighed and stood up. And brushing sand from her dress, she took his hand, helping him to his feet. "Shall we go and be with my mother . . . grandfather?"

Now his smile was broad indeed – a smile he showed only to close intimates – which displayed his small, sharp, fish-like teeth. And:

"Grandfather?" he said. "Ah, no. In fact I'm your *father's* great-great-grandfather! And as for yourself, Anne . . . well you must add another great."

And hand in hand they walked up the beach to the house. The young girl and the old – the *very* old – man . . .?

RAMSEY CAMPBELL

The Winner

RAMSEY CAMPBELL'S CURRENT projects include a slightly revised version of his novel *Secret Stories* from Tor Books under the title *Secret Story*, and his latest novel *The Communications*, now retitled *A Grin in the Dark*.

He is currently working on a novel-in-progress, *Thieving Fear*, and along with his regular column in the magazine *All Hallows*, he has added another, "Ramsey's Rambles", to *Video Watchdog*.

And so to the author's second contribution to this volume. As he explains: "'The Winner' was written for Kealan Patrick Burke's themed anthology, *Taverns of the Dead*.

"I've been in pubs as unnerving as this one, and perhaps they've lodged in my shadowy subconscious. The worst was in Birkenhead – a pub where as soon as you walked in you felt as if you'd announced your Jewishness at a David Irving book launch."

U NTIL JESSOP DROVE ONTO THE WATERFRONT he thought most of the wind was racing the moonlit clouds. As the Mini left behind the last of the deserted office buildings he saw ships toppling like city blocks seized by an earthquake. Cars were veering away from the entrance to the ferry terminal. Several minutes of clinging grimly to the wheel as the air kept throwing its weight at the car took him to the gates. A Toyota stuffed with wailing children wherever there was space among the luggage met him at the top of the ramp. "Dublin's cancelled," the driver told him in an Ulster accent he had to strain to understand. "Come back in three hours, they're saying."

"I never had my supper," one of her sons complained, and his sister protested "We could have stayed at Uncle's." Jessop retorted inwardly that he could have delayed his journey by a day, but he'd driven too far south to turn back now. He could have flown from London that morning and beaten the weather if he hadn't preferred to be frugal. He sent his windblown thanks after the Toyota and set about looking for a refuge on the dock road. There were pubs in abundance, but no room to park outside them and no sign of any other parking area. He was searching for a hotel where he could linger over a snack, and realising that all the hotels were back beyond the terminal entrance, when he belatedly noticed a pub.

It was at the far end of the street he'd just passed. Enough horns for a brass band accompanied the U-turn he made. He swung into the cramped gap between two terraces of meagre houses that opened directly onto the pavement. Two more uninterrupted lines of dwellings so scrawny that their windows were as narrow as their doors faced each other across two ranks of parked cars, several of which were for sale. Jessop parked outside the Seafarer, under the single unbroken street lamp, and retrieved his briefcase from the back seat before locking the car.

The far end of the street showed him windowless vessels staggering about at anchor. A gust blundered away from the pub, carrying a mutter of voices. The window of the pub was opaque except for posters plastered against the inside: THEME NIGHT'S, SINGA-LONG'S, QUIZ NIGHT'S. He would rather not be involved in any of those, but perhaps he could find himself a secluded corner in which to work. The lamp and the moon fought over producing shadows of his hand as he pushed open the thick shabby door.

The low wide dim room appeared to be entangled in nets. Certainly the upper air was full of them and smoke. Those under the ceiling trapped rather too much of the yellowish light, while those in the corners resembled overgrown cobwebs. Jessop was telling himself that the place was appealingly quaint when the wind used the door to shove him forward and slammed it behind him.

"Sorry," he called to the barman and the dozen or so drinkers and smokers seated at round tables cast in black iron. Nobody responded except by watching him cross the discoloured wooden floor to the bar. The man behind it, whose small eyes and nose and mouth were crammed into the space left by a large chin, peered at him beneath a beetling stretch of net. "Here's one," he announced.

"Reckon you're right there, cap'n," growled a man who, despite the competition, would have taken any prize for bulkiness.

"You'd have said it if he hadn't, Joe," his barely smaller partner croaked past a hand-rolled cigarette, rattling her bracelets as she patted his arm.

"I'm sorry?" Jessop wondered aloud.

She raised a hand to smooth her shoulder-length red tresses. "We're betting you went for the ferry."

"I hope you've staked a fortune on it, then."

"He means you'd win another, Mary," Joe said. "He wouldn't want you to lose."

"That's so," Jessop said, turning to the barman. "What do you recommend?"

"Nothing till I know you. There's not many tastes we can't please here, mister."

"Jessop," Jessop replied before he grasped that he hadn't been asked a question, and stared hard at the beer-pumps. "Captain's Choice sounds worth a go."

He surveyed the length of the chipped sticky bar while the barman hauled at the creaking pump. A miniature billboard said WIN A VOYAGE IN OUR COMPETTITTION, but there was no sign of a menu. "Do you serve food?" he said.

"I've had no complaints for a while."

"What sort of thing do you do?"

"Try me."

"Would a curry be a possibility? Something along those lines?"

"What do you Southerners think goes in one of them?"

"Anything that's edible," said Jessop, feeling increasingly awkward. "That's the idea of a curry, isn't it? Particularly on board ship, I should think."

"You don't fancy scouse."

"I've never tried it. If that's what's on I will."

"Brave lad," the barman said and thrust a tankard full of brownish liquid at him. "Let's see you get that down you."

Jessop did his best to seem pleased with the inert metallic gulp he took. He was reaching for his wallet until the barman said "Settle when you're going."

"Shall I wait here?"

"For what?" the barman said, then grinned at everyone but Jessop. "For your bowl, you mean. We'll find you where you're sitting."

Jessop didn't doubt it, since nobody made even a token pretence of not watching him carry his briefcase to the only unoccupied corner, which was farthest from the door. As he perched on a ragged leather stool and leaned against the yielding wallpaper under a net elaborated by a spider's web, a woman who might have been more convincingly blonde without the darkness on her upper lip remarked "That'll be a good few hours, I'd say."

"Can't argue with you there, Betty," said her companion, a man with a rat asleep on his chest or a beard, which he raised to point it at Jessop. "Is she right, Jessop?"

"Paul," Jessop offered, though it made him no more comfortable. "A couple, anyway."

"A couple's not a few, Tom," scoffed a man with tattoos of fish and less shapely deep-sea creatures swimming under the cuffs of his shabby brownish pullover.

"What are they else then, Daniel?"

"Don't fall out over me," Jessop said as he might have addressed a pair of schoolchildren. "You could both be right, either could, rather."

Resentment might have been a reason why Daniel jerked one populated thumb at a wiry wizened man topped with a black bobble cap. "He's already Paul. Got another name so we know who's who?"

"None I use."

"Be a love and fish it up for us."

At least it was Mary who asked in these terms, with a hoarseness presumably born of cigarettes. After a pause Jessop heard himself mumble "Desmond."

"Scouse," the barman said – it wasn't clear to whom or even if it was an order. Hoping to keep his head down, Jessop snapped his briefcase open. He was laying out papers on the table when the street door flew wide, admitting only wind. He had to slap the papers down as the barman stalked to the door and heaved a stool against it. Nobody else looked away from Jessop. "Still a student, are you, Des?" Betty said.

He wouldn't have believed he could dislike a name more than the one he'd hidden ever since learning it was his, but the contraction was worse. Des Jessop – it was the kind of name a teacher would hiss with contempt. It made him feel reduced to someone else's notion of him, in danger of becoming insignificant to himself. Meanwhile he was saying "All my life, I hope."

"You want to live off the rest of us till you're dead," Joe somewhat more than assumed.

"I'm saying there'll always be something left to discover. That ought to be true for everyone, I should think."

"We've seen plenty," Daniel grumbled. "We've seen enough."

"Forgive me if I haven't yet."

"No need for that," said Mary. "We aren't forgivers, us."

"Doesn't it make you tired, all that reading?" Betty asked him.
"Just the opposite."

"I never learned nothing from a book," she said once she'd
finished scowling over his words. "Never did me any harm either."

"You'd know a couple's not a few if you'd read a bit," said Joe.

"Lay off skitting at my judy," Tom warned him.

For some reason everybody else but Jessop roared with laughter.
He felt as if his nervous grin had hooked him by the corners of his
mouth. He was wobbling to his feet when the barman called "Don't
let them scare you off, Des. They just need their fun."

"I'm only . . ." Jessop suspected that any term he used would
provoke general mirth. "Where's the . . ."

"The poop's got to be behind you, hasn't it?" Betty said in gleeful
triumph.

Until he glanced in that direction he wasn't sure how much of a
joke this might be. Almost within arm's length was a door so
unmarked he'd taken it for a section of wall. When he pushed it,
the reluctant light caught on two faces gouged out of the wood,
carvings of such crudeness that the female was distinguishable from
her mate only by a mop of hair. Beyond the door was a void that
proved to be a corridor once he located a switch dangling from an
inch of flex. The luminous rotting pear of a bulb revealed that the
short passage led to an exit against which crates of dusty empties
were stacked. The barred exit was shaken by a gust of wind and, to
his bewilderment, what sounded like a blurred mass of television
broadcasts. He hadn't time to investigate. Each wall contained a
door carved with the rudiments of a face, and he was turning away
from the Gents before the image opposite alerted him that the man's
long hair was a patch of black fungus. He touched as little of the door
as possible while letting himself into the Gents.

The switch in the passage must control all the lights. Under the
scaly ceiling a precarious fluorescent tube twitched out a pallid glow
with an incessant series of insect clicks. There was barely enough
space in the room for a pair of clogged urinals in which cigarette
butts were unravelling and a solitary cubicle opposite a piebald slimy
sink. Beneath the urinals the wall was bearded with green mould.
High up beside the cubicle a token window was covered by a rusty
grille restless with old cobwebs. Jessop kicked open the cubicle door.

A watery sound grew louder – an irregular sloshing he'd attributed
to the cistern. He urged himself to the seatless discoloured pedestal.
The instant he looked down, only the thought of touching the
encrusted scabby walls restrained him from supporting himself

against them. Whatever was gaping wide-mouthed at him from the black water, surely it was dead, whether it had been drowned by someone or swum up the plumbing. Surely it was the unstable light, not anticipation of him, that made the whitish throat and pale fat lips appear to work eagerly. He dragged one sleeve over his hand and wrenched at the handle of the rickety cistern. As a rush of opaque water carried the mouth into the depths, Jessop retreated to the first urinal and kept a hand over his nose and mouth while he filled the mouldy china oval to its lower brim.

He dodged out of the fluttering room and was nearly at the door to the bar when he faltered. A confusion of angry voices was moving away from him. A clatter of furniture ended it, and a hoarse voice he identified as Betty's ordered, "Now stay there." He was wishing away the silence as he eased the door open a crack.

The bar seemed emptier than when he'd left it. Two considerable men who'd been seated directly ahead no longer were. The stool hadn't moved from in front of the exit. Could the men be waiting out of sight on either side for him? As he grew furious with his reluctance to know, the barman saw him. "Food's on its way," he announced.

Mary leaned into view, one hand flattening her scalp, to locate Jessop. "Aren't you coming out? This isn't hide and seek."

When embarrassment drove Jessop forward he saw that Daniel had changed seats. He was penned into a corner by the men from the abandoned table, and looked both dishevelled and trapped. "He was trying to see your papers, Des," Betty said.

"Good heavens, I wouldn't have minded. It isn't important."

"It is to us."

As Jessop resumed his corner Tom said, "Got a sweetheart abroad, have you? Was she the lure?"

"His bonnie lies over the ocean," Mary took to have been confirmed, and began to sing.

"No he doesn't," Jessop retorted, but only to himself while he busied himself with his tankard, which had been topped up in his absence. Once the chorus subsided he said guardedly "No, they're over here."

"How many's that?" enquired Joe. "Bit of a ladies' man, are you?"

"A girl in every port," said Tom.

"Not in any really," Jessop said, risking a laugh he hoped was plainly aimed at himself.

"Same with us," Daniel said and gave his fellows an ingratiating look.

The microwave behind the bar rang as if signalling the end of a round, which let Jessop watch the barman load a tray and bring it to him. Once the bowlful of grey stew had finished slopping about, Jessop had to unwrap the fork and spoon from their tattered napkin. He was spooning up a blackened lump when Betty said "What do you make of that then, Des?"

This struck Jessop as the latest of several questions too many. "What would you?"

"Oh, we've had ours. We gobbled it."

"Sup up, Des," Daniel advised. "You'll get plenty of that where you're going."

Was the dish Irish, then? Jessop seemed to have no option other than to raise the dripping lump to his mouth. It was either an unfamiliar vegetable or a piece of meat softened beyond identification, presumably in whatever pot had contained the communal dinner. "Good?" Mary prompted as everyone watched.

"Gum." At least the mouthful allowed him not to answer too distinctly. He swallowed it as whole as an oyster, only to become aware that his performance had invited however many encores it would take to unload the bowl. He was chewing a chunk that needed a good deal of it when Joe declared "If you're not a student I'm saying you're a teacher."

Jessop succeeded at last in downing and retaining the gristly morsel. "Lecturer," he corrected.

"Same thing, isn't it?"

"I wouldn't say quite."

"Still teach, don't you? Still live off them that works, as well."

"Now, Joe," Mary interrupted. "You'll have our new mate not wanting to stay with us."

Jessop could have told her that had happened some time ago. He was considering how much of his portion he could decently leave before seeking another refuge from the gale, and whether he was obliged to be polite any longer, when Tom demanded "So what do you lecture, Des?"

"Students," Jessop might have retorted, but instead displayed the Beethoven score he'd laid out to review in preparation for his introductory lecture. "Music's my territory."

As he dipped his spoon in search of a final mouthful Mary said "How many marks would our singing get?"

"I don't really mark performances. I'm more on the theory side."

Joe's grunt of disdainful vindication wasn't enough for Tom, who said "You've got to be able to say how good it is if you're supposed to be teaching about it."

"Six," Jessop said to be rid of the subject, but it had occupied all the watching eyes. "Seven," he amended. "A good seven. That's out of ten. A lot of professionals would be happy with that."

Betty gave a laugh that apparently expressed why everyone looked amused. "You haven't heard us yet, Des. You've got to hear."

"You start us off, Betty," Daniel urged.

For as long as it took her to begin, Jessop was able to hope he would be subjected only to a chorus. Having lurched to her feet, she expanded her chest, a process that gave him more of a sense of the inequality of her breasts than he welcomed, and commenced her assault on the song. What was she suggesting ought to be done with the drunken sailor? Her diction and her voice, cracked enough for a falsetto, made it impossible to judge. Jessop fed himself a hearty gulp of Captain's Choice in case it rendered him more tolerant as she sat down panting. "Oh," he said hurriedly, "I think—"

"You can't say yet," Daniel objected. "You've got to hear everyone."

Jessop lowered his head, not least to avoid watching Mary. Betty's lopsidedness had begun to resemble an omen. The sound of Mary was enough of an ordeal – her voice even screechier than her friend's, her answer to the question posed by the song even less comprehensible. "There," she said far too eventually. "Who'll be next?"

As Joe stood up with a thump that might have been designed to attract Jessop's attention, he heaped his spoon with a gobbet of scouse to justify his concentration on the bowl. Once the spoonful passed his teeth it became clear that it was too rubbery to be chewed and too expansive to be swallowed. Before Joe had finished growling his first line, Jessop staggered to his feet. He waved his frantic hands on either side of his laden face and stumbled through the doorway to the toilets.

The prospect of revisiting the Gents made him clap a hand over his mouth. When he elbowed the other door open, however, the Ladies looked just as uninviting. A blackened stone sink lay in fragments on the uneven concrete beneath a rusty drooling tap on a twisted greenish pipe. Jessop ran to the first of two cubicles and shouldered the door aside. Beyond it a jagged hole in the glistening concrete showed where a pedestal had been. What was he to make of the substance like a jellyfish sprawling over the entire rim? Before he could be sure what the jittery light was exhibiting, the mass shrank and slithered into the unlit depths. He didn't need the spectacle to make him expel his mouthful into the hole and retreat to the corridor. He was peering desperately about for a patch of wall not too stained to lean against when he heard voices – a renewal of the television sounds beyond the rear exit and, more clearly, a conversation in the bar.

"Are we telling Des yet?"

"Betty's right, we'll have to soon."

"Can't wait to see his face."

"I remember how yours looked, Mary."

It wasn't only their words that froze him – it was that, exhausted perhaps by singing, both voices had given up all disguise. He wouldn't have known they weren't meant to be men except for the names they were still using. If that indicated the kind of bar he'd strayed into, it had never been his kind. He did his best to appear unaware of the situation as, having managed to swallow hard, he ventured into the bar.

More had happened than he knew. Joe had transferred his bulk to the stool that blocked the street door. Jessop pretended he hadn't noticed, only to realise that he should have confined himself to pretending it didn't matter. He attempted this while he stood at the table to gather the score and return it to his briefcase. "Well," he said as casually as his stiffening lips would allow, "I'd better be on my way."

"Not just yet, Des," Joe said, settling more of his weight against the door. "Listen to it."

Jessop didn't know if that referred to the renewed onslaught of the gale or him. "I need something from my car."

"Tell us what and we'll get it for you. You aren't dressed for this kind of night."

Jessop was trying to identify whom he should tell to let him go – the barman was conspicuously intent on wiping glasses – and what tone and phrasing he should use when Daniel said, "You lot singing's put Des off us and his supper."

"Let's hear you then, Des," Joe rather more than invited. "Your turn to sing."

"Yes, go on, Des," Mary shrilled. "We've entertained you, now you can."

Might that be all they required of him? Jessop found himself blurting "I don't know what to perform."

"What we were," Joe said.

Jessop gripped his clammy hands together behind his back and drew a breath he hoped would also keep down the resurgent taste of his bowlful. As he repeated the question about the sailor, his dwarfed voice fled back to him while all the drinkers rocked from side to side, apparently to encourage him. The barman found the glasses he was wiping more momentous than ever. Once Jessop finished wishing it could indeed be early in the morning, if that would put him on the ferry, his voice trailed off. "That's lovely," Betty cried, adjusting her fallen breast. "Go on."

"I can't remember any more. It really isn't my sort of music."

"It will be," Daniel said.

"Take him down to see her," Betty chanted, "and he'll soon be sober."

"Let him hear her sing and then he'll need no drinking," Mary added with something like triumph.

They were only suggesting lyrics, Jessop told himself – perhaps the very ones they'd sung. The thought didn't help him perform while so many eyes were watching him from the dimness that seeped through the nets. He felt as if he'd been lured into a cave where he was unable to see clearly enough to defend himself. All around him the intent bulks were growing visibly restless; Mary was fingering her red tresses as though it might be time to dispense with them. "Come on, Des," Joe said, so that for an instant Jessop felt he was being directed to the exit. "No point not joining in."

"We only get one night," said Tom.

"So we have to fit them all in," Daniel said.

All Jessop knew was that he didn't want to need to understand. A shiver surged up through him, almost wrenching his hands apart. It was robbing him of any remaining control – and then he saw that it could be his last chance. "You're right, Joe," he said and let them see him shiver afresh. "I'm not dressed for it. I'll get changed."

Having held up his briefcase to illustrate his ruse, he was making for the rear door when Mary squealed "No need to be shy, Des. You can in here."

"I'd rather not, thank you," Jessop said with the last grain of authority he could find in himself, and dodged into the corridor.

As soon as the door was shut he stood his briefcase against it. Even if he wanted to abandon the case, it wouldn't hold the door. He tiptoed fast and shakily to the end of the passage and lowered the topmost crate onto his chest. He retraced his steps as fast as silencing the bottles would allow. He planted the crate in the angle under the hinges and took the briefcase down the corridor. He ignored the blurred mutter of televisions beyond the door while he picked up another crate. How many could he use to ensure the route was blocked before anyone decided he'd been out of sight too long? He was returning for a third crate when he heard a fumbling at the doors on both sides of the corridor.

Even worse than the shapeless eagerness was the way the doors were being assaulted in unison, as if by appendages something was reaching out from – where? Beneath him, or outside the pub? Either thought seemed capable of paralysing him. He flung himself out of their range to seize the next crate, the only aspect of his surroundings he felt able to trust to be real. He couldn't venture down the dim corridor past the quivering doors. He rested crate after crate against the wall, and dragged the last one aside with a jangle of glass. Grabbing his briefcase and abandoning stealth, he threw his weight against the metal bar across the door.

It wouldn't budge for rust. He dropped the case and clutched two-handed at the obstruction while he hurled every ounce of himself at it. The bar gave a reluctant gritty clank, only to reveal that a presence as strong as Jessop was on the far side of the door. It was the wind, which slackened enough to let him and the door stagger forward. He blocked the door with one foot as he snatched up the briefcase. Outside was a narrow unlit alley between the backs of houses. Noise and something more palpable floundered at him – the wind, bearing a tangle of voices and music. At the end of the alley, less than twenty feet away, three men were waiting for him.

Wiry Paul was foremost, flanked by Joe and Tom. He'd pulled his bobble hat down to his eyebrows and was flexing his arms like thick stalks in a tide. "You aren't leaving now we've given you a name," he said.

A flare of rage that was mostly panic made Jessop shout "My name's Paul."

"Fight you for it," the other man offered, prancing forward.

"I'm not playing any more games with anyone."

"Then we aren't either. You won."

"Won the moment you stepped through the door," Tom seemed to think Jessop wanted to hear.

Jessop remembered the notice about a competition. It was immediately clear to him that however much he protested, he was about to receive his prize. "You were the quiz," Paul told him as Joe and Tom took an identical swaying pace forward.

Jessop swung around and bolted for the main road. The dark on which the houses turned their backs felt close to solid with the gale and the sounds entangled in it. The uproar was coming from the houses, from televisions and music systems turned up loud. It made him feel outcast, but surely it had to mean there would be help within earshot if he needed to appeal for it. He struggled against the relentless gale towards the distant gap that appeared to mock his efforts by tossing back and forth. He glanced over his shoulder to see Paul and his cronies strolling after him. A car sped past the gap ahead as if to tempt him forward while he strove not to be blown into an alley to his right. Or should he try that route even if it took him farther from the main road? The thought of being lost as well as pursued had carried him beyond the junction when Betty and Mary blocked his view of the road.

They were still wearing dresses that flapped in the wind, but they were more than broad enough to leave him no escape. The gale lifted Mary's tresses and sent them scuttling crabwise at Jessop. "Some of us try to be more like her," Mary growled with a defensiveness close to violence. "Try to find out what'll make her happier."

"Lots have tried," Betty said in much the same tone. "We're just the first that's had her sort on board."

"Shouldn't be surprised if her sisters want to see the world now too."

"She doesn't just take," Betty said more defensively still. "She provides."

Jessop had been backing away throughout this, both from their words and from comprehending them, but he couldn't leave behind the stale upsurge of his dinner. When he reached the junction again he didn't resist the gale. It sent him sidling at a run into the dark until he managed to turn. The houses that walled him in were derelict and boarded up, yet the noise on both sides of him seemed unabated, presumably because the inhabitants of the nearest occupied buildings had turned the volume higher. Why was the passage darkening? He didn't miss the strip of moonlit cloud until he realised it was no longer overhead. At that moment his footsteps took on a note more metallic than echoes between bricks could account for, but his ears had fastened on another sound – a song.

It was high and sweet and not at all human. It seemed capable of doing away with his thoughts, even with his fleeting notion that it could contain all music. Nothing seemed important except following it to its source – certainly not the way the floor tilted abruptly beneath him, throwing him against one wall. Before long he had to leave his briefcase in order to support himself against the metal walls of the corridor. He heard the clientele of the Seafarer tramp after him, and looked back to see the derelict houses rock away beyond Mary and Betty. All this struck him as less than insignificant, except for the chugging of engines that made him anxious to be wherever it wouldn't interfere with the song. Someone opened a hatch for him and showed him how to grasp the uprights of the ladder that led down into the unlit dripping hold. "That's what sailors hear," said another of the crew as Jessop's foot groped downwards, and Jessop wondered if that referred to the vast wallowing beneath him as well as the song. For an instant too brief for the notion to stay in his mind he thought he might already have glimpsed the nature of the songstress. You'd sing like that if you looked like that, came a last thought. It seemed entirely random to him, and he forgot it as the ancient song drew him into the enormous cradle of darkness.

STEPHEN JONES & KIM NEWMAN

Necrology: 2005

MORE THAN EVER, WE ARE MARKING the passing of writers, artists, performers and technicians who, during their lifetimes, made significant contributions to the horror, science fiction and fantasy genres (or left their mark on popular culture and music in other, often fascinating, ways) . . .

AUTHORS/ARTISTS/COMPOSERS

Veteran artist **Frank Kelly Freas** (Francis Sylvester Kelly), "The Dean of Science Fiction Illustrators", died in his sleep after a long illness on January 2nd, aged 82. He began his career in 1950 with covers for the classic pulp magazine *Weird Tales* and went on to illustrate for *Astounding Stories*, *Analog*, Gnome Press, *MAD* magazine, Ace Books, DAW Books, Starblaze and Laser Books, amongst many other markets. Over the years his book and magazine work earned him eleven Hugo Awards as Best Artist and he was a founder of the Illustrators of the Future Contest. Collections of his work include *Frank Kelly Freas: The Art of Science Fiction*, *Frank Kelly Freas: A Separate Star* and *Frank Kelley Freas: As He Sees It*. Freas also spent seven years as the major cover artist for *Mad* magazine (where he created "Alfred E. Newman") and designed the "Skylab 1" shoulder patch for NASA.

87-year-old comic book legend **Will**(iam) [Erwin] **Eisner** died following complications from quadruple heart bypass surgery in Florida on January 3rd. Following his comic strip debut in 1936, Eisner was drafted into the Army during World War II, where he created the *Joe Dope* strip to teach Jeep maintenance. His most famous creation was crime-fighter *The Spirit*, who appeared in twenty Sunday newspapers with a circulation of five million from 1940–52. He later became one of the most respected and influential writers and artists in the graphic novel field (having established the genre with *A Contract with God* in 1978), and the Eisner Awards are presented in his honour each year at the San Diego ComicCon.

58-year-old British children's author **Humphrey** [William Bouverie] **Carpenter**, whose "Mr. Majeika" series was adapted by BBC-TV in the 1980s, died of heart failure following a long illness on January 4th. Author of *The Oxford Companion to Children's Literature* (with his wife Mari Prichard), *Secret Gardens: The Golden Age of Children's Literature* and *The Inklings: C. S. Lewis, J. R. R. Tolkien, Charles Williams and Their Friends*, Carpenter was also a prolific broadcaster, playwright, jazz musician and controversial biographer (including J. R. R. Tolkien and Dennis Potter).

British literary agent **Gerald** [John] **Pollinger**, who represented such SF and fantasy authors as John Wyndham, James Blish and Eric Frank Russell during his more than fifty years with the Laurence Pollinger agency, died on January 5th, aged 79.

Prolific American author **Bruce B.** [Bingham] **Cassiday** died from complications from Parkinson's disease on January 12th, aged 84. A pulp author for such titles as *Dime Mystery* and *Shock*, he edited *Argosy* from 1954–73 and in 1971 became the last fiction editor of *Adventure*. Cassiday wrote the 1975 novelization *Flash Gordon: The War of the Cybernauts* (as "Carson Bingham"), co-wrote *The Illustrated History of Science Fiction* (1989) and edited *Modern Mystery, Fantasy, and Science Fiction Writers* (1993).

Diane Gail Kelly Goldberg, who published horror fiction as "d. g. k. Goldberg", died of cancer on January 14th. A former psychotherapist and the author of around fifty short stories, her novels include *Skating on the Edge*, published as a print-on-demand title, and *Doomed to Repeat It*. At the time of her death, she left behind a sequel to her first novel and a collection of short stories entitled *Wrong Turn*.

Canadian-born "cozy" mystery writer **Charlotte** [Matilda] **Mac-Leod** (aka "Alisa Craig"/"Matilda Hughes") died in Maine the same day, aged 82. Her novels *The Curse of the Giant Hogweed*, *The Wrong Rite* and *The Grub-and-Stakers House a Haunt* include fantasy and supernatural elements.

British-born composer and arranger **Albert Harris** died in New Zealand on January 14th, aged 88. Arriving in the US in 1936, he worked on such films as *Kiss Me Deadly*, *Master of the World*, *The Raven* (1963), *Dr. Goldfoot and the Bikini Machine*, *The Ghost in the Invisible Bikini* and the *Curse of Dracula* segment of the 1979 TV series *Cliffhangers*.

Canadian-born **Dan Lee** (Danny Wei-Ping Lee) died of lung cancer on January 15th, aged 35. Described as one of America's "brightest and most promising" animation designers, Lee joined Pixar Animation Studios in 1996 where he created major characters for *A Bug's Life*, *Toy Story 2*, *Monsters Inc.* and *Finding Nemo*.

German author, editor, translator and literary agent **Walter Ernsting** (aka "Fred McPatterson") died in Austria the same day, aged 84. In the 1950s and 1960s he edited and wrote for *Utopia-Magazin* and *Galaxi* while, as "Clark Darlton", he co-founded the hugely successful "Perry Rhodan" franchise with Karl-Herbert Scheer in 1961.

Swedish SF author, poet, playwright, editor and translator **Sven Christer Swahn** also died on January 15th, aged 71. He had spent the previous three months in a coma. Swahn translated around 300 books into Swedish, and his own titles include *13 Stories of Ghosts and Other Things*, *My Dearly Departed* and *A Monster's Memories: A Ghost Story of the 20th Century*.

Bookseller and publisher **Stephen Gregg** died of a degenerative disorder of the nervous system on January 18th, aged 50. During the 1970s he published the SF semi-prozine *Eternity*.

Theatre composer **Dick Gallagher**, whose credits include *Have I Got a Girl for You: The Frankenstein Musical*, died on January 20th, aged 49.

British author, publisher and antiquarian book dealer **Geoffrey Palmer** died on January 22nd, aged 92. With his long-time partner Noel Lloyd he wrote a number of children's ghost stories which appeared in such collections as *Ghosts Go Haunting*, *A Brew of Witchcraft*, *Ghost Series Around the World*, *Moonshine and Magic*, *The Obstinate Ghost and Other Ghostly Tales* and *Haunting Stories of Ghosts and Ghouls*. They also collaborated on a biography of E. F. Benson and another about his father, and published a series of chapbooks under the Hermitage Books imprint.

British SF fan **Ken Lake** died of liver cancer on January 24th. His reviews, articles and letters appeared in BSFA publications from the early 1980s onwards.

Bookstore owner **Beverly J.** (Jean) **Mason**, who ran the wonderful Toad Hall Records and Books in Rockford, Illinois, with her late husband Larry, died on February 3rd, aged 68.

Country music singer and songwriter **Merle Kilgore**, who was also manager for Hank Williams, Jr, died in Mexico after a long battle with cancer on February 6th, aged 70. He wrote the hit "Wolverton Mountain" for Claude King and teamed up with June Carter to co-write "Ring of Fire", which became a signature tune for Carter's husband, Johnny Cash.

Pulitzer Prize-winning American playwright, screenwriter and author **Arthur** [Asher] **Miller**, who is probably best remembered for his marriage (1956–61) to Marilyn Monroe, died of congestive heart failure on February 10th, aged 89. Miller's 1953 play *The Crucible* was set during the seventeenth-century witch trials in Salem, but was in reality a veiled attack on Joe McCarthy and his House Committee on Un-American Activities. It was filmed in 1997, starring Miller's son-in-law, actor Daniel Day-Lewis.

American songwriter **Jack Segal**, who wrote "Scarlet Ribbons", died of heart failure the same day, aged 86.

American SF and fantasy author and editor **Jack L.** [Laurence] **Chalker** died of lung and kidney failure after several surgeries on February 11th, aged 60. When only fourteen years old he started publishing his Hugo-nominated fanzine *Mirage*, and he later founded the Baltimore Science Fiction Society with a high school friend, which led to the regular Balticons. He was the author of more than sixty books, including *A Jungle of Stars* (1976), *Dancers in the Afterglow*, *A War of Shadows* and *The Moreau Factor*. His best-known series include "The Well of Souls" novels, "The Four Lords of the Diamonds" quartet, the "Soul Rider" quintet, the "Change-winds" trilogy, and the "Dancing Gods" and "Rings of the Master" sequences. Also the founder of Mirage Press, he also produced such non-fiction studies as *The New H. P. Lovecraft Bibliography* (1962), *In Memoriam: Clark Ashton Smith*, *The Necronomicon: A Study* and *The Index to the Science-Fantasy Publishers: A Critical and Bibliographic History* (both with Mark Owings), and *An Informal Biography of Scrooge McDuck*.

American fan and reviewer **Gary S. Potter**, who co-published and introduced the 1993 chapbook *Voyages Into Darkness* by Stephen Laws and Mark Morris, died on February 13th, aged 46. His horror fanzine *The Point Beyond* was published since 1989.

British writer, scriptwriter and anthologist **Richard Davis** was found dead of an apparent heart attack at his home on February 14th, aged 60. During the 1960s and 1970s he was extremely active in the horror field, making his fiction debut in 1963 in *The Pan Book of Horror Stories*. In 1966 he became assistant story editor on the BBC-TV's second series of *Out of the Unknown* and was also story editor on the 1968 series *Late Night Horror*. He edited *The Tandem Book of Horror Stories No. 2* and *No. 3*, and the *Space*, *Spectre* and *Armada Sci-Fi* anthology series for younger readers. He began Sphere Books' annual *Year's Best Horror Stories* series in 1971 which, after three volumes, was taken over by other editors and American publisher DAW Books. Davis attempted to continue the series as *The Orbit Book of Horror Stories*. He also worked as a scriptwriter on the 1974 BBC World Service radio series *Price of Fear* starring Vincent Price, which formed the basis of the 1976 anthology of the same name.

American SF short story writer and poet **Sonya Dorman** [Hess] died on the same day, aged 80. She won a Rhysling SF poetry award in 1977 and her fiction appeared in *Amazing*, *The Magazine of Fantasy and Science Fiction*, *Orbit* and *Dangerous Visions*. *Planet Patrol* (1978) was a young adult fix-up novel.

SF author **F. M.** (Francis Marion) ["Buz"] **Busby** died after a lengthy intestinal illness on February 17th, aged 83. Winner (with his wife Elinor) of the 1960 Hugo for Best Fanzine for *Cry of the Nameless*, he made his fiction debut in 1957 in *Future SF* magazine. His best-known novels include *Cage a Man*, *All These Earths*, *The Breeds of Man*, *Arrow from Earth* and the "Rissa Kerguèlen", "Demu" and "Dynas" series. His short fiction is collected in *Getting Home*.

"Gonzo" American counter-culture journalist **Hunter S.** (Stockton) **Thompson** killed himself with a self-inflicted gunshot wound to the head on February 20th, aged 67. Well-known for his prolific drug use and eccentric and acerbic behaviour, his cult 1972 book *Fear and Loathing in Las Vegas* was filmed in 1998 with Johnny Depp as Thompson, and Bill Murray played him in the semi-biographical film *Where the Buffalo Roam* (1980). Thompson also briefly appeared in the pilot episode of TV's *Nash Bridges*, which he co-created with star Don Johnson. The model for the character of "Duke" in Garry Trudeau's comic strip *Doonesbury*, he once famously described President Richard Nixon as "America's answer to the monstrous Mr Hyde. He speaks for the werewolf in us". Thompson's ashes were fired from a cannon on August 21st during a fireworks ceremony, which Depp reportedly picked up the $2 million-plus tab for.

75-year-old Polish artist **Zdzislaw Beksinski** was found dead from multiple stab wounds in his Warsaw home on February 22nd. Two teenagers were charged with murder. Some of his work was collected in *The Fantastic Art of Beksinski* (1998).

Paperback cover illustrator **James Avati** died on February 27th, aged 92. His realistic style appeared on such titles as Harry Harrison's *Deathworld* titles, *Doc Savage: Meteor Menace* and the original cover for J. D. Salinger's *The Catcher in the Rye*. A documentary, *James Avati: A Life in Paperbacks*, was released in 2000.

American SF writer **Raylyn Moore**, the first woman to publish a story in *Esquire* (1954), died the same day, aged 77. Her books include the novel, *What Happened to Emily Goode After the Great Exhibition* and the 1974 study of L. Frank Baum, *Wonderful Wizard, Marvelous Land*. Her short fiction appeared in *The Magazine of Fantasy and Science Fiction*, the *Orbit* anthologies and elsewhere.

Pianist **Martin Denny**, credited with creating the jungle sounds of "exotica" or "tiki" music in the 1950s, died in Honolulu on March 2nd, aged 93.

Walt Disney animator and character designer **Vance Gerry** died of cancer on March 5th, aged 75. He began working at Disney in 1955 and was a layout artist on *101 Dalmatians* and *The Sword in the Stone* before moving on to other roles on such titles as *The Jungle Book*, *The Aristocats*, *The Black Cauldron*, *The Great Mouse Detective*, *Hercules*, *Fantasia 2000* and many others.

Radio and TV scriptwriter **Gertrude Fass** who, with her husband George (who died in 1965), wrote episodes of *Science Fiction Theater* and *Sherlock Holmes*, died on March 6th, aged 95.

British novelist, screenwriter and playwright **Willis Hall** died on March 7th, aged 75. His TV work included many scripts for *Worzel Gummidge*, starring Jon Pertwee. His books for children include the "Vampire/Henry Hollins" series beginning with *The Last Vampire* (1982), and his ghost stories appeared in such anthologies as *The Midnight Ghost Book* and *The After Midnight Ghost Book*.

American cartographer and illustrator **Karen Wynn Fonstad**, who created *The Atlas of Middle-Earth* (1981), died of breast cancer on March 11th, aged 59. Her other fantasy and SF map books include *The Atlas of Pern*, *The Atlas of the DragonLance World* and *The Forgotten Realms Atlas*.

Scriptwriter **William Cannon** died on March 12th, aged 67. He wrote such films as *Skidoo*, *Hex* and the 1980 TV movie of *Brave New World*.

93-year-old SF and fantasy author, poet and editor **Andre Norton** (Alice Mary Norton) died in her sleep of congestive heart failure after a long illness on March 17th at her home in Murfreesboro, Tennessee. A former reader at Gnome Press (1950–58), her first book,

The Prince Commands, was published in 1934. Norton's more than 130 novels, many aimed at young adults, included such titles as *Star Man's Son 2250 A.D.*, *Star Guard*, *Sargasso of Space* (as "Andrew North"), *The Time Traders*, *Catseye*, *Steel Magic*, *Operation Time Search*, *Fur Magic*, *Exiles of the Stars*, *High Sorcery*, *Dragon Magic*, *Shadowhawk*, *Dare to Go A-Hunting*, *Mirror of Destiny*, *The Solar Queen* and the popular "Witch World", "Time War", "Beast Master", "Mark of the Cat", "Solar Queen" and "Trillium" series. Her 170th book, *Three Hands for Scorpio*, was published posthumously in 2005. She also collaborated with a number of writers and editors, among them, Robert Adams, Robert Bloch, Marion Zimmer Bradley, Martin H. Greenberg, Mercedes Lackey and Julian May. The author of nearly 100 short stories and editor of numerous anthologies, including the ghostly *Small Shadows Creep* and the *Cat Fantastic* series, she became the first female SFWA Grand Master in 1984 and received a World Fantasy Lifetime Achievement Award in 1997. The SFWA Andre Norton Award for young adult novels was inaugurated in 2006. She arranged to be cremated along with copies of her first and last books.

Old-time fanzine publisher **Art Rapp** died of Alzheimer's disease on March 24th. Between 1947 and 1950 he produced forty issues of *Spacewarp*, and continued the title into the late 1990s with issue #204.

Film and TV writer **Paul Henning**, who created the hit 1960s shows *The Beverly Hillbillies* and *Petticoat Junction* and executive produced *Green Acres* for CBS-TV, died on March 25th, aged 93. He also wrote the *Hillbillies* theme song, "The Ballad of Jed Clampett", sung by Jerry Scoggins.

American writer and film-maker **Robert F. Slatzer**, who wrote two books about Marilyn Monroe and claimed to have briefly married the actress in 1952, died after a long illness on March 28th, aged 77. A scriptwriter for such studios as Monogram, Republic, Universal, MGM, Columbia and Paramount, Slatzer also wrote and directed films, including *Bigfoot* (1969), starring John Carradine.

Scriptwriter **Dave Freeman**, whose credits include *Rocket to the Moon* and episodes of TV's *The Avengers*, died on March 28th, aged 82.

Songwriter **Jack Keller**, who composed the theme song to the 1960s sit-coms *Bewitched* and *Gidget*, died of acute leukaemia in Nashville on April 1st, aged 68. His songs include "Everybody's Somebody's Fool", "Venus in Blue Jeans" and the Monkees' "Your Auntie Grizelda". Keller was also credited as a producer on the Monkees TV theme and first record album.

Comic strip writer and artist **Dale Messick** (Dalia Messick), whose long-running *Brenda Starr, Reporter* ran in 250 newspapers during its peak in the 1950s, died on April 5th, aged 98, after suffering a series of strokes. Messick was pressured by her syndicate to retire in 1985, and she received the National Cartoonist Society's Milton Caniff Lifetime Achievement Award in 1997. Movie versions of *Brenda Starr* were filmed in 1945, 1976 and 1987, while the US Postal Service issued a Brenda Starr stamp in 1995.

Canadian-born author **Saul** (Solomon) **Bellow** died at his home in Massachusetts the same day, aged 89. The Nobel laureate and Pulitzer Prize-winning author wrote more than a dozen novels, at least two of which are genre-inspired: *Henderson the Rain King* and *Mr. Sammler's Planet*. He appeared in Woody Allen's *Zelig* as himself.

Bibliographer and book dealer **Leonard A.** (Angus) **Robbins**, who compiled the six-volume set *The Pulp Magazine Index* for Starmont House (1989–91), died from ALS (Lou Gehrig's Disease) and pneumonia on April 5th, aged 84.

Animation designer **Gene Hazelton** died on April 6th, aged 85. He worked on *Invitation to the Dance*, *The Flintstones*, *Tom and Jerry* and the credits for *I Love Lucy*.

Disney background artist **Bill Layne** died on April 7th, aged 94. His many credits include *Sleeping Beauty*, *101 Dalmations*, *The Sword in the Stone*, *Mary Poppins*, *The Jungle Book*, *Bedknobs and Broomsticks* and *Robin Hood*.

Feminist author **Andrea Dworkin** died on April 9th, aged 58.

Terri Pinckard, whose article "Monsters Are Good for My Children" appeared in *Famous Monsters of Filmland*, died after a long illness on April 10th, aged 75. Her short stories appeared in the *Year's Best Horror Stories*, *Fantasy Book* and *Vertex: The Magazine of Science Fiction*, and were anthologised by Forrest J Ackerman in such volumes as *Dr. Acula's Thrilling Tales of the Uncanny* and *Sci-Fi Womanthology*.

Australian-born author, magazine columnist and movie expert **John** [Raymond] **Brosnan** was found dead in his London flat on April 11th after friends were unable to contact him. He had reportedly died some days earlier of acute pancreatitis. Brosnan, who was aged 57, published several books on genre cinema, including *James Bond in the Cinema*, *Movie Magic: The Story of Special Effects in the Cinema*, *The Horror People*, *Future Tense: The Cinema of Science Fiction* (aka *The Primal Screen: A History of Science Fiction Film*), *Hollywood Babble On*, *Lights! Camera!*

Magic!, *Scream: The Unofficial Companion to the Scream Trilogy*) and *The Hannibal Lecter Story*. His novels include such SF and fantasy titles as the "Skylords" series (*Skyship*, *The Midas Deep*, *The Skylords*, *War of the Skylords* and *The Fall of Skylords*), *The Opononax Invasion*, *Damned & Fancy*, *Have Demon Will Travel*, *Mothership* and *Mothership Awakening*, along with a number of horror novels under the acronymic pseudonyms "Harry Adam Knight" and "Simon Ian Childer" (often in collaboration with Leroy Kettle) and "James Blackstone" (with John Baxter), including *The Fungus*, *Tendrils*, *Worm*, *Torched*, *Carnosaur*, *Slimer* and *Bedlam* (the latter three all filmed). Brosnan apparently suffered from acute depression and, according to close friends, simply lost the will to live after years of health problems. He was cremated along with a plastic dinosaur and a Czech translation of one of his novels to the James Bond theme.

American fanzine editor **Bill** (William) [Lawrence] **Bowers** was found dead at an assisted living facility on April 18th, aged 61. He probably died of complications from emphysema. From the 1960s–90s he edited such fanzines as the Hugo-nominated *Double Bill* (with Bill Mallardi), *Xenolith* and five-times Hugo nominee *Outworlds*. A Fan Guest of Honour at the 1978 Worldcon, as a drafting engineer he also helped design some of the early *Star Wars* toys from the Kenner Toy Company.

Canadian-born composer **Robert Farnon** died on April 21st, aged 87. His credits include the TV shows *Quatermass II*, *The Prisoner* and *The Champions*, along with such movies as *Road to Hong Kong* and *Expresso Bongo*.

Czechoslovakian satirical SF author and psychiatrist **Josef Nesvadba** died on April 25th, aged 78. His collections include *The Death of Tarzan* (1958, filmed in 1962), *Einstein's Brain*, *Vampires Ltd.* (filmed as *Upir z Feratu* in 1981), *The Last Journeys of Captain Nemo* and *In the Footsteps of the Abominable Snowman* (aka *The Lost Face*).

Disney artist and writer **Joe Grant** died of a heart attack at his drawing table on May 6th, aged 96. Starting with *Mickey's Gala Premiere* (1933), he worked at Disney designing the evil Queen/Witch in *Snow White and the Seven Dwarfs*, was co-story director on *Fantasia*, co-scripted *Dumbo* and conceived *Lady and the Tramp*. His other credits include *The Reluctant Dragon*, *Pinocchio*, the Oscar-winning short *Der Fuehrer's Face*, *Alice in Wonderland*, *Beauty and the Beast*, *Aladdin*, *The Lion King*, *Mulan* and *Fantasia 2000* (the flamingo yo-yo ballet) and he came up with the title

Monsters, Inc. At the time of his death he was still working four days a week at Walt Disney Feature Animation.

Jeff Slaten, who sold some stories to Atlas Comics in the mid-1970s, died of a heart attack on May 7th, aged 49. He also co-wrote the 1979 SF novel *Death Jag* (with Albert C. Ellis) and collaborated with Robert E. Vardeman on a story.

Television writer **Stanley Silverman**, whose credits include *Science Fiction Theatre*, *The Green Hornet* and *Land of the Giants*, died on May 9th, aged 90.

Disney animator **Brian Wesley Green** collapsed and died on May 12th. He worked on *The Hunchback of Notre Dame*, *Atlantis the Lost Empire*, *Dinosaur* and *Fantasia 2000*.

Low budget screenwriter, playwright and film critic **Ed Kelleher** (aka "Edouard Dauphin") died of a degenerative brain disease on May 14th, aged 61. His screenplay credits include the 1970s cult favourites *Invasion of the Blood Farmers* and *Shriek of the Mutilated*, along with *Lurkers*, *Prime Evil*, *Madonna* and *Voodoo Dolls*. Kelleher also wrote six horror novels in collaboration with Harriette Vidal, plus biographies of punk rock performance artist Wendy O. Williams and David Bowie. From 1979 to 1986 he was the tour manager and publicist for the singer-songwriter Melanie.

Comics artist **Paul H. Cassidy**, one of the first illustrators to draw *Superman* and credited with adding the "S" to the Man of Steel's cape, died on May 15th, aged 94. He began working in Joe Schuster's studio in 1938 and was a ghost artist on the strip for the next two years.

29-year-old composer/orchestrator **Linda Martinez**, whose credits include the 2002 TV remake of *Carrie*, committed suicide on May 19th.

SF editor **Samuel H.** (Herbert) **Post** died of inoperable cancer on May 20th, aged 81. During the 1950s and 1960s he was paperback editor at MacFadden-Bartell, where he published Philip K. Dick, Damon Knight, A. E. van Vogt, Poul Anderson and others. He edited (uncredited) the 1960s anthologies *The 6 Fingers of Time and Other Stories* and *The Frozen Planet*.

57-year-old American SF writer and elementary school teacher **Pat** (Patricia) **York**, who was nominated for a Nebula Award in 2001, died on May 21st in Columbus, Ohio, when a bus collided with the car in which she was a passenger. Her short stories appeared in *Full Spectrum*, *Realms of Fantasy* and other publications, and she was twice a finalist in the Writers of the Future competition.

Fanzine editor **Noreen Shaw** (Noreen Mary Kane), who edited the

Hugo-nominated *Axe* with her husband, SF editor Larry Shaw (who died in 1985), died on May 25th, aged 74. She also co-chaired the 1955 Worldcon with her first husband, Nick Falasca.

Television writer **Frank Barton**, who worked on TV's *The Invaders*, died on May 31st, aged 87.

Composer **Jaime Mendoza-Neva** died of complications from diabetes the same day, aged 79. His many credits include Edward D. Wood's *Orgy of the Dead*, *The Witchmaker*, *The Brotherhood of Satan*, *Legacy of Blood*, *Legend of Boggy Creek*, *Grave of the Vampire*, *Garden of the Dead*, *The House on Skull Mountain*, *A Boy and His Dog*, *The Town That Dreaded Sundown*, *Creature from Black Lake*, *Shadow of Chikara*, *Vampire Hookers*, *The Evictors*, *Psycho from Texas*, *Mausoleum* and *Terror in the Swamp*.

American science fiction and fantasy novelist and poet **Warren [Carl] Norwood** died of liver and kidney failure on June 3rd, aged 59. His books include *The Windhover Tapes: An Image of Voices* and its sequels, *Midway Between*, *Polar Fleet*, *Final Command*, *Shudderchild* and *True Jaguar*. With Mel Odom he collaborated on three "Time Police" novels (*Vanished*, *Trapped!* and *Stranded*), and he was a John W. Campbell Award finalist in 1983 and 1984.

Minneapolis bookseller and collector **Peder D. Wagtskjold** died of acute liver and renal failure on June 6th, aged 41. He began his career as a bookseller in 1985 at DreamHaven Books, where he worked for almost twelve years. He then started his own mail-order venture, PDW Books, and was associated with small press publisher Fedogan & Bremer for a number of years.

American *Dungeons & Dragons* artist **David C. Sutherland III** died on June 7th, aged 56.

Former SF short story writer, turned playwright and screenwriter, **Michael R. Farkash** was found dead after a long illness on June 9th, aged 53.

Composer **David Diamond** died on June 13th, aged 89. His credits include *Zombies of Mora Tau* and *20 Million Miles to Earth*.

British scriptwriter **N. J. Crisp** died on June 14th, aged 81. He wrote the TV movie *The Masks of Death* (with Peter Cushing as Sherlock Holmes) plus episodes of *Orson Welles' Great Mysteries* and *Doom Watch*.

Film and TV writer **Samuel Roeca** died on June 17th, aged 85. His credits include *Sabu and the Magic Ring*, *The Night Visitor* and episodes of *Tarzan* and *Land of the Lost*.

British experimental composer and drummer **Basil Kirchin**, whose film credits include the 1971 film *The Abominable Dr. Phibes* starring Vincent Price, died of cancer on June 18th, aged 77. He also contributed scores to *The Shuttered Room* and *The Mutations* (aka *The Freakmaker*).

Comics publisher and dealer **Bruce Hamilton** died after a long illness the same day, aged 72. In the 1980s he founded the Gladstone Publishing Co. to publish Walt Disney characters. An early advisor to *The Overstreet Comic Book Price Guide*, he also worked with Disney artist Carl Barks to produce limited edition lithographs.

Television writer **Richard Tuber** also died on June 18th, of a heart attack, aged 74. During the 1950s and 1960s he often worked for TV producer Ivan Tors and his credits include *Around the World Under the Sea* and episodes of *Science Fiction Theater*.

Comic book artist **Sam Kweskin** (aka "Irv Wesley") died on June 23rd, aged 81. He started at Atlas Comics (later Marvel) in the early 1950s, working on such titles as *Adventures Into Terror*. After a stint in advertising and commercials from 1957 onwards, he returned to comics in the early 1970s to draw for *Daredevil*, *Sub-Mariner* and *Dr. Strange*.

Cartoonist and animator **Rowland B.** (Bragg) **Wilson** died of heart failure on June 28th, aged 74. Named Playboy's Cartoonist of the Year in 1982, he was also a layout designer on such Disney cartoon films as *The Little Mermaid*, *The Hunchback of Notre Dame*, *Tarzan* and *Hercules*.

Book dealer and collector **John** [Kevin] **McLaughlin**, whose Book Sail specialised in rare books and artwork, died at his home in California on June 30th, aged 63. In 1984 he purchased the only surviving final draft typescript of *Dracula* (under the original title *The Un-Dead*), bearing numerous corrections in Bram Stoker's own hand. The manuscript failed to reach its $1 million reserve at a Christie's auction on 2002, but subsequently sold to an anonymous buyer for $944,000.

Hollywood author/screenwriter/producer/director **Ernest Lehman**, whose credits include Alfred Hitchcock's *North by Northwest* and *Family Plot*, died of a heart attack on July 2nd, aged 89. In 2001 he was the first screenwriter to receive an honorary Academy Award.

SF and fantasy author **Chris** (Christopher) [Renshaw] **Bunch**, who often collaborated with his brother-in-law Allan Cole, died of chronic obstructive pulmonary disease on July 4th, aged 61. A Vietnam war veteran and former combat correspondent, his numerous books include the popular eight-volume "Sten" series with Cole plus such titles as *The Far Kingdoms*, *The Wind After Time*, *The Darkness of God*, *The Empire Stone*, *Storm of Wings*, *The Last*

Battle and *The Dog from Hell*. Bunch and Cole also scripted a number of TV series, including episodes of *The Incredible Hulk*, *Werewolf* and *The A-Team*. In 1997, Bunch shot a squatter during an argument, but the killing was judged "justified and excusable" homicide.

Evan Hunter (Salvatore A. Lombino), who also published police procedural novels under the name "Ed McBain", died of cancer of the larynx on July 6th, aged 78. His many books include *The Blackboard Jungle*, *Lizzie* (the story of Lizzie Borden), *Tomorrow's World* (as by "Hunt Collins") and the popular "87th Precinct" police procedural series, which he began publishing in 1956 and which has become the longest-running crime series in print, comprising fifty-five titles. His anthology *Transgressions*, published two months before his death, included new novellas by Stephen King, Joyce Carol Oates, John Farris and others. As well as having his own work filmed, he also adapted Daphne du Maurier's short story, "The Birds" into a screenplay for Alfred Hitchcock (the author detailed the experience in his 1997 memoir *Me and Hitch*). He was named a Grand Master by the Mystery Writers of America in 1985 and in 1998 was the first American to be honoured with the Cartier Diamond Dagger Lifetime Achievement Award presented by the Crime Writer's Association of Great Britain.

55-year-old Lewis Carroll enthusiast and chairman of the H. G. Wells Society **Giles Hart** was killed in the London suicide bus bombing on July 7th. He was due to give a talk that evening on Carroll's lesser-known works. Born in Sudan, Hart was posthumously awarded a Knight's Cross of the Order of Merit by the Polish president on July 22nd for his prominent support of the Polish Solidarity movement during the 1980s.

Book packager, publisher and editor **Byron** [Cary] **Preiss** died of injuries sustained in a car accident in East Hampton, New York, on July 9th, aged 52. Preiss launched Byron Preiss Visual Publications in 1974, publishing fantasy, science fiction and graphic novels. After embracing digital publishing in the early 1990s with Byron Preiss Multimedia, he founded iBooks in 1999. He was responsible for such titles as the graphic novel of *The Stars My Destination*, *The Illustrated Harlan Ellison*, the *Isaac Asimov Robot City* and *Weird Heroes* shared world series and such theme anthologies as *The Ultimate Dracula*, *The Ultimate Frankenstein*, *The Ultimate Werewolf*, *The Ultimate Zombie*, *The Ultimate Alien*, *The Ultimate Dinosaur*, *The Ultimate Dragon* and *The Ultimate Witch*. Preiss also wrote such books as *Dragonworld* (with J. Michael Reaves), *The Little Blue Brontosaurus* and *The Vampire State Building*.

British-born critic, author and Oscar-nominated screenwriter **Gavin Lambert**, whose best-known novel is *Inside Daisy Clover*, died of pulmonary fibrosis on July 17th, aged 80. A former editor of the BFI's *Sight and Sound* magazine (1949–55), he emigrated to Hollywood in the 1950s and worked as an assistant to director Nicholas Ray (with whom he had a brief affair). Lambert contributed additional dialogue to *Whoever Slew Auntie Roo?* and his short fiction was collected in a number of volumes, beginning with *The Slide Area: Scenes of Hollywood Life* (1959). He also wrote biographies of Natalie Wood, Lindsay Anderson, George Cukor and Norma Shearer, amongst others.

Disney animator **Ruben Apocaca** died the same day, aged 73. He worked on *Sleeping Beauty*, *Mary Poppins* and *The Jungle Book*, as well as such TV shows as *The Flintstones* and *Alvin and the Chipmunks*.

Self-taught comics artist **Jim** (James) [Nicholas] **Aparo** died after a long battle against cancer on July 19th, aged 72. He started out at Charlton in the early 1960s, and during his almost thirty years with DC Comics he illustrated the adventures of Batman, Green Arrow, Aquaman, the Phantom Stranger and The Spectre, amongst others. He had been retired for around four years.

American radio and TV scriptwriter **Shirley Thomas Perkins**, who created the 1950s series *Men in Space*, died of cancer on July 21st, aged 85.

Reclusive American film collector **Alois F. Dettlaff** was found dead at his home in Wisconsin on July 26th. He was 84. In 1980, Dettlaff revealed that he had the only known surviving print of Thomas Edison's long thought lost *Frankenstein* (1910). He finally made it available to other collectors on home video in 2003.

American composer and lyricist **Robert Wright** died on July 27th, aged 90. His collaborations with George Forrest (who died in 1999) include the score for the Tony Award-winning 1953 Broadway musical *Kismet* and the movies *I Married an Angel* and *After the Thin Man*. His hits include "Stranger in Paradise" and "I've Been Working on the Railroad".

British film critic, author, TV and radio presenter and scriptwriter **Tom Hutchinson** died in his sleep after a long illness on August 3rd, aged 75. For many years the chief film critic of *The Sunday Telegraph*, he also worked for *Picture Guide*, *Mail on Sunday*, *The Guardian* and *Radio Times*. Hutchinson was the author of *Horror &*

Fantasy in the Cinema and *The Horror Film,* and he contributed many of the horror star entries to Kim Newman's *The BFI Companion to Horror.* His other books included biographies of Marilyn Monroe and Rod Steiger.

German-born Hollywood composer-arranger **Lyle "Spud" Murphy,** who transformed "Three Blind Mice" into the theme for *Three Stooges* shorts at Columbia, died of surgery complications on August 5th, aged 96. His composing process, the Equal Interval System, was adopted by hundreds of professional musicians.

DreamWorks animator **Timothy Gruver** died of a grand mal seizure on August 9th, aged 33. He worked on *Shrek, El Dorado* and *Prince of Egypt.*

UFO sceptic **Philip J.** [Julian] **Klass** died of prostate cancer the same day, aged 85. His seven books include *UFO Abductions: A Dangerous Game* (1989), and for many years he offered a reward of $10,000 to anyone who could provide scientific evidence of alien visitations. The money was never claimed.

45-year-old **Joe Ranft,** the Oscar-nominated co-writer of *Toy Story* and story supervisor at Pixar Animation Studios, was one of two people killed on August 16th when their vehicle veered off the highway in Mendocino County, California, plunging 130 feet into the Pacific ocean. Ranft's other credits include *The Nightmare Before Christmas, The Little Mermaid, Beauty and the Beast, The Lion King, A Bug's Life, Toy Story 2, Monsters Inc.* and *Cars.* As a voice actor he portrayed Heimlich the Bavarian caterpillar in *A Bug's Life* and Wheezy the penguin in *Toy Story 2.*

Children's author **William Corlett** died in France the same day, aged 66. Best known for his "Magician's House" sequence – *The Steps Up the Chimney, The Door in the Tree, The Tunnel Behind the Waterfall* and *The Bridge in the Clouds* (the first three dramatized by the BBC, 1999–2000) – his other books include *The Summer of the Haunting.*

Legendary German-born portrait photographer **Horst Tappe,** whose subjects include Pablo Picasso, Salvador Dali and Alfred Hitchcock, died after a long battle with cancer in Switzerland on August 21st, aged 67.

French SF editor and anthologist **Daniel Riche** died of cancer the same day, aged 56. Starting in the 1960s, he edited and published the fanzine *Nyarlathotep* before going on to become a book and magazine editor. In the 1980s he edited the "Gore" line of splatterpunk novels for Fleuve Noir, while *Le Livre d'Or de Richard Matheson* was a "Best of" collection of the author's work. He also appeared as a demon in the 1991 film *Ma vie est un enfer (My Life is Hell).*

Disney imagineer **Fred Joerger** died on August 26th, aged 91. He helped create the models and art direct such attractions as Sleeping Beauty's Castle, Pirates of the Caribbean, Submarine Voyage and EPCOT.

American composer **Richard Loring** died of cancer on August 28th, aged 86. His credits include *House on Haunted Hill*.

Animator **Marty Scully** died of Lou Gehrig's disease on August 30th, aged 42. He worked on *Mr. Magoo*, *The Pagemaster* and *Rugrats Go Wild*.

Philippines-born comic book artist **Fred Carrillo** also died in August, aged 79. He worked on such titles as *The Phantom Stranger* and *Swamp Thing*.

Polish artist **Henryk Tomaszewski**, who is credited with creating the distinctive post-war Polish Poster School style, died in Warsaw from a progressive nerve degeneration on September 11th, aged 91.

French-born author **Vladimir Volkoff** died on September 13th, aged 72. Although best known for his spy fiction, he published a couple of SF novels in the 1980s and won the 1963 Jules Verne Award for *Metro Pour L'Enfer* (*Metro to Hell*).

67-year-old film and Broadway composer **Joel Hirschhorn**, who won an Academy Award for Best Song for co-writing "The Morning After" from *The Poseidon Adventure*, died of a heart attack on September 17th after breaking his shoulder in a fall the previous day. His other credits, usually in collaboration with Al Kasha, include *The Towering Inferno* (another Oscar winner for the song "We May Never Love Like This Again"), *Freaky Friday* (1976), *Dorothy Meets Ozma of Oz*, *Pete's Dragon*, *All Dogs Go to Heaven* and *The Giant of Thunder Mountain*.

89-year-old science fiction author and US patent attorney **Charles L. (Leonard) Harness** died on September 20th, following a stroke earlier in the year. He published his first story in 1948, and his relatively small number of books include *Flight Into Yesterday* (aka *The Paradox Man*), *The Ring of Ritornel*, *Wolfhead*, *The Catalyst*, *Firebird*, *Redworld*, *Krono*, *Lurid Dreams* and *Lunar Justice*. Harness' short fiction is collected in *The Rose* and *An Ornament to His Profession*, and in 2004 he was named an "Author of Distinction" by the SFWA.

Nazi hunter **Simon Wiesenthal**, who was the inspiration for Laurence Olivier's character in *The Boys from Brazil*, died on September 20th, aged 96.

Popular British children's author **Helen Cresswell** died of ovarian cancer on September 26th, aged 71. The author of more than 120 books, including *Snatchers*, *The Bongleweed*, *Moondial*, *Bag of Bones*, six witchy *Lizzie Dripping* fantasies (assembled from the BBC-TV series *Jackanory* in the 1970s) and "The Bagthorpe Saga", beginning with *Ordinary Jack* and adapted as a TV series in 1981. Cresswell's TV scripts include an adaptation of *Five Children and It*, *The Phoenix and the Carpet* and *The Demon Headmaster*, and she received The Phoenix Award in 1988 for *The Night-Watchmen*.

American puppeteer and Emmy Award-winning scriptwriter **Jerry** (Jerome) [Ravn] **Juhl** died of complications from cancer on September 27th, aged 67. He joined the Jim Henson Company in 1961 and from 1977–81 was head writer on *The Muppet Show*. He also worked on five *Muppet* spin-off movies, various specials, and the TV series *Sesame Street* and *Fraggle Rock*. Guests were given funny noses at his memorial service.

Shakespearean scholar and biographer **John** [Charles] **McCabe** [III], who created the Sons of the Desert organisation honouring screen legends Laurel and Hardy, died of congestive heart failure the same day, aged 84. His 1961 book on the comedy duo is widely considered the definitive work, and his other volumes include biographies of James Cagney, George M. Cohan and Charlie Chaplin.

Screenwriter **Louis A. Garfinkle** died of complications from Parkinson's disease on October 2nd, aged 77. Nominated for an Academy Award in 1977 for *The Deer Hunter*, he also wrote and produced *I Bury the Living* and *Face of Fire*.

73-year-old scriptwriter **Dennis Murphy** died on October 6th. His credits include *The Todd Killings* and *Eye of the Devil* (aka *13*).

Film and TV writer and producer **Devery Freeman** died of complications from open heart surgery on October 7th, aged 92. A veteran of the "Golden Age" of American television, in 1954 he helped create the Writers Guild of America and as a negotiator won the right for the union to decide how writing credits were displayed on screen.

Mountain climber **Michael Ward**, who was part of the 1953 Everest expedition, died the same day, aged 80. Two years earlier he photographed a thirteen-inch, three-toed footprint in the Himalayas that is purportedly that of a yeti.

Songwriter **Baker Knight** (Thomas Baker Knight, Jr), whose work was recorded by Elvis Presley, Frank Sinatra, Dean Martin, Paul McCartney and Ricky Nelson, amongst others, died on October 12th, aged 72. His best-known songs include "The Wonder of You", "Somewhere There's a Someone" and "Lonesome Town".

Chicago advertising executive **Jack Mathis** died on October 13th, aged 73. His book on the Republic serials, *Valley of the Cliffhangers*, was published in 1975, and he followed it with *Republic Confidential: The Players* and *Republic Confidential: The Studio*, the first two volumes in a proposed trilogy.

French-born artist and fan **Bernie Zuber** died of complications from pneumonia in California on October 14th, aged 72. The original vice-president of the Mythopoeic Society from the late 1960s to the early 1970s, he was the first associate editor of the society's journal, *Mythlore*. As founder and president of the Tolkien Fellowships, he edited the newsletter *The Westmarch Chronicle*. His professional career included working on Disney's *Sleeping Beauty* and doing publicity for the animated *Lord of the Rings*. Zuber suffered from bipolar disorder and during the late 1980s was homeless for five years before subsequently losing most of his possessions.

Cartoonist **Tom Gill** died of heart failure on October 17th, aged 92. He began his career drawing cartoon strips for the *New York Daily News* and the *New York Herald Tribune* before joining Dell/Gold Key Comics, where he was the artist on *The Lone Ranger* for twenty years (1950–70) and such other titles as *Hi-Yo Silver* and *Bonanza*.

TV scriptwriter **Stephen Katz** died of prostate cancer on October 18th, aged 59. He received an Academy Award nomination in 1978 for Best Short Film, and he scripted episodes of *Knight Rider* and *Friday the 13th The Series*, plus the 1990 movie *Satan's Princess*.

Comedy scriptwriter **Fred S. Fox** died of pneumonia on October 23rd, aged 90. Beginning in 1939, he worked with such Hollywood legends as Bob Hope, Bing Crosby, George Burns, Red Skelton, Lucille Ball, Jack Carson, Jackie Gleason, Doris Day, Spike Jones and Jerry Lewis. Fox worked as a gag writer on the *Road* movies with Hope and Crosby and co-wrote *Oh God! Book II* for Burns.

Swedish science fiction author **Denis Lindbohm**, who published more than a hundred stories since 1945, died of cancer on October 24th, aged 78. He was considered a founder of Swedish SF fandom.

Two-time Chesley Award-winning fantasy artist **Keith [Arlin] Parkinson** died on October 26th, four days after his 47th birthday, following a sixteen-month battle against leukaemia. The role-playing game *Everquest* was created around his designs, and his work appeared on numerous TSR books, video game covers, magazines, calendars and even pinball machines. His work is collected in *Knightsbridge: The Art of Keith Parkinson*, *Spellbound: The Kieth Parkinson Sketch Book*, and *Kingsgate: The Art of Keith Parkinson*.

New Zealand-born scriptwriter **Bruce Stewart** also died in October, aged 80. After moving to the UK in the early 1950s, he scripted episodes of TV's *Out of This World*, *Out of the Unknown*, *Timeslip* and *Sherlock Holmes*, along with the 1960s vampire movie *The Hand of Night* (aka *Beast of Morocco*).

Television writer and creative executive **Michael Piller** died of cancer on November 1st, aged 57. An executive producer (1990–94) and writer on *Star Trek: The Next Generation*, he co-created *Star Trek: Voyager* and *Star Trek: Deep Space Nine*. He also co-created the 1995 UPN series *Legend* and, with his son Shawn, created the USA Network series *The Dead Zone*, based on the novel by Stephen King. In 1998, Piller scripted and co-produced *Star Trek: Insurrection*, the ninth film in the popular franchise.

The death of 89-year-old Hollywood scriptwriter **Jerome Gottler** was announced the same day. He wrote a number of *Three Stooges* shorts, including *High Society*, for which he was mistakenly nominated for an Academy Award when it was confused with the musical of the same title.

Composer and songwriter **Rick Thodes**, whose credits include *Mars Attacks!*, died of brain cancer on November 2nd, aged 54.

British-born science fiction author **Michael G.** (Greatrex) **Coney** died of lung cancer, caused by exposure to asbestos, in Canada on November 4th, aged 73. His first story was published in 1969, and his books include *Mirror Image*, *Syzygy*, *Friends Come in Boxes*, *The Hero Downstairs*, *Winter's Children*, *The Jaws That Bite the Claws That Catch* (aka *The Girl With a Symphony in Her Fingers*), *Hello Summer Goodbye* (aka *Rex*), *Charisma*, *The Ultimate Jungle*, *Neptune's Cauldron*, *Cat Karina*, *The Celestial Steam Locomotive*, *Gods of the Greataway*, *Fang the Gnome*, *King of the Sceptre'd Isle* and the collection *Monitor Found in Orbit*. When diagnosed with terminal cancer, Coney posted three unpublished novels online for free.

Reclusive British author **John** [Robert] **Fowles** died after a long illness on November 5th, aged 79. A middle-class rebel best known for his best-selling novel *The French Lieutenant's Woman*, he also wrote *The Collector* and *The Magus*, both of which were filmed. His final novel, *A Maggot* (1985), included aspects of SF, Gothic horror and detective fiction.

Italian composer **Francesco de Masi** died of cancer on November 6th, aged 75. His many film scores include *Toto vs. Maciste*, *Lo Spettro*, *Triumph of Hercules*, *An Angel for Satan*, *Three Fantastic Superman*, *Murder Clinic*, *Orgy of the Living Dead*, *The New York Ripper*, *Invaders of the Lost Gold*, *Thor the Conqueror* and *Bronx Warriors 2*.

Film historian **Dave Holland** (David Thomas Holland) died on November 14th, aged 70. Best known as the founder and director of Alabama's annual Lone Pine Film Festival, he was also the author of the 1989 study *Out of the Past: A Pictorial History of the Lone Ranger*.

Television writer and producer **Edward Gruskin** died of Alzheimer's disease on November 15th, aged 91. He began his career writing for the 1940s *Doc Savage* comic book and went on to produce a radio show based on the character. Gruskin also wrote and produced the 1950 *Flash Gordon* TV series starring Steve Holland.

Maurice Zimm (Maurice Zimring), who wrote the original screen story for the Universal classic *Creature from the Black Lagoon*, died on November 17th, aged 96. He scripted a number radio plays, TV shows and films before moving to Hawaii in 1960 to work in real estate development.

American fantasy author **Jay** (Mark) **Gordon** died after a long battle with ALS (amyotrophic lateral sclerosis, or Lou Gehrig's disease) on November 18th, aged 61. A former IT specialist, his first novel, *The Hickory Staff*, the first book in the "Eldarn Sequence", written in collaboration with his son-in-law Robert Scott, was published by Gollancz in 2005. The pair delivered a second volume, *Lessek's Key*, just prior to Gordon's death and had almost completed a first draft of the final book in the series, *The Larion Senate*.

Playwright and TV scriptwriter **Robert Sloman** died aged 79. With producer Barry Letts, he scripted the 1970s *Doctor Who* serials "The Daemons" (under the pseudonym "Guy Leopold"), "The Time Monster", "The Green Death" and "Planet of the Spiders".

Animation designer **Charles McElmurray**, whose credits include *A Boy Named Charlie Brown* and *Magoo's Arabian Nights*, died on December 5th, aged 84.

American science fiction writer **Robert Sheckley** died of a brain aneurysm on December 9th, aged 77. He had been hospitalized in April with an upper respiratory infection during a visit to Ukraine and subsequently returned to the United States after a local businessman paid his medical costs. However, he was not well enough to attend the 2005 World Science Fiction Convention in Glasgow, where he was scheduled to be a Guest of Honour. A prolific short story writer whose career began in 1951, his short fiction is collected in *Untouched by Human Hands*, *Citizen in Space*, *Store of Infinity*, *Shards of Space*, *The People Trap*, *The Robot Who Looked Like Me*,

Dimensions of Sheckley and *Uncanny Tales*. Sheckley's novels include *Immortality Inc.* (aka *Time Killer*, filmed as *Freejack*), *The Status Civilization*, *Journey Beyond Tomorrow*, *Mindswap*, *Dimension of Miracles*, *Options*, *The Alchemical Marriage of Alistair Crompton* and the film novelisation *The Tenth Victim* (based on his 1953 short story "Seventh Victim"). He also collaborated on books with Harry Harrison and Roger Zelazny, and wrote tie-in novels for *Aliens*, *Star Trek: Deep Space Nine* and *Babylon 5*. He produced the 1966 radio series *Behind the Green Door*, narrated by Basil Rathbone, scripted fifteen episodes of the 1953 *Captain Video* TV series, and had his work adapted on *Armchair Theatre*, *Out of the Unknown* and *Monsters*. His novel *The Game of X* became Disney's *Condorman*, while *Prize of Peril* was also filmed in 1983. From 1980–82 Sheckley served as fiction editor of *Omni* magazine, and in 2001 he was named "Author Emeritus" by the Science Fiction and Fantasy Writers of America.

Horror author and anthologist **J. N. Williamson** (Gerald Neal Williamson) died on December 8th, aged 73. A published author since the 1960s, his first novel, *The Ritual*, appeared in 1979 and he followed it with more than thirty more, including *Horror House*, *The Evil One*, *Playmates*, *Babel's Children*, *Evil Offspring*, *Dead to the World*, *The Black School*, *Hell Storm*, *The Night Seasons*, *The Monastery*, *Bloodlines*, *The Haunt* and *Affinity*. His short fiction is collected in *The Naked Flesh of Feeling* and *Frights of Fancy*, and he also edited five volumes of the *Masques* series (1984–2006) of original anthologies. Williamson's non-fiction books include *The New Devil's Dictionary: Creep Cliches and Sinister Synonyms* and *How to Write Tales of Horror, Fantasy & Science Fiction*, and in 2003 he was awarded a Lifetime Achievement Award by the Horror Writers Association.

American children's author **Margaret Hodge** (Sarah Margaret Moore) died of heart disease and complications from Parkinson's disease on December 13th, aged 94. The author of more than forty books, including the Caldecott Medal-winning *St. George and the Dragon*, her other titles include *Merlin and the Making of the King*.

Prolific British science fiction, fantasy and comics author [Henry] **Kenneth Bulmer** died after a long illness on December 16th, aged 84. Starting in 1952, he wrote numerous short stories and more than 180 novels under a wide variety of pseudonyms in numerous genres. These include such titles as *Space Treason* (with Vince Clarke), *Encounter in Space*, *City Under the Sea*, *The Secret of ZI*, *The*

Earth Gods Are Coming and *Worlds for the Taking*. His most popular series, the "Dray Prescott" space opera sequence, was published over more than fifty volumes by DAW Books (and later German publisher Heyne) under the by-line "Alan Burt Akers". With Robert Holdstock he collaborated on most of *The Professionals* TV tie-ins as "Ken Blake", and he edited eight volumes of the *New Writings in SF* anthology series. For the UK comics industry Bulmer worked for Amalgamated Press during the late 1950s and '60s, churning out "novel-length" war stories for War Picture Library as well as contributing strips to such titles as *Lion* ("Jet-Ace Logan"; "Karl the Viking"), *Hurricane* ("Worst Boy in School"), *Buster* ("Gladiator"; "The Drowned World"), *Boys' World* ("The Angry Planet") and *Valiant* ("The Steel Claw"). A former Honorary President of the British Fantasy Society, he was awarded a Special BFS Award in 1998.

American novelist **Rona Jaffe** died of cancer in a London hospital on December 30th, aged 74. She began her career as an associate editor at Fawcett Publications before writing her first best-seller, *The Best of Everything* (1958). Her novel *Mazes and Monsters* became a TV film in 1982 starring Tom Hanks.

American book dealer, editor, convention organiser and fan "Big-Hearted" **Howard DeVore** died after a long illness on December 31st, aged 80. He compiled *A History of the Hugo, Nebula, and International Fantasy Awards* (with Donald Franson) in 1978, which was revised twice. A member of First Fandom, DeVore was set to be the Fan Guest of Honour at the 2006 World Science Fiction Convention in Los Angeles.

PERFORMERS/PERSONALITIES

American actress and comedienne **Thelma White** (Thelma Wolpa), who starred as Mae, the drug-dealing blonde in the cult favourite *Reefer Madness* (1936), died of pneumonia on January 4th, aged 94. A former child star in carnivals and vaudeville, she became a contract player at RKO Radio Pictures during the 1930s and later, after appearing in some *Bowery Boys* films, developed a second career as an agent and producer. Her clients included James Coburn, Dolores Hart, Debbie Reynolds and Robert Blake. She reputedly had affairs with both sexes, including Marlene Dietrich.

Martial arts specialist and film stuntman **Stuart Quan** died after losing consciousness in a car returning from a snowboarding trip on January 8th. He was 43. Quan appeared in *Big Trouble in Little*

China, Licence to Kill, The Shadow, Fist of the North Star, Escape from L. A. and *Hulk*.

Spencer Dryden, drummer with 1960s American rock band Jefferson Airplane and '70s group New Riders of the Purple Sage, died of colon cancer in California on January 10th, aged 66. He was the son of British actor Wheeler Dryden, half-brother of Charlie Chaplin.

Jimmy Griffin, co-founder of the 1970s group Bread, died of lung cancer on January 11th, aged 61.

Bollywood actor **Amrish Puri**, who played the evil villain "Mola Ram" in Steven Spielberg's *Indiana Jones and the Temple of Doom*, died in Bombay of a brain haemorrhage on January 12th, aged 72. Puri appeared in more than 200 films over three decades.

American actress **Ruth Warrick** died of complications from pneumonia on January 15th, aged 88. Best known for he role as Emily, the first Mrs. Kane, in Orson Welles' *Citizen Kane*, she also appeared in *The Corsican Brothers* (1941) opposite Douglas Fairbanks, Jr, *Journey Into Fear*, Disney's controversial *Song of the South, How to Steal the World, The Returning* and *Deathmask*. In later years she moved to TV and starred in *Peyton Place* and the daytime soap operas *As the World Turns* and *All My Children*.

Hollywood leading lady **Virginia Mayo** (Virginia Clara Jones) died of pneumonia and heart failure on January 17th, aged 84. Initially plucked from the chorus line, the curvaceous blonde actress appeared in such films as *Wonder Man, The Secret Life of Walter Mitty* (with Boris Karloff), *The Story of Mankind* (as Cleopatra), *Castle of Evil, Haunted* and *Evil Spirits*, along with an episode of TV's *Night Gallery* ("The Diary").

31-year-old American actor **Lamont Bentley**, who appeared in *Tales from the Hood* (1995), died when he was thrown from his vehicle outside Los Angeles on January 19th.

Cal Bolder, who portrayed the bald-headed "monster" in *Jesse James Meets Frankenstein's Daughter*, died of cancer the same day, aged 74. He also appeared in episodes of TV's *Star Trek, The Man from U.N.C.L.E.* and *The Girl from U.N.C.L.E.*

American-born soul singer **Solomon King** (Allen Levy) died on January 20th, aged 74. After touring with Billie Holiday and singing with Elvis Presley's backing group, the Jordanaires, he moved to Britain in the 1960s and had hits with "She Wears My Ring", "When We Were Young" and "Say a Little Prayer".

American actor and voice-over artist **Steven Susskind** died after an automobile accident in Mission Hills, California, on January 21st.

He was 62. Susskind was heard in *Monsters, Inc.*, and the TV series *Challenge of the GoBots* and the animated *Batman* (as "Maxie Zeus"). He also appeared in *Friday the 13th Part III*, *Terminator 3: Rise of the Machines*, *Witch Hunt*, *Star Trek V*, *House* and *F/X 2*, along with such TV series as *Weird Science*, *Teen Angel*, *Tales from the Crypt* and *Alien Nation*.

British comedienne **Patsy** (Patricia) **Rowlands** died of breast cancer on January 22nd, aged 71. Best remembered for her supporting roles in nine *Carry On* films (1969–75), she also appeared in *Vengeance* (aka *The Brain*) and *The Fiendish Plot of Fu Manchu*. On TV she co-starred as "Netta Kinvig" in Nigel Kneale's 1981 SF series *Kinvig*, and was featured in episodes of *Out of the Unknown*, *The Avengers* and *Raven*.

Comedian and talk show host **Johnny Carson**, whose signature introduction "Heeere's Johnny" was used to memorable effect by Jack Nicholson's character in Stanley Kubrick's *The Shining*, died of emphysema on January 23rd, aged 79. An Academy Awards host, from 1962–92 he hosted *The Tonight Show* for NBC-TV, reputedly earning $10 million a year by the end of his third decade.

Texas-born singer **Ray Peterson**, best known for his 1960 death ballad "Tell Laura I Love Her", died of cancer on January 25th, aged 69. He also had a hit with "The Wonder of You".

Actor **Paul A. Partain**, who portrayed the crippled "Franklin" in the original *Texas Chain Saw Massacre* (1974), died of cancer on January 27th, aged 58. His other credits include *Race with the Devil* and *Return of the Texas Chainsaw Massacre*.

Drummer and song-writer **Jim Capaldi**, co-founder of the 1960s British rock group Traffic, died of stomach cancer on January 28th, aged 60. Traffic's hits include "Paper Sun", "Hole in My Shoe" and "Here We Go Round the Mulberry Bush", and Capaldi had a solo hit in 1975 with "Love Hurts". He left an estate of just over £2 million to his wife.

31-year-old adult film star **Karen Bach** committed suicide on January 28th.

American character actor and prolific cartoon voice artist **Ron Feinberg** died on January 29th. He appeared in *A Boy and His Dog* (as "Fellini") and the TV movies *Dying Room Only* and *The Man in the Santa Claus Suit*.

Former US airman **Dave Lerchey**, the first white singer with the Del Vikings, died of cancer the same day, aged 67. Baritone and tenor Lerchey sang on the 1950s hits "Come Go with Me" and "Whispering Bells". The group's songs were featured in the movies *The Big Beat* and *American Graffiti*.

Eric Griffiths, who played guitar with John Lennon and Paul McCartney in the Quarry Men, before they became the Beatles, died in Scotland of pancreatic cancer on January 29th, aged 64.

New York actor **Fred Borges** died of a heart attack on January 31st, aged 45. He appeared in such low budget independent horror films as *Weasels Rip My Flesh* and *Long Island Cannibal Massacre*.

Canadian-born actor **John Vernon** (Adolphus Raymondus Vernon Agopsowicz) died on February 1st, following complications from heart surgery. He was 72. Best remembered as "Dean Wormer" in *National Lampoon's Animal House*, during the 1970s and '80s he turned up regularly on TV as a villain in such series and films as *Tarzan*, *Search*, *Kung Fu*, *The Six Million Dollar Man*, *The Greatest American Hero*, *The Powers of Matthew Star*, *The Invisible Man* (1975), *Automan*, *The Phoenix*, *Knight Rider*, *Alfred Hitchcock Presents*, *War of the Worlds*, *Ray Bradbury Theater*, *Tales from the Crypt*, *Escape*, *The Questor Tapes* and *The Fire Next Time*. His other credits include the 1956 film of *1984* (as the uncredited voice of "Big Brother"), *Chained Heat*, *The Uncanny* (with Peter Cushing), *Herbie Goes Bananas*, *Heavy Metal*, *Curtains*, *Blue Monkey*, *Killer Klowns from Outer Space* and *Batman: Mystery of the Batwoman*.

87-year-old film and stage actor and human rights activist **Ossie Davis** (Raiford Chatman Davis) was found dead on February 4th in a Miami hotel room. Honoured with a Lifetime Achievement award by the Screen Actors Guild in 2001, he directed and co-wrote the 1970s Blaxploitation film *Cotton Comes to Harlem* and appeared in *Shock Treatment*, *Avenging Angel*, *Joe versus the Volcano*, *Doctor Dolittle* (1998) and *Bubba Ho-Tep* (based on the story by Joe R. Lansdale), along with the TV movies *Night Gallery* and *The Soul Collector*, plus the mini-series of *Stephen King's The Stand*. Davis was married to actress Ruby Dee, and they celebrated their 50th wedding anniversary in 1998 with the publication of a dual autobiography, *In This Life Together*.

Keith Knudsen, who joined 1970s band the Doobie Brothers as drummer on their fourth album, died of pneumonia on February 8th, aged 56. He played on their 1980 #1 hit "What a Fool Believes".

1970s soul singer **Tyrone Davis**, who had hits with "Can I Change My Mind" and "Turn Back the Hands of Time", died after being hospitalized for a coma on February 9th, aged 66.

American football player-turned-actor **Chuck Morrell** died of a cerebral haemorrhage on February 10th, aged 67. After leaving the Washington Redskins in 1959, he appeared in a number of movies and TV shows. In 1988 he produced and appeared in *Grotesque*, starring Linda Blair. Morrell underwent a heart transplant in 1995.

American actor **Brian Kelly**, who starred as "Ranger Porter Ricks" in the 1960s TV series *Flipper*, died of pneumonia on February 12th, aged 73. He appeared in a number of films, including *Around the World Under the Sea*, until a motorcycle accident in 1970 left him with a permanently paralyzed right arm and leg. After winning a settlement from the accident, Kelly turned to producing, buying the rights to Philip K. Dick's novel *Do Androids Dream of Electric Sheep?* He executive produced the subsequent film adaptation, Ridley Scott's *Blade Runner*.

Guyana-born British actor **Harry Baird** died of cancer on February 13th, aged 73. He made his debut in Carol Reed's *A Kid for Two Farthings* (1954) and appeared in *Tarzan the Magnificent* and *Road to Hong Kong* before becoming a *peplum* star in Italy with such films as *Taur the Mighty Warrior* and its sequel *Thor and the Amazon Women*. He also appeared in *The Oblong Box* (with Vincent Price and Christopher Lee) and *Castle Keep*. In 1957 he portrayed Rhodes Reason's bearer "Atimbu" in the low-budget TV series *White Hunter* (1957), and as "Lt Mark Bradley" was a regular on *U.F.O.* (1972–73).

American actress **Nicole DeHuff**, who appeared in *Suspect Zero* with Ben Kingsley, died of pneumonia on February 16th, aged 30.

85-year-old Irish-born actor **Dan**(iel) [Peter] **O'Herlihy** died of heart failure on February 17th in Malibu, California, following a long illness. After starting his career at Dublin's Abbey Theatre, he appeared in such films as Orson Welles' *Macbeth*, *Invasion USA.*, *The Cabinet of Caligari* (scripted by Robert Bloch), *Fail-Safe*, *Halloween III: Season of the Witch*, *The Last Starfighter*, *RoboCop* and *RoboCop 2*, plus such TV movies as *The People*, *Good Against Evil*, *Death Ray 2000* and *Artemis 81*. He also appeared in episodes of *Alfred Hitchcock Hour*, *The Man from U.N.C.L.E.*, *The Bionic Woman*, *Battlestar Galactica* and *Ray Bradbury Theater*, and was a regular on *A Man Called Sloane* and *Twin Peaks*.

American actor **Richard Lupino**, a member of the theatrical family, died of non-Hodgkin's lymphoma on February 19th, aged 75. He appeared on TV in episodes of *Alfred Hitchcock Presents*, *Twilight Zone*, *Thriller* ("Trilogy of Terror") and *The Evil Touch*.

Former model turned actress **Sandra Dee** (Alexandra Zuck) died of complications from kidney disease on February 20th, aged 63. She had lifelong battles with sexual abuse, anorexia, alcoholism and drug addiction. Best remembered as the teenage star of *Gidget* and the

Tammy series, and the wife (1960–67) of singer Bobby Darin (who died in 1973), Dee also appeared in *Portrait in Black*, *A Man Could Get Killed*, the 1969 movie of H. P. Lovecraft's *The Dunwich Horror*, the pilot TV movie for *Fantasy Island* and episodes of *Night Gallery* ("Tell David" and "Spectre in Tap Shoes") and *The Sixth Sense* ("Through a Flame, Darkly"). The song "Look at Me, I'm Sandra Dee" was featured in the musical *Grease*, and she was played by Kate Bosworth in Kevin Spacey's recent biopic of Darin, *Beyond the Sea*.

Musical theatre actor **John Raitt**, the father of singer Bonnie Raitt, died of complications from pneumonia the same day, aged 88. He created the role of carnival barker "Billy Bigelow" in Rodgers & Hammerstein's *Carousel* on Broadway and appeared in episodes of TV's *Third Rock from the Sun* and *The X Files*.

Flamboyant Californian TV preacher **Gene Scott** died of a stroke on February 21st, aged 75. Christopher Plummer's character in the 1987 film *Dragnet* was reportedly based on him.

French-born actress **Simone Simon** died in Paris on February 22nd, aged 94. A former model who was brought to Hollywood by studio head Darryl Zanuck, she is best known for her role as "Irene Dubrovna", a Serbian-born fashion artist haunted by the fear that she is a were-panther, in the two Val Lewton productions *Cat People* (1942) and *The Curse of the Cat People* (1944). She also appeared as the Devil's seductive emissary "Bella Dee" in *All That Money Can Buy* (aka *The Devil and Daniel Webster*). Her last film was in 1973.

25-year-old South Korean actress **Lee Eun-ju** hanged herself in her apartment dressing room the same day. Her film credits include *Hello! UFO* and *Bloody Beach*.

American singer **Harry Simeone** also died on February 22nd, aged 94. His hits included "The Little Drummer Boy" in 1958 and the Christmas song "Do You Hear What I Hear" four years later.

Edward Patten, a singer with Gladys Knight & the Pips from 1966–89, died of a stroke on February 25th, aged 66. The group's hits include "I Heard it Through the Grapevine" and "Midnight Train to Georgia".

Singer and drummer **Chris Curtis** (Christopher Crummey), who had a number of hits with 1960s "Merseybeat" group the Searchers (named after the 1956 John Ford Western), died of complications from diabetes on February 28th, aged 63. The Searchers had a #1 hit with "Sweets for my Sweet" in 1963, followed by "Sugar and Spice", "Needles and Pins" and "Don't Throw Your Love Away". After leaving the group in 1966, Curtis joined the session group the Flower-pot Men on the psychedelic anthem "Let's Go to San Francisco".

Canadian actress **Guylaine St-Onge**, who played the murderous alien "Juda" in Gene Roddenberry's *Earth: Final Conflict* (2001–02), died of cervical cancer on March 3rd, aged 39. Her other credits include the 1991–92 series *Lightning Force* and episodes of *War of the Worlds*, *Alfred Hitchcock Presents*, *The Outer Limits* and *Mutant X*.

Melanie McGuire, who starred in the low-budget horror film *Deadly Scavengers*, died the same day, aged 42.

Academy Award-winning Hollywood actress [Muriel] **Teresa Wright** died of a heart attack on March 6th, aged 86. Replaced by Loretta Young in *The Bishop's Wife* (1947) when she became pregnant, Wright is best known for her role as "Charlie", opposite Joseph Cotton's murderous namesake in Alfred Hitchcock's *Shadow of a Doubt* (1943). Her other credits include *Track of the Cat*, *The Search for Bridey Murphy*, *The Elevator*, *Crawlspace*, *Somewhere in Time* and the TV movies *The Enchanted Cottage* and *The Miracle on 34th Street* (1955) and *Flood!*. From 1942–52 she was married to novelist Niven Busch (*Duel in the Sun*), and in 1959 married Robert Woodruff Anderson, author of *Tea and Sympathy*. They divorced and later remarried.

American character actor **Sandy Ward**, who played "Sheriff Bannerman" in *Cujo*, also died on March 6th, aged 79. His many other credits include *The Velvet Vampire*, *Earthquake*, *Wholly Moses!* and the TV movies *Good Against Evil* and *The Golden Gate Murders*.

British radio disc jockey and prolific voice-over artist **Tommy Vance** died of complications from a stroke on March 6th, aged 63.

German actress **Brigitte Mira** died on March 8th, aged 94. She made her film debut in 1948 and her credits include Ulli Lommel's *The Tenderness of the Wolves*.

Versatile British stage and screen actress **Sheila Gish** (Sheila Gash) died of cancer on March 9th, aged 62. Her infrequent film appear-ances included playing the ageing girlfriend of immortal Connor MacLeod in *Highlander* (1986). She returned to the series fourteen years later in the third sequel, *Highlander Endgame*. Gish's second husband was actor Denis Lawson.

Popular Irish comedian **Dave Allen** died in London on March 10th, aged 68. He collected his favourite supernatural stories in the 1974 anthology *A Little Night Reading*.

Danny Joe Brown, lead singer with Molly Hatchet, died of diabetes the same day, aged 53.

Italian actor **Guglielmo Spoletini** (aka "William Bogart"), who appeared in numerous "spaghetti Westerns", died on March 12th. His credits include *The Amazing Doctor G*, *Night of the Serpent* and *The Omen*.

American character actor **Jason Evers** (Herbert Evers) died of heart failure on March 13th, aged 83. Best known as the mad scientist in *The Brain That Wouldn't Die* (as "Herb Evers"), he also appeared in *The Illustrated Man*, *Escape from the Planet of the Apes*, *Claws* and *Barracuda*, while his last film before he retired was *Basket Case 2*. On TV Evers guest-starred in episodes of *The Green Hornet*, *The Invaders*, *The Wild Wild West*, *Star Trek*, *Fantastic Journey*, *The Bionic Woman*, *Fantasy Island* and *Knight Rider*.

Don Durant, who starred in Roger Corman's *She Gods of Shark Reef*, died of cardio-pulmonary failure on March 15th, aged 72. He had been battling chronic lymphocytic leukaemia and lymphoma. Durant composed the music for the 1950s Western series *Johnny Ringo*, and also appeared in episodes of TV's *Twilight Zone* and *Alfred Hitchcock Presents*, before leaving acting in the 1960s to pursue a career in real estate.

American actor **Anthony George** (Ottavio George), who replaced Mitchell Ryan as "Burke Devlin" on TV's *Dark Shadows* in 1967 and remained on the show as "Jeremiah Collins", died of complications from emphysema on March 16th, aged 84.

American character actor **Barney Martin**, best known as Jerry Seinfeld's father "Morty" on the sit-com *Seinfeld* (1991–98), died of cancer on March 21st, aged 82. His many credits include the TV movies *Splash Too* and *I Married a Monster*.

Rod Price, guitarist with the blues band Foghat, died of a heart attack on March 22nd, aged 57.

British character actor **David Kossoff** died of liver cancer on March 23rd, aged 85. The son of Russian parents, he worked as a draftsman and furniture designer before appearing in such films as *Svengali* (1954), *The Angel Who Pawned Her Harp*, *The Bespoke Overcoat*, *1984*, *A Kid for Two Farthings*, Hammer's *The Two Faces of Dr. Jekyll* (aka *House of Fright*) and *The Mouse on the Moon*. His scenes were deleted from *The Private Life of Sherlock Holmes*. Kossoff's son Paul, guitarist with the rock band Free, died at the age of twenty-five as a result of drug abuse.

92-year-old Memphis TV horror host **Sivad** (Watson Davis) died of cancer the same day. From 1962 to 1970 Davis (actually an advertising director for a local cinema chain) hosted "Fantastic Features" on Channel 13 WHBQ as a fanged and caped vampire.

He also made numerous live appearances and had several local hit records.

Paul Hester, the 46-year-old drummer and co-founder of Australian band Crowded House, apparently committed suicide by hanging himself from a tree in a Melbourne park on March 26th. A former member of New Zealand group Split Enz, Hester formed Crowded House in 1985 with singer Neil Finn and bass player Nick Seymour. Their hits include "Don't Dream It's Over" and "Weather With You".

American celebrity attorney **Johnnie L. Cochran, Jr**, best known for his successful defence of football star-turned-actor O. J. Simpson on murder charges in 1995, died of a brain tumour on March 29th, aged 67. Over the years, Cochran also represented Jim Brown, Todd Bridges, Tupac Shakur, Snoop Dogg and Sean "P. Diddy" Combs.

Japanese-born musician **Hideaki "Billy" Sekiguchi** (aka "Bass Wolf") died of a heart attack in New Orleans on March 31st, aged 38. Co-founder of the band Guitar Wolf in the early 1990s, he appeared in local film-maker John Michael McCarthy's science fiction film *The Sore Losers* (1997) and starred with fellow band member Seiji in Tetsuro Takeuchi's zombie movie *Wild Zero* (2000).

German actor and singer **Harald Juhnke** died after a long battle with alcoholism on April 1st, aged 75. He appeared in Fritz Lang's *The Testament of Dr. Mabuse* (1962) and in later years made a career out of covering Frank Sinatra's hits in German and dubbing Marlon Brando.

72-year-old American actress **June Easton**, who was married to actor and dialect coach Robert Easton, died after a long battle with lupus on April 2nd. She appeared in *Abbott and Costello Go to Mars* and *Son of Sinbad*.

The death was announced the same day, during the BBC's live broadcast of *The Quatermass Experiment*, of 84-year-old Polish-born **Pope John Paul II** (Karol Wojtyla) from heart and kidney failure in Rome, Italy. At twenty-six years, he was one of the longest-serving Pope's in history. A former actor and playwright, two of his plays were adapted into movies.

American actress **Debralee Scott**, who was a regular on such TV series as *Welcome Back Kotter* and *Mary Hartman Mary Hartman*, died on April 5th, aged 52. She appeared in *Earthquake*, *The Reincarnation of Peter Proud*, *Pandemonium* and the TV movie *Death Moon*.

British character actor **John Bennett** died on April 11th, aged 76. His numerous credits include Hammer's *The Curse of the Werewolf*,

The House That Dripped Blood, *The House in Nightmare Park*, *Watership Down*, *The Plague Dogs*, *Merlin of the Crystal Cave*, *Sherlock Holmes and the Leading Lady*, *Split Second* and *The Fifth Element*, along with episodes of *The Avengers*, *Doctor Who*, *Survivors*, *Blakes 7* and *Roald Dahl's Tales of the Unexpected*.

Johnny Johnson, the pianist on many Chuck Berry hits, died on April 13th, aged 80.

British stage and screen actress **Margaretta Scott** died on April 15th, aged 93. She appeared in *Things to Come* (1936), *Percy* and Hammer's *Crescendo* (replacing Bette Davis). She was the last surviving signatory of the document that established the British actors' union Equity in 1934.

John Fred Gourrier, lead singer with John Fred and His Playboy Band, who had a hit in 1968 with "Judy in Disguise (With Glasses)", died of complications from a kidney transplant the same day, aged 63.

London-born character actress **Kay Walsh** (Kathleen Walsh) died on April 16th, aged 93. Her films include *Vice Versa* (1947), *Dr. Syn Alias the Scarecrow*, *A Study in Terror*, Hammer's *The Witches* (aka *The Devil's Own*), *Scrooge!* (1970) and *The Ruling Class*. She was married to David Lean for nine years, and received a screenplay credit on his version of *Great Expectations* (1946).

Mexican leading man **Jaime Fernández** died of a heart attack related to chronic diabetes the same day, aged 67. The brother of director Emilio and singer and actor Fernando, he appeared in more than 180 films, including *El Zorro escarlata*, *El regreso del monstruo*, *La venganza del ahorcado*, *Santo vs. the Vampire Women*, *La huella macabra*, *Blue Demon el demonio azul*, *Blue Demon contra el poder satánico* and *La sombra del Murciélago* before becoming general secretary of the actors' union A.N.D.A.

Oscar-nominated Hollywood actress **Ruth Hussey** (Ruth Carol O'Rourke) died of complications from an appendectomy on April 19th, aged 93. Under contract with MGM from 1937–42, her credits include the classic ghost film *The Uninvited* and episodes of TV's *Science Fiction Theatre*, *Alfred Hitchcock Presents* and *Climax!*

British character actor **Norman Bird** died on April 22nd, aged 81. His numerous credits include *Man in the Moon*, *Night of the Eagle* (aka *Burn Witch Burn*), Hammer's *Maniac*, *The Mind Benders*, *The Black Torment*, *Hands of the Ripper*, *Doomwatch*, the animated *Lord of the Rings* (1978, as the voice of "Bilbo Baggins"), *The Slipper and the Rose*, *The Medusa Touch* and *The Final Conflict*, plus many TV shows.

Veteran Oscar-winning British actor Sir **John Mills** (Lewis Ernest Watts Mills) died following a chest infection on April 23rd, aged 97. His more than 100 film and TV credits include *The Ghost Camera*, David Lean's *Great Expectations*, *The Rocking Horse Winner* (which he also produced), *Around the World in Eighty Days* (1956 and 1989 versions), *Trial by Combat* (aka *Dirty Knights' Work*), *Dr. Strange*, *The Masks of Death* (as "Dr. Watson"), *When the Wind Blows*, *Frankenstein* (as the blind hermit, 1992), *Deadly Advice* (as Jack the Ripper) and *Hamlet* (1996). He portrayed the eponymous scientist in Nigel Kneale's four-part miniseries *Quatermass* (aka *The Quatermass Conclusion*, 1979), and was also the first person to sing Noël Coward's "Mad Dogs and Englishmen" on stage. His widow, stage actress, playwright and author **Mary Hayley Bell**, died on December 1st, aged 95. She had been suffering from Alzheimer's disease. The Shanghai-born Lady Mills' best-known work is the novel *Whistle Down the Wind*, which was filmed in 1961 starring their daughter Hayley. The couple's other daughter, Juliet, stars in the daytime soap opera *Passions*.

Austrian-born Swiss actress **Maria Schell** (Margarete Schell) died of pneumonia on April 26th, aged 79. The sister of actor Maximilian Schell, her credits include Jess Franco's *99 Women* and *The Bloody Judge* (aka *Night of the Blood Monster*), *Superman* (1978) and the TV miniseries of Ray Bradbury's *The Martian Chronicles*.

Dependable character actor **Mason Adams** died the same day, aged 86. He appeared in such films as *Demon* (aka *God Told Me To*), *Revenge of the Stepford Wives*, *The Final Conflict*, *The Kid with the Broken Halo*, *The Night They Saved Christmas*, *F/X*, *Not of This Earth* (1999), *Northstar* and *Who is Julia?*. He was also in an episode of TV's *Monsters* and was a regular on *Lou Grant*.

John Mills' former wife, **Aileen Raymond**, the mother of actor Ian Ogilvy, died on April 28th, aged 95.

British character actor **Brook** [Richard] **Williams**, who played the doctor hero in Hammer's *Plague of the Zombies*, died on April 29th, aged 67. His other credits include *Hammersmith is Out*, *The Medusa Touch* and TV's *The Avengers*. The son of Emlyn Williams, he was mentored as an actor by family friend Richard Burton and one of his godparents was Noël Coward.

21-year-old adult film actress **Britney Madison** was killed in a car accident on May 2nd.

American character actress **Elisabeth Fraser** [Jonker], who played Sgt. Bilko's girlfriend "Sgt Joan Hogan" on TV's *The Phil Silvers Show*, died of congestive heart failure on May 5th, aged 85. She also appeared in episodes of *The Addams Family*, *Bewitched*, *The Monkees* and *The Man from U.N.C.L.E.*, while her film credits include *The Hidden Hand* and *Seconds*.

Actress **June Lang** (aka "June Vlasek") died on May 16th, aged 90. She was featured in *Chandu the Magician* (with Bela Lugosi), *Nancy Steele is Missing!*, *Ali Baba Goes to Town* and *Flesh and Fantasy* before her marriage to reputed mobster Johnny Roselli ended her career in the mid-1940s.

American actor and impersonator **Frank Gorshin** died from lung cancer, emphysema and pneumonia on May 17th, aged 72. Best known for his Emmy Award-winning role as "The Riddler" in the 1966–68 TV series *Batman* and the 1966 spin-off film, he was nominated for another Emmy as Commander Bele in the original *Star Trek* episode "Let That Be Your Last Battlefield" and also appeared in such films as *Hot Rod Girl*, *Dragstrip Girl*, *Invasion of the Saucer Men*, *Death Car on the Freeway*, *Goliath Awakes*, *Beverly Hills Bodysnatchers*, *Midnight*, *Meteor Man*, *Twelve Monkeys*, *Back to the Batcave: The Misadventures of Adam and Burt* and *The Creature of the Sunny Side Up Trailer Park*. Gorshin was on the *Ed Sullivan Show* the night the Beatles made their American TV debut in 1964, and his final appearance was in Quentin Tarantino's *CSI: Crime Scene Investigation* fifth season finale, "Grave Danger", aired two days after his death.

British musician and composer **Keith Miller** died of a brain haemorrhage the same day, aged 58. In 1966 he appeared as a guitarist with soul band St Louis Union in *The Ghost Goes Gear*. After establishing his own studio in London he worked on *Star Wars* and TV's *Blakes 7* and *Red Dwarf*.

Canadian-born actor **Henry Corden**, whose credits include *The Secret Life of Walter Mitty*, *The Black Castle* and *Abbott and Costello Meet Dr. Jekyll and Mr. Hyde* (all with Boris Karloff), died of emphysema on May 19th, aged 85. Corden also appeared in episodes of *Superman*, *Thriller*, *Twilight Zone*, *My Favorite Martian*, *I Dream of Jeannie* and *Land of the Giants*, and in 1977 he took over as the voice of cartoon character Fred Flintstone from Alan Reed.

American-born character actress **Harriet White Medin** died after a long battle with Parkinson's disease on May 20th, aged 91. After World War II she moved to Italy, where she worked as a dialogue coach and appeared in numerous films (often as a creepy housekeeper), including *The Horrible Dr. Hichcock*, *The Ghost*, *Black Sabbath*, *The Whip and the Body*, *Blood and Black Lace* and *The*

Murder Clinic. She returned to the US in the 1960s, where her credits include *Schlock* (under the pseudonym "Enrica Blankey"), *Season of the Witch* (aka *Hungry Wives*), *Death Race 2000*, *The Bermuda Triangle*, *Blood Beach*, *The Terminator* and *The Witches of Eastwick*.

American actor **J. D. Cannon**, best known as Sam McCloud's irascible boss "Chief Peter B. Clifford" in the NBC-TV movie series *McCloud* (1970–77), died the same day, aged 83. His credits include *McCloud Meets Dracula* (1977), Disney's *Beyond Witch Mountain*, and *Raise the Titanic*, along with episodes of *Alfred Hitchcock Hour*, *Voyage to the Bottom of the Sea*, *The Wild Wild West*, *The Invaders*, *The Hardy Boys/Nancy Drew Mysteries*, *Fantasy Island*, *Blake's Magic* and *The Highwayman*.

Comedy actor and TV director **Howard Morris** died of a heart ailment on May 21st, aged 85. Best remembered for his role as hillbilly "Ernest T. Bass" on *The Andy Griffith Show*, he also appeared in *The Nutty Professor* (1963), *Way . . . Way Out*, *High Anxiety*, *Splash*, *The Munsters' Revenge*, *Transylvania Twist*, *It Came from Outer Space II* and *The Wonderful Ice Cream Suit*, along with episodes of *Thriller*, *Alfred Hitchcock Presents*, *Twilight Zone* and *Fantasy Island*. Morris also directed the pilot episode of Mel Brooks' *Get Smart* and provided the voice for such animated characters as Atom Ant, Beetle Bailey, "Dr. Sivana" in *Legends of the Superheroes* and all the young monsters in *The Groovy Goolies*.

Thurl Ravenscroft, the voice of Kelloggs' "Tony the Tiger" Frosties ads and various Disney characters, died of prostate cancer on May 22nd, aged 91. His voice was also used in *Dr. Seuss' How the Grinch Stole Christmas* ("You're a Mean One, Mr. Grinch"), *The Hobbit* (1977) and *The Brave Little Toaster* and its sequels.

Veteran American screen and radio actor **Eddie Albert** (Edward Albert Heimberger), best known for the TV series *Green Acres* (1965–71) and *Switch* (1975–76), died of pneumonia on May 26th, aged 99. A leading environmental conservationist and recipient of the Bronze Star for rescuing 142 Marines during World War II, he was one of the first actors to ever appear on television, in an experimental 1936 transmission for NBC. During his seventy-five-year career in Hollywood, his numerous film credits include Disney's *Escape to Witch Mountain*, *The Devil's Rain*, *Dreamscape*, *Brenda Starr*, *Terminal Entry* and TV's *The Borrowers* (1973), *The Word*, *The Demon Murder Case*, *Goliath Awaits*, *The Girl From Mars*, *Beyond Witch Mountain* and *The Barefoot Executive* (1996). He also played "Winston Smith" on a *Studio One* adaptation of *1984* in

1953, and was the voice of "The Vulture" on the animated *Spider-Man* TV series. In 1946, Albert produced the controversial sex education films *Human Beginnings* and *Human Growth* for US schoolchildren. He married Mexican actress Margo (Maria Marguerita Guadelupe Boldao y Castilla) in 1945 (she died in 1985), and his son Edward is also an actor.

Irish-born stage and film leading man **Geoffrey Toone** died on June 1st, aged 94. His film credits include Hammer's *Terror of the Tongs*, *Dr. Crippen*, *Captain Sinbad* and *Dr. Who and the Daleks*, and he appeared in episodes of *Alfred Hitchcock Presents*, *Matinee Theatre* ("The Invisible Man"), *One Step Beyond*, *Doctor Who* and *The New Avengers*.

Austrian-born character actor **Leon Askin** (Leo Aschkenasy) died in Vienna, Austria, on June 3rd, aged 97. After fleeing persecution by the Nazis and serving with the US Army during World War II, he appeared in such films as *Road to Bali*, *Son of Sinbad*, *The Terror of Doctor Mabuse*, *Sherlock Holmes and the Deadly Necklace*, *The Maltese Bippy*, *Hammersmith is Out*, *Dr. Death Seeker of Souls*, *The World's Greatest Athlete*, *Genesis II*, *Young Frankenstein* and *The Horror Star*. A regular on *Hogan's Heroes* (as "General Albert Burkhalter") his other TV credits include episodes of *Superman*, *The Outer Limits*, *My Favorite Martian*, *It's About Time*, *The Man from U.N.C.L.E.*, *The Monkees* and *The Hardy Boys/Nancy Drew Mysteries*: "The Hardy Boys and Nancy Drew Meet Dracula". Askin became a resident of Vienna in 1994, and he was decorated with one of the city's most distinguished prizes, the Gold Medal of Honour.

British film and TV actor **Michael Billington** died of cancer the same day, aged 63. From 1972–73 he played "Colonel Paul Foster" on TV's *U.F.O.* and as Soviet assassin "Sergei Barsov" he tried to kill Roger Moore's James Bond in *The Spy Who Loved Me*. Billington, who reputedly screen-tested for the role of James Bond more often than any other actor, also appeared in episodes of *The Prisoner*, *The Greatest American Hero*, *Fantasy Island* and *The Quest* (as regular "Cardinay").

71-year-old actor **Terry Doyle** died of a heart attack during a stage performance of Disney's *Beauty and the Beast* on June 3rd. He also appeared in *Prom Night III* and *Teenage Psycho Killer*.

American character actress **Lorna Thayer**, best known as the waitress in the chicken-salad sandwich scene with Jack Nicholson in *Five Easy Pieces*, died on June 4th, aged 86. She also appeared in Roger Corman's *Beast with a Million Eyes*, *The Andromeda Strain*, *Rhinoceros* and the TV movie *The Aliens Are Coming*.

29-year-old adult film star **Chloe Jones** died of liver failure the same day while awaiting a transplant.

Oscar- and two-time Tony Award-winning actress **Anne Bancroft** (Anna Maria Louise Italiano, aka "Anne Marno") died of uterine cancer on June 6th, aged 73. Best known for her iconic role as Mrs Robinson in *The Graduate* (1967), her credits also include the 3-D *Gorilla at Large* (1954), *Lipstick*, *The Elephant Man*, *Love Potion No.9* and *Antz*. She married actor/director Mel Brooks in 1964 and had a cameo as a gypsy in his 1995 comedy, *Dracula Dead and Loving It*.

American character actor **Dana Elcar** died of complications from pneumonia the same day, aged 77. His numerous credits include *Fail Safe*, *The Fool Killer*, *The Boston Strangler*, *The Maltese Bippy*, *The Nude Bomb* (as "Chief"), Disney's *Condorman*, *All of Me* and *2010*, as well as such TV movies as Richard Matheson's *Dying Room Only* and *The Gemini Man*. He was a regular on *Dark Shadows* (1966–71, as "Sheriff Patterson") and as spy boss "Peter Thornton" on ABC TV's *MacGyver*. Elcar also appeared in episodes of *Way Out*, *The Invaders*, *Get Smart*, *The Sixth Sense*, *The Six Million Dollar Man*, *The Incredible Hulk*, *Galactica 1980*, *Voyagers!*, *Knight Rider* and the revived *Dark Shadows*.

American-born leading man **Ed(ward) Bishop** (George Victor Bishop) died of a virus caught in an English hospital on June 8th, aged 72. Best known for his role as "Commander Ed Straker" in twenty-six episodes of Gerry Anderson's TV series *U.F.O.*, for which he dyed his dark hair blond, he also provided the voice of "Captain Blue" in Anderson's 1967 puppet series *Captain Scarlet and the Mysterons*. Bishop's film credits include *The Mouse on the Moon*, *The Bedford Incident*, *Battle Beneath the Earth*, *Doppelgänger* (aka *Journey to the Far Side of the Sun*), the James Bond adventures *Diamonds Are Forever* and *You Only Live Twice*, *Saturn 3*, *Twilight's Last Gleaming*, *Whoops Apocalypse*, *The Fifth Missile*, *Young Indiana Jones and the Curse of the Jackal* and *2001: A Space Odyssey*, although most of his performance as a Pan Am shuttle pilot in the latter was cut.

Actress **Trude Marlen**, who appeared in *Sherlock Holmes and the Grey Lady* (1937) died on June 9th, aged 92.

Dependable "B" movie actor **Robert Clarke** died of complications from diabetes on June 11th, aged 85. Best known as the star, writer and producer of *The Hideous Sun Demon* (1959), his numerous other credits include *The Enchanted Cottage*, *The Body Snatcher* (with Karloff and Lugosi), *Zombies on Broadway*, *Bedlam*, *A Game* *of Death*, *Genius at Work*, *Dick Tracy Meets Gruesome*, *The Man from Planet X*, *Captive Women*, *The Astounding She-Monster*, *The Incredible Petrified World* (with John Carradine), *From the Earth to the Moon*, *Beyond the Time Barrier* (which he also produced), *Terror of the Bloodhunters*, *The Brotherhood of the Bell*, *Frankenstein Island*, *Midnight Movie Massacre*, *Alienator*, *Haunting Fear* and *The Naked Monster*. Clarke appeared on TV in episodes of *Science Fiction Theater*, *Men Into Space*, *Kolchak: The Night Stalker*, *Fantasy Island* and *Knight Rider*. His 1996 autobiography (written with Tom Weaver) was entitled *To "B" or Not to "B": A Film Actor's Odyssey*.

Australian-born actor **Ron Randell** died of complications from a stroke in Alabama the same day, aged 86. He made his Hollywood film debut in 1947, and his film credits include Monogram's *Bulldog Drummond at Bay* and *Bulldog Drummond Strikes Back* (as the eponymous hero), *Captive Women*, *The She-Creature* (1956), *The Most Dangerous Man Alive*, *Kiss Me Quick* and the TV movie *Mandrake*. He also appeared in episodes of *One Step Beyond*, *The Outer Limits*, *Alfred Hitchcock Hour*, *Betwitched* and *Wild Wild West*, and starred in *Sherlock Holmes* on Broadway.

Britain's original 1960s rock chick, **Krissie Wood**, was found dead of a suspected drug overdose in a West London bedsit in early June, aged 57. She had apparently been suffering from depression. She reportedly had affairs with Eric Clapton, Jimmy Page, George Harrison and John Lennon, and from 1964–78 she was married to Small Faces and Rolling Stones guitarist Ronnie Wood.

69-year-old American character actor **Lane Smith**, who played *Daily Planet* editor Perry White on *Lois & Clark: The New Adventures of Superman* (1993–97), died on June 13th of complications from ALS or Lou Gehrig's disease. He also appeared in such films as *Man on a Swing*, *Red Dawn* and *Prison*, the TV movies *Dark Night of the Scarecrow*, *Bridge Across Time*, *Duplicates*, *Alien Nation: The Udara Legacy* and *WW3*, and he was a regular on *V* (1984–85, as "Nathan Bates") and *Good & Evil* (1991, as "Harlan Shell").

British actor **Jonathan Adams**, best remembered for his role as the uptight "Dr Everett Scott" in *The Rocky Horror Picture Show*, died the same day of a stroke, aged 74. He had played the Narrator in the original London Stage production of Richard O'Brien's horror-musical at the Royal Court's Theatre Upstairs. His other credits include the 1989 stage production of *Metropolis*, the 1990 horror film *Two Evil Eyes*, *Eskimo Nell* and TV's *The Invisible Man* (1984) and *Star Cop* (as regular "Alexander Krivenko").

Singer and voice actress **Robie Lester** died of cancer on June 14th, aged 75. A Disneyland Story Reader on a number of record sets, she performed the title song of *The Three Lives of Thomasina* and was the singing voice for Eva Gabor in *The Aristocats* and *The Rescuers*. Lester also appeared in *Sword of Ali Baba* and sung on the 1966 Sandpipers' hit "Guantanamera".

American actress **Cay Forrester** died of pneumonia on June 18th, aged 83. She appeared in *Brenda Starr, Reporter* (1945), *Strange Impersonation, Queen of the Amazons* and the psycho-thriller *Door-to-Door Maniac* (starring Johnny Cash), that she also scripted.

Tatsuo Matsumura, who appeared in *The Human Vapor, Secret of the Telegian* and *King Kong vs. Godzilla*, died of heart failure the same day, aged 90.

British character actress **Imogen Claire**, who appeared in a number of films for director Ken Russell, died on June 24th, aged 58. Her credits include *Tommy, The Rocky Horror Picture Show, Lisztomania, Flash Gordon* (1980), *Shock Treatment, Salome* and *The Lair of the White Worm*.

Eddie (Edward) **Smith**, co-founder of the Black Stuntman's Association in 1967, died after a long illness the same day, aged 81. He worked on the *Planet of the Apes* sequels, the Bond film *Live and Let Die, Earthquake, Dr. Black Mr. Hyde, The Sword and the Sorcerer, Predator 2* and the 1996 remake of *The Nutty Professor*.

American character actor **Jack Kosslyn** died on June 24th of complications from a stroke, aged 84. His many credits include *The Amazing Colossal Man, Attack of the Puppet People, Earth vs. the Spider, War of the Colossal Beast, The Magic Sword, High Plains Drifter, Play Misty for Me* and *Empire of the Ants*.

Ventriloquist and voice artist **Paul Winchell** (Paul Wilchen) died in his sleep the same day, aged 82. Best known as the Grammy-winning voice of Walt Disney's bouncing Tigger in the *Winnie-the-Pooh* cartoons, he also voiced Dick Dastardly in *Wacky Races*, Fleagle in *Banana Splits*, Gargamel in *The Smurfs*, The Chinese Cat in *The Aristocats* and Boomer in *The Fox and the Hound*. Amongst other inventions, Winchell patented an artificial heart in 1963, a disposable razor, a flameless cigarette lighter and an invisible garter belt.

American character actor **John Fiedler**, who was the voice of Piglet in Disney's *Pooh* films from 1968 until 2005, died of cancer the following day, aged 80. His other credits include *The Deathmaster, Mystery in Dracula's Castle, The Shaggy D.A., The Rescuers, The Fox and the Hound* and episodes of *Tom Corbett Space Cadet* (as semi-regular "Cadet Alfie Higgins"), *Twilight Zone, Thriller, The*

Munsters, *Bewitched*, *Star Trek* (as the Jack the Ripper character in "Wolf in the Fold"), *Kolchak: The Night Stalker* (as regular "Gordy Spangler"), *Fantasy Island*, *Amazing Stories* and *Tales from the Darkside*.

R&B singer **Luther** [Ronzoni] **Vandross** died on July 1st, aged 54. After struggling with weight problems, diabetes and hypertension for many years, he suffered a stroke in April 2003, from which he never fully recovered. A former back-up singer for David Bowie, Barbra Streisand, Bette Midler and others, his hits include "Here and Now", "The Best Things in Life Are Free" (with Janet Jackson) and "Power of Love", and his most recent studio album, *Dance with My Father*, won a number of Grammy Awards. Vandross had a small role in the 1993 comedy *The Meteor Man* and also had a cameo on TV's *Touched by an Angel*.

69-year-old singer **Renaldo "Obie" Benson**, a member of the legendary Motown R&B group the Four Tops for five decades ("Standing in the Shadows of Love", "Reach Out [I'll Be There]"), died the same day of lung cancer. Benson wrote many of the group's hits and is also credited as the writer of Marvin Gaye's 1971 classic "What's Going On".

American character actor **Harrison Young**, who appeared as "Palmer Harper" on the daytime TV soap opera *Passions* in 2001, died on July 3rd, aged 75. His many credits include *Waxwork II: Lost in Time*, *Children of the Corn IV: The Gathering*, *Humanoids from the Deep* (1996), *Reptilian*, *The Adventures of Rocky and Bullwinkle*, *Crocodile*, *Starforce*, *Bubba Ho-tep* and *House of 1000 Corpses*.

Veteran TV actor **Kevin Hagen**, best known as "Doc Baker" in *Little House on the Prairie*, died of oesophageal cancer on July 9th, aged 77. A semi-regular on *Land of the Giants* (as "Inspector Kobick"), he also appeared in episodes of *Twilight Zone*, *Thriller*, *Voyage to the Bottom of the Sea*, *Lost in Space*, *Time Tunnel*, *The Man from U.N.C.L.E.*, *The Wild Wild West*, *Amazing Stories* and *Fantasy Island*.

Actress **Ann Loring** died on July 10th, aged 90. Her credits include TV's *Tales of Tomorrow*, and she later became an author. Among her books is the horror novel *The Mark of Satan*.

British actor **Derek Aylward** died the same day, aged 82. He appeared in *The Ghost of St. Michael's*, *The House in Marsh Road* and TV's *The Adventures of Charlie Chan* and *Quatermass II*. Aylward later became the star of such British porn films as *The Playbirds*, *Cool it Carol* and *School for Sex*.

British character actress **Gretchen Franklin**, best-known as "Ethel Skinner" in the long-running BBC-TV soap opera *Eastenders*, died on July 11th, aged 94. Her many film credits include *Help!* with the Beatles, *Monster of Terror* (aka *Die! Monster, Die!*) with Boris Karloff, *Twisted Nerve* and *The Night Visitor*. She also appeared in "The Beckoning Fair One" episode on *Journey to the Unknown*, *Quatermass* (aka *The Quatermass Conclusion*) and the BBC's 1980 version of *Dr. Jekyll and Mr. Hyde*.

Irish-born stage and screen actress **Geraldine Fitzgerald**, who was nominated for an Academy Award for her role as "Isabella Linton" in *Wuthering Heights* (1939), died of Alzheimer's disease on July 17th, aged 91. Her later credits include *Bye Bye Monkey*, *Lovespell*, *Diary of the Dead*, *The Link*, *Poltergeist II The Other Side* and episodes of *Suspense* and Alfred Hitchcock's TV series. After spurning the advances of British author Patrick Hamilton, he reputedly portrayed her as murder victim "Netta Longdon" in his 1939 novel *Hangover Square*.

Canadian-born character actor **James** [Montgomery] **Doohan**, better known as chief engineer Montgomery "Scotty" Scott from the original NBC-TV *Star Trek* series (1966–69) and the series of seven spin-off films, died of pneumonia and Alzheimer's disease on July 20th, aged 85. His ashes were fired into space in December aboard a commercial rocket. Doohan was also a regular on the 1978–80 series *Jason of Star Command* (as "Commander Canarvin") and his other credits include *The Satan Bug*, *Pretty Maids All in a Row*, *Knight Rider 2000*, *Bug Buster*, *Through Dead Eyes*, *Skinwalker* and *Curse of the Shaman*, along with episodes of *The Twilight Zone*, *The Outer Limits*, *Voyage to the Bottom of the Sea*, *Bewitched*, *The Man from U.N.C.L.E.*, *Fantasy Island* and *Star Trek: The Next Generation*. He collaborated with S. M. Stirling on a series of military SF novels, including *The Rising*, *The Privateer* and *The Independent Command*, and his autobiography, *Beam Me Up, Scotty* (a phrase that was never actually used in the TV show) was published in 1996. He received a star on Hollywood's Walk of Fame in 2004. Doohan's ninth child was born in 1980, when the actor was 80 years old.

64-year-old British-born Blues singer-songwriter [John William] **"Long John" Baldry** died in Canada on July 21st, after suffering from a severe chest infection for four months. The six-foot, seven-inch tall singer, whose hits include "Let the Heartaches Begin" and who is credited with discovering Rod Stewart, reportedly died penniless. As a voice actor, he was Sonic the Hedgehog's evil nemesis

Dr Robotnik. Elton John (aka Reginald Dwight) derived half his name from Baldry's.

88-year-old American stage and screen actor **George D. Wallace** died on July 22nd in Los Angeles of complications from injuries sustained during a fall while on vacation in Pisa, Italy. He had been hospitalized for five weeks in the city before he was sufficiently stabilized to return to the US Wallace appeared in more than twenty-five Westerns, including several Hopalong Cassidy films, but is best-remembered as "Commando Cody, Sky Marshall of the Universe" in the 1951 Republic serial *Radar Men from the Moon*. He also appeared in *Ghost Buster, Forbidden Planet, Retik the Moon Menace, Night of the Hunter, The Six Million Dollar Man* pilot, *Prison, The Haunted, Defending Your Life, Multiplicity, Bicentennial Man* and *Minority Report*. On TV he was in episodes of *Planet of the Apes, Fantasy Island, Monsters, Star Trek The Next Generation, Early Edition, The X Files* and *Buffy the Vampire Slayer*.

Eugene Record, lead singer of soul group the Chi-Lites (best remembered for their hit "Oh, Girl"), died of cancer the same day, age 64.

Prolific American film and TV actor **Ford Rainey** died of a series of strokes on July 25th, aged 96. He made his (uncredited) debut in *White Heat* (1949), and went on to appear in such films as *The Andromeda Strain, Halloween II* and *The Cellar*, along with the made-for-TV movies *The Man from the 28th Century, A Howling in the Woods, Strange New World* and *Manhunter*. He also appeared in episodes of *Remar of the Jungle, The Outer Limits* ("I, Robot"), *Lost in Space, Get Smart* ("Weekend Vampire"), *The Time Tunnel, The Invaders, The Wild Wild West, The Immortal, Night Gallery* ("The Phantom Farmhouse"), *Search* and *The Six Million Dollar Man*. He played the US President on several episodes of *Voyage to the Bottom of the Sea* and was "Jim Elgin" in *The Bionic Woman*.

British actor **David Jackson**, best known for his roll as "Olag Gan" in BBC-TV's *Blakes 7* (1978–79), died of a heart attack the same day, aged 75. He was also in Hammer's *Blood from the Mummy's Tomb, Killer's Moon* and an episode of *Space: 1999*.

78-year-old British stuntman **Alf Joint** also died on July 25th. His credits include the Bond films *On Her Majesty's Secret Service* and *Goldfinger, The Projected Man*, Hammer's *The Lost Continent, Witchfinder General, The Keep, An American Werewolf in London, Return of the Jedi, Lifeforce* and *Superman II*. On TV he plunged over the waterfall in *The Adventures of Sherlock Holmes*.

Transsexual Brazilian porn star **Camilla de Castro** died on July 26th after jumping off a balcony while on a drug binge.

Singer **Loulie Jean Norman**, who performed with everyone from Spike Jones to Frank Sinatra, died on August 1st, aged 92. She sang the original *Star Trek* TV theme and was the high-pitched soprano on "The Lion Sleeps Tonight".

American stage and screen actress **Ileen Getz** died of cancer on August 4th, aged 44. She portrayed the humourless "Judith Draper" on the TV series *Third Rock from the Sun*.

Mary Amadeo Ingersoll, who portrayed a reporter in the 1990s TV movies *Alien Nation: The Enemy Within* and *Alien Nation: The Udara Legacy*, died of breast cancer on August 8th, aged 52.

American film and TV actress **Barbara Bel Geddes** (Barbara Geddes Lewis), best known for her Emmy-winning role as matriarch "Miss Ellie" in CBS-TV's *Dallas* (1978–90) died of lung cancer on August 8th, aged 82. Blacklisted following her testimony before the Un-American Activities Committee during the McCarthy era, her credits include *The Long Night* (with Vincent Price), Hitchcock's *Vertigo*, *The Todd Killings* plus episodes of *Alfred Hitchcock Presents* ("Lamb to the Slaughter"), *Dow Hour of Great Mysteries* ("The Burning Court") and Hammer's *Journey to the Unknown*.

Seven-foot, six-inch actor **Matthew McGrory**, who played the gentle giant "Karl" in Tim Burton's *Big Fish*, died of natural causes on August 9th, aged 32. At the time of his death he was working on a biopic of wrestler-turned-actor André the Giant (who died in 1993). McGrory, the tallest actor in the world, also appeared in *Bubble Boy*, *Men in Black II*, *The Dead Hate the Living*, *Shadow-Box*, *Constantine*, Rob Zombie's *House of 1000 Corpses* and its sequel *The Devil's Rejects*, along with episodes of TV's *Charmed* and *Carnivàle*.

Actor and puppeteer **Carl Harms** died after a short illness on August 11th, aged 94. He began his career as a walk-on in Fritz Lieber, Sr's repertory Shakespearean Theater in 1930. He appeared on an early TV adaptation of *The Tempest* with Roddy McDowell, worked on the popular children's show *Howdy Doody* and had a supporting role in the live-action series *Johnny Jupiter*. Harms also helped create replica models for NBC's coverage of several Gemini and Apollo space missions.

British leading man **James Booth** (David Geeves-Booth) died the same day, aged 78. His film credits include *The Secret of My Success*, *Revenge*, *Airport 77*, *Avenging Force*, *Programmed to Kill*, *Moon in*

Scorpio, Deep Space, Inner Sanctum II, The Breed and *American Ninja 4: The Annihilation*. Booth also appeared in an episode of the 1950s TV series *The Invisible Man* and he played former convict "Ernie Niles" in David Lynch's *Twin Peaks* (1990–91).

British actor **Peter Porteous**, who played "Petrov" in the TV series *Space: 1999*, died on August 12th. He also appeared in *The Shuttered Room, Venom, Lifeforce* and the Bond films *Octopussy* and *The Living Daylights*.

Actor and stuntman **James Gavin** died on August 13th, aged 70. His credits include *The Werewolf* (1956), *The Nude Bomb* and *Blue Thunder*.

American stage and screen actress, singer and political activist **Herta Ware**, who was married to blacklisted actor Will Geer (who died in 1978), died on August 15th, aged 88. She appeared in *Dr. Heckyl and Mr. Hype, Critters 2: The Main Course, 2010, Cocoon: The Return, Species* and episodes of TV's *Amazing Stories, The Munsters Today, Eerie Indiana* and *Star Trek: The Next Generation* (as "Maman Picard").

Actress **Eva Renzi**, who portrayed the killer in Dario Argento's *Bird with the Crystal Plumage*, died of cancer on August 16th, aged 60. She also appeared in *Funeral in Berlin* and *Bite Me Darling*.

Veteran American character actor and director **Mel Welles** (Ernst von Theumer) died of heart failure on August 19th, aged 83. Best remembered for creating the role of "Gravis Mushnik" in Roger Corman's original *The Little Shop of Horrors* (1960), his numerous other credits include *Abbott and Costello Meet the Mummy, The Undead, Hold That Hypnotist, The 27th Day, Attack of the Crab Monsters, Revenge of the Blood Beast, Dr. Heckyl and Mr. Hype, Chopping Mall, Wolfen, Invasion Earth: The Aliens Are Here* and *Wizards of the Lost Kingdom*. He also directed *Blood Suckers* (aka *Man-Eater of Hydra*) and *Lady Frankenstein*.

American character actor **Brock Peters** (George Fisher, aka "Broc Peters") died of complications from pancreatic cancer on August 23rd, aged 78. His films include *Soylent Green, The Big One: The Great Los Angeles Earthquake, Alligator II: Mutation, Cosmic Slop, Ghosts of Mississippi*, and he played "Admiral Cartwright" in both *Star Trek IV The Voyage Home* and *Star Trek VI The Undiscovered Country*. Peters also appeared in episodes of TV's *Girl from U.N.C.L.E., Night Gallery* ("Logoda's Head"), *The Bionic Woman, Battlestar Galactica* and *Star Trek: Deep Space Nine* (in the recurring role of "Joseph Sisko"). He portrayed Darth Vader in the National Public Radio adaptations of the *Star Wars* trilogy, and voiced

"General Mi'Qogh" in the *Star Trek: Starfleet Command III* video game. Peters also performed background vocals on the Harry Belafonte hit "Banana Boat Song (Day-O)".

British leading man **Terence Morgan** died of heart failure on August 25th, aged 83. A discovery of Laurence Olivier, his film credits include *Hamlet* (1948), *Svengali* (1954) and Hammer's *The Curse of the Mummy's Tomb*.

French character actor **Jacques Dufilho**, who portrayed the ship's captain in Werner Herzog's *Nosferatu* (1978), died on August 28th, aged 91. His other credits include the 1956 *Hunchback of Notre Dame*.

British character actor **Michael Sheard** (Michael Perkins) died of cancer on August 31st, aged 67. He played "Admiral Ozzel" in *Star Wars: The Empire Strikes Back* and was also in *Raiders of the Lost Ark* (most of his scenes as a U-boat Captain were cut) and *Indiana Jones and the Last Crusade* (as Adolf Hitler). His other appearances include episodes of *Adam Adamant Lives!*, *Space: 1999*, *The New Avengers*, *The Tomorrow People* (as Hitler again), *Blakes 7*, *Roald Dahl's Tales of the Unexpected* and *The Invisible Man* (1984), and he appeared with more Doctors in *Doctor Who* than any other actor.

American TV comedian **Bob** (Robert) **Denver**, who played shipwrecked first mate "Gilligan" in the CBS series *Gilligan's Island* (1964–67) and spin-off movies, died of complications from cancer on September 2nd, aged 70. He had undergone quadruple heart transplant surgery earlier in the year. Denver also appeared in several films, including *The Invisible Woman* (1983), and such TV series as *Far Out Space Nuts* (1975–76), *Back to the Beach* (1987) and episodes of *I Dream of Jeannie*, *Fantasy Island* and *ALF*. The iconic *Gilligan's Island* included a number of genre episodes featuring spoofs of vampires, Sherlock Holmes and Dr Jekyll and Mr Hyde, while the 1980s cartoon spin-off *Gilligan's Planet* gave the show a SF theme.

Actress and stuntwoman **Tomi Barrett**, who worked on the choreography for Brian DePalma's *The Phantom of the Paradise*, died of lung cancer on September 8th, aged 54.

Former stripper and night-club entertainer **Honey Bruce** (Harriett Jolliff) the former wife of comedian Lenny Bruce (who died in 1966) from 1951–57, died of complications from colitis in Honolulu the same day, aged 78.

British character actor **Ronald Leigh-Hunt** died on September 12th, aged 88. He appeared in *Colonel March Investigates* (and the TV series *Colonel March of Scotland Yard*, with Boris Karloff),

Curse of Simba (aka *Curse of the Voodoo*), *Where the Bullets Fly*, *The Omen* and the 1992 TV movie of *Frankenstein*.

40-year-old British actor and stuntman **Malcolm Xerxes** died of a self-inflicted gunshot wound in Toronto, Canada, on September 13th. He was being pursued by police as a suspect in the non-fatal shooting of his girlfriend. Xerxes appeared in several low budget movies and episodes of TV's *Relic Hunter*, *Witchblade* and *Veritas: The Quest*.

American leading lady and singer [Mary] **Constance Moore**, who portrayed heroine "Lieutenant Wilma Deering" in the 1939 serial *Buck Rogers*, died of heart failure after a long illness on September 16th, aged 85. She also appeared in *The Missing Guest*.

American leading man **John Bromfield** (Farron Bromfield) died of kidney failure on September 18th, aged 83. Best remembered for playing lawman "Frank Morgan" in the TV series *The Sheriff of Cochise* (1956–58) and *U.S. Marshal* (1958–60), he also appeared in *Curucu Beast of the Amazon*, *Manfish* and Universal's Gill Man sequel *Revenge of the Creature*. He was married to French actress Corinne Calvet for five years.

Adult film star and fetish model **Eva Lux** died of a heroin overdose on September 20th, aged 32.

Character actor **Gregg Martell**, who portrayed the friendly caveman in *Dinosaurus!*, died of Parkinson's disease on September 22nd, aged 87. His other credits include *Space Master X–7*, *Return of the Fly*, *Valley of the Dragons* and *The Three Stooges Meet Hercules*.

26-year-old adult film star **Julie Robbins** was killed in a single car accident the same day.

Lanky British character actor [David] **Roger Brierley** died of a heart attack on September 23rd, aged 70. His many credits include playing the head Cyberman in *Doctor Who* opposite Colin Baker, *Superman II*, *Young Sherlock Holmes* and the 1985 TV movie *A Very British Coup*.

Tommy Bond (Thomas Ross Bond), who played "Butch" the bully in dozens of "Our Gang" and "The Little Rascals" films during the 1930s, died of complications from heart disease on September 24th, aged 79. He later appeared as boy reporter Jimmy Olsen in the 1948 serial *Superman* and the feature *Atom Man vs. Superman*. He retired from acting in 1951.

American comic actor **Joseph "Jojo" D'Amore** died of emphysema and cancer the same day, aged 74. A friend of fellow stand-up comedian Lenny Bruce, he appeared in *Mansion of the Doomed*, *Dracula's Dog*, *Alligator* and *The Sword and the Sorcerer*.

TV comedian **Don Adams** (Donald James Yarmy), who won three Emmy Awards for his performance as the bumbling CONTROL Agent 86, "Maxwell Smart", in the NBC sci-spy series *Get Smart* (1965–70), died of bone lymphoma complicated by a lung infection on September 25th, aged 82. Typecast in the role, Adams recreated the character in the 1980 spin-off film *The Nude Bomb*, the TV movie *Get Smart Again*, a brief 1994 revival of the show and a 1999 series of Canadian TV commercials for the Buck-a-Call long-distance phone service. In 1983 he became the voice of cartoon character *Inspector Gadget*, a role he continued until the late 1990s.

Adult gay film actor **Troy Steele** (Scott Saunders) died of complications from AIDS on September 26th, aged 43.

Ukrainian-born bit-part player and regular Mickey Rooney stand-in **Sig** (Siegfried) **Frohlich**, who played the Wicked Witch of the West's blue monkey that flew off with Dorothy's dog Toto in the 1939 classic *The Wizard of Oz*, died of pneumonia on September 30th, aged 97. He was believed to be the last survivor of the film's thirteen winged monkeys. Frohlich also appeared as a soldier in Ming the Merciless' army in the original *Flash Gordon* serial, and his other credits include *The Atomic Kid*, *How to Stuff a Wild Bikini* and *Clue*.

British-born character actor and folk singer **Hamilton Camp** (aka "Robin Camp") died of a heart attack after suffering a fall near his home in California on October 2nd, aged 70. Best remembered for his recurring role as a time-travelling H. G. Wells in *Lois & Clark: The New Adventures of Superman*, his credits also include such films as *Bedlam* (with Boris Karloff), *The Son of Dr. Jekyll*, *Heaven Can Wait* (1978), *Starcrash*, *Evilspeak*, *Eating Raoul*, *Twice Upon a Time*, *Arena*, Disney's *The Little Mermaid*, *Dick Tracy* (1990), *Doctor Dolittle* (1998), *Wishcraft*, the TV movies *It Came Upon a Midnight Clear* and *Attack of the 50ft Woman*, plus episodes of *Bewitched*, *Mork and Mindy*, the revived *Twilight Zone*, *Star Trek: Deep Space Nine* and *Star Trek: Voyager*. Camp was also a prolific voice actor on numerous *Scooby-Doo* cartoons and other series.

Comedian and actor **Nipsey Russell**, who played the "Tin Man" in *The Wiz* (1978), died of stomach cancer the same day, aged 81. He also appeared in the children's fantasy *Dream One* (aka *Nemo*).

22-year-old actor **Jacob Reynolds** also died on October 2nd after being involved the day before in an automobile accident in Houston, Texas. His film credits include *Voodoo Doll* (2005).

Popular British TV comedian, scriptwriter (as "Gerald Wiley") and character actor **Ronnie Barker** died on October 3rd, aged 76. He had suffered from heart problems for some years. After beginning his career in radio, Barker teamed up with fellow comedian Ronnie Corbett for the long-running BBC series *The Two Ronnies*, which ended with Barker's premature retirement in 1987. "The Phantom Raspberry Blower of Old London Town" was a classic Jack the Ripper-inspired sketch performed by the duo on the show. Barker also appeared in the films *A Ghost of a Chance*, *The Magnificent Seven Deadly Sins* and *Robin and Marian*, while his TV credits include episodes of *The Avengers* and *The Saint*, and he played "Bottom" in a 1971 production of *A Midsummer Night's Dream*.

Mike Gibbins (Michael Gibbins), drummer and singer with the late 1960s band Badfinger, died in Florida on October 4th, aged 56. As protégés of the Beatles (they were the first act signed to Apple Records), the group's hits included "Come and Get it" (used in the film *The Magic Christian*), "No Matter What" and "Day After Day" before the band broke up and two of its members committed suicide.

56-year-old American actor and comedian **Charles Rocket** (Charles Claverie) was found dead in his backyard of his Connecticut home on October 7th after apparently committing suicide by cutting his throat. A regular on *Saturday Night Live* in the early 1980s (before he was fired for saying "fuck" on air), his credits include *Earth Girls Are Easy*, *Delirious*, TV's *Wild Palms*, *Hocus Pocus*, *Charlie's Ghost Story*, *Titan A. E.* and episodes of *Max Headroom* (as regular "Ned Grossberg"), *Touched by an Angel* (in the recurring role of "Adam"), *Quantum Leap*, *Lois & Clark: The New Adventures of Superman*, *Star Trek: Voyager*, *The X Files* and *3rd Rock from the Sun*. As a voice actor, Rocket contributed to *Batman: Gotham Knights*, *Men in Black*, *Superman* and *Batman Beyond*.

30-year-old Bollywood sex symbol **Anju Gill Raj** committed suicide by self-immolation on October 8th.

American comedian and character actor **Louis Nye** died of lung cancer on October 9th, aged 92. After a career in theatre, night-clubs and radio, he joined Steve Allen's TV show in 1956. Nye's credits include *Sex Kittens Go to College* (aka *Beauty and the Robot*), *Zotz!*, *Full Moon High*, the 1985 TV movie of *Alice in Wonderland* (as the Carpenter), and as horror host "Zombo" in the eponymously titled episode of *The Munsters*. During the 1980s and '90s he also contributed various voices to the *Inspector Gadget* cartoon show.

British actress **Jan Holden** (Valerie Jeanne Wilkinson) died after a long illness on October 11th, aged 74. She was the lead in Hammer's *Stranglers of Bombay* and also appeared in *Fire Maidens from Outer Space*, *Quatermass II* (aka *Enemy from Space*), *The Camp on Blood*

Island, The Haunted House of Horror (aka *Horror House*) and episodes of TV's *The Avengers* and *Journey to the Unknown*. Her first husband was the actor Edwin Richfield.

94-year-old American actress **Mildred Shay**, who lived in London for many years, died of a stroke on October 15th, while visiting her daughter in California. She began her film career in the early 1930s, and her credits include *Roman Scandals, I Married an Angel, Superman III, Labyrinth* and *Little Shop of Horrors* (1986). She also dubbed Greta Garbo's voice in *Grand Hotel* (1932).

British TV and film actress **Barbara Keogh** died the same day, aged 76. She appeared in *The Abominable Dr. Phibes* (with Vincent Price), *Wuthering Heights* (1978), *The Quatermass Conclusion, Whoops Apocalypse* and *Paperhouse*, plus episodes of *Hammer House of Horror, Hammer House of Mystery and Suspense* and *Highlander*.

British stage and screen actress **Ursula Howells** died on October 16th, aged 83. She played a werewolf in *Dr. Terror's House of Horrors*, and her other credits include *The Oracle, Torture Garden*, the psycho thriller *Mumsy Nanny Sonny and Girly* (aka *Girly*) and the TV movie *The Cold Room*.

Eugene Lee (Gordon Lee) who, as a child actor, portrayed Spanky McFarland's younger brother "Porky" in more than forty of MGM's *Our Gang* (aka *Little Rascals*) comedy shorts (1935–39), died after a long battle with lung and brain cancer the same day, aged 71. He retired at the age of six and never acted again.

American entertainer **Elmer** ("Len") **Dresslar**, who recorded the "Ho, ho, ho" part of the "Jolly Green Giant" advertising jingle back in 1959, also died on October 16th, aged 80.

Veteran character actor **John Larch** also died on the same day, aged 91. His credits include *The Wrecking Crew, Play Misty for Me, Future Cop, The Amityville Horror*, TV's *Future Cop* and *Fire in the Sky*, along with numerous Westerns.

Bald-headed British actor **John Hollis**, who portrayed the villain "Kaufman" in the 1960s TV serials *A for Andromeda* and *The Andromeda Breakthrough*, died after a long illness on October 18th, aged 74. He also appeared in such films as *Casino Royale, Captain Kronos Vampire Hunter, The Adventures of Sherlock Holmes' Smarter Brother, Superman, The Empire Strikes Back, Flash Gordon* (1980), *Superman IV The Quest for Peace* and the James Bond film *For Your Eyes Only* (as "Ernst Stavro Blofeld"). Hollis' other credits include the 1981 BBC adaptation of *Day of the Triffids* and episodes of *Out of the Unknown, The Avengers* (including "The Cybernauts"), *Adam Adamant, Doctor Who, The Tomorrow People* and *Blakes 7.*

79-year-old **Reggie Lisowski,** a professional wrestler who appeared in the ring under the name "The Crusher" from the 1949 until the 1980s, died of complications from surgery to remove a brain tumour on October 22nd.

Texan-born character actor **William "Bill" Hootkins** died of pancreatic cancer in Santa Monica on October 23rd, aged 58. Based for many years in England, his numerous credits include *Star Wars* (as rebel pilot "Red Six"), *Twilight's Last Gleaming, Sphinx, Flash Gordon* (1980), *Raiders of the Lost Ark, Dream Child, Biggles, Haunted Honeymoon, American Gothic, Superman IV The Quest for Peace, Batman, Hardware, Dust Devil, The NeverEnding Story III, Death Machine, The Island of Dr. Moreau* (1996), *The Omega Code, The Breed* and the 1987 TV movie *The Return of Sherlock Holmes.* Hootkins also appeared in *Hammer House of Mystery: Black Carrion* and more recently he portrayed Alfred Hitchcock in the London stage production of *Hitchcock's Blonde.*

Best remembered for his suave villains, Canadian-born actor **Lloyd Bochner** died of cancer in Santa Monica on October 29th, aged 81. In a film and TV career that spanned more than five decades, he appeared in William Castle's *The Night Walker, The Dunwich Horror, Crowhaven Farm, Satan's School for Girls* (1973), *A Fire in the Sky, The Golden Gate Murders, Rona Jaffe's Mazes and Monsters,* the *Manimal* pilot, *Millennium, Legend of the Mummy,* the animated *Batman: Vengeance* and episodes of *Thriller, Twilight Zone* (the classic "To Serve Man", based on the story by Damon Knight), *Voyage to the Bottom of the Sea, The Man from U.N.C.L.E., Wild Wild West, The Green Hornet, Girl from U.N.C.L.E., Tarzan, Bewitched, The Starlost, The Six Million Dollar Man, The Bionic Woman, The Amazing Spider-Man, Fantasy Island, Battlestar Galactica, Darkroom, Highway to Heaven, Superboy* (as a vampire) and the 1992–94 *Batman* cartoon series (as the voice of "Mayor Hamilton Hill"). In 1998 Bochner co-founded the Committee to End Violence to look at the impact of violence in film and television on popular culture.

Stage and screen actress **Paula Laurence,** who played "Hannah Stokes" in TV's *Dark Shadows,* died of complications from a broken hip the same day, aged 89.

1950s Rockabilly singer **Barbara Pittman** died of heart failure in her Memphis home also on October 29th, aged 67. She recorded for Sam Phillips' Sun Records and later dated Elvis Presley. She toured with Jerry Lee Lewis and The Righteous Brothers, and was lead singer with Barbara and the Visitors, and The Thirteenth Committee. Best known for "I Need a Man", she also performed the title song for the Vincent Price film *Dr. Goldfoot and the Girl Bombs* (1966), directed by Mario Bava.

81-year-old British actress **Mary Wimbush** died of a stroke on Hallowe'en after collapsing at the BBC's Birmingham studios shortly after recording an episode of Radio 4's *The Archers*. Her credits include *Fragment of Fear*, Hammer's *Vampire Circus*, the 1981 *Doctor Who* spin-off *K-9 and Company* and *Century Falls*. She was married to actor Howard Marion Crawford (who died in 1969).

American actress **Jean Carson** died of a stroke on November 2nd, aged 82. Her credits include *I Married a Monster from Outer Space* and episodes of *Inner Sanctum* and *The Twilight Zone*.

British character actor **Geoffrey Keen** died on November 3rd, aged 89. Best known for his role as "Sir Frederick Gray", the stuffy Minister of Defence, in such later James Bond films as *Moonraker*, *The Spy Who Loved Me*, *For Your Eyes Only*, *Octopussy*, *A View to a Kill* and *The Living Daylights*, he also appeared in *Seven Days to Noon*, *Meet Mr. Lucifer*, *The Malpas Mystery*, *Horrors of the Black Museum*, *The Mind Benders*, TV's *The Scarecrow of Romney Marsh*, *Berserk!*, Hammer's *Taste the Blood of Dracula*, *Doomwatch* and *Holocaust 2000*.

American actress **Sheree North** (Dawn Bethel) died of complications from surgery on November 4th, aged 72. Originally groomed by the studios as a replacement for Marilyn Monroe, she later became an accomplished character actress in such films as *Destination Inner Space*, *The Trouble with Girls* (with Elvis and Vincent Price), *Maneater*, *The Cloning of Clifford Swimmer*, *Telefon* and *Maniac Cop*. On TV she appeared in episodes of *Future Cop*, *Fantasy Island* and *Freddy's Nightmares*.

American rock guitarist **Link Wray** (Fred Lincoln Wray, Jr.), whose best-know hit was the 1958 instrumental "Rumble", died in Copenhagen, Denmark, on November 5th, aged 76. Later hits included "Jack the Ripper" in 1962 and a version of the "*Batman* Theme" three years later. His music was also used on the soundtracks of *Streets of Fire*, *Pulp Fiction*, *Twelve Monkeys* and *Independence Day*, amongst other films. Jimi Hendrix, Jeff Beck, Pete Townshend, Marc Bolan, Bob Dylan, Neil Young and Bruce Springsteen are amongst those who cited him as an influence.

Stuntman, character actor and professional wrestler **The Great John L** (William H. Clark) died on November 6th, aged 80. He made his movie debut as a stuntman in the 1958 *Journey to the Center of the Earth*, and was one of Burt Lancaster's beast-men in *The Island of Dr. Moreau* (1977).

Character actress, singer and comedienne **Avril** [Florence] **Angers** died of pneumonia on November 8th, aged 87. A pioneer in post-war British television comedy, her infrequent film appearances include *The Brass Monkey* (aka *The Lucky Mascot*), *The Green Man* and *Devils of Darkness*.

American actress **Pamela Duncan**, who starred in Roger Corman's *Attack of the Crab Monsters*, died of a stroke on November 11th, aged 73. Her other film credits include Corman's *The Undead* and *Girls! Girls! Girls!* before her retirement from the big screen in 1962 to concentrate on TV work. She also appeared in episodes of *Captain Video*, *Rocky Jones Space Ranger* and *Thriller*.

Leading man **Keith Andes** (John Charles Andes) was found dead at this Californian home the same day, aged 85. He had committed suicide by asphyxiation after suffering from various physical ailments in recent years. Andes played "Dr. Barnett" in the 1973 TV series *Search* and was "Akuta" in the original *Star Trek* episode "The Apple". His other credits include episodes of *The Outer Limits* and *Buck Rogers in the 25th Century*.

Actor **Rik Van Nutter**, who portrayed James Bond's friend, CIA agent "Felix Leiter", in *Thunderball*, died of a heart attack on November 12th, aged 75. His other credits include *Uncle Was a Vampire* (with Christopher Lee) and *Assignment Outer Space*.

Former child actress **Ruthi Robinson** (Ruth E. Poe), who played "Little Red Riding Hood" in *The Wonderful World of the Brothers Grimm* (1962), died on November 15th, aged 55.

Radio writer and announcer **Ralph Edwards**, who created and hosted the NBC TV show *This is Your Life* (1952–61), died of heart failure on November 16th, aged 92. Boris Karloff was the subject of a 1957 episode. Emmy Award-winning Edwards' other successful shows include *Truth or Consequences* and *The People's Court*.

American character actor **Harold J. Stone** (Harold Hochstein) died on November 18th, aged 93. His film credits include *The Invisible Boy*, *X – The Man with X-Ray Eyes*, *Girl Happy* (with Elvis), *The Greatest Story Ever Told* and *The Werewolf of Washington*. He also guest-starred in more than 150 TV shows, including *Alfred Hitchcock Presents*, *Alfred Hitchcock Hour*, *Twilight Zone*, *Voyage to the Bottom of the Sea*, *The Man from U.N.C.L.E.*, *Get Smart* and *Highway to Heaven*.

American actress **Carolyn Kearney**, who starred in *Hot Rod Girl* and *The Thing That Couldn't Die*, died of complications from heart problems on the same day, aged 75. After appearing in just four feature films, she moved to TV, where she appeared opposite Boris Karloff in the *Thriller* episode "The Incredible Doktor Markesan", along with episodes of the *Twilight Zone* and *Alfred Hitchcock Presents*. It is reported that Hitchcock considered Kearney for the role in *Psycho* that eventually went to Vera Miles.

Actress [Dolores] **"Dodo" Denney** died after a short illness on November 20th, aged 77. She began her career playing "Marilyn the Witch" in *The Witching Hour* on local television, and her other credits include *Willy Wonka & the Chocolate Factory* (as "Mrs Teevee"), *Splash* and *Ride with the Devil*.

Mexican-born **Luz Potter**, one of the last eight surviving Munchkins from *The Wizard of Oz* (1939), died of Alzheimer's disease on November 21st, aged 90. A former circus performer, she also appeared in the Universal comedy *Ghost Catchers* (1944); played Violet, a midget, in *The Incredible Shrinking Man* (1957) and, billed as "Luce Potter", portrayed the creepy tentacled head of the Martian Intelligence in the classic *Invaders from Mars* (1953).

Veteran American-born stage and screen actress **Constance Cummings** [Levy] CBE (Constance Halverstadt) died in London on November 23rd, aged 95. A long-time UK resident after her marriage to British playwright Benn W. Levy (who died in 1973), her first film credit was Howard Hawks' *The Criminal Code* (1931), also featuring Boris Karloff. She went on to appear in *Behind the Mask* (also with Karloff), James Whale's *Remember Last Night?*, *Blithe Spirit* and "The Scream" segment of *Three's Company*.

American singer and actress **Beverly Tyler** (aka "Beverly Jean Saul") died of a pulmonary embolism the same day, aged 78. Her film credits include *Voodoo Island* (with Boris Karloff), before she retired from the screen in the 1960s.

73-year-old Japanese-American character actor **Pat Morita** (Noriyuki Morita) died of heart and kidney failure on November 24th, while awaiting a kidney transplant. After being released from an internment camp during World War II, he became a stand-up comedian before getting his big break as "Arnold" in the TV series *Happy Days*. Along with his Oscar-nominated role in *The Karate Kid* and its three sequels, he appeared in *When Time Ran Out*, *Full Moon High*, *Slapstick (of Another Kind)*, *Alice in Wonderland*, *Babes in Toyland*, *Spy Hard*, *Do or Die*, *Auntie Lee's Meat Pies*, *Timemaster*, Disney's *Mulan* and *King Cobra*, plus episodes of *Man* *from Atlantis, The Incredible Hulk, Space Rangers* and the 1990s *Outer Limits*.

Actress, singer and dancer **Adele Lamont** (Adele Thompson), who appeared in *The Brain That Wouldn't Die* as the model whose torso is selected by mad scientist Jason Evers, died the same day, aged 74. A singer with Xavier Cugat's band, she was also in an Off-Broadway production of *He Who Gets Slapped* with Robert Culp.

Jocelyn Brando, the older actress sister of brother Marlon (who died in 2004), died on November 25th, aged 86. She appeared in the TV movies *Dark Night of the Scarecrow* and *Starflight: The Plane That Couldn't Land*, along with episodes of *One Step Beyond, Alfred Hitchcock Presents, Alfred Hitchcock Hour* (Ray Bradbury's "The Jar"), *Thriller* and *Darkroom*.

Veteran character actor, scriptwriter, film director and former opera singer **Marc Lawrence** (Max Goldsmith), best known for his many gangster roles, died of heart failure on November 26th, aged 95. In films since 1932, his numerous credits include *The Spider's Web, Beware Spooks!, S.O.S Tidal Wave, Charlie Chan on Broadway, Charlie Chan in Honolulu, Charlie Chan in the Wax Museum, The Monster and the Girl, Hold That Ghost, Hurricane Island, My Favorite Spy, King of Kong Island, Diamonds Are Forever, Pigs* (aka *Daddy's Deadly Darling*, also wrote, produced and directed), *Dream No Evil, The Man with the Golden Gun, Night Train to Terror, Donor, Cataclysm, From Dusk Till Dawn, End of Days* and *Looney Tunes: Back in Action.* Lawrence was subpoenaed to appear before the House of un-American Activities Committee in 1951, where he admitted that he had once been a US Communist party member. After reluctantly implicating several co-workers (including Jeff Corey, Sterling Hayden, Lionel Stander, Larry Parks and Anne Revere) as alleged communist sympathisers, he was blacklisted and moved to Italy for six years. Lawrence's autobiography, *Long Time No See: Confessions of a Hollywood Gangster*, was published in 1991.

New Orleans band leader, singer and producer **Joe Jones** died on November 27th, aged 79. He is best remembered for his song, "You Talk Too Much", which was recorded in 1959 but did not become a hit until it was featured in Barry Mahon's *The Dead One* (aka *Blood of the Zombie*, 1960). Originally released by New Orleans label Ric, it was picked up by New York-based Roulette who took it to #3 in the US charts. Jones also discovered the Dixie Cups ("Chapel of Love") at a talent show and got them signed with Red Bird records.

62-year-old drummer **Tony Meehan**, a founding member of Cliff Richard's backing group The Shadows, died on November 28th from head injuries sustained in a fall at his home in London. He played on such hits as "Living Doll", "The Young Ones" and "Apache" before leaving the group in 1961 to become a producer at Decca Records.

Austrian-born character actor **Joseph Furst** died on November 29th, aged 89. Based in the UK for many years, he appeared in *Theatre of Death* and *The Brides of Fu Manchu* (both with Christopher Lee), *Diamonds Are Forever*, *Inn of the Damned* and episodes of *One Step Beyond*, *Doctor Who* and *Doom Watch*.

47-year-old American actress and comedienne **Wendie Jo Sperber** died the same day after a long battle with breast cancer. She starred in the 1980s TV series *Bosom Buddies* with Tom Hanks and also appeared in Steven Spielberg's *1941* and the first and final episodes of the *Back to the Future* trilogy (as Marty's kid sister "Linda McFly"). After being diagnosed in 1997, Sperber founded the weSPARK Cancer Support Center in Sherman Oaks, California.

American leading lady **Jean Parker** (Luise Stephanie Zelinska, aka "Lois Mae Green"), who starred opposite John Carradine in Edgar G. Ulmer's *Bluebeard* (1944), died of complications from a stroke on November 30th, aged 90. Her many film credits include *Rasputin and the Empress*, *Gabriel Over the White House*, *Murder in the Fleet*, *The Ghost Goes West* (1935), *Beyond Tomorrow*, *Dead Man's Eyes* (with Lon Chaney, Jr.) and *One Body Too Many* (featuring Bela Lugosi). Parker was married to her fourth husband, actor Robert Lowery, from 1951–57, and in later years she worked as an acting coach before becoming something of a recluse.

71-year-old actor and teacher **Jack Colvin**, best known for his recurring role as investigative reporter "Jack McGee" in the TV series *The Incredible Hulk* (1978–82), died on December 1st after suffering a stroke in October. He also appeared in *The Terminal Man*, *Embryo* and *Child's Play*, the TV movies *The Spell*, *Exo-Man* and *The Incredible Hulk Returns*, plus episodes of *The Six Million Dollar Man*, *The Bionic Woman* and *The Invisible Man* (1975).

Radio actor **Anthony Georgilas**, whose credits include *The Lone Ranger* ("Who was that masked man?") and *The Green Hornet*, died on December 3rd, aged 78. He was also a production manager on TV's *The Twilight Zone*.

Voice actor **Gilbert Mack**, who began his career in vaudeville, died on December 5th, aged 93. He was heard on such radio shows as *Inner Sanctum* and *Dick Tracy* and contributed to numerous cartoon TV shows, including *Johnny Jupiter* (as the title character), *Astro Boy* (as "Mr. Pompus"), *Gigantor* and *Godzilla*.

American radio newscaster and announcer **George Walsh** died of congestive heart failure on December 5th, aged 88. Best known as the announcer for the *Gunsmoke* radio and TV series during the 1950s, his voice was also used in the "Smokey the Bear" forest fire prevention campaign and the now-closed Disneyland rides Flight to the Moon and Mission to Mars. In June 1947, while working as a programme director at a radio station in Roswell, New Mexico, he broke a story about a UFO being captured by the local Air Force that has passed into folklore.

Character actor, production associate and acting mentor **Beach Dickerson**, best known for his roles in Roger Corman movies, died on December 7th, aged 81. He made his debut in Corman's *Attack of the Crab Monsters* (1957), for which he also worked on the special effects. Subsequent credits include *War of the Satellites*, *Teenage Caveman*, *Visit to a Small Planet*, *Creature from the Haunted Sea*, *The Trip*, *The Dunwich Horror*, *School Spirit*, *Deadly Dreams* and *Future Kick*.

Russian actor **Georgy Zhzhyonov** died of complications from a broken hip on December 8th, aged 90. He appeared in *Planet of Storms*, which was re-edited in the US as *Voyage to the Planet of Prehistoric Women*.

Stand-up comedian and character actor **Richard Pryor** (Richard Franklin Lennox Thomas Pryor III) died of a heart attack on December 10th, just days after his 65th birthday. In 1980 he received third-degree burns over half of his body when he set himself alight while either freebasing cocaine or trying to commit suicide (reports vary). Six years later he was diagnosed with multiple sclerosis, and in the early 1990s he underwent quadruple bypass surgery. Married seven times, Pryor was paid $4 million to appear in *Superman III*. His other credits include William Castle's *The Busy Body*, *Wild in the Streets*, *The Phynx*, *Some Call it Loving*, *The Wiz* (as the title character), *Wholly Moses!*, *The Muppet Movie*, *Lost Highway* and "The Night of the Eccentrics" episode of TV's *The Wild Wild West*. Pryor was married six times to five women and had seven children. His autobiography, *Pryor Convictions*, appeared in 1994.

Character actress **Mary Jackson** died the same day, aged 95. A former school teacher, she was a regular on TV's *The Waltons* (1972–81, as "Miss Emily Baldwin") and also appeared in *Targets* (with Boris Karloff), *Terror House* (aka *The Folks at Redwood Inn*), *Audrey Rose*, *Big Top Pee-Wee* and *The Exorcist III*.

Veteran character actor **Norman Leavitt** died on December 11th, aged 92. His numerous credits include *The Spider Woman Strikes*

Back, *Harvey* (1950), *M* (1951), *The Ten Commandments*, *Teenage Monster*, *Cinderfella*, *The Three Stooges in Orbit* and *Day of the Locust*. He retired from the screen in the mid-1970s.

Danish-born actress **Annette Vadim** (Annette Stroyberg) died of cancer in Copenhagen on December 12th, aged 71. A former fashion model, she married director Roger Vadim in 1958 and he cast her as the vampire "Carmilla" in *Blood and Roses*. The couple separated soon after, but she went on to appear in a handful of films, including *The Testament of Orpheus* and *Agent of Doom*, before retiring from the screen in the mid-1960s.

American actor **John Spencer** (John Speshock) best known for his Emmy Award-winning role as vice president candidate "Leo McGarry" on TV's *The West Wing*, died of a heart attack on December 16th, aged 58. His other credits include *WarGames*, *Sea of Love*, *Ravenous* and TV's *Touched by an Angel*, *F/X: The Series*, *Early Edition*, *Lois & Clark: The New Adventures of Superman* and the new *Outer Limits*.

Japanese actor **Fujiki Yuu** died of a pulmonary embolism on December 19th, aged 74. His credits include *Throne of Blood*, *King Kong vs. Godzilla*, *Atragon*, *Godzilla vs. Mothra*, *Yog: Monster from Space* and *Ghost Man*.

Texas attorney **William Bryan Jennings**, who played a police officer in the 1966 cult movie *Manos: The Hands of Fate*, died the same day, aged 86.

Argentinean-born actress and radio interviewer **Argentina Brunetti** died in Rome on December 20th, aged 98. She was brought to Hollywood in the late 1930s to dub the voices of Jeanette MacDonald and Norma Shearer into Italian, and appeared in numerous films and TV shows, including *It's a Wonderful Life*, *Ghost Chasers*, *7 Faces of Dr. Lao*, *The Venetian Affair*, *Blue Sunshine* and episodes of *Alfred Hitchcock Presents*, *The Veil*, *One Step Beyond*, *Thriller*, *The Invaders*, *Wonder Woman*, *Fantasy Island* and *The Quest*.

Veteran American leading man **Myron Healey** died of respiratory failure on December 21st, aged 82. He was featured in the US footage in *Varan the Unbelievable*, and his other film credits include *Crime Doctor's Manhunt*, *Down to Earth*, *Batman and Robin*, *Panther Girl of the Congo*, *Jungle Moon Men*, *The Unearthly* (with John Carradine), Disney's *The Computer Wore Tennis Shoes*, *Claws*, *The Incredible Melting Man*, *Ghost Fever* and *Pulse*. On TV he appeared in episodes of *Ramar of the Jungle*, *The Veil* (with Boris Karloff), *Men Into Space*, *The Alfred Hitchcock Hour*, *Land of the Giants*, *Ghost Story*, *Kolchak: The Night Stalker*, *The Incredible*

Hulk, The Amazing Spider-Man, V and *Knight Rider*.

Brazilian actress **Aurora Miranda,** the sister of Carmen Miranda, died of a heart attack on December 22nd, aged 90. A popular singing star in her native Brazil, she also appeared in Robert Siodmak's *Phantom Lady* (1944) singing the song "Chica-Chica-Boom-Boom" and danced with Donald Duck in *Disney's The Three Caballeros* the same year.

Character actor **Michael Vale,** best known for his portrayal of Dunkin' Donuts' "Fred the Baker" in a fifteen-year advertising campaign, died of complications from diabetes on December 24th, aged 83. He was also in *Marathon Man* and *The Psychic Parrott*.

Droopy-eyed American character actor **Vincent Schiavelli** died of lung cancer at his home on Sicily on December 26th, aged 57. He lent his distinctive features – often in comedic roles – to such films as *The Return, Schizo, The Adventures of Buckaroo Banzai Across the 8th Dimension, Ghost, Batman Returns, Lurking Fear,* Clive Barker's *Lord of Illusions,* the Bond film *Tomorrow Never Dies, Escape to Witch Mountain* (1995), *Casper Meets Wendy* and the Hallmark TV movie *Snow White*. He also turned up in episodes of *Shadow Chasers, Star Trek: The Next Generation, Shades of L.A., Tales from the Crypt* ("Mournin' Mess"), *Eerie Indiana, Highlander, The X Files, Buffy the Vampire Slayer, Sabrina the Teenage Witch* and the 1981 pilot *Comedy of Horrors,* and was the voice of the magician "Zatara" in the animated *Batman*. An accomplished chef, Schiavelli also wrote three cookbooks and award-winning food articles.

Veteran character actor [Joseph] **Patrick Cranshaw** died on December 28th, aged 86. He began his film career in 1955, and appeared in *The Amazing Transparent Man, Curse of the Swamp Creature, Mars Needs Women, Sgt. Pepper's Lonely Heart's Club Band, Pee-Wee's Big Adventure, Quantum Leap, Alien Avengers II, Ed Wood* and Disney's *Herbie: Fully Loaded*.

Teresa E. Victor, who was *Star Trek* actor Leonard Nimoy's assistant for almost twenty years, died after a long illness on December 29th, aged 62. She was the computer voice in *Star Trek: The Wrath of Khan* and *Star Trek III: The Search for Spock,* and also had a small role in *Star Trek IV: The Voyage Home*.

American stripper **Candy Barr** (Juanita Phillips), an associate of Jack Ruby, died of pneumonia on December 30th, aged 70.

* * *

FILM/TV TECHNICIANS

British cinematographer turned director **C. M. Pennington-Richards** died on January 2nd, aged 93. He shot such films as *Scrooge* (1951), *1984* (1956) and *Tarzan and the Lost Safari* before going on to direct Hammer's *A Challenge for Robin Hood*, *The Oracle*, *Sky Pirates*, *Danny and the Dragon* and episodes of TV's *The Invisible Man*.

68-year-old Japanese director **Koji Haasjimoto** (aka "Koji Hashi-moto"), whose credits include *Godzilla 1985* and *Sayonara Jupiter*, died on January 9th from injuries sustained in a mountain climbing accident. He was an assistant director on *Ghidrah the Three-Headed Monster*, *King Kong vs. Godzilla*, *Frankenstein Conquers the World*, *Monster Zero*, *Godzilla's Revenge*, *Tidal Wave* and *Latitude Zero*.

Jack Kine, who co-founded the BBC Visual Effects Department in 1954, died on January 14th, aged 83. With Bernard Wilkie he worked on the TV productions of *1984*, *Quatermass II*, *Quatermass and the Pit*, *Doctor Who* and *Caves of Steel*, plus the 1966 movie *Invasion*.

American writer-producer **Philip DeGuere, Jr** died of cancer on January 24th, aged 60. He scripted, executive produced and directed the 1978 pilot movie *Dr. Strange*, created the CBS-TV series *Simon and Simon* (1981–88), and also produced *The New Twilight Zone* and *Max Headroom*.

British film editor **Alfred Cox** also died in January. He worked on many classic Hammer horror films, including *Brides of Dracula*.

80-year-old Italian film composer **Franco Mannino** died on February 1st of complications following surgery. His many credits include *Beat the Devil*, *I Vampiri*, *Lo Spettro*, *Hercules Prisoner of Evil* and *Murder Obsession*.

Cinematographer **Joan Weidman** died of cancer on February 6th. Her credits include the documentary *SPFX: The Empire Strikes Back* (1980). She was a producer on several films, including *The Giant of Thunder Mountain*, before overseeing *Wishmaster* and other movies as president of a major completion bond company.

American TV director **John Patterson**, whose credits include episodes of *Project U.F.O.*, *MacGyver*, *Early Edition*, *The Invisible Man*, *Carnivàle* and every season finale of *The Sopranos*, died of prostate cancer on February 7th, aged 64. He also directed the TV movies *The Spring*, *Grave Secrets: The Legend of Hilltop Drive* and *Robin Cook's Harmful Intent*.

50-year-old French film producer **Humbert Balsan** committed suicide on February 10th. He started his career as an actor, playing

Sir Gawain in Robert Bresson's *Lancelot of the Lake*, and went on to produce more than sixty films, many by Arab film-makers.

Stills photographer **Robert Marshak**, who worked with Steven Soderbergh on the remake of *Solaris* and John Sayles on *The Brother from Another Planet*, died of pancreatic cancer on February 13th, aged 53.

Austrian-born film producer **Otto Plashkes** died of heart failure in London on February 14th, aged 75. He worked on *Tarzan's Three Challenges* as a production manager, and during the early 1980s he produced the Sherlock Holmes films *The Hound of the Baskervilles* and *The Sign of Four* starring Ian Richardson for British TV.

Japanese film director **Kihachi Okamoto** died of cancer of the oesophagus on February 17th, aged 82. He was best known for his *jidai-geki* films, such as *The Sword of Doom* and *Zatoichi Meets Yojimbo*.

British-born **Peter Foy**, who refined the flying harness for the 1954 Broadway stage musical of *Peter Pan*, died in Las Vegas the same day, aged 79. His creation of the Multi-Point Balance Harness for the film *Fantastic Voyage* is still used today.

Jef Raskin, who headed the team that developed the Apple Macintosh computer and gave it its name, died of pancreatic cancer on February 26th, aged 61.

Japanese director **Hiroyuki Nasu**, best-known for the *Bee Bop High School* series of films, died of liver cancer on February 27th, aged 53. He also directed the 2004 horror movie *Devilman*.

Television producer **Shelley Hull**, the son of actor Henry Hull (*WereWolf of London*) died of pneumonia the same day, aged 85. His many TV films include *Death at Love House*, *Return to Fantasy Island* and *Return of the Mod Squad*.

Director and actress **Pam Carter** died of a heart aneurysm on February 28th, aged 50. She directed episodes of the cartoon series *Archie's Weird Mysteries* and Nickelodeon's *20,000 Leagues Under the Sea* along with the 2003 TV film *Time Kid*.

Former Universal marketing executive **John Hornick** died on March 4th, aged 50. He joined MCA/Universal Studios in 1983, where he became VP of marketing and merchandising, designing toys and product tie-ins for such movies as *E.T. The Extra-terrestrial*, *Jurassic Park*, *The Flintstones*, *Casper* and the classic Universal Monsters. He was also involved in the design and planning of the Universal Studios theme parks and the Universal City Walk.

Hollywood producer **Debra Hill**, who co-wrote the 1979 film

Halloween with John Carpenter, died of cancer on March 7th, aged 54. Hill and Carpenter returned for *Halloween II*, and were also credited of several of the later sequels. *Halloween 9* was reportedly in production at the time of her death. Her other credits include *The Fog* (and the 2005 remake), *Escape from New York*, *The Dead Zone*, *Clue*, *Big Top Pee-Wee*, *The Fisher King*, *The Lottery* and a series of B-movie remakes for HBO (including *Attack of the 50ft. Woman*). Hill was born in Haddonfield, New Jersey, the name of the fictional Illinois town in the *Halloween* films.

Four time Oscar-winning British film production designer and art director **John** [Allan Hyatt] **Box** died the same day, aged 85. Best known for his work on big budget epics, his credits also include *The Gamma People*, *Rollerball*, *The Keep* and *First Knight*.

Film editor **Sydney Gottlieb**, whose credits include *The Creature from the Black Lagoon*, died after a minor fall on March 10th, aged 100.

Veteran animator **Hal Seeger** died on March 13th, aged 87. He began his career at the Fleischer Studios in the 1930s, working on *Popeye* cartoons and *Hoppity Goes to Town*. After forming Hal Seeger Productions in New York City in the late 1950s, he produced such TV series as *Out of the Inkwell* (1962), *The Milton the Monster Show* (1965) and *Batfink* (1966).

American entrepreneur **John** [Zachary] **DeLorean**, whose firm designed the eponymous gull-winged DMC–12 car used in the *Back to the Future* trilogy, died of complications from a stroke on March 19th, aged 80. Only around 8,000 vehicles were built before the company collapsed in 1982. DeLorean was arrested later the same year by the FBI in a drug sting, and he declared bankruptcy in 1999. Married four times, his wives included actresses Kelly Harmon and Cristina Ferrare.

Film editor **Warner Leighton**, who began his career as a sound editor on the first Cinerama production *South Seas Adventure* before cutting such TV cartoons as *The Flintstones*, *Space Ghost*, *Secret Squirrel*, *Moby Dick and the Mighty Mightor*, *The Fantastic Four* and *Birdman and the Galaxy Trio*, died on March 20th, aged 74. He also edited the animated features *Hey There It's Yogi Bear* and *A Man Called Flintstone*.

Film producer **Julian "Bud" Lesser**, the son of producer Sol Lesser, died of cancer on March 22nd, aged 90. An assistant producer on his father's *Tarzan and the Mermaids*, he produced a number of films during the 1940s and 1950s including *Whispering Smith vs. Scotland Yard*, *Jungle Headhunters* and *The Saint's Girl Friday*.

Producer and director **Eddie Saeta**, whose credits include *Dr. Death, Seeker of Souls* and episodes of TV's *The Man from U.N.C.L.E.*, died on March 26th, aged 90. He also worked as a 2nd unit director on *The Invisible Ghost* (with Bela Lugosi), *One Dark Night, Jungle Moon Men, 20 Million Miles to Earth* and *The Three Stooges in Orbit.*

Special effects designer **Anton Rupprecht** committed suicide on March 27th, aged 42. He worked with The Character Shop and his credits include *Friday the 13th A New Beginning, Night of the Creeps, House, The Puppet Masters* and *Bride of Chucky.*

65-year-old Canadian director and producer **Robin Spry**, whose Telescene Film Group made such series as *Big Wolf on Campus, The Hunger* and *The Lost World* until it filed for bankruptcy protection in December 2000, died in a car accident in Montreal on March 28th. His other credits include *Witchboard III The Possession, Dr. Jekyll and Mr. Hyde* (1999), *Nightmare Man, Student Bodies* and *Matthew Blackheart: Monster Smasher.*

Film and TV casting director **Judith Weiner** died of ovarian cancer on April 5th, aged 58. Her many credits include *The Howling* and *Jekyll and Hyde. . . Together Again.*

American film editor **Robert Golden** died on April 6th, aged 93. His many credits include *The Whip Hand, The Corpse Vanishes, Spooks Run Wild* and *Invisible Ghost* (all three with Bela Lugosi), *Doomed to Die* (with Boris Karloff) and *Night of the Hunter.*

Canadian-born Broadway and Honorary Oscar-winning film choreographer **Onna White** died on April 8th, aged 83. A featured dancer in the original stage cast of *Finian's Rainbow*, she choreographed a revival of the show as well as the Disney film *Pete's Dragon.*

Italian-born film writer-director and rare book collector **George P. (Pan) Cosmatos**, best known for *Rambo: First Blood Part II* and *Tombstone*, died of lung cancer in Canada on April 19th, aged 64. A writer for *Sight and Sound* magazine, his other directing credits include *Of Unknown Origin* and the underwater SF adventure *Leviathan.*

Claymator **Bob Gardiner**, who worked on the Oscar-winning short *Closed Mondays*, committed suicide on April 21st, aged 54.

Veteran make-up artist **Bob Schiffer** died of a stroke on April 26th, aged 88. He worked on numerous films, including *She* (1935), *The Devil Doll* (1936), *The Hunchback of Notre Dame* (1939), *The Wizard of Oz, The 5,000 Fingers of Dr. T, Kiss Me Deadly, Around* *the World in 80 Days, The Amazing Colossal Man, Whatever Happened to Baby Jane?* and *Castle Keep.* In later years he moved to Disney, where his credits include *Now You See Him Now You Don't, Mystery of Dracula's Castle, Charley and the Angel, The Island at the Top of the World, Escape to Witch Mountain, Bedknobs and Broomsticks, Pete's Dragon, Herbie Goes to Monte Carlo, Return to Witch Mountain, Tron, The Shaggy DA, The Cat from Outer Space, The Black Hole, Herbie Goes Bananas, Splash, Baby Secret of the Lost Legend, Frankenweenie* and *Something Wicked This Way Comes.*

American producer **Charles A. Pratt**, whose credits include *Willard, You'll Like My Mother, The Reincarnation of Peter Proud, Ben, Arnold* and *Terror in the Wax Museum*, died of lung cancer on April 27th, aged 81.

Art director **Sherman Loudermilk** died of Alzheimer's disease on April 30th, aged 92. His credits include *The Devil's Hand* and TV's *Galactica 1980.*

Visual effects designer and stop-motion animator **Phil Kellison**, who worked on *The Giant Behemoth* (with Willis H. O'Brien), *Jack the Giant Killer* and *Dinosaurus!*, died on May 13th.

Emmy Award-winning TV producer and Broadway composer **Richard Lewine** died on May 19th, aged 94. In 1957 he produced Rodgers and Hammerstein's *Cinderella* starring Julie Andrews for CBS-TV, and his other credits include Cole Porter's *Aladdin* (1958) and a CBS special of *Blithe Spirit* featuring Noel Coward.

British art director **Lucy Richardson** died of breast cancer on June 1st, aged 47. Her credits include *The Princess Bride, The Secret of Roan Inish, Spider, Ella Enchanted, Star Wars Episode I: The Phantom Menace* and George Lucas' TV series *The Young Indiana Jones Chronicles.* A production manager on the 1997 Canadian anthology series *The Hunger*, Richardson was reportedly the inspiration for John Lennon's 1967 song, "Lucy in the Sky With Diamonds".

Independent record producer **Simon Waronker** died on June 7th, aged 90. In 1955 he founded Liberty Records and signed such talent as Johnny Burnette ("You're Sixteen"), Eddie Cochran ("Summertime Blues"), Jan and Dean ("Surf City") and Julie London ("Cry Me a River"). However, his biggest act was probably Ross Bagdasarian, better known as "Dave Seville" of Alvin and the Chipmunks (Alvin, Simon and Theodore), whose first single sold four million copies in the first month.

Hungarian-born film producer **William G. Reich**, who produced the 1975 Italian horror film *The Night Child* (aka *The Cursed Medallion*), died of heart disease in Florida on June 12th, aged 91.

Film and TV editor **Joseph T. Dervin**, who received an Emmy Award in 1966 for his work on *The Man from U.N.C.L.E.*, died on June 20th, aged 90. He also edited such shows as *The Ghost and Mrs Muir* and *Kung Fu*, and was responsible for creating the feature film versions of *The Man from U.N.C.L.E.*, including *The Spy With My Face*, *The Spy in the Green Hat* and *The Helicopter Spies*.

Film sound editor **Richard Sperber**, who worked at Twentieth Century Fox for many years, died on June 21st, aged 88. His credits include *Fantastic Voyage*, *The Omen*, *Damnation Alley*, *High Anxiety*, *Damien: Omen II*, *The Boys from Brazil* and the TV movie *Good Against Evil*.

Special effects model-maker **Michael Cuneo** died of a brain tumour on June 24th, aged 41. He worked on the TV series *Star Trek: The Next Generation* and *Star Trek: Deep Space Nine*.

62-year-old **Chet Helms**, "Father of the Summer of Love", died of complications from a stroke in San Francisco on June 25th. He famously discovered singer Janis Joplin.

Film and TV director **Bruce Malmuth** died of oesophageal cancer on June 28th, aged 71. His credits include episodes of the revived *Twilight Zone* series and *Beauty and the Beast*.

Norman Prescott, chairman and co-founder of Filmation Studios, died on July 2nd, aged 78. In 1959 he supervised the music and post-production for the Embassy Pictures' release of *Hercules*, and he later independently produced the animated features *Pinocchio in Outer Space* and *Journey Back to Oz*. Prescott started Filmation with Lou Scheimer in 1965 after acquiring the rights from DC Comics to produce the *The New Adventures of Superman* TV series. The animation studio went on to produce the 1973 Emmy-winning *Star Trek* cartoon series, along with such shows as *Fantastic Voyage*, *The Batman/Superman Hour*, *Sabrina and the Groovie Goolies*, *The New Animated Adventures of Flash Gordon* and the live-action *Shazam!*, *The Ghost Busters*, *Isis*, *Ark II* and *Space Academy*.

Film producer **Charles Okun**, whose credits include *The Legend of the Lone Ranger*, *The Sentinel* and *Dreamcatcher*, died of cancer on July 3rd, aged 80.

Australian-born British costume designer **Jocelyn Rickards** died on July 7th, aged 80. As well as designing costumes for such classic 1960s films as *The Knack*, *Morgan A Suitable Case for Treatment* (aka *Morgan!*) and Antonioni's *Blow-Up*, she also worked on the second James Bond film, *From Russia with Love*. She was married to film director Clive Donner.

Russian-born Hollywood art director and production designer **Alexander Golitzen**, who shared an Academy Award for his work on Universal's 1943 *Phantom of the Opera*, died on congestive heart failure on July 26th, aged 97. He worked on more than 300 movies, including *Arabian Nights*, *Cobra Woman*, *The Climax* (with Boris Karloff), *Abbott and Costello Go to Mars*, *Abbott and Costello Meet the Mummy*, *Revenge of the Creature*, *This Island Earth*, *Cult of the Cobra*, *Tarantula*, *The Creature Walks Among Us*, *Francis in the Haunted House*, *The Mole People*, *The Incredible Shrinking Man*, *The Deadly Mantis*, *Man of a Thousand Faces*, *The Land Unknown*, *The Monolith Monsters*, *Touch of Evil*, *Monster on the Campus*, *Curse of the Undead*, *The Leech Woman*, *Midnight Lace* (1960), *The Brass Bottle*, *The Night Walker*, *The Sword of Ali Baba*, *The War Lord*, *The Ghost and Mr. Chicken*, *Munster Go Home!*, *Let's Kill Uncle*, *The Reluctant Astronaut*, *Games*, *Eye of the Cat*, *Colossus: The Forbin Project*, *The Beguiled*, *Slaughterhouse-Five*, *Play Misty for Me* and *Earthquake*. Golitzen won two more Oscars for his work.

Gerry Thomas, the man who invented the frozen TV dinner in 1954 while working as a salesman for a food firm in Nebraska, also died in July, aged 83. Although more than ten million frozen meals were sold in the first year, Thomas received a small pay rise and a $1,000 bonus for his idea.

62-year-old film producer **Terry Carr**, whose credits include *Predator 2*, was found dead in his car along with his daughter on August 1st.

Oscar-nominated American costume designer **Donald Brooks** (Donald Marc Blumberg) died of a heart attack the same day, aged 77. His stage and screen credits include the Barbra Streisand fantasy *On a Clear Day You Can See Forever* and *The Terminal Man*.

British film and TV director **David Tomblin**, who co-created and produced the cult 1967 series *The Prisoner* with Patrick McGoohan, died on August 4th, aged 74. Starting out as an assistant producer on such shows as *The New Adventures of Charlie Chan*, *The Invisible Man* and *One Step Beyond*, he filled the same role on such movies as Hammer's *Taste of Fear*, *The Haunting* (1963), *Night Must Fall* (1964), *The Adventures of Sherlock Holmes' Smarter Brother*, *The Omen*, *Superman*, *Star Wars*, *Superman II*, *Raiders of the Lost Ark*, *Return of the Jedi*, *Never Say Never Again*, *Indiana Jones and the Temple of Doom* and *Indiana Jones and the Last Crusade*. After writing and directing several episodes of *The Prisoner*, Tomblin went on to work on *U.F.O.* and *Space: 1999*.

Japanese writer and director **Teruo Ishii** died of cancer on August 12th, aged 81. His credits include *Atomic Rulers of the World* and the *Super Giant* series.

Italian cinematographer **Tonino** (Antonio) **Delli Colli**, who worked with Sergio Leone, Pier Paolo Pasolini, Federico Fellini and Roman Polanski, amongst other directors, died of a heart attack in Rome on August 16th, aged 82. His many credits include *Black Magic*, *The Thief of Bagdad* (1961), *Ghosts – Italian Style*, *Spirits of the Dead*, *F/X 2* and *The Name of the Rose*.

American cinematographer **Meredith Nicholson**, whose credits include the low budget movies *She Demons*, *The Amazing Transparent Man*, *Frankenstein's Daughter*, *The Devil's Hand* and *Missile to the Moon*, died on August 18th, aged 92.

American music pioneer Dr **Robert A. Moog**, who developed the electronic synthesiser that carried his name, died of an inoperable brain tumour on August 21st, aged 71. In the mid-1960s, his invention revolutionized the music industry and was used by the Beatles, the Doors, Yes, Pink Floyd, Emerson Lake and Palmer and numerous other bands. A Moog was also used on the soundtrack for Stanley Kubrick's *A Clockwork Orange* and many other SF films.

TV writer and producer **Herbert J. Wright**, best known for creating the villainous Ferengi in *Star Trek The Next Generation*, died on August 24th, aged 58. After being mentored by Japanese film-maker Akira Kurosawa, Wright started out in the mailroom of Universal Studios and worked his way up to writing, producing or directing for such shows as *Night Gallery*, *The Six Million Dollar Man*, *Space Rangers*, *War of the Worlds* and the Emmy-nominated children's programme *Through the Magic Pyramid*.

American TV executive and director **Perry Lafferty** died of complications from prostate cancer on August 25th, aged 87. He directed three episodes of the original *Twilight Zone* series.

Fred Joerger, who helped create the models for Disneyland attractions such as The Haunted Mansion and Sleeping Beauty's Castle, died on August 26th, aged 91.

Actor turned writer and director **Wyott Ordung** died on August 28th, aged 83. After appearing in films and on TV in the early 1950s, he scripted the cult classic *Robot Monster* (1953), *Target Earth* and Roger Corman's *Monster from the Ocean Floor* (in which he also appeared as superstitious fisherman "Pablo"). The 1959 SF film *First Man into Space* was based on his original story, and Ordung was assistant director on *The Navy vs. the Night Monsters* and *The Mummy and the Curse of the Jackals*.

Movie art director and character actor **Roger Pancake** died of oesophageal cancer on September 10th, aged 71. He was art director on *Creature from Black Lake* (in which he also played the monster) and *Mansion of the Doomed*, and had small roles in *The Cat from Outer Space* and *Dracula's Dog*.

Film editor-turned-Oscar-winning director **Robert Wise** died of heart failure on September 14th, four days after celebrating his 91st birthday. Best known as the director of such musicals as *West Side Story* and *The Sound of Music*, Wise began his career as an editor at RKO Radio Pictures, cutting such films as *The Hunchback of Notre Dame* (1939), *The Devil and Daniel Webster* and *Citizen Kane*. He made his uncredited debut as a director re-shooting scenes for Orson Welles' troubled *The Magnificent Ambersons* before taking over *Curse of the Cat People* for producer Val Lewton in 1944. His other films include *The Body Snatcher* (with Karloff and Lugosi), *A Game of Death*, *The Day the Earth Stood Still*, *The Haunting* (1963), *The Andromeda Strain*, *Audrey Rose* and the first of the successful *Star Trek* movie franchise. In 1996 he made his only cameo appearance as an actor in John Landis' *The Stupids*. Martin Scorsese described Wise as "the Steven Spielberg of his time".

British cinematographer-turned-writer/producer/director **Guy Green** O.B.E. died of heart and kidney failure in Los Angeles on September 13th, aged 91. In 1947 he became the first British director of photography to win an Academy Award, for *Great Expectations*, and his directing credits include Hammer's *The Snorkel* and the John Fowles adaptation *The Magus*. Green reportedly turned down the offer to direct *Dr. No*.

TV director **Henry Kaplan**, whose credits include the 1960s Gothic soap opera *Dark Shadows*, died on September 14th, aged 79.

Film producer **Sid Luft**, the former manager/husband (1952–65) of Judy Garland and stepfather to Liza Minnelli, died of a heart attack on September 15th, aged 89.

Director and cinematographer **Richard E. Cunha** died of heart failure on September 18th, aged 84. Born in Honolulu, he is best known for his horror and SF films of the 1950s, such as *Giant from the Unknown*, *She Demons*, *Missile to the Moon* and the delirious *Frankenstein's Daughter*, which were made on shoestring budgets. In the early 1960s Cunha also photographed *Bloodlust*.

American film producer **Gordon Carroll** died of pneumonia on

September 20th, aged 77. Among his credits are *Alien*, *Blue Thunder*, *Aliens*, *Aliens³*, *Alien Resurrection* and *Alien vs. Predator*.

Japanese special effects director and cinematographer **Teisho Arikawa** (aka "Sadamasa Arikawa") died of lung cancer on September 22nd, aged 80. His credits include the original *Godzilla* (*Gojira*), *Gigantis the Fire Monster*, *Rodan*, *The Mysterians*, *The H-Man*, *Battle in Outer Space*, *Mothra*, *Gorath*, *King Kong vs. Godzilla*, *Varan the Unbelievable*, *Attack of the Mushroom People*, *The Lost World of Sinbad*, *Atragon*, *Dagora the Space Monster*, *Ghidrah the Three-Headed Monster*, *Godzilla vs. the Thing*, *Frankenstein Conquers the World*, *Monster Zero*, *War of the Gargantuas*, *Godzilla vs. the Sea Monster*, *King Kong Escapes*, *Son of Godzilla*, *Destroy All Monsters*, *Latitude Zero*, *Yog Monster from Space* and *The Mighty Peking Man*. Arikawa also directed the special photographic effects on the 1960s *Ultraman* TV series and he directed the 1983 film *The Phoenix* (aka *War of the Wizards*).

78-year-old American film producer **Joseph Wolf** who, with Irwin Yablans, helped launch the successful *Halloween* franchise through their Compass International Pictures, died on September 22nd from complications from a fall. Made for just $325,000, *Halloween* grossed more than $100 million. After launching Media Home Entertainment, he was a partner with New Line Films on the first *Nightmare on Elm Street*. Wolf also served in various producer categories on *Fade to Black*, *Hell Night*, *Blood Beach*, *Children of the Living Dead* and *HellBent*, as well as *Halloween II* and *Halloween III Season of the Witch*.

TV producer **Bruce Johnson**, whose credits include *Mork and Mindy*, died of heart failure on September 27th, aged 66.

Kenyan-born film producer and director **Raju Patel** died of cancer in Los Angeles on October 9th, aged 45. In the mid-1990s he teamed up with Disney to produce a live-action version of *The Jungle Book* and went on to produce a sequel, *The Second Jungle Book*, for Columbia-TriStar. Patel's other credits include *Cyborg 2*, *The Adventures of Pinocchio* and *The New Adventures of Pinocchio*.

Actor-turned-director **Bernard Carr** died on October 18th, aged 94. He was assistant director on *One Million B.C.*, *Turnabout* and *Topper Returns* and directed the 1948 old dark house comedy *Who Killed Doc Robbin?*.

German-born film director and screenwriter **Wolf** [Peter] **Rilla** died in England on October 19th, aged 85. The son of character actor Walter Rilla, he is best remembered for the 1960 film *Village of the Damned*, based on John Wyndham's book *The Midwich Cuckoos*.

Irish-born film producer **Tony Adams** died of an aneurysm on October 22nd, aged 52. He had suffered a stroke two days earlier during a meeting about the *Spider-Man* Broadway musical. After starting as John Boorman's assistant on *Deliverance*, Adams later became president of Blake Edwards Entertainment, producing a number of the *Pink Panther* movies.

British scriptwriter, playwright, producer and novelist **Alfred [James] Shaughnessy** died of complications from a stroke on November 2nd, aged 89. A veteran of Ealing Studios in the early 1950s, he directed the 1957 film *Cat Girl* starring Barbara Shelley and scripted Hammer's *Crescendo*, *The Flesh and Blood Show* and the TV movie *The Haunting of Cassie Palmer*. Shaughnessy also worked on such TV series as *The Saint*, *Journey to the Unknown* and *The Adventures of Sherlock Holmes*.

75-year-old American cinematographer **Steven Larner** died after an accident at his Californian vineyard on November 6th. His numerous credits include *The Student Nurses*, *The Night God Screamed*, *Twilight Zone: The Movie*, *Curse of the Black Widow*, *World War III*, *V: The Final Battle* and the TV series *Beauty and the Beast*.

Canadian-born visual effects producer **C. Marie Davis** died of breast cancer on November 9th, aged 47. She began her career working as an assistant to cartoon voice actor Mel Blanc. Moving to CIS Hollywood, she worked on *The Blob*, *Scrooged*, *The Abyss*, *Total Recall*, *Ernest Scared Stupid*, *Batman Forever*, *Star Trek: Generations*, *The Muppet Christmas Carol*, *Contact*, *Deep Impact*, *Practical Magic*, *Mission to Mars*, *Cats & Dogs*, *Scary Movie 2*, the remake of *Planet of the Apes*, *Kate & Leopold*, *Spider-Man*, *S1m0ne*, *The Tuxedo* and *Star Trek: Nemesis*. As vice-president of production services at Sony Pictures Imageworks, she was responsible for such films as *The Matrix Reloaded*, *The Polar Express*, *Spider-Man 2*, *Zathura* and *The Chronicles of Narnia: The Lion, The Witch and The Wardrobe*.

75-year-old film director **Moustapha Akkad**, the executive producer of all eight *Halloween* films, died in hospital on November 11th from injuries sustained in the Amman, Jordan, hotel bomb blasts three days earlier. His 34-year-old daughter Rima Akkad Monla was killed immediately in the terrorist suicide blast that claimed the lives of fifty-seven people attending a wedding reception. A US national, the Syrian-born Akkad also produced the 1985 horror film *Appointment with Fear*.

British sound recordist **John W. Mitchell** died on December 17th, aged 88. He worked on *The Thief of Bagdad* (1940), *Hamlet* (1948), *The Rocking Horse Winner*, *Moby Dick*, *Billion Dollar Brain*, *Chitty Chitty Bang Bang*, *Murder by Decree* and the Bond films *From Russia with Love*, *Casino Royale*, *On Her Majesty's Secret Service*, *You Only Live Twice* and *Live and Let Die*.

Walt Disney film executive **Irving Ludwig**, who was instrumental in the creation of Buena Vista Distributors, died in Santa Monica on November 26th, aged 95. The Russian-born Ludwig was a movie theatre manager before joining Disney in 1940 where he oversaw the releases of such films as *Fantasia*, *The Shaggy Dog*, *The Absent Minded Professor*, *Mary Poppins* and *The Love Bug*.

E. Cardon "Card" Walker, who rose through the ranks from the mailroom to eventually becoming CEO and chairman of the Walt Disney Co. following the death of co-founder Roy O. Disney, died of heart failure on November 29th, aged 89. He helped create such attractions as It's a Small World, Pirates of the Caribbean and The Haunted Mansion, and launched EPCOT at Walt Disney World, Tokyo Disneyland and the Disney Channel.

87-year-old veteran American film director **Herbert L. Strock** died of heart failure on November 30th, following a car accident. Best known for his three teenage horror films for AIP in the 1950s, *I Was a Teenage Frankenstein*, *Blood of Dracula* and *How to Make a Monster*, the former publicist, writer and editor also directed *The Magnetic Monster*, *Donovan's Brain* and *Riders to the Stars* (all uncredited), the 3-D *Gog*, *The Devil's Messenger* (with Lon Chaney, Jr) and *The Crawling Hand*, along with numerous episodes of *Science Fiction Theatre* and the 1950s Boris Karloff TV series *The Veil*. Strock was also assistant editor on MGM's *Gaslight* (1944), edited *Psycho Sisters*, *Witches' Brew* and *Night Screams*, and wrote the screenplay for *Monster* starring John Carradine. His autobiography, *Picture Perfect*, appeared in 2000.

Hollywood set designer **John S. Detlie** died of lung cancer the same day, aged 96. His credits include *I Married an Angel*, *A Christmas Carol* (1938) and *On Borrowed Time*.

British TV producer **Leonard Lewis** died on December 2nd, aged 78. His credits include *Adam Adamant Lives!*, *Tales of the Unexpected* and the BBC miniseries *Jack the Ripper*.

42-year-old American film producer **Gregg Hoffman**, founder and partner in Twisted Pictures with Oren Koules and Mark Burg, died on December 4th, after being admitted to hospital complaining of neck pain. A former vice president of production at the Walt Disney Co., in 2003, he brought the script and an eight-minute demo of *Saw* to Twisted, who financed the picture for $1.2 million. It subsequently grossed $102 million worldwide. The sequel, *Saw 2*, took $108 million, and a third film in the series was in development at the time of Hoffman's death, as were such other low budget horror productions from Twisted Pictures as *Catacombs*, *Silence* and *Crawlspace*.

Influential British cinematographer **Adrian Biddle** died of a heart attack on December 7th, aged 53. He began his career in 1969, at the age of sixteen, working uncredited with the underwater camera crews on the James Bond film *On Her Majesty's Secret Service* and *Captain Nemo and the Underwater City*. After rising to focus-puller on Ridley Scott's *Alien*, he was promoted to director of photography for James Cameron's sequel, *Aliens*, and worked again with Scott on the Apple Computers launch commercial "1984". Biddle shot twenty-six films in nineteen years, and his other credits include *The Princess Bride*, *Willow*, *Judge Dredd*, *101 Dalmations* (1996), *The Butcher Boy*, *Event Horizon*, *The Mummy* (1999), *The World is Not Enough*, *102 Dalmations*, *The Mummy Returns*, *Reign of Fire*, *An American Haunting* and *V for Vendetta*, which reportedly included the biggest urban night shoot ever attempted.

49-year-old independent film producer **Robert F. Newmyer**, whose credits include *The Santa Clause* (1994) and its two sequels, died of heart failure triggered by an asthma attack on December 12th, while working out in a Toronto gym.

Editor turned director **Ed Hansen** died of bladder cancer on December 16th, aged 68. Hansen edited *Nightforce*, *Skeeter*, *The Elf Who Saved Christmas* and other films, and directed *Cyber-CHIC*, *Takin it Off* and *Takin it All Off*.

Jack Wiener, who produced *F/X*, *F/X2* and *Vampira*, died of a heart attack on December 26th, aged 79.

USEFUL ADDRESSES

THE FOLLOWING LISTING OF organisations, publications, dealers and individuals is designed to present readers and authors with further avenues to explore. Although I can personally recommend most of those listed on the following pages, neither the publisher nor myself can take any responsibility for the services they offer. Please also note that the information below is only a guide and is subject to change without notice.

—The Editor

ORGANISATIONS

The Australian Horror Writers Association <www.australianhorror.com> is a non-profit organisation that was officially launched in July 2005. AHWA is the focal point and first point of reference for writers and fans of the dark side of literature in Australia. AHWA aims to spread the acceptance and improve the understanding of what horror is in literature to a wider audience, and in doing so gain a greater readership for established and new writers alike. The organisation offers new writers mentor programmes, critique services, competitions and information about how to get published. The website includes many links and articles.

The British Fantasy Society <www.britishfantasysociety.org.uk> was founded in 1971 and publishes the bi-monthly newsletter *Prism* and the magazine *Dark Horizons*, featuring articles, reviews, interviews and fiction, along with occasional special booklets. The BFS also enjoys a lively online community – there is an e-mail news-feed, a discussion board with numerous links, and a CyberStore selling various publications. FantasyCon is one of the UK's friendliest conventions and there are social gatherings and meet-the-author events organised around Britain. For yearly membership details, e-mail: <secretary@britishfantasysociety.org.uk>. You can also join online through the Cyberstore.

The Friends of Arthur Machen <www.machensoc.demon.co.uk> is a group whose objectives include encouraging a wider recognition of Machen's work and providing a focus for critical debate. Members get a hardbound journal, *Faunus*, twice a year, and also the informative newsletter *Machenalia*. For membership details, contact Jeremy Cantwell/Correspondence Secretary, 78 Greenwich South Street, Greenwich, London SW10 8UN, UK.

The Ghost Story Society <www.ash-tree.bc.ca/GSS.html> is organised by Barbara and Christopher Roden. They publish the superb *All Hallows* three times a year. For more information contact PO Box 1360, Ashcroft, British Columbia, Canada V0K 1A0. E-mail: <nebuly@telus.net>.

The Horror Writers Association <www.horror.org> is a worldwide organisation of writers and publishing professionals dedicated to promoting the interests of writers of Horror and Dark Fantasy. It was formed in the early 1980s. Interested individuals may apply for Active, Affiliate or Associate membership. Active membership is limited to professional writers. HWA publishes a monthly Newsletter, and organises an annual conference and the Bram Stoker Awards ceremony. Apply online or write to HWA Membership, PO Box 50577, Palo Alto, CA 94303, USA.

World Fantasy Convention <www.worldfantasy.org> is an annual convention held in a different (usually American) city each year, oriented particularly towards serious readers and genre professionals.

World Horror Convention <www.worldhorrorsociety.org> is a smaller, more relaxed, event. It is aimed specifically at horror fans and professionals, and held in a different city each year. In 2007, it moves out of North America for the first time and will be held in Toronto, Canada <www.whc2007.org>.

SELECTED SMALL PRESS PUBLISHERS

Beccon Publications, 75 Rosslyn Avenue, Harold Wood, Essex RM3 0RG, UK. E-mail: <beccon@dial.pipex.com>

Burt Creations <www.burtcreations.com>, 29 Arnold Place, Norwich, CT 06360, USA.

Cemetery Dance Publications <www.cemeterydance.com>, PO Box 943, Abingdon, MD 21009, USA.

Crowswing Books <www.crowswingbooks.co.uk>, PO Box 301, King's Lynn, Norfolk PE33 OXW, UK.

CSfG Publishing <www.csfg.org.au>, PO Box 89, Latham ACT 2615, Australia. E-mail: <orders@csfg.org.au>.

Earthling Publications <www.earthlingpub.com>, PO Box 413, Northborough, MA 01532, USA. E-mail: <earthlingpub@yahoo.com>.

Elder Signs Press, Inc. <www.eldersignspress.com>, PO Box 389, Lake Orion, MI 48361–0389, USA.

Endeavor Press <www.endeavorpress.net>, PO Box 4307, Chicago, IL 60680–4307, USA. E-mail: <info@endeavorpress.com>.

Eraserhead Press <www.eraserheadpress.com>, 205 N.E. Bryant, Portalnd, OR 97211, USA.

Fantagraphics Books <www.fantagraphics.com>, 7563 Lake City N.E., Seattle, WA 98115, USA.

Gray Friar Press <www.grayfriarpress.com>, 19 Ruffield Side, Delph Hill, Wyke, Bradford, West Yorkshire, UK. E-mail: <g.fry@blueyonder.co.uk>.

Hill House, Publishers <www.hillhousepublishers.com>, 491 Illington Road, Ossining, NY 10562, USA. E-mail: <peterschneider@hillhousepublishers.com>.

Infrapress <www.writers.com/publishing>, 87 South Meadowcroft Drive, Akron, Ohio 44313–7266, USA. E-mail: <publishers@writers.com>.

Midnight Library <www.midnightlibrary.com>, Fountain Valley, CA, USA. E-mail: <gschloss@midnightlibrary.com>.

MonkeyBrain Books <www.monkeybrainbooks.com>, 11204 Crossland Drive, Austin, TX 78726, USA. E-mail: <info@monkeybrainbooks.com>.

Nemonymous <www.nemonymous.com>.

Night Shade Books <www.nightshadebooks.com>, 3623 SW Baird St, Portland, OR 97219, USA. E-mail: <night@nightshadebooks.com>.

NonStop Press, PO Box 981, Peck Slip Station, New York, NY 10272–0981, USA. E-mail: <nonstop@compuserve.com>

Northern Gothic, "Fenham View", 6 Studley Terrace, Arthur's Hill, Newcastle-upon-Tyne, NE4 5AH, UK. E-mail: <chaz@chazbrenchley.co.uk>

Pendragon Press <www.pendragonpress.co.uk>, PO Box 12, Maesteg, Mid Glamorgan, South Wales CF34 0XG, UK.

Prime Books <www.prime-books.com>.

PS Publishing <www.pspublishing.co.uk>, Grosvenor House, 1 New Road, Hornsea, East Yorkshire HU18 1PG, UK. E-mail: <editor@pspublishing.co.uk>

Raw Dog Screaming Press <www.rawdogscreaming.com>, 5103 72nd Place, Hyattsville, MD 20784, USA.

Sarob Press <www.home.freeuk.net/sarobpress>, "Ty Newydd", Four Roads, Kidwelly, Carmarthenshire SA17 4SF, Wales, UK. E-mail: <sarobpress@freeuk.com>.

Savoy Books <www.savoy.abel.co.uk>, 446 Wilmslow Road, Withington, Manchester M20 3BW, UK. E-mail: <office@savoy.abel.co.uk>.

Small Beer Press <www.smallbeerpress.com>, 176 Prospect Avenue, Northampton, MA 01060, USA. E-mail: <info@smallbeerpress.com>.

Subterranean Press <www.subterraneanpress.com>, PO Box 190106, Burton, MI 48519, USA. E-mail: <subpress@earthlink.net>.

Tachyon Publications <www.tachyonpublications.com>, 1459 18th Street #139, San Francisco, CA 94107, USA. E-mail: <jw@tachyonpublications.com>.

Telos Publishing Ltd <www.telos.co.uk>, 61 Elgar Avenue, Tolworth, Surrey KT5 9JP, UK. E-mail: <feedback@telos.co.uk>.

Tartarus Press <www.tartaruspress.com>, Coverley House, Carlton-in-Coverdale, Leyburn, North Yorkshire DL8 4AY, UK. E-mail: <tartarus@pavilion.co.uk>.

Twilight Tales <www.sales@twilightTales.com>, 2339 N. Commonwealth 4C, Chicago, IL 60614, USA.

Undaunted Press <www.undauntedpress.com>, 761 Tree Top Ridge Drive, Valley Park, MO 63088, USA. E-mail: <cthulhuzilla@sbcglobal.net>.

Wheatland Press <www.wheatlandpress.com>, P.O. Box 1818, Wilsonville, OR 97070, USA.

Wildside Press <www.wildside.com>, 9710 Traville Gateway Drive #234, Rockville, MD 20850, USA.

DVD DISTRIBUTORS

EI Independent Cinema <www.SeductionCinema.com> produces low budget horror (Shock-O-Rama Cinema) and erotic genre movies (Seduction Cinema). 10 Park Place, Building 6A, 2nd Floor, Butler, NJ 07405, USA. E-mail: <eicinema@aol.com>.

Mondo Macabro <www.mondomacabrodvd.com> distributor of obscure European and other foreign horror and exploitation movies. Boum Productions Ltd., PO Box 3336, Brighton BN2 3GW, UK. E-mail: <video@boumproductions.com>.

SELECTED MAGAZINES

Alan K's Inhuman Magazine is an attractive digest fiction publication with an old-time pulp feel. For more information (no unsolicited manuscripts) e-mail: <outreart@aol.com>

Apex Science Fiction & Horror Digest <www.apexdigest.com> is a new digest magazine edited by Jason B. Sizemore. Subscriptions are available from: Apex Publications LLC, 4629 Riverman Way, Lexington, KY 40515, USA. E-mail: <jason@apexdigest.com>.

Black Gate: Adventures in Fantasy Literature <www.blackgate.com> is a nicely designed magazine devoted to the best in epic fantasy. For sample issue and subscription rates check their website or write to: New Epoch Press, 815 Oak Street, St. Charles, IL 60174, USA. E-mail: <john@blackgate.com>.

Black Static <www.ttapress.com> is the new title for *The 3rd Alternative*. Subscriptions payable by cheque or credit card (accepted in sterling, euros or US dollars) to: TTA Press, 5 Martins Lane, Witcham, Cambs CB6 2LB, UK.

The Bulletin of the Science Fiction and Fantasy Writers of America <www.sfwa.org> is published quarterly by the Science Fiction and Fantasy Writers of America, Inc. You do not need to be a SFWA member to subscribe, and the magazine features many interesting and important articles aimed at professional genre authors and would-be writers, including market reports. Single copies or a full year's subscription are available from: SFWA Bulletin, PO Box 10126, Rochester, NY 14610, USA. You can sample articles or purchase back issues and subscriptions on the magazine's website <www.sfwa.org/bulletin/>. E-mail: <bulletin@sfwa.org>.

Cemetery Dance Magazine <www.cemeterydance.com> is edited by Richard Chizmar and Robert Morrish and includes fiction up to 5,000 words, interviews, articles and columns by many of the biggest names in horror. For subscription information contact: Cemetery Dance Publications, PO Box 623, Forest Hill, MD 21050, USA. E-mail: <info@cemeterydance.com>.

Dark Wisdom: The Magazine of Dark Fiction <www.darkwisdom.com>, attractive Lovecraftian digest magazine edited by William Jones and published three times a year by Elder Signs Press, PO Box 389, Lake Orion, MI 48361–0389, USA.

Locus <www.locusmag.com> is the monthly newspaper of the SF/fantasy/horror field. Contact: Locus Publications, PO Box 13305, Oakland, CA 94661, USA. Subscription information with other rates and order forms are also available on the website. Sterling equivalent cheques can be sent to: Fantast (Medway) Ltd, PO Box 23, Upwell Wisbech, Cambs PE14 9BU, UK. E-mail: <locus@locusmag.com>.

The Magazine of Fantasy & Science Fiction <www.fsfmag.com> has been publishing some of the best imaginative fiction for more than fifty years, now edited by Gordon Van Gelder. Single copies or an annual subscription (which includes the double October/November anniversary issue) are available by US cheques or credit card from: Fantasy & Science Fiction, PO Box 3447, Hoboken, NJ 07030, USA, or you can subscribe online.

PostScripts: The A to Z of Fantastic Fiction <www.pspublishing. co.uk> is an excellent new digest magazine from PS Publishing. Each issue features approximately 60,000 words of fiction (SF, fantasy, horror and crime/suspense), plus a guest editorial, interviews and occasional non-fiction. Issues are also available as a signed 150-copy hardcover edition. For more information contact: PS Publishing Ltd., Grosvenor House, 1 New Road, Hornsea, East Yorkshire HU18 1PG, UK. E-mail: <editor@pspublishing.co>.

Rue Morgue <www.rue-morgue.com>, is a glossy bi-monthly magazine edited by Jovanka Vuckovic and subtitled "Horror in Culture & Entertainment". Packed with full colour features and reviews of new films, books, comics, music and game releases. Subscriptions are available from: The Rue Morgue House of Horror, 2926 Dundas Street West, Toronto, ON M6P 1Y8, Canada, or by credit card on the web site. E-mail: <info@rue-morgue.com>. *Rue Morgue* also runs the Festival of Fear: Canadian National Horror Expo in Toronto, and you can log on to Rue Morgue Radio at: <www.rue-morgue.com>.

SF Site <www.sfsite.com> has been posted twice each month since 1997. Presently, it publishes around thirty to fifty reviews of SF, fantasy and horror from mass-market publishers and some small press. They also maintain link pages for Author and Fan Tribute Sites and other facets including pages for Interviews, Fiction, Science Fact, Bookstores, Small Press, Publishers, E-zines and Magazines, Artists, Audio, Art Galleries, Newsgroups and Writers' Resources. Periodically, they add features such as author and publisher reading lists.

Space and Time <www.cith.org/space&time>, the magazine of fantasy, horror and science fiction is published twice a year by editor-in-chief Gordon Linzner. Single issues are $5.00 plus $1.50 shipping (USA). Subscriptions are available by US postal money order or cheque to: Space and Time, 138 West 70th Street (4B), New York, NY 10023–4468, USA. In the UK order from BBR Distributing, PO Box 625, Sheffield S1 3GY, UK.

Supernatural   Tales   <www.chico.nildram.co.uk/Supernatural

Tales.html> is an annual small press magazine of stories and occasional non-fiction edited by David Longhorn. Three-issue subscription (no foreign cheques) from: Supernatural Tales, 291 Eastbourne Avenue, Gateshead NE8 4NN, UK. E-mail: <davidlonghorn@hotmail.com>.

Talebones <www.talebones.com> is an attractive digest magazine of science fiction and dark fantasy edited and published by Patrick and Honna Swenson. For a four issue subscription (US funds only or credit card) write to: 5203 Quincy Avenue S.E., Auburn, WA 98092, USA. E-mail: <info@talebones.com>.

Video Watchdog <www.videowatchdog.com> is a full colour monthly review of horror, fantasy and cult cinema on tape and disc, published by Tim and Donna Lucas. Described as "The Perfectionist's Guide to Fantastic Video", an annual twelve-issue subscription is available in US funds only or VISA/MasterCard to: Video Watchdog, PO Box 5283, Cincinnati, OH 45205–0283, USA. E-mail: <orders@videowatchdog.com>.

Weird Tales <www.wildside.com> is the latest large-size incarnation of "The Unique Magazine". Edited by George H. Scithers, Darrell Schweitzer and John Gregory Betancourt, it is published by Wildside Press LLC, in association with Terminus Publishing Co., Inc. Single copies or a six-issue subscription is available (in US funds only) from: Wildside Press, 9710 Traville Gateway Drive #234, Rockville, MD 20850, USA. Submissions should be addressed to Weird Tales, 121 Crooked Lane, King of Prussia, PA 19406–2570, USA. An e-mail version of the magazine's writers's guidelines (no electronic submissions) is available from <weirdtales@comcast.net>. You can also visit the message board at <www.wildsidepress.com>. In the UK contact: Cold Tonnage Books, 22 Kings Lane, Windlesham, Surrey, GU20 6JQ, UK <andy@coldtonnage.co.uk>.

BOOK DEALERS

Bookfellows/Mystery and Imagination Books <www.mysteryandimagination.com> is owned and operated by Malcolm and Christine Bell, who have been selling fine and rare books since 1975. This clean and neatly organised store includes SF/fantasy/horror/mystery, along with all other areas of popular literature. Many editions are signed, and catalogues are issued regularly. Credit cards accepted. Open seven days a week at 238 N. Brand Blvd., Glendale, California 91203, USA. Tel: (818) 545–0206. Fax: (818) 545–0094. E-mail: <bookfellows@gowebway.com>.

Borderlands Books <www.borderlands-books.com> is a nicely designed store with friendly staff and an impressive stock of new and used books from both sides of the Atlantic. 866 Valencia Street (at 19th), San Francisco, CA 94110, USA. Tel: (415) 824–8203 or (888) 893–4008 (toll free in the US). Credit cards accepted. Worldwide shipping. E-mail: <office@borderlands-books.com>.

Cold Tonnage Books <www.coldtonnage.com> offers excellent mail order new and used SF/fantasy/horror, art, reference, limited editions etc. Write to: Andy & Angela Richards, Cold Tonnage Books, 22 Kings Lane, Windlesham, Surrey GU20 6JQ, UK. Credit cards accepted. Tel: +44 (0)1276–475388. E-mail: <andy@coldtonnage.com>.

Ken Cowley offers mostly used SF/fantasy/horror/crime/supernatural, collectibles, pulps, videos etc. by mail order at very reasonable prices. Write to: Trinity Cottage, 153 Old Church Road, Clevedon, North Somerset, BS21 7TU, UK. Tel: +44 (0)1275-872247. E-mail: <kencowley@blueyonder.co.uk>.

Dark Delicacies <www.darkdel.com> is a friendly Burbank, California, store specializing in horror books, toys, vampire merchandise and signings. They also do mail order and run money-saving book club and membership discount deals. 4213 West Burbank Blvd., Burbank, CA 91505, USA. Tel: (818) 556–6660. Credit cards accepted. E-mail: <darkdel@darkdel.com>.

DreamHaven Books & Comics <www.dreamhavenbooks.com> store and mail order offers new and used SF/fantasy/horror/art and illustrated etc. with regular catalogues (both print and e-mail). Write to: 912 West Lake Street, Minneapolis, MN 55408, USA. Credit cards accepted. Tel: (612) 823–6070. E-mail: <dream@dreamhavenbooks.com>.

Fantastic Literature <www.fantasticliterature.com> mail order offers the UK's biggest online out-of-print SF/fantasy/horror genre bookshop. Fanzines, pulps and vintage paperbacks as well. Write to: Simon and Laraine Gosden, Fantastic Literature, 35 The Ramparts, Rayleigh, Essex SS6 8PY, UK. Credit cards and Pay Pal accepted. Tel/Fax: +44 (0)1268–747564. E-mail: <sgosden@netcomuk.co.uk>.

Fantasy Centre <www.fantasycentre.biz> shop (open 10 a.m.–6 p.m., Monday to Saturday) and mail order has used SF/fantasy/horror, art, reference, pulps etc. at reasonable prices with regular bimonthly catalogues. They also stock a wide range of new books from small, specialist publishers. Write to: 157 Holloway Road, London N7 8LX, UK. Credit cards accepted. Tel/Fax: +44 (0)20–7607 9433. E-mail: <books@fantasycentre.biz>.

Ghost Stories run by Richard Dalby issues semi-regular mail order lists of used ghost and supernatural volumes at very reasonable prices. Write to: 4 Westbourne Park, Scarborough, North Yorkshire YO12 4AT, UK. Tel: +44 (0)1723 377049.

Kayo Books <www.kayobooks.com> is a bright, clean treasure-trove of used SF/fantasy/horror/mystery/pulps spread over two floors. Titles are stacked alphabetically by subject, and there are many bargains to be had. Credit cards accepted. Visit the store (Wednesday-Saturday, 11:00am to 6:00pm) at 814 Post Street, San Francisco, CA 94109, USA or order off their website. Tel: (415) 749 0554. E-mail: <kayo@kayobooks.com>.

David Wynn's **Mythos Books LLC** <www.mythosbooks.com> is a mail order company presenting books and curiosities on Lovecraftiana, Cthulhu Mythos, horror and weird fiction releases with regular e-mail and web site updates. Write to: 351 Lake Ridge Road, Poplar Bluff, MO 63901–2177, USA. Major credit cards accepted. Tel/Fax: (573) 785–7710. E-mail: <dwynn@LDD.net>.

Porcupine Books offers regular catalogues and extensive mail order lists of used fantasy/horror/SF titles via e-mail <brian@ porcupine.demon.co.uk> or write to: 37 Coventry Road, Ilford, Essex IG1 4QR, UK. Tel: +44 (0)20 8554–3799.

Kirk Ruebotham <www.abebooks.com/home/kirk61/> is a mail-order only dealer, who sells out-of-print and used horror/SF/fantasy/ crime and related non-fiction at very good prices, with regular catalogues. Write to: 16 Beaconsfield Road, Runcorn, Cheshire WA7 4BX, UK. Tel: +44 (0)1928–560540 (10:00am–8:00pm). E-mail: <kirk.ruebotham@ntlworld.com>.

Shocklines <www.shocklines.com> is described as "your one-stop shop for horror". This online resource mostly deals in small press titles and limited editions, and offers many signed editions. Credit cards accepted.

Bob and Julie Wardzinski's **The Talking Dead** offers reasonably priced paperbacks, rare pulps and hardcovers, with catalogues issued regularly. They accept wants lists and are also the exclusive supplier of back issues of *Interzone*. Credit cards accepted. Contact them at: 12 Rosamund Avenue, Merley, Wimborne, Dorset BH21 1TE, UK. Tel: +44 (0)1202–849212 (9:00am–9:00pm). E-mail: <books@ thetalkingdead.fsnet.co.uk>.

Ygor's Books specializes in out of print science fiction, fantasy and horror titles, including British, signed, speciality press and limited editions. They also buy books, letters and original art in these fields.

You can contact them at: PO Box 40212, Mesa, AZ 85274, USA. Tel: (480) 897–0981. E-mail: <ygorsbooks@earthlink.net>.

MARKET INFORMATION AND NEWS

DarkEcho <www.darkecho.com> editor Paula Guran sends out periodic, personal e-mails whenever time and whim allows. It doesn't cover horror news comprehensively or list market news, but it's still worth subscribing to for free by e-mailing: <subscribe@darkecho. com>.

The Gila Queen's Guide to Markets is an e-mail newsletter detailing markets for SF/fantasy/horror plus other genres, along with publishing news, contests, dead markets, anthologies, updates, etc. For a sample copy or subscription (US funds only, credit card or PayPal), contact: Kathryn Ptacek, PO Box 97, Newton, NJ 07860-0097, USA. E-mail: <GilaQueen@worldnet.att.net>.